ess Mowry

he Trees

of the Night

Way Past Cool

Way Past Cool

by Jess Mowry

Farrar Straus Giroux

New York

Copyright © 1992 by Jess Mowry

All rights reserved

Printed in the United States of America

Published simultaneously in Canada by HarperCollins*CanadaLtd*

First edition, 1992

Library of Congress Cataloging-in-Publication Data

Mowry, Jess.

Way past cool / Jess Mowry.

I. Title.

PS3563.0934W3 1992   813'.54—dc20   91-42050   CIP

To Susan Daniel

for taking the chance.

And for Jeremy

just 'cause that's what it is

Way Past Cool

"Gordon! GUN!" screamed Curtis, diving off his skateboard onto trash-covered concrete.

Gordon dove from his board too, all 180 pounds rolling and skidding then scrambling warp-seven behind a dumpster as a full-auto fired from a battered black van. Velcro ripped and his backpack burst open. Books and a binder tumbled out. Another gun joined the first, a rhythmic steely stutter of Uzis in chorus. Bullets pocked brick, sending chips whizzing and spattering to a whine of ricochets that sounded just like the movies. The dumpster rang dully as silver dents stitched its rusty sides.

Gordon was a born leader, first to risk his butt, with a natural balance of brains and balls tempered by a healthy helping of fear. As with all good leaders, his decisions came fast under fire; if they happened to be the right ones, so much the better. But there were times when a gang leader had to do stupid things—like jumping to his feet and offering his head and shoulders as an easy target while he cupped his hands to his mouth and bawled, "DOWN, suckers!"

The warning wasn't needed: the other boys had already scattered among garbage cans, their boards abandoned and darting away as if seeking cover too. Gordon's stupidity would be remembered later as cool, though he never considered that. In another sort of war he might have won a medal.

The auto-fire cut off: thirty-two-round magazines emptied fast at 550 rounds per minute, as most kids in West Oakland knew. It was as if somebody had switched on silence. Gordon jerked the old .22 pistol from the back of his jeans and got off three quick shots in the van's general direction before the worn-out little gun jammed. Its popping sounded weak and wimpy after the 9mm Uzi snarls.

But the van peeled away, rubber screeching and blue smoke blasting from rusty chrome side pipes. Gordon cursed and beat the gun's butt on the dumpster lid. It fired again, once, defiant now in the sudden morning stillness. Brick dust puffed from a building across the street, and a window nearby slammed shut. The van's engine roar faded up the block. Tires squealed as the van got sideways around the corner.

"Motherfuckin piece of SHIT!" raged Gordon. He almost whacked the gun again, but caught himself in time and looked around instead while wiping a skinned and bloody elbow on his jeans. "Yo! Anybody hit?"

Four heads poked up from behind a ragged row of garbage cans: Ric and Rac, the twins, identically flat-topped and wide-eyed, Curtis with his long, ratty dreadlocks, and Lyon's fluffy bush, like an Afro gone wild.

"Hey!" squeaked Curtis, his expression amazed. "I got myself shot in the back!"

Beside him, Lyon lifted Curtis' tattered T-shirt, plain and faded black like the other boys' . . . gang colors. "Yeah? Well, you for sure be takin it cool, man. Let's check it out."

Curtis squirmed, trying to look over his shoulder. "Well, how the fuck I sposed to take it?"

The twins squeezed close too, their mouths open in duplicate wonder and tawny eyes bright with curiosity.

Gordon walked over, carrying the gun muzzle-down.

Lyon glanced at the fat boy over Curtis' head. "That thing gonna go off again, Gordon?"

Gordon spat on the garbage-slimed concrete, holding the pistol like a snapping rat by its tail. "Now how the fuck I know, man? Piece of shit jam up just when you needin it, an then go off when you don't! How many goddamn times I say we gotta save back for some kinda better gun?"

He scowled at the other boys, and pointed. "An how many motherfuckin times I gotta tell you dudes *not* to hide a'hind stupid ole garbage cans in a firefight?" He aimed a finger at one can bleeding yellow goo. "Dumpster steel mostly stop bullets. *Them* don't!" His eyes, obsidian hard in a coffee-colored face, softened slightly and his voice gentled down. "So, how Curtis?"

Lyon dabbed at Curtis' shoulder blade with the tail of his own tee. "Stop that silly wigglin, sucker!" Spitting on his fingers, Lyon wiped more blood. The scent of it was coppery, like new pennies. Finally, he smiled and patted Curtis' arm. "It be only a cut. Like from a chunk of flyin brick or somethin. Nowhere near his heart. That be all what matter."

Curtis tried to reach around to his back, but couldn't. "Well, it for sure *feel* like I been shotted!"

Gordon wedged his bulk between the cans and peered at the wet ruby slice across the smaller boy's honey-bronze skin. He snorted. "Shit. Don't signify nuthin, man. You ever get yourself shot for real, you fuckin well know it! We all check out how way past cool you handle it, then!"

The twins exchanged identical glances and snickered in stereo. "Best believe, sucker!" said Ric. "Gordy been shot! He give it a name! Word, you, Curtis!"

"Yeah!" giggled Rac. "In the butt, he shot! Yo, Gordy, show us again!"

Lyon had a funny V-shaped smile that looked mostly smart-ass even when it wasn't. "Bein shot sposed to mean you way past bad." He turned his smile on Gordon. "Course, gettin butt-shot just don't tell the same, huh?"

Gordon chewed his lip a moment, then growled. "Pend a lot on whose butt you talkin, don't it?" He jabbed Rac in the chest with a finger. "An stop callin me Gordy, goddamnit!" Squatting with a grunt, he started picking up his garbage-stained papers.

"Well," said Ric, "I get myself shot, I want it be in the arm, Gor-DEN!"

"Word!" agreed Rac. "Wear a tank top all the time. Look way past cool, believe!"

Gordon spat again, barely missing Rac's Nikes. "Yo, raisin-brain! Gettin shot more like to make you way past DEAD! Ever hear of somebody bein actual shot in the arm real-time? That ain't nuthin but TV dogshit, sucker!" He glared at the gun, then looked up at Lyon. "I feel like dustin this goddamn thing, man. Prob'ly end by killin one of us someday stead of doin any good."

"So?" asked Ric. "What you spect for twenty dollars, dude?"

"Word!" added Rac. "K mart blue-light-special kinda gun, all that is! Deek even say."

Gordon's nostrils suddenly flared. "Deek, huh? Listen

up, suckers! Deek talk a fly out shit, he wanna! Only a motherfuckin fool figure he gots somethin to say worth the ghost of a dog! Next time he come by curb-preachin you, tell him to fuck off!"

"Well," said Rac, "spose he get pissed an tell his bodyguard to shoot me?"

Lyon grinned. "Then ask him if he do you in the arm."

"Just shut up, Ric," said Gordon. "For once."

"I'm Rac," said Rac. "*He's* Ric."

Gordon sighed. "Whatever." He stood and shoved the pistol at Lyon. "Here, man, see if you can fix this piece of shit again."

Lyon looked closely at the gun. "Mmm. I see what happen. Rimfire bullets be most like to jam. That cause the primer stuff be in the rim, an with cheapo bullets like these it don't all the time go clear around. Then the firin pin hit a empty spot an you end up with jack."

"Or a dirt nap," growled Gordon. "Shit! I don't wanna hear all that stuff, man! Like we gonna be pop-quizzed on gun fixin in school or somethin! It the onliest goddamn gun we got, an the onliest goddamn gun we 'ford right now, so's just make it shoot again an stop rattlin my goddamn chain, huh!"

Gordon heaved another sigh and stared around the alley mouth at the wreckage; scattered skateboards, books and binders, and more sheets of somebody's homework fluttering in the gentle morning breeze. He scowled when he recognized them as his own. "Shit an goddamnit to hell! Ain't this a motherfuckin BITCH!"

Lyon watched as Gordon snatched up the papers and tried to wipe them clean, then gave up and stuffed them into his pack. "Yo, Gordon, tell the teacher you got em all dirty gettin drive-byed."

"Too fuckin funny, man! Ain't one of them stupid teachers gotta live around here. Not know from nuthin what is. Shit, this my goddamn English story too . . . how I gonna spend my motherfuckin summer vacation! Been bustin my goddamn ass over it all cocksuckin week, an now ole Crabzilla gonna kill me for sure!" Gordon scowled at the twins' grins. "You two! Get your asses busy pickin up your own goddamn shit! We gonna be late an get tardies out the wazoo!"

Ric and Rac moved as one. They were wiry, hard-muscled, Hershey-brown boys of thirteen, wearing tight black tees faded to gray, ragged 501s with ripped knees, and big battered Nikes. Their eager, snub-nosed faces made them look like African imps. Their mother had named them from some old book about kids who made fools out of grown-ups. A desperate teacher had once pleaded with them to dress differently so she could tell them apart. They'd shown up next day with their initials Magic Markered on the front of their shirts.

Curtis was still trying to touch his own back. He was the smallest of the gang, twelve and childlike, with the prominent tummy and smooth-lined body of a little boy. A lot of kids figured him for the mascot. His dad was white, and Curtis could gleam like polished bronze when clean. His parents were trying to save enough money to move to Jamaica someday.

Lyon laid the gun on a dumpster lid and wiped Curtis' cut a final time, then dangled his long bloody fingers in Curtis' face. Curtis winced. Lyon grinned. Everything about Lyon was long; narrow, lean-jawed face with high cheekbones, and tall slender body more delicate than skinny. His teeth looked too large for his mouth. His ebony eyes were tilted up at the corners and, like his V smile, always seemed a little sly. He had a funny loose way of holding or moving his hands that made them look like paws. He read books because he wanted to, and could fascinate or terrify with magic tricks or spooky stories. Lyon appeared fragile but most kids left him be.

Lyon licked his fingers. "Mmm. Way cool blood, homey. Maybe I take me some more. Tonight. When the moon be full."

Curtis went very still. His voice broke. "Not funny! Maaaan, don't be sayin them kinda things!"

Rac snickered. "Yo! That time of month already, Lyon-o? Hey, what you call a used Kotex?"

"Vampire tea bag!" answered Ric.

Curtis glared. "Eat shit an die, suckers! So there!"

"You two your very own HBO, ain't ya?" said Lyon.

"Everybody just shut the fuck up!" roared Gordon. "Goddamn honky show here!"

"Donkey show," said Lyon.

"Whatever." Gordon tugged at his pack straps, then faced Curtis. "An you stop actin like a goddamn puss! Spose you wanna go to 'mergency, now?"

Curtis considered that.

"Way past fun," Lyon told him. "Get to sit on your butt an wait for hours, aside all kinda cool people what been shot an stabbed, ODin an pukin all over the place. Yo, they prob'ly give you stitches. Leave a hot scar. Like Frankenstein."

"Um . . . naw, I don't wanna," murmured Curtis.

Lyon's eyes lost some of their slyness. "Well, it gonna be bleedin some, open like that. Better take off your shirt so's it don't stick."

Gordon nodded. "Good idea." He peered at the cheap digital watch on his wrist. "Shit! Now we for sure late!" He studied the watch, frowning and flicking it with a finger. "Shit, I think it busted."

"Yo," said Ric. "Hold it up to your ear, man."

"To check if it still tickin," added Rac.

Gordon did, and the twins burst into laughter.

Gordon, a month shy of fourteen, was the oldest. He was a big, heavy-breasted boy with a belly that hung over his jeans and bobbed whenever he moved. For all his jiggly softness there was muscle buried beneath the fat, like a small tank wrapped in foam rubber. His T-shirts never covered his middle, and his jeans sagged so low that his bullet scar usually showed. His hair was a natural bush, and his flat-nosed, heavy-lipped face made him look dense unless you paid attention to his eyes. He kicked the squatting Ric in the butt with the toe of his ancient Airwalk, sending both brothers sprawling. "Shove it in *your* ear, asshole! There! Now you know what time it is, fool!"

"Well," said Curtis, coming out from behind the cans and stripping off his shirt. "Don't feel up for sittin in class bleedin all goddamn day. Mom an Dad both at work. Maybe I just bail myself on home an watch TV or somethin."

The twins got up and examined his back again. "Um, yo," asked Rac. "What that shiny white shit way down inside there?"

"Bone!" said Lyon, slapping Rac's hand away. "An keep your goddamn dirty finger outa it!"

"Mondo gross!" said Ric. He shook a finger at his brother. "Can't touch that!"

Curtis turned to Lyon, his eyes widening. "No shit? You mean my skelenton showin?"

Lyon laid a paw on his shoulder. "It be okay, man. Leave a cool scar for later on. *Better'n* just a pussy ole shot in the arm, any day."

Curtis looked thoughtful, then puffed his little chest almost as far out as his tummy and made a face at the twins. He strutted to the alley mouth and peered cautiously up the deserted street. "Wonder if them motherfuckin gangbangers still motorin round here?"

Lyon glided up beside him and gazed toward the corner where the van had gone. Oily smoke mixed with streamers of gray-white gunpowder still drifted in the cool air. The sun was spilling over the roofline and down the buildings, turning grimy orange brick into gold. The faint breeze was still stirring in from the Bay, as yet untainted by garbage stink and exhaust fumes, smelling of salt and hinting of faraway places. Lyon's long delicate hand clasped Curtis' shoulder again. "I come home with ya, homey. Patch you up good as new. Gots any peroxide at your place?"

"Nuh-uh. Gots Bactine, I think."

"That do. Keep them ole maggots from hatchin." Lyon flipped a finger at the empty street, then glanced at the rusty little .22 he'd brought with him. "Showtimes! There be them big dudes with their full-auto Uzis, an go bailin warp-seven cause Gordy gots the balls to shoot back with *this!*"

Ric moved close to Gordon. "Yo! Gordy gots 'dustrial-strength balls! Word!"

Rac stepped to Gordon's other side. "Believe! That why he lead!"

Gordon shrugged. "Don't call me Gordy." He jerked his jeans up a little and eyed his watch again with a frown. "Well, I don't figure it cool for us to scatter right now. Three blocks back to Curtis' place, or bout the same to school. We better decide which one we goin for, an keep together. Yo, Lyon! Maybe you should oughta fix that gun right now, man. Ain't a good idea to be skatin round with a bullet stuck in the chamber." He stared at his watch once more, then whacked it.

"So, what in hell you spect for two ninety-eight at K mart, man?" asked Ric. "A goddamn Seiko or somethin?"

Rac poked his brother. "Shut up, doofus! His mom give him that for his goddamn birthday! It a *heart thing* . . . like Lyon always talkin bout. Yo, sucker, what *your* mom ever give you from the heart?"

Ric snickered. "YOU, sucker! I the first, 'member?"

"BFD! By one stupid little minute! So, shoot bullets through me, why don't ya!"

Lyon fingered the gun. "Well, what I sposed to fix this with, my dick? I need me somethin like a screwdriver for poppin out the bullet."

Gordon tore the watch from his wrist and flung it into a garbage can. "Mmm, s'prised you can't magic it fixed, man." He pulled a switchblade from his pocket and thumbed the button. Nothing happened. "Shit!" Gordon pried it open with his fingernail. "Try this. An please don't bust it."

Handing the knife to Lyon, he dropped his hands to the roll of fat where another boy's hips would have been and scanned the street. "Shit, we so goddamn late now them school doors is prob'ly locked! Best we all just bail on back to Curtis' place an hang."

Curtis looked happy, until the twins faced him and demanded, "Yo! Gots any food?"

"Um, well, it gettin kinda close to the end of the month. Gots bread . . . an this big new bottle of ketchup."

The twins made identical faces and turned on Gordon. "Yo! We don't score school lunch . . ." Ric began.

"We don't get nuthin all goddamn day!" Rac finished.

Gordon sighed once more. "I gots enough food for everybody. Mom workin steady again. Best we go my place, stead of Curtis' . . . I spose."

"Better," said Rac.

"Word," added Ric. "You ain't sposed to leave your dudes go hungry."

Rac nodded. "Word up! By rules!"

Muscle hardened somewhere in Gordon's chest. He clenched big fists. "Shut up! Don't need me no 'minders bout the rules from you two suckers! Curtis! Quit fuckin with your goddamn back! Get busy an snag all our boards fore some car come by an run 'em into street pizza! Yo, Lyon! Get that gun fixed so's we can bail the hell outa here!"

Gordon faced the street again. His forehead creased. "Goddamn if that dint look like the selfsame ole van what done a drive-by on us a couple days ago." He glanced at Lyon. "Same sorta big dudes . . . least sixteen. But why in hell they tryin to do us?"

Lyon returned to the nearest dumpster and laid the gun on the lid. He eyed it a moment, then poked the knife point into the ejection port. "They pass some sorta new law say you gotta have a reason for shootin black kids?"

Curtis returned with his arms full of boards and started standing them upright against the dumpster. "Oughta be a rule bout it, anyways."

"Word!" said Ric. "Give it a name!"

"Straight up!" added Rac. "Law say black kids eat shit an die!"

Gordon snorted. "Yeah, next you be tellin me there salt in the goddamn sea! Swear you two gots one little brain between ya, an trade it off." He ran a finger across Curtis' back, then drew bloody zeros on the twins' foreheads. "Yo! That there all what the world figure you worth, suckers! Shit, it say all the time on TV how people like otters an little white rats better'n you. Leave them nuthins on till I say you take em off. Make you 'member what is an what ain't."

Lyon rapped while he worked on the gun. "You ain't furry an cute, so's you way cool to shoot, be a whale or a seal, then you got some appeal." He pried out the misfire round, tossed it away, then worked the gun's action a few times, slapped the clip back in, and handed it to Gordon. "Should be workin now, man. You be figurin the Crew got somethin up with these drive-bys?"

Gordon scratched his head, which made him look like a stupid fat boy. "Cross my mind, man, but goddamn I figure how . . . or why. Ain't none of em ole enough for drivin', an even they rousted that van, for sure weren't them in it. Nor the time last neither. An, hey, you tell me how they ever score the buck for *one* Uzi, never mind deuce. Shit, all they gots be that ole snub .38, an it ain't much better'n this!" He flipped the little pistol in his palm.

"Well," suggested Curtis. "Maybe they pay some big dudes to do us?"

Gordon snorted again. "Uh-huh. With what, man, Wesley's looks?" He paused a moment. "Less they done cut some sorta deal with Deek . . ." He shook his head. "Naw. Don't figure, man. We most never fight with em no more. Not since we all little ole kids. Shit, why should we? Hood they got no better'n ours."

Gordon snagged his board, a street-scarred Steadham full-size, and decked easily despite his mass. But then a siren sounded in the near distance, and he froze. His eyes shifted to Lyon.

The slender boy's head came up. His face turned skyward and his hands dangled loose in their pawlike way. The other boys waited, watching him. At times like these his ears almost looked pointy. "Two blocks up an three over," he murmured. "Comin this way, warp-seven. Ain't no ambulance nor fire truck neither."

Gordon's eyes calculated. "Most nobody call the cops over some shootin." He glanced in the siren's direction and fingered his jaw. "Course, if they come, it with their screamer full-on, just like now. That give whoever gots the full-auto plenty of time to bail. Best we chill our own fire." He buried the pistol under a sackful of sodden garbage in the dumpster, then wiped his hands on the tail of Rac's tee.

"Shit, man!" squeaked Rac. "Shoot bullets through me, why don't ya!"

Gordon grinned. "I know. It ain't fair. Shut up." He jerked his jaw toward the street. "Let's motor. Be cool."

The boys grabbed their boards, decking and following Gordon out of the alley and down the sidewalk. They rolled fast in file, Lyon second on his pug-nosed Chris Miller, then the twins on identical Hammerheads. Curtis brought up the rear on his ancient flat-deck Variflex. The siren's yelping came closer, beating between the buildings and echoing through the canyons of brick and concrete. The boys had almost reached the lower corner when the cop car skidded around the intersection behind them, fishtailed, recovered sloppily with screeching rubber, and blasted down the block. The boys neither looked nor altered their pace.

The car braked suddenly at the alley mouth, its nose diving as if scenting the gun smoke, but then the boys were spotted and it dropped ass and squeaked off after them, slewing sideways into the intersection just as Gordon reached the curb, tires smoking as it slid to a stop. Its engine almost strangled, shaking the whole car, but struggled back to a loping idle that slowly smoothed out. Its siren blipped silent on a rising squeal but the rooftop strobes kept firing. Inside, the radio spat catfight sounds.

The boys tailed their boards and bunched together behind Gordon, waiting. Their faces switched on expressions of stupid, dull-eyed sullenness while their hands hung loose and open at their sides. The car doors burst simultaneously wide, one cop, white, on the passenger side, crouching behind, shotgun leveled at Gordon's chest through the open window. The other, black, gripped his gun double-handed over the car's roof. Strobe fire glinted ruby and indigo off his chrome-silver sunglasses.

Gordon yawned and hitched up his sagging jeans.

It was a long half second. The cops poised, tense. They were bulky, big-bellied men in gunmetal-blue uniforms. Their shirts were stretched tight over bulletproof vests, and they were belted by black leather that creaked with the weight of cuffs and clubs, walkie-talkies, and strangely shaped pouches packed with state-of-the-art stuff for survival in a hostile environment. Helmeted in stark white, they looked like intergalactic mercenaries grounded on a planet whose native inhabitants hated their guts. The strobe lights fought a losing battle against the gold of the climbing sun. The scents of hot rubber and steel, of leather and plastic, polyester and polish, radiated out from the car. The engine settled into an indifferent idle, its exhaust ghosting steam in the cool morning air. The radio hissed and spat its alien language.

On the sidewalk stood small black, brown, and bronze figurines that a moment before had been living and laughing. Now, the only hint of humanness was the blood seeping down Curtis' back. A big fat fly lazily circled his shoulder, sparking metallic iridescence in the sun like a tiny high-tech toy.

The cops' faces could have come from the same sort of action-figure mold as an old He-Man, Master of the Universe. It was even hard to tell them apart. "Against the wall!" ordered the black, a dusty line from any movie. "Spread!" he added, never doubting these kids wouldn't know the script by heart.

The figurines moved, little androids now, automatically obeying alien orders. Backpacks, books, and binders hit the sidewalk like so many weapons. Skateboards were left where they stood. The cops' eyes shifted uneasily behind their chrome mirrors, studying rooflines and blank windows above for an ambush. Finally, the cops moved after the boys, who were lined against grimy brick, their backs and balls vulnerable. The scene—the kids, the two big men, the shotgun wary while the black cop holstered his pistol but left the snap undone—would have looked bogus on network TV, like a parody of something from a long time ago. The black cop considered the row of little sculptures, then squatted with a grunt and creak of leather and tore into the backpacks like a gorilla who smelled a banana. He seemed about as disappointed when he didn't find one. Finally he stood with another grunt and rubbed his back. A shiny black boot freed homework to the breeze and sent Lyon's board skittering into the street. A smile crossed the white cop's mouth as a garbage packer swung ponderously around the corner and bore down on the board. The driver, black and tired-looking, took the scene at a glance and didn't seem to find it a parody of anything. His heavy-gloved hands moved gently on the big wheel, guiding twenty tons and ten huge tires in a delicate dance around the skateboard. The truck rumbled away. The cop's smile clicked off.

The black one began searching the boys, slapping where

he should have patted, and jerking arms back to check out their undersides like junk-shop merchandise that nobody could make you buy if you broke. For some reason he passed over Lyon and started with the twins, looking slightly confused as if he hadn't counted right. "You two. Turn around. Well, ain't that cute."

Four tawny eyes stared through the man.

"What're those marks on their foreheads?" asked the white cop. His eyes narrowed. "Looks like blood."

"Is," muttered the black one. "Initiation rite. Back against the wall."

The twins exchanged glances and secret smiles nobody else could see before turning and spreading again.

Moving to Gordon, the cop found the blade and yanked it out, raised it and an eyebrow to his partner with an I-told-you-so smirk, then thumbed the button. Nothing happened. He frowned. "Cheap shit from Taiwan." He shoved it in his pocket.

Reaching Curtis, he fingered the small boy's dreadlocks, then wiped his fingers on Curtis' jeans and studied his back. "Got us a little Rasta mon here. Peace, love, an ganja. So what happened to you, Ziggy?"

Curtis' voice carried all the emotion of an ATM terminal. "I fall down." He thought a moment. "In busted glass."

"Uh-huh," said the cop. "Say somethin for me in Rasta, mon." The fly had settled and was busy sucking blood. The cop smacked it flat with his palm.

"Pussy clot!" hissed Curtis.

"Welcome to a kinder, gentler America, boy." The cop turned to face the row of backs, dropping his hands to his belt. The white cop lowered the shotgun slightly. "Anybody hear some shootin a few minutes ago?"

"No," said Gordon.

The black cop gave the white another smirk and stepped back to Gordon, nudging the boy's feet farther apart with his boot. "Uh-huh. Figured you did the talkin, fat boy. Only kids packin that much lard around here are the ones makin a profit. So what's your gang dealin, fat boy? Rock? Ice? Or you the kind sell hospital garbage to little kids?"

Gordon said nothing.

"Uh-huh. So what you call yourselves, fat boy?"

"Friends," said Gordon.

"Uuuuh-huuuuh." The man thunked the back of Gordon's head with his knuckles. "C'mon, fat boy. We seen you dudes always hangin out together. Gangs always got baaaad names, like the Crew. So what's yours, fat boy?"

Gordon sighed, tensing for what would come next. "I just tell you."

Knuckles made a watermelon sound on Gordon's skull. "Uh-huh. More like smart-mouth little niggerboys. So who shot your Rasta 'friend,' lard-ass?"

"He fall down. In busted glass."

"Uh-huh. Maybe you can't take no name cause the Crew come an smoke your butts? Word say they some real bad-ass dudes."

"Uh-huh," Gordon murmured.

The cop whacked Gordon's head against the wall. "You gonna go far with that mouth of yours, niggerboy! How come you ain't in school?"

Gordon took a breath. The shotgun's muzzle lifted a little. "We takin our Friend home. Cause he fall down. In busted glass."

The cop snapped his holster strap. "Yeah. Right. You

oughta get a medal! Ain't gonna catch me cryin when the Crew come down an show you what time it is!" He scattered skateboards with his boot.

Lyon murmured something, so softly that only Curtis next to him heard. There was a small metallic click.

"GODDAMNIT!" bawled the black cop, grabbing at his pants pocket where the point of Gordon's blade poked through. Startled, the white brought the shotgun up, ready.

Cursing, the black cop carefully pulled out the knife, ripping his pants a little more, then laid it anglewise in the gutter against the curb and broke it with his bootheel. There wasn't a sound from the kids, but quivering shoulders revealed silent snickers. Chrome eyes watchful, the cops slid back into their car. The white racked the shotgun, then the car clunked into gear and squeaked away. "Get a life, suckers!" the white spat back.

"I take mine over yours any day, motherfucker!" Gordon muttered. He turned from the wall, rubbing his brick-bruised forehead, and hesitated because the car was only halfway down the block. But he felt the other boys' eyes on him and flipped the finger anyhow.

Like a broken spell, the hard little sculptures softened and became kids once more. The twins sidled up to Gordon with grins. Rac squeezed the fat boy's biceps. "Yo! *There* the rock!"

Ric giggled and draped his arm over Gordon's broad shoulder. "An ice! Maaaan, Gordon total cool like it under fire! Way cool. Way past cool!"

Gordon smiled a little. "Uh-huh. You can go an rub them zeros off now. Cops gots a way of turnin everbody into nuthin."

"Give it a name," said Rac, dabbing at the tail of his tee with his tongue and wiping his brother's forehead with it.

"Word!" agreed Ric, doing the same to Rac's forehead. "Like the ghost of a dog!"

Curtis moved close to Lyon and gazed up into the slender boy's face. "Um, you done that knife thing, huh, man?"

"Done what?" the twins demanded.

Lyon shrugged, his narrow eyes sly as usual. "Just a coincidence, homey."

"Did Lyon make a curse?" asked Rac. "How he do that anyways?"

"Who know," said Ric. "Fuck that. What's a 'incidence?"

Gordon's eyes shifted between Lyon and the broken knife, but he said nothing, just nudging the twins and pointing to the mess on the sidewalk.

Curtis searched Lyon's face again, then smiled and darted into the street to rescue Lyon's board as a car rounded the corner. It honked at Curtis, and all the boys fingered it and bawled curses. The car laid a patch and warped away. Maybe its driver would spread the word he'd been attacked by a youth gang. Curtis returned, grinning and panting, and gave Lyon his board. Lyon turned him around to wipe blood and smashed fly from his back. Gordon and the twins gathered up their school stuff and repacked their packs.

Curtis knelt down beside Gordon. "Um, you figure what them asshole cops say is true? Bout the Crew gonna smoke us?"

Gordon shuffled his wrinkled papers. "Naw, that just dogshit, man. Cops always sayin stuff like that. They *like* seein us fight. Hope we kill each other."

"Why?"

"Save them the trouble," said Lyon. "One time I read this book. Tell where back in the olden days some of them

KKK dogfuckers liked to get us fightin so's they could watch an laugh over it."

Curtis rose and came back beside Lyon. "Well, shit. Seem like we be pretty fuckin stupid to go puttin on showtime for them assholes!"

Lyon nodded. "Mmm. You say it, homeboy."

The morning breeze had given up, beaten back to the Bay by the reek of overflowing dumpsters, alleys slimed by the walking dead, fumes and smoke from worn-out engines, leaking drainpipes, stopped-up sewers, and the sour sweat of too many people backed into too few corners. There were other smells, homey ones, of breakfasts cooking, bathroom steam, and the soapy-clean scent of new-washed laundry. But, like the antiseptic of hospital halls or the heavy perfume of funeral flowers, they were never enough to cover the stink of something sick or something forgotten that crumbled and rotted with its bones poking through.

The blue of the sky was yellowing as a black Trans-Am swung into a Burger King lot and cruised around to the drive-up window. It was ten years old, big and sleek, muscle sheathed in sheet metal. Its glistening polish, blood-crimson striping, and mirror-chrome Centerlines told of regular care by a megabuck detailer. Panther-footed on fresh low-pro Goodyears, arrogant as hell and expensive to feed, it was the kind of kid's car most kids dreamed of but could never afford if they lived to be ninety.

But the driver was just six years older than the dream, and looked one less behind the wheel. Still, he handled the power with casual cool, always aware of the envy eyeing him from the sidewalks. A lot of white dudes in the better parts of town might wonder how Deek lived the dream. Most black kids knew, but more than a few envied him anyway. Engine rumbling a deep bass beat, CD deck pumping a Too Short rap, Deek idled his 'Am up to the order window. The slim, dark girl in her lame-looking uniform felt the big muscle-car's jungle-cat purr as it circled the building and glided to a stop, and pretended she didn't give a shit.

Markita was the same age as Deek, but had a two-year-old son at home in her mother's small apartment, and her weekly wage wouldn't have paid for one of Deek's tires. She remembered a crack dealer back in school, a dude she *could* have gone with if doing the right thing hadn't seemed so important, and imagined for a moment how she'd look now beside this boy in that way bad machine.

Deek himself didn't look particularly bad. He was mainframed for something small, quick, and lean, so what would have been beef on a bigger-boned boy quivered on him like chocolate pudding. Markita didn't see him that often; maybe once or twice a month and never this early in the day, but each time he showed up his designer jeans strained tighter on his butt while his soft boy-breasts got floppier and his belly hung farther out of his T-shirts. She doubted if he could have run a full block or lifted anything heavier than a sixer of beer, but then the game's name was survival and Deek seemed to be fully equipped for that.

His clothes were always fresh, like they'd never been

sweated in, and his top-line L.A.s never seemed to see side-walk. He wore enough gold around neck, wrists, and fingers to pay a month's wages to a whole Burger King crew. Mar-kita had to admit that if she had only one word to describe his chubby-cheeked, double-chinned face she'd have to go with "cute"—like the Beaver might have looked at sixteen if he'd been black and pigging for years on junk food—though his golden eyes glinted as hard as the real thing. His hair was sheened and sparkly, and long in the old Michael Jackson style, like he could care about being hip or trendy.

Sunlight struck fire from Deek's pudgy hand as he leaned from the car window. Markita blinked behind bulletproof glass. Her own slender fingers were bare of even that single signifying band. The shine of her short curls had already been dulled by the frying-fat fumes, and just the thought of another long day made her feet ache. Her voice came out knife-edged and bitchy, surprising her. "May I take your order, please?"

Her eyes shifted to the shadowy figure beside Deek, half hidden by the car's low roofline and camouflaged by the black-on-black interior. She wondered who rode shotgun with the chubby little street prince: some ebony airhead, or maybe a blond bubble-brain to show the poor niggers that drug bucks could buy what you couldn't score with a high school diploma or a hard-muscled bod. Deek without money would still have been cute, like something that squeaked when you squeezed it. But Markita had stopped sleeping with that sort of stuff a long time ago. She bent for a better look, pretending to straighten a napkin stack.

It was another boy: the bodyguard, and a necessary ac-cessory. He was gunmetal black, and built so wiry and hard that Markita doubted there was an ounce of fat on him anywhere. He was tall and long-limbed with what some old people called "African" features, like Markita's, though his hair was razored crisp and flat. He had big buck teeth behind loose lips that probably never quite closed, eyes like warm obsidian that some might call soulful, and the sort of long-backed build where T-shirts made in Taiwan for "normal" kids would always leave his belly button bare. Even in new 501s and black satin tank top he seemed out of place in the high-tech machine, reminding Markita of a *National Enquirer* photo showing a Kenyan jet pilot posed in his cockpit clad in just a loincloth. This dude would have looked way past cool in a loincloth. Fact was, he would have been righteous with a bone in his nose. Next to him, Deek should have been wearing a beanie with a propeller on top. The boy was slumped bonelessly in the seat with a beer bottle clasped upright in his crotch. He looked either half drunk or all the way bored. Markita felt her heart warming toward him for some reason.

Deek thumbed down the CD and gave Markita a cute smile. "I have me a big breakfast an a extra order of Tater Tenders, girl." He glanced at the other boy. "Yo! Ty!"

Ty seemed to come back from somewhere else. "Huh? Oh. A egg-a-muffin, I spose."

"This ain't McDonald's, stupid!"

The tall boy bent over the console and peered up at the order window. Seeing Markita, he gave her a smile that looked low-tech and harmless and infinitely patient. Markita didn't think that the short snap of "Ty" fit him at all. She couldn't imagine those thick homely lips ever being self-programmed to say it. They'd more likely mumble a shy "Tyler" or "Tyrone" and then relax back into a good-natured goofy grin once more. She pictured his walk, planting one huge Nike flat on the pavement at a time in no particular hurry to get anywhere. He probably couldn't rap to save his life, or give a particular shit about it. He wore no gold that Markita could see, though there was a fine silver chain around his neck and some sort of small, quarter-sized medallion hanging from it under his shirt between the starkly defined plates of his chest.

"Um?" he asked. "Where the menu?"

Markita felt warmth again. She made a little movie in her mind. Ty was the kind of boy who, had he stayed in school, would have plodded to graduation on a solid C average and gone with an "African" sort of girl like . . . well, like herself. She would probably have to teach him the mechanics of love, but he would have always known the meaning. He would marry the girl and go to work for a scrap yard, confident at the iron controls of a 1930s-technology crane but uneasy with a pocket calculator and intimidated by an ATM. Markita's eyes strayed to the small, tight nipples on his chest, like tiny buds beneath the black satin. They'd be the same color as the rest of him: hardly noticeable. He'd be a gentle savage in bed, patient and caring to his family, and in a few years they'd be able to afford a house with a yard in a good East Side neighborhood. Eventually their children, maybe Markita's own son, whom Ty would be just as proud of as the others he'd father, would teach him Nintendo games and how to program the VCR. Markita couldn't have explained why she seemed to know all this, she just felt as if she did—now that it was too late.

"The fuckin menu was back there on the goddamn post, stupid!" Deek rolled his golden eyes at Markita and added a hopeless shrug. "Give him the same's me, girl."

Markita watched as Ty slumped back in the seat and took a gulp from his bottle. The beer was Heineken dark, she noted. Only prime shit for Deek. She turned away from the window to a skinny, slope-shouldered boy who lounged at the grill and stared into space. His name was Leroy, and he looked like one. Bib overalls would have fit him just fine. He was finishing high school at night, after dropping out for about a year to deal on corners. He'd made pretty good buck for a while, until he'd tried to collect a credit from a cracked-out sixth-grader who'd opened him up with an old Denny's steak knife. He was taking a computer course too, hard to believe as that was. He'd asked Markita out a few times but she hadn't accepted . . . yet. She hoped he would ask her once more. "Two breakfasts, Leroy." She lowered her voice, though the window glass was a full inch thick. "Make one a special."

Leroy giggled—Markita was getting used to that—and snagged his spatula. "One mega-size booger comin up! So who givin the lady some shit this early in the mornin?" He glanced out the window, then whistled and turned back to the grill. "Mmm, MMM! You really playin with power there, homegirl!"

Markita moved to the hot racks and took down two boxes of Tater Tenders. "Just do it, Leroy. Or I will. An you make sure I know which's which so the fat little showtime get what comin to him." She added gently, "An don't be callin me homegirl."

Leroy giggled again. "That one a lot more'n showtime, girl. Show you first, maybe, but then he *tell* you what time it is, best believe!" He grabbed his crotch. "Yo, gimme a second an I add some secret sauce."

Markita made a face. "Leroy, you so gross!" Then she noticed a fly flat-backing it on the floor. She smiled and knelt to pick it up. "I hope it usually take you longer'n a second."

Leroy turned, momentarily confused, then smiled too. He had nice eyes.

A few minutes later the Trans-Am nosed into a parking space at the back of the Burger King lot, easing up to a fence whose battered boards seemed held together only by the layers of spray-painted words and symbols and gang marks. Deek revved the engine once, then cut the ignition and it died with a snarl. The rap thumped softly on, its bass beat a feeling more than a sound. Deek yawned and stretched. "Feel like shit, gettin up so early, man." He glanced at the big gold watch on his wrist. "You *believe* it only ten fuckin o'clock?"

Ty was gazing out the window, watching as a mother led her two small children across the street. They sucked on Popsicles. Ty tried to remember the last time he'd had one. Grape was his favorite. "Seem funny, don't it . . . seein other dudes goin to school?"

Deek coughed up something and spat it out the window. "Naw, it don't. What the fuck they learnin there anyways?" He jerked a thumb toward the restaurant building. "Just enough to be spendin the rest of they goddamn lifes workin in one of them grease-bomb factories, that what!" He gave Ty a smirk. "Stop watchin em, stupid. Hell, I seen you standin there at the window some mornins. It like pickin a goddamn scab. Leave it be an it heal."

Ty said nothing. He opened the sack and passed a boxed breakfast to Deek. Deek had his own apartment in an ancient three-story building where the owner didn't give a shit what happened as long as the rents were paid. The city had wanted to knock what was left of it down after the earthquake, but the owner had written a letter to the Oakland *Tribune*, pleading that his poor people would have nowhere to go, and their "plight" caught the ass end of a brief burst of black unity. He'd gotten by with bolting a few four-by-fours over the biggest cracks, and the structure was now officially quakeproof. Deek had one room, top floor front, but it had its own bath . . . sort of. Mostly it was in the same kind of nuke-attack mess as any other sixteen-year-old boy's.

For Ty and Deek the days usually ended long past midnight, often after spending the last hours watching the VCR or old TV movies, with pizza and beer or ribs and beer, or beer all by itself. Deek smoked a little dope sometimes, but it only gave Ty headaches. Deek would zone out on the ratty old sofa and Ty would finally drag him to bed and strip off his clothes. Deek slept till at least noon and treated everybody like shit until about five or six in the evening. Ty was used to that. Deek did three things well: eating, sleeping, and dealing. Ty covered most everything else.

Midmornings, Ty weighed and measured and chopped and packed. It was mostly rock, though ice was becoming a volume seller, and there was a little coarse coke for the rich kids . . . dogshit grade, nothing near the quality of what went up the noses of whites across town. It was simple, mindless work, like digging a ditch or boxing burgers or punching a keyboard. Deek bought from a good supplier, didn't cut any more than it already was, and sold full weights—or at least never bitched that Ty packed full weights. Ty supposed it was pretty good shit, considering, and tried not to think about who it was for.

Sometimes Ty mopped party puke from the floor, unstopped the greenish-orange thing in the bathroom that passed for a toilet, or swabbed out the rusty shower stall with Pine Sol. Once in a while he changed the sweaty gray bedsheets and did the laundry when there were no more clean socks. Since he didn't have a license, he rode his skateboard to run messages and check on or collect money from the street-corner dealers. Most were boys younger than himself, and not all carried guns or were good with their blades, so it wasn't too much of a prob when some got greedy or tried the same old shit each thought was original and Ty had to beat them up. He did it with cool efficiency and no particular anger. He had a big .45 Army pistol and generally just flashing it kept the kids chilled and shit to a minimum. Deek had once told him that the dudes who managed paper boys probably got more trouble. Ty had had to shoot a few times, but never hit anyone he knew of. He also brought back the takeout food and cigarettes and scored the beer from the store where Deek had an account.

The oldest of five brothers and sisters, with a mother who worked long days and sometimes into the night, and a father who was kind in his way but who never came home anymore, Ty knew how to cook and often did on the apartment's crusty old three-burner range. He also shopped for groceries. Other kids just figured he rode beside Deek all the time and smoked butt. Ty didn't care what anybody thought; he knew this was the best job he'd ever get, and it depended on keeping Deek alive.

Once in a while he went home, sometimes for dinner but really for love. His mom had finally started accepting the money he brought, mostly because the younger kids needed stuff, and life wasn't getting any cheaper. If there were points of light beaming out like the TV talk said, none seemed to be shining in Oakland. His mom could have gotten more from welfare than her job—most mothers could— but pride had a way of backing you into funny corners sometimes. Ty suspected she prayed for him; at least there were moments late at night when he felt as if somebody was, and who else would? Ty supposed there was a God, somewhere, but He didn't seem to like kids very much, and black ones not at all. If Ty ever wondered why he still wore the little silver St. Christopher medal, he figured it was because his mother had given it to him when he was about three. Ty never stayed long on his visits; he hated lying about what he did to the younger kids as much as the gleam of knowing pride in his twelve-year-old brother's eyes. The boy knew what is, and it wouldn't be long. Going home made Ty sad. It was funny that, no matter how drunk he got every night, he'd still wake up early like he had to be in school. Often he'd stand at the window and watch the other kids on the sidewalk below. If there was a future, Ty had figured out a long time ago that it wasn't something he wanted to think much more about than who those little bottles and packets were for.

"Naw," said Deek, shoving back the box. "The other one, man. With the X on it. Girl say it made fresh. This one been on the racks for a hour."

Ty shrugged and switched boxes. "She, um . . . she kinda nice, huh?"

Deek flipped back the lid and ripped open a packet of plastic silverware with his teeth. "Stupid cramp, man! She just like I tellin you, be workin in there time she forty . . . same's all them other suckers shaggin off to school ever goddamn mornin. Pitcher *your*self washin cars or bussin tables, man. That all they gonna let a stupid Buckwheat-lookin niggerboy like you do, don't matter you got a fuckin diploma or not!"

Deek started to shovel pale scrambled eggs into his mouth, alternating with gulps of beer. He frowned as Ty clicked the door handle. "Where in hell you goin?"

"Gotta piss."

Deek glanced back at the restaurant and smirked again. "Shit, maaaan! Don't go wastin your time on *her!* Last I seen a face like that was on a goddamn clock, an a fuckin

cuckoo come outa it! You feelin the need, we score us somethin nice tonight. Jesus, ain't you learned nuthin yet cept
how to slide on a rubber?"

Ty's lips clamped over his teeth, something that seldom
happened, as if it cost him too much to make his harmless
face hard. Deek had girls up all the time . . . minks that
would never have looked twice at Ty in school or on the
street. Some were older than Ty or Deek, a few were
younger, but they all seemed practiced at doing anything
to, with, and for a dude except talking to him. Ty had
learned a lot about sex in the past few months but little
more about love than he already knew. Sex was something
that felt so good for a few minutes you could die happy
right there inside the silky wet lips of a cunt. But when it
was over, you had nothing left but a fast-fading memory
. . . maybe a lot like crack. You panted and sweated, searching for something right up until that last intense second,
but then there was only emptiness and the same sort of
something-wasted feeling he'd had when he was his little
brother's age and beat off in the bathroom. He'd been surprised at first to feel like that after "real" fucking; thinking
that maybe he just didn't know enough. But now he'd had
all the variations he wanted—including one night alone with
Deek when just for the hell of it they'd checked *that* stuff
out—and fucking was just something he did when he needed
to; better than beating off but nothing at all like he'd imagined love would be.

He'd thought about that a lot, mornings packing bottles,
and decided that love was what you gave and got from your
family. Sex didn't seem to have much to do with it. The
real mystery was how you could start a family of your own
to love and be loved by when all you got from the world
was hate or indifference.

Lately, Deek bought only one girl at a time. Ty got sloppy seconds. It didn't matter; he'd sit out on the fire escape and smoke Kools until it was his turn. Sometimes Deek liked to watch. Ty didn't give a shit about that either . . . it was only fucking, after all. Sometimes the girl would stay all night, and Ty would make her breakfast while Deek slept. A few seemed to think that was funny as hell. Those who talked then, and actually said something, just told the same stories of drugs or unwanted babies or busted-up families and running away that Ty had already heard a million times before. But most just figured they could score something extra, probably because Ty looked so stupidly dense at the stove in just his jeans, or padding his big bare feet across the worn-out linoleum to put plates on the table. The last girl to spend the night was one of Deek's bargains, picked up at the bus station. She seemed to have dropped three years off her "fifteen" in the slanting gold sunlight of morning. She'd run from Mississippi to the fabled "City of the Black," and Ty pictured her with her hair full of little bows in a gingham dress . . . whatever the hell that was. He'd given her the bus fare home and fifty dollars more. He often wondered if she'd gone.

Deek preferred to sleep alone. That meant with Ty beside him. Ty didn't mind that either. It was no different from sleeping with his brothers except for the gun beneath the pillow. After that one night when they'd tried boy stuff together, both had decided it wasn't worth the effort. But, more than once, Ty had wakened to find Deek holding tight to him in sleep.

Ty pushed open the door. "I not talkin to nobody, man. Just tellin you I gotta piss, that all."

Deek shook his head. "Yo! Them dudes gonna show anytime now. You stay. You my goddamn bodyguard, ain't ya? How it look?"

"You askin me, look goddamn stupid, your bodyguard wettin his pants. *That* how it look!"

"So? Stupid your thing, an you do it good. Piss here, you can't hold it. Ain't nobody around wanna see your black dick anyways."

Ty let out a sigh. He stood and pissed on the car's front tire. If Deek noticed, he pretended not to. Ty got back in and quietly forked scrambled eggs.

"Stop drinkin so goddamn much an you wouldn't gotta be pissin ever motherfuckin time you turn around," Deek advised. He studied the tall boy a moment and his golden eyes warmed a little. "Maybe you drinkin too much, Ty?"

Ty's lips had relaxed so his teeth showed again, but his own eyes stayed cool. "Gots a prob with that too?"

"No." Deek's tone hardened. "Long's you don't stay so drunk you can't do you job. Had me another body-guard . . ."

Ty sighed again. "I hear part of that story a'fore. So what happen him?"

Deek glanced at his clean pink fingernails. "Sucker got into shootin up. Stuff I don't sell. Guess he got hold of some bad shit one night. Cold stone dead on my goddamn floor. I drug his ass downstairs, load him in my trunk, drove out by the Bay, an dump him in the mud. Whole paragraph bout him three days later. Page six of the *Trib*, man."

"I do my job. Do it good. Just like you say."

Deek nodded. "Course you do, man." He smiled and slapped Ty's thin shoulder. "Fact is, I don't know what I do without ya."

The morning sun beat on the midnight-black car. Heat ghosts shimmered up from its sheet metal. Deek pulled off his shirt and went back to eating. Ty glanced at him, thinking of half-melted chocolate Easter bunnies, then poked at his own breakfast. Suddenly, Deek stiffened. "FUCK!"

Ty turned. "Now what I done?"

Deek shoved a Tater Tender under Ty's nose. "Check *this* shit!"

Ty had to cross his eyes to see. Then he grinned. "So? Ain't you never seen no little ole fly a'fore? Can't hurt you none. Already dead. Be thankful it ain't no rat turd. What my mom always say."

"Yeah, right! Musta been nuthin but nonstop terminal tee-hees growin up in your family! Like Little House in the Ghetto!"

Ty shrugged. "There some good times, spite all. Guess it don't take much for makin you happy when you little."

"Or stupid!" Deek flung the potato patty out the window, then carefully checked out the rest of the box before stuffing another in his mouth and muttering around it. "Least your folks *wanted* you." He swallowed, and added. "Even if you was a retard." He eyed the tall boy like he had the Tater Tenders. "You stink when you sweat, know that? An you sweat all the fuckin time, like now. An, if I been born with a face like yours, I shoot my ownself. Stop that goddamn smilin, asshole! Why you gotta go smilin all the goddamn time?"

Ty went on eating. "Easier'n not, I spose."

"My ass!" Deek glared at his food, then toward the restaurant. "You figure that dribble-lip cunt done it on purpose?"

"I think there a law 'gainst givin people unnatural stuff."

"Too funny, asshole!"

Ty munched a Tater Tender. "Naw, she not do that to you. Be ascared."

"What *that* sposed to mean, stupid?"

Ty shrugged again. "Mean what I mean it to mean, that all."

A dented Dodge van, over twenty years old and painted a streaky charcoal black with spray cans, humped into the lot and rattled to a stop beside the Trans-Am. Its brakes squealed and its engine dieseled on a few moments after the ignition cut, farting blue smoke before it finally died. Heat wavered out of the snaggle-toothed grille along with greenish wisps of antifreeze steam. Ty slipped his .45 out from under the Heineken sixer at his feet, flicked off the safety, and laid it on his leg. "Check me out. I doin my job. See?"

Deek scowled. "Oh, shut up, stupid!"

The van's driver was a muscle-bulked boy of about seventeen. Wrenching the outside handle, he shouldered open the door and slid out. He wore heavy old work boots, one torn toe showing bright steel, dirty Levi's, and a ragged T-shirt that used to be white and clung to the solid slabs of his chest and washboard belly like a coat of paint. He wore a satin black bandana around his head. Another boy, slimmer, but not much, clad the same but minus his shirt, stayed in the van and watched Ty watching him as the driver walked to Deek's side of the car. Both boys had Ty's gunmetal tone, though theirs seemed dusty and dull with the half-wild scruffiness of junkyard dogs. The driver stopped at Deek's window and offered a cautious grin: a guard dog in daylight who suspected a petting. He sniffed the air. "Breakfas time, huh? Lotta hungry folks these days." His voice was as solid as his body and seemed just as hard to keep leashed.

Deek's mouth was full, and he casually chewed and swallowed before snagging a box of Sherman browns off the dash. He fired one, then held out the box to the big dude. "TV say everthing only gettin better all the time."

The big boy carefully took a thin cigarette in his thick callused fingers. His forehead furrowed a little as he leaned in for the flame. "Cain't trus' nuthin they say, brother. We come up the coas', through this rich little town call Sanna Cruz. Seen people on the street holdin signs sayin they work jus fo food. WHITE people! Shit, you *know* thangs gotta be some bad when white folks start livin like niggers!" His eyes ran over Deek's rolly body with a curious kind of envy. "Course, you be doin all right fo yo'self, brother. *That* I seein wit my own eyes!"

Deek blew smoke. "Word. Well, now you dudes afford a Burger King breakfast too. Maybe."

The big boy stiffened slightly. His frown deepened. "What you sayin, 'maybe'?"

Ty held the .45 in his lap, his finger on the trigger. His eyes stayed steady on the other boy in the van. He could smell the dude at Deek's window, a rough mix of oil and leather and sweat that made him think of his dad for some reason. Except for the Night Train fumes. "Yo, brother," Ty called softly. "I like to see your hands, man. Both em, okay?"

The big boys exchanged glances over the car's roof, then the one in the van shrugged and kicked back in the seat, hands clasped comfortably behind his head. There might have been a hint of respect in his eyes.

Deek smiled. "Did you do one?"

Smoke snorted from the big boy's wide nostrils. He straightened, chest expanding. "Hey, man! You never say nuthin bout doin one! You . . . you never even say nuthin bout *hittin* one! Now, what you tellin me?"

Deek grinned, cute enough to cuddle. "Aw, chill out, big brother. It cool. You totally right. All I say was to give em another major-nasty full-auto drive-by. But, hell, I gotta make sure, don't I?" He spread his pink palms and his golden eyes scanned the big boy's smoldering ebony. "An you done it . . . didn't ya?"

The big boy dropped his hands to his hips. His deep voice went high. "Well, COURSE we done it, man! It like . . . like I give you my *word!* Bof clips this time! We *earn* our money!"

Deek looked hurt. "Did I say you didn't, man?"

The big boy looked confused. His hands slid to his sides. "No . . . no you dint." He searched the asphalt at his feet. "Folks jus talk dif'rent here, that all it is. Half time you never know if they sayin what they meanin."

Deek grinned again. His chubby brown hand touched the hard black of the big boy's forearm. "Yo, it all cool, brother. Word." He took two Heinekens from between Ty's feet and pressed them into the big boy's hand. "Here, man. An for your homey too."

Ty watched the other boy, who was looking as confused as the first one had sounded. Ty had the picture in his mind; the first dude would be standing with the bottles in one hand and the cigarette in the other. Ty heard the rip of Velcro as Deek pulled a roll of bills from his belt pouch. Deek would hand the big boy a fifty. Holding money out in the open usually freaked anybody a little, and the dude would have to stick the Sherman in his mouth to pocket the half-buck. The smoke would probably water his eyes. Deek was MC Control in these situations, though why he was bothering to run the whole number on these dudes, Ty couldn't figure . . . unless it was just to keep in practice. Ty almost felt sorry for the big boys.

Deek had spotted them a few days before, about sundown, standing by their van, which was dead in the street with a flat front tire. Both boys had worn helpless expressions, saying they knew their spare was flat and there was no one to call. Deek had offered them a ride to a gas station. Their faces had lit with stunned hope and wonder at the glistening ebony dream coming to their rescue. Ty had casually checked out the van while the dudes were getting in each other's way in their rush to take off the wheel. The tangled blankets in back, scattered work clothes, soup cans, and the smell of unwashed males and dirty socks said it all. Eager as puppies in the Trans-Am's back seat, they'd started bragging about their new Uzis before a block had rolled by. Deek had scored them a room and gotten them flat puking drunk that night while Ty had gone through all their things and confirmed the Uzis. They were semis converted with mail-order parts: the select-fire switches had three positions but only the letters S and F. The clips were the standard 32s, though Ty was surprised that these sort of dudes coming to the "big city" wouldn't have brought along the bigger 50s. But then they were probably low on cash after scoring the guns.

"Uh," said the big boy, pulling the cigarette from his lips and wiping his eyes. "Thanks, brother. I, uh, spose you ain't gonna be needin us no more?"

Deek killed his bottle, slipped it back into the sixer, and patted his belly with a satisfied sigh. "Mmm. You brothers gonna be hangin town a while?"

The big boy nodded hard. "Sho. This kinda work what we come fo."

Deek twisted a finger in his neck chain, the gold clicking softly. "Mmm. Well, I might gots another job you could do . . . Same thing, dif'rent kids."

The big boy grinned, again nodding hard. "Sho, man! Sho! We do it, best believe!" He suddenly looked shy. "We wuz lookin at some cars a while ago. Cool ones. Course, nuthin in this here class." His grin widened. "Maaaan, you sho nuff got some foxes in this here town!"

"They cost."

"I hear that, brother! Course, what don't?"

Deek snickered. "An I hear that." He reached to the console and picked up a Polaroid picture. It was a trifle fuzzy, but showed five boys practicing curb moves on skateboards. He handed it to the big dude. "Them. Today. Same street, but about four blocks east. They get outa school round three-thirty an always ride together. Pick your own place, you wanna, but they usually cut behind one block that mostly truck shops an stuff an fuck around for a while like they doin in the pitcher."

The big boy studied the snapshot. "Sho!" He walked quickly back to the van and handed the picture and bottles to the other boy, then bent and looked past Ty to Deek. "Uh . . . you be wantin us to *do* one?"

Deek sighed out smoke with a patient sound. "Accidents happen. But no more'n one, hear me? Bunch of dead kids no good to nobody. I get the money to you back in your room tonight." He grinned. "Course, you trust me, man?"

"Sho we do, brother! Hell, you been nuthin but good to us!" The big boy hesitated, his forehead creasing again. "Jus . . . well, we jus figure this kinda stuff pay mo better, y'know? Special when *this* happen." He pointed to a little hole just behind the doorframe. "What I sayin is, you never tole us them little ole kids got guns! You spect these here little shits got em too? I mean . . . well, like I sayin, you coulda tole us . . ."

Deek choked on Sherman smoke. His voice broke. "*Told* ya!" he squeaked. "TOLD ya!" He kicked open the door and stomped around to the big boy, his belly bobbing. He jammed a chubby finger against a chest like armor plate. The big dude stepped back a pace. The top of Deek's head came about level with the big boy's chin. Deek leaned back and glared upward. "Where the fuck you comin from, nigger?"

"Uh . . . Bakersfield."

Deek looked blank for a second, then laughed. "Shit! Well, what they do down there anyways, grow motherfuckin *cotton* or somethin? Jesus Christ, boy, listen up! MOST little shits in this town got guns, so don't you come bitchin to me bout some snot-nose seventh-grader poppin your ass with a wimpy .22! Shit! I could get this done for half what I payin you . . . for a goddamn dime bag of rock if I want some other little snot to do it! Get real or die, sucker!"

Deek spun on his heel and stalked back to the car. "I get the buck to your room tonight," he shot over his shoulder, then added a grin across the car's roof. "Twenty fuckin dollars do *both* you dudes. Little kids work cheap. 'Member that!"

"Bakers-fuckin-field!" snorted Deek, watching in the mirror as the van pulled into the street and chugged away, trailing smoke.

Ty thumbed on the .45's safety and took another swallow of beer. "Mmm. Matter of fact my mom tell me one time they do grow cotton down there."

Deek shrugged, firing the engine with a roar. "Times I figure *you* be happy in a cotton field, stupid."

"Yo! Touch my tee an die!" squalled Ric, dancing away from Gordon.

"Can't touch this neither!" snickered Rac, in step with his brother.

Gordon gave the garbage-glopped gun and the twins a pair of equally disgusted glances, then crooked a finger at Curtis. "Gimme yours, man. You ain't wearin it anyways."

"Hey!" squeaked Curtis, sidling behind Lyon. "Not fair! All kinda shit already happen to me this goddamn mornin!"

Gordon flicked slime from his hands. "Sure it fair, sucker. Wasn't for you an your goddamn back them cops wouldn't of slapped us around so much. Now, give!"

Curtis clung to Lyon's hand, peering hopefully up at the slender boy. "Yo, do I gotta, man?"

Lyon slipped an arm around Curtis in a quick hug. "Well, it gonna need washin anyhow. Then your mom gots to sew it." He grinned. "Sides, callin that sucker a pussy clot not be helpin us one helluva lot. Make for Gordon takin your heat, what it is."

"But it was a cool thing to say anyways," said Rac.

"Word!" added Ric. "Way cool! One to ten, that be a eight. Believe!"

"An takin heat be Gordon's job," finished Rac. "Word by rules!"

Lyon squeezed Curtis' shoulder. "Seem like all dogshit takin be poor Gordon's job sometimes. Aw, let him use it, Curtis. We just might be needin our gun again pretty soon. Never know."

Curtis untied the T-shirt from around his waist and tossed it to Gordon. "Pussy clot," he whispered, twining his fingers in Lyon's.

Gordon sighed. "I heard that." He wiped off the pistol and spat. "Life ain't nuthin but a goddamn Popsicle course."

"Obstacle course," said Lyon.

"Whatever."

Meantime, the twins were ranging farther up the alley, poking into dumpsters and cans like a mongoose team on *Wild Kingdom.* They weren't so much looking for something as just not able to stand the thought of missing anything. Suddenly Rac stiffened, rising on tiptoes and peering intently over a dumpster toward the alley's far end. Ric instantly joined him, then both turned and beckoned to the other boys. "Yo, Gordy!" hissed Rac, finger to his lips.

Carrying their boards, Gordon, Curtis, and Lyon ran to the twins, all taking cover behind the dumpster. Ric pointed. "Yo! Check this out!"

Morning shade still filled the alleyway, but silhouetted against the sunlit street at the opposite end were the figures of two boys. The smaller was backed against the wall while the other, bigger, made jabbing motions at him with a gun. The smaller boy squatted. It looked like he was untying his shoes.

Lyon leaned across the dumpster lid, straining forward, his eyes narrowed to bright black slits. "The little dude be Marcus Tibbet. Third-grader. Live in my buildin. Never seen the other, but he not wearin Crew colors, nor nobody else's look like, neither."

"I can see that much!" growled Gordon. "An I don't give a shit if he *was* somebody! He in our ground now. By rules, his ass ours! So, what kinda gun? An I already check it chrome-plated."

"Prob'ly nickel."

"Whatever."

"Um?" whispered Ric. "You mean, like money nickel?"

Rac poked him. "Shut the fuck up, doofus!"

"*Both* you shut the fuck up, goddamnit!" hissed Gordon.

"Mmm," murmured Lyon. "Some kind small 'volver. Like the pawnshop man be callin a lady's gun."

Gordon gave a short nod. "Yeah? Well, bullets still come outa them little holes fast enough for dirt-nap time."

"Dude look nervous as a bitch cat havin a litter," said Lyon. "Check how he keep on lookin out at the street."

Curtis pressed against Lyon. "Yo, maybe he gots him a watcher out there?"

"Naw," said Gordon. "Then he not need to keep checkin for himself." Gordon considered a moment, then shed his backpack. "Okay! We gonna take him! Leave all your boards an shit here. Spread wide. Get busy!"

With Gordon leading, gun up and ready, the boys fanned out among the rows of cans and dumpsters. They darted silently up the alley, each checking for places to hide as they ran. As Lyon had said, the bigger boy with the gun was splitting his attention between the smaller kid and the street entrance. It was the little boy, Marcus, who first noticed the Friends coming. Instead of staying cool, he just stared stupidly.

The big boy, tall and lean but no older than Gordon, saw where Marcus was looking. He spun around, his eyes first widening in surprise, then slitting as he tried to aim at all five running shadows at once. By then Gordon was only about a hundred feet away, and dove behind a dumpster, then leaped up and aimed his own gun two-handed the way cops did. The other boys scattered for cover. Orange flame spat from the muzzle of the tall boy's gun. An instant later came the sound, a flat crack echoing between the alley walls and the thunk of the bullet denting the dumpster. Gordon's .22 popped no louder than a cherry bomb. Twice. One shot flew wild into the street beyond, barely missing a beer truck and pocking a building on the far side. The second tore into the tall boy's thigh.

He screamed and crumpled to the pavement as if he'd been hit in the heart. His gun clattered on the concrete as he cried and clutched at his leg with both hands while curling into a ball. The Friends were on him in seconds, the twins grabbing his arms, Lyon and Curtis a leg each. The boy screamed again as he was jerked flat on his back. He howled and twisted until Gordon jammed the .22's muzzle against his forehead. "Shut up, sucker! Or you dead! Word!"

The boy's eyes crossed for a second as he stared at the gun. Then he went limp as laundry. The twins began dragging him into the shadow of a doorway. He only whimpered now. Tears ran down his cheeks. A ruby stain spread slowly on his faded jeans over the bullet hole. Lyon picked up the small shiny revolver and checked it out carefully. Curtis danced here and there, trying to help the twins but mostly getting in the way. Gordon finally grabbed his arm. "Yo! Watch the street!" Curtis darted for the alley mouth.

Ric and Rac had the tall boy pinned against a steel-plated door, his legs sprawled out on the pavement while they held his arms. The bloodstain was still spreading, but not very fast. Gordon yanked up his jeans, which were slipping low from the run, then walked over and put the pistol to the boy's head again. "You keep shut up, sucker! I get back to you!" He handed the gun to Rac, who immediately stuck the muzzle into the boy's ear.

Gordon went across to Marcus, who still squatted wide-eyed, crying harder than the boy who'd been shot. His fingers seemed frozen to his shoelaces. He wore an old Hammertime tee, purple shorts, and brand-new Cons. He started to blubber as Gordon and Lyon stared down at him. His voice came out high and squeaky. "Fucker tryin to steal my goddamn SHOES, Gordon! Say he gonna kill me if I not give em him!"

Gordon was still panting from the run. He yanked at his jeans again and wiped sweat from his face. Across the alley the tall boy started to moan. Marcus slumped against the wall, pulled up his knees, buried his head between, and choked and sobbed. Lyon broke open the revolver and flashed it to Gordon: there were only three cartridges in the cylinder counting the one already fired, and all were green with age. Gordon shrugged, then half turned to the tall boy. "I tellin you to shut up, sucker!"

"Jesus, man, it fuckin HURTS! I gonna bleed to death here!"

Gordon scowled. "You hear me, asshole? Second warnin's for good cops an bad movies! Lyon! Go an check him out."

Lyon went to the boy and crouched beside him. He snapped the gun shut, spun the cylinder to a live round, and gave it to Ric. Ric poked the muzzle into the boy's other ear. The dude went still, clenching his teeth and squeezing his eyes tight shut. Lyon bent close and studied his thigh. Long delicate fingers probed. The boy whimpered again but kept his eyes closed. Then Lyon rocked back on his heels, wiped his fingers on the cuff of the boy's jeans, and crossed his arms on his knees. He studied the tall kid, then asked, "Yo. Gots a name, man?"

The boy's eyes opened, narrowly."Keeja."

Lyon's smile flickered. "We all be just regular niggers here, man. Your slave name be cool."

The boy studied Lyon, then closed his eyes once more. "Justin."

"Mmm. Well, Justin, fact is, I seen dudes hurt worse eatin shit off their boards. Shit, I prob'ly pick that little ole bullet out with my fingers, cept you scream an scare everbody. You live, whatever that worth . . . longs you stay shut up. Word."

Gordon was just standing and staring down at the little boy, looking partly pissed but mostly confused. Lyon returned to kneel beside the crying kid and lay a gentle hand on a small quivering shoulder. "Yo. Marcus-homey. Chill it, man. You be okay, so stop all that baby-ass shit. Nobody got no time for it."

Gordon squatted with a grunt and lifted the little boy's chin. "Hear Lyon-o, man? Chill out. *Now*. What the fuck good cryin gonna do ya? Wipe your goddamn face an get you ass up out that garbage. You a *man* goddammit, act like one!" He glanced at the boy's new shoes, big as moon boots. "Cocksuckin eighty-dollar Cons! What in hell you spect to happen? That sucker run em past some used-clothes place an score him enough for a bag an a half."

Lyon helped Marcus to his feet, sniffling and choking, snot shiny on his lip. "My mom just give em me yesterday. My goddamn *birthday*, Gordy!"

"Don't call . . . Oh shit! What the fuck *that* got to do with nuthin?" Gordon roared. "Figure the world give a shit cause your mom love you an it your motherfuckin birthday? Yo! Maybe your mom don't know what is . . . but you goddamn well do!" Grabbing the little boy's shoulders, Gordon shook him like a flour bag full of chicken parts. "NOW STOP THAT CRYIN OR I WHACK YOU UPSIDE THE HEAD!"

Marcus quieted. He stared up at Gordon and wiped his eyes with savage swipes. He puffed his little chest. "I cool, man!"

Lyon smiled and high-fived the boy. "Course you be, man. Way past cool."

Gordon crossed his arms over his chest and nodded. "Mmm. That more better. Ain't no boys in this hood. Spose you know it gonna cost ya? Rules don't come for free."

Marcus sniffled a few more times, but dug in his pocket. "Gots . . . um . . ." He counted in his little palm. "Two dollars an . . . um . . . forty-seven cents. That enough, man? I can sco' some more tomorrow."

Gordon took the money and shoved it in his jeans. "Yeah. You covered, man." He glanced over his shoulder. "We runnin a special on assholes today."

Marcus followed Gordon's eyes. "Yo! You gonna do that sucker, Gordy? Shit, I pay extra to see that, man. Word! I seen a dead kid once, but I never seen nobody get iced!"

Gordon frowned. "Ain't nuthin cool bout killin somebody, stupid. An don't call me Gordy! You pay for rules, rules 'tect ya. Nuff said! Anyways, why ain't you in school?"

"Oh, I wuz just goin. What it is, my mom take me to the doctor this mornin. Got me a ear affection. Wanna see my excuse?"

"No. Get cruisin. An keep your mouth shut, hear me?"

The little boy nodded hard. "Word up, Gordon! Straight! I cool!"

Lyon led the kid to the alley entrance. "Yo, Marcus-man. Rub some dirt over them shoes. Soon's you can."

"Oh, shit, Lyon! My mom have a total cow!"

Lyon nudged Marcus up the sidewalk, exchanging glances with Curtis, who stood at a corner wall. "Listen up! You be figurin your mom wanna see you wearin a little dirt, or nappin in a whole lot? Cool dudes use their minds, man. Stay alive. Now get your butt off to school."

Marcus hunched his shoulders and started up the street. "Okay, Lyon. But I *still* hope you waste that mother-fucker!"

Lyon gave Curtis a shrug, then returned to the alley. Gordon was squatting in front of Justin, between his sprawled legs. There was blood smell in the air, but the stain on Justin's jeans wasn't much bigger. Flies circled hopefully. Justin's long-muscled body had that hollowed gauntness of never having enough to eat. His plain white tee, jeans, and Nikes were ragged and dirty, and his un-tended hair was matted. He was sweating even though the morning was still cool, and his scent was strong and sour. His teeth were still clenched and he breathed through them in shallow sips. His half-open eyes were dull and hopeless.

Gordon checked the boy's earlobes; the left was pierced but hadn't had a ring in it for a long time. There were no holes in his arms, but Gordon spread his unresisting fingers and found burns. In Justin's pockets were only a pipe and a switchblade and eighty cents. Gordon shoved the coins in his own pocket, and checked out the knife, which was better than his own had been.

Justin's voice sounded the way his eyes looked. "Please don't kill me. I dint know this was anybody's ground. Swear to God. Let me go. I never come back here. Please."

Gordon snorted."Shit! You sayin you never seen our marks?"

Justin's eyes lifted slightly to search Gordon's face. "Swear to God I dint, man! I only seen where the Crew's ground end. That all!"

"He lyin," said Ric in a cheerful tone. He twisted the gun a little.

"Like a motherfuckin doggie," added Rac, poking his gun deeper into Justin's ear.

Justin winced, and his eyes dropped to stare at nothing.

"Keeja."

Justin looked up at Lyon.

"One time you had pride, man," the slender boy said. "An a heart." Then he shrugged. "Don't tell me the story. I hear it all a'fore."

Gordon bent forward and slipped the knife blade into Justin's left nostril. "Member what I say bout second warnins? Real time mostly give you none. This here your first, last, an onliest!" He flicked the blade, slicing a quarter-inch slit in the boy's nose. Justin's body went steel-hard for an instant but he stayed quiet. Blood trickled over his lips to spatter his chest.

"That mind you we gots us rules here," said Gordon. He rose and turned to Lyon. "Figure he walk?"

"Hurt like hell, your bullet in there, but he walk he be wantin to bad enough."

Gordon studied the knife again, then sighed and dropped

it between Justin's legs. "You hear? You walk! You get your crack-ass the fuck out our hood!"

Gordon stepped back. The twins hauled Justin to his feet. He yelped and clutched his thigh as weight came on his leg, and would have fallen but for Gordon grabbing him. "Ahhhuuuggg!" he squalled. "I can FEEL it in there! I CAN'T walk, man!"

The twins moved back, their guns still pointed. Justin's face seemed to melt into that of a lost little kid. He slumped against Gordon, tears and blood dripping down Gordon's shirt. "What I do, man?" he sobbed. "Got no home. Nobody give a shit! Now I shot! I don't wanna die, man!" He buried his face on Gordon's broad shoulder.

Gordon's forehead creased. His hand drifted to Justin's back and made a few pats. The twins looked uncertain as they held their guns, flicking tawny glances at Lyon. Curtis peered around the corner. Lyon picked up the knife and slipped it into Justin's pocket. "You shoot us first, member?"

Justin kept his face hidden on Gordon's shoulder. "But it *hurts*!" Then he jerked up his head and stared at Lyon. "Make it stop, man! Take it out! Please! I hear you say you could."

The twins' eyes widened and locked on Lyon. Their guns now pointed at the pavement. Gordon shifted uneasily, his hand still wanting to pat Justin's back. "Um, can you, Lyon? I mean, if that what he really want?"

Lyon scanned Justin's eyes. "Mmm. It gonna hurt, man. More'n you ever dream. Listen up. There be a kid-center place three blocks over an bout four east. They not no Boys'an Girls' Club or nuthin. Not ask no stupid questions, nor tell no cops neither. They fix you. Feed you. Help you get clean, but only if you really want."

"But I can't *walk*, man!" Justin's eyes hardened. "What your motherfuckin rules say over *that*, sucker? Say, leave me here to die? Say call the cops to kick me, put their dogs to bite me, then lock me up cause I got no home? Nobody *want* black kids, man! I been there! The places they put you, even you ain't done nuthin, be just like prison, man! You locked in! Gimmie a chance, man! Take it out. PLEASE!"

Lyon looked into Justin's eyes a moment more, then nodded. He pulled the blade from Justin's pocket, flipped it open, and tested the edge on his thumb. "Kay, man. But I warn ya." He pointed. "Ric, Rac! Take him back in the doorway. Hold him like you was. Curtis-homey! Yo! Come take a leg here. Gordon, you take the other one. Hold him tight."

Quickly, the boys took their positions, pinning Justin against the rusty steel door again. Lyon was moves, wasting no time. Kneeling, he sliced Justin's jeans open over the wound. Justin watched, his thin chest heaving, but there were no more tears. Lyon nodded to himself, then wiped the blade and his fingers on his shirttail. His eyes lifted to Justin's. "You sure, brother?"

Justin squeezed his eyes shut. "Just do it!"

"Um?" asked Curtis. "Maybe we should give him a bullet to bite on?"

"Don't be a goddamn fool!" muttered Lyon. He sucked a breath, then his long slender fingers moved fast. The blade flashed. Justin screamed once, but the other boys held him down. Lyon's quiet voice cut the silence that followed. "Game over."

Justin's eyes fluttered open. He stared at Lyon's bloody fingers and the little chunk of ruby-dripping lead they held.

"Want it, man?" asked Lyon.

Justin's eyes closed. "No."

Lyon shrugged and flipped the bullet toward the alley mouth. Rac patted Justin's shoulder. "You got balls, man. That musta hurt." Ric nodded. "Yeah, Justin, you musta been a pretty cool dude one time."

"You gots a good heart, man," said Lyon. "Be listenin to it more." Stripping off his shirt, Lyon tied it tight around Justin's thigh. Ric and Rac helped the boy to his feet. He tried his leg, winced, but nodded to Lyon. "Um, thanks, man. Three blocks back an four east, you was sayin?"

"Word . . . Keeja." Lyon folded the knife and handed it to the boy.

Justin limped toward the alley entrance. He stopped, bent painfully down and picked up the bloody little bullet, then slipped it into his pocket before going on.

Gordon gripped Lyon's slim shoulder as if it were something fragile and easily broken. "What he callin himself, that African name? It don't change nuthin."

Lyon shook his head. "No. It don't. Sometimes bad be sad."

Gordon sighed. "Times I don't unnerstand you at all, Lyon."

Curtis moved to Lyon and shyly slipped an arm around his slender waist. "That cause he magic. Ain't sposed to unnerstand magic shit, just believe an get your ass out the way an let it work!"

Rac made smacking sounds with his lips. "Aw, kiss him, why doncha, Curtis!"

"Word!" added Ric. "We all *know* you wanna!"

"Assholes!" bawled Gordon. "Shut the fuck up an gimme them goddamn guns fore you go an shoot yourselfs in THE brain!" He snatched both guns from the twins.

Ric shrugged. "Well, leastways we score ourselfs a new bang-bang, huh?"

"Yeah," said Rac. "So what kind is it, Lyon-o?"

Lyon took the revolver from Gordon and peered closely at the tiny letters. "Iver Johnson. What ole people call a Sat'day-night special. Top catch, see? Obsolete. Can't say how big . . . maybe a .34 or 37.50 or somethin else they ain't made in a million years. Prob'ly be a pain in the butt findin bullets for it . . . why Justin only packin three." He glanced at Gordon. "Maybe the pawnshop man tell us more when we go by for scorin them .22 bullets."

Gordon frowned and shoved the automatic back in his jeans. "Ain't s'prised. If that sucker had him a decent gun he'd prob'ly sold it to buy more rock." He considered. "Well, we gots but two shots left in the .22, an deuce more in that Ivy-Jackson thing. Maybe we better go by an see the pawn man fore we take Curtis home. Case more shit happen. Shit come in piles, y'know? Might be a cool idea to re-up our marks too. I gots some paint, home."

"But we hungry, goddamnit!" squalled the twins.

"An Curtis here still be bleedin some," added Lyon.

Shaking his head, Gordon started back down the alley. Lyon moved to follow but the twins barred his way.

"Yo! So who get to carry the nickel gun now?" demanded Rac. "The Ivory-Jason?"

"Yeah," said Ric. "You gots your magic, don't need no gun. Give it me!"

"No, ME," yelled Rac, shoving his brother. "I say so first!"

Lyon smiled his V and handed the revolver to Curtis. The small boy made a face at the twins and slipped the gun carefully into his jeans, like Gordon. "It a Iver Johnson. An both you be pussy clots. So *there!*" He and Lyon walked together after Gordon, Curtis with his little chest puffed, and strutting. Ric and Rac stomped along behind; they didn't weigh much and it was hard for them to stomp loud enough to be noticed.

"Dint want the motherfuckin thing anyways!" muttered Rac. "Goddamn wienie-dude gun, all that is!"

"Yeah!" agreed his brother. "Bozo-leted Ichy-whatsis!"

"Um?" Curtis murmured to Lyon. "Gordon way past cool shot, huh? For to just hit the dude in the leg like that. Just like a movie, huh, Lyon?"

Lyon let out a soft snicker. "Gordon be lucky he hit him anywheres. Almost do a beer truck, case you didn't see."

"Oh yeah. But what if he accident'ly kill the dude?"

Lyon shrugged. "Justin be tryin to do Gordon, weren't he? Sides, what is, is. What ain't, ain't worth nuthin. Magic always do the right thing. Believe."

Back at the other end of the alley the boys picked up their school things, shouldered packs, and decked their boards, then rolled in file down the block once more. There were more cars moving in the street now, and people on the sidewalks. As always, a siren sounded somewhere in the distance, and the faint jangle of a burglar-alarm bell carried from blocks away. The Friends skated casually, weaving around people, dodging the legs of wineheads and zoners sticking from doorways, eyed occasionally by other kids but generally ignored by adults as if they didn't exist at all. They reached Gordon's block and were almost to the steps of his building when the fat boy cut suddenly into the deep-set doorway of a burned-out storefront. The other boys followed instantly, tailing and peering with Gordon down the street. A gleaming black Trans-Am was curbed on the opposite side. A cop cruiser was double-parked behind it, strobes firing.

Gordon laughed. "Yo! Them's the same two cocksuckers slapped us around! Let's check how Deek sucker like bein treated niggerboy style! Maaan, he always got shit in that car . . . everbody know! Maybe them cops do some actual good . . . bust his ass fore he kill somebody else!"

"Mmm," murmured Lyon. "Maybe, one time, we see the law work."

"Wish I had me a camera," said Curtis.

Ty was thinking about going home for supper; he could stop at a market and buy as many groceries as he could carry . . . maybe a pack of Popsicles for the kids. His brother Danny wanted a new pair of Nikes, the major-buck kind. Ty wondered what his size was now . . . the little dude was growing so fast. Then Ty saw Deek's eyes flick up to the mirror.

"Shit!" Deek muttered.

Ty glanced in the outside mirror in time to see the cruiser light its strobes, remembering Danny calling it "popping cherries." The .45 was in Ty's lap, along with a half-empty Heineken. He slipped the bottle back into the sixer, laid the gun on top, and covered all with Deek's T-shirt. Deek's face had paled slightly as he swung the car to the curb and stopped. Ty noticed that he cut the front wheels back out again and left the engine running with his foot on the clutch. Maybe it was the beer, but Ty felt cool, even though the Trans-Am's trunk packed mega trouble. Deek was a good driver, and the 'Am had twice the acceleration, cornering grip, and top speed of any city cop car. It was also registered to a blind post-box number. Ty knew Deek wouldn't hesitate a second to abandon it if he had to. The chase might even be fun . . . like an Eddie Murphy movie. The picture of Deek bailing his jiggly lard across some trash-choked vacant lot almost brought a smile to Ty's lips. But then Deek gave a snort of disgust.

"It just *them* suckers! Shit! Hard to believe it been a week already, huh?"

Ty shrugged. "Time warp fast when you havin fun, I spose." He glanced in the mirror again, seeing the white cop waiting in the car. The man's face behind his chrome glasses wore the same sly, shit-eating expression that Danny had put on the day Ty had caught him shoplifting in Pay Less Drugs . . . a goddamn Speak 'N Spell, of all the stupid things to steal! Ty had bought it for him anyway.

The black cop ambled up to Deek's window. Deek ripped open his belt pouch and dug out five hundred-dollar bills. A few people on the sidewalk had slowed their pace as they passed, watching the scene with eyes that were curious, hopeful, or hostile. But Deek's chubby fingers moved fast, hidden between his legs, as he folded the bills and sandwiched them into the Trans-Am's papers.

The big cop leaned casually against the car, his voice pitched to sound routinely bored, but loud enough for the people on the curb to hear. "License, registration, and proof of insurance, please."

The sidewalk people moved on, one or two looking disappointed. A bag lady with a cartful of cans and crap stayed, but she hardly counted as human. Wordlessly, Deek handed the stuff to the man.

Ty's gaze drifted across the street to the burned-out

building. He'd seen the skate kids cut in to the doorway, and watched them now as they peered from the shadows behind broken window glass. Ty didn't know much about them . . . just another young dogshit hood gang. The big fat boy was the leader, though he didn't look too bright and it was a miracle he could ride at all. The twins were born followers, hyper to the max and probably a bitch to keep under control, but they'd be fearless and loyal to whoever they respected. There was the small kid with his childlike potbelly and long, tangled dreads: maybe half white, judging by his features and the yellow-brown tones in his hair, and no doubt the mascot who took all the shit and got the dirtiest jobs. Both he and the tall, slender boy were shirtless, and all were cutting school. Ty couldn't blame them much; it had probably been one hell of a morning. Ty tried to get a better look at the slim graceful boy with the big puppy feet and the loose, pawlike hands. For some reason Ty had always been curious about him; it was strange how hard it seemed to see him clearly. Like a ghost in a movie, he never appeared as solid and real as the other boys. Ty sometimes wondered if his pure blackness could somehow shimmer the air around him like heat waves from asphalt. He couldn't really be called girlish, yet was almost more pretty than handsome, and, without a shirt, looked too delicate and fragile to survive in this neighborhood. Of course, the other gang members would protect him. Ty frowned slightly: some boys that age would use a pretty dude until they got the facts of life straight. But Ty didn't think that was happening here. The fat kid might lead, but the slender boy hovered ever at his elbow, and Ty suspected he was the one really in control.

Ty smiled a little, recalling how blown-away those two big boys had been that these kids had shot back. He could guess the gang's thoughts as they peered from behind glass fangs; they would be figuring that the cop had gone back to his car to run Deek's license. They'd be hoping that the 'Am would get searched, found full of rock, and that he and Deek would be slapped around, maybe whacked a few times with the cops' clubs, then handcuffed and hauled away forever. Ty knew this because when he was their age he'd have prayed for the same. He suddenly wanted another beer, but fired one of Deek's Shermans instead and ignored the wistful look the bag lady gave him. One hand strayed to the little medallion on his chest.

Ty closed his eyes, sucking smoke deep and holding it. He remembered back to when Deek was first scheming him out as a bodyguard. They'd been cruising in the 'Am, just sipping beer and listening to some old Rick James on the CD, when these cops had pulled them over. Till then, Ty wasn't sure about taking the job, as if some small part of him, only half real like a ghost, still stood on the sidewalk clutching his scarred old skateboard and watching the gleaming car pass him by. But seeing Deek casually slip money to the cop, Ty had felt something crumble inside him, and the hungry young ghost on the curb had faded forever.

Now he gazed over at the other young boys and felt only a worn-out sort of sorrow . . . like finding a favorite T-shirt after losing it for months only to discover it just wouldn't fit anymore. In a way those kids were a kind of last defense. Ty felt sympathy, knowing that what they were fighting was so huge and powerful and so far beyond their understanding that they might as well have been trying to stop a tank with BB guns.

Ty himself didn't understand much more, except that there *was* something, and he figured whatever that something was for sure didn't want to be understood. He'd seen a TV special once about the Great Pyramids, and that's how he visualized it: he and Deek were just a couple of bricks on the bottom. On the next level up was the older black dude with the Mercedes and Afro-yuppie suit who Deek scored from about once a week. Above that was only a rumor of a white man uptown. And beyond that the pyramid towered into the clouds and Ty could only imagine what might be hidden up there. Lying awake at night, Ty tried to forget what the pyramid was built on—enough to know what it was made from; power and money and greed. Its cement was probably hate and fear and hopelessness. Ty always pictured the bottom bricks as black.

To Ty, these cops were on no higher a level than his own . . . more likely one row down. Under them were the kids who sold for Deek in the parks and streets and schools. There were about thirty at any time, though the exact number changed almost daily as new ones came in and others got out. Some were busted . . . usually the new ones and often in their first week. Others just quit, and a few just stopped . . . or, as that old anti-smoking commercial on TV went, *actually, technically, they died.* Below them were the kids who dealt only to use. Math had never been easy for Ty, but he figured a conservative estimate of 30 × 5 for them. They just *stopped* a lot, more often at the hands of their own burned customers than what they put into their own bodies. And the foundation for the whole structure was the kids who crouched in doorways or stairwells with their pipes and papers and points, begging on the streets for money to "get something to eat," fucking it for the kids who were really starving and *had* to beg, and breaking into cars and apartments and preying on all those younger or weaker . . . or alone.

Without friends.

Ty smoked and watched the boys, thinking how funny it was that everybody outside places like this should be so stupidly amazed that kids wanted guns and banded together in gangs. What in hell else were they supposed to do, go it alone and get picked off one by one? Trouble was, gangs, like individuals, could be bought and used by those smarter and more powerful.

Ty frowned and idly fingered his medallion. Like now. Like those kids over there had no idea how Deek was fitting them into the pyramid . . . the one that was black on the bottom but white on the top.

Ty flipped his half-smoked cigarette out the window, watching as the bag lady scrambled for it. Hell, he thought, didn't those kids watch anything on TV but cartoons? For sure, the facts and figures on the news were mostly lies, but after a while you could *see* them! If you paid attention. If you didn't fuck up your mind. It was plain as dogshit on the sidewalk that if you were rich and white and got caught doing drugs you had a *dependency problem.* You went on TV and told everybody how sorry you were and checked into a place for rich fuckups. A poor black kid with burns on his fingers got dragged into an alley by the cops and beat to a pulp before being hauled off to jail. When are you ever gonna get real, little brothers!

The cop came back to Ty's window and handed him the papers without a word. His face was expressionless behind his chrome mirrors. Ty could see Deek's reflection in silver. It was funny how a dead expression was also a childlike one. Deek said nothing; there was nothing to say that wouldn't have been an even bigger joke. Deek let out the clutch and swung the car away from the curb, not bothering to signal because the cop car stood guard for him.

Ty studied the gang boys as the Trans-Am purred past. Four faces showed sullen hatred for what they couldn't understand. Ty knew the feeling well. It was what would eventually cement them into the pyramid after they were beaten down by banging their heads against it for a few more years. Ty had seen that look in so many eyes for the last few months that he hardly noticed it anymore, even though he knew that, given half a chance, those kids wouldn't waste a second killing Deek and himself on the spot. But there was something different in the fifth face: the fragile features of the slender boy. Maybe it was the shadows, or the way he always seemed so hard to see. It made Ty uneasy.

Deek saw where Ty was looking. His foot came off the gas and his eyes flicked to the mirror as the cruiser made a squeaky U-turn and dwindled down the block.

"Yo, stupid! How come you never say nuthin? Shit, this's *perfect!*"

Ty shrugged. He picked up his beer and chugged it while Deek cut the car across the street and pulled to the curb, facing the wrong way, directly in front of the gang. Ty could feel the tenseness of the younger boys, trapped as they were in the doorway. He snagged the .45 and flicked off the safety as the fat one reached behind his half-bare butt and the others automatically spread out as wide as they could between the walls. The hate was still there, maybe tempered a little by fear, but the fat boy's jaw was set and the twins' tawny eyes like frozen gold. Only the smallest kid looked uncertain. He pressed against the slender boy, who just seemed to watch with no expression at all. Ty caught a flash of something silver passed from the small kid to the older one, whose long, loose paw closed over it. Ty gave the block a quick checkout; traffic was light, and the cops wouldn't be back. Most people on the sidewalk, at least those under forty who had more than Jell-O for brains, seemed to have found some excuse to cross over to the other side of the street. Only an old lady with a grocery bag walked obliviously between the car and the doorway. Ty slipped out fast and stood, his door left half open while he leaned against the car. His big hands were clasped casually on the roof, cradling the pistol so the boys could see what is. He didn't exactly point it at them, just close enough to signify. Ty knew about their .22, but the silver glint in the slender boy's paw bothered him. He wished that Deek had given him time to snag the short-barreled Uzi carbine from the back seat. Even drunk or stoned Deek was no fool, and he hadn't lived to sixteen by taking these kinds of stupid chances. Ty supposed, as always, he had a reason.

Despite the Heinekens, Ty's senses were sharp, aware of the street life around him. The sparse traffic, both ways, would slow momentarily until the drivers read the word, then speed up to get past. On the opposite sidewalk people were doing the same. Nobody wanted to witness. Even the crazy bag lady moved on, her shopping cart's wheels squealing rustily.

Deek leaned from his window. "Yo, Gordy! What's up, dude?"

Ty saw uncertainty creep into the fat boy's eyes: he might have been ready to die but Deek's cheerfulness took him off guard. The hand hovering back by his butt came slowly to his side. For a moment he hesitated, then took a breath and stepped from the shadows. Even sheathed in rolls of fat his chest was impressive. He came halfway across the sidewalk, warily, like a rat in the open. "So, what you want, Deek? An don't call me Gordy, I hate that!"

Deek put hurt in his voice. "Hey, I'm sorry, Gordon. Didn't know. Just cool to see all you dudes okay."

Ty watched the fat boy's eyes narrow in suspicion. "Why not we be okay, Deek?"

Deek shrugged. "Shitty world, man. That all."

Back in the doorway, Ty noted the twins easing closer to the sunlight, curious now. Only the slender boy remained deep in shadow, his half-naked body blending into the background, hard to see. He seemed to be studying Deek. He'd slipped one arm around the smaller kid, keeping him back too. His other paw half concealed what Ty now saw was a little silver gun. It was aimed from the hip full at Deek. Ty wondered how good a shot he was. Though small, the gun was bigger than a .22. Ty gave a mental shrug; he'd done the best he could to cover Deek's ass. The rest was in God's hands. That thought caught him by surprise . . . funny thing to think.

As always in these situations Ty felt as if time had slowed. Little details stood out sharp. The sun creeping down the storefront had warmed the broken window glass and a tiny triangle dropped from the frame and hit the concrete with a musical note that seemed loud. The fat boy tensed again. The twins' eyes shifted for an instant. Only the slender dude's gaze never wavered.

There was stubbornness in the fat boy's tone. The words came out like they tasted bad. "This *our* ground, Deek! Why you come schemin round here?"

Ty watched the fat boy. There was a hollow triangle in his T-shirt where the twin rolls of chest fat overlapped his belly. That would be a good target, close to the heart, but he'd have to shoot the slender kid first. That wouldn't be easy. Then, to Ty's amazement, Deek popped the door and got out, stretching casually and wiping at the wet under his armpits just like any other kid. Gordon was probably heavier than Deek, and Deek was a good head taller, but Gordon probably had bigger bones. Some kids seemed meant to be fat and looked almost cool that way. Deek wasn't one of them.

Deek's voice was soothing. "Yo, Gordon, I fucked up, okay? Jeez, shoot bullets through me!" He made a vague wave down the street. "What I sayin is, I was just motorin through. How the hell I know them cocksuckin cops gonna curb me? I *sorry*, man. Shit, you *know* I wouldn't try sellin round here without your permission an a righteous cut besides."

Gordon's forehead creased slightly. Two vertical lines appeared over his nose. Ty recalled his mother saying once that those kinds of lines meant a person spent a lot of time trying to figure things out. Somehow you never imagined a fat kid doing much thinking.

Gordon seemed to search for words. He hitched up his sagging jeans. "Well . . ."

Behind him, their toes over the sunlit line, the twins edged forward, eyebrows up, breathing through their mouths. The slender boy stayed where he was. His grip tightened on the small kid. The gang's scent came to Ty's nostrils: dirty jeans, old sport shoes, oily hair, and the bittersweet tang of kid sweat. For a second Ty thought he caught a trace of blood smell, but couldn't be sure.

Gordon finished with a lame "Gots no goddamn right bein here at all, man."

Deek spread chubby pink palms and moved closer to Gordon. "Hey, I hear you, man. An I promise it ain't gonna happen again. Swear to God."

Father of lies, thought Ty. That's what the Bible called the devil.

Gordon seemed to feel the eyes of his gang. His back, curved by the weight of his belly, straightened a little. "Yeah, well . . ."

"Listen up, dude," Deek went on. "Word. I just had to make a little ole detour. What it is, Wesley wanna talk to me."

Gordon was instantly alert. "Bout what?"

Deek's palms spread wider. His own jeans were slipping. Compared to Gordon's big boy-butt Deek had an ass like a girl's, Ty thought.

"Hey, Gordon, you a leader too. You know I can't say. Be breakin the rules, what it is." Deek seemed to think a moment, then stepped even closer to Gordon and laid a big-brother hand on his shoulder. Ty barely heard him whisper. "The Crew maybe havin some drive-by probs, man. Seem Wesley needin some major bucks for scorin himself a decent gun."

Even the twins, closest to Gordon, couldn't have heard. But Ty saw the slender boy's eyes narrow to slits. Gordon looked uncertain for a few seconds, then demanded. "So, what you callin a decent gun, man?"

Ty stiffened as Deek turned with a smile, stepped to the car, and snagged the Uzi from the back seat. All the gang boys tensed. Gordon's hand darted behind his back. The little silver gun gleamed in the slender dude's dark, delicate fingers.

But Deek only held the carbine up sideways for a second or two. "Somethin like this decent enough for ya?"

The twins' eyes went wide as surprised panther cubs. "WAY cool!" breathed one. "PAST," sighed the other. "Word!"

Deek grinned, then casually tossed the gun back into the car. "Word up, you dudes *never* need worry bout nuthin no more, packin one of them! Yo, Gordon, I could make it happen for ya. Straight."

Gordon's mouth had opened slightly. Now it shut with a snap. He snorted. "Uh-huh. Cept how we 'ford bullets for the goddamn thing?"

Deek shrugged. "Aw, there's always ways, man. But what can I say? You just seen the future." He snickered. "State of *the* art. Believe. Just think on it, that all." He smiled again and took the keys from the ignition. "Anyways, like I sayin, I sorry as hell bout crossin your ground out askin first." He walked back and keyed the trunk lid. "Yo! I pay you dudes for me fuckin up."

Gordon came slowly to the rear of the car. The twins crowded close behind him, all caution gone, expecting more wonders. As if on display against the soft black carpet in the Trans-Am's trunk, next to the grocery boxes holding the real merchandise, were two cases of Heineken.

Deek waved a gold-ringed hand as though performing a magic trick. "Hell, they even still cool, Gordon. Shit, I know you an your dudes don't do nuthin else. They both yours, just for lettin me motor through. Deal?"

Ty watched. Street pride was a funny thing; you never knew what rule it would follow, but it was based a lot on practical logic. He caught the flick of the fat boy's eyes to the slim kid's, and saw a slight nod in the shadows. That confirmed what Ty had always suspected about who did a lot of the gang's real thinking, though Ty's respect for the fat boy's brain had risen a point or two. The twins were trembling like eager puppies.

Gordon stepped back and crossed his arms over his chest. "Okay, Deek. One time, *this* time. An that all it for, hear?"

Grinning, Deek moved aside as the twins scrambled for the beer. "Oh, for sure, Gordon. But I just sayin that my offer always open to ya. Course, that just business, you understand?"

"Mm. Spect I unnerstand a lotta shit, man. We let you know, but don't go holdin your breath or nuthin."

The twins carried the cases back to the sidewalk. Still grinning, Deek slammed the trunk lid. "Word. I think hard, I was you, man. Specially if the Crew go an score some major fire." Deek paused a moment, then bent close to Gordon. "Word up, there some big dudes schemin your hood, man. WAY bad dudes! We talkin Gorilla an Cripps class, little brother! Hope you got mega bullets for them two pop toys of yours, man!"

"Shit," muttered Gordon. "Four third-graders kick *anybody's* ass! Little bullet go through big dude easy as small dude! Save your preachin for somebody who give a shit!"

Deek shrugged and twirled his key ring. "Yo! That was for free, Gordon. Everbody gots to have friends!"

"Mmm. I could say somethin, but I won't."

Ty waited until Deek was back in the car before sliding in himself. He watched the slender boy all the while. Their eyes met again for an instant. Ty picked up another beer and popped it as Deek swung the 'Am into the street and squeaked away.

Deek's beeper sounded as they reached the next block. He pulled up next to a corner phone booth that was smothered in spray paint and surrounded by a glittering pool of its own shattered glass. It was still working, though, because Deek talked for a few minutes, then returned to the car looking almost happy for so early in the day.

"Gots a new one wantin a job," he snickered, sliding back into the seat. "Told him to meet us tonight at the Burger King. Always helps to pig em out first, specially the hungry ones." He released the parking brake and shifted into gear, then glanced at Ty. "You figure that black-ass bitch gonna be there?"

Ty frowned and shrugged. "Naw. Too many hours. Child-labor law. Even if she black as sin." He took a swallow of beer, then added, "Like me."

Deek snickered again and shook his head. "Maaaan, it just too fuckin bad there ain't no more Panthers around. You be a natural. Yo! Black pride an brotherhood be a long time dead, stupid, case you ain't figured it out yet. Only black asses you got to worry over is mine an yours!"

Early evening was hotter than hell in Gordon's apartment as the sinking sun beat on the building's back side. The small front room was dim, lit ruddy red through the single window's pulled-down shade like the sullen glow from a furnace door's glass. That wall was bare brick, graced only by a faded wood-framed picture of Martin Luther King and John F. Kennedy that had once belonged to Gordon's grandmother. There was also a new glossy eight-by-ten of a young Huey Newton in sixties Panther battle gear, and a pair of African spears crossed over a shield, cheap imitations that only looked real from a distance and the sole reminder that Gordon had a father somewhere. Mortar crumbled constantly from between the bricks and dusted the worn-out carpet. From afternoon to sunset the wall radiated heat like a barbecue pit. The window itself was painted solidly shut, and the transom above the triple-locked hallway door was nailed over with plywood. Now the trapped air was a steamy soup of sweating kids, cigarette smoke, and the sharp winey scent of Heineken dark. A ratty old couch sat in the center of the room. It faced the hall door and a TV on a card table. The TV's screen flickered blue-white with a Little Rascals episode. The soundtrack sputtered, chunks of it missing, and the background music was ancient beyond understanding. But the boys sat on the floor with their backs to the couch and watched with more interest than they usually showed for cartoons.

Gordon, Curtis, and Lyon wore only their jeans, their shoes and socks scattered wherever they'd been kicked. The twins were naked and drunk. Gordon had his 501 buttons mostly popped open so his belly spilled free into his lap. A beer bottle stuck up between his wide-spread legs. A Kool dangled from his lips as he carefully copied his English composition onto fresh binder paper with ponderous strokes of a first-grader's huge pencil in between glances at the TV. He frowned as he tried to ignore the twins' constant chatter. Ric and Rac had killed almost a case by themselves and their normally flat stomachs bulged drum-tight and awkward like pictures of wild jungle boys. Gordon flicked ashes into a tuna can and looked over at Lyon, who was sitting beside him. Lyon was blowing smoke rings and sipping his sixth beer. Nobody had ever seen him drunk.

Gordon rolled his eyes toward the twins. "Maybe they pass out soon. I hope."

Lyon smiled his smile and puffed another perfect smoke ring. "When it come by beer, they be like the rats on that ole anti-coke commercial."

"Word. Hell, they be like that with everthing. Gotta have it all *now*. 'Member that time we find the dumpster unlocked 'hind KFC, an them two stuff down chicken till they can't even skate?"

Lyon sent a small smoke ring chasing a larger and piercing

it. "Tigers burn bright. But I think panthers brighter."

"Huh? That some kinda magic talk, man?"

"Naw. Forget it."

Gordon leaned forward and thumbed up the TV as the twins chattered on in their own special language of mostly half-finished sentences. Then Gordon turned to Lyon once more. "Figure that pussy little sucker gonna smoke Miss Crabtree into marryin him? Shit, she way too fine a lady for that schemin prick, anybody see! She a way cool teacher too, best believe. Wish we had somebody like that in our school, huh?" He took a gulp of beer. "Spose she long dead anyways, huh? Or maybe recycled into somebody else."

"Reincarnated, man."

"Whatever." Gordon blew smoke and straightened his homework papers. "Yo, Lyon, do white folks ever get . . . carnationed into black?"

"Mmm. Only the good ones. What it is, being black a major 'sponsibility. It way hard to do right. That why so many fuck it up an forget why they here. Yo. 'Member back when the paper tell bout M. C. Hammer scorin himself a six-million-dollar house an bail Oakland? That sorta what I sayin. I mean, who in hell *need* a six-million-dollar house? You say what you want, man, but way I see it, ain't nobody gonna be happy nowheres till everbody happy everwheres, no matter what color they be."

Rac swung around to face Lyon. "Yo! So what happen to *bad* white people?"

"They come back as dogs nobody want, so they end up street-pizza or gettin put to sleep."

"Oh. Guess that why a dog's ghost signify less'n nuthin, huh?"

"Give it a name."

"Well," said Ric, aiming his Kool at the screen. "Black

or white, Gordy right, I for sure wish we had us Miss Crabtree 'stead of ole Crabzilla! But I think she needin somebody, know what I mean?"

"For poppin her cherry," added Rac.

"Shut up," said Gordon. "An stop makin ever goddamn thing dirty all the time!"

"Well," said Lyon. "Don't be worryin over her. Best believe Spanky an his gang be seein right through that slimy little sucker like glass. Him an Buckwheat be smokin his butt anytime now. Word."

Gordon frowned slightly. "Spose you seen this one a'fore too?"

"Course. Wanna know what happen?"

"No."

Curtis had been busy back at the kitchen counter and now came padding over to the couch. He carried a beer in one hand, and his own tummy was puffed like a balloon from trying to pace the bigger boys. He concentrated on keeping to a straight line, and carried a plate balanced carefully in his other hand. "Yo! Ketchup sandwiches comin up!"

Ric and Rac, slumped shoulder to shoulder on the other side of Gordon, their chins and chests glistening with spilled beer, snickered out Kool smoke. "Don't ya gotta eat em first for that to happen?" asked Rac.

"Shit!" said Ric. "You mean that all what left we can eat here?"

"Well," sniffed Curtis. "You both be pussys so why don't you go an eat yourselfs?"

The twins exchanged glances. "That pretty cool," giggled Ric. Rac considered. "For Curtis." Both snagged two of the drippy red-and-white things and chewed messily. "No goddamn napkins?" demanded Rac.

"SHUT UP!" roared Gordon.

Putting the plate on the couch, Curtis sat clumsily down next to Lyon. The gash on his back had been covered by gauze stuck to him by Big Bird Band-Aids. His hand shyly found the slender boy's.

Ric gulped beer and giggled. "Yo, Curtis! Ask if Gordon let ya use his crib!"

"Word!" snickered Rac. "Give it a name! Kiss him now, why don't ya?"

Gordon clenched a big fist in front of Rac's nose.

The twins exchanged glances of innocence. Suddenly, Ric grabbed his brother and wrestled him flat on his back, scrambling on top and pressing him down. "Oooooh, Lyyyy-on! You make me go all squishy inside like ketchup sandwiches!"

Rac squirmed and wiggled, both boys gleaming and slip-pery as seals. "You can tear off all my clothes but you can't make me pant!"

"Hey!" giggled Ric. "My mom say that!"

"No shit? Mine do too! Ain't that a 'incidence!"

"Stop that!" bawled Gordon. "It dirty an gross! An this here my mom's goddamn 'partment!"

Snickering, the twins staggered to their feet, their arms going over each other's shoulders. Snagging their bottles, they stumbled, laughing, for the bathroom.

Curtis scowled. "Prob'ly gonna go an beat-off!"

Gordon spun around and glared after them. "You do, you goddamn well gonna clean it up! Ain't gonna have my mom thinkin I done it!"

Lyon grinned. "They prob'ly couldn't even find their dicks now with all four hands an a flashlight."

Gordon set his homework pages on the couch, flipped his pencil across the room, and turned back to the TV. "Well,

I like how Buckwheat an Spanky always workin together like brothers. An that was a long time ago when black an white kids wasn't sposed to hang together. They was a way cool gang, huh?"

Lyon nodded. "That the way gangs oughta be, man, good, but not takin no shit off nobody neither." A shadow crossed his face. "So, what you be thinkin bout Deek, man? You be figurin it worth a couple cases now an again for lettin him motor our hood?"

Gordon stared at the TV and shrugged. "Not now, man. I mean, we sposed to be kicked-back an partyin, ain't we? Just forget the goddamn street a while."

Lyon blew a last smoke ring before crushing out his Kool. "Mmm. That be the one thing most hard to forget. There time for partyin, an frontin an maxin, an time for fightin. Seem like we don't got much time for thinkin."

"School time sposed to be for thinkin, man."

"Well, there thinkin, an then there *thinkin* with your own mind."

A commercial came on for the Ninja Turtles' new pizza machine gun, the colors starkly bright in the room's sullen shadows. Gordon sighed and took another gulp of beer. "Mmm. Well, you figure Deek talkin anywheres close to straight bout Wesley an his dudes workin for him to score themselves a good gun? I mean, the Crew always up for keepin their ground clean. Same's us."

Lyon combed long fingers gently through Curtis' dreads to take out the tangles. "Could be . . . *if* Deek talkin straight, specially bout them big dudes schemin. After all, man, guns be the only way we got a chance with somebody twice our size. I ain't sayin Deek don't lie like a dog most times, but if the same kinda shit what happen to us this mornin come down on the Crew, just might be they gettin scared enough to try goin for some of Deek's dirty bucks." Lyon gazed into space for a while, his fingers moving slow and careful. Curtis lay with his head on Lyon's leg, his eyes closed and a smile on his bronze little-boy face. Lyon looked back at Gordon. "Main prob to my mind be, if the Crew score themselves a Uzi, it turn out just like the TV always sayin bout that Middle East shit. Balance of power gonna get fucked up. Word."

Gordon frowned and glanced over to his narrow bed near the kitchen counter where the two small guns lay atop the gray USN blanket. "Well, the pawnshop man tell us he can still special-order bullets for that ole Michael-Jackson."

"Iver-Johnson. But what good that gonna do us up against a Uzi, man?"

"Yeah. Shit." Gordon fingered his jaw. "But why Wesley even wanna put moves on our hood, Lyon? Word come to me say he gots enough probs in his own."

Lyon shrugged a slender shoulder. "Uzi change things. Same's why Deek always be schemin round here when he already gots more money than God." Untangling his fingers from Curtis' hair, Lyon jerked a thumb toward the bathroom doorway. "It be the same sorta reason them twins go an drink they fool selfs to death, you let em. Gettin more shit always make you *want* more shit, man. Don't know why, but that what it is." Curtis was asleep. Lyon gazed down at the small boy's peaceful face. "There be this too, Gordon. We start lettin Deek cruise round here, little kids gonna see him. Some gonna start creamin their jeans over that goddamn car. Others gonna want to buy what he sellin. That make us workin for Deek any way you figure it, man. Hell, you see that."

Gordon pulled up his knees and dropped his chin into his hands. "Yeah. Spose I do. Maybe I just waitin to hear you say it in that real-time way you got. Well, all what I know is, if the Crew come by a better gun than us, we gonna have probs. An ain't no way we ever gonna score our own-selfs some major fire without we find us some mega money." He met Lyon's eyes. "So, magic-boy, you tell me where we gonna score that kinda buck, cept by some sucker like Deek? An, even Wesley stay cool, what about them big dudes, man? Bet your ass *they* got Uzis or Tens or somethin else way past bad. Like you say, how small dudes like us gonna keep equal?"

Gordon sighed again and nodded toward the TV. "Musta been way past cool, bein a kid back in them olden days. Even if we did gotta ride the butt end of buses." His eyes narrowed as he turned back to Lyon. "Yo. Y'all thinkin somethin again. I can always tell cause you get that magic look."

Lyon smiled and drained his bottle. "Ghost of a dog, man. Just thinkin I wish we knowed more bout Deek. Anyways, let it chill. Tomorrow another day."

Gordon nodded. "Yeah. But I totally outa ideas, man. Course, I could do me some schemin on Wesley at school. Times he talk free when his dudes ain't around."

Lyon grinned. "Special when he be sweatin to copy some-body's homework." He glanced at the binder sheets on the couch. "That story of yours all done over, man?"

"Close enough for Crabzilla. Times I get to wishin I knew me more big words, like you. But then I gots more on my mind than goddamn homework right now, best believe. Like keepin us all alive. THAT how I gonna be spendin my motherfuckin summer vacation! Word!" Gordon killed his beer and reached for another. "Lyon? Was things always this shitty for kids?"

Once more Lyon shrugged. "It the way things be *now* what matter."

The Little Rascals ended by saving the day, and the news

came on. There were two million homeless people in the United States and eight million predicted by the year 2000. The President was giving ten million dollars to Czechoslovakia, and aid to the kinder, gentler U.S.S.R. was being considered in Congress. Gordon leaned forward and turned off the TV. The sun was gone, and the room went dark as the screen dwindled to a single tiny point of light. Gordon got to his feet, his unbuttoned jeans slipping low, and switched on a dim, yellow-shaded floor lamp by the couch. He stood for a moment looking down at Lyon and Curtis. "Um . . . you *can* use my crib, y'know? Anytime."

"Huh? Oh, thanks, Gordon, but I ain't sleepy."

"Um . . ." Gordon pointed to Curtis. "I mean . . . well, y'know? You an him?"

"Mmm? Curtis gonna be spendin the night with me again. I call his mom so's she don't worry. His parents don't like seein him drunk."

Gordon flushed. "I mean, for you AN him."

Lyon laughed. "Oooo." He looked down at the small sleeping boy, then grinned up at Gordon. "Now shit, here I figure you know me better'n anybody, man. But, what it is, I spose me an Curtis love each other, but not *that* way."

Gordon plopped down on the couch, crinkling his homework sheets. "Oh. Um . . . well . . . shit. Course I never ask, but this last couple years I just figured you was . . ." He swallowed. "Um . . . gay."

Lyon grinned. "Mean, Christmas mornin an all that shit, man?"

Gordon grabbed a bottle and took several big gulps. "Well, times you mind me of Michael Jackson."

Lyon looked thoughtful. "What it is, Michael Jackson's a werewolf, man. That why he be lonely an nobody understand him. I mean, check it out, he hang with kids, do cool things for em, an try an make em happy, an all them radio assholes make jokes, say, get real, Michael. HE the real one! Word!"

Gordon took another swallow of beer. "Well, it just that you all the time so . . . gentle, man. What I sayin is, somebody dint know you, figure you maybe for a puss."

"Mmm. So, what you really sayin is, black dudes ain't spose to be gentle?" Grinning again, Lyon stood and puffed his slender chest, making the fine muscles stand out. He pumped a biceps and posed. "Maaaan, I gonna smoke me some butt tonight! Jo mama!"

Gordon snickered. "That look just plain stupid, man. Somethin Wesley do."

"Well, what I sayin is, everbody be half boy an half girl."

"WHAT?"

"Figure. You gots a mom an a dad, don't ya?"

Gordon considered that a long time. Finally, he nodded. "Mmm. So, what you tellin me is everbody gots a gentle part an a hard part, an the girl part's the gentle one?"

Lyon grinned again. "Not always, man. Ever hear of Lucrezia Borgia or Lizzie Borden?"

"They do stuff like Madonna?"

"Times I think Madonna want to do stuff like them. Anyways, ain't no rule say a dude got to be bad . . . least when there no reason to be. Yo. Even a bad-ass ole panther take time out to be gentle to its cubs, huh. So, here Michael Jackson bein gentle for kids an all them stupid suckers sayin he ain't cool cause he ain't bad. That total dogshit, man! Now you see what I sayin?"

"Maybe after I think on it some more." Gordon rolled the bottle between his palms and looked at the floor. "But I never seen you schemin a girl, man."

"Well, I never seen you neither."

"Um . . . you ever figure I get a girl to like me, Lyon?"

"Course! Yo! Lisa Thompson in fifth period all the time peekin you out, man! Mean to tell me you never even notice? An she ain't the only one, best believe. Thing is, girls come at you sorta sideways most times. You gotta pay attention. It like lookin for magic signs."

Gordon reached for the last sandwich. "Sound more like some kinda game to me."

"Mmm. That be givin it another name, man. Take up a lot of your time, you start in playin it, best believe."

"So how come you ain't playin it? For sure you gots the looks."

"Don't gots the time."

Gordon glanced down at himself. "Shit. Check me out. I just a stupid-lookin fat boy, man."

"You ain't stupid. An bein fat in this hood show you some kinda survivor. Lotta hungry kids give they left nuts to be your size. Word."

Gordon was quiet while he finished the sandwich, then he looked up at Lyon again. "What it is, man, I never even kiss nobody a'fore. I mean, cept my mom, course, but that a different thing."

Lyon smiled. "It come natural."

"You mean, *you* been kissin girls, man?"

"Done me a lot more'n kiss, best believe. Rubbers I carry in *my* wallet never get all dry an crackly."

"Well, how come you never say?"

"Nobody never ask. Sides, ain't nobody keepin score, an whose business it be but my own?"

"Yeah. That right, huh, man? Well, um, how you do it a'zactly . . . I mean just the kissin stuff with your tongue an all?"

"Same's you skate. Or do anythin else. Your own personal style."

"Mmm. Spose that mean gentle work for you?"

"Lotta girls *like* gentle. You be s'prised, man."

"Well, guess you fuck all the time then, huh?"

Lyon shrugged and waved a careless paw. "Tell you a secret of the universe, Gordon. Word. *Any* doofus can fuck. It real lovin what seem to come so hard." He frowned. "It most like, well, if you ain't loved when you little, it major hard to learn lovin at all."

Gordon nodded slowly. "Yeah. I think I hear that, man." Still looking thoughtful, he glanced at the clock atop the TV. "Mmm. Seven-thirty. My mom be home in bout a hour an a half."

Lyon snagged an empty bottle from the floor. "Well, I help you clean up all this shit. What you wanna do bout them twins? They prob'ly zoned in the bathtub or somethin."

"Aw, I drag em out by my bed an throw a blanket over em. Go down an call their mom to say they spendin the night again." Gordon frowned and looked back over his shoulder. "SHIT! Them suckers in my MOM'S room!" Stumbling to his feet, jerking up his jeans and almost tripping over Curtis, Gordon roared, "What the fuck you doin in there?"

Rac's grinning face appeared around the doorframe. "Tryin on cheap jewelry. Yo, check it out! We gonna be *gentle* niggerboys!"

He and Ric staggered into the room wearing necklaces, bracelets, and earrings. Curtis sat up, stared, and rubbed his eyes. Lyon hid a grin behind a long paw. Gordon's face turned purple. "You motherfuckin . . . PERVERTS!"

There was a knock on the hallway door.

For a second, all the boys froze. Then, jewelry jingling, bellies jutting, the twins dashed to Gordon's bed and grabbed the guns. Even drunk they still moved like an attack team, flanking the hall door with their guns up and ready. Gordon eased to the peephole, keeping his big body clear of the door panel. Lyon glided silently to the kitchen. He slipped two long knives from a drawer and passed one to Curtis, then both boys took up positions beside the twins.

"It Tunk," whispered Gordon, his eye to the peephole. "One of Wesley's dudes. He packin his board. Don't see nobody else." He turned to Lyon. "What you figure, man?"

"You sure he alone?"

"How in hell I know? Could be the whole goddamn Crew all up an down the hall and I couldn't see em through this motherfuckin thing!"

"Oh, shit," Curtis whispered, clutching his butcher knife, its blade dripping crimson ketchup. "What if they already score emselfs that Uzi an come for to do us?"

"Shush!" hissed Gordon. "Don't borrow trouble!" He thought a moment, then peered back out through the peephole. "Yo, Tunk! You alone?"

The voice from the hallway was high and punctuated by squeaks. "Word, Gordy. Wes send me, man. 'Bassador. Rules!"

Gordon glanced at the twins; both were breathing hard and deep, shiny with sweat and swaying a little on their feet. But their tawny eyes burned bright. Ric had the safety off on the .22, and Rac held the revolver's hammer back with a thumb. Both gripped their guns double-handed, and their teeth gleamed in their dusky faces.

"Okay," called Gordon. "Rules, man. But I gonna open this door fast, an I want you fly your ass in here warp-seven! Get by the TV, an then you CHILL! We gots TWO guns, man! Leave your board outside."

Tunk's voice got even squeakier. "Nuh-uh! No WAY, José! Not my goddamn board! Ain't no rules bout boards, Gordy! There a fuckin ole junkie cruisin your second floor, if ya wanna know. Ain't losin my board to some stinkin ole needle sticker!"

Gordon gritted his teeth and eyed the twins again. "You two better chill! Same's the cops sposed to do, till you actual SEE somethin in his hand! You go an blow him away by accident we gonna have World War III all over the hood! Word!"

Rac snorted. "We cool, Gordy!"

"Yeah!" said Ric. "Go for it, man!"

"Okay," called Gordon. "Board cool, Tunk. But you *move* your ass!"

Gordon unsnapped the locks and yanked back the door. A small boy burst like a blur into the room. He landed solidly in his oversize Nikes near the TV, then spun around as Gordon slammed the door and shot the bolts. But Ric and Rac jammed a gun muzzle in each of Tunk's ears and he froze, clutching his skateboard over his balls.

"Rules, Gordy, rules!" Tunk squeaked. "'Bassador! No goddamn guns in my ears!"

Tunk was no bigger than Curtis, with the same childlike body, but soft velvet black like a moonless midnight. He was loose-lipped and pug-nosed with eyes big and bright under long silky lashes. He wore old 501s with one knee ripped open, a huge gold earring and wrist chain that had to be fake, and a camouflage Army shirt, sleeves rolled up and so big that he looked like a caricature of a street kid in a Little Rascals episode. His board was a battered old Tony Hawk, and his big eyes got even bigger when he saw Curtis' knife dripping red.

"Oh, shut up, man," growled Gordon. "Nobody even touch you!" He checked the peephole once more, then pressed an ear to the door panel and listened. Finally, he sighed. "An don't call me Gordy, goddamnit!"

Tunk puffed a little. "How bout just Gordy?"

His V smile flickering, Lyon stepped over to Tunk. Curtis hovered near with the knife. Unbuttoning Tunk's shirt, Lyon ran his hands up the small boy's ribs, patted his pockets, and checked the tops of his shoes. "He be clean, Gordon." Lyon jerked his thumbs in opposite directions and the twins moved back and lowered their guns.

Tunk dropped his board on the floor and flapped his huge shirt like a caped crusader to reveal the rest of him. "*Course* I clean, suckers! Rules!" He puffed his chest again, sniffed, then buttoned his shirt's top button, which came about to the height of his tummy.

Gordon yanked up his jeans and brushed sweat from his forehead. "Yeah, yeah. You safe, man. Prob'ly a lot safer than in that hall. Chill out. Wanna beer?"

Tunk's face brightened. "For sure!" He strutted to the couch and plopped down on top of Gordon's homework. Curtis handed him a bottle. Ric and Rac stayed close by, still watchful. Tunk tilted back the bottle, expertly chugged almost half, then burped, wiped his mouth, and grinned. "*Kickin!* You score this from the Deeker, huh?"

"Rules," muttered Gordon.

"Oh, yeah." Tunk snagged a Kool pack off the couch's arm. "Yo! These anybody's?"

Gordon waved a palm.

"Thanks! My brand!" Tunk popped a cigarette into his mouth. Curtis fired it with his Bic. Tunk sucked smoke, then blew out a satisfied cloud and studied the twins. "Way cool look, bros. Like MTV."

Ric and Rac dropped the guns to their sides, looked at each other, and giggled.

Tunk chugged more beer, smacked his lips, and eyed Curtis' knife. "Shit, dude, you do somebody tonight?"

Curtis looked shy. Lyon took the knife and licked the blade. "In the shower."

Tunk snickered and made stabbing motions. "I get it! Eee, eee, eee!" He watched as the twins sat down on the carpet and reached for fresh beers, then pointed. "Yo! So where y'all score that way cool chrome gun?"

"Nickel," said Curtis.

"Rules," said Gordon. He frowned. "So, I spose you here to tell us the Crew gonna start workin for Deek sucker soon?"

Tunk made a face. "Gimme a break, man. Rules." He killed the bottle and burped again. "But it's 'portant, Gordon. Word up!" He eyed the last sixer on the floor.

"Go for it," said Gordon.

"Way cool!" Tunk popped another bottle and again chugged half. "Shit! That taste megalicious! No lie! Oh, an if you wanna know, we gots a test tomorrow in Crabzilla's class. Maaan, she EVER on the rag today! Believe, believe!"

Lyon smiled. "She been like that ever since Toto 'scape out her bike basket."

"Huh? Oh." Tunk giggled. "Word! So how come you dudes wasn't in school? Cop come round talkin the big-buddy program. Got to kick back a whole half hour for that."

Gordon snorted. "We already been big-buddied. Anyways, maybe we just not feel up for goin today. So why you here, Tunk?" He pointed to the clock. "My mom be home soon, an we gots a junkie to clear out the buildin . . . less you lie?"

Tunk lay back and gulped more beer, then lazily waved a hand. "No lie. Word. Wes wanna meet. Neutral ground."

Gordon's eyes flicked to Lyon's. "Yeah? This bout Deek?"

Tunk killed the second bottle, burped again, and sighed happily. "Rules. But you gettin warm. Wesley askin, so's you get to pick the place. Long's it neutral, y'know."

Gordon snorted again. "I know by rules, man."

Tunk felt beneath him, pulled out Gordon's homework composition, and studied the first page a moment. "Yeah? Too bad you don't know there ain't no K in vacation."

Gordon turned surprised eyes to Lyon. The slender boy shrugged. "You dint ask."

Lyon sat down close to Tunk. "Yo. 'Bassador be 'portant job, man. Look like you get yourself major thirsty warpin all the way down here too." He popped another bottle and handed it to the small boy.

Tunk grinned and slumped deeper into the couch. "Gotta say, this here shit's my weakness, man. My mom tell it be the death of me!" He giggled. "Least I go happy, huh? Course, I can't get too wasted . . . gotta skate all the way home, an your hood turn mega-mean this time of night. Couldn't pack my blade on account of this 'bassador stuff, y'know."

Lyon cocked an eyebrow at Gordon. "That be cool, Tunker man. Me an Curtis 'scort you back to your marks after the talkin done. Be your very own bodyguards. Here, this last Heinie got your name all over it."

Tunk gulped again. "Maaan, you dudes way past cool! Know how to treat your bros. One up the rules even. Ain't no wonder we don't fight. Um, gots another smoke too?"

Lyon shook another Kool from the pack, fired Curtis' lighter for Tunk, and handed him the last bottle. Ric and Rac had slumped together, their backs against the couch. They were nodding, the guns loose in their hands.

"Rules be mostly for street time," said Lyon. "Here, we all be like regular homeys." He took Curtis' shoulder and turned him around. "Yo. Check this out, Tunker. Here why we not be in school today. Drive-by. Full-autos in deuce. This for free, man."

Tunk carefully checked out Curtis' back. "Mmm. There some word on that."

Gordon's eyes shifted to Lyon, then back to Tunk. "What word?"

Tunk looked uneasy before shrugging. "Rules, Gordon. Sides, lots of word go round don't mean dogshit." He finished the third bottle, set it aside, then picked at the label of the fourth for a few seconds. "But I tell you this, man. For free. Same a'zact thing happen to us today. After school. This ole black van come rippin by an spray us! Two full-autos, uh-huh, uh-huh! Just like you say!" He jammed a thumb to his chest. "*I* say they Uzis. Tell by the sound, if you wanna know. Wes not so sure, but he shoot back an that motherfuckin van bail its butt, best believe!"

Gordon sat down on the arm of the couch, picked up his homework, frowned at the pages a moment, then set them carefully aside. "Any your dudes get hit?"

Tunk considered, taking a gulp from the bottle. "Mmm. I don't figure I should oughta say, man. Rules again. But all our dudes actin like dogs gone hyper an bout to piss on the floor, uh-huh. Word up, there some big gang schemin-out both our hoods."

"Mmm," said Lyon. "Word up, by Deek, what you really tellin us, huh?"

Tunk nodded, then frowned and studied the bottle. "Shit! Now I so fuckin wasted I just now gone an told you stuff I shouldn't, huh?"

Lyon smiled and gripped the smaller boy's shoulder. "Yo, brother, we cool. We not be sayin nuthin to nobody. Sides, we just went an told you some free stuff by us, 'member?"

"Did ya?" Tunk thought hard, then solemnly nodded. "Oh yeah. You did." He slumped deep in the cushions, unbuttoned his shirt and slapped his belly. "Aw, what the fuck, dudes. I drunk. I happy. Shoot bullets through me. So, Gordon, where ya wanna meet?"

"How bout that ole car wash? The one what been closed since way back in the earthquake? After school tomorrow. Say, bout four?"

Tunk tilted up his bottle and chugged the whole thing, then giggled and wiped his mouth. "Gonna do it, do it good, I say! For sure Gordon. Fact is, we was hopin you pick that place . . ." He held up his palms. "I mean, don't go gettin paranoid or nuthin . . . you can pick another one. It just bout the best place around for a meet, that all."

Gordon glanced at Lyon, who nodded. "Sure, man," said Gordon. "The car wash."

Tunk let out a big burp, then struggled to his feet, making it on the second try. He gave Gordon a clumsy high-five. "Done deal, dude."

Curtis handed Tunk his board. "Yo. Hot ole Hawk, Tunk! How's it cruise on them Rat Bones?"

"Aw, nuthin nuclear, man, but it get me there. Y'all still skatin that ole Variflex, huh? Always wanted to check me out one of them antique flat-deckers."

Curtis picked up his own board. "Well, you prob'ly miss the kicktail at first. Most dudes do. But it a way cool street cruiser. Word up, I gonna score me a Steve Steadham full-size in Jamaica! Yo, wanna trade for the ride back tonight?"

"Shit yeah, dude! Let's do it!" Tunk grinned. "If I can still ride at all with my tank fulla Heinie." He swapped boards with Curtis as Lyon sat down and started putting on his socks and shoes. Curtis went searching for his own. Gordon handed Lyon his T-shirt. "Here, man, Curtis can wear Ric's."

"That be Rac's."

"Whatever. Ain't neither of em goin nowhere more tonight, believe." Squatting beside the sleeping twins Gordon began taking off the jewelry.

Lyon shrugged into Gordon's tee, so big it draped him like a poncho, then knelt and slipped the revolver from Rac's limp fingers. "We run that junkie off on the way out so's he don't be hasslin your mom comin home." Tucking the gun into the back of his jeans, he faced Tunk. "You dudes gonna be packin all your fire to the meet?"

Tunk snickered. "Gimmie a break, man! 'All' our fire! Meanin that puss-pop .38?" He slapped his forehead. "Aw, shit! I just went an done it again, huh?"

Lyon patted his shoulder. "Yo. That just be your heart talkin, brother. We cool. Sides, you could score yourself some points by Wesley, tellin him we gots two guns now."

"Mmm. Figure I should, man? Wes hyper to the max already."

Gordon glanced up. "Might scare him into callin off the meet. An best believe we *need* to talk bout this shit."

Tunk considered. "Well, I don't know. Seem I gots 'sponsibility by my homeys, man. For sure Wes ain't gonna be stoked over hearin you dudes one gun up on us." Tunk's eyes shifted between the fat boy and Lyon. "Maybe . . . maybe I just won't tell him less I figure it need to be said." Tunk searched Gordon's face. "It . . . like a trust thing, y'know? I stickin out my ass here. You could hurt us bad with that other gun, we dint know you gots it."

Lyon patted the small boy's shoulder once more. "Yo. What it is, we leave the tellin or not tellin up to you, man. Like you say, it be a trust thing. More, it be a heart thing."

Tunk nodded. "You dudes way past cool. Make me wish I live a block closer so's I be in your hood."

"Well," said Curtis, straightening from his shoes. "You can still come over an hang . . ." He looked at Gordon. "I mean, to trade moves an stuff . . ." He turned to Lyon. "Y'know? Just like a regular kid?" Spreading his palms, he faced Gordon again. "Can't he?"

Gordon slid the bracelets off Ric's wrist and shook his head. "Rules, man."

Tunk nodded slowly. "Yeah." He fingered Curtis' board. "What it is, first thing happen, you dudes start figurin I schemin on ya. Or Wesley think I schemin *for* ya. Just can't work, man. Rules make things hard sometimes."

Lyon touched Curtis' arm. "We ain't, none of us, regular kids, man."

Curtis stared at the floor. "Yeah. I think I just now figure what that really mean." He looked up at Lyon. "Things be all cool in Jamaica, huh?"

Lyon smiled. "Believe."

Curtis slipped into Rac's tee, then went to the door. He stood on tiptoes to peer through the peephole. He stiffened. "Yo, Tunk! That there the junkie you was tellin us about?"

Tunk came over by Curtis, stumbling a little, and stood on his toes too. "Word! That the ole rag bag, for sure!" He looked over his shoulder to Gordon. "Yo! Anybody home cross the hall, man? Sucker checkin out the door, if ya wanna know. Listenin for people inside."

"Shit!" spat Gordon. He dropped the double handful of jewelry on the couch. "That ole Mrs. Washington's 'part-ment. She cook nights at some hospital. Way cool lady. Sometimes bring home cookies an shit for us. Hell, she gots nuthin in there but a goddamn ancient Sony! Black an white!"

Tunk had his eye to the peephole again. "Yeah? Well, that sucker just pull a little crowbar, if ya wanna know. Nice lady gonna lose her Sony, best believe, ya don't get busy, man."

"Shit! What a motherfuckin day!" Gordon grabbed Ric by the shoulders and shook him hard. The boy stayed limp as laundry. Shaking Rac brought only a mumbled curse.

"Shit!" Gordon snatched the pistol from Ric's hand and flicked off the safety. "Wanna help us, Tunk? Nuthin in the rules say you gotta."

Tunk grinned. "Bet your ass I help, man! Be fun! But I tellin ya, that sucker out there gots the terminal twitchies. Never know what they gonna do like that. Maybe gots a blade sides that bar. Ya gonna shoot him?"

Gordon moved to the door and stared through the hole. "Not if we don't gotta. Somebody might go an call the cops an then there be some great big huge donkey show right when my mom come home all tired. Shit. There enough of us here to take that sucker even with them twins drunk on their goddamn asses!"

Curtis snagged the two knives off the TV and offered the bigger to Tunk. Tunk tried the edge on his finger, then grinned and shoved his shirt sleeves higher. "Word up, man! *Course* we take that cocksucker! Shit, I turn him into deli slices with this! Extra thin! See if I don't!"

"Well," said Gordon. "Try not an hurt him any more'n you gotta, man. We don't want no goddamn blood all over the fuckin place, if there any way other. Special not *his* kind. Prob'ly all fulla AIDS."

Lyon suddenly snapped his fingers. "Yo, Gordon! You mom gots any sheen? In a spray-can?"

"Huh? Yeah. In the bathroom."

Lyon nudged Curtis. "Toast time, homey!"

"Word! Just like Michael Jackson!"

"Huh?" said Tunk.

Lyon shoved the revolver into Tunk's hands and darted for the bathroom. Tunk put down the knife and checked out the gun. "Whoah! Way cool fire, Gordy! Yo! What kinda gun is it anyways?"

"Pull the trigger, bullets come out. But there only two, so don't waste 'em. An don't call . . ."

"Sorry. I forgot. Um, look like you trust me, huh, man?"

"Mmm. Guess we do." Gordon turned to Curtis, who had pulled out his Bic lighter and was turning up the valve. "You know what the fuck you doin, man?"

Curtis' little-boy face beamed. "For sure, Gordon! Me an Lyon done this lotsa times!"

Tunk broke open the revolver and checked the two bullets. "Shit, man, these things all green an yucky! Figure they even go off?"

"Dude try an do me with one this mornin. Shoot just fine for him . . . cept he miss."

"Oh." Tunk snapped the gun shut again.

Lyon came running back with the can of hair sheen. "Yo, Curtis! Get busy!"

Across the hall, a tall, thin dude in dirty jeans, sweatshirt, and ragged old-style Cons levered at the doorframe above the dead bolt with a small shiny crowbar. He was probably twenty but looked twice that, with his gaunt face, gray-toned skin, and the bruiselike smudges under his eyes. His movements were stiff and jerky like those of an animated movie-corpse and he shook all over like something wound too tight and ready to snap its spring. He let out a screech and whirled around as Gordon's door burst open, whipping up the crowbar and taking a wild swing at the two small shadows that sprang at him.

Lyon ducked the bar, twisted on his toes, and aimed the spray can. His delicate finger jammed down the button and held it, shooting sheen all over the dude's face. The dude cursed and clapped one hand over his eyes as he stumbled back, the other slicing the air with the sharp steel bar. In the next instant Curtis landed crouching beside Lyon. He jerked up the Bic with both hands and fired it into the spray stream.

There was a muffled FOOM. Yellow-blue flame exploded around the dude's head, blinding bright in the dim-lit hallway. The can recoiled in Lyon's hands but he kept his finger pressed tight on the button. Fire hissed like a blowtorch from the nozzle. The dude's hair crackled.

The dude screamed. The crowbar clattered on the bare board floor as he clawed and beat at his flaming face and hair. He twisted frantically to get out of the fire stream. He staggered back, slammed into a wall, tried to run, and crashed face-first into the other. He stumbled in circles for a few moments, then finally broke into a blind lope for the stairwell. Blood gushed out of his nose from hitting the wall. His screams echoed down the narrow hall. Lyon followed him, cutting off the spray, but pale yellow flames still flickered and crackled in the dude's matted hair. The smell was sickening. Lyon kept the can aimed, urging the dude on with curses and yells as loud as the screams. Curtis trotted at his side, the lighter clutched ready. Gordon and Tunk trailed behind, adding their own bawling and shouts to the noise, guns held up in case the dude tried to fight.

Other doors creaked cautiously open on chains for a second or two, then slammed shut again. Peepholes darkened as eyes watched. The big dude lurched to the head of the stairs. The flames were dying out, but his hair still smoked and stank. He ground his fists into his eyes, blinking hard, lashes charred, trying to see his attackers. Suddenly, Gordon drove between Curtis and Lyon in a football block, slamming his loose bulk into the big dude's body. Another scream echoed in the hall as the dude went over backward down the steel-edged steps in a tangle of arms and legs, animal cries, and fleshy thuds. He hit the landing below with a crash that seemed to shake the whole building. Then there was silence except for the panting of the boys.

They crowded together at the top of the staircase, teeth gleaming and eyes glittering in the dimness. The bulb was gone in the stairwell, and they could see only a black smoking bundle on the landing below.

"Fuuuuuck!" came Curtis' awed whisper. "Maybe we done him anyways?"

Then there were low moans, whimpers, and a curse. The still-smoking shape struggled to its hands and knees and started to crawl away.

Tunk snickered and puffed his chest. "Stick him with a fork, dudes, he DONE!"

Gordon hitched up his jeans, cupped his hands to his mouth, and roared down the stairwell, "An don't come back, sucker! This FRIENDS ground! Next time, you DEAD!"

Behind the boys, another door opened. They turned to see a tired-looking man in dusty work clothes. He asked, "You get the bastard, Gordon?"

"Yo, Mr. Franklin. Spect we did."

The man nodded. "Your mother home yet, son?"

"No sir. Bout another fifteen minutes, I spect. But my friends here just now leavin. They make sure that sucker gone fore my mom come in."

The man smiled a little. "How you doin in school, boy?"

Gordon kicked a toe at the banister. "Um, mostly C's. Gots me one B, though. In English. Mostly cause Lyon here help me."

The man looked where Gordon pointed, seeming puzzled for a moment. He blinked, then smiled again. "Hard to see

him in the dark. Well, keep them grades up, son. Onliest
way you gonna get somewheres. You boys be careful now."
The door closed.

The boys walked back up the hall. A stink like burned
chicken feathers still hung heavy in the air. Lyon, Tunk,
and Curtis got their boards. Tunk gave the revolver back
to Lyon. "Maaaan, you dudes way past BAD! Word up!
Yo, gots any more hot moves like that?"

Lyon grinned. "Rules." He turned to Gordon. "Sorry I
can't stay an help you clean up some of this shit."

Gordon put the pistol on top of the TV and began gathering bottles. "Aw, no prob. Um, but how you spell vacation, man?"

Lyon spelled it for him, then added. "An best you get
that story done right, or Crabzilla kill ya for sure."

Gordon stood in his doorway as the other kids walked
back to the stairs. "You boys be careful now," he called.

"What it is," said Deek, flipping away his Sherman as he locked the 'Am and armed the alarm. "Black kids just keep on gettin stupider an stupider!" He turned to Ty and counted on chubby fingers. "What juvie most full of? Black kids! What jail an prison most full of? Black kids! An, that ain't enough for ya, what color the kids cuttin an shootin each other in the streets?" He snickered. "Gonna deny some more, stupid? It just like that ole sayin . . . battle of brains an *you* gots no ammunition!"

Ty tugged on the tail of his brown leather bomber jacket to make sure it covered the .45 in the back of his jeans. The Trans-Am was parked prominently beneath the brightest light in the Burger King lot like a showpiece on display. Which it was, thought Ty. He checked his watch: eight-seventeen. The new kid they'd been supposed to meet at eight would probably be sweating bullets; thinking he'd blown it somehow and Deek didn't want him after all. That was part of the plan. While there was no shortage of kids creaming their jeans to work for Deek, even Ty had to admit that the majority were too stupid—though "stupid," like "funny," could mean a lot of things that had nothing to do with intelligence.

Deek was careful in choosing his kids. Some, especially those who already had guns and were way past streetwise, came on so showtime bad that they blew their chances in the first minute no matter how smart they really might be. It totally disgusted Ty to see some ten- or eleven-year-old with wax in his ears and snot on his lip bragging over his piece or how many times he'd used it. Most were lying, desperately begging recognition from anybody that they lived and breathed, or at least adding one zero to the number of times they figured they'd done something way bad or cool. But none of that shit got by Deek or impressed him. The trouble with showtimes was that they wanted to *look* like dealers, dressing the part like pint-sized pimps till they flashed on the street like neon. Besides, showtimes always had the biggest mouths and the tiniest balls, and broke like glass if busted. Deek preferred the quiet kids: the lean and ragged and hungry ones. It was funny to Ty how those always seemed the darkest too, like himself. They blended into the background, hard to see, but that had little to do with their color. They were more like small and sad-eyed ebony ghosts, haunting the sidewalks or hovering half invisible in doorways or drifting past bars late at night, sighing a soft, almost shy chant of rock, rock, rock, no louder than a breeze stirring trash in the gutter. And no one but the buyers seemed to see them, or hear. Ty also thought it funny how loyal most of them were, like they'd finally found something to believe in after a long, lonely search through a rotting world of hunger and lies, where everything good and everything beautiful was guarded by bars and glass. Sometimes it was hard to tell if the bars locked you in or out. And then there was that magic kingdom sealed inside a TV screen.

Many of the kids dealt for "good" reasons: to feed smaller brothers or sisters, or to support unemployed or unemployable parents. A few were even sent to Deek by mothers or fathers or foster-home people, though those were usually rejected on sight because they were fucked up or unwilling anyway. There were no solid rules, but Deek's instincts were generally right. That was good, because handling them later was mostly Ty's job.

Deek pocketed the keys and started for the building. The evening air was chill with a taste of fog to come, and he wore a black leather jacket with the cuffs rolled back to show his gold wrist chains. The jacket was almost new—a Michael Jackson style with a lot of zippers, and expensive as hell, but cut for a Michael's slim body—and already too tight for Deek to zip up. Ty figured to score it soon for his brother. Sometimes Ty tried to picture Deek as a thin hungry kid. He couldn't, though he often suspected that Deek had been one, once.

Maybe because Deek had had to get up earlier than usual that morning, he was a little loose from drinking all day. Ty kept careful watch on the shadows as he followed Deek across the lot. Ty's own stomach felt heavy with beer, but the alcohol seemed to fire his senses and heighten his wariness. Deek hadn't let him go home like he'd wanted, and the combo of beer and the cops on top of confronting the gang of young boys had stretched even his patience thin. More, the vision of that strange slender boy in the shadows, his eyes meeting Ty's twice in what might have been sympathy, kept scratching at the back of Ty's mind. Ty's mom sometimes went to see an old lady who did weird things with bones and claimed to tell fortunes. Ty mostly figured that was ten dollars down the toilet. He didn't believe much more in magic than in God . . . at least he wasn't sure . . . but it was easy to see that that slim kid believed in *something*, and it probably had more to do with bones than the Bible. Ty fingered his medallion once again.

"Black kids hungry, man!" Ty suddenly blurted to Deek's back. "An it ain't only for food!"

Deek stepped up on the sidewalk that surrounded the restaurant building. This brought his face almost level with Ty's. Ty figured Deek was going to be pissed now; there had been a few times when Deek had hit him, though he always apologized soon after. But Deek only laughed and tapped a finger against Ty's chest, rattling the medallion on its cheap silver chain. "Oh, get real, stupid. Shit, you been there, so stop tryin to smoke yourself. You know same as me that to them little fucks bein BAAAAD is the only thing in the world what matter . . . all the time braggin bout their blade scars or bullet holes, strippin off their shirts to show em. Black kids got nuthin else on their tiny little brains. An all the time the real world is laughin at em cause they locked up in places like this where all they can do is be 'bad' to each other!"

Deek laughed again and patted the top of Ty's head. "What your prob is, you born bout thirty years too late. Ain't no more Panthers, my man. Ain't nobody fightin to make nuthin better. An all them little suckers think it so way fuckin past cool to be endin up dead or spendin their lifes in cages like animals cause they figure it the badge of bein black. Yo. See the joke, man? Them little shits stuck behind the bars of whitey's cage an thinkin *that* make em bad!"

Deek swung around and aimed a finger through the window. "That there our new boy, man. Wanna bet me it ain't? He make you proud? He give you hope? Shit! Check him out, stupid . . . just one more little black sucker!"

Ty looked through the glass. At this hour on a weekday night the restaurant was almost empty; just two high school couples laughing and talking together at one table and, at another near the door, an old dude in dusty coveralls who might have been a janitor. The rest of the business was mostly drive-throughs. A velvet black boy, black as Ty and maybe twelve, tall for his age so he seemed even thinner, sat alone in a corner booth. His elbows were on the table and his face buried in his hands, so Ty couldn't see him too well; just an uncut fluff of hair and a puppyish body about twenty pounds lighter than it should have been. Though worn and faded, his clothes were clean, signifying he still had somebody who cared. His jeans were a year too tight, and his Nikes were banded with electric tape to hold them together. There was a pattern to the banding, like he'd tried turning it into a decoration too. Pride was a funny thing. There was a scarred old skateboard under the table: the reason his toes were so heavily taped and his shirt was only a black satin tank top despite the evening cold. It was too big, probably a castoff, and one strap had slid from his shoulder and dangled at his elbow. The boy's posture said the rest. A small cup of coffee, the shadow line showing it was still half full, though no steam rose, sat in front of him. Smoke curled from a cigarette in a tinfoil ashtray that held another three butts. The boy looked like he could have been crying . . . could've been in love for the first time and torn up about it, or could have had an overdue homework assignment. But Ty knew what that lost and lonely look really signified.

He'd be perfect, thought Ty. One more brick for the

bottom of the pyramid, and so right for the job that he even looked familiar. In his mind Ty compared him to the fighting stances and defiance of the gang boys that morning. Once, maybe this kid had been a fighter too. But twelve years of fighting had worn out his heart.

Deek snickered and draped an arm over Ty's shoulder. "Yo. That YOU, man! Prob'ly just how you look four, five years ago. Come to think on it, that still sorta how you look sometimes, when you figure nobody watchin. I ain't always asleep when you stand by that goddamn window in the mornin's." Suddenly Deek stiffened. "SHIT! You *believe* it that selfsame dribble-lip cunt!"

Behind the counter's bulletproof glass Ty saw the same dark girl who had served them that morning. Though long-limbed and slim, and draped in the baggy fast-food uniform, her body showed pride in breasts carried high, and a soft curve of hips in perfect proportion to the slenderness of her waist. Her hair was cut short in tight, natural curls, accenting what some old people would call the Africanness of her features . . . nose wide but small-bridged, fierce cheekbones, and full-lipped mouth. She wore the lame little cap shoved far back from her smooth forehead as if in contempt, the way a cheetah might treat a circus costume. She was the kind of pure black girl who would never appear in any McDonald's or Burger King commercial or be pictured playing with Barbie dolls beside some blond child on TV. Ty wondered if she, like himself, had ever envied the Arnolds and Websters and Cosby kids of the world. But there was a sort of defiance in her very blackness—the way she wore her hair and the way her sleeves were rolled high past her elbows to bare strong, slim arms—that made Ty suddenly regret his own razored head. He pictured himself in that Afro-ish bush of the boy's, recalling his mom saying once that the style *had* been called a natural way back in the sixties. Ty noted the grace of the girl's moves, and the cool caution with which she kept watch on the customers. She might hate this city as much as he did, but she'd learned to survive in it.

Ty saw the slight softening of her long-lashed black eyes as they lit on the solitary boy. She seemed to hesitate a moment, then drew a small cup of coffee from the machine, scooped a handful of cream and sugar packets from a tray, picked up a cloth, then disappeared around the racks. She came into the customer area a few seconds later through a steel door back by the bathrooms. The cup and packets she carried in one hand, the cloth in the other. Ty watched as she went to the boy's booth and set the coffee near his elbow, then spread the packets with a fan of her fingers like a magic trick to please a small child. She smiled, her teeth large and white against skin as velvety midnight as the boy's. Her hand hovered near the boy's shoulder as if wanting to lift the strap of his shirt back up to where it belonged. It was something a mother would do; a little automatic gesture of love. Ty knew because he'd seen his own mom do those things. She murmured something, and the boy looked up, suspicion changing to surprise that anyone would be nice without a reason.

"DAMN!" Ty's long frame jerked rigid. Blood seemed to burn in his veins like battery acid. Fists clenched, teeth bared, he tore away from Deek and ran to the restaurant door. The old dude in coveralls looked up as the spring-closer screamed under the force of Ty's shoulder, waited until Ty stalked past his table, then got quietly up and left. The high school couples went silent, the girls clutching their bright nylon totes while the boys eyed Ty with cautious hostility.

Ty's Nikes were noiseless as panther paws crossing the polished tile. Automatically, he noted the high school boys, probably seniors, one average-sized and uncertain, the other muscle-bulked with his big jaw set in suspicion. Ahead, the dark girl glided away from the boy's booth, graceful and wary as a slim cat herself, her hand clenching the wet cloth like a weapon. Ty figured she would dart to the kitchen to tell the manager or call the cops. He didn't care. She didn't seem afraid of him—and even furious as he was, he found he didn't want her to be—but he gave her only a glance before his eyes locked with the boy's.

The boy had turned when Ty slammed through the door, searching Ty's face first with hope, and then his expression had hardened into the narrow-eyed sullen look little kids wore when they were scared shitless but trying to be cool. The boy swallowed once, like a cartoon character, then squeaked, "Yo, Ty." It came out half question.

Ty's lips curled back from his big teeth. "You stupid little NIGGER!" He grabbed his brother's arm.

In the kitchen, Leroy looked up from scraping the grill as Markita slipped through the door and slammed it behind her. The room was hot despite the rumbling vent fan; the building's original design probably hadn't considered bulletproof glass at the counter. Leroy was stripped to a wide-mesh black tee, his uniform shirt and the hat he righteously hated flung in a ball in a corner. The long knife slash shone pale down his body. The manager wouldn't be back until nine, when Leroy would leave for his night school, and the chances of a field inspector showing up in that neighborhood after dark were pretty slim. The manager was white, but trusted Markita and Leroy completely. Besides, they worked every hour they could get without him having to show overtime on the books.

Like Markita, Leroy was bone-weary but snapped alert when he saw Markita's face. "What up, girl? We gettin hit again?"

Markita ran up front to the racks and peered around them into the customer area. "That dealer, from this mornin! He outside! His bodyguard just now come bustin in an grabbed some little boy! Maybe I better call the cops!"

Leroy flung down his scraper and ran up beside Markita. He squinted between the burger slides, seeing Ty yank a smaller boy out of a booth. The kid was cussing up a storm, twisting and squirming in Ty's grip, and stubbornly bracing his Nikes on the floor. They squeaked as Ty tried to drag him away.

Markita made a move toward the wall phone, but Leroy took her arm. "Best you keep yourself clear, girl! It be way past game over, time the cops even get here. Then they be pissed at us for callin em! Manager ain't gonna be too stoked neither. You know it for a fact!"

Markita shook her arm free. "Goddamnit, Leroy! Nobody NEVER does nuthin! That why this stuff always happenin!"

Leroy gripped Markita's arm again as she turned for the phone, holding her back. "Wait, girl! Chill a minute! Check it! There the dude lettin the little kid snag his skateboard."

"So?"

Leroy held on to her arm. "Listen up! If the dude was gonna do the kid, he sure as hell wouldn't be lettin him bring his board along! LOOK! How them two actin 'mind me more of tryin to get my little brother in the bathtub on a Sat'day night. Damn if it don't!"

Markita stopped trying to pull away. She had to admit that's exactly what the scene looked like. It would have almost been funny if she hadn't known what Ty was and who he worked for. She watched the tall homely boy drag the smaller one toward the door in a series of squeaky jerks. The kid was still struggling wildly, and tears glittered on his cheeks, but he seemed a lot more pissed off than scared he was going to be murdered. Markita saw the big high school dude stand as Ty skidded the kid past the table, but Ty muttered something, swinging around for just a second and flipping up the tail of his jacket. The big dude paled and sat down fast. Ty kicked the door partway open, shouldered it wider, then flung the young boy into the night. Markita felt Leroy's hand gentle on her arm.

"Leave it go, girl," Leroy murmured. "Whatever it is, be a black thing, an ain't nuthin nobody can do."

Deek was waiting outside near the doorway, Sherman in his lips, jacket collar up against the chill. Fog was creeping thick from the distant Bay, oozing through the gap-toothed board fence at the back of the lot like spirits on *Ghostbusters*. Deek raised his eyebrows, his expression more curious than anything else as Ty flung the kid out the door. The small boy stumbled, almost falling, and dropped his board. It rolled toward Deek. Deek put out a toe and stopped it, then leaned against the wall, arms crossed over his chest, to watch.

The kid recovered at the edge where the concrete dropped off to the asphalt of the drive-through lane. He spun around, his Nike sole squealing, and straight-legged a kick at his big brother's crotch. Ty had half expected that; he knew all the moves that boys his little brother's age would make. Those he hadn't done himself at twelve he'd learned of fast in the months of handling Deek's dealers. Dodging, Ty grabbed the boy's outflung foot and yanked. The kid crashed flat on his back, his breath wuffing out. "Fucker!" he gasped. He jerked back his leg and tore free of Ty's grip, then scrambled up, eyes squinted with tears and face twisted in rage. "I fuckin KILL ya!" he hissed, going for Ty with small fists swinging.

Almost casually, Ty flipped out a long arm and whacked the kid across the mouth with his open hand. The boy staggered backward, slipping off the edge of the sidewalk, arms windmilling, feet scrabbling for balance. He recovered, shaking his head in wonder while spitting blood from a split lip. But he leaped for Ty again, eyes slitted in little-kid fury, teeth bared behind curled-back lips, and sobbing out sounds from deep in his throat.

Deek flicked ashes from his Sherman. "What IS this shit?" he demanded.

Ty snagged a fistful of the kid's huge tank top, big and loose because it was an old one of his. He held the boy at arm's length, beyond the range of furious kicks and small flailing fists. "It a family thing. Nuthin to do with you. I want the night off, Deek."

"*What?*" Deek scowled and flipped his cigarette away. "Yo! You know goddamn well we gotta meet them Bakersfield suckers at ten!"

"Goddamnit, Deek, this Danny! My BROTHER!"

Deek's eyebrows shot up. "*That's* Furball?"

Ty's patient eyes narrowed. Danny's street name came from the scrawny little cat on the *Tiny Toons* TV show, the one with the rag bandage around his tail and a notch in his ear and the perpetual bad luck. Danny's left ear had been nicked in a knife fight when he was eight.

"Yo!" Deek yelled. "He gots a . . ."

Distracted, Ty heard the snick of the switchblade too late. It was Taiwanese junk, but Danny kept the cheap steel sharp. There wasn't much pain as the blade slashed through Ty's leather sleeve, just a sort of burning drag across his forearm and the sudden wet warmth of welling blood.

"DAMN!" Ty cursed himself. He'd known that Danny always carried the knife, just as he knew the boy was now fighting on instinct. None of Deek's dealers could have pulled that move on him! Ty's hand flashed, clamping on Danny's thin wrist and twisting hard. The boy screamed, and the knife hit the concrete with a tinny sound.

Blood seeping from the slash in his sleeve, soaking the cuff and running ruby down his wrist, Ty grabbed Danny again and shoved him backward across the drive-through lane and into the oncoming fog. The rotten fence shook its whole length as Ty slammed his brother against it. A board popped loose behind the boy's back. Danny's teeth suddenly gleamed stark in the darkness. He tried to tear into Ty's bloody wrist. Ty cracked the boy under the jaw, snapping his head up, then clutching his shirt one-handed and savagely shaking the kid. "Stop it, Danny! Fore I gotta hurt you! Game over, man!"

The boy went limp, his knees buckling, held only by Ty's grip on his shirt. His eyes shifted past Ty. Wary of a trick, and scared the boy might try biting again, Ty risked only a quick glance over his shoulder. Through the fog he caught a glimpse of the restaurant's interior, warm-lit and safe-looking, its bright decorations making it a world apart behind glass. Like life, Ty thought, all the good things locked behind glass. The high school kids had gone, but Ty saw the dark girl peering out through a window, a hand shading her eyes as she tried to pierce the fog. She clutched a mop the way Zulu warriors on TV held their spears. Ty hoped she would stay inside. Eyes flicking back to the boy, Ty saw a strange sort of desperate hope in Danny's face. Then Ty realized that Danny wasn't looking at the girl at all but to Deek, who was coming over carrying the skateboard and knife.

Danny made a sudden move, wiggling out of his shirt and

darting under Ty's grab. Ty spun to catch him, but Danny only skidded to his knees on the fog-slicked pavement in front of Deek.

"Please, man!" Danny sobbed. "I wanna work for you. I got to! PLEASE!"

Deek gave the kneeling boy a one-sided smile, then reached down and patted his head. "Chill, boy. You see yourself this never fly."

Danny jerked his face around, fresh tears on his cheeks. His finger flashed to point at Ty like a blade. "HE gots no say over me! He don't give a shit bout me! It MY life, man! MINE!" He spat bright blood at Ty.

Deek folded the knife shut, then dropped it and the board in front of Danny. Ignoring the boy, Deek looked over to Ty. "Ain't this a bitch, man? Motherfuckin family shit do you every goddamn time. Word! Listen up, stupid. I *need* ya tonight!" Scowling, he glanced at his watch. "Look. We gots about a hour. Can you get this goddamn mess cleaned up by then?"

Ty was staring down at his brother. Danny was still kneeling at Deek's feet, sobbing with his head lowered. The boy's thin body glistened with fog-wet, his shoulder blades standing out stark under black velvet skin, his sides heaving as he panted steam. The soles of his Nikes were worn through. Ty's own breath came suddenly hard through a thickness in his throat, but blood still pounded hot in his veins; he could feel its pressure behind the steaming wet oozing from the slash in his arm. He saw the knobby ridge of his little brother's backbone, bent now, and so fragile he could have broken it with a kick. Rage flared in Ty. He *wanted* to kick the boy . . . wanted to systematically beat the shit out of him just like any other of the stupid, snot-nosed little niggers he had to handle. But there was more; he *wanted* to hurt this boy! It was like he *cared* about hurting this boy!

Why?

Ty found himself wondering over that, and his rage leaked away like what was flowing from his arm. He saw that his little brother was shivering. Ty bent down and took Danny's arm, lifting him gently to his feet. He handed the boy his shirt, though expensive black satin was no shelter from cold. He noted that the girl behind glass was still watching. "Put it on, Danny. You catch the sniffles." Ty's voice hardened before he knew it. "Don't you *never* go down on your knees for nobody, nigger! I . . . I fuckin *kill* ya, ever you do that again!"

Then Ty suddenly knelt. He pulled the boy tight against him. "I love you, Danny!"

Deek cocked his head and let out a snort. Ty ignored him. Danny's chin started to quiver as tears ran free down his cheeks. Ty stood, unzipping his jacket and gathering the boy beneath it. He saw the girl turn from the window and walk away slowly, dragging the mop like a mop once more.

Ty leveled his eyes at Deek over Danny's head. "Can't clean up in a hour what this motherfuckin world done to him in twelve years."

Deek's scowl deepened. "Look! We drive him home, then meet them dudes. After that you can take all rest of the fuckin night . . . all fuckin tomorrow too, if you gotta. But I need to know if they done the Crew . . ." Deek's mouth snapped shut and his eyes flicked to Danny. "If it a done deal. Anyways, I can't have them cotton suckers hangin round here when I don't need em no more. They stupider'n a goddamn dozen little kids put together, an that goddamn van stick out like a big black dick! They talk, best you believe! Be showtimin all over town! Prob'ly end in jail, when they broke again. You seen that little sucker Wesley . . . he fixin to fold any second. Hittin em after school today just maybe snapped his little mind. IF them cocksuckin field niggers done it right!"

Deek eyed Danny once more as if not liking what he saw. But then he smiled and leaned down, nudging the skateboard closer to the boy. He didn't seem to notice Ty stiffen when he dropped a hand on Danny's shoulder. "Yo, Furball. Wanna make yourself a *whole* half-buck tonight, dude? All you gotta do is be cool an let us motor you home. Then stay there. Word! Shit, man, that only what your big brother want for ya anyways, ain't it? An, hey, now you even gonna get paid for bein cool!"

Danny studied Deek, peeking from under Ty's jacket and shivering. Deek grinned and waved a palm toward the 'Am. "Yo, dude, bet you never ride in nuthin like that a'fore, huh?"

Ty clasped the boy tighter. "Never rode in no car his whole life, I know bout. But you best believe he ain't gonna ride in *that* one!" Ty locked eyes with Deek and hid Danny's face in his jacket. "World don't pay you for bein good, man. Or cool. Danny ain't takin no goddamn money for doin what he sposed to do anyhow. If that stupid, then that just what it is!" Ty lowered his eyes and sighed out steam. "I get my board. Me an Danny take the bus home. Got us some talkin to do. I ride my board back. Meet you front of your place soon's I can. So what we late? Be the selfsame goddamn trick you just pull on my brother! Sides, I ain't so stupid but I can't see them dudes goin nowhere till they gots their money!"

Deek's eyes had narrowed but he seemed to consider Ty's words. A moment passed, then he shrugged. "Mmm. Maybe you right, man. Well, so how's I just cruise on over your place an pick you up when you done your little heart-to-heart?"

Ty's lips closed over his teeth. His voice came from low in his throat. "Don't you *never* come by my family's place, man! NEVER!"

Deek and Ty regarded each other over Danny's head, but Deek finally gave a short nod. "What it is, I guess. Family shit like that." He glanced at Ty's dripping arm. "Blood. My ass!" He spun on a toe and started for the car. "I get your goddamn fuckin skateboard toy, stupid!" Then he paused and looked back. "Word! You get this here shit covered, man! Total! An you make goddamn sure that little . . . That your brother keep his mouth shut!" Deek snorted and walked on.

Ty waited until Deek was only a ghost in the fog, then pulled a black bandana handkerchief from his jacket pocket and handed it to his brother. "Here, Danny. Wipe your face. It, um, it cool I still call you Danny?"

The boy nodded solemnly. "Yeah. *You* can."

Danny dabbed at his face, then blew his nose with a comical little-kid honk. "Um, I sorry as hell I cut you, Ty. Is it bad?"

Ty flexed his arm, wincing when more blood dribbled from his sleeve. "Naw. Fact is, I hurt myself worse just fallin off my board when I was your age."

Danny studied Ty's arm, looking doubtful, but then smiled. "Yo. That 'your age' stuff sound like what daddy used to say sometimes. When he come home." He gingerly touched Ty's arm. "Done a total number on your cool jacket. Yo! Maybe Mom could sew it? She way good at fixin shit like that." He hesitated. "Or maybe you just wanna go an score yourself a new one. You can, huh? For cause you got the buck. Um, Ty? You do that, maybe you gimme that one, huh? I always want me a cool jacket like that."

Ty pressed his sleeve together to slow the bleeding. "No,

Danny. This not fit for you. Look like just somebody's throwed-away shit. Tomorrow, you an me, we go shoppin . . . right uptown at the 'spensive mall. We score you any kinda jacket you want. One what fit you proper so everybody *know* it yours only. An we get you some new clothes. Whatever you want, man. An the bestest goddamn Nikes they gots. Maybe you help me buy some stuff for the other kids too?"

Danny's eyes widened. "Word, Ty?"

"Best you hear, man. Cause . . . well, cause I love you."

"It sound funny you sayin that, Ty. I don't mean bad-funny, just funny, y'know?"

"Yeah. Well, maybe true stuff . . . stuff from your heart . . . sometime sound uncool. But, anyways, I gonna be comin home more. You an me, we do us some movies, check us out some arcades. You oughta be kickin on games, man, fast as you was with your blade."

Danny's face broke into a sudden grin. Kids' faces were like that, thought Ty, their expressions never still, always changing. Hate or fear could vanish in a second and never leave a trace, to be replaced by wonder or hope . . . or love. Only when they got older did kids' faces harden to reflect the world around them.

"Aw," said Danny. "That only for cause you wasn't watchin when you shoulda. Deek 'stracted ya. That weren't cool at all, man." He slipped his hand into Ty's. "Um, is it okay I hungry, Ty? There weren't much for supper again, an I just barely 'forded myself that coffee so's I could sit inside an wait." Danny hesitated once more. "Um, that there Deek kinda a asshole, ain't he?"

Ty glanced toward the fog-shrouded Trans-Am. "Yeah. That a fact." Ty looked down at his brother again. "But you just forget all bout him, Danny man. I mean that now. Word up."

Danny giggled. "Or you kill me?"

Ty's bloody fingers tightened on Danny's hand. "I . . . don't know what I do. An that the God's honest truth. But I love you always more in my mind if you dead than seein you livin doin shit like just now. That, um, sound kinda stupid, huh?"

Danny searched Ty's face. "I don't know. But *you* doin bad shit, Ty."

Ty shook his head and shrugged. "I don't know what the fuck I doin no more, Danny. An that the God's truth too. Seem like everthin round here all backwards. Like a picture negative."

"Huh?"

Ty shook his head again. "Yo, I just a stupid niggerboy, man. Maybe we all just picture negatives. Forget it." He smiled and brushed fog droplets from Danny's hair. "Yo. I hungry too." He wiped blood from his watch. "We gots us bout a half hour fore the next bus past home. Let's you an me get usselfs somethin to eat, man."

Danny grinned, his face childlike and eager once more. He tugged on Ty's hand, not seeing the pain it caused. "Word up, Ty! Yo! That girl in there, she give me a *free* coffee, man! Just like that! Shit! Maybe she peek you out an like what she see an give you somethin too!"

Ty glanced toward the restaurant, doubting very much if the girl had liked what she'd seen.

As they started back to the building, Deek rolled up beside them in the 'Am and shoved Ty's board out the window. Danny darted to catch it before it hit the ground.

Deek's golden eyes speculated on Ty. He muttered, "'Member, man. I had me another bodyguard." He popped the clutch and the big car snarled off into the fog.

A family of six was just gathering around a table as Ty and Danny came in. There were four kids, boys and girls, the oldest about eight. They were giggling and maxing the way kids do in restaurants because they know their parents won't yell at them. The mother was only half seriously shushing them while their father balanced a huge tray of food in one hand like a waiter and made a game of passing it out to the children. The man gave Ty and Danny a careful glance as they walked to the counter, but Ty had his arm around his brother and his bloody sleeve pressed to his side. The man smiled at them. Ty tugged at his jacket to make sure the .45 stayed covered.

Markita's eyes were wary as the two boys came up to the glass. She noted the small kid's split lip, puffy eyes, and the tear streaks on his face. She'd seen most of the fight, if it could've been called that, including the flash of the knife. She winced now at the sight of Ty's slashed sleeve and blood-covered hand. Keeping her face closed, she silently took Ty's order for cheeseburgers, fries, and drinks, not repeating it to Leroy because he was hovering just behind the racks and heard every word. She felt Ty's gaze on her as she scooped up fresh fries—even though there were packs already on the rack—but pretended not to notice.

The smaller boy had gone back to the corner booth and sat expectantly as Markita put the food on a tray and slid it into the pickup slot. She waited while Ty pulled out his nylon wallet with his bloody hand and dug for bills. It seemed to hurt him to move his arm and, despite herself, Markita felt sympathy for the dark, homely boy. And that was so stupid it brought a following flash of anger, especially when she recalled how scared she'd been of him minutes before. She snatched the money as he pushed it into the slot, ignoring the blood on it, then shoved the tray through and stared full into his eyes. "Proud of yourself, nigger?"

For a moment the dark dude looked totally confused. Then he lowered his patient eyes and fumbled the tray out the other side. His arm seemed to hurt him like hell. If he'd looked up he would have seen sudden pain mirrored in Markita's face. But he didn't look up. "That my brother," he murmured, almost sadly, as he turned away.

Markita watched, bewildered now, as Ty carried the tray over to the booth. She didn't notice Leroy beside her until he touched her hand.

"Ain't life a bitch, girl?"

Still watching the boys in the booth, Markita spoke softly. "They're *brothers*."

"Mmm," said Leroy. "I heard." He snorted and shook his head. "Ain't no wonder whitey figure we all stone-cold crazy!"

Lyon woke with Curtis' beer-scented breath in his face. The smaller boy's warm body was pressed to his own beneath the wool Army blanket. Lyon slept lightly, waking often in the night, and restless whenever the moon neared full. And tonight it was; he could sense its pull inside him as it rose beyond the ceiling of his tiny windowless room and far above the fog that chilled the air and stilled the city sounds.

He felt as if he hadn't slept for long. Sitting up in total darkness, he confirmed it from the ember-red numbers of his clock. It was just 10:13. He and Curtis had gotten back from escorting Tunk at nine. Curtis had gone right to sleep, drunk as he was, and his breathing now was slow and peaceful. He'd escaped the city until morning, and Lyon envied him that. A siren sounded in the distance, and there were some gunshots, but Curtis, like all city kids, would dream right on through it.

Lyon eased from the narrow mattress on the bare board

floor, kneeling a moment to tuck the blanket tighter around his friend. Then he stood with hands on slim hips and scanned the blackness as if he could see every detail. Even with light there wasn't much to look at.

Lyon had his own room, across the hall from his mom's place. The three-story brick building had originally been built for offices, and the eleven apartments now shelled inside were all different shapes and sizes. The wiring was always overloaded and blowing fuses, and the nigger-rigged plumbing was a leaky stinking joke even when it worked. Lyon's room had probably been for maintenance, but little of that was done anymore. It was about twelve by twelve, its ceiling gridded with pipes that groaned and thunked and flaked insulation. The walls, where not covered by posters of rockers, rappers, movie monsters, and collages made of magazine pictures, showed more lath than plaster. Opposite the hallway door was a huge deep sink, revealing rusty iron where chunks of porcelain were chipped, that often did duty as a bathtub and sometimes a toilet. On a shelf to one side squatted a crusted double-burner hot plate that Lyon had tapped to a gas line himself, and where he cooked most of his meals. In cold weather a big clay flowerpot turned upside down over one burner furnished heat. A shelf above held a battered collection of dumpster-salvage pots and pans. To the other side of the sink, a fifties GE refrigerator completed Lyon's kitchen. It was all streamlines and girlish curves with sleek chrome handles and trim like an Art Deco space capsule. It worked perfectly despite being rescued from a condemned building, skidded by the gang down four flights of stairs, pushed six blocks on skateboards, and then battled and cursed up here to the third floor. Lyon had painted it black. It was funny how nobody ever imagined a black fridge.

In the center of the room stood a table and two chairs, survivors of a chrome dinette set. The Formica was cracked and yellowing, and the seats patched with electrical tape. The plating was mostly peeled from their rusty legs. Over the table a bare bulb dangled from wires with a little rubber bat spreading its wings from the pull string. Lyon's few clothes and special things were stored in a bashed-up three-drawer filing cabinet. His many books and stacks of magazines were neatly arranged against one wall on board-and-brick shelves. To anyone breaking in—lucky enough to get past the fire ax suspended ready to swing from above—Lyon's TV would look like an ancient black-and-white model of water-warped wood, and not be worth a second glance. Actually, there was a good Sanyo color set mounted inside. Lyon was good with tools, and his toolbox was one of his proudest possessions.

For all practical purposes, Lyon had lived alone since about age seven. His mom paid the half-buck a month for his room, occasionally gave him some money to buy clothes and food, signed his report cards, and remembered him with a present on Christmas and sometimes his birthday. Since she worked independently, and often had customers in her two-room apartment, this arrangement seemed fine to both her and her son.

Lyon, when he thought about it at all, supposed his mother loved him just as much as any kids on TV were loved, and knew for a fact more than a lot of kids in the neighborhood, even though he'd been an unwelcome accident that never should have happened. But, as his mother had sometimes reminded him when he'd been bad, she *could* have just left him in the dumpster. In fact, the dumpster-baby story had been told to him so much at bedtime that it was more like "Goldilocks and the Three Bears" by now.

His mom was only twice his age anyway. Lyon figured the reason she didn't know jack about kids was that she'd never been one herself.

Lyon put his hand out in the darkness, his fingers finding the little bat on the first try. But then he flicked it away. He didn't want to wake Curtis. And yet he wished he had someone to talk to. This was going to be one of those nights when sleep wouldn't come. He wished he had a lot of beer. That was the only thing that might work. He considered begging a bottle of Night Train off his mother—there was no reason *not* to drink himself to sleep, now that the day's hassles were done—but she might have a customer. With a sigh, he slipped into his clothes, shoved the Iver-Johnson in back of his jeans, picked up his board, deactivated the ax, and quietly opened the door. Finding a winehead passed out with a partly full bottle was a good possibility. Putting his head out first, Lyon checked up and down the corridor. Only one weak bulb burned in the stairwell, but it was enough to see that the shadowy hall was deserted. He stepped out, easing the door shut behind him until the locks clicked, then bent to the baseboard where he'd drilled the two tiny holes. He pulled on the piece of picture-frame wire sticking a half inch out of the left-hand hole. The ax was now on guard again. Anyone opening the door without first pulling the right-hand wire would get the ax blade in the face, neck, or chest, depending on how tall they were. A kid about Curtis' size was safe, and the other gang members always ducked anyway.

Carrying his board by its front truck, Lyon silently descended the stairs, pausing at the second-floor landing to check out the hall and the dark steps below. The only light here was the ruddy glow of an EXIT sign; any other bulbs got stolen as fast as they could be replaced, their filament wire being just the right size for reaming the #25 needles junkies liked best. The building was still except for muffled TV and radio sounds from some of the apartments, and nobody with any real business or brains would linger long in these halls after sundown.

On the ground floor, the street door had a small window of thick glass embedded with wire. It was starred and cracked from being beaten with bottles and so layered with spray paint that the streetlight outside filtered through like something from a church. Tonight the door was locked, though the latch was often jammed open with wadded-up paper for various reasons. Lyon peered out the one little section that was still mostly transparent to make sure no one lurked beyond in the entry. He'd just stepped out, his nose wrinkling at the stinks of shit, piss, and puke, when the rattle of skate wheels carried from down the block, coming fast.

Lyon hesitated, a hand darting first to his pocket to feel the door key, then touching the worn butt of the gun. Head cocked, ears erect, he listened. Whoever the skater was, he rode hard wheels, maybe Bullet or Rat Bone 97s . . . noisy, rapid-wearing, and expensive. Only rich kids skated that type wheel; the gang and the neighborhood dudes went with softer stuff like Powell 85s or Variflex Street Rages. Lyon's own board glided silent as cat feet on ancient 70mm Kryptonic Reds. Staying in shadow, Lyon moved closer to the steps to get a good peek-out when the skater passed by. The dude—not very many girls rode, and never at night —had a definite destination and was shredding to the max to reach it, his wheels snapping over the cracks and buckled sidewalk slabs or ripping like machine-gun fire across iron access plates and sewer covers. The dude was a good skater too, Lyon thought; hard wheels were bad news on slippery wet pavement. The space between kicks told Lyon it was an older dude with long legs.

The skater shot past in a second, but Lyon's eyes caught him like a camera: tall, long-bodied, new jeans and Nikes, and megabuck bomber jacket, sharp razored hair, and ebony face like a cold starless midnight, gleaming with sweat and fog-wet. He rode a serious Sword and Skull plank, and his panting trailed puffs of steam that drifted behind like a jet plane's trail.

It was Deek's bodyguard.

Rage flared in Lyon. He leaped the steps, landing silent on the sidewalk, gun ready in hand. By rules he should shoot the sucker on the spot, but he didn't take aim. There was logic in the rules, and to shoot the dude dead right there wasn't logical to Lyon. The rules also let you use your brain and your heart to do the right thing. Not like what the cops and the TV called laws. Maybe the rules seemed hard sometimes, like not letting Curtis and Tunk hang together. But if the rules didn't make sense, what kid would obey them?

Lyon lowered the gun, watching the dude's shadow fade into the fog. He scented the strong, older-boy sweat, curious because there was blood in it too. He knew Deek's bodyguard lived somewhere a few blocks west of Friends' ground. Since Lyon's building was on the east-border block, that meant the dude was probably shortcutting through. Gordon could decide what to do in the morning. Anyway, there were just the two bullets in the revolver, and Lyon had seen the .45 when the bodyguard's jacket lifted on a long kick. The rules gave no time to fools.

Then Lyon heard the crack of another skateboard slapping a curb down the block behind him. He whirled and scrambled up the steps, just melting into the dark entry once more when the second skater shot by. Again, Lyon's quick eyes caught all.

Except for his worn-out clothes and wild puff of hair the second dude could have been a young clone of the first. He rode a fan-tailed Rob Roskopp, first series, almost as old as Curtis' Variflex, rolling on the sort of soft no-name wheels that came on toy boards and could be scored for a dollar apiece from the poor box at most skate shops. One of his bearings ran loose and dry, and his truck bushings creaked when he kicked. The boy wore only an oversized black satin tank top, and his thin body glistened and steamed in the cold. He panted low urgent sounds like sobs in his throat, breath rasping, maybe from smoking too much, and trailing vapor behind. He seemed desperate not to lose sight of the older dude. He also looked sort of familiar. Lyon wondered if he'd seen him at school.

As soon as the boy was past, Lyon leaped back down on the sidewalk. All thoughts of drinking himself a six-hour death burned away. Something hot was up tonight, along with the blood in the air and the full moon above. If anything was worth being black and thirteen in Oaktown, what it is was this!

Besides, he told himself, decking and kicking off after the two boys, the gang needed all the data scoreable on Deek and his schemes. Lyon slipped the gun back into his jeans as he rolled. Gordon's huge tee covered it easily. Ghosting the dudes wouldn't be hard; even hidden in the fog the rattle and snap of the bigger boy's wheels came clear through the night. The main prob would be not running up on the younger dude. Lyon felt a slight stab of uncertainty as he neared the next corner: the Crew/Friends borderline. Wesley sometimes put a dude on night patrol to check who was dealing after dark. But then Lyon heard the wheel

sound swing right, up the cross street into unclaimed territory. He saw the faint figure of the younger boy follow,
his wheels as silent as Lyon's own. Lyon wondered if he
also had a gun. Maybe he was after Deek's bodyguard to
do him? But the boy was maintaining his distance, and the
logical place for a kill would have been back in the darker
western blocks. Lyon considered: Deek covered a lot of
ground in his car; it was likely that some other gang was
interested in him too, and had put out a scout. It was too
goddamn bad that gangs couldn't work together on this sort
of shit, but then the cops would do their damnedest to bust
it up. Lyon rolled on.

There were people and traffic farther up this street, cars
cruising, their headlights like pale cones in the mist, their
boom music beating deep. The streetlamps were haloed,
and the neon signs swam from the fog as Lyon ripped past.
He dodged the figures that materialized in his path, and
cut cautiously around the clusters of men and mid-teen
boys, some with their ladies and most of them drunk or
otherwise fucked, who hung by the bars and liquor stores.
There were a few taunts, but most from dudes close to his
own age; the older people didn't seem to see him as well.
A bottle whistled past his head once and shattered in the
street. Two bigger boys on boards tried to pace him, so
drunk they kept getting in each other's way, but he lifted
his shirt for a moment and they checked the gun and
dropped back, laughing and howling for him to do the motherfucker. Lyon wasn't sure who they had in mind. A woman
in a doorway flashed her tits when Lyon looked twice to
make sure it wasn't his mom. They weren't bad for an old
lady's. His wheels crunched often through broken glass,
and he skidded one time in a puddle of puke, but managed
to maintain his distance with the second skater, who seemed

to be tiring fast, his kicks getting ragged, and just barely clearing the curbs on his ollies. Lyon wondered how much longer the boy could keep matching the older dude's pace. Whatever else Deek's bodyguard did, Lyon had to respect his skating.

Lyon's own breath was burning his throat; one of these days he'd cut down on Kools. His T-shirt was soaked now and clammy with fog-wet and sweat. His knees were beginning to ache. The Iver Johnson's big old-fashioned front sight was chafing a spot on his butt. A bunch of small boys zoned in a doorway with crack pipes stared openmouthed as he passed. Glimpses of the dude ahead when he rolled under lights showed him to be just about dusted; he'd fallen back so far that Lyon couldn't hear the older boy's wheels anymore. It was beginning to look like Deek's bodyguard was headed all the way uptown, and Lyon considered dropping the chase. Then he saw the small boy cut into a side street.

Lyon slowed, coasting a moment, then tail-skidding to a stop beneath a dead streetlamp. A golden glow pooled on the sidewalk from a bulb behind the barred windows of a closed-up corner market. A girl's laugh echoed softly in the store's shadowed doorway. "They done gone thataway, pardner."

Lyon's smile flickered as he fought back his breath. "Yeah?" he panted. "Then maybe I head em off at the ole pass, huh?"

The girl laughed again, a good open laugh, and her tone was friendly. Must be a slow night, thought Lyon.

"It way past ten, boy," said the girl. "Your mom know where her children are?"

Lyon's smile faded, and he turned away. "I not know where she be neither."

The girl was silent a few moments, then she sighed. "Mmm. Well, sympathy spread pretty thin around here, boy."

Lyon frowned. "Don't 'member me askin for none. Special from the likes of you! Anyways, I bet you just got that outa some ole book."

The girl sighed once more. "Used to read me a lot of books, boy. An not just them they make you in school. Got no time, no more . . . no time for nuthin but eatin an sleepin an workin, seem like." Her voice trailed off and she seemed to study the slender boy. "Look to me like you on some kinda quest." She sniffed. "Bet you don't even know what that mean."

Lyon snorted. "Your ass I do, girl! Quest be a seekin thing . . . for justice an truth an that sorta shit. Nobody go on em no more. So there!"

Again, the girl was quiet a time. Finally she nodded. "Keep on seekin, little warrior."

Lyon decked. "An you take care, sister. Night." He rolled down the side street.

It was narrow, dark, and silent after the blocks of bars and noisy fucked-up people. The crumbling old buildings seemed to lean over the sidewalks. More than half looked abandoned, their windows and doorways blanked with boards and spray-painted plywood. The others, mostly small shops and garages at ground level, had their windows defended by bars or big screens. The echo of the bodyguard's wheels had been swallowed in the fog. Lyon skated carefully, his ears alert, eyes straining to pierce the mist, and nostrils flared as if to scent danger. Garbage and trash lay everywhere, and a few stoves and refrigerators had been shoved from windows above, and looked it. The curbs were lined with a zombie parade of dead cars without wheels, their hoods, doors, and trunk lids gaping open like mouths, glass all smashed and strewn in sprays of icy glitter. Most were stuffed with more garbage, all were spray-painted, and some showed bullet holes. Rats scuttled in and out of them, a few sitting up and eyeing Lyon as if it were only a matter of time. One had its doors shut even though its glass was all gone. Lyon heard a child's cough as he rolled by. It was a lonely sound. There was also an occasional big battered truck, its hood secured by a padlocked chain or cable to protect its battery. Only the city's overglow, heightened by the hidden moon above, lit the block. A sick orange flicker farther down indicated a dying streetlamp at the next intersection. A half dozen upper windows in buildings showed lights, but these only seemed to strengthen the darkness.

The trash made skating treacherous, and the glass crunching under his wheels set Lyon's teeth on edge. Fearful of the noise, he tailed and strained his ears for sounds from the other boys. Nothing. Picking up his board, he stood a moment while sweat chilled on him, shivering and trying to decide what to do. He must have lost the dudes . . . they could have gone into any of those buildings farther down the block. He found he wasn't disappointed; he'd had his night's adventure—quest—and even if he hadn't learned anything to help his gang, he'd be so dusted by the time he got home that he'd probably sleep like the dead. He glanced around; there were gang marks on the cars and buildings, but too many of them and all different. Still, this might be somebody's ground; at least the kids would all go to a different school, so nobody would know him. Maybe he could score a cigarette from the girl on the corner before he started back. She might be able to say if he was in somebody else's territory so he could watch his ass on the return run.

Gordon's black tee was technically colors, piss-poor maybe, but he could always strip it off. It suddenly seemed like a long way home.

He was just about to turn and deck once more when the parking lights of a car winked on toward the end of the block. They looked like the amber eyes of some huge jungle cat. Then a voice carried to his ears; an older boy's, sounding slightly drunk and pissed to the max. "C'mon, stupid! It way fuckin past get-busy time! I don't wanna *hear* no more bout your motherfuckin family shit!"

Lyon froze. The voice was Deek's.

A shiver, this one of fear, went down Lyon's spine. For sure he'd wanted to find Deek, but wanting was something like dreaming, and dreams didn't usually end the way you'd hoped. He hesitated. Still, anything he could learn about the dealer would be good for the gang, and might give them an edge over the Crew at tomorrow's meet. If nothing else, just knowing where Deek cribbed could be a major advantage. Lyon decided, since he'd come this far, he might as well check things out.

Stepping off the sidewalk, he eased between two abandoned cars and moved slowly down the line of vehicles on the street side. The panther-eyed stare of the Trans-Am's parking lights disappeared behind a big old box-bodied truck as Lyon neared, but the murmur of voices sharpened with each step closer until he could hear every word. Deek was doing most of the talking and seemed mega-pissed at his bodyguard.

"You stupid shit! It almost *eleven* now an them dudes just might be lame enough to go out cruisin an start askin everybody in sight if they seen us! Fuck that cocksuckin little brother of yours, man! Blood mean nuthin cept trouble! Tell me you can't handle no skinny-ass little twelve-year-old! What in hell you figure you gettin paid for, stupid? Babysittin?"

Then came the bodyguard's voice, hard and sulky. "Call MY brother no cocksucker, man! Danny ain't one of yours! An he ain't never gonna be! So just shut up your goddamn mouth, Deek!"

Deek's voice dropped low, and that somehow made it dangerous. "You best think long an hard fore you tell *me* to shut up again, nigger. An shit! What the fuck make you figure I even want him? Word, stupid! I seen a zillion Dannys! An he's figured out what it is, man . . . oh yes he has. An you a even bigger fool for denyin it! Buck, what it is, stupid! An not you an not nobody gonna stop him from tryin for some now, best believe! Cause he KNOW for a fact he just a rag-ass little niggerboy without none!" Deek snorted. "Blood don't mean nuthin to him no more. You deny that, then what the fuck runnin down your arm right this minute, sucker?"

Lyon edged around the burned-out hulk of a Honda Civic. The big truck loomed ahead, parked facing up the street. Deek's car was behind it, in front of what looked like a tall, narrow apartment building. Stopping beside the Honda, Lyon studied the truck: it would be no prob climbing over the cab to the flat roof of the van box. He could crawl to the rear and see and hear everything. He slipped his board onto the charred front seat of the Honda where he could snag it fast.

Then another thought hit him, so intense that he shivered again. Deek and his bodyguard caught unaware! A gun and two bullets! Lyon's hand found the Iver Johnson and pulled it from his jeans. The law checked Deek's license and let him go on killing kids. The rules said different!

Then Lyon thought about the bodyguard . . . who had a

twelve-year-old brother named Danny. Lyon knew enough about love to recognize it when he heard it in somebody's voice. His long fingers clenched tight on the gun butt. The ancient revolver was warm from his skin. If he killed Deek, would the bodyguard's duty be done? Or would his loyalty hold beyond death? Maybe there was a rule about that too?

Lyon eased along the Honda's flame-blistered fender, the gun gripped two-handed and ready. He remembered the green-crusted cartridges. Well, one had fired that morning; there was a good chance both of these would too . . . even better odds that at least one would go off. He recalled the bodyguard's .45. Maybe the dude loved his brother enough to see that this had to be done?

Deek's voice suddenly raged, breaking in the middle. There was a soft thunk that sounded like a fist against flesh and a short wuff of breath. "Don't fuck with me, man! NEVER!"

Lyon pictured Deek's chubby fist and the tall boy's lean washboard belly.

"NOW where the fuck you goin, stupid?"

The bodyguard's voice sounded strained, but stubbornly patient. "Got to tie somethin round this arm. Bleedin won't stop."

"Aw, SHIT! Know what? You losin it, man . . . lettin some little sucker slice you like that! For chrissake, nigger, shag your ass!"

Lyon heard the wet squeak of Nike soles as the bodyguard ran up the building's steps. Now Deek was alone! The lock clicked on the building's front door. There was a squeal from a spring as it opened. Lyon felt his heart thumping in his chest. Tensed, trembling, the gun gripped in hands gone suddenly cold, Lyon stepped to the front of the Honda. He'd give the bodyguard another thirty breaths to get deep inside the building or up the stairs. There'd be plenty of time to do Deek, grab his board, and roll before the dude could get back out again. Lyon poised on his toes, ready.

Lyon scented the boy before he saw him. The second skater! He was crouched on the curb side of the truck, pressed to the huge front tire, peering around it at the building. Wisps of steam curled from his thin body and bushy hair. One strap of his tank top hung at his elbow, and his shoulder blade stood out knife sharp under his skin above the ridges of his ribs. His board lay beside him, its nose aimed for the street.

Lyon froze. The apartment building's door clacked shut. Lyon tried to still his shivering. What in hell was happening? Who the fuck *was* this kid? Lyon was almost positive now he'd seen him before at school—not in any of his classes, just a face in the hall or cafeteria. Pale light flashed on in a third-floor window. It threw enough glow down onto the street to show the notch in the boy's left ear. Furball! He had a name with his knife but belonged to nobody. Was this the same boy the bodyguard had called Danny . . . his brother?

Lyon's mind replayed what he'd just heard: if Danny was Furball, then he must be the kid who wanted to work for Deek. And his big brother didn't want him to. So what the fuck was he doing here? And, Lyon wondered, what was *he* going to do now?

On TV the hero would creep up behind some unsuspecting dude, press the gun to his head, and whisper something showtime like "Freeze, sucker!" Prob was, that didn't really work. In real time the dude would likely give a yell. It was a human reflex. For sure the hero might also clunk the dude over the head with the gun butt. Then he'd always stay out just long enough for the hero to do whatever heroics needed to be done. Maybe that would work if you had a lot of practice thunking dudes on the head, knowing how hard to hit them and exactly where. Maybe cops did, but Lyon didn't. Besides, Lyon had seen Gordon get clunked with a Night Train bottle one time in a fight. The fat boy had only cursed and proceeded to kick the sucker's ass.

Now, Lyon thought a string of curses, wishing he knew what to do. Finally, he just stepped into the space between the truck and the Honda, aimed the gun one-handed at the boy, put a finger to his lips, and softly shuffled his Nikes.

The boy's head snapped around. "Uuuuuh!" His eyes popped wide, flicking, one, two, from the gun to Lyon's face. His jaw started to drop, but then comprehension flashed over his features, and he relaxed slightly, breathing out a vapory sigh. Lyon took a step nearer, then knelt, keeping the Iver Johnson aimed. "Furball?" he whispered.

Furball scanned Lyon's face, his own expression a mix of fear and mounting anger. "Yeah? So what, man?" he whispered back. He studied Lyon again, then his eyes narrowed. "I seen you. At school. You Lyon. You belong to the Friends. Word say you magic. I don't believe none of that shit. Yo! An you a fuckin homo!"

"Chill out an shut the fuck up!" hissed Lyon. "Else you be tellin everybody round school tomorrow how a blow boy kick your butt!" Lyon jerked his jaw in the direction of Deek's car. "Spose you know who *that* be?"

Furball's eyes turned suspicious. "Shit stink? What it by ya?" He spat near Lyon's feet. "An I ain't ascared of no pussy little faggot gun neither!"

Lyon's V smile clicked on. "Pussy little faggot gun be shootin pussy little bullets, meanin dirt-nap time for assholes what don't shut the fuck up. An here be some magic for ya, man. I know Deek not wantin you workin for him.

An your brother not neither. Maybe cause he love ya, sucker." Lyon's smile faded. "Best you believe us Friends ain't too stoked over it our ownselfs."

Furball looked uncertain a second, but then his eyes hardened. "I don't live in your ground, man. You dudes got no say over me." A new thought seemed to hit him. "Yo! How you know Ty my brother?"

"Could be by magic. Could be I just know he love you, man . . . don't wanna see you sellin yourself to the likes of Deek. Like a blow boy."

"Fuck your magic, sucker! An Ty gots no say over me. Not no more . . ."

Lyon cut Furball off with a jerk of the gun as the light went out in the window above. That meant the body-guard—Ty—would be back in less than a minute! Lyon stood, still covering Furball with the gun. Was there enough time left?

Furball stared at the upper window, then turned back to Lyon. There was fear in his eyes once more. "You come to *do* em, man? Dint ya?" He trembled like something trapped. "No!" he hissed. "Not my brother, man! PLEASE!" He jumped to his feet, a hand darting for his pocket. Lyon whipped the gun up in a two-handed aim. But Furball ignored it. He stared straight into Lyon's eyes. "No! I ain't gonna let ya!"

Desperate as the seconds ran out, Lyon tried a fake. "So I kill you too, sucker!"

Furball's own magic was the knife appearing out of no-where in his hand. "I don't care! C'mon, nigger, do me, ya gots the balls! Ty hear. Then he kill YOU!" Furball's chest puffed as he sucked breath for a yell. The building's front door creaked open.

Lyon lowered the gun. "Okay, man. Your game. Word."

For a long moment the two boys just stood facing each other. Ty came down the steps and crossed the sidewalk. The Trans-Am's engine snarled to life. Finally, Furball let his knife hand drop to his side. "C'mon, Lyon. I don't want Ty seein me. We slide round the truck when Deek pull out. 'Kay, man?"

The Trans-Am's tires fried rubber. Its headlights slashed the fog. Furball and Lyon barely made it around the truck's front fender before the car shot past up the street, tires still smoking as it burned away. The fog flared blood red for an instant as Deek tapped the brakes at the corner but ran the stop sign. Rubber screamed again as the car slewed right and disappeared.

"Seem like Deek gots plans for somebody," murmured Lyon.

Furball was just staring after the car. His eyes were slitted and his lips pulled back from his teeth. "Motherfucker gots no right callin Ty stupid, man! Or all them other sucker names!" He swung around to Lyon. "Cocksuckin fat-ass prick HIT Ty, man!" His knuckles paled as he clenched the knife. "I should kill him for that!"

Lyon glanced once at the knife, then lowered the Iver-Johnson's hammer. "You gots no chance in hell 'gainst Deek with nuthin but a blade, man. What the fuck you figure I doin here?"

Furball looked Lyon up and down. "Yeah? Well, you was gonna kill my brother too, wasn't ya?"

Lyon let the gun hang at his side, its muzzle down in his long loose paw. His uptilted eyes beneath their soft lashes held a calculating curiosity. "Not less he make me."

Furball's knife hand whipped out. The blade was suddenly at Lyon's throat. "Cheer me up, sucker!"

Holding the other boy's eyes, Lyon spread his arms wide

and slowly sank to his knees. The blade followed him down so he ended, head back, throat offered, gazing up into Furball's face. Seconds passed. Bitter smoke from the Trans-Am's tires drifted across the sidewalk. Finally, Furball sighed out steam. His lips clamped shut over his teeth. He jerked the knife away and folded it closed against his leg, then stood proud with arms crossed and chest puffed. "Get up, man. Don't never go down on your knees for nobody, nigger. My brother say that."

Lyon rose. "Your brother give it a name. That why Friends not be workin for Deek sucker, nor no others like him."

Furball snorted as he pocketed the knife. "Yeah? So try an eat names, asshole! Know what? Way I see, the whole fuckin world tryin to keep you on your goddamn knees when you ain't gots no money!" He spat on the sidewalk and yanked his tank-top strap back up. "So give THAT a name, magic boy!"

Lyon slipped the gun into his jeans. "So world always be tryin, man. That somethin new? Don't mean you gotta eat shit, just cause it shoved in your face."

Furball gave Lyon a long look. The shirt strap slipped off his other shoulder. "Yo! You done that a'purpose just now, huh? Shit. You ain't stupid! You never leave yourself open like that by accident! Why?"

Lyon shrugged. "Wish I had me a smoke."

"Huh? Oh. I gots a couple Kools here." Furball dug in his pocket and pulled out a squashed pack. "Gots no fire, though."

A Bic appeared in Lyon's paw.

"See?" said Furball. "I knowed all the time you was fast!"

Lyon smiled, and the two boys leaned together to fire their cigarettes. Their eyes met over the flame. Lyon asked, "You love your brother, man?"

Furball snorted smoke. "What a fuckin stupid question! COURSE I do!" Then he turned away and picked a scab of paint from the truck's fender. "But *he* work for Deek. Gots him a gun an everthing. A *real* gun, not some piss-ass little toy like yours! Dudes respect him! Want me some of that!"

Lyon let smoke trickle from his nostrils. "Respect not be the same like you scared of somebody, man."

"Shit! I know that. Like, who respect cops?"

Lyon nodded. "Mmm. So you figure your brother respect Deek?"

"Huh? Well . . . *course* not! Deek treat Ty like shit, man! You *hear* what that sucker call Ty just now? An he HIT him, man! Hard's he could! I SEEN it, man!" Furball's chest puffed again. "But know what? Ty just stand there, man! Like, hard's that motherfucker hit him weren't jack, man! Word!"

Lyon took another hit on his Kool. "So what you sayin is, Ty don't respect Deek, an Deek don't respect Ty. So what kinda shitty job that be? I askin ya, man."

Furball fingered his cigarette. "Well . . . well, he just doin it for cause to help my mom. Maybe that all the respect he need. I mean, I ain't sayin he don't got lotsa way cool clothes an shit. But know what, Lyon? Most all his buck come home, uh-huh! Yo! Him an me? We goin UPtown mall shoppin tomorrow! Gonna score our whole goddamn family all kinda clothes an food an shit we need, man. Word! THAT why Ty takin Deek's shit, man . . . doin it for cause he love us all!"

Furball's eyes suddenly slitted. "But YOU dint know none of that, did ya? Yo! All you seen was some dude to kill!" He flipped his cigarette away and clenched his fists. "Shit! Why I dint do ya just now, I don't even know!"

Lyon sat down on the truck's running board. "Cause you

be knowin what is, inside like, even you smoke you ownself that you don't." He met Furball's eyes. "Word. I COULDA killed your brother, man. Just now! Listen up. Can't you be seein how total easy it happen? Give it a name, man. You ain't stupid. You figure me an who I belong to be the onliest ones waitin on a clear shot at your brother?"

Furball watched as Lyon crushed out his Kool. It made a soft hiss on the wet rusty steel. Furball stared down at his ragged Nikes and kicked a taped toe on the concrete. "Spose I never think it like that a'fore. I never belong to nobody."

Lyon shrugged. "Man, you don't *need* to belong to nobody but yourself. I say this, dude, bet your ass your HEART knowed it all along."

Furball looked down at his chest, half bared where his shirt had slid off. "My heart know my little brother an sisters hungry, man. An walkin round wearin ole raggedy-ass Salvation Army clothes what white people throwed away." He looked up at Lyon. "So maybe my heart DO know, man . . . what gonna happen to Ty. So what I do? My mom scared. I can tell for cause sometime she cry in the night. She scared for Ty, an I think she scared what happen not havin the money Ty bring us home. Somebody got to take up the slack, man. Why I come here tonight. I figure to talk Deek alone, out my brother bein round."

Furball frowned. "You fuck that for me, man." He shrugged. "All what you tellin me? Bout hearts an shit? Sound magic. Gotta be magic for cause I don't unnerstand. Like churchy shit. I don't believe none of that neither. Tell you this, man. Word up! There a God, he be white. Believe it! Anybody with eyes see that! Nigger kids got no God, man! He cost too fuckin much!"

Furball kicked at the concrete again. "Aw, what it is,

man. Shoulda knowed none of this shit work out for me!" He touched his left ear. "Dudes think my name come from this." He snorted. "Me? I figure it come from bein borned unlucky. Or black. Shit. Maybe mean the same, huh?"

Lyon nodded. "Mmm. Sometime seem that way."

"Well, I gotta say that one way cool name you got yourself. Lion. There *power* in that, man. Somethin you can respect. Word!"

Lyon smiled. "It *be* my name. With a *y*. See, my mom leave me in a dumpster, night I be born. Cold as hell, she say. Then, long bout mornin time she . . . well, she say she hear a callin. In her mind, like. Say she be thinkin bout me all them hours. So, she goes running down. Frost all over everthing. Say she lift up that lid, figurin I be total history. But there I was, she say, smilin right up at her like shit don't stink . . . like I knowed all along she be comin back." Lyon looked suddenly shy. "She tell me only a lion live through that."

"Jesus," breathed Furball. "Man, that musta totally sucked! Shit! Wonder you gots a heart at all!"

Lyon shrugged. "Well, only real lions left be in cages."

"Yeah. Guess so, huh? Shit, I'd hate bein caged, man."

"Mmm. Word say it go with bein black. Mean you way past bad."

"Word fulla shit sometimes. Just for cause it black don't mean it true." Furball was quiet a time, kicking at the old truck's tire. He pulled up his shirt strap but it slid right off again. He frowned and fingered it a moment but let it hang. "Um, Lyon? Wanna get drunk with me tonight? I talkin DEAD, man! Shit. Way I feel now, 'most wish I dead for real!"

"Mmm," said Lyon. "I hear that. But best not be wishin bad shit. There enough of it floatin round already." Lyon

smiled. "I be proud to die with you, man. You got somethin
by?"

Furball puffed his chest once more. "Word! Gots me a
whole motherfuckin quart of Jack D. That do us both till
mornin, believe! It in a 'bandoned buildin on my block.
Better keep your gun ready on the ride back past them
bars, man. That street only get badder, night go on."

Lyon stood up and pulled his tee over the gun. "For sure,
man. An this time you gots permission to be shortcuttin
Friends' ground."

Furball grinned. "Oh! So's you ghosted me, huh? Shit,
I shoulda knowed. That the onliest way you find this place.
Nuthin magic bout that."

"Word. But followin your brother be the onliest way *you*
find this place too. An I woulda ghosted him anyways. So,
just maybe you being here save your brother's life tonight.
Tell me there not no magic in *that*, man. Shit. What you
spect, rabbits outa hats?" Lyon's face hardened a little and
he pointed to the building's upper windows. "Yo. Now I
know where Deek be cribbin. Mornin come, all the Friends
know too. Dudes like Deek get done cause of little ole fuckups like that. Last word from me." Lyon went around the
Honda and pulled out his board, then studied Furball
across the car's blistered roof. "So, you gonna be tellin
your brother Deek gettin schemed on?"

Furball's eyes shifted from Lyon to the window above.
"Word, you ain't gonna try an kill Ty, man?"

Lyon shook his head. "You know for a fact I can't be
promisin nuthin like that, man. You know it be Ty's job to
cover Deek's ass. Word, we try not to hurt your brother if
there be any way other. You know, by rules, it the best I
can give. So?"

Furball stared down at the sidewalk. "If I say I gonna
tell, mean you gotta kill me right now, huh?"

Lyon sighed. "No, man. You coulda done me with your blade, but you didn't. By rules, I owe you. But that not what it is, man. I trust you. Your heart. Forget all that good an bad an magic an churchy shit. Just listen to your heart. Black hearts be strong an good all by theyselfs, deep down." Lyon thought a moment. "You tell your brother this, word up. Say you hear Deek playin with power where he gots no right. Even the ghost of a dog gots teeth."

"So, you trust me, man?"

"So, I trust your heart, brother."

Furball nodded. "Okay. Done deal. An you owe me nuthin, man. You coulda killed me first with your gun an then gone right ahead and done Deek an Ty. So, maybe I see a little what you talkin hearts."

Lyon thought about the two bullets, wondering what he would have done if he'd had more. But that didn't matter. Now. He smiled. "Done deal, dude."

Furball grinned. "So, let's go die, brother."

"So, what it is with Furball, man?" asked Deek, steering with one hand, the other steadying the beer bottle between his legs as he slid the Trans-Am, tires crying, around a corner. "Did you go an smoke his little butt?"

"No." Ty stared straight ahead through the misted windshield into fog, his body braced as Deek recovered the fishtailing car with a twist of the wheel and a jab on the gas. "Danny home in bed. Where he belong. Put him there myself. Need his sleep for school tomorrow."

Deek gave Ty a glance, and grinned. "He get good grades, man?"

"Yeah."

"Them an seventy-five cents score him a cup of coffee anytime."

"Don't fuck with me, Deek. I ain't in no mood."

"Yo, stupid! Better GET in the motherfuckin mood! Nuther few minutes an you just might be facin a couple a Uzis! Ain't nuthin more dangerous than makin a payoff . . . special if it the last one!"

Deek eyed the tall boy, then sighed. "Aw, I sorry I hit ya, man. Did I hurt ya?"

"No."

"Well then, don't pout. With your lips it just make ya look . . ."

"I know," said Ty.

"Mmm. Well, if them cotton suckers went an hosed down the Crew like they sposed, Wesley gonna be on his little ole niggerboy knees BEGGIN enough work for to score him some fire." Deek grinned again. "Just maybe I surprise the little sucker with a present. Show my good faith, what I sayin."

Ty shrugged. "I do my job. Leave the thinkin to you." Then he turned. "What you sayin, *present?*"

"Done me some of that thinkin, man. While you was babysittin. Listen up! I give the Crew a Uzi—now what I even need the Friends for? The Crew hold em down, best believe. Or just do em all. I could give a shit which."

Ty frowned. "Mean, you gonna hand them kids a one-grand gun, just like that?"

Deek snickered. "What I say, man? My good faith! Kids LIKE to be trusted. Shit, you of all people should oughta know that!"

Ty glanced at the back seat where the carbine lay. Deek saw him and smiled. "Naw. Not that one. It almost new. I get em another. At a discount."

Deek hunched over the wheel, peering ahead through the mist, then swung the car into a shabby old gas station. It was closed for the night, its pumps protected by plywood panels chained around them. Accordion bars were drawn across the front of the rusty steel building. A small bulb burned inside the office section, revealing bare shelves and a wide-open cash-register drawer. A sputtering fluorescent tube over the service-bay door lit an ancient RICHFIELD sign. Deek drove carefully around behind the building, threading the 'Am through piles of bald tires and junked auto parts. The headlights swept past several gutted car bodies and a mountain of dead batteries along the back fence. Deek eased the 'Am to the building's far side so that it was facing the street once more. He killed the lights but left the engine running.

"What up?" asked Ty as Deek set the parking brake.

"Nuthin. Just gotta piss."

Automatically, Ty flicked off the .45's safety and moved to get out.

"Naw," said Deek, pushing open his door. "Place a total graveyard. I'm cool." He swung the door shut and walked back around the building.

Ty watched a moment in the mirror as Deek disappeared into mist. Why was he going so far just to piss? It probably had something to do with the lame-looking little dance he did to get his zipper zipped again under his sagging sack of lard. Another six months and Deek wouldn't be cruising the designer racks anymore . . . just plain old fat-boy 501s like Gordon wore. But then Gordon carried himself with pride.

Six months. Ty scanned the shadows. Six months seemed an eternity. Coldly, Ty considered if he'd even live that much longer, especially the way Deek was maxing things lately. Ty thought of Danny: he *had* to stay alive for the boy! What Danny needed was a man, but Ty decided he'd have to do.

Ty noticed another stack of old batteries piled against the station wall; probably saved back until the price of scrap lead went up again. Word said the major dealers sometimes did that with their shiploads of shit. He remembered how his dad had tried scrap salvaging for a while; same as he'd tried almost everything else a poor, honest black man could do to make a living for his family. Ty had helped, prowling with him through the back streets and alleyways in a rattly old '58 Ford flatbed, picking up every stray piece of rusty scrap iron, digging in dumpsters for aluminum cans, and snatching dead batteries out of empty lots and junk cars. They'd been worth about a dollar apiece. On a good day they might score a whole half dozen.

Ty gazed at the batteries now, noting the fluffy white fuzz grown thick on their terminals from oxidation. He'd been just about Danny's age then; same miserably thin body and underfed muscles, struggling to heft those heavy goddamned things the four feet up to the truck bed, but mentally counting each as one more dollar for his family. Chump change for sure, yet there'd been a proud sort of feeling at the end of the day; maybe like one rag-ass niggerboy who couldn't be beaten down.

Ty flexed his slashed arm, wincing a little. Six months of that and he'd been wiry as a cheetah he'd seen on *Wild Kingdom*. He pulled up his shirt and ran a palm over his belly. Deek's punch hadn't hurt him, but all the beer and riding in this goddamned car was starting to show. Deek could afford to get sloppy and fat. A bodyguard had to stay hard and fast, and right now Ty didn't feel much of either.

Deek used to have another bodyguard.

Ty shrugged and popped another Heineken. You gonna die, nigger, die happy. He looked at the batteries again, recalling how that fuzzy shit used to burn in the cuts on his hands. He remembered how, in the hot afternoons, after they'd sold their day's earnings at the scrap yard, he and his dad would sit dusty and sweaty and shirtless in the truck and split a quart of Colt .45 before going home. Ty used to like the malt liquor with a grape Popsicle. They'd talk about all sorts of stuff, things a dude just no way could ask his mom. And supper had always tasted so goddamn *good* with a half quart of Colt already inside him. Ty remembered his dad's strong man-smell. Danny needed something like that.

Ty's mind drifted. He could get a license. They charged now for the driver training course at school—another advantage rich kids had over poor—but coming up with the buck would be no problem now. There were lots of old flatbed trucks scoreable for under a grand. He'd put in a CD for sure; it would make the work go smoother. He suddenly realized he could make it all happen in only a month more of working for Deek. One motherfucking little month! Why in hell hadn't he thought of this before? Maybe you had to know what you wanted before you could try for a grip on it.

Deek returned and slid back into the car. Ty stayed silent as they headed out to the street. In the city you learned young to keep your dreams to yourself. It was funny, thought Ty, that now more than ever he'd have to cover Deek's ass.

The old motel was way over east, off Foothill; a two-story shoe box of cracked, scabby stucco and peeling pastel paint. Its second-floor landing was railed by rusty wrought iron. The neon sign flickered half dead, and more of the yellow bug-light bulbs by each door were burned out or broken than working. The shabby black van looked totally at home in the parking lot, among bashed-up, wanna-be-bad sixties and seventies 'Stangs, Cams, and GTOs. There was also a tricked-out Vee-dub, and a battered, big-pig station wagon that probably belonged to some homeless family who'd checked in for one night of showers, warmth, and black-and-white TV.

Deek parked the 'Am facing out toward the street. Ty made sure his .45 was cocked, safety off, and nestled it carefully in the back of his jeans. He noted the cautious movement of curtains in several of the motel windows, and felt eyes on him for a second or two. Pale light shone from behind faded shades in the second-floor room of the Bakersfield dudes, but no one was doing a peek-out from up there. Deek left the car unlocked and didn't arm the alarm.

Ty moved in front of Deek as they neared the stairs. "I go first," he murmured. "I knock, an you keep way 'hind me."

Deek grinned, puffing up the staircase at Ty's heels. "Times like this make up for all the shit you cause me, man."

Once more Ty was aware of eyes behind curtains as he moved along the landing. Some of the peephole glasses darkened. A lot of those people were waiting for something, and it probably wasn't Domino's pizza. Most of the TVs seemed tuned to the same channel: likely this place had no cable. The low voices of happy children came from the room next to the Bakersfield boys. It didn't take much to make kids happy, Ty thought. Food, love, and a warm place to sleep counted most.

Reaching the dudes' door, he heard TV sound in there as well, news noise, something about Iran or Iraq and sending them guns or money. Motioning Deek to stay back, Ty stepped to the panel and rapped softly with his knuckles while keeping his other hand on the .45's butt.

For a minute, nothing happened. Finally, the voice of the older dude called out. He sounded drunk on his ass again, but his tone was surprised and eager. "Hang on, I comin', bra."

"Why Santa ain't got no kids," Ty muttered.

"*What?*" whispered Deek.

"Cause he don't come but once a year, an then it down the chimney."

Deek gave him a strange look, but Ty had relaxed, sighing out vapor. The hand that had hovered on the gun slipped to his side. "Danny tell me that."

Deek frowned. "It gettin so's I can't tell when you drunk or not no more, man."

Ty only smiled slightly as the door locks clicked open. The big boy wore just his filthy 501s, half unbuttoned and slipping so low that curls of hair showed and he walked on the cuffs. Despite all his muscle his body seemed slack, belly out from drinking and powerful arms dangling loose at his sides. A Night Train bottle hung loose in his hand. He swayed on his feet and stumbled forward so that Ty had to catch him. The big boy laughed and crushed Ty's slim body to the solid slabs of his chest. Ty felt a moment of panic, but the big dude only focused red-rimmed eyes on Ty and laughed again. "Yo, bra! I jus now sayin to Lionel here you not be leavin your bros out in the col'!" He lifted Ty off his feet and swung him into the room. "Bring your asses in here where it warm, niggers!" He set Ty down and offered him the bottle.

Ty took a gulp of warm wine laced with spit to be polite, even though he hated Night Train, then scanned the room at a glance, missing nothing. The big boys had been here for days now, with Deek paying the rent and some extra bucks for food, which went mostly for Train. The motel maid had probably gotten disgusted a long time ago and given up trying to clean. Train bottles and empty KFC buckets lay everywhere, along with pizza boxes and empty potato-chip bags. What few clothes the dudes owned were all on the floor. The sooty Panel-Ray heater was cranked full-on, and the air was a smothering stew of wine sweat and old socks, and murky as the fog outside with Lucky Strike smoke. The sheets of the one double bed trailed gray on the dirty beige carpet even though a stack of fresh ones was dumped by the door. The other boy was sprawled on the bed, wearing just a pair of Jockey shorts so ragged that they showed as much skin as cotton. He held a Train bottle about ready to spill on his stomach, and a cigarette smoldered forgotten in his fingers. He didn't look as if he realized yet that company had come.

The old Zenith TV atop the dresser-desk was advising people to buy their Toyotas now while the dealers were eager to deal. The light in the center of the ceiling was one of those energy-saving fluorescent rings. It threw a sick bluish glow that turned the tan walls the color of puke and tinged the gunmetal skins of Ty and the big boys a cold, corpselike violet. Ty had seen too many of these goddamned rooms in the last few months. For some people they might have been a beginning; for most they meant the end was near. He remembered a thing he'd heard in history class one time: black death. It was a sickness.

One chair stood cockeyed in a corner, its plastic cushions patched with silver duct tape. Both Uzis lay on it. Ty gave Deek a short nod, signifying all was way past cool. These dudes were nothing but overgrown children trying to play a game whose rules took a lifetime to learn. As he had that morning, Ty felt sorry for them. He found himself hoping they'd have the sense to go home when their money ran out. He also hoped they hadn't killed any of those young boys, so maybe, in time, this whole thing would fade to a sad little joke.

Deek had come in and eased the door shut when the big boy had let go of Ty. Ty watched his eyes find the guns and a smile curl his lip. The second boy, Lionel, had finally figured what is and was struggling to get to his feet. He spilled the Train on the bed, and would have fallen on his face but for the first boy clapping a huge arm around him and pulling him close. Ty wondered if they were real brothers.

The first boy's face was all eagerness now as he towered over Deek and held the other dude. Ty thought of those twins when they'd scrambled for the beer.

"We done it, man!" the first boy laughed. "Done it good, best believe!" He stopped and pondered a moment. "Well, we dint get none, you was spectin that. But, maaan, we ever scare the holy shit outa them little bastards!"

Deek studied the boy for one quick second, then grinned and slapped a massive shoulder. "Way cool, bro! I knowed I could trust ya. Yo! Sit down, crew. Gots a bonus for ya. Word!"

Ty watched the big boys drop heavily back on the bed. Their faces were totally childlike now, their eyes bright with the pleasure of Deek's praise. Ty's nose wrinkled; the Train taste in his mouth was sickening. Ripping open his pouch, Deek pulled out a hundred and slapped it into the first boy's callused palm. "An that only a part what I gots for ya, bros."

Ty's eyes narrowed. He wondered what was up. Was Deek going to get these dudes to really do somebody— maybe that other gang, the Friends?

The big boys exchanged happy grins, each holding a corner of the bill. Ty suddenly wanted to kick them. It was like some ancient nigger joke; Rastus and Remus getting their woolly little heads patted by the massah. Flinching at the pain in his arm, he dug in his pocket for his Kools; anything to get that goddamn sick taste out of his mouth.

Ty saw Deek pull something else from his pouch. A moth-erfucking watermelon wouldn't have surprised him. His eyes narrowed again as Deek produced something small wrapped in Kleenex. Deek unfolded the tissue to reveal a pair of plastic syringes, the kind the anti-AIDS people gave away on the street to junkies. Ty saw the sudden flicker of uncertainty in the big boys' eyes.

The first dude swallowed, shying slightly back from Deek's offered palm. "Uh . . . we don't us do nuthin like that there, man. Don't wanna get ourselfs hooked on no heroin."

Deek chuckled. "Hey, no, brother! Yo, what it is be just coke . . . but some super major shit. No way you get hooked, man! Hell, you dudes ain't stupid. You figure I want any-body workin for me full-time what on somethin?"

Lionel was too drunk to be very doubtful of anything. And Deek's voice could *soothe*. Still, he asked. "But, um, what I sayin, don't coke get snorted up you nose?"

Deek grinned and patted his shoulder. "Not when it THIS good, my man, best believe!" Then he seemed to consider a moment, bouncing the barrels in his open hand. "Look, bros. What it is, this sorta like my blood thing. Hear what I sayin? My *test*, sorta, for dudes what I thinkin bout takin on, long-time. Shit, you tellin me you can't handle it?"

The first boy took several huge gulps from the bottle, then passed it to Lionel. "Sho! We up for some good stuff, best you believe!"

Lionel tilted the bottle back and killed it, then nodded hard. "Like he say, man, we up fo it. Uh . . . you gonna show us how it done, right?"

"Word," said Deek.

Ty had slipped the Kools back in his pocket. He took a step closer, his eyes slitted and his lips clamped over his teeth as Deek pulled a little cellophane packet from his pouch. Ty had seen enough of those, he packed them, but Deek's coke was no way in hell fit for shooting. Ty remembered his job, and kept himself from going any closer. But he scowled when he saw that the stuff was pure white, almost luminous under the bluish ceiling light. He dug out his Kools once more and fired one fast, sucking smoke deep and holding it long. Some sort of new shit? he wondered. Like a test-market thing? He didn't like the idea. Some people on TV didn't want stuff tested on white rats and rabbits. Ty flicked ashes on the floor. Well, it was Deek's game. Maybe he did have some other plans for the dudes. And even if the stuff was the purest China white, the boys were way too drunk to get anything out of it. Fact was, they'd probably puke up their Night Train-soaked guts and never try anything like that again. Maybe that was Deek's plan.

Deek went into the bathroom and returned with a bottle cap of water. His voice was gentle. He could coax a bat into hell when he wanted. The big boys watched, fascinated, as Deek's Bic furnished a flame. Ty moved back by the door and quietly smoked, though his eyes missed nothing. The shit *was* pure, whatever it was. It melted instantly in the water. Deek didn't use cotton to strain it, just loading the barrels right out of the cap. Ty's gaze shifted: with all their muscles the big boys had beautiful veins.

Something scratched at the back of Ty's brain. He wished he hadn't been drinking all day. He was going to have to stop that, especially now. He tried to force some of the fuzz from his mind. Only the finest coke would have melted that way. But this shit had no sparkle. The best street smack he'd ever seen had never been that snowy white, and still needed straining.

Deek wiped the gleaming points with a flourish of the

Kleenex, reminding Ty of the Burger King girl's touch of magic with the sugar packets for Danny; something to please a small child. The two big boys bent forward to cautiously take the needles from Deek. Lionel looked about ready to pass out anyway, but struggled to concentrate as Deek pointed out good veins and warned about poking all the way through. Almost together the needles went in. Both boys winced and bit on their lips. They had to be brothers, Ty thought. Work-callused thumbs pressed plungers . . .

Then Ty remembered. "NOOOO!"

It was a story his dad had told on one of those hot afternoons laid-back in the truck. Ty recalled the sun slanting orange through the city haze and the grimy windshield; the taste of grape Popsicle and Colt .45, sour-sweet with an ass-kicking bite like Night Train. Back then he'd thought Train was way past bad. It was just the cool kind of story you'd never get from your mom—no ghost stuff at bedtime to scare little kids—an old junkie revenge trick. That white fuzzy stuff that grew on junk batteries had the same look and texture as the sort of smack sold back in those days. It dissolved exactly the same in a spoonful of water.

But, shot into your body, it was pure death in a second!

Ty sprang for the bed even as the two big boys crumpled forward, the needles still stuck in their arms. Deek had stepped back to give them room to hit the floor. He watched with the same sort of interest he might have shown for a school science experiment. He spun around when Ty screamed, looking more annoyed than anything else. Ty thought, if he could only catch the boys, yank out the needles, they'd somehow be good as new again. Those big black bodies could never be *that* easy to kill!

Deek grabbed one of Ty's outflung arms, the one that Danny had slashed, grabbed it with both chubby hands.

For all his slack muscles, Deek clamped on like a pit-bull bite, twisting viciously like little kids gave Indian burns. Ty felt his skin rip open. Pain lashed up his arm and exploded in his brain. He screamed again, in agony now, and dropped to his knees, hitting the dirty carpet in sync with the thuds of the two big bodies. Blood gushed from his sleeve.

Rage tore through Ty's mind, smashing back at the blackness that roared in like a wave to drown him. It was like being slammed in the stomach or kicked in the balls: he couldn't get air. His sight blurred and dimmed down like a dying TV screen, to a tiny point of light with darkness crushing it out. He fought the black, the tears in his eyes as hot as the blood pumping from his arm. Somehow he forced strength to his legs. He struggled up from his knees. His free hand searched for the gun.

Then Deek's voice filtered through the hurt and fury. "Game over, Ty."

Vaguely, Ty realized that Deek had let go of his arm. The pain still cut him in razor-edged ripples. He sucked a breath through clenched teeth, and again the blackness tried to smother him. He sank back to his knees. The hand that had sought the gun now clutched at his bleeding arm. He tasted puke but choked it down. Finally, head lowered, panting for breath, he managed to whisper, "Why?"

Deek's voice came fuzzy, like from far away. The words were a bad joke from a million old movies. "They knew too much."

Deek's tone went soothing. Ty felt himself being helped to his feet, then led to the chair. There was a double clunk of the Uzis hitting the floor and then he was slumped on crackly old plastic. A bottle was shoved in his blood-covered hand. More Train? Ty didn't care, he tilted it up and drank.

Slowly, his vision came back into focus. He found he was shaking. He drank again, hating the shit but needing it bad. He saw Deek wrapping both Uzis in one of the dead boys' T-shirts. His eyes found the bodies and shied away fast. He gulped the rest of the bottle like Kool-Aid, then looked back at the boys.

Wasted was another word for dead. And that's what a kid's death was. Maybe they *had* known too much, but in another way they hadn't known enough. Kids playing TV games for keeps. Was the whole motherfucking world nothing but kids playing parts? And who in hell wrote the scripts? Black kids played at being bad. And died for it. What did white kids play, keeping nigger kids in their cages?

Clutching his arm, Ty lurched to his feet, forcing his eyes from the figures on the floor. The TV was talking about someone getting sentenced to prison for shooting a sea otter. A child's laughter carried from the room next door. Black death meant nothing to nobody.

Deek's hands glistened with Ty's blood. He wiped them on the bundled T-shirt, then snagged the one-buck bill from the floor and folded it back into his pouch. "Sorry, man. Didn't know it was gonna freak ya like that. Yo. You cool now?"

Black and cool, thought Ty. I the motherfuckin iceman, the iceberg, the coolest nigger breeze you ever done seen, sucker! What in hell was wrong with being black and *warm?* He pressed his torn sleeve tight so no more blood would drip on the carpet. A month, he thought . . . one more motherfucking month and he'd get himself free of this trap. Fuck cool! Fuck cool forever! He'd be warm and stupid for the rest of his goddamned life! Let Deek find some other cool fool to pimp pain and death to black kids! He'd already had another bodyguard . . .

Ty's eyes found the dead boys again. Then he raised them to Deek's . . . warm obsidian facing frozen gold.

Deek's gaze was calculating. "Yeah, well, you deserve a day off, man. Tell you what. I handle things alone tomorrow. You an Danny go an have a real cool time. Yo. Danny a way cool little dude, man. I really hope nuthin ever happen to him. Seem like kids get wasted so easy, an just nobody give a good shit. Know what I sayin?" Deek nudged the bigger boy's body with his toe. "So what you figure they rate, man? Tomorrow, next day, a few stupid lines on the *Trib*'s back page? Just another couple niggerboys found dead. Gang, drug killin?" Deek pointed to a ragged nylon wallet half sticking out of the boy's back pocket. "Wanna know his name, man? Maybe he gots pitchers of his family?"

Ty suddenly shivered in the hot steamy room. "No. I . . . cool."

Deek smiled. "Yeah. You are." Bundle under one arm, he moved to the door. Glancing first out the peephole, he opened it slightly and checked up and down the landing. Finally he stepped out, pulling another Kleenex from his pocket and draping it over the inside knob. Ty wiped it carefully before following Deek, then, gripping the outside knob with the tissue, he started to ease the door shut behind him. Just before the lock clicked, he tensed. Darting back into the room, he wiped the Night Train bottle. He glanced at the other empty, then remembered that the boy had wrapped his big hand around it again. He supposed that was a cool thought. He caught sight of one more full bottle as he turned to leave, hesitated a second, then slipped it into his jacket pocket, eased out on the landing, where Deek waited, and closed the door, making sure that the lock caught.

Deek grinned at him. "Way past cool, dude. I lucky I

got ya." Then he frowned slightly. "Yo. Can't you hold your arm like it ain't hurt? Case anybody watchin us leave. An careful you don't drip no more blood."

Gritting his teeth against the pain, Ty shoved his hand into his jeans so the blood would run into his pocket. He followed Deek back along the landing and descended the stairs. Their shoe soles were silent, and Ty didn't feel any eyes as they crossed the weedy parking lot to the 'Am. A breeze was stirring from the distant Bay, and the fog seemed to be thinning, but Ty doubted if anyone could have read the car's plate as they drove away. In a place like this it wasn't likely that anyone would even try.

Deek swung off Foothill onto 64th, rolling slow through a quiet neighborhood of old but well-kept houses, each with its own small yard. Trikes, Big Wheels, balls, and a few big Tonka toys lay here and there on wet lawns. Only the age of many of the cars and pickups parked in the driveways hinted at a black community. Here, Ty thought, was peace and pride . . . at least for now. Ty remembered this was where his mom had always talked of moving someday.

Instead of taking East 14th toward downtown, Deek cut back up to 73rd, then out to 880, where the traffic was still heavy. Once northbound, cruising casually among the rumbling semis, Deek stopped checking the mirrors so often.

"Yo, Ty? How your arm, man? Shit, I sorry I had to do ya like that, but you almost freak on me back there, y'know."

Ty's arm throbbed and felt twice its size but the bleeding had almost stopped. He shrugged, pulling out the bottle, twisting off the cap, and taking a long hit. "I live. Only the bad die young."

Deek arched an eyebrow. "Well, I woulda told you the plan, cept I didn't know myself till I sure them suckers done what they sposed." He glanced over again. "Yo. Could you handled it if I'd told ya first?"

Ty took another drink. It wasn't so bad. He could learn to live with it. "I don't know. Weren't there no way other?"

"Never trust nobody, man. Yo. You ain't pissed or nuthin?"

Ty felt only a dull aching sadness that seemed to throb through him like the pain in his arm. He swallowed more Train. It eased the hurt a lot better than Heineken. "No," he murmured. "Not no more. I just tired, Deek. I wanna go home."

"Cool, man. I drop ya."

"No. I get out down by that late-night market. Wanna pick up some stuff for breakfast."

Deek drifted the car onto an exit ramp, still studying Ty. "Now you *sure* you chilled, man? What I sayin is, this shit ain't gonna come back an freak ya later on?"

"I just too fuckin tired to be freaked by nuthin no more."

"Mmm. Well, I seen you look a lot better, man. An that arm of yours still bleedin. People in that store might see."

Ty stared straight ahead. "Nobody in that hood gonna pay no 'tention to some niggerboy bleedin, even he lay dead on the sidewalk."

Markita came out of the grocery store, moving quickly away from the bright white fluorescence and standing in shadow so her eyes could adjust to the night. She carefully scanned the small parking lot, and then the dark foggy tunnel of the three-block walk back home. It was an obstacle course she hated and feared. On nights like this with the fog drifting thick between the crumbling old buildings, some abandoned and boarded, the city seemed to close down on her like one of those funnel traps on nature shows. There was some small relief on the second block, where the weedy asphalt of a shut-down car wash offered no cover for night-lurking things. She always breathed a little easier when passing it, knowing she might be able to dodge and play a desperate game of hide-and-seek in and out of the wash bays if chased. But then the third block would close in once more and cut off her options. And it had its own special terror.

She glanced at her K mart watch: 12:23, and sighed at

the thought of having to be at work again in just five and a half hours. She shifted the small grocery bag in one arm: a quart of orange juice, another of milk, and a box of oatmeal for her son. Though she ate for free at the Burger King, and brought leftovers home for her mom, Markita had vowed she'd be damned if she raised her son up on junk food. J'row was going to need every muscle and mind cell to survive, and Markita didn't believe jack about all that fast-food "leaner and lighter" dogshit.

She stared down the gloomy blocks again, then pulled the little spray can of Mace from the pocket of her old Navy-surplus peacoat and nested it atop the groceries. Her mother had scored her the stuff. You were supposed to be eighteen and have a license or something to carry it, and Markita supposed she could be fined or go to jail if caught. Of course, when you were poor, being fined was only a joke *before* you went to jail, as if having no money was a crime in itself. It seemed like, sooner or later, if you didn't have money you ended up in a cage. And the law made protecting yourself a crime too, even though it never did a goddamn thing to help you.

Lately, Markita had been considering a gun, something small and semiautomatic. Leroy would know what was best. She decided to ask him about it in the morning. After what had happened tonight, the bodyguard boy, Ty, dragging the younger kid out of the restaurant right under everybody's noses, Markita no longer felt safe anywhere. The fact that the boys had been brothers didn't do much to cheer her up. Fear was like that; you went from being scared of what did happen to living in terror of what *might* happen. And from what Markita had seen of life, it seemed to get worse as you got older.

She glanced at the Mace can again. Well, like her mother

often said, just as well be hung for a sheep as a lamb. They were one and the same when you were black and poor. If trying to save your own life and protect those you loved was a crime, there wasn't much hope left anyhow. She remembered reading something in a Charles Dickens book at school: "If the law says that, then the law is a ass!"

Looking once more down the street, she turned up her coat collar and started for home, putting pride in her stride. She met no one on the first block, and the only traffic was a lone pickup chugging past, missing on one cylinder and trailing oil smoke, with garbage cans rattling in back. She crossed the side street, hurrying clear of the corner lamp's light cone. They've turned us into children of the night, she thought. A little of the fear left her now: fifty percent home free. The breeze was strengthening, thinning the fog into swirls, and she could just make out the steps of her own building up near the next corner. A newspaper page fluttered past like a little ghost, making her jump. The last ordeal was an alley mouth midway up the block. For her, crossing it at night was like some ancient child's story of whistling past a graveyard. Even safe on the other side she always felt as if someone had slid out to follow her the last hundred yards home. She would hunch her shoulders and plead with herself not to run, afraid to turn and look and just as scared not to.

She deepened her breathing as she neared the black gap, storing up oxygen—she supposed—in case she did have to bail her behind. Screaming for help would be one total waste of breath. She fingered the door keys in her pocket. Then, just a few feet from the tunnel of fear, she stopped so suddenly that her Reebok soles squeaked.

Over the years, Markita had heard a lot of things going on in that alley; snatches of slurred talk from wineheads and cracked kids, screams, fighting, gunshots, and even the carefree laughter of children. She remembered playing there herself; one time sitting and giggling on the slashed front seat of an abandoned car, watching through the shattered windshield while her friends acted and danced on the hood. They'd called it their drive-in movie game. Bodies had been found: stabbed, shot, OD'd, or just with their hearts worn out at fourteen. Once there'd been a baby stuffed in a dumpster and, last summer, a little homeless boy who the cops said had been killed and half eaten by rats.

But Markita had never heard crying come from in there before . . . at least not like she was hearing it now. If there was such a thing as pure misery it would sound like this, she thought. And it was all the stranger for being boy-crying. She'd always thought a child's cough in night silence was the loneliest sound in the world: now she wasn't so sure. The sobbing echoed softly between the walls in the same sort of lost-soul keening she might have imagined coming out of some cemetery crypt in a Friday Frights movie.

Ain't no concern of yours, girl, she told herself. Sympathy spread too goddamn thin around here as it is. She stood a moment, recalling she'd said something close to the same to a young boy on a skateboard while she'd been on an errand for her mother a couple of hours ago. Usually she kept those kinds of things to herself, but, then, it hadn't seemed to matter. The kid probably thought she was a whore anyway. Lady of the night? How fucking poetic! He'd been a strange sort of boy, so delicate-looking yet so totally self-sufficient; like a prototype of something new or a re-program of something very old that was better equipped to survive. Evolution in action. The shape of things to come. Shape changers. Weren't werewolves called children of the night?

Markita shoved those thoughts aside. Whoever was in the alley crying couldn't have been too far up, judging by the nearness of his sound. And he couldn't have had many options left to suffer alone in such a place. Anybody who was past caring about himself wouldn't be very concerned about others, and it took a hell of a lot more than a silver crucifix or a bunch of wolfbane leaves to ward off evil in this neighborhood. Markita glanced across the street, wondering if a short detour might not be the coolest move up next. Instead, she found herself edging closer to the alley mouth.

This ain't gettin it, girl, warned a part of her mind. You bein a goddamn fool, all you are! Somebody else's busted-up heart be no business of yours, best believe, specially when your own barely Scotch-taped together. She remembered Leroy's words; about it being a black thing and not nothing nobody could do.

Well, she thought, reaching the corner of the last building and pressing her back to cold brick. If black don't do nothing for black, who in hell will? She listened a little longer, feeling strangely cool. You didn't often hear big boys cry, and this had to be one . . . a kid would have blubbered, and no grown-up man would cut his own heart out like that. It was so . . . *uncool.* Markita frowned, her lips forming the words "Shut up, fool!" She recalled an old thing her mother sometimes said when life seemed to go seven ways to hell: "What did I ever do, to be so black and blue?" Finally, Markita set the grocery bag down and pulled out the Mace. Finger poised ready on the little button, she sucked a breath and stepped around the corner.

Only the fog-filtered glow of a light at the alley's far end penetrated the passage. Markita realized too late she'd silhouetted herself against the openness behind her. But the lonely sobbing went on without pause. The breeze was growing stronger, twisting the mist into tortured shapes and wafting the smells of sodden garbage and wet cardboard into her face. She scented boy-sweat, and the familiar fumes of Night Train. And something else. She suddenly shivered, catching the coppery bite of fresh blood. She almost bolted then, half turning to run for home and leaving her food forgotten. The Mace seemed no more protection than a cross in the hands of a doubter. But the fog slit open above and the silver face of the moon swam out of it, casting a ghost-glow that glimmered off the weeping walls and glistening dumpster lids. The boy hadn't gone very far, as if not even trying to hide. Markita saw his huddled form, back to the wall, long legs pulled up like a little kid's, arms crossed on top, and face buried against them. Something blue-black and metallic hung loose in the fingers of one bony hand. Markita took a step closer before realizing it was a gun.

Part of her saw the picture she must be making, standing there, stupidly, with her silly can of Mace, while not ten feet away crouched a boy with a gun, his mind gone from drinking by the smell of him, and who looked long past caring about anybody's life. Yet, Markita remembered something else her mother often said . . . that black women always seemed to find the strength to carry on while their men were beaten down. Markita had always wondered if black women were really stronger, or was it just that the men and boys wore themselves out so fast by shaking the bars of their cages?

Without thinking, Markita let the hand holding the Mace drop to her side. She took another step toward the boy, his male sweat strong in her nostrils above the smells of wine and blood. A skateboard lay beside him, next to a fog-limp paper bag. He might have been older than her, or just tall for his age, but there was something familiar about him.

Maybe it was the expensive leather jacket with its own distinctive scent, somehow male in itself. Markita's jaw thrust forward in the way her mom always scolded as "boy-scaring" and not at all ladylike. She said the first thing that came to mind . . . said it loud and proud.

"Hush yourself, boy!"

The boy's head snapped up, and the moonlight fell full on his harmless, gunmetal features. Big teeth and tear streaks glittered. Recognition flashed across his face even as Markita spoke his name.

"Ty?"

Like a little kid, he almost melted back into tears once more. But then his big loose lips stopped quivering, his lean jaw set, and sudden determination iced his eyes. Slowly, his gaze locked on Markita, he raised the heavy pistol and jammed the muzzle against his head.

Markita froze in horror. It seemed to take every bit of strength in the boy's thin body to hold the gun. His finger trembled on the trigger as if that slim piece of metal between him and death was beyond his power to pull. Then, as if the weight was just too much, his arm fell back and the gun butt clunked on the pavement. Ty's chin shook and fresh tears flooded his cheeks, ice blue in the moonlight.

"I . . . can't!" he sobbed, and hid his face once more.

Markita's moves were deliberate. She shoved the Mace into her coat pocket, dropped her hands to her hips, and stared down at the boy. She could have been surveying some little mess her son had made.

"Ohhh . . . SHIT! All that tell me is you still got some sense left in your goddamn head!"

Ty's head came up again, his mouth opening and eyes widening until he looked like Buckwheat with a flattop.

"Some," Markita went on. She found she was shaking

her finger just like her mother. It was so lame yet she couldn't stop. "But not one hell of a lot, best believe!" She saw the Train bottle and kicked it spinning up the alley. "What the matter, boy? Killin yourself with that shit ain't fast enough for you? Tell you this for a fact, you just keep on sittin there, bawlin your goddamn heart out for all the world to hear, an somebody be comin right directly along happy as hell to do it for you! Yes, they will!"

Ty's mouth shut with a clop. Leaving the gun where it lay, he crossed his arms on his knees once again. Markita saw him wince. His expression grew sullen, and he stared at the alley's opposite wall. "I not that lucky," he muttered. He glanced up at Markita from the corner of his now narrowed eyes. "An what it to ya anyways, girl? Shit, you not know from nuthin what it is!"

Markita's finger jabbed the air to her right. "Oh, don't I, boy? Who in hell you figure you talkin to, nigger? All my goddamn life I livin just three door up that way! What you tellin ME I don't know from nuthin? Shit! Gots me a two-year-old at home know ten *time* more bout what it is than you!" She stamped her foot, something her mother did too. "You! With all them way cool clothes, an all your money-bucks, an your gun, an all your . . . all your goddamn motherfuckin BAD! So, what in hell it get you, boy? Not a goddamn friend in the world, am I right? An here you sittin on your drunk-ass black butt in the garbage an wet just like any other little ole throwed-out kid got no home!"

Ty rested his chin on his arms. His long steamy sigh sounded as tired as Markita felt. "You don't know what I just gone an done, girl." He considered, glancing up at her. "Else you run screamin all the way home. Word."

Markita tensed a little, but then her arm fell to her side and her shoulders sagged under the heavy coat. "Mmm.

Well, I might run but I wouldn't waste my time on screamin. Spose you went an shot somebody?"

Ty squinted his eyes shut. Fresh tears squeezed out anyhow. His lean body shook with choked-back sobs. "There a difference tween a killin an . . . an a murder. Killin a thing the world make you do. Somethin you *got* to do when there ain't no way other. Murder . . ." He shut his mouth and set his jaw, turning away from Markita to watch a rat that had scented his blood and was creeping close. "You just now tellin me you know from jack? Then you know I can't say no more."

Markita had felt ice down her spine when Ty had said the word. It was a word you didn't hear too often, strangely enough, on the streets where it happened all the time. People got "done," "smoked," "iced," "wasted" . . . little kids talked of "dirt naps." But it just didn't seem cool to use the M-word. Part of her did want to run home now. She realized that she didn't actually know jack about this boy . . . that all her feelings toward him and recent thoughts about him were mostly made up in her mind. Ty looked so basically gentle and harmless—even uncool—yet she'd watched in fear as he'd dragged his own brother into the night and hurt him just hours ago. Killing to defend himself, maybe even protecting that slimy sucker Deek, she could accept as just a part of this goddamned life. But that other word—even in this place it still sounded evil. She was being some kind of fool, she thought. If she had any goddamn sense at all she'd get the hell away from this crazy, drunken niggerboy just as fast as she could and pray God she'd never see him again. Maybe a while later, home safe and in bed, she'd hear that single gunshot.

But still she stood there, gazing down at the boy who'd treated his little brother to burgers and fries and sat talking to him with love in every look and gesture. Markita shoved her hands in her pockets and shuffled her Reeboks. "Murder a . . . evil word."

Ty seemed to be watching the rat edge closer. But he nodded. "Yeah. That say it all. Mean a cold killin without no good reason. An what difference it make if you the one actual pull the trigger or just stand by with your head up your ass an let it happen?"

Markita sifted Ty's words in her mind. In a way it was like trying to get a confession out of her own son—that he'd done some way naughty thing; but maybe not quite as naughty as he thought. Ty had buried his face once more. Suddenly, Markita moved to him and knelt. She lay a gentle hand on his shoulder. "Tell me. It can't hurt."

Ty looked up. "It . . . it put you in a bad way, girl . . . knowin."

"Put *you* in a worse way keepin it all inside, look like to me. An, it Markita."

"What is?"

"My name."

"Oh." Ty wiped his face with his sleeve. "So how come you know mine?"

"I hear Deek callin you." Markita settled herself next to Ty. "Now. What it is, I ain't leavin till I get the story, an till I sure in my mind you ain't gonna go an do somethin stupid."

Ty glanced over at the rat again. It was sitting up, whiskers quivering, its little eyes black and cold. Ty sighed out wine-scented steam. "Stupid my thing, an I do it good. I tell, could put you in shit, Markita."

Could put *you* in deeper shit, thought Markita. For all you know I go runnin to the cops. But Ty didn't seem to have considered that. Markita shrugged. "You let it keep eatin you all by yourself, you gonna be spendin a lot of lonely nights holdin that there gun to your head."

Ty spat, hitting the rat full in the face. It squealed and scuttled away.

A few minutes later, Markita's hand found Ty's bloody one and held it. "But you didn't *know*," she said. "What that evil bastard Deek was gonna do. An by the time you read him, it was too late. Yes it was." She shook her head. "An all for a couple of goddamn guns."

Ty wiped new tears from his cheeks, flinching when he lifted his arm. He hadn't told the girl what the Bakersfield boys had been hired to do. Now he found himself wondering if he would have felt any differently over their deaths if they had killed one of the young gang kids. But what would give him any right to feel differently? After all, he did know Deek's plan for the younger boys—and he'd been ready to shoot at least one of them himself that morning. Or at least he'd thought he was. He sighed steam once more. "It funny, what it is. I mean, if I coulda got to my gun, right there in that room, I'da killed Deek. Word! But now it like I gone all cold an nuthin inside. It like a cage he make for me, an now I caught in it. Anything happen to Deek, come from that, happen to me too. Seem like life here ain't nuthin but some long line of cages. You step in the first one, all you hear from then on be them bars clankin shut 'hind your black ass. An them cages keep on gettin smaller an smaller."

Ty went silent, just staring over at the opposite wall.

Markita pressed Ty's bony hand, thinking how cold it was. "That a way cool little brother you got."

Ty's face twisted like he might cry again. "No. He a *warm* boy, right on the edge of goin cool." Ty turned to Markita. "He at the age where he standin at the door of that first cage . . . sniffin the sucker bait. An it smell so GOOD!" He waved his bloody hand. "So way past good 'pared to what he see all round him here. Eleven, twelve, thirteen . . . them's the magic ages. Don't care what they tell me in high school, bout futures an career shit. You start choosin you life bout time your own dick wake up . . ." Ty glanced quickly at Markita. "Um, sorry." His arm fell back and he gritted his teeth. "What I sayin is, Danny could still be saved. Cept it don't look like there gonna be nobody round to save him. Like, there ain't nobody in the whole fuckin world even figure he *worth* savin! Cept Mom, course. But what she do? World make it so she all the time bustin her butt just tryin to keep food on the table an rent money in some sucker's hand. Leave her no time for *bein* with her kids. Everthing Danny learnin bout life come from right here off these motherfuckin streets. Tell him the only shit what matter be money, an bad . . . an cool." Ty shrugged. "An it funny, that maybe I gotta stay in a cage to keep Danny outa one."

Markita sighed now. "I don't know. An I never knew nobody what did . . . not for real. Maybe, like everbody say when they can't figure somethin out logical, it just a black thing." She leaned close and gently lifted Ty's arm. "Mmm. You been cut bad."

There was a funny note of pride in Ty's voice. "Danny done that." Then he turned away. "My cool little brother." Ty made a sound that was too cold for a laugh. "Show he bout up for life in the hood, don't it?" Ty looked back at his arm. "TV say all these kids ain't nuthin but wild little animals. Well, maybe I just gotta tame Danny down. I gotta try." He glanced at the gun on the pavement. "Maybe that why I can't do my ownself. It like, when I put up the gun, this voice come to mind, whisper, 'Don't, sucker.' " Ty's forehead creased. "Young voice." He shook his head. "Shit.

Only crazy-ass people sposed to hear voices! Like them old niggers what holler all day in the street."

"I don't think you hurt when you crazy," said Markita. "I think goin crazy the onliest way some folks got to make the hurtin stop." She pressed his hand again. "You got other family? I mean, sides your mom an your brother?"

"Nuther brother, eight. Two little sisters." Ty turned to Markita once more. "Say you gots a son?"

"J'row. He two."

Ty looked away. "Oh. Then that mean . . ."

"Mean I gots a son, what it mean."

"Oh . . . Sorry."

"Don't be. I ain't." Markita pulled her coat a little tighter, then pointed. "So, what's in the bag?"

Ty dropped his chin back on his arms. "Nuthin."

"Now, what you tellin me, nuthin? I see Popsicles, gonna melt, an Cocoa Puffs an stuff gettin all foggy-wet. Shoulda got plastic."

"Huh?"

"You know? Paper or plastic?"

"Oh. Well, I can't never member what best. Ain't paper sposed to save the 'vironment or somethin?"

"Shit, boy, what good all that stuff do when you can't even put food on your table fit to eat?"

"Yeah. Guess you right."

"Mmm. Ain't no normal dude gonna be thinkin bout that sorta stuff, anyways."

Ty sighed steam once again. "Yeah. Spose it ain't cool. I was gonna take Danny uptown shoppin tomorrow. Score stuff for the other kids too, clothes an shoes an nice shit like that. Hell, I prob'ly mess it all up, same's I do everthing else."

"Oh, stop makin yourself out a fool! Ain't that just the

main trouble with you dudes! Facin down guns an knives don't scare you a bit, but just the thought of pickin out little girls' clothes get you actin like Norman Bates on Mother's Day! You know their sizes?"

"Uh-uh."

"Course you don't! Listen up, boy! Get your mom to write em down for you. She *can* write, can't she?"

Ty frowned. "Course she can."

"An you can read?"

"COURSE! Well, good enough for that kinda shit."

"Mmm. I spect she know all about what them little brothers an sisters of yours be dreamin an wishin for. Ask her."

Ty nodded slowly. "Yeah . . . yeah, spose I could go an do that. Shit, I just now think on me an Danny lookin through little girls' clothes. Bet he like to die!"

"Well, it be a warm thing for you dudes to be doin, wouldn't it? An, yo. You really wanna help them kids, you best start by keepin to your word. Ain't nuthin cut a kid deeper'n gettin promises busted." Markita gathered up the groceries, mindful of the sodden sack. She got to her feet and gazed down at Ty, her jaw jutting once more. "You just c'mon now, boy . . . up outa that goddamn garbage an wet fore you catch your death. Spose you too goddamn drunk to walk?"

"No, I ain't!"

"Well, get your ass up, then. An stop lookin like you just found out you engaged to a lizard or somethin. I live right on the next corner. Got me a nice big plastic Mervyn's bag I been savin by. We put all your stuff in that." Markita hesitated, then added. "An I take me a good careful look at that arm of yours too. Bad-ass niggerboy like you gonna get himself enough hate stares in them uptown stores out lookin like you fresh from a gang fight!"

Five minutes later, Ty was following Markita into the warm dimness of her second-floor apartment. His skateboard dangled from the fingers of his bloody hand. Markita carried both grocery bags, which was cool, because Ty had fallen a few times.

Automatically, he scanned the little room as he eased the door shut behind him. It was cluttered. A streetlight's glow through the single window showed old but well-kept furniture: a comfortable-looking couch and two matching chairs, end tables with lamps, and a coffee table stacked neatly with magazines. Against the wall by the hallway door was a massive chest of drawers with a small TV and lots of framed snapshots on top. Ty saw several of Markita and a baby, and there were a couple of a smiling woman who was probably Markita's mother. Ty caught himself searching for pictures of boys her age. There were none.

On the opposite side of the doorway was a big bookshelf lined with paperbacks and what looked like a set of encyclopedias. Off to the left, beneath the window, was a single bed, still made up, with a frilly sort of spread. In the wall across from the bed was another door, closed, and beside it an old wooden baby crib. On the wall above it hung a framed picture of Martin Luther King. Scotch-taped close by were some child's drawings in crayon and a Ninja Turtles comic book cover. The floor space remaining was mostly covered by throw rugs of every size, shape, and color. Where bare boards showed, polish gleamed. A long counter separated the kitchen area. A narrow door, standing open to darkness back beside the fridge, probably led to the bathroom.

Markita pointed to the door by the crib. "Mom," she whispered.

Ty nodded. The room's warmth was a comfort after the

street's wet cold. The apartment had a background scent of cleanliness and lemony polish that was somehow defiant. It reminded him of his own home. He thought he could catch a faint trace of perfume above fresh-laundered sheets and pillowcases. There was also the warm, sleepy smell of a small child that seemed to stir some sense of protectiveness in him. The deep bass of music beat softly from another apartment, soothing like a heart. Blocks away a siren howled, but that only seemed to make the room more peaceful and secure. Ty noticed a few bright toys beneath the crib, and then coloring books given equal importance with the magazines on the coffee table. What looked like a baby version of a Speak 'N Spell computer lay beside them. Ty scanned the room once more, slower now, taking in more detail. Only the hurt in his arm remained to remind him of the world beyond these walls.

Putting a finger to her lips, Markita moved silently to the crib and motioned Ty to follow. He stood for a moment, looking down. The little boy lay on his back, pure ebony against the pale sheet. The blanket had slipped below his round tummy. The baby chub padding his chest and out-spread arms promised muscle to come. His hands were half open as if undecided between offerings or fists. The tiny fingers of children always looked so perfect. Ty reached to touch one, then saw the dried blood on his own and jerked back his hand. He turned away, murmuring, "Maybe I catchin a cold, like you say." He wiped at his nose.

Markita had been watching Ty, wondering how this could be the same boy who'd just seen two others die. "His name's J'row," she whispered.

"It a good name. Strong. It African?"

"I don't know." Markita smiled, looking back down at her son. "I kinda made it up. Sound a little African, though, don't it?"

A woman's sleepy voice called from behind the closed door. "Markita?"

"Yo, Mom. Everthing cool."

"It's so late, honey. You need your sleep."

Markita smiled at Ty. "I still gotta take me a bath yet, Mom. Good night."

"Sweet dreams, child."

Gently taking Ty's hand, Markita led him around the counter and set down the groceries. She slipped the orange juice and milk into the fridge, and Ty's pack of Popsicles into the freezer section. Then she motioned him through the bathroom door, following as he felt his unsteady way into the darkness. She shut the door behind her and pulled the light chain. The naked bulb was small, but Ty blinked as it came on. The little bathroom was so totally female that he felt like some big, clumsy, wet animal. He didn't move for fear of soiling something. He just stood, stupidly, skateboard clutched in one hand, waiting for whatever the girl had planned to do.

The walls were painted a pale peach color, and the toilet tank top and lid were fitted with fluffy lavender covers that matched the bath mat beside the big claw-footed tub. The chrome was half gone from faucets and pipes but the brass winked like gold wherever it showed. The air was scented with talcum powder and Dove. A long, flower-papered shelf above the sink was lined with all those mysterious bottles and jars that women and girls seemed to find so important. Staring around, mouth open, Ty could hardly imagine that just a few inches of ancient brick separated this fragile little world from what lay outside. Here too was a kind of defiance.

Markita's movements were casually cool; she shrugged off her coat and hung it on a hook, then took Ty's board and stood it by the door. Ty wasn't surprised that she seemed so at home here; what came to his mind was how confident she'd looked sitting beside him in the alley.

Besides her Levi's and Reeboks, Markita wore just a faded purple T-shirt. Ty saw her proud breasts strain the thin cotton as she reached high to hang her coat. It took effort for Ty to shift his eyes away. Like words in a book, her slim, supple body and graceful movements made him think of young panthers. He caught a glimpse of himself in the cabinet mirror and decided he looked like something washed from a flooded graveyard. Markita was studying him now, for the first time in light, but if she thought as he did she gave no sign. She aimed a commanding finger at the toilet lid. "Sit."

Ty's jeans were wet and slimed with garbage. He perched uneasily on the edge of the fluffy cover and kept his eyes on the floor. He suddenly noticed his big sloppy footprints on the spotless bath mat, and felt his face flush. None of Deek's paid girls, innocent or otherwise, had ever made him feel this uncool, as stupid as Deek always called him. But Markita was all flowing coolness as she bent close to examine his arm. Ty stole another glance at her: as he'd thought, she wore nothing beneath the T-shirt. With breasts like those, so firm and high, she didn't have to. Her nipples tilted up slightly, standing tight beneath the soft cloth. From the cold? he wondered. He thought first of Hershey's kisses, but those were common candies. Then he remembered the heart-shaped box he'd bought for his mother on Valentine's Day, each fine chocolate nestled within a cup of gold foil. There had been some like kisses, but larger, rounder, and made of some smooth creamy sweetness that melted in your mouth like cocoa-brown magic.

Ty felt the warmth of Markita's body so near to him now, and a heat of his own stirred restless in his loins. Her scent was honestly female from a long day of work. Ty breathed it deeply, his nostrils flaring to pull it all in. He let his eyes run down her legs: her Levi's old and shaped to her girl-muscled curves, hugged low on her hips, cuddling her behind, and snuggled to the soft swells of her thighs. He imagined the satiny feel of her skin, and the strength hidden beneath it. He dropped his gaze to the floor again, noting that one of her shoelaces had come undone. He resisted the stupid urge to reach down and tie it.

Markita frowned as her fingers lightly probed the slash in Ty's sleeve. Her lips pressed together like a pout when he winced. She hadn't missed his quick, almost shy peek-out of her, and heard him suck air through his nose. Her own eyes flicked to the tight crotch of his jeans and noted the wakening there. She glanced at his feet: the big clunky Nikes made them look huge. There was a saying about that. Was it a black thing? Of course, she'd seen some puppy-footed white boys too . . . but never one naked, and she doubted she ever would. And, for that matter, girl, she told herself, what's got you thinkin you ever gonna see Ty that way?

"Goddamn jacket linin all stuck to you there," Markita muttered. "Most god-awful mess I ever did see!" She clicked her tongue. "Let's try an get this thing off you, out hurtin too much."

Fussing, Markita helped Ty shed his jacket, turning the bloody sleeve inside out and peeling the clotted satin lining away from the wound. Ty clenched his teeth and tried to flow cool. It hurt like hell. The gash looked hideous when bared to the light. Danny had done a way cool job with his cheap little blade, and Deek had ripped it deeper when he'd twisted. Dried blood, black and sullen, caked around the six-inch slash. Flakes of it fell when he flexed his wrist.

Bright crimson still oozed from within, and clotted ruby caked the edges like sticky spilled wine. Ty tasted copper in his mouth through the numbness of Night Train. He chewed his lip, his eyes shifting once to Markita's and seeing worry and pain. She kept hold of his arm. There was a quaver in her voice when she spoke.

"This really 'mergency-room stuff, Ty. Best you believe it oughta get stitched. You be lucky as hell not comin down with infection."

Ty looked sulky and made a halfhearted move to pull away. But Markita held on and he gave up because it hurt too damn much. "Never get me no goddamn affection in my life," he snorted.

He looked up in time to catch a smile flickering on Markita's face. "I'm sure you did," she said. "Maybe you just don't remember. Hush now, an don't you go fightin me. Let's get that shirt off too. Then we see bout cleanin this up."

There was no reason to take off Ty's skimpy tank top to tend to his arm. But Markita had her own reasons, and Ty didn't seem to consider them, letting her slip the shirt over his head and guide his arm out of the strap. He felt suddenly vulnerable, half naked and hurting in this girlish little world. But heat still flowed into his loins, and he watched Markita from beneath lowered lashes. Her gaze felt like warm water washing over him. She seemed to have trouble looking away. He scented something else in the air, half familiar, and shifted uneasily on the edge of the lid. He felt his dick harden and strain his tight jeans.

Markita scented it too, grateful that Ty was staring at the floor so she could scan his body. His long wiry frame was just as she'd imagined that morning: each muscle sculpted clean, and the squared plates of his chest sharply defined as if they'd been added after his skin was already fit. His nipples were tiny black buds, almost invisible, and sexy as hell for some reason. The slender chain around his neck and the delicate, dislike little medallion suspended between hard-edged muscle shone stark against his gunmetal tone. It seemed to tremble on its fragile chain . . . to the beat of his heart? Markita wanted to touch the small silver thing, to hold it and know what it was. It would be warm. A sheen of sweat made Ty glow like polished midnight, but the scent of it told of too much beer and bad food. Markita's eyes drifted down the arch of his rib cage and the ripples of belly muscle to the softness that showed at his waist. She thought of a young panther, caged and dying slow, and not caring any longer to test the bars.

She drew back a little, letting his shirt slip from her hand to the floor by his jacket. Her voice came out husky. "Got to wash that clean with peroxide. Shoulda been done hours ago." She moved to the medicine cabinet above the sink and took down a big brown bottle. "Gonna hurt."

She thought she saw a little boy's fear flash for an instant in his eyes. But then his gentle face set hard. There were pictures of African warriors' masks in her mother's encyclopedias.

He shrugged, then looked up at her. "Markita. That a real pretty name. Sound African too."

"Sposed to be." Markita took out a box of cotton, then added, "Shit. Ain't nobody round here care bout no 'African,' cept some old doctor man my mama know who teachin her Swahili. Can't figure why, less he lonely for someone to talk to. Don't know why she troublin neither. Spose she gots a thing for the man." Markita's eyes narrowed a little, and her jaw jutted. "She only thirty. Ain't *dead*, y'know?"

Ty spread his palms. "What I done now?"

Markita's eyes softened again. "Nuthin. Sorry."

"Well," said Ty carefully. "Doctor be 'portant. Seem like to me your mom . . . do a lot worse?"

Markita shrugged. "He ain't 'lowed to do no real doctor stuff. Not here in the U.S.A. He from real Africa. South. Only went to nigger doctor college there or somethin. Can't help no white folks." She frowned again. "So, *there* be all the goddamn 'African' you need to know."

"Um, can you say somethin in Swahili?"

"Taka-taka."

"What that mean?"

"Polite way of sayin shit, what it mean. Yo. You figure white schools teachin CAUCASIAN heritage or somethin? Shit, *cho*-boy, what in hell good it gonna do you knowin your umpteenth great-grandfather ran round in his birthday suit chuckin spears at lions an tigers an bears? Hey, that stuff gonna help you survive in this *here* jungle? Gimme a break, boy! You want 'African'? Go an get yourself a dose at one of them Muslim meetins or that there black social thing they got way over East. Go an listen to 'em speechin-down bout how they gonna MAKE them white suckers pay US back IN spades for all the shit they done to us two hundred years ago! My ass! Yo. They even GOT some white folks there, lookin humble as hell an all shit-eatin sorry over what *their* great-grandfathers prob'ly never even done in the first place, an ready to kiss YOUR black butt cause of it! Bout like to make ME puke, best believe!"

Ty's eyes had widened as the girl spoke her mind. And that was giving it a name for sure! But she *had* a mind to speak, he realized. His loins had cooled a little, but it was somehow worth it. He nodded slowly, trying to make his own mind come up with words that made sense. For the first time he could remember he found himself wanting a girl to be more impressed with what was in his head than in his wallet, or between his legs. "Um, well, don't you never think it might be whites what . . . well, *controllin* all this shit?"

Markita looked at him as if he was a rat on Rollerblades. "Boy, case you ain't figured what is an what ain't yet, white folks runnin the whole goddamn world! I can't see where they doin such a cool job of it myself, an our turn gonna come one day, best you believe. But what scare the holy shit outa me is that it sure ain't lookin so far like we gonna run the zoo any goddamn better! Special if this here part of Oaktown be any example!" She sighed then, as if she'd been through this before. "Listen up, boy. How in hell you spect me to go worryin over what some dogfuckin skinheads or KKK cocksuckers or just plain greedy-ass white moth-erfuckers gonna do to me when I scared half to death just takin my two-year-ole son out on the sidewalk at broad-daylight noontime in my very own pure black neighbor-hood? Shit, boy, make bout as much sense as YOU worryin over paper or plastic while you bleedin to death. Word!" She thought a moment. "*Uhuru*, my ass! Ain't got ME no goddamn *uhuru* round here, an that a fact, jack!" She cocked her head. "Yo! Spose YOU think *uhuru* mean that soulful-eyed lady on *Star Trek?*"

Ty had, so said nothing. He sighed out a tired sound. The warmth had almost totally gone from his loins now. Thinking took energy too. And it was hard to think about love when you hurt. Still, he watched the proud profile of Markita's body show itself under her T-shirt again as she reached back to the top shelf of the medicine cabinet. The tee's purple color was perfect against her dark skin. The shirt climbed as she stretched on tiptoes, revealing the concave of her stomach which had just enough baby chub to shape and beautify her navel. Ty noted how the jeans slid low on her hips, and thought her as perfect as J'row's tiny fingers. Lieutenant Uhura had never been his idea of perfect. Anyway, they'd never even let *her* kiss Captain Kirk.

He blinked to find Markita standing over him once more, the peroxide bottle in one hand and a blue box of cotton fluff in the other. He thought he heard another little quiver in her voice, so different now from just moments ago when he'd asked something stupid and got a good talking to. A smile tugged at his lips: a girl who *could* talk! About as rare in his life as a roller-skating rat.

Markita ordered him to scoot back on the toilet lid.

"Can't," he said. "This goddamn gun be pokin my butt."

Markita tried to put impatience into her voice, like when some Burger King customer dawdled over the menu while people piled up behind. "Well, pull it out, boy."

Ty stood, and a little smile broke into that kind of goofy grin Markita had always imagined on his face. She flushed, thinking what a stupid thing to say. She stepped back. She could have stepped farther back. Ty laid the .45 on the side of the sink, then met Markita's eyes. Warm, he thought. Funny he'd never noticed before how hard it was for ebony eyes to look cold.

That exciting scent of two bodies and minds who wanted and needed each other flared in his nostrils once more. He felt the pull . . . like playing with the little magnets his mom kept on the refrigerator door. You brought them close and that mysterious force that drew them together grew stronger and stronger until they met like magic no matter how hard you tried to keep them apart. He felt power pulsing between his legs again, throbbing hot and hard. He forgot the pain in his arm, and his big bony hands clasped Markita's slim waist. He lowered his face to hers and whispered her pretty African name.

Markita felt the same magic force, even as she sensed the new heat in Ty's body and smelled his longing for her in the air. This was a time she seemed to have been dreaming of for years. It was almost funny to realize that she'd gone from a dream to the dreamed-for reality in less than a day. She set the cotton and bottle beside Ty's .45 as his hands found her body and pulled her close to him. She let her eyes run freely over him now. Her fingertips traced the squared plates of his chest and lingered a moment on one tiny nipple. That seemed to send a shiver through him, surprising her; she hadn't known boys were sensitive there. She touched the little silver medallion, curious, but that could wait. Then she lifted her gaze to a face that could only be kind. Ty bent his head and his lips brushed hers, almost shyly at first. He held her as if she was some fragile and pretty thing he was scared he might break. And that made her *feel* pretty and fragile . . . the way she'd always wanted to feel, except that this world tore fragile things apart. Ty's tongue quested but didn't force. She let him in a little at a time so that she would always remember this moment. It must have hurt as he gathered her tighter against him. She felt new blood soaking her shirt, but his eyes were at peace. His tongue explored, bringing the taste of him into her mouth; a sensation of sweat and blood, and the taint of too many cigarettes and too much drinking . . . a sad, sick taste, but that of every boy she'd ever known. It was frightening in a way, and yet she wanted him all the more because of it.

For Ty, Markita had a sweetness he'd always imagined a girl should have. Her full lips were soft, made for slow kissing, and the click of her teeth against his sounded somehow fierce and clean. Their first kiss lasted long, and then Ty released her to slip the shirt over her head. He stepped back to see her, smiling, maybe stupidly, but he no longer cared. A powerful backbone she had, he thought, to carry those beautiful breasts so proudly like that above a waist so slim. He thought of candies again, velvety smooth and the darkest chocolaty brown this side of midnight. He bent and kissed each nipple and heard her breath quicken. Then her hands were at his jeans, her fingers fast and sure as she undid the buttons. Once more he kissed her nipples, teasing their tips this time with his tongue so they stood tight and hard. His hands slipped down her body to the buttons of her Levi's as she slid his off his own narrow hips. Her hands found and cradled his maleness, making him moan in his throat and shiver again. She, like himself, wore nothing beneath her jeans. He pressed his lips to hers, sliding his hands to her smooth-muscled behind and pulling their bodies together.

They stayed like that, minutes passing, their eyes closed, exploring each other by touch, taste, and smell so they seemed to melt into one. Outside in the street a siren screamed past and gunshots sounded a few blocks away. But nothing could hurt them here. Ty's arm was bleeding again, and Markita was soon streaked with crimson. The room seemed to warm with the heat of their bodies. Ty glistened now, and his breath came hard, but he didn't try to enter her. Markita had seen his ebony shaft before taking it into her hands. This part of him too was all she'd imagined, throbbing with power to the beat of his heart, unsheathed and *bad*. She wanted to feel him surging inside her . . . wanted this drunk and bleeding and dying niggerboy more than anything else in the world.

And yet, close to the edge, he still held himself back.

Markita took hold of him, to guide him into her or thrust her own body onto him. Why didn't he take her? she wondered. Had she been so totally right in her dream . . . that this gentle, savage boy had yet to learn the physical moves of love? Then she saw his eyes, desperate for her even as he pulled away, and she suddenly knew the reason.

The room seemed to chill. A coldness washed over her. Was this time she'd dreamed of, like so many of her dreams, ended before it had really begun? Nigger dreams; grab what you can while you can, *now*, because the good things went around but never came around again. Selfish thoughts flashed through her mind, hateful and cruel: he would die, just as all the other boys like him would die. He'd be shot or stabbed in the heart, OD'd, or just drink himself to death before another time came around like this. It wasn't fair!

Yet, as she saw the love for her in his eyes, Markita's feeling of loss faded a little. Ty *did* love her! Yes, he did! His denying her now when it would be the cool thing to do, even expected of him to go on, surely proved that.

Didn't it?

Markita's eyes narrowed. Ty had backed away, panting, gleaming, his lean chest heaving. He still stood straight and solid, clutching himself with one hand as if to ease the weight of his throbbing power. Had she been a fool one more time? Markita wondered. Was the end of the dream really: *down on your knees and suck, bitch, lotta bad shit goin round?*

Then she saw him clearly through her doubt, and knew for a fact that he loved her. She cursed herself for not preparing on the chance that a dream would ever come by. Since J'row, she'd been living on dreams a lot. What cool dude wanted anything but a fuck from a bitch with a kid? What cool dude even *liked* kids? Maybe that was a black thing too—God help all niggers if it was. And Markita had been fucked over too much to care about that kind of fucking. Even stupid dreams were better than that, and besides, she could always dream up the happy endings. Of course, there was Leroy, but lame as it sounded, Leroy was a *friend*; he could make her laugh, probably even in bed, calling it something like "jumping her bones." He *would!* She *could* love Leroy, and be happy with him . . . and *he* had a future. Maybe the trouble with dreaming was that you began to believe you really had choices.

Frantic thoughts ran around in her head: the market would be closed, the nearest liquor store was blocks away. Ask a neighbor? At this hour? *Don't be a fool!* And in spite of herself, Markita could see the funny part of it . . . so motherfucking STUPID!

Markita saw Ty's eyes widen with a surprised look. Good Jesus Christ, had she said that out loud? But he suddenly looked shamefaced, his cheeks way too dark to show much of a blush, though Markita could see it. Then came that wonderful goofy grin once more—did he ever do that when he wasn't drunk?—and he dug in his jeans for his wallet. "I, um, I forgot I got one," he murmured.

Savage and gentle, loving and dangerous, jeans off his butt and his shaft thrust out fierce like a weapon, he made such a picture that Markita broke up. She moved to him quickly before he could misunderstand, hugging him tight while tears of laughter ran down her cheeks. "Ty, you just so way past cool, you FLOWIN cool!"

He grinned again and blushed again, fumbling out the little foil packet with big bony fingers. "It, um . . . actually it Theodore."

"*Theodore!* But how you get Ty outa that?"

"Well, um, like I sayin, I the oldest. An you know how

little kids' shoelaces forever comin undone? Seem like most my life I bein followed round gettin called to like that."

Markita busted into laughter once more and kissed him long. "I like the sound of it, now that I know." She looked down at both their blood-smeared bodies. "Christ, what a mess we make of everything!" She turned from him and opened the bathtub faucets, full-on. Ty grinned again. Markita popped the stopper into place as Ty sat back on the fluffy lid cover to take off his shoes and jeans. Markita sat on the mat, beside the splashing water, to take off her own.

The ancient tub was huge and deep, its bright whiteness a fierce contrast to the glistening ebony bodies of Ty and Markita as they faced one another, entwined within. Ty was big, but that was a fact he seemed to know in the same way he'd be careful of his feet. He entered her slowly, gently, and that made it all the more pleasurable for her as she parted to him. She locked her strong legs around his lean hips and pulled herself even tighter onto him. His power was the surging, loving savagery inside her that she'd dreamed it would be, so stone hard and straight it was almost like the intense, tearing pleasure-pain of the first time. She bit her lip to keep from crying out. Steam rose around them like wispy little ghosts. The warm water was soon pink-tinted with Ty's blood, ebbing and flowing to the rhythm and pulse of their movements. Markita nuzzled Ty's face, tasting again the desperate sadness of his life and maybe the foreshadow of his death. But he shared all his love with her freely, every sensation and pleasure . . . patient and caring and making his search her own. She could feel when he held back for her, waiting until she climbed with him. And when they found that place at last, it was together, and he held her there so the dream-moment lasted a long, long time.

So *this* was love, Ty thought at that instant . . . a thing of two parts. There was this one intense and beautiful moment, and then there was knowing you could never be happy yourself when those you loved were not. Even a stupid nigger could figure that out.

A time later, Ty and Markita stood naked, hand in hand, gazing down at the small sleeping child. They nibbled grape Popsicles. No words were needed. Markita bent to tuck the blanket up around J'row's chin and then kissed his forehead. Ty reached down a long gunmetal finger to touch a tiny perfect one. The little hand curled over it, tightly. Ty leaned close and kissed the child where Markita had.

A clock on the TV showed almost 3 a.m. Markita's hand pressed Ty's, and she looked over toward her bed. "You could stay," she whispered.

But Ty was thinking of Danny; how the boy would look peacefully sleeping beside his smaller brother on the big old mattress with room enough for three. Ty thought how Danny had looked a few hours ago, naked and climbing sulkily into bed. Ty wanted to be home, to ease himself under the blankets between the two younger boys and feel their warmth against him as he had for so many years. He and Danny could talk about stuff before school, any sort of shit, just like they used to do. They'd scheme out the day ahead, the years ahead. Ty would tell him about the truck. Maybe it would sound lame to Danny at first—chump change and uncool—but they'd split a quart of Colt .45 after the shopping was done, sitting together someplace quiet in the sun with their shirts off, and somehow Ty would make him see it was right.

"No," said Ty. "But, um, thanks." He smiled. "Maybe tomorrow. I gotta get them groceries home so's the kids got somethin sides mush for breakfast. But you keep the other Popsicles for J'row." He glanced at his arm, bandaged now with gauze and hospital tape. "An thanks, Markita. For everthin."

Their arms went around each other, and they kissed again. Then Markita sat on the edge of the coffee table and watched while Ty began putting on his clothes.

"I could get off early," she said. "That is, if you figure you an Danny might want some help with them little-girl things."

Ty hesitated, shirtless on the floor, his hands on his shoe-laces. This too was love, he realized, making choices and praying to a God who never seemed to listen that they were the right ones. Danny was just twelve, and though he already knew a lot about life, the idea of sharing his brother with this girl might be more than his heart could handle, especially since Ty had been out of his life for so long. *Long?* Ty wondered. Yeah. At twelve a few months seemed years. It might be a hard fight to win Danny back. Ty felt a chill in Markita's warm apartment, wondering if he'd have to give up his love for this girl for the love of his brother.

Markita saw Ty's hesitation, and knew the reason. Ty had told her more about Danny while she was bandaging his arm. He'd also told her of the truck he hoped to buy, and how he'd have to suffer with Deek at least another month to do it. Markita had been around enough younger kids to know how fierce and jealous Danny would feel toward his brother's attention and time. A twelve-year-old in this place might even kill to keep love. But Markita didn't think about that. What frightened her was the thought of losing Ty to save a young boy she didn't even know . . . a boy who might already be way past saving.

Markita knelt down in front of Ty, putting on a smile and leaning close. "I understand. It just boy stuff you two gotta do together."

"Yeah. That what it is. But, yo. We come by the Burger

King soon's Danny get out of school, fore we go uptown."

Ty smiled. "Danny tell me tonight, sorta, that he figure you cool. Spose it mostly cause of that free coffee you give him. But he smart. Smarter'n me, best believe. I think he be gettin to like you soon."

Ty stood, and the little medallion glinted in the streetlight glow from the window. Markita touched it, warm from his body as she'd known it would be. She bent close to study it in the dimness, but the detail looked half worn away.

Ty smiled again. "Oh, that just a silly ole thing my mom give me way back a long time ago. Don't signify nuthin . . . cept her givin it me, course. Don't even know why I still wearin it." He shrugged. "Hell, who know, maybe it lucky. Sposed to be St. Christopher."

Markita let go of the little silver disk. Its warmth seemed to linger a moment on her palm. "I seen em in cars sometimes. St. Christopher sposed to be lucky for travelers, I guess."

Ty's smile widened to a grin. He reached for his jacket and shirt. "That case, can't see it doin me no good. I sure as hell goin nowhere."

Markita helped Ty put his shirt on over his stiff bandaged arm, and then held his jacket while he slipped into it. "I read bout him one time, sorta by accident when I was lookin through my mom's cyclopedias over there. I think he sposed to be lucky for somebody sides travelers too. He carryin somethin on his shoulder."

Ty nodded as Markita zipped his jacket and tucked its tail carefully over the .45. "Yeah. Cept you can't see what it is cause it too wore out."

"You Catholic, Ty?"

"Nuh-uh. I a nuthin. Mom try to raise us up some kinda churchy stuff, but it never rub off on me." Ty's smile faded.

"Nor Danny neither, look like. Guess it come down tween money an God round here, an God lose. Ain't no wonder He don't give a shit." Ty chewed his lip a moment. "How bout you, Markita?"

She shrugged. "Guess you could say the same. My mom a regular churchgoer, but I don't bother much more bout what God gonna or not gonna do than them bad whites an skinheads we was talkin before."

Ty nodded again. "Mmm. Spect that right." He snagged his board and took the plastic bag of groceries from the counter. Markita opened the hallway door. Ty automatically checked the hall before stepping out, then turned and gave Markita a last long kiss.

She stood watching until his shadow faded down the stairwell, then whispered, "Please don't let him die."

■ "Yo, Lyon!"

Lyon spun around. He was still wearing Gordon's old T-shirt that looked like a tent on his slender body and totally concealed the Iver Johnson in the back of his jeans. One pawlike hand darted for the gun while the other brought his skateboard up to shield off a knife. Beside him, Curtis' books thudded on the floor as the smaller boy also whipped his board into defense position. Around them, the laughter and shouting and rowdy roar of kids in the school hallway died down. The tinny slam of locker doors and the rattle of cheap combo locks cut off. Kids nearby slipped quickly out of the line of fire.

Then Lyon saw it was Furball with his binder and board under one arm. The boy had frozen, looking surprised at the reaction he'd caused, his free hand hovering automatically near his knife pocket. Not far behind Furball, Lyon noted the twins at their shared locker. Their eyes were still red-rimmed and puffy from last night's drinking, but they'd come instantly alert and were measuring the distance to Furball in case Lyon needed backup.

Lyon and Furball broke into grins. Both wore black shades to cover the aftermath of a quart of JD and talking together all night until they'd watched the sun rise from a mud flat down by the ship channel. Tenseness faded from the air. There were some snorts and muttering among the other kids, a few who'd been hoping to see some sort of fight, but most relieved they wouldn't be dodging bullets or blades. The casual savagery of another school day's end echoed through the hall once more, mixed with the smells of kid sweat, hair sheen, girls' powder and perfume, and hundreds of pairs of well-worn sport shoes. Furball came up to Lyon, and Lyon lowered his board and tucked his tee back over the gun. Curtis and the twins relaxed, but still watched both boys with suspicion.

Furball's grin vanished as he faced Lyon. He shed his shades, narrowing his eyes with a message and shifting them briefly to Curtis, who had bent to pick up his books. "Um, can we talk, man? I mean, some more?"

Lyon took his own glasses off and glanced at Curtis. Curtis nodded and moved away, but brushed the dreads from his eyes and kept close watch on Furball. Lyon flashed his V smile at the twins, who'd been slowly advancing down the hall. They stopped, exchanged tawny-eyed looks of speculation, then shrugged in stereo and returned to their locker, where they usually did a good business selling Kools on credit. Curtis checked Lyon a final time, then started walking down the hall to the front doors.

Lyon looked back at Furball and raised an eyebrow.

"Bout last night," said Furball. "What it is, I done me some thinkin all day. Bout bein 'bad,' what I sayin . . . an how you tellin me dudes like Deek go down from little fuckups sometimes. I been thinkin bout my brother too, man. Like, how he might could get done right longside that dog-sucker Deek." Furball searched Lyon's face. "What I sayin here, Ty a *good* dude, Lyon. Word. Know what? Yo, he come home this mornin with all kinda cool food an shit. Flintstones vitamins too! Make everbody do one. Even Mom. Tell us we gotta, ever day from here on, for cause to stay strong. You hearin this, Lyon?"

Lyon nodded and smiled, but looked past Furball to where Gordon was coming out of the boys' room struggling to button his jeans at least halfway. As usual, the T-shirt he wore didn't near cover his belly but he had a shiny black nylon jacket, its tail long enough to hide the .22.

Lyon's eyes came back to Furball, and his smile warmed. "It cool to be hearin you say them things, man." His fore-head creased a little. "But I don't gots much time to be talkin right now. There somethin by."

Furball looked uncertain and scanned the fast-emptying hall. The twins had stopped Gordon; all three boys mur-mured together and flicked occasional glances at Lyon. Cur-tis stood by the open front doors as the last of the other kids poured through, also keeping watch on Lyon. Furball looked down at his Nikes and kicked a toe on the faded tile floor. "Yeah. Word up, you an the Crew gonna meet."

Lyon's eyes cooled slightly. "Mmm. Word say, huh? Well, you tell me yourself lotsa word go round don't signify dogshit."

Furball shrugged, still staring at his shoes. "Yeah, I know, but . . ." He seemed to choose his words carefully. "Listen, man. I gonna meet my brother soon. At Burger King. For cause of that shoppin thing I was tellin you last night."

Lyon could see impatience on Gordon's face. "Yo. Better

cut to the chase," he told Furball gently. "What it is, you be tellin me you thinkin on changin your mind bout givin your brother word we find Deek's crib."

Furball's mouth opened. "Shit! You really *can* read minds like magic, Lyon!"

Slyness flickered at the edges of Lyon's uptilted eyes. He smiled his V and touched a delicate finger to Furball's chest. "What it is, readin hearts be easier. They most never lie."

Furball shifted uncertainly under Lyon's soft touch. His face hardened. "What I sayin is, I ain't gonna let nuthin happen to my brother, man. What it takes!"

"Mmm." Lyon's fingertip gently traced muscle as if measuring something. "That ain't hard to hear at all, man." He lowered his hand, palm open. "But you know inside yourself Deek's shit gotta be chilled. Maybe below zero. What it take be what it is."

Furball squeezed his eyes tight shut and sucked a breath.

"Tap your Nikes together three time," said Lyon. "Who know, might even work."

Furball's eyes snapped open. "Huh? Oh." Then his gaze leveled cold. "Oh, shut up an listen to me, sucker!" He flicked a glance toward Gordon and the twins, then dropped his voice to almost a whisper. "Yo! Last night, fore you show, I hear some shit Deek tellin my brother. It bout you an the Crew. I not unnerstand a'zactly meanin all, but he talkin drive-bys an . . ."

Gordon's voice cut him off. "Yo, Lyon! C'mon, man. It gettin way past get-busy time."

Furball ignored the fat boy, who had come quietly close, the twins following. Furball gripped Lyon's arm. "Word, man! This crucial!"

"Gordon . . ." Lyon began.

But Gordon shook his head. "No! Gots no TIME now!

What up too goddamn 'portant for dickin round with!" He eyed Furball. "Who this dude anyways?"

"A friend," said Lyon. "Listen up . . ."

Gordon clenched big fists. "NO! Goddamnit, Lyon, *I* talkin now. An what I sayin is we gots no time for dudes what don't count. Not today. Maybe I listen to your magic shit too much anyways. What it gettin us? I say one time more, man, c'mon."

Lyon sighed, but nodded, then touched Furball's shoulder. "Seem Gordon be right, man. But you was too, bout the word. Gangs meetin an talkin be major 'portant shit . . . special bout THIS sorta shit. But you know where I live now. You come over tonight. We talk more. Word." He turned to Gordon. "Yo. Give him a pass. Total an forever."

"*What?* Goddamnit, Lyon, you don't tell ME bout rules!"

Lyon's voice changed, turned strange and menacing. "Just do it!"

Gordon blinked, staring at the slender boy as if just seeing him for the first time, but the twins only watched in curiosity. Gordon's eyes shied away. His big body sagged loose. He nodded to Furball. "Okay, dude. Whoever the fuck you are, Lyon trust ya. You pass. Anytime."

"Yo! How come?" demanded Ric.

"Yeah!" piped Rac. "What this shit?"

"Shut up!" roared Gordon. He grabbed Furball's shoulders and spun the thin boy around to face the twins. Surprised, Furball's hand darted for his knife, but Lyon touched his arm and he didn't pull.

"You see him?" demanded Gordon. "You hear me?"

The twins nodded sulkily.

"Word." Gordon snorted and let go of Furball, then moved for the hallway doors. "Let's bail!"

Lyon followed the other boys, but looked back once.

Furball still stood by the lockers. He'd slipped his shades on once more, way too big and half hiding his face, but looked fierce and determined just the same.

"Yo! Lyon-o! What by?" asked Rac, close behind the slender boy as they ran down the steps and out the school gates.

"Yeah," puffed Ric. "We gots Furball in Crabzilla's class. He pretty cool. Gots a name with his blade. Yo, he wantin to be a Friend?"

Lyon slammed down his board, decking and kicking away after Gordon, who was already ripping up the sidewalk. "He be already a friend," said Lyon. "A friend alone."

"Must be more magic shit, he meanin," muttered Ric to his brother as they decked and rolled after Lyon.

"Yeah," agreed Rac. "Or what. Don't unnerstand none of it!"

Curtis caught up and spat between their boards. "Yo! COURSE it a magic thing, suckers! Magic by the heart. Ain't no wonder in hell YOU two can't unnerstand. Shit! Prob'ly gots only one pussy little heart tween ya both. So THERE!" He kicked hard, shooting between the twins, dreads flying, to roll beside Lyon.

Ric and Rac made a few kissy noises but shrugged to each other.

"Yo, Lyon," Curtis panted as they rounded a corner. "I seen you *change* back there in the hall! Sometimes, when I stayin with you an it's late an you figure I sleepin, I swear I see you do it then, in the dark. But *this* was daytime!"

Lyon grinned, cutting around a sewer cover. "What kinda crazy talkin that be, homey? You seen too many movies. An you been readin my spooky books too."

"Don't mean jack, Lyon! Gordon seen you, an he like to shit! An Gordy ain't scared of nuthin! So there."

"Prob'ly cause Gordon gots more 'portant shit to be

scared over than what he *think* he see. An same by you.
Or oughta be."

Curtis frowned. "Well . . . you was out last night. ALL
night. Yes, you was! I woke up alone. There was a moon
just comin clear out the fog. I went to the hall window an
looked. You went somewheres to do magic shit, huh, Lyon?
Know what? I bet you gonna magic that Deek motherfucker
to death."

Lyon grinned again, his big teeth gleaming. "Yo, homeboy. Why for you be askin me all this silly-ass shit?"

"Cause. Hey, I know you a lot better'n you think I do,
man. Cept, times I don't unnerstand you at all. I known
you all my goddamn life, but sometimes it seem like you
somethin else."

Lyon smiled. "Some*body* else, man."

"Nuh-uh! SomeTHING else! Shit, I know what I wanna
say!"

Lyon and Curtis separated to pass a cluster of people in
front of a funeral parlor. All the boys studied the coffin
with interest as the bearers carried it down steps. It wasn't
a full-sized one. Curtis cut back beside Lyon again, and the
slender boy said, "Well, homey, that maybe make two of
us what don't always unnerstand." Lyon's jaw set and he
skated on in silence. Gordon was keeping up a killer pace
for all his extra weight, and the old car wash was only a
few blocks away now. Curtis was about to drop to his usual
place in the rear of the file when Lyon spoke again.

"Times I get thinkin my life ain't my own, man. Like
. . . like really I die that first night in the dumpster. But
then somethin come along . . ."

Curtis kicked close once more, his eyes widening. "No!
SomeBODY, man. Don't say someTHING!"

Lyon stared ahead at Gordon's back. "What it is, man.

Somethin. There's times in my dreams when I can almost see him. There musta been a moon that night. Funny, though, I can't never 'member nuthin bout him cept he look so goddamn sad."

"Nuh-uh!" cried Curtis. "No way in hell you 'member shit like that, man! You was a goddamn little baby!"

Lyon didn't seem to hear. "He had this big sack, all shiny black like Gordon's jacket there. Only, it was sorta all rainbowy too . . . like a puddle on the street."

"No. No! NO! You motherfucker! It was just some ole winehead trollin for cans, what it was! Now shut the fuck up, sucker! I don't wanna hear no more of this shit!"

Lyon smiled. "Yo. You figure everthin out on them streets at night be just wineheads or junkies, man? Or *people?*"

"Not funny, Lyon! Look, I ain't even listenin to you!" Curtis clapped his hands over his ears, almost losing his balance for a second.

"There be *collectors*," said Lyon.

"What?" Curtis dropped his hands. "Well, *course!* What I just say."

"But not *them* kind. See, these here collectors I talkin bout been round a long, long time. Like, before there was even a Oaktown. Or America."

"Um . . . Did they come from Africa? All chained up in ships?"

"Ain't nobody chain up *these* dudes, man. For sure, once, in ever long while, people might catch one, but then they try an kill it. The collectors be all over the world, man. But mostly where kids die a lot. See, they go round at night, collectin up all the spirits of dead kids."

Curtis stubbornly shook his head. "Nuh-uh! No way! Dead kids go to heaven! Like the one in that box back there."

"Shit, I thought they be goin to Jamaica, mon."

"Not funny, asshole!"

"Well, anyways, this collector had himself a whole sackful of kid spirits, an he stuck em all in me."

"No, he didn't! Why would he do that for? Goddamnit, there ain't no motherfuckin thing as collectors! Same's Draculas an werewoofs!" Curtis considered a second. "Well, I think they do got some werewoofs in Pennsylvania . . . but that clear cross the goddamn ocean! Stop tryin to freak me with your spooky talk, Lyon. Not even in daytime."

Lyon grinned once more. "Dint your mom never tell you that nuthin be there at night what ain't in the day?"

"She weren't talkin no collectors an werewoofs!"

Lyon shrugged and kicked harder to keep pace with Gordon. "Then don't be askin me questions if you can't handle the answers, man. Maybe all dogs go to heaven, but kids sposed to get REAL lives first. That why there be collectors."

"Oh, yeah, right, man! An them collectors is what ole people call werewoofs! Uh-huh, uh-huh, I'm sure!"

Lyon shrugged again. "So, you tell me who be better for the job? They black an scary an nobody fuck with em much."

"So, what happen to all the kids get collected?"

"Don't know. Maybe they get new hearts an another chance to be kids somewheres. Hell, GOT to be a place where kids wanted." Then Lyon smiled and reached out to touch Curtis' arm. "Yo. We almost there, homey. Story time over. Best be savin back your breath case we end up gotten to fight. Heart magic be good strong stuff, but there just ain't enough of it goin round yet."

"Um, you figure there ever gonna be, Lyon?"

"Believe, homey. But it gotta START with kids. Most

people lose the good part of their hearts when they get older."

The twins had been skating close behind, both shirtless now, and gleaming. Ric murmured to his brother, "Yo. Figure Lyon a good dude, or just a crazy niggerboy?"

"Don't know," said Rac. "Shit, you prob'ly be crazy too, spendin your first-borned night in a motherfuckin dumpster, man."

"Shit. Spendin MY first-borned night with YOU prob'ly done me!"

Rac only held a palm to his chest for a moment, then to his brother's. "Well, say this, we still gots ours."

Ric did the same. "Yeah. Hey, figure we oughta make Curtis get his butt back behind us where he belong?"

"Mmm. Maybe we should let him cruise with Lyon from now on. They sorta just like you an me, even if they ain't. You can watch our ass."

"No, you. I the first, 'member?"

"Shit! How I forget, you 'mindin me ever goddamn day of my life! Flip ya for it?"

Ric flashed a finger. "Flip THIS, niggerboy!" He glanced over his shoulder. "Anyways, who in hell be followin us, doofus?"

"Yeah? Well, if a werewoof sneak up an do ya, an you get your ass collected, don't come cryin to me, sucker!"

Deek was right, God damn his soul to hell! Ty shoved the *Tribune* away and smashed out his Kool in a little foil ashtray already brimming with butts. Elbows on the table-top, he dropped his face to his hands and squeezed his eyes tight shut until points of light danced in the darkness. There was a single short paragraph on the paper's back page: two youths found dead in an East Oakland motel room of an apparent drug overdose. Details were being withheld pending further investigation. Ty wondered how much "investigation" would really be done. They were young, they were black, and they were dead: end of story.

A story he'd helped write.

His slashed arm was stiff and hurt to move but he deliberately used it so it hurt all the more, digging in his jacket pocket for cigarettes. He fired one, sucking smoke deep, then hissing it out in sadness and disgust; sadness for the boys—he *would* have stopped Deek if he'd known—and disgust for himself and the world he had to live in. The paper's front pages were filled with details of some humpback whales that had beached themselves in the Bay. A massive rescue operation was underway to save them. Ty took a swallow of cold coffee, not tasting that it was, then looked at his watch. Danny was late; really late. He should have been out of school over an hour ago. Maybe he'd gotten detention? His grades were good but he didn't take shit from other kids or his teachers, so it would probably be for fighting one or speaking his mind to the other. The boy was proud. Was there such a thing as being too goddamn proud . . . or just proud about the wrong sort of things? Was this what black pride had—Ty searched for the word, Markita had used it once when they'd been talking last night: *evolved*. Was this what black pride had evolved into? There was another word; Ty couldn't bring it to mind, *de-*something.

He glanced over at the girl; she was busy behind bullet-proof glass but still managed to give him a smile whenever she caught his eye. Ty found himself wishing he knew more about life, stuff the street couldn't teach. Did black kids hold life so cheap because they couldn't see any future in it? Was the whole fucking world evil, or just this city? Ty remembered a Bible story his mom had told him a long time ago: about how God had destroyed an evil city. Ty had never liked the story: hadn't there been any children in that place? Some God! Ty fingered his medallion and watched Markita boxing burgers. He recalled her joke about the Muslim center: they said God was black, or Jesus was; something like that. Well, so fucking what! Black, white, or every goddamn color of a motherfucking rainbow, *He* didn't seem to give a shit about kids either! So, what in hell was there left for them to believe in? Whatever color Christ had been, he'd got his fool self nailed to a cross for nothing!

Ty studied Leroy, who was busy at the broiler. His shirt

sleeves were shoved high up his wiry arms and he'd squashed and shaped his stupid little hat so it looked like something Bobby Brown might wear. In a world of cool Leroy was a loser: working days in a Burger King, finishing high school at night, and taking a computer course on top of it all. Ty knew a lot of bad dudes who would say that Leroy had sold out, gone Oreo . . . *incognegro*. But who in hell was the joke really on? Ty wondered again what Danny would think of busting his butt hauling scrap iron when dudes years younger than him could fill up a goddamn truck with money. Maybe *that* was the color of God: black on one side and green on the other! How much was love worth in a place where money bought life and death?

Ty glanced at his watch again, flicking away more dried blood. Where in hell *was* the boy? Ty decided he'd wait another fifteen minutes, then skate over to the school. Time was running out. Deek would want him back on the job tonight, and he *had* to go. Ty crushed his half-smoked Kool and dropped his face back into his hands.

There was a soft touch on his shoulder. Ty looked up to find Markita beside him with a fresh cup of coffee. He noticed that Leroy was now at the counter, taking orders. The customers all seemed to be kids just out of school, most toting binders or wearing backpacks stuffed with books and homework. Ty met Leroy's eyes for a second, and the dude nodded. It was funny; Ty had expected him to be pissed; it was plain he had a thing for Markita. But there was only a sad sort of understanding in Leroy's eyes, like he'd been to hell and burned his wings but was satisfied to have come back alive. There was something cool in that. In a way, Leroy was badder than Deek would ever be. He'd chosen a life that didn't hurt anybody. That took real balls. You could dress up a lion in a clown suit and make it jump through hoops, but it would still be a lion.

"How's your arm?" asked Markita.

Ty shrugged as if it didn't bother him, but added, "Hurt some. Inside-like."

"Always gotta hurt some to get better."

Then the room seemed to darken as if the gunmetal uniforms of the two cops just entering had sucked up the light. Ty tensed, and felt Markita's grip tighten on his shoulder as the big men neared. It was the pair who helped hold up the pyramid. Ty scented leather and gun oil and aftershave. A coldness flowed through him, but he felt no fear. If the cops had come for him because of the two boys, then somebody else was going to die. There was no way Ty would let himself be locked in just another kind of cage.

"Move away slow," he murmured to Markita. "Get clear of me. Back inside the kitchen."

Markita hesitated.

"Do it, girl!" Ty hissed.

She obeyed, coolly, walking casual toward the steel door. Ty shifted on the slick plastic seat so he could get at his .45. The cops wore bulletproof vests but were carrying their helmets like the football players they'd probably been in high school. Ty wished he'd had more practice with his gun. And now his arm was stiff and clumsy . . . and the motherfucking room was full of kids!

When he'd been about Danny's age, Ty had seen a seventeen-year-old cornered in a parking lot and surrounded by twenty cops. The boy had only a cheap little revolver. Yet he'd brought the gun up and aimed, knowing full well what would happen. He'd smiled . . . Ty was sure of it! The paper said he'd been hit by seventeen bullets and a shotgun blast. And his own gun had been empty all the time! Ty suddenly knew why the boy had died smiling: he'd finally escaped from the cage.

Ty's hand found the .45. But there was no sign of interest

or even recognition as the cops' eyes passed through him. All Ty could sense was the mutual hate that somehow bound him and the two men together. The white one yawned, saying to the other, "Christ, I hate these fucking rotations!"

Rotate on *this*, sucker! Ty thought, flipping the finger under the table.

"Hey, girl," called the black one to Markita as she passed by. "What's the chance of getting breakfast?"

Markita snorted. "Bout the same's a Popsicle in hell. An I damn sure ain't your girl!"

The cop flushed slightly, but strode to the order window in silence. A few kids snickered and flashed signs to Markita. The white cop squeezed his creaking bulk into a booth with his back to Ty.

Ty wanted to leave then, to get out fast and onto his skateboard and be a kid again for just a few minutes. But he stayed. To leave now wouldn't be cool.

Wesley, the Crew leader, was one of those beautiful boys who were usually displayed in commercials or movies as the one cool black who hung with a bunch of uptown whiteys. Girls of any color would want to cuddle him, and dudes of any race would at least envy his build. He wasn't muscled to the point of awkwardness; just perfectly proportioned like some sort of coffee-colored model of God's ideal thirteen-year-old boy. No one blamed him much that he knew it; dressing in short cutoffs even when it rained, and wearing only skintight tank tops or mesh tees when he wore a shirt at all. Word said that a perv-shop owner had once paid him a bill to pose in black leather for a magazine, holding a whip over some old white sucker in a KKK suit.

His hair was a natural bush—why fuck with perfection?—and the massive gold-plated chain with its heavy medallion slapping his solid, square-slabbed chest looked like something he'd won in a war. He never just stood but he posed, but he was so way past cool to look at that you could forgive him for it. If he'd been a sculpture in a park, nobody would have spray-painted him.

He was posing now atop the rusty tin roof of the pressure-pump shed behind the peeling, sheet-metal bays of the closed-up car wash. He watched, coolly, as the Friends rolled across the weedy, trash-strewn asphalt. His feet in big megabuck Cons were spread wide apart, and his hands rested half curled on his narrow hips. The fingers of one held a smoldering Marlboro, the other the stick of a strawberry Popsicle.

Three other boys sat on the roof: two, a tall, thin ebony dude and a chocolate-brown boy of average build, on one side of Wesley, and skinny little Tunk on the other. All were shirtless in the hot afternoon sun, and dangled their faded-jeaned legs over the edge, swinging Nikes and Reeboks in the air. All had cigarettes and half-eaten Popsicles. Each had his skateboard beside him: Wesley's lay between his feet. Tunk was the only one smiling, as if you couldn't be bad and suck on a Popsicle at the same time. A fourth boy, round-faced and roly-poly with a chest like a pair of water balloons, sat on a battered vacuum unit at the back of the car-wash lot, munching his Popsicle and eyeing the Friends. His shirt lay beside him, wadded up and covering his other hand. Gordon gave him a long glance as he tailed about thirty feet from the wash-bay structure. "Bet Game-Boy there gots the gun," he murmured to Lyon. "He look like some kinda chocolate marshmallow, but he badder'n hell when he don't gotta move much. Ain't nobody never smoke his ass on Nintendo."

"Mmm," said Lyon. "Sound like my kinda dude. I watch him." He gazed around. Behind the vacuum box, a six-foot chain-link fence ran along the back of the lot. It was the saggy kind without a pipe rail on top, and hard to climb.

Beyond was a narrow strip of dry weeds and then a concrete-lined ditch about four feet deep and twenty wide. Its bottom was covered with what looked like black Jell-O pudding that stank like everything slimy and rotten. The blank back sides of buildings lined the ditch's opposite shore. There were no hiding places.

"Wesley gots him *five* dudes," said Lyon. "Seem he be down one today."

"Um," whispered Curtis. "Maybe one got shot or somethin yesterday?"

"Tunk woulda told us a major thing like that," said Gordon.

"Well, then maybe he home sick? Happen to bad dudes too, y'know?"

Lyon smiled a little, but shook his head. "Yo. Wesley gots him a brain in that way cool bod. He be holdin back a reserve, best believe." Lyon scanned the lot again: all four of the wash bays were empty, except for a junked Ford Pinto in one. The metal door to the pump shed was chained and padlocked shut. "Well, there be Tunker, Brett, an Ajay up on the roof side Wesley, an Game-Boy on the vac. Even money say Turbo be coverin us from somewheres."

Ric and Rac moved close. "Thought Gordon say Game-Boy gots the gun?" whispered Rac.

"Yeah," said Ric. "Yo. Anybody see there somethin under his shirt there."

Lyon frowned. "An it might just be nuthin but his fist, sucker."

Gordon wiped sweat from his face and scowled. His T-shirt was soaked from the warp-seven ride and stuck to him like a coat of paint under his jacket. "Yeah. An if the Crew already done score that Uzi from Deek, an Turbo gots it, we all dogmeat right now! Spread the fuck out! You goddamn know better'n to be bunchin all up like one easy target!''

The boys moved apart. Gordon looked at Lyon again. "Well, Game-Boy major hot shootin Space 'Vaders, but I don't know how he handle a real gun. Ask me, he ain't the one gots it. Keep a good watch for Turbo. I seen *him* shoot. You figure Tunk tell Wes bout our chrome gun?''

Lyon glanced up to the small skinny boy on the roof. "Mmm. Don't know. But best we be keepin it iced long's we can. Don't be showin yours neither, less you gotta.''

"Yo! Gordy!" Wesley called. "You look hotter'n hell with that there jacket on, man. G'wan, take it off, you want. Shit, I know you packin the fire." He grinned. "An you late, man. We save by some Popsicles for ya, but they start in meltin, so's we hadda eat 'em. Oh well." He bit off the last chunk and flipped the stick away.

Gordon glanced at Game-Boy again, then shifted slightly so the .22 in the back of his jeans wouldn't be seen as he peeled off his jacket. Facing Wesley, he stripped his shirt off too and wiped under his arms with it. "So, where Turbo?''

Wesley shrugged. "His mom take him to the dentist after school.''

"Uh-huh." Gordon yanked up his jeans, squinting because Wesley had the sun at his back. "This meet sposed to be by rules, Wes. Everbody need to be here.''

Wesley took a last hit off his cigarette and flicked it away. He spread his hands. "Yo. Dude gots a Popsicle habit. Don't brush his goddamn teeth or somethin. Can I help that?''

"Mmm." Gordon planted his feet wide apart and crossed his arms over his chest. "Say we let that slide, man. I still gots a prob with you dudes bein up on that roof while we on the ground. Wanna be cool, best you come down with us." He pointed to the wash bays. "An we all be cooler kicked back in the shade, man." He jerked a thumb sideways. "Shit. Check out poor Game-Boy, there. He lookin like to melt. Yo, don't you give a shit over your dudes, Wes?"

Wesley frowned. "My ass! Why you figure I ain't got em all packed together so's some motherfuckin ole black van come by an spray em dead?!"

Gordon pointed. "Street gate chained up, man. An I *know* you smart enough to check out it locked." He scowled. "Or maybe it ain't really locked, huh? Maybe you gots Turbo standin by ready to drop it an let that cocksuckin van in on US?"

Wesley considered a minute, then his face softened a little. "Chain locked, Gordon. Word, man. You wanna, send one of your dudes to check it out." He waited, and when Gordon did nothing, looked down at Tunk. "Yo, Gordy, my 'bassador tell me y'all get yourselfs sprayed too. Least that what he say YOU say. My prob is, how I for sure know that?"

Gordon nodded to Curtis, who pulled off his shirt and turned around to show the bandage on his back. "You come down," said Gordon, "You see we both gots the same prob, man."

Wesley exchanged quiet words with Tunk before facing Gordon again. "Yo! Let's see your gun, Gordy."

Gordon recrossed his arms, and snorted. "You first! An don't call me Gordy, man! I hate that!"

"Goddamnit, Gordon, stop fuckin around! Yo! I let you copy my goddamn English homework last week!"

"BFD! An I told Coach you was in the fuckin nurse's office when you went an cut PE!"

Up on the roof, Brett and Ajay snickered. Wesley shot

them a look, then stabbed a finger toward the back of the lot. "Game-Boy gots it! Never figure you was that blind, Gor-DEN!"

Gordon turned. The fat kid on the vacuum box slipped a little black snub-nosed revolver from under his shirt and held it pointed to the sky.

"So there!" sniffed Wesley. "Now you!"

Gordon's eyes went to Lyon, who nodded. Slowly, Gordon pulled the pistol from his jeans and held it muzzle-down.

Wesley nodded. "That thing still jam up, man?"

"Naw. We got it fixed a way long time ago."

"Uh-huh. Well, why not ya give it to one of them clones an he slide on over an shoot shit with the Gamer. Then we come down. Okay?"

Gordon exchanged glances with Lyon, who nodded again, then held the gun out to one of the twins. "Yo, Ric."

"I'm Rac."

"Whatever. Just do it."

Rac took the gun and strutted over to Game-Boy, who had put his revolver back under the shirt again. Ric's eyes carefully tracked his brother. Wesley snagged his board and leaped from the roof with the other boys close behind. All landed lightly, then spread wide and advanced warily to within ten feet of the Friends. Curtis stood patiently as Wesley came forward to study his back. The Crew leader nibbled his lip for a moment, then faced Gordon. "Mmm. Gotta say, man, all I see's some Big Bird Band-Aids an gauze stuff. Hell, that there red shit be ketchup, all I know."

"Yeah?" said Ric. "So put some on your wienie, dude."

"Shut up, asshole!" hissed Gordon.

Curtis clenched his teeth. "Take it off, man."

Gordon looked at the small boy, then smiled. "Yo, Wes, go for it. Don't faint or nuthin."

For a few seconds Wesley looked uncertain. Then he gingerly took hold of the top of the bandage.

"Um," said Tunk, moving close. "Do it fast, man. So's it don't hurt him so much."

"Shut up! I know bout goddamn Band-Aids!" Wesley ripped the bandage loose. Curtis sucked air but stayed silent. Tunk, Brett, and Ajay crowded close to check out the gash, which had started to bleed.

"Um, sorry, man," murmured Wesley.

"S'cool," muttered Curtis.

"Black van," said Gordon. "Shitty paint job. Ole Dodge with a two-piece windshield. Yesterday mornin, fore school. Deuce Uzis."

"An the second motherfuckin time!" added Curtis.

Wesley dropped the sticky bandage to the ground, and nodded. "Okay. So's we gots the same prob. But who it is, an why they wanna do us? Deek say . . ."

"Shit!" said Gordon. "Lemme guess, man. Deek tellin ya it some big dudes wanna move our grounds. An he wantin to front a Uzi to work for him."

"Word," said Wesley. "Or give him a dealin pass."

"Dint know you sold em, man."

Wesley scowled. "We don't! Dint know *you* did, man!"

"We don't! Gots enough motherfuckin probs in the hood without that shit!"

Wesley met Gordon's eyes a moment, then sighed. "Mmm. Maybe we do too."

Gordon thought for a second, glanced at Lyon, then said. "Well, just maybe we gots us a handle on somethin, man. Leastways over Deek sucker."

Wesley scanned Gordon's face. "Yeah?" He fingered his

jaw, then waved toward the wash bays. "Yo. Maybe you right bout the shade bein the place, man. Let's us all slide in an be cool while we talk some. Maybe we let Game-Boy an Ric catch theyselfs a tan a while?"

"I'm Ric," piped Ric.

Tunk and Curtis snickered. Wesley smiled. "Whatever."

The boys were just turning toward the wash structure when suddenly there were yells and fighting sounds from around one side. "Wes-LEEEE!" screamed a voice. "LYON!" bawled another.

"Turbo!" yelled Wesley, spinning toward the sounds.

"Furball!" shouted Lyon.

Wesley whirled back to face Gordon. "You lyin motherfucker!"

"YOU the liar, cocksucker!" Gordon roared back.

Ajay and Brett whipped out their knives. Tunk hesitated a few seconds, then unhappily pulled his. Ric and Curtis snatched up their boards and clutched them like clubs. Gordon and Wesley both spun toward the back of the lot. Rac had the .22's muzzle buried in Game-Boy's chest. Game-Boy was staring down at it. Wesley's hand went for his pocket. Brett and Ajay circled their blades in the air and took steps toward Curtis and Ric. Tunk was holding back, looking miserable. Gordon jerked up his own board. Then the bright little gun flashed like magic in Lyon's dark paw, aimed square at Wesley's heart. There was a loud click as he thumbed back the hammer: ancient as it was, the little gun had a solid steel sound. All the boys froze.

Wesley's face twisted in rage. "You SHIT!" he screamed at Gordon. "You fucked over the rules!"

Gordon glared back. "YOU fucked em first, cocksucker! You lie bout Turbo!"

"You lie bout your gun, motherfucker! What Rac got

there? A toy?" Wesley whirled to point at the wash structure. "An who you gots tryin to do Turbo, you lyin sucker?"

"Both you shut up!" Lyon bawled. He jabbed the gun at the Crew boys. "Ajay! Brett! Tunk! Bail them blades! Nice an far! NOW!"

The three boys shifted their eyes to Wesley as the fighting sounds got louder from around the wash bay: struggling bodies slamming loose tin, yells and panted curses.

Wesley gritted his teeth. "Just do it!"

Three knives glittered bright arcs through the air, hitting the asphalt about thirty feet away.

"Rac!" shouted Lyon. "Get Game-Boy over here! Then watch all these dudes!" he jabbed the silver gun again. "Gordon! Wes! C'mon! We all gots enough probs now, out we doin each other, goddamnit!" He darted for the wash structure, not looking back.

Wesley and Gordon stared at one another for a few seconds, then followed on the run. The other gang boys regarded each other uneasily, their eyes shifting to Game-Boy as he came slowly across the lot with Rac holding the pistol to his head, then all turned to gaze in wonder after their leaders and Lyon.

Turbo was a dark, wiry dude. Furball had him flat on his back on the gravelly pavement, crouching on the boy's chest, knife point at his throat. Turbo clutched a snub-nosed revolver jammed to Furball's cheek. Both boys gleamed and panted hard, their bodies scratched and dirt-streaked, and little chunks of gravel sticking to their skin. Close by lay their boards, wheels in the air like dead things. Lyon rounded the corner and skidded to a stop. Gordon and Wesley almost crashed into him.

"Furball! Chill!" yelled Lyon.

Furball's eyes were wild. "He do me, I back off! He do me, Lyon!"

Lyon spun to Wesley. "Call your man! Fast! Or we lose em both!

Wesley just stood for a second, fists clenched, chest heaving, looking like a kid about to explode. His eyes seemed to seek escape but couldn't find any. Finally he sucked a breath. "Game over, Turbo."

Turbo's eyes were huge and scared, showing white all around, and rolling. He swallowed and a thread of crimson appeared on his throat beneath the knife point. "Wh . . . what you tellin me, man? How I know he not . . . ?"

Wesley shot Lyon a glare, but growled, "Cause *I* tellin ya, man! So just do it!"

Turbo choked back a sob, then cautiously lowered the gun, letting his arm fall back on the ground. Furball's eyes flicked to Lyon.

"Heart," Lyon murmured.

Furball drew back the knife and got to his feet. His thin body started shaking. Lyon nodded, then turned to face the gang leaders. Both were looking more confused than anything else. Raising an eyebrow, Lyon let down the Iver Johnson's hammer. Then he tucked the gun back into his jeans and moved to Furball. The skinny boy's tank top had slipped from both shoulders and hung at his waist. Lyon began brushing gravel off Furball's back. His touch seemed to calm the boy.

Wesley had been watching all Lyon's moves, alert for some trick. His eyes now shifted to Gordon, unarmed except for his board, and seemed to consider if he could take the fat boy. Then he looked down to Turbo, who still had the revolver in his hand. He seemed to feel Lyon's eyes on him, and raised them to the slender boy. Finally, he muttered,

"Get up, Turbo. Chill out. Be cool, man. You done good."
Then he faced Gordon. "Yo! This here suck somethin way
total, man! What IS this shit . . . gots yourself another
dude hid by an he go an jump my man! Yo, not fair! Word!"

Gordon was just staring at Furball. "But he ain't . . ."
Lyon coughed.

Gordon read. "Well . . . shit, Wes! You keepin Turbo
hid by! Not fair neither, man!"

Wesley puffed a chest that didn't need it. "Yo! Just 'tectin
my dudes, what it is, man. I gots a right! If that ain't a
rule, then it for sure the fuck oughta be!"

Furball was watching Turbo get up, one finger restless
on the knife handle. Turbo kept the gun muzzle pointed
down. Furball suddenly snorted, puffing his own little chest.
"Yo! I not jump nobody, man! This here sucker come round
an try an grab me from a'hind!"

"Call ME no sucker, you skinny-ass motherfucker!"
Turbo spat.

Wesley slammed a fist into Turbo's chest. "Yo! You tellin
me you jump him with a gun, an he only gots a piddly-ass
knife, an HE get YOU grounded like that? SHIT!"

Turbo sputtered, but Lyon smiled and touched his arm.
"Yo! Furball be way past bad with his blade. Hell, everbody
know. Ain't Turbo's fault."

Turbo nodded sulkily. "Goddamn right it ain't!"

Gordon searched Lyon's face, then gave Wesley a nudge.
"Yo. I rent him to ya for givin your dudes lessons, man.
Twenty bucks a hour."

"My dick!" Wesley clenched his fists again, but finally
relaxed and shrugged. "Oh, too funny, man." He glared at
Turbo. "Put that goddamn gun by fore you go an hurt
yourself!" He turned back to Gordon. "Yo! Not fair you
gots yourself two guns an not say!"

"Get out my face, Wesley! YOU gots two guns an not say neither!"

"I tole you, goddamnit, gotta 'tect my dudes, man! Whole motherfuckin world gone total apeshit!"

"Well, you got that right anyways. Word up now, Wes, no more shit tween us. Okay? We talk real-time. Straight."

"Mmm. Okay." Then Wesley grinned. "Sides, it a squirt gun painted black. Gotcha, Gordy."

"Huh?" Gordon stared at the revolver Turbo was slipping into his jeans.

"WHAT THIS SHIT?" squalled Furball. "Mean I almost do a dude over a goddamn motherfuckin squirty gun?!"

Lyon grinned with Wesley and gripped Furball's shoulders with both hands. "Maybe that be why white folks on TV don't want their kids playin with war toys."

Turbo brushed gravel from his arms, and puffed. "Yo, sucker. MINE for real, believe! It Game-Boy gots the water gun!"

"Oh," said Furball. "Well, I guess you'da done me after all."

Turbo touched his throat, then looked at his bloody fingertip. "Shit. Prob'ly been my last game, man. Your reflexes stick the blade in even after you dead."

Furball cocked his head. "Word up? Jeez, I never knew that. Yo, man, I sorry over your neck. It bout stop bleedin now."

Turbo shrugged. "Hell, I live, man. S'cool."

Wesley scowled. "Fuck no, it ain't cool, goddamnit!" He spun to Gordon. "Yo! Rules! Check it out, your man draw blood!"

"Aw, shit, Wes!" Gordon groaned. "You callin rules on a fuckin little ole pussy scratch like that?"

"What it is, man." Wesley crossed his arms. "You just

now say we gonna follow the rules. Yo. That mean only rules fit you?"

Lyon's grip tightened on Furball's shoulders. "Give Turbo your blade, man."

"*What?*"

"Trust me. Rules gotta be followed. What else we got?"

Furball shifted the knife in his hand. Turbo started to step toward him, then saw his eyes and hesitated.

"Well?" said Wesley. "We ain't gots all fuckin day, y'know?"

"Do the heart thing," whispered Lyon.

Carefully, Furball reversed the knife and offered it handle-first to Turbo. Turbo cautiously slipped it from Furball's fingers, then slowly brought the blade tip up against Furball's throat.

"Well?" Wesley demanded. "S'matter, Turbo? Blood puss ya out or somethin?"

Locking eyes with Furball, Turbo flicked the knife point, drawing a thin line of blood. Furball didn't flinch. All the boys relaxed. Turbo gave back the knife. Furball folded and pocketed the blade, then reached out a tentative hand and wiped a streak of dust and gravel bits off Turbo's back as the boy turned away. Turbo grinned and let himself be cleaned. "Ahhhh, little mo to the lef', bra."

Gordon gave Wesley another nudge. "Cool?"

Wesley looked thoughtful. "Mmm. Game-Boy's squirt gun be full of battery acid, Gordon. That for free."

"Jesus, Wes!"

Wesley shrugged. "What I say, man? World get shittier, mean you gotta do shittier things to live. Word. C'mon, man, best we get our dudes chilled down for somethin really nasty happen."

Gordon nodded and moved with Wesley around the corner. "Y'know, Wes, word we meet seem like all over at school today, fuck if I know how. Prob'ly be up an down the hoods, come mornin."

"Or what," agreed Wesley. "An if Deek sucker true talkin bout some big dudes schemin round, might just make em put the moves on us, speed of light. Know what I sayin?"

"Yeah. We best get busy, man."

Wesley signaled for Turbo to follow as he and Gordon walked away. Lyon kept a hand on Furball's shoulder and stayed where he was. Gordon glanced back at them, his forehead furrowing once more. Lyon crooked a finger at him.

"Um . . . Yo, Wes," said Gordon. "Gimme a minute, huh, man?"

"Mmm. Well, no more tricks. Word?"

"Up."

" 'Kay. I get everbody together inside. Set a watch. Who for you?"

"Use Curtis."

Wesley nodded and moved on, Turbo following.

Gordon stalked back to the other boys. "All right. What the fuck IS this shit anyways? Lyon, you gone total crazy, bringin some strange sucker to a meet? You coulda got dudes killed!"

Furball twisted free of Lyon's hand. "Sucker yourself, man! An Lyon dint bring me! I follow ya!"

Gordon spat on the ground. "Then YOU the crazy one! What in hell you thinkin . . . wanna try an join up or somethin? So you way bad with that blade, for sure you go an choose the world's shittiest time for showin it!"

Furball puffed his little chest. "Fuck that! Don't need ME no gangs an pussy rules! Know what? I only wanna tell you somethin . . . a thing maybe save YOUR ass! But, oh no, big, bad, 'PORTANT gang man got no time for me what don't count!"

Furball's outthrust jaw began to quiver. "Nobody gots no goddamn time for me!" His shoulders sagged and a tear squeezed from one eye. "Fuck you, man! You don't even know what I give up for cause just to come here!" More tears ran down his cheeks. He wiped at them savagely, then spun to Lyon. "YOU done this, fucker!" Furball began beating with both fists on Lyon's slim chest. Lyon just stood, his slender body taking it.

"Homo!" Furball blubbered. "Motherfuckin dumpster baby! I wish you woulda died!"

Suddenly, Lyon caught both of Furball's fists and just held them. Furball struggled for a moment, then slumped against the slender boy, crying like a little kid. "I wanna go *home!*"

Gordon had stood silent, watching first with anger, then uncertainty as Furball cried. Now he moved to the smaller boy and turned him around. "Stop it, man! Just . . . oh, STOP cryin, goddamnit! Listen up! You CAN'T go home! Case you not figure, you in deep shit now. Hell, even if I let you go, Wesley won't." Gordon grabbed Furball's shoulders and shook him gently. "*Think*, dude! What happen if Wesley find out you ain't one of us? Bad blade or no, you one dead sucker! Be cool now, cry all you wanna when you out of this shit."

Understanding suddenly flooded Furball's face. Then fear. He turned to Lyon, who laid a hand on his shoulder once more. "Listen, brother," Lyon said. "You gotta trust us now. There be no runnin home to Mom no more when the game get scary an you don't wanna play."

Lyon gathered the smaller boy to him as his crying faded to sobs, then looked at Gordon. "Last night, when I tole you I find Deek's crib? Furball was there fore me. He hear things Deek be sayin bout us an the Crew."

Gordon's eyes hardened. "What things?"

Footsteps sounded from around the corner, crunching gravel. Wesley's voice called. "Yo, Gordon! We ready up."

Gordon glanced quickly over his shoulder, then pressed close to Furball. "Listen, dude!" he whispered. "You hang right by Lyon, an you do a'zactly what he say, when he say it! Keep your mouth shut, an hope to hell my dudes gots enough cool to cover ya! Just maybe you come outa this with your ass!"

A few minutes later, both gangs were sitting in a ragged ring on the cool concrete floor of a wash bay. Cigarette smoke swirled like fragile blue ghosts over their heads as the breeze sighed through. A loose strip of roofing tin creaked softly above, occasionally lifting to let a sunbeam stab into the center of the circle, where it spotlighted a dance of dust motes. The air was thick with kid sweat and concentration. Curtis stood at one end of the bay holding the little .22, and Tunk kept watch at the other with the Crew's .38. Gordon and Wesley sat together, their backs to the sheet-metal wall below a control box that had been beaten with a sledgehammer until its empty coin tray stuck out like a mangled tin tongue. Lyon sat to Gordon's right, legs drawn up, arms crossed atop, and chin resting on them. His uptilted eyes under his soft puff of hair seemed to take in everything without looking long at anything. Furball crouched close to him like a lean little cat, his eyes scanning brightly and small muscles tight. Ric and Rac were next, pressed shoulder to shoulder as if charging each other's batteries by contact. Their tawny eyes stole cool, curious glances at Furball's tear-streaked face, not missing the thread of blood at his throat or the matching one on Turbo's. Wesley's dudes completed the circle; Game-Boy beside Rac, kicked back in the soft, sagging pose of a fat kid who knew he was and didn't give a shit. Then came Ajay, Turbo, and Brett. Wesley had called the meet, so was obligated by rules to lay out the reason; the details of the drive-by shooting and Deek's offers and threats were no major news to anybody. Gordon's story followed; basically the same, with Curtis called into the sunbeam spotlight to show his wound once more.

Then came the discussion. Rules were simple; raised hands signaled questions, speakers recognized by mutual consent of the gang leaders. If an adult had been listening he would have probably figured the boys were just following a form learned in school. But the ritual was ages older . . . older than Oaktown, Lyon would say, older than America. If the circle of boys had been gathered in darkness around a fire, and if the setting had been a jungle glade or forest grove, and the boys clad in lion skin or chain mail, the rules would have been the same.

Wesley flipped away his Marlboro and blew out smoke. "Deek know too much."

Nobody snickered.

"He come an curb us yesterday mornin," Wesley went on. "Bout a block from the school. He talkin same ole dogshit bout how we just rag-ass little niggerboys, gots no hope in hell without bucks. Then he start in bout some big dudes schemin on the hood. An then he come sorta sideways—like bout somethin mighta happened to you dudes, Gordon, over the same sorta shit. Well, course we hear some auto-fire over your way, but hell, you hear *that* all the goddamn time an get so's you don't pay it no mind no more."

"Less it aimed at you," added Turbo.

"Go without sayin, man," Wesley murmured.

Gordon's face was thoughtful. "Mmm. That when Deek make you a offer for a Uzi?"

"Yeah. Course, he done that a'fore. Only, this time, he sound in my ear more . . . um . . ."

"Sincere?" murmured Lyon.

"Uh-huh. You good with them big words, man. An you ain't no puss bout it . . . make em come cool. Anyways, Deek talkin us up way you do by cops . . . sayin what you figure they wanna hear . . . tellin us all bout how word say you dudes movin up your hood, wantin more ground."

Gordon snorted Kool smoke out of his nose. "Shit, man. Why we wantin more ground? Gots enough probs hangin on to what we hold now."

"Yeah. My own mind tellin me that too, all the time Deek talkin. But he talk so motherfuckin *cool*, man . . . like Lyon might could if he want. Say how *you* might just be doin a deal with him . . ."

"My ass!"

Wesley held up palms. "I know, man, but you wasn't *there*. Know what I sayin? Deek come on with how you score yourself some major fire, you get to believin you some-body, man . . . stead of just another little Buckwheat gang. All of a sudden you way past baaaad. Gotta take more ground. Get some respect."

"Shit," said Gordon. "An just tell me what that really get you, man? You gots more ground, mean you gotta cover it. An that take more dudes . . . dudes what you dint grow up with an don't know. Then, more dudes an ground you got, more deals an shit you gotta do to keep em. Pretty soon you gots no fuckin time for doin nuthin but gang stuff." His eyes drifted past Lyon's. "An tell me how you go to a dance with a girl, tryin to come cool, when there a goddamn gun stickin out your ass?" He snorted again. "Sides, a Uzi shoot bout five hundred fifty goddamn 'spensive bullets a minute, man. Know what that cost?"

Wesley smiled. "Ain't Popsicle money, for sure. Hell, man, here we just tryin to save by for scorin usselfs a CD boomer. Yo. What I sayin is, *we* been figurin the same shit too, man. And sound like to me, we come to the same . . . um . . ." He looked expectantly at Lyon.

"Conclusions, man."

"Yeah! But then here come Deek sucker motorin by like shit don't stink, tryin to tell us, if you dudes gettin drive-byed, you just might start in thinkin it were us settin it up. That when I say myself, this here shit gone far as it goin, I sendin 'bassador Tunk over cross the line for some real-time talk." Wesley considered a moment. "Seem like to me Deek goin round shit-disturbin, what it is. An he too puss to go messin with the big dogs, so he schemin on us. Shit, man, I take that motherfucker down myself, cept he ain't never out that bodyguard of his, an word say that dude one way bad sucker."

Furball stiffened at that but only Lyon noticed. Then Lyon's pawlike hand went up. The other boys stared at him for a second like he'd just materialized from the *Enterprise*'s transporter deck.

"Man," said Wesley. "How in hell you do that? It like you only get seen when you wanna! That a thing come in handy for sure!"

Lyon smiled. "Mostly it a quiet thing, I guess. Anyways, rewind a little, Wes man. You just now tellin us that when Deek curb you yesterday mornin he seem to already know we been drive-byed. That a little passin strange, ain't it? Our hood mostly quiet mornin times. An for sure we'd marked *his* car cruisin three blocks away, so he wasn't there, so he couldn't seen nuthin, yet you tellin us that he know."

"Mmm," said Wesley. "Well, I not sayin he actually come out an word up. But, one to ten, I give him a eight for knowin shit he shouldn't."

"I give him a ten for *bein* in places he shouldn't!" growled Gordon. "An I just like you, Wes. Gots enough goddamn probs comin round without no motherfuckin dealer movin in full-time."

The twins shot their hands up together. "Too bad Deek sucker don't live round here," said Ric.

"Word!" added Rac. "Then we could just do him an his bad-ass bodyguard an everthin be way past cool again!"

Game-Boy grinned. "Leastways, close enough for Oaktown, huh?"

"Raise your goddamn hand next time, man," muttered Wesley.

Furball had stiffened again at the mention of Deek's bodyguard. Lyon laid a hand on his shoulder and leaned close, whispering, "Be almost time for you, man. See the words in your heart fore you let your mouth make em."

Lyon put up an open palm. "I know where Deek be cribbin out."

Murmurs buzzed among the boys until Gordon glared around the circle and Wesley snapped his fingers. Wesley cocked his head, gave Lyon an uncertain look, then shifted suspicious eyes to Gordon. "So, how long you dudes know this, man?"

"Chill out, Wes," said Gordon. "Not till just this mornin when I see Lyon at school. He ghost Deek's bodyguard last night."

Wesley studied the slender boy. "Mmm. Ghost be the word when you talkin bout *him*, for sure! I see that with my eyes, man! Big words, big balls, an spooky like somethin sittin on a tombstone!" He smiled. "Bet cops come round messin with you, they end up not knowin if to shit or go blind, man." Then his smile faded. "So, where this place of Deek's?"

Lyon told. Nobody seemed to notice that he kept a hand on Furball's shoulder, just as no one seemed to notice Furball was shaking. When Lyon finished, Gordon turned to Wesley. "That anybody's ground over there? Deek could be payin for 'tection."

Wesley shrugged. "Nobody's I hear bout. Course, wanna get technical, all this here part of Oaktown sposed to belong either Gorillas or some other major-time gang. But that sorta like sayin cops there to 'tect ya. None of them big-dude gangs give a shit bout no little rag-ass niggerboys like us, or what we do to each other over a few dogshit blocks. Long's we don't get in their way. Even Deek ain't nuthin but chump change to them, an he keep a pretty low pro, considerin." Wesley thought a moment, then added, "Maybe . . . if we all knowed totally an for sure that it Deek sucker puttin schemes on us, we hang together an take the motherfucker down."

Gordon glanced at Lyon. "Spose we try warnin him off first. Like to let him know we know what it is. We could trash his 'partment."

"An leave a dead rat in his bed," added Tunk from the end of the bay.

Curtis giggled at the other end. "Leave him a rat-meat pizza with a note!"

"Naw," said Turbo. "Just tie a note to the rat's tail."

"Shut up," said Wesley. "All you! Got no time for little-kid shit! Yo, Gordon! You always sayin second warnin's for good cops an bad movies. Well, way I see it, we both been givin Deek all kinda warnin's to keep off our hoods, man, an then we turn right round an let him buy off little chunks of our asses with beer. What I sayin is, we settle this shit right now, man. If Deek really puttin drive-bys on us, then we do the sucker cold, NOW, fore we start losin dudes!"

Silence followed. The boys all stared at one another. Cigarettes were fired. Wesley looked around, his nostrils flaring, then spat into the sunbeam. "Well? Ain't nobody gots nuthin to say all a sudden? Seem like, second ago, y'all was chippin your goddamn teeth bout dead rats an pizzas like a bunch a third-graders at recess time!"

"But we still not know for sure if it Deek puttin the moves," said Tunk.

No one saw Lyon gently nudge Furball, but all the boys turned when Furball's hand went slowly up like it took all his strength to lift. Silence settled once more around the circle. The loose tin creaked softly overhead, strobing the sunbeam. Gordon and Wesley both nodded to the small boy. Furball sucked a breath, then got to his feet so the dusty sun spotlight played over him. One of the shirt straps slid off his shoulder but he just let it hang. He looked like a kid on his first day at a new school who'd been forced by the teacher to introduce himself to the class. Eleven pairs of eyes scanned him; those of the Friends more curious than the Crew's, except for Lyon. For a few seconds Furball seemed to be judging his chances of escape, of getting past Curtis or Tunk even though both boys had guns. Furball's knife hand hovered near his pocket, but he pulled it away and picked up his skateboard instead. Finally, he locked eyes with Lyon and spoke as if only to him.

"I was there, last night, front of Deek's buildin, fore Lyon come. I hear things Deek tellin my . . . his bodyguard."

Wesley's gaze could have cut glass, and his voice slashed like it. "You ghost him too, man? Why?"

Gordon tapped Wesley's knee. "Chill, man. Wait. Furball recognized now, let him talk."

Furball's eyes shifted to Gordon. He took another breath. "Deek know all bout you Friends gettin drive-byed yesterday mornin. Word, man. Just like Wesley say, only a lot more. Words an music, man. He even knowed you shoot back an put a bullet in the van."

"I *did?*" said Gordon.

"Shut . . . shush!" hissed Wesley.

Furball turned to the Crew leader. "An Deek know all bout how you dudes get sprayed after school yesterday, man. Time an place."

Wesley's eyes went to slits. "Yo, Tunk! You tell Gordon the place when you see him last night?"

"Um . . . don't think so."

"He didn't," said Gordon.

Wesley nodded. "Mmm. An I never did, just now." He looked back at Furball. "What place, dude?"

Furball swallowed. "Backside the truck shops."

Wesley nodded again. "That where it happen. Word. So, what else Deek say bout us, man?"

Furball swallowed once more and took another breath. "He say . . . say you gonna meet him here, tonight . . . for cause to do a deal on a Uzi."

Gordon jerked around to face Wesley. "Well, ain't that a goddamn bitch, man!"

Wesley shrugged and looked sulky. "Oh, chill, Gordon. Ain't nuthin been cut. Yo. Why the fuck you figure I call for this here meet anyways? Hey, you figure I WANNA deal with that sucker? Shit, I gotta keep all my options open, man. Just like you. Everybody gots to have options. What it is." He shrugged again and looked back at Furball. "What else, man?"

Furball hesitated. His eyes drifted down to Lyon's. "Deek was raggin on my . . . his bodyguard . . ."

"Yo!" said Gordon. "What all this 'my' shit?"

"Chill," said Lyon. "You all be makin him feel like Buckwheat at a skinhead concert."

"Yeah," agreed Turbo. "What it is. Let the man breathe."

Furball's fists clenched, and he got out the rest with a cracked voice. "Deek was raggin on his bodyguard bout bein late for some kinda payoff clear cross town. It was to some dudes sposed to done a drive-by!"

Furball's knees seemed to give. He sank down close to Lyon and stared at the greasy concrete. "That . . . all what I know."

"Shit!" yelled Turbo. "That plenty enough for ME, best believe!"

Both gangs exploded into voice, cursing Deek, until their leaders shouted them down. Wesley twisted around to Gordon and demanded, "Yo! You not even know this shit till right this minute, huh? Don't lie to me, man, I can read faces most good as Lyon!"

Gordon glanced at Lyon, then shrugged. His voice came out careful. "I know bout Lyon . . . an my new dude, Furball . . . findin Deek's crib. But not what Furball just now say. Word, Wes."

Wesley looked doubtful. "Your 'new dude, Furball,' huh? Tell me, man, just how long Furball been a Friend?"

Gordon's face turned stubborn. "That my own goddamn business, sucker!"

Wesley puffed a moment, then relaxed and let out air.

"Uh-huh." He snagged a Marlboro pack from the floor and shook up a cigarette. Ajay fired it with a Bic. Wesley pulled in smoke and blew it carefully away from Gordon's face. It smogged the sunbeam now slanting orange in the late afternoon. "Somethin ain't gettin total told here," he muttered. "Like my mom always sayin, I can feel it in my bones. But, like Turbo just now say, we gots more'n enough reason for takin Deek down." Wesley sucked more smoke, then pointed his cigarette. "An Furball was right over what he say he hear. We sposed to be meetin Deek here at nine to do a deal for a Uzi." He turned back to Gordon. "My option, case this meet with you went dogshit, man. Know what I sayin?"

Gordon nodded. "Seem like we cut it fine, brother."

"Mmm. Got that right, homey." Wesley's eyes roamed the circle. "Well, guess that mean we into makin a plan together for doin Deek sucker, huh? Best time to my mind be when he show here tonight."

Gordon was also searching the faces around him. "Word. Spect that gonna mean takin down his bodyguard too."

"NOOOO!" Furball's cry beat between the tin walls, so sudden that all the boys froze for a second. Furball leaped to his feet and whirled to run. He might have made it . . . Curtis and Tunk were just staring at him openmouthed, their guns hanging loose in their hands. But Furball took extra seconds to whip out his knife and throw it in fury at Lyon's chest before trying to get away.

Days later the word would go around how Lyon had caught the glittering blur out of the air, and no one would doubt he'd used magic. But now the other boys scrambled, yelling, for Furball, piling onto the small skinny boy and dragging him down.

Furball fought like a panther cub as both gangs tried to

pin him to the floor. He kicked and clawed and bit, small
fists flailing. Ajay screamed, kicked in the balls, and staggered back to double over and puke. Ric stumbled out of
the fight, his nose gushing blood, then Brett backed away
with a hand torn open by Furball's teeth. Tunk and Curtis
still stood, guns at their sides, not knowing whether to leave
their positions. Once, Furball almost escaped, his shirt
ripped off and left dangling in Game-Boy's hands. But Gordon grabbed his Nike and yanked him back down again.
Even then Furball almost got free by kicking off the shoe,
but Wesley leaped in front of him and smashed a fist into
his face. Furball wavered a moment on his elbows and
knees, shaking his head, trying to clear it, bloody mist
spraying from his mouth and nose as he panted for breath.
Then Rac darted forward and kicked him in the stomach.
Furball collapsed on the greasy concrete, and the other
boys massed in to grab arms and legs.

A minute later Furball lay gasping for air, half choking
on his own blood, his nose streaming it and his battered
face a mask of it. His jeans were torn half off, and his thin
body was streaked with dirt and scratches. He'd been
dumped back against the tin wall beneath the bashed-up
control box. Rac and Game-Boy each held an arm while
Lyon and Turbo pinned his legs. For a little while the only
sounds were Furball's strangled gasps, the panting of the
other boys, and Ajay's moans as he lay curled on the floor
with both hands clasping his crotch. Gordon and Wesley
stood shoulder to shoulder staring down at Furball. Gordon's own jeans were about to slide off, and his lip was split
and puffing. Wesley's wrist oozed blood where Furball had
bitten him.

Wesley shifted his eyes from the small boy to Gordon,
his nostrils flaring and his voice low and dangerous as he

demanded. "Okay, man. Game over! Now who the fuck is he?"

But it was Lyon who spoke, holding Furball's leg and not looking up. "Deek's bodyguard be his brother."

Furball struggled weakly, then spat in Lyon's face. "I gonna kill you!" he sobbed. "Word!"

The day was dead. Only a faint ruddy glow lingered in the sky across the Bay as Ty tailed his skateboard by a corner phone booth. He thought of San Francisco somewhere over in that direction; of the Golden Gate Bridge and the cable cars he'd only seen in movies or on TV. The news always made San Francisco sound so clean . . . and Oakland so dirty. But then the TV lied about a lot of things. Maybe, he thought, he'd take Danny over on a BART train someday and they could ride a cable car; maybe check out Chinatown, where everybody always said you could score firecrackers no prob. Danny liked them, but they were hard for kids to get. Ty wondered if Markita might want to go too.

Ty stepped into the booth, then scowled. There was no phone, though there had been one just a few days ago. Now there was only a blank metal mounting where the phone had been, with a few colored wires dangling down like veins from a chopped-off arm in those gross little Garbage Pail Kid cards he used to collect when he was Danny's age. A sticker was slapped on the mount, already half covered by graffiti, gang marks, and anger. What little of it Ty could read said something about public nuisances and how the phone company in cooperation with law enforcement was concerned with serving and protecting the community.

What it translated to was drug dealing.

For a minute Ty just stood and stared stupidly at the stark steel plate the way a person whose home had been robbed might stare at the empty places where belongings had been. Ty was tired; bone-weary as never before in his life. The evening air was cool, but sweat sheened his face. His arm was swollen, and the knife slash burned beneath Markita's bandage. Rage flickered inside him as he stared at the useless phone booth; rage trying to spark off a flame like the tiny flash of a cigarette lighter's flint. Images drifted through his mind of somebody hurt, or sick, or lost. He thought of Markita again; of how she had to walk these blocks alone at night because the bus had been routed away from danger, and now even the last chance of a phone call for help had been denied her. He thought too of Danny: being chased, or stabbed, or shot, and dragging himself to this booth only to find a nightmare of nothing inside. Ty's knuckles paled as he clenched his fists and thought about a race of people, and a whole generation within that race, being punished for the sins of a few. The rage kept sparking inside him, trying to fire off something bigger. Ty recalled Danny trying to make a hand grenade by taping a firecracker to a Bic lighter.

And who were that few . . . *really?* Were they the hungry or unwanted kids who'd never had anything good in their lives and saw no future ahead? Or were they the unseen white tip of the pyramid who sucked up the profit from it all?

Ty remembered things from the TV news: of people shot and killed for nothing but looking at somebody the wrong way, or flipping a finger, or cutting into someone's parking space. The safe, clean, well-fed world behind the TV's glass always acted so shocked and disgusted that people could kill for such tiny insults. But Ty knew why it happened: it was all those little sparks of anger, constantly firing day by day, week on week, month on month, and building to years of held-back rage that finally exploded.

Ty dug out his Kools, wincing at the fire in his arm. He remembered a sixth-grade health book that showed a cartoon picture of antibodies dressed up like cops and battling an infection gang clad in chains and black leather jackets with skulls and crossbones on the backs. It was funny to imagine there was a war going on right here inside him. He slipped a cigarette between his lips and fired his lighter, having to spark it several times because the fuel was getting low. The butane in the lighter was a liquid under pressure. It could only be held captive and kept under control by constant pressure. Take off the pressure and it would escape . . . become a free vapor. Danny's Bic hand grenades hadn't worked. Maybe because, once the little plastic prison was shattered, the butane would rather be free than explode?

Ty recalled an antidrug commercial: some famous black basketball player telling kids that if they used drugs they were garbage and *he* didn't want garbage in his neighborhood. *Yo, boys and girls, you're garbage! Nothing to do with garbage except bury it—no hope for you at all!* How way past fucking cool, thought Ty, like offering a drowning man a glass of water. Hell, why not just come right out and tell the kids to go ahead and kill themselves and each other because they were just garbage anyway and nobody gave a shit!

Ty sighed out smoke. Even garbage could be recycled, if somebody gave a shit.

His rage sparked again but nothing exploded. His fuel was too low. He turned from the booth and gazed up the darkening street. It was that quiet time between day and night. Traffic was light. Day people were home, and the night prowlers and concrete cannibals were just waking up, arming and armoring themselves for the jungle hours ahead. Streetlights were coming on: sodiums flaring sulphur yellow, mercury-vapors glowing dull, sullen purple until they warmed. Traffic signals winked like pirate-movie jewels along the blocks, and the headlights of passing cars seemed to leave the sidewalk a little darker each time they swept by. The afternoon breeze had died, and there was no scent of fog in the burned-out air. The night would be clear with a big full moon.

Carrying his board, Ty walked a little ways, wondering for probably the thousandth time why Danny hadn't come. The boy hadn't been kept late at school: Ty had managed to slip past the security guard and checked at the office. Danny hadn't gone home; Ty had checked that out too. Ty had considered going back to the Burger King to ask Markita if Danny had finally shown up, but didn't want to risk getting her in trouble with the manager by hanging around. Instead, Ty had skated a weary grid of blocks in the hope of finding his brother. Maybe, he thought, that was why he seemed so tired now. He stopped in the middle of the sidewalk: goddamnit, Danny had been way past stoked about going uptown for new clothes; what in hell could have happened to make him change his mind? It hurt to think that something else in Danny's young life could be more important than hanging a while with his big brother. Maybe it *was* too late for the boy.

It was for Ty: his time was up. Deek wanted him, and like a lost soul who'd been bitten by a vampire or a zombie under a spell, Ty had to serve his master. Just ahead, an old neon sign struggled to light above a cafe doorway, sputtering and buzzing as it flickered to life. Ty knew the place: a rib shop run by a Vietnamese family where Deek often sent him for takeout orders. There was a pay phone inside.

Ty stepped to the door. Pain jabbed dull needles through his arm as he reached for the handle. A small sound of hurt escaped from his throat. His vision blurred. Blackness hovered at the edges. He swayed a little, his hand clutching the cold brass handle for support. Its ornate old design made him think of coffins. The cigarette slipped from his lips and hit the sidewalk with a burst of bloody sparks. He blinked his eyes and looked into the face of a corpse.

A scream tried to tear out of his throat, but in the next instant he realized that it was his own reflection in the door glass. The fitful blue neon above had eaten his face, cutting stark hollows under his cheekbones, shadowing his eyes into empty sockets, and tinging his dark skin a sick rotting violet. The scream came out as a sigh of relief—like a little kid waking up from a nightmare to find he was home safe in bed. Still, icy sweat chilled Ty's body. He forced himself to study his living-dead image, deciding he was just tired as hell, and that he was going to let his hair grow out naturally into an Afro or a Buckwheat or whatever the fuck anybody "cool" wanted to call it. Fuck being cool! Who in hell needed the latest look for digging through dumpsters and loading scrap iron? Just being black and somehow fighting free of the trap was all the identity he needed. Let the suckers decorate their cages; chains were still chains even if solid gold! Ty waited until the chill and dizziness had passed, then pushed open the door and went in.

The tunnel-like room stretched back into smoky dimness, higher than it was wide. A narrow counter with a row of chrome-pillared stools, their worn red leatherette seats patched with silver crosses of duct tape, ran along one side. Behind the counter were the grill, sinks, and barbecue pit. A line of tall, old-fashioned booths, their backs at least six feet high and their padding the same sort of cross-patched plastic as the stools, took up the opposite side of the room. The ceiling was black as midnight with soot, and lost in shadow. Three bare little bulbs dangled from ten-foot wires, but most of the useful light came from a pinkish fluorescent tube hanging from grease-caked chains over the grill. A few beer signs, one showing a pretty mountain waterfall, shone bright colors along the wall above the booths.

For all its ancient shabbiness the little cafe was still some-how friendly. The air was thick and steamy with food smells and people like a big family's kitchen on a Sunday dinner night. The solid old wood of the counter and booths, the massive Art Deco Hamilton shake machine beside the grill, the chrome-smothered Seeburg jukebox by the door—"high-fidelity," whatever the hell that meant—and the neat little clusters of sauce bottles, ketchup squeezers, sugar jars, and nickel-plated napkin holders on the counter and tables gave the place a homey kind of kicked-back atmo-sphere that all of McDonald's or Burger King's showtime plastic and high-tech Formica could never match. Markita would like it here, he was sure. He could almost picture himself and the girl together in one of those dim-lit old booths. Even Danny might think this cafe was cool in a funky sort of way, even if there were no games.

The space behind the counter couldn't have been much

more than three feet wide, yet the whole Vietnamese family seemed to work happily together the way Ty had always imagined a family should. The father tended the pit, the mother polished and stacked the silverware, and a small slim boy about Danny's age with silky black hair flowing midway down his back, dressed in jeans and a sleeveless half-tee, scrubbed dishes in the sink while a wrinkled old woman who could have been his grandmother or great-grandmother sat by the new IBM cash register and carefully read some kind of Vietnamese newspaper. Did they lie in that language too? Ty wondered. The boy had Walkman headphones clamped over his ears and moved to what might have been rap. The old woman had a beat-up little AM pocket radio near her elbow that was tuned low and wailed what was probably a song but sounded more to Ty like cats being swung by their tails. Ty supposed the only reason he heard it was that he always listened whenever he came in, and it always seemed to be the same song. He'd sometimes wondered what real African music sounded like . . . probably as alien to him as that tortured-cat stuff was to that boy.

There were only two customers at the counter, both older men, who could have been garbage-truck drivers and appreciated kickin' barbecue. Both glanced once at Ty, marked him as trouble to be carefully ignored, and went back to eating. Ty paid no attention to the people in the booths, though he heard the cheerful squabbling of kids and a mother half trying to get them chilled down. The Vietnamese man was watching the news on a greasy little six-inch Sony that sat on a shelf above the pit as he tended a rack of ribs. He turned and, recognizing Ty as a steady, gave him a smile and a nod. The boy, either noticing his father or feeling the chill from the door, glanced around too. He had the faintest smudge starting on his upper lip. His expression showed he knew who Ty was but didn't live in the same world, so wasn't impressed. That was way past cool as far as Ty was concerned.

The phone was on the back wall by the dark little hallway that led to the bathrooms and the alley door beyond. Above it, Scotch-taped over the scratched and scribbled numbers, messages, and doodles, was a small square of cardboard with NO DEALING neatly printed in blood-red Magic Marker. Somehow Ty knew that the young boy had put it there. Why didn't Danny have that same sort of pride? Ty felt the eyes of the Vietnamese boy bore into his back as he dropped a quarter in the slot and punched up the number of Deek's service . . . carefully because his fingers seemed stiff and clumsy. Behind him, Ty heard money clunk into the Seeburg and then an old M. C. Hammer song, "Pray," begin. He gave the Vietnamese boy a quick glance: the dude was washing dishes once more but had the headphones hanging around his neck while he listened to the jukebox. Ty noticed what looked like a school book propped open on a shelf above the sink.

The answering-service girl sounded cheerful and white. Hell, thought Ty, for all she knew Deek was a doctor. Maybe he was. The kind who made megabucks treating the symptoms and not the disease, the sort whose operations were always successful even though the patients died. Ty gave the girl Deek's code, then hung up and leaned against the wall, waiting for the phone to ring. The room seemed to have gone hot and hazy. Ty wiped sweat from his forehead and unzipped his jacket. Maybe it was all the barbecue smoke. He gazed over at the beer sign showing a cool mountain waterfall splashing down between snow-covered rocks. Were there really places like that? The jukebox beat seemed to throb in time to the ache in his arm. "We got to pray just to make it today . . ." You tell it, Hammer, Ty thought. Maybe you was voted Oaktown's prime booster or something like that, but you made your bucks and got your ass out! He closed his eyes, feeling dizzy again. Maybe it was the food smells? He remembered he hadn't eaten anything all day except a bowl of Cocoa Puffs with his family that morning, and yet he wasn't really hungry.

"Yo, dude! What kinda fire you gots?"

Ty opened his eyes and saw nobody. For an instant a chill hit him again. Then he blinked and looked down. There was a fat little boy, maybe eight, who had probably played the jukebox. He had a flattop and wore a Bart Simpson T-shirt with a black Bart saying, "Yo, don't have a cow, man." It seemed painted on the kid, and a roll of chocolate-brown chub hung out underneath. His hands and face were smeared with sauce.

Ty tugged at his jacket, but the gun was well covered. The little sucker had spotted it anyway. Evolution in action?

"A .45," sighed Ty.

"Yeah. Them's way kickin, but I want me a .357," said the kid.

Why? Ty wanted to ask. The little boy's clothes were clean and new, he was stuffed to the max and obviously loved. But Ty only shrugged. "Yeah," he murmured.

The kid flashed a sign from one of the major gangs and waddled on back to the bathrooms. At eight, that was still funny, even cute, but in a couple more years the kid could get shot for something like that. Ty recalled a passage from his mother's Bible reading . . . something about when I was a child I thought as a child and spoke as a child but when I became a man I put away childish things. So when did that happen? When they'd been talking in the tub last night, mostly about Danny, Markita had mentioned that in primitive societies a boy became a man when he could father other children. That made Danny a man. But "father" seemed too responsible a word somehow . . . Our Father who art in heaven . . . our father who deserted his children! No wonder some whites call us *boys!*

The phone rang. Ty almost jumped. He picked it up, aware again of the Vietnamese boy's hostile eyes. "Yo!" said Deek's voice when Ty answered. "It bout way past motherfuckin *time*, stupid! Where the fuck are ya? We gotta cover us some street fore we meet with the Crew."

Ty closed his eyes again. His throat felt hot and dry. He wished he had a Popsicle. "Don't have a cow, man," he murmured.

"*What?* Hey, you drunk again?"

"On life," said Ty. He told Deek where he was.

"'Kay, man. I there'n less'n five. Be out front." Deek hung up.

Automatically, Ty checked the coin return, found nothing, which was what he had expected, then walked back out to the street. A mercury-vapor was burning bright now in front of the cafe, but Ty slipped into the shadows of a boarded-up storefront next door. It seemed only a minute before the arrogant thunder of the Trans-Am's engine echoed down the block . . . or maybe the reverb was only in Ty's head; he wasn't sure. The streetlight's glare hurt his eyes, and the bluish-white globe seemed to have a fog halo around it. Only there wasn't any fog tonight. Ty moved to the curb as the big car cut close. He noticed the fat little boy watching wistfully from the window as he slid into the seat. Wrong movie, Ty thought. It's the dude washing dishes that's going somewhere. "Don't pay no 'tention to the man 'hind the curtain," Ty mumbled.

Deek studied him. "Shit! You look like warmed-over death, man! Yo! You sick or somethin?"

Ty wiped more sweat from his face, then tossed his board in back. "Maybe the vampire what bit me gots rabies."

"What the fuck's THAT sposed to mean, asshole? You talkin like some kinda crazy ole street nigger!" Deek swung the car away with a squeak of rubber.

"Just tired," said Ty.

"Mmm." Deek studied Ty once more, then groped on the floor and handed Ty a bottle. "Here, man, you *need* this."

Ty took the bottle of Train. It was cold. Sighing, he twisted off the cap and drank. It soothed his throat.

"Just take it slow, man," said Deek. "I need you full-up tonight."

"Yeah. After that I go back in my box again."

Deek gulped Heineken and burped. "Oh, shut up, stupid!"

Deek had an old Too Short disk in the deck: the "raw and uncut" album that white boys played loud while mall cruising in their jacked-up Japanese four-by-fours. Maybe raps like that were supposed to tell the world how bad black dudes were, but after you'd told everybody to go fuck themselves, their mother, their dog, and their hamster about ten million times, it just sounded stupid . . . like a little kid who'd just learned a naughty word and was running it by everybody in sight to check out what sort of reactions he got. As far as Too Short's sex life, Ty sometimes wondered if the dude was trying to cover with words what his name might really signify. If the message was supposed to be that blacks were big and loud and knew how to fight and fuck, then maybe they should take a lesson from the Vietnamese, who were small and quiet but had won a war and, judging from the size of their families, were way past kickin cool at fucking. More, they seemed to know how to love each other—besides serving up some bad-ass barbecue.

"You been bit girl, what it is."

"Huh? Oh." Markita turned to find Leroy beside her. She was on the sidewalk behind the Burger King, just outside the steel-plated back door. Over to the east a huge full moon was rising, ivory like the top of an old skull, and shining through the skeleton of a distant water tower so it seemed to be beaming from behind bars. Markita found herself holding the handles of a big black plastic garbage can she'd been going to empty in the dumpster. She wondered how long she'd been standing there staring at the moon like some sort of loony lizard.

She smiled. Leroy was a friend. You could say off-the-wall things to a friend. "Could be. I spose you gonna go an run me a line from some ole movie now?"

Leroy looked like he was working up one of his goofy giggles. Instead, he pulled the stupid little hat from his head and mashed it as if he'd considered dropping it into the garbage atop some leftover burgers and fries that had mummified on the hot racks. Company rules said, politely, that all such unsold food should be disposed of in a proper and hygienic manner. That translated to churning it into a sickening mess with paper and coffee grounds and floor sweepings until it would gag a maggot, and keeping the dumpster padlocked. Markita had forgotten that disgusting ritual tonight. She saw Leroy's eyes shift across the drive-through lane to where a pair of small shadows were hovering near the dumpster: a boy and girl, maybe six or seven. They had to be new to the street not to know the word on company policy.

Leroy looked away and sighed. "You talkin some ole Western . . . bout good women always goin for gunfighters?"

"Somethin like that, I guess."

"Mmm." Leroy shaped his hat into something else he wasn't satisfied with, but put it back on anyway. "Look like to me a lot of you girls go wastin half your lives tryin to make somethin outa dudes what ain't. Can't figure why in hell you call that love. Ask me, it more like takin in some sorta sick wild animal and then cryin your fool heart out cause it bite your hand an run right away again soon's it get well."

Leroy sighed once more and fiddled with his hat, while watching the two small figures by the dumpster and looking unhappy. "But since you askin, girl, sideways like girls do, I don't figure you wastin your time on that dude." Leroy squared his hat and turned back to the door, then stopped and added, "Just don't never let him get to thinkin he in some kinda cage. Even a nice one." Leroy giggled. "Shit, he a lot like me . . . just ain't figured it out yet."

Markita turned and gave the lanky boy a sudden kiss on the mouth. He blushed, and Markita smiled and touched his arm. "That a way cool thing to say, Leroy. An you right. He is just like you."

Leroy giggled again. "Mmm. World's chump-change

champeen. Well, girl, you tell him, he don't 'preciate the prize, I gon' smoke his butt!'"

Markita's eyes drifted back to the rising moon. "Y'all figure the manager get pissed off if I go on home early? I like to tuck J'row in my ownself for a change. Seem like I never got no time to be with him."

Leroy grinned. "Hell, girl, hours you been workin, I tell the sucker he can put his pissed-off in one hand, shit in the other, an check which one fill up first! You get your ass on home to that son of yours now. I dump that ole trash."

"That's okay, Leroy. I'll do it. An thanks." Markita hefted the heavy can and lugged it over to the dumpster. The two small shadows shied from her but watched with big sad eyes as she keyed the padlock. She hesitated, then snapped it shut again and walked away, leaving the can behind and not looking back as the little kids scrambled for it.

Headlights swept around the building as Markita reached the door. She turned, seeing the children's eyes glitter as they looked up from eating. It was a cop car, and the kids were frozen between fear and hunger as it stopped. Markita faced the car, her feet apart and her hands dropping to her hips. She recognized the cops as the pair who'd wanted breakfast served in the middle of the goddamn afternoon. The manager might have obliged, figuring it might be good for business to have cops as regular customers, but in this neighborhood it would probably have the opposite effect. What cop talk she'd overheard in the past seemed to class people into three categories . . . cops, civilians, and garbage. These two didn't act like they thought any "civilians" lived around here.

The black one leaned from the window and jerked a thumb at the kids. "You shouldn't be doin that, girl."

Markita felt like spitting. She wished she wasn't wearing that goddamn stupid hat. And, for a moment, she was also afraid that if she spoke her mind these cops would check up on the hours she worked. They always had *ways*, she thought, another dusty old movie line. But hadn't Ty said something last night about going down on your knees?

Her voice came out cold. "Why not? It the exact selfsame sorta garbage you gonna get served up hot out the window. Stuff outlast the box it come in!" She sniffed. "Or you gonna be big brothers an buy them kids a meal?"

The men exchanged glances. Finally, the black one shrugged. "Try raisin up a family of your own on *my* salary, girl, an see how much sympathy you got left over."

Markita snorted. "I sure as hell like to give it a try!" Spinning on her heel, she stalked back into the restaurant and slammed the steel door behind her.

Again the cops exchanged glances. Then the white one looked over at the little kids who were grabbing food as fast as they could and stuffing their shirtfronts full in case they had to run.

"Jesus!" said the white cop. "What in hell's it gonna be like around here when *they* get to be her age?"

The black one dropped the car into gear and squeaked off for the drive-through window. "You best believe I ain't stayin that long to find out!"

■ Lyon stood alone on the pump-shed roof, a slender sil-
houette against the golden globe of the rising moon, somehow too fragile and fine to survive the world that
surrounded him. From a wash bay below came the quiet
murmur of kid voices, subdued and serious, their scents
edgy and tense, and the smell of Marlboro and Kool smoke.
At the front of the lot, invisible in shadow except for his
cigarette ember, Turbo stood watch for Deek's car. Wesley
hadn't lied to Gordon about the entrance chain being
locked; he'd just not mentioned at the time that the iron
pipe post at one end could be pulled out of the ground.

Wesley had said that the Crew had met with Deek in this
place before, around back of the wash structure so as not
to be seen from the street. One of the gang always stayed
at the entrance, replacing the pipe once Deek's car was in
so the dropped chain wouldn't be noticed by any cruising
cops, but ready to pull the post again to let Deek out. But
plans were being made, and there was a chance that Deek

wouldn't be leaving this place tonight—or ever. But what
about Ty? And then, what about Furball? Ty was good at
his job—way too good—Lyon had seen that on the street
yesterday morning. If Deek could be done, shot dead with
no doubt, then the bodyguard's job would be over. He'd
be free, and might be spared. But the talk in the bay below
still went around and around without figuring a way to get
past Ty to the dealer except to kill him first.

Lyon gazed at the moon. Its light was turning silver as it
climbed. Lyon looked past it to the few stars strong enough
to pierce the city's glow. But no answers came from out
there. They never did. On cold concrete, other young minds
struggled with the problem like high-powered computers
fed insufficient data. Furball was tied up and gagged with
strips of his shirt. It was done every day on TV. Of course,
detailed instructions never came with the model . . . like,
exactly how tight? The reality for Furball was probably too
tight. Lyon decided he'd check the boy soon to make sure
there was still circulation in his hands.

Or would that even matter in a little while?

Lyon was tired; getting old, he supposed, all the drinking
and smoking and nights without sleep finally wearing him
down until he felt like something that *should* be sitting on
a tombstone. It would be a peaceful job, he imagined, like
a hall monitor for dead kids: check their passes and point
them in the right direction. He'd left the council a few
minutes ago to be alone and to think. He felt the moon's
pull but, for the first time he could remember, there seemed
little power in it. It was just a cold, dead ball of rock that
didn't even shine with a light of its own but only reflected
the unseen sun. If Furball's brother was killed tonight, the
dude wouldn't run to the cops; that wasn't the way. Even
if, gasping for breath and spitting blood a couple of hours

ago, he hadn't already vowed it before both gangs, Lyon had seen in his eyes that the boy would hunt them down and kill them one by one, or until he was killed himself. *That* was the way, and it went by the rules.

Lyon sighed. The trouble with rules or laws seemed to be that once they became a system they stopped being justice. Lyon recalled the old *Moby Dick* movie, and Captain Ahab's little black cabin boy, Pip. The Great White Whale hadn't given a shit that Pip was innocent; just one woolly little head smashed down beneath the waves because some raging white monster had a harpoon up its ass.

There were scrabbling sounds, and Lyon turned to see Curtis' baby face peering at him over the eaves. "Um, can you help me, Lyon?"

Lyon came silently across the loose tin, took the smaller boy's hand, and pulled him up.

"Um," said Curtis. "I dint mean to corrupt ya or nuthin . . . I mean, if you was doin magic or somethin?"

Lyon smiled. "That cool. You never corrupt me, homey. I just be tryin to think. The reg'lar kind."

"Oh. Um, wanna smoke, man? Nobody down there can figure out nuthin."

"Yeah. I was kinda 'fraid of that."

Curtis pulled a couple of slightly bent Kools from his pocket and fired his Bic. The two boys sat together and gazed silently at the moon for a while. Finally, Curtis blew smoke. "Wes an Gordon wanna talk to you in a minute, man. Bout the plan . . . an I guess over Furball too."

Lyon breathed out a moon-silvered sigh. "Yeah. I figure they would. Mostly bout Furball. It be my own fuckin fault the little dude follow us." Lyon stared at the stupid, smiling moon face. "Seem like listenin to your goddamn heart be way past hazardous to your health round here."

A tear glistened like a drop of chrome in Curtis' eye. "Yo! How can we just go an kill him, man? Ain't nobody down there WANT to! They don't even wanna think bout it, I can tell."

Lyon nodded. "Yeah, I know, homey. Spect that what Gordon an Wes be wantin me to handle."

Curtis' eyes went wide. The tear left a glittering trail as it rolled down his cheek. "*You?*" he whispered.

Lyon stared at the stars, so clean and pure and forever out of reach. "By rules it be my 'sponsibility, man." His long hands clenched into fragile-looking fists, and he spat at the moon. "Hearts an magic! Motherfuckin dogshit, man!" He suddenly faced Curtis, his lips pulled back from big teeth. "What fuckin good a heart do ya here, man? This goddamn world twist love all round so even *it* kill ya!"

Curtis shrank away, but then reached out a hand to touch Lyon's arm. "Don't talk like that, man. Please. I mean, if you wanna go an grow fur an claws an stuff, it ain't gonna scare me. But don't change inside, okay?"

Lyon shook off the smaller boy's hand. "Oh, get real, you little puss! I ain't no different from any other stupid niggerboy! All I done was jack myself off in my mind . . . like everthin was gonna be all way past cool just cause I believe in somethin I figure was good. But it don't work once you been down with what real, man!" He stabbed a finger skyward. "There be no goddamn power up there, man! Nuthin what give a motherfuckin shit! Onliest power be HERE!" He waved a hand around. "An it evil!"

Lyon swung back to face Curtis, his uptilted eyes narrowed to ebony slits. "Yo, sucker! Can't you *feel* it, man? It comin right up outa the goddamn ground . . . from the stinkin dirt what been shit on an tore open an shoved round till when some of it show through a crack in the concrete it don't even look like no real dirt no more! I'm sick of this place, man! I wanna go home!"

Curtis took the slender boy's arm again. "Um, maybe you can come to Jamaica with me? I can ask my mom an dad."

Lyon grabbed Curtis' shoulders and shook him hard. "Yo! Grow the fuck up, you stupid little sucker! You ain't never goin nowhere! It be all fuckin lies, man! The TV lies, the school lies, the cops lie, an the worst lies of all be them what you tell your ownself!"

Tears ran down Curtis' cheeks to spatter silver spots on the rusty tin roof. He lowered his head, grabbing handfuls of hair and yanking them over his face. "I am so goin to Jamaica, man!" he sobbed. "Someday! Just long's I keep wearin dreads an believe it!" He jerked up his head and shoved his locks aside. "So THERE, sucker! That heart shit an magic too, man! My own! An it don't make no fuckin difference to me if YOU stop believin or not! THAT what it is, man! Get your ass down there an check out Furball! HE still tryin to fight! An know what else, sucker? You CAN'T go home till you done your job! So just do it, Lyon! Shit, if you can't save Furball, ain't nobody can, an I ain't gonna be your goddamn homey no more, pussy clot!"

For a long time Lyon just stared at the smaller boy. Then he finally flipped away his Kool and looked back at the moon. It was still pretty, even if it wasn't good for anything. "Mmm. Maybe I see you in Jamaica someday, homey."

Curtis wiped his face and sniffled. "It a island, y'know? We gonna fly there on a airplane."

Lyon nodded. "That be way past cool, mon." He glanced at the moon once more. "Wonder what it look like there."

Curtis smiled a little. "Same moon, mon. Shit, even I know that."

Lyon fingered his jaw. "Mmm. Deek gonna be here at

nine. Don't leave us a lotta time for much more figurin. Let's get busy, dude." Lyon rose and leaped from the roof, landing lightly on the weed-buckled asphalt below. Somewhere, he thought, down in that dead-looking dirt, the seeds of young growing things were still fighting through no matter how much shit got dumped on them.

Eyes glittered from the dark wash bay, and the ruby points of cigarettes glowed. The two gangs were gathered by the back entrance, leaving Rac with the .22 watching Furball, whose small shape was huddled on the floor beneath the control box. Game-Boy giggled as Lyon appeared to drop from the sky. "He's baaa-aaak!"

Even in the soft moon shadow Wesley seemed all muscle and hard angles, making Gordon beside him just a tired-looking fat kid, Game-Boy a shapeless mass of lard, and the other dudes skinny and frail. Wesley was standing in his usual pose, hands on hips, while the other gang members were scattered around on the floor. Some sat on their boards. Wesley had tensed when Lyon landed close, but covered with a short cough of Marlboro smoke. "Shut up, man," he muttered automatically to Game-Boy. He gave Lyon a glance, then faced the other dudes again.

"So," said Wesley, as if summing up a school report. "We ain't nuthin but goddamn fools if we try an take Deek down with just the pussy little pops we got us now. Sides, there just six bullets in the .38, seven in the .22, an"—he jerked a thumb at Lyon—"only two in that there ivy-what-sis. We know Deek's bodyguard gots a .45, and that Deek pack least one full-auto Uzi in his car, sides the one he sposed to deal us tonight. So"—Wesley spread his palms —"what I sayin is, we be cool to wait till we gots that Uzi in our hands. Then we hose both them suckers down. Game over!"

Under the control box, hands tied behind his back, Fur-

ball made savage sounds through his gag and struggled until
Rac stuck the .22's muzzle in his ear. The other boys darted
glances at Furball, but none tried to meet his eyes.

"What it is, be a piss-poor plan, man," Lyon said quietly.

Wesley puffed. "Yeah? So, you gots a better one, magic
boy?"

"Bet your ass!" called Curtis, climbing down from the
roof and moving close to Lyon.

Wesley flipped away his cigarette, then turned to glare
at Gordon.

Gordon shrugged. "Lyon talk, mostly cool to listen."

Lyon stepped into the shadows of the bay. All eyes shifted
to him. Furball's felt like laser beams focused to burn
through steel. "Wesley here be a doin kinda dude," said
Lyon. "Take things head-on. Kickin bad."

Wesley relaxed a little.

"But that be like tryin to take on the law, man," added
Lyon. "Yo. You just can't fight it that way. Got to dodge
an twist an lie to it same's it be all the time doin to you.
Word. You ain't no fool, Wes. But you don't figure Deek
gonna be one neither? You think he gonna hand you a
loaded Uzi? Uh-uh! Yo. Maybe he deal you that gun tonight,
but you best be believin he hold by the clip another day."

Murmurs started among the other boys. There were nods
in the shadows. Furball had gone totally still, his head
cocked, listening. Wesley didn't look too happy but finally
nodded. "Yeah. Got to say you right, man. Shit! What the
fuck we gonna do now?"

Tunk nudged Ric. "Yo, Rac," he whispered. "That Lyon
chill you out fast, huh?"

"I'm Ric. Word, man! Lyon always like that. Even when
we was little an playin some make-believe game, like *Star
Trek* or somethin. Then here come Lyon along an shoot it

all fulla holes . . . like you can't breathe the air on Venus
or somethin like that. Who knew?"

"Well," added Rac, taking the gun out of Furball's ear.
"Been lotsa times Lyon-o keep US from gettin shot fulla
holes with the stuff he know."

"Shush!" said Gordon. He looked up at Wesley. "Well,
there go one *more* motherfuckin idea down the toilet."

Wesley frowned. "Yo! You hear me arguin, man? I say
he right, know I say it cause I feel my lips move when I say
it!" He turned to Lyon. "So, what we gots to work with
now? Shit, we all been curbed by Deek enough to know his
moves . . . bodyguard come out the car first with his .45
ready-up. Hell, that chill everthin from first level on! Deek
only spectin us Crew here tonight. Mean you Friends gotta
stay hid by. Deek careful. Word. He gonna park his car
way out in the open, best believe. Then he wanna see our
.38 all the time. An him or his guard gonna keep on countin
heads so's to make sure nobody come or go while we dealin."

Gordon nodded, then looked up at Lyon. "So, us gonna
stay cool in here, man. We wait our chance . . . maybe
when the guard gots his gun down helpin Deek or somethin.
Then we hit them suckers full-on with the .22 and the
chrome gun. You an me the best shots, man. Tween us, we
oughta be able to take out the guard. Meantime, Wes do
Deek with the .38. The other dudes gonna keep screamin
an yellin and throwin shit to keep Deek an his man all
confused. We even use the squirt gun for a . . . a . . ."

"Decoy," said Lyon. He considered. "Mmm. Could work.
But there be a good chance some of us gonna get hit. An
what if the guard come out the car with a Uzi stead of his
.45?"

Wesley shrugged. "Goddamnit, Lyon, we already thought
bout that. But, hey, what the fuck ELSE can we do, man?

They bigger'n us, an maybe smarter, an gots more firepower for sure."

"Get the bodyguard out the way first."

Gordon snorted. "Yeah? How, man? You gonna magic him to sleep, or throw some kinda spell so he just drop down his gun an walk away?"

"I need to talk to Furball. Alone."

Wesley's eyes turned suspicious. The other boys all swung around to stare at the small figure tied up on the floor. Finally, Gordon shrugged. "Go for it."

"Chill out!" Wesley barred Lyon's way, then glared down at Gordon. "What's this shit, man? There too much fuckin smoke in the air tonight."

Gordon got to his feet and faced the other leader. Muscles showed under their padding of chub. "No. YOU chill, sucker!" He jabbed a finger at Furball. "Yo! You figure I let one of my own dudes get the shit kicked out him like that over some sorta stupid trick?" He spat at Wesley's feet. "Hey! You think that, then we best just call down this whole goddamn donkey show right here an now, man! Hell, you go for it, score yourselfs that motherfuckin Uzi! Sell yourselfs to Deek like cheap little blow boys! Yo! Maybe we get a Uzi too. Maybe a Mac or a Galil, or somethin else BETTER than an Uzi! Maybe then we take YOU on! Listen up, man! That what you want? What it is, we don't take Deek down together, here an tonight, we just end up fightin each other while Deek an any other suckers like him keep right on shittin all over us an killin our little hood kids!"

Wesley took a deep breath and let it out slow. His own massive muscles seemed to sag. "Okay," he sighed. "Go for it, Lyon. I just hate to die a fool, that all."

"Dead be dead," said Lyon. "Cool death be just the same as fool death. You mom cry. Maybe your homeys run you a rap that be forgot in a week, but nobody else give a shit if you was cool or a fool."

Furball was quiet as Lyon moved to him and knelt at his feet. Black-ice eyes bored into Lyon's with suspicion, but a little uncertainty too. Lyon took Furball's knife from Rac. He cut the strip of satin that bound the boy's ankles, then slipped Furball's Nike back on and tied it. Furball's face was a mask of caked blood, his lips split and swollen, and one eye half shut, though no less wary than the other. Lyon helped the smaller boy to his feet and held his tied hands while he struggled for balance. Both gangs watched in silence as Lyon led Furball away. Rounding the corner of the pump shed, the two boys walked down to the last wash bay. Inside lay the gutted corpse of a Ford Pinto wagon, its shattered glass, small parts, and puffs of slashed upholstery scattered all over. Lyon pointed, and Furball sat stiffly down on the front fender. Lyon gazed into the other boy's eyes as he flicked open the blade.

"I still trust your heart, man," said Lyon. "Could be you don't trust mine no more, but I gots to know."

Furball didn't flinch when the knife flashed, slicing first the gag then the strip of shirt that bound his hands. He said nothing, just sitting and rubbing his wrists.

Lyon went on, "You already hear what been decided, man. You know for a fact that Deek gonna die tonight. An, less you an me get back trustin each other again an do us some figurin, fast, your brother an some other good dudes prob'ly gonna die too."

Lyon gave Furball the knife and stepped close, his hands at his sides. "Course, there be another way you might save your brother, man. Spect you know. Do me now an run. You be half up the block fore Turbo know what is. You can spot Deek's car an stop him fore he get here."

Furball fingered his knife. His voice came out husky.
"You weird sucker! How come you always gotta make easy
shit hard?" He jerked up the blade so the point poised
against Lyon's chest. "Know what? I *know* you let me do
ya, man! It like you *like* puttin your stupid life in somebody's hands . . . like you checkin to see if they know what
it worth." He shrugged. "Christ, man, cool as you are, ain't
you figured a life like yours ain't worth shit? Hell, for all
I know, you just plain crazy stead of good. Sometimes it
hard to tell . . . make you 'spicious why somebody treat
you nice, know what I sayin? Shit, man, now you go an do
it again! Put it on ME! Like a magic curse! Here you say,
go to Deek, save my brother, when all the time I knowin
what Deek gonna do to you dudes later on. An it worse for
cause he makin my own brother be part of it, man! You
make me know that killin Deek the onliest way I get my
brother back!"

Furball coughed and spat blood on the floor. He held the
knife so its point poked through Lyon's shirt but hadn't cut
him yet. "Shit," Furball rasped, "somethin busted inside
me. I can feel it."

"You heart?" Lyon asked softly.

"Get real, sucker!" Furball coughed again. "That got
busted a long, long time ago!" Then he sighed and wiped
his mouth with the back of his free hand. "Okay, magic
boy. I play this game with you. But if Ty get killed tonight,
you gonna stand to me just like you doin right now an I
gonna cut YOUR fuckin heart out forever so's it don't go
givin nobody else no stupid ideas. Deal, man?"

"Word," said Lyon. He smiled his V. "An it be on the
left side, man."

"What is?"

"The heart."

"I know."

"*My* left, not yours."

"Oh." Furball shifted the knife momentarily, then lowered and folded it. "Funny, huh? Seem somehow like it oughta be on the right."

The kid was cornered, cracked to the max, and lying like a dog. Ty had him backed into the deep, dark doorway of a dusty-windowed junk shop, cowering against rusty accordion bars which weren't even locked because there was nothing behind them worth stealing. The small, lean-muscled boy, maybe eleven or twelve, was so wasted from smoking his own profits he could barely stand. Mostly he pleaded, but threw in a threat now and then. His begging bought no sympathy from Ty's tired heart, and his threats were as empty as the blackness at his back where not even a night light burned. Ty felt the way he had in the phone booth; weak and sick yet with something inside that sparked feebly without finding fuel to catch flame. Images kept drifting through his mind, blurring what should have been solid and hard; like the time last year when he'd had the flu and a fever so bad that for two days he hadn't known if the comings and goings of his family around him were real or just in his head. He remembered having a serious talk with

Danny about sex . . . while all the time the boy had been in school. Now he thought of those piles of old batteries, their cells dead and empty, and the plates that had once produced power all warped and dry and falling apart.

The small boy's lying and babble seemed to filter through a dirty fog. It didn't matter: Ty had heard it all before, too many times for it to touch him anymore. In a way it was like *being* a battery . . . a jumper battery that had had its juice sucked down so often trying to start worn-out engines that it would never hold a full charge again. It was funny, though, with the world all hazy around him, that smells could stand out so sharp: the small boy stank with a sourness that reminded Ty of a motor struggling to burn the rotten old gas his dad had siphoned out of abandoned cars. Their truck would barely run on the stuff, smoking and spitting and sometimes stalling dead with its filter clogged with rust and varnish. Even a big old truck engine needed clean fuel. His dad had joked that the siphoned shit from the wrecks would be pure poison to the new little motors made today.

Not long ago, maybe a month, this kid had been one of the showtimes: designer jeans, moon-boot Reeboks, three-bill bomber jacket bought to match Ty's, and a do so sharp it needed biweekly tuning. That kind of kid burned out fast but brought in big bucks while he lasted. Ty tried to remember what the boy had looked like when he'd first started; ragged, underfed, and hungry as hell for all those good things locked behind bars and glass. Danny's face drifted through Ty's mind, but he made it go away. Besides, this boy looked nothing like Danny, and had gotten everything a way cool little black dude would want. And now the ride on Santa's magic sleigh was over.

"Straight up, Ty! Word, man! I got jumped! Just now!

Big suckers . . . bigger'n you, even! Rousted all my buck! Swear to God, man!"

Ty wiped a hand over his forehead. It came away wet. He forced his eyes to focus on the kid, not even sure if he'd heard his exact words. It didn't matter; whatever the boy was saying would sound something like that. What it translated to was . . . *taka-taka*: a thousand dollars' worth of shitty fuel burned up by a fine-tuned little engine that had finally stalled in rush-hour traffic.

"Swear to God," Ty repeated in a murmur. "What make you figure He give a shit?"

The boy gave him a strange look. "Huh?"

Ty shook his head slowly. "I give you a jump start just last week. A warnin, an one more chance. What it is, my own battery almost dead. Cars pilin up behind you. Onliest thing left to do is shove you out the way."

"*Huh?*" The kid was staring now, his eyes red and wild but suddenly scared despite all the shit in his brain.

Ty went on, listening to his own voice as if it were somebody else's. "Deek want you stripped for parts. Left in the gutter on blocks to show others what happen to burned-out junk."

The little boy tried to look fierce and bad. "Shut up, sucker! I ain't ascared of you!" He stabbed a finger at the Train bottle half sticking from Ty's jacket pocket. "You drunk! I can take you, man!"

Ty sighed. He pulled out the bottle, drank the rest, and tossed it over his shoulder, hearing it smash on the sidewalk behind him. The shatter of glass made the little boy wince. Ty studied him through the fog in his mind: at least Danny's old Nikes, 501s, and castoff tank top had a dignity of sorts, never having been much to begin with. But nothing looked worse than expensive, cool clothes turning into dirty rags.

There was still a gold chain, and an earring glinted . . . half the price, thought Ty, of a ton-and-a-half truck. The boy would have cash in his pockets, or probably stashed somewhere on him in what he figured was an original hiding place. And there was the little .32 Colt pistol in the back of his jeans, worth an easy two bills, and which the kid would try to do him with very soon now. Crack was intense, but cruelly quick. On top, where the boy had been a minute ago, you were pumped to the max, and it wouldn't have surprised Ty if the little kid had gone for him with only his fists. The kid's eyes still glittered with danger, but snot glistened on his lip. His fingers, small and perfect, twitched, and one hand was already inching toward the gun. The fall from grace was fast; into pure hell and paranoia where everyone was THE ENEMY and wanted you dead or worse. It was funny how, for these kids, that was often the real truth.

Seconds passed as Ty tried to make his tired mind work. Through the fog that wasn't real he could scent the dank mustiness of the junk-shop merchandise piled behind cracked windows that were held together by bolted plywood patches. The small boy's breathing was shallow and fast. Ty could swear he heard the kid's heartbeat above the low rumble of the Trans-Am idling at the curb. They were on a shadowy side street just around the corner from a block of bars and nightclubs where the boy did most of his business, and the deep bass boom of rap seemed to vibrate the concrete underfoot. Then, from light-years away, Ty heard the faint, sweet singing of angels. For a second, Ty forgot the dangerous little boy and his gun. He was suddenly six again, and sitting beside his mother in church.

Then he remembered the shabby storefront up near the next corner with its childish painting of a dark-skinned

Jesus in one dirty window. He should have known there would be no miracles in Oakland; that nobody was going to die for his sins except himself.

The little kid went for his gun.

He wasn't Danny, and Ty was up for the move. The Colt was almost new, nickel-plated and ivory-gripped, a bright shiny toy for a cool niggerboy. It flashed in the shadows as Ty grabbed the kid's wrist and twisted. The gun clattered on the pavement just like Danny's knife. But this boy wasn't Danny, and he didn't scream as Ty twisted harder. He had his own dirty fog to muffle his mind. This boy wasn't Danny, and Ty wrenched his wrist until there was a soft snap of bone. Then the boy screamed, but only for a second until Ty's fist smashed into his mouth.

Ty didn't pull his own gun; the kid was beyond threats. If he had to use the .45 there would be only one reason. A broken wrist would have stopped any normal twelve-year-old, but this boy hardly realized he was hurt. For the first few seconds Ty felt fear as punches that would have put older dudes on their knees just rocked the kid around like one of those rolly-bottomed toys that always bounced back for more. The boy beat and kicked savagely back at Ty, even using his slack-wristed hand. Old horror movies played in Ty's mind; of fighting the living dead who couldn't feel pain. It was almost a surprise to see and smell bright fresh blood instead of something rotten and green gushing from the boy's mouth and nose. And tears on his cheeks . . . corpses couldn't cry.

The kid choked on blood. It sprayed dark and glistening as Ty hit him in the stomach once, twice, and again with all the strength in his own body. He felt the knife slash rip open beneath the bandage. He remembered a scrap-yard crane, its throttle jammed wide open and engine running wild, screaming in iron agony until the operator had ripped off his shirt and smothered its air intake. Even a heartless machine needed air. Ty stepped warily back and let the kid fall to his knees, where he doubled and puked something that didn't seem much like food.

Behind the diamond pattern of bars, Ty saw Deek's reflection in the door glass. He was sitting in the car, arms crossed on the windowsill, chin resting on top, and that same science-class expression on his face as when watching the two big boys die.

"Kick him," Deek advised.

But Ty only gazed down at the kid while his own chest heaved for breath and his heart struggled like a water pump sucking air. The pain in his arm seemed to lash him like fire when he saw the way the boy's hand was hanging. Ty shook his head hard to clear the fog, then bent and snagged the Colt, automatically snapping on the safety before slipping it into his jacket. He leaned down again and pulled the gold chain over the boy's lowered head.

"Yo! The earring too!" Deek called. "Was my mother-fuckin buck bought it. Just tear it out, man."

But Ty undid the tiny catch, almost gently even though his fingers felt numb, and eased the ring from the boy's earlobe. Then he straightened and waited a few moments more, but the boy's brain had finally got word that the body it lived in had been badly hurt. No fight was left as Ty took the kid under the arms and hauled him to his feet, then propped him like a dead thing back against the bars. A tiger-striped nylon wallet Ty pulled from the boy's pocket held two bucks and some ones. There was also a Boys' and Girls' Club card, a school picture of a pretty girl, and an old faded one that was probably his mom and little sister. And a Trojan. Ty closed his eyes, wondering why the beautiful memory of last night's lovemaking with Markita was playing in his mind. The boy was still bent over, clutching at his stomach with his good hand while the other hung useless at his side. He whimpered, dry-heaving and spitting more blood, thick little bubbles of it frothing from his nostrils. Slowly, he slid down again, his shirt riding up so the rusty bars raked his back, to sit in the stinking puddle he'd made. The babyish smell of piss-wet jeans drifted in the air.

Kneeling, Ty pulled off one of the kid's Reeboks and checked it and the sock for money. Nothing. He did the same with the other, not much surprised when the result was the same . . . the boy was too smart for that. Ty sighed once more, and rocked back on his heels. Faintly from up the street, above the booming of rap and the soft sullen purr of the 'Am's idling engine, the choir singing carried.

"Yo!" came Deek's voice cutting through. "Little shit owe me a grand, man! Get your ass busy, stupid!"

The boy's retching had stopped, and he just sobbed and moaned while his nose bubbled blood. His body was still numbed by the crack, but that little mercy would be gone all too soon, leaving him alone on the dark street with a broken bone and maybe, as hard as Ty had hit him, something else smashed up inside. There were things in the night who would prey on even what little was left. Ty felt rage sparking, throwing off fire like a Chinatown pinwheel. "Maybe," he murmured, "I leave you your soul."

He reached to the kid's crotch and pulled open the zipper. The boy wore shorts, a luxury denied Ty and his brothers. The rage kept sparking as Ty felt in the warm and wet where only a few sparse curls had sprouted. He found the wad of bills. The boy's earthly debt was paid. Jamming the money into his jacket atop the gun and the gold, Ty stood. Suddenly, he cocked back his foot for a kick.

Then he saw Deek grinning in the glass. "Do it, nigger!"

The choir voices soared up out of the city on the wings of a note as pure and sweet as a young child's laughter. Dark angels, thought Ty, as the sparking pinwheel spun. He whirled around and stalked to the car, where he wordlessly yanked the two hundreds from the kid's wallet, added them to the mass of cold metal and warm wet money, and flung the whole handful past Deek and onto the floor.

"Hey!" yelled Deek.

But Ty had turned away. He went back to the junk-shop door and jerked the boy to his feet by his good hand. The kid whimpered but didn't resist. Ty stuck the wallet into his jeans.

"What's this shit, man?" Deek demanded.

Ty only shook his head. "Claimin his soul ain't my motherfuckin job."

Ty pulled the boy a few paces up the sidewalk. The kid stumbled on his bare feet through the glass of Ty's bottle, crying "No!" in a voice without hope. Then his legs gave and he fell to his knees. Ty gathered him up and slung him over one shoulder. Deek's curses echoed in the empty street as Ty walked on. Through the fog, Ty heard the car pull away and pace him. Deek's shouts of rage were muffled. Only the angel song carried clear.

The storefront church was a pitiful parody of God's house on earth. The angels had heard of Ty's coming, and fled. Ty blinked in the glare of one big naked bulb as he kicked the door open. Its glass pane shattered with a jagged kind of music. There was one small room, high-ceilinged and narrow like the rib shop. The walls were bare Sheetrock with a few African Bible pictures Scotch-taped to them like the torn-out magazine images of rock and rap groups that kids always worshipped. The floor was cracked and curling linoleum, and a long way from clean. The altar was a kitchen table draped in cheap crimson velvet, and the sweaty-faced preacher behind it looked like a fat-assed Uncle Remus from the Disney cartoon. On the wall at his back hung a picture of what could have been a black Jesus or a nigger faggot. There were a few rows of battered folding chairs. Besides the preacher and the six choir members, there were maybe a dozen other people: mostly old women, a few old men, and two wide-eyed little girls about four and five.

The sweet singing had shattered to jagged pieces like the door glass when Ty busted in with his bloody stinking burden. Metal chairs creaked like old bones as people turned to stare. Outside, Ty heard Deek's car pull up and stop.

Ty glared around the now silent, shabby room. The .45 was in his hand before he knew it. He jabbed the gun toward the fat preacher, and the man paled and slumped against the wall beneath the black Jesus.

"LIAR!" bawled Ty. He desperately searched faces but found only fear. "How much?" he demanded of the people. "How much you payin him to lie to you?"

There was no answer, and Ty had expected none. The ceiling above didn't split open. No lightning bolt struck him down. The little girls began to cry. Ty was sorry for that. "Suffer, little children," he softly said.

Staggering under the boy's weight, Ty stumbled up what passed for an aisle. Blood, the young boy's and his own, dripped a trail behind. Reaching the velvet-draped table, he knocked the preacher's big Bible to the floor with a sweep of the gun barrel and laid the boy gently down. The people were watching but nobody moved. In no face did Ty find compassion, least of all the preacher's . . . except, strangely enough, in the little girls'. Only their eyes seemed to see the bleeding boy and not the gun. The preacher cowered back against the wall. Ty spat at his feet, and the man flinched. The boy on the altar had curled into a sobbing ball of pain. Ty faced the people once more, and pointed with the gun. "HE the one dyin for your sin, suckers!"

Spinning around, Ty straight-armed the pistol above the preacher's head. The .45's blast beat from the walls and echoed loud in the little room as Ty emptied its clip into the heart of the picture. The preacher sank down to a quivering mass on the floor below it. He hid his face in his hands.

Ty jammed the smoking gun into his jacket, then stabbed a bloody finger at the boy. His rage was draining away, leaving him cold and empty. His voice, when it came, was quiet and sad. "Save *him*, niggers. That the onliest way you save yourselfs."

Ty walked back out on the street and got into Deek's car.

Deek smoked rubber, peeling away fast, and eyeing Ty all the while with real amazement. "Hell, man!" he muttered, awe in his tone. "I never knowed you had *that* kinda power in ya!"

"Jesus," snickered Deek as he eased the 'Am around a corner. "I mean, whatever possessed ya, man?"

Ty said nothing. Deek had produced another bottle of Train, and Ty was just holding it in his hands. Now he twisted off the cap and drank.

"Stuff make ya chase your mother," said Deek.

Ty recapped the bottle, then concentrated on reloading the .45's clip from a box of bullets in the glove compartment.

"Well. Check. It. Out. My man," said Deek, pointing with his Sherman. "Tell me that ain't Miss Rwanda 1992! Hell, she so totally African she still cook with flies!"

Ty hardly heard Deek. He shook his head to thin the fog. Maybe he'd been listening inside his mind for angels— *real* angels—coming after him and pissed as hell. In a way that would be a relief. Then Ty saw Markita across the street, trudging home, her hands buried in the pockets of her old Navy coat, its high, upturned collar hiding her face.

Ty slipped the pistol back into his jeans. "Leave her be, man," he said as Deek started cranking down his window to yell something.

Deek swung around with a scowl as they passed the girl. She didn't look up, though Ty knew she'd marked the car and probably guessed he was in it.

"Yo! What in hell's wrong with you tonight?" Deek demanded. "You sick or somethin, stupid?"

Ty drained the bottle in a few gulps and dropped it on the floor. "Somethin stupid," he repeated in a murmur while gazing at the outside mirror. He watched the girl melt into the darkness and wished he'd seen her face.

Deek snorted. "Yo, sucker! What the fuck's THAT sposed to mean? Hey, check yourself, man . . . all sweaty an smelly. An for Christ sake DO somethin bout that goddamn blood fore it get all over my motherfuckin car!" He punched Ty in the shoulder, his scowl deepening when Ty hissed and clenched his teeth. "Yo. It your fuckin arm, ain't it, man? That stupid sucker brother of yours give you affection!"

Ty nodded slowly. "Yeah . . . yeah, got to be what it is. First time in my goddamn life I get some an it got to come from him. Funny."

"Ain't nuthin funny bout it, stupid." Then Deek's face softened slightly. "Mmm. Sorry, Ty. I didn't know." He peered ahead to where the car-wash lot made an empty gap in the next block of buildings like missing teeth in an old dog's snarl. "But this one fuck of a time to go an get sick on me, man. I ain't spectin no shit from Wesley an his little rag-asses, but it for sure gonna make me look like a goddamn fool if you go an pass out or somethin." He turned to study Ty. "Yo. Can you hang together another hour, man?"

"Hell," Ty mumbled. "I hold together another month."

"Huh?" Deek gave him a strange look, then dug a tiny bottle from his jacket pocket. "Here, dude. Take a snort. It fly your ass through."

Ty glanced at the white powder and suddenly shivered. "No. I . . . cool, Deek. Let's just get it done, okay?"

Deek nodded, and slipped the bottle back into his pocket, then pulled out a Hershey bar. He snapped it in two, handed half to Ty, then gently patted Ty's shoulder. "Yo, homeboy, soon's this deal done I takin you uptown to one of them duty-doctor places. They make you all better again, believe."

Ty met Deek's eyes, remembering even Lucifer had once been a handsome young prince. If God were really all-loving and all-merciful, did it mean that even the Prince of Darkness had only to go down on his knees to Him and beg forgiveness to be saved?

But then who would run hell?

Deek popped the last of the candy bar into his mouth and licked his fingers. "Better pack the Uzi tonight, man. Show em where we comin from. Sides, way you look, you prob'ly couldn't hit jack with that .45 if them little suckers try some shit."

Ty took Deek's carbine from the back seat, leaving the pair Deek was going to deal Wesley, both minus their magazines. Up the street, Ty saw a lanky boy standing at the car-wash entrance. The boy flashed a hand signal to others unseen, then pulled the chain post from the ground. Ty caught a flicker in the mirror: a car was rounding a corner a couple blocks behind. Its headlights silhouetted Markita's slim figure, still back on the last block. Deek noticed the lights too. His eyes shifted between the mirrors and the lot. The lanky boy had dropped the chain and stood waiting.

Ty knew that Deek was debating whether the cool move would be to cruise on past and circle around once more so as not to be seen pulling into the lot.

"Shit!" muttered Deek. "Yo. Figure that car back there a cop, man?"

Ty turned and squinted through the rear window. "No way to tell from here. But it ain't movin very fast. Cops cruise like that."

"Mmm. Yeah. But so do any car fulla dudes lookin for action or trouble." Deek checked the mirrors again. "Naw. Can't be no cops, man. Car slowin down back by your African queen." He grinned. "Hope they don't give her no shit."

Ty remembered the night before, Markita coming up the alley alone with just her silly little can of Mace. "She be cool," he said, hoping it was true.

"Mmm. Look like you been bit, my man. You two make a way cool couple, like prom night in the Congo or somethin." Then Deek grinned. "Shit, who am I to stand in the way of true love, man." He cut the car into the lot, killing the lights as they passed the watcher boy, who moved quickly to replace the post.

Ty put the last bite of candy into his mouth, tasting blood from his fingers on the chocolate. He scanned the wash bays as Deek motored along the front of the structure before swinging around to the rear. The moon was high, and its light didn't penetrate far into the four short tunnels. From what he could see they seemed empty except for the corpse of a car in the last one. He checked the Uzi, making sure the stock was locked open, the clip fully seated, and the select-fire switch all the way forward to A. He cocked the bolt, and caught himself whispering a prayer that he wouldn't have to shoot any kids. That thought was funny, sad, and frightening all at the same time. Who in hell did he figure could be listening anyhow?

The wash structure's shadow stretched halfway across the back of the lot. Beyond the moonlit strip of weedy asphalt that glittered here and there with broken bottle glass was a six-foot chain-link fence and then a big storm-drain channel. There was water in it tonight, glinting like gunmetal under the moon. Ty supposed it had something to do with tides in the Bay. Anyhow, the water left no place outside the fence for anyone to hide. Ty turned his attention back to the wash bays. It took effort to keep his mind clear and concentrate on his job, but everything—his own escape from the cage, Danny's future, and maybe even Danny's life—depended on protecting Deek. Ty glanced toward the fence again, noting the low square shape of a battered vac-uum box. One small kid might conceal himself behind it, but why? Even these young boys wouldn't be stupid enough to try an ambush with just one kid hidden there. Besides, the only fire the Crew had was an old snub-nosed .38 like TV detectives carried. A short-barreled revolver like that was only good at close range, and then only in the hands of an expert shot. A kid would hardly be able to hit anybody with it over thirty feet away, except by stupid blind luck. And Ty saw that all the gang were gathered in plain sight at the edge of the moon shadow, strictly by rules.

Except for Wesley, Ty didn't know their names but there were five boys here, which left the sixth watching the gate, just like the other times when Deek had met them in this place. Wesley was even holding the .38 up by its barrel. Ty relaxed as much as he dared without letting the fog flood back into his mind, but scanned the wash bays once more as the Trans-Am growled to a stop and its engine settled into a silky-smooth idle. From this side of the structure there was a clear view through to the moonlit street beyond. The junk car's roof was mostly caved in, so there wasn't much chance of anybody hiding inside. And yet Ty couldn't shake the feeling that there were other eyes watching him besides those of the five boys standing in the moonlight. It had to be in his head, he decided. He studied the kids, thinking how they looked like ebony sculptures . . . somehow pure and fine in the cold silver glow. It was sad to know that some would be dead in just a few years, crushed beneath the pyramid, a structure that stood only by keeping the best and strongest bricks on the bottom to hold up the old rotten ones on top. What would happen if those bottom bricks just slipped out from under? That thought made a funny cartoon picture in Ty's mind.

Deek slapped the stick into neutral, pulled the parking brake, and then snagged one of the empty Uzis from the back seat. "Yo, Wes man!" he called, holding the gun up sideways. "Check out your future, dude!"

Ty popped his door and slid from the car. He saw the kids' eyes widen a little when they checked that he carried the carbine. They would know from the clips that his was loaded while the one Deek would deal them wasn't. Ty noted that they were careful to keep from bunching together, but at this range, with a full-auto, they would also know that it wouldn't much matter.

Deek opened his door and got out. "Yo, Wes. What it is, why don't you just go an put that there little toy of yours on my hood, an let's all be ground-floor cool." He snickered. "Careful bout my paint, man."

Wesley stepped forward and laid the .38 on the 'Am's hood, where it vibrated lightly to the engine's idle. Ty hardly glanced at the gun, except to note how cheap and toylike it looked . . . like a Taiwanese copy of a Colt. But, mostly, he scanned the boys' faces: even street-hardened kids like these hadn't yet learned to completely cover their quick-changing emotions. Still, their expressions stayed guarded and cool, eyes watching Deek with wild-animal wariness and shifting sometimes to Ty's Uzi to check where it pointed. That was normal enough, yet something *was* different tonight: Ty could feel it; almost like walking into a room where some other dudes had been talking you down or telling a joke that you missed. The kids were avoiding his eyes instead of flashing occasional glares of challenge to show they were bad and not scared of him. If he were in school, Ty would have checked for a tack on his seat or a sign Scotch-taped to his back saying: KICK ME.

But he wasn't in school. This was real-time, where missing the joke could mean death. His voice came out rusty, and he coughed to clear his tight throat. "Maybe I better search em, Deek? This here neutral ground, we gots the right."

Wesley snorted contempt. He wore no shirt anyway, but nodded to his dudes, who stripped off theirs and turned around slow, arms out, while Ty watched. Tight jeans showed worn spots on pockets, and bulges that were probably blades, but Ty wasn't worried about knives. The kids didn't look like fine little sculptures anymore, just dirty, snot-nosed, rag-ass niggerboys. Ty expected more contempt to flash on Wesley's face, but seemed to get speculation instead. Whatever the joke was, he'd missed it again. He scanned the roly fat boy, whose apron of loose lard hung even lower than Deek's. Stepping to the kid, he felt below his belly where there was plenty of room to hide a small gun.

The boy giggled. "Yo! Tickles, man."

Deek grinned as Ty moved away and the boys slipped back into their shirts. "Ty here take good care of me, huh, dudes?"

Ty's finger curled tense on the Uzi's trigger as Deek handed the empty carbine to Wesley. One of the other kids, a skinny little boy whose huge Army Desert Storm shirt made him look like a camouflaged bat, suddenly let go a loud and childish germ-spraying sneeze. Ty's finger jerked tight at the sound. He wanted to slap the little sucker the way his own mom would have whacked him at Danny's age for something like that. Newspaper words floated through his mind: TWELVE-YEAR-OLD SHOT FOR SNEEZING.

"Ty! Help!" screamed a voice. It was Danny!

The gang boys froze, but their eyes flicked to the vacuum box. Ty couldn't tell if their faces showed rage or fear. He clutched the Uzi, covering the kids, ready to fire, and feeling the trigger spring tighten behind his finger. Nobody moved. Danny's voice called again, sounding hurt. "Ty! Hurry!"

Deek's head whipped back and forth between Ty and Wesley. "What's this shit?" he bawled.

Ty was staring toward the fence: Danny had to be behind the vac box. Rage blasted the fog from Ty's brain so things stood out sharp-edged and stark the way they had in the church. He jabbed the Uzi one-handed at the gang while jerking the .45 from his jeans. "Nobody move!" he shouted. "You God DAMN little animals! You hurt my brother, I fuckin kill you all!" Snapping off the .45's safety, he skidded the Uzi across the car's hood to Deek.

Deek snagged the gun and covered the kids. He flashed Ty a furious glare. "That motherfuckin little BASTARD! I tell you an tell you blood mean nuthin but trouble, but you too goddamn stupid to listen!" He stepped forward and jammed the gun muzzle to Wesley's chest. "All you suckers! Move close together! Way slow!"

Ty dashed for the vac box, his .45 up and ready. Wesley's scared voice quavered in his ears as he ran, pleading with Deek now, all cool gone. "It that cocksucker Furball, man!

What make all this shit! He come here to do ya, Deek! Swear to God, man!"

But Ty didn't hear any more. His Nikes skidded on the rotten asphalt as he rounded the box and stopped, dizzy, sweating and panting even though the distance was less than fifty feet. Danny lay on his back in the narrow, shadowed space between the box and the fence. He was half naked, hands behind him, his knees drawn up, and his ankles tied together with what looked like strips of his shirt. Another satin strip hung loose at his neck like a gag he'd managed to work free. Even in the soft moonlight Ty could see that his brother had been badly beaten: his face puffy and caked with dried blood, lips swollen and split, and scratches all over his body. Fury flamed inside Ty. He *would* kill them! *All* of them! Slamming the pistol down on top of the box, he dropped to his knees at his brother's feet. From over at the car, Wesley's pleas carried to his ears. "Yo, Deek! *Listen*, man! He *follow* us, man! We *catch* him! Tie his ass up. Word! He say he come to *kill* you, man! I swear it!"

Lies! thought Ty, as he bent over his brother. Lies as stupid and childish as those of the snot-nosed dealer boy he'd dumped in the church. All these goddamned kids were lost! Save them? What a motherfucking joke! They should be exterminated like the dirty, garbage-eating little black rats they were! Yet, though raging inside, Ty's voice came out a sob. "Danny!" He reached to gather the boy against him.

Something silver flashed in the moonlight. Suddenly Danny was sitting up, his arms free, and kicking the loose strip of satin off his legs while he pressed the muzzle of a shiny little revolver to Ty's heart. Ty froze. A cry choked off in his throat. Tears burned his eyes like battery acid. "No!" he whispered. "Not you, Danny. Jesus, not you too!"

Danny's eyes locked on his brother's, desperate and pleading. "Don't move, Ty! PLEASE! I love you, man! I swear it! But don't move!"

The fire in Ty flickered and died. Cold seemed to cover him, and he shivered, no longer sure what in the world was real anymore. Deek's voice could have come from the moon, calling, "Ty! What the fuck's goin on?"

Ty's mind wandered, lost in his own skull. His gaze drifted to the little gun in his brother's hands: it looked somehow familiar. The words came out stupid, like most of his words seemed to do. "What you swear it on, Danny?"

Ty saw tears glisten in Danny's eyes too. The boy's chin quivered and his ragged lips moved as if in prayer. "You, Ty. I swear it on you. I gots nuthin else, man."

Ty's hands were still outstretched and open. Slowly, he turned his head, looking past the pistol which lay just a foot from his face. At the car, the gang was still bunched together under Deek's gun. Deek's face and stance showed uncertainty. Wesley was still talking fast, pleading like a little kid caught doing something naughty, trying to explain what Danny was doing here and tied up. It sounded all too true in Ty's ears. He realized suddenly that Danny had come to save him. What a joke! But why was Danny holding a gun to his heart?

"Please, Ty," Danny whispered. "You gotta trust me, man! Listen! Last night, you say you love me so much you could kill me. I *know* what that mean now! An I love YOU that much, man! Believe. *Please!*"

Deek's voice cut through Danny's whisper. "TY! Goddamnit, what's up?"

Ty looked at the tears running down Danny's cheeks. He closed his eyes, but the fog flooded in and tried to smother him. He blinked and shook his head in confusion, and shivered once more, scenting his brother's fear over the smells of sweat and blood and sour saltwater from the storm channel. "Danny," he murmured. "I got to get you out of here." He turned toward Deek. "It . . . true. Danny been half smoked an tied up."

The Uzi wavered in Deek's chubby hands. He eyed Wesley a few moments more, then lowered the gun. "Mmm. Sorry, my man. Look like you done me a favor." His eyes flicked over to Ty, and he spat on the ground. "Just too motherfuckin bad you dudes didn't go all the way with that little sucker. Maybe we talk more bout it another day." Letting the gun hang one-handed, he faced Ty and called, "Yo, stupid! Get that little shitball out here so's we get this deal done! You an me, man, we gots some major talkin to do later on!"

Wesley grinned as he fingered the unloaded carbine. "Yo, Deek! We come a cunt hair close to doin that dude already. Word! Hey, you oughta go on over an check him out, man. Major street pizza or what!"

"Yeah?" Deek looked back toward the box. A smile spread slow over his face. "Mmm. Yo, Ty! Just chill there a minute, man!" Deek gestured casually to the gang with the gun muzzle. "Yo, Wes. Just you leave you little ole toy there on my hood an you an your way cool dudes come with me, huh?"

Deek was all moves, Ty thought: he kept the kids in front of him as they came across the lot. The gang boys were snickering and grinning now, puffed and proud of what they'd done to Danny, practically pissing themselves like puppies under Deek's praise. Heartless little animals, all of them . . . lost. And the Bible said, "A little child shall lead them!"

Ty tensed then: what would happen when they saw that

Danny had a gun? Ty noted Wesley's .38 left lying on the Trans-Am's hood. The vibration of the engine was inching it forward. In a moment it would slide off and hit the ground. It was such a cheap-looking thing it might even fall apart. But what would that matter? These little animals would leave here tonight with an Uzi. One day, maybe they'd turn on Deek. "I got to get you out of here, Danny," Ty whispered again.

It was almost a surprise when Ty felt the gun still pressed to his chest. He looked down at it, and suddenly knew why it seemed familiar: he'd seen it last in the pawlike hand of that strange-eyed slender boy. Ty's mind began running around in his skull like something trapped. How had Danny gotten it? Why? Deek and the smaller boys were nearing. "No, Danny!" Ty hissed. "Don't do it, man! You gots no chance alone . . . an we *need* Deek!"

Tears still flowed down Danny's face, silver in the moonlight. "No, we don't!" he whispered back. "That a lie, man! We all dyin for cause we believe that lie! You an me, man, we DON'T need his kind!"

Ty looked up again. The .45 atop the box was so close! But what could he do with it now? Then he caught a movement at one end of the wash structure: it was the lanky boy from the gate. He was easing carefully through the shadows, and he had a gun . . . *another* snub-nose revolver! He crossed a patch of moonlight. The gun's blue steel glinted cold. Ty stared back at the .38 on the hood. It had no metallic shine, and now it slipped off and fell, and the sound of it hitting the asphalt was so small that Ty heard it only because he was listening . . . a hollow, *plastic* clatter! The gang's snickering and boasting around Deek drowned the tiny noise. *There* was the joke, stupid! These little suckers had fooled him with a toy!

Danny was watching his brother's face. He seemed to read Ty's thoughts, and saw him suck breath for a warning yell to Deek.

Ty felt the gun muzzle rake across his chest, heard Danny's words, "I love you, man." Then Danny pulled the trigger.

Being killed was like nothing Ty had ever imagined. On TV it looked heroic and cool: in real-time fast and final. But it always happened to somebody else. The sound, with the gun jammed tight to his skin, hardly seemed more than a grunt. He saw orange fire spit back from the loose-fitting cylinder. Its flash lit Danny's face, but Ty couldn't read his brother's expression. There was no pain, only a slam to his side that knocked him over backward. It seemed almost funny being killed by such a pussy little gun. Danny had killed him because he loved him: child logic, but the same thing he'd said to the boy only last night. It made about as much sense as anything else in this twisted-up world. Ty knew he was dead before the pavement rushed up to crash against his back; knew it because he saw angels at last. They were small, dark angels, like bare-chested boys. And they glistened like ebony sheathed in crystal-clear fire. Beads of ice-flame, like molten chrome drops, scattered from their bodies as they came for him. All wore expressions of vengeance. It was funny that they had no wings, that they had to climb the fence like ordinary kids. But maybe God didn't give wings to little black angels.

A half block away, Markita heard the shots through a red fog of fury. The two cops, the black and the white who would rather see kids starve than let them eat garbage, were just getting back in their car, laughing. They'd searched her, alone there on the deserted street, searched her body with warm loving care. It wasn't rape, but rape would have left her feeling this same way. She was sure. They'd taken her Mace: she too could legally be turned out to die under the law's loving protection. They'd told her she was lucky she wasn't spending the night in jail. Maybe she imagined it, but she wondered now if they would have taken it if she'd been more cooperative. Translate: a good, submissive little niggergirl while they were feeling her up.

"Thing about Oakland," the black one was telling the white, "it's a real *cop's* town, know what I sayin?"

"I hear that, brother," chuckled the white, tossing Markita's Mace can onto the dash.

Then the shots had crackled up the street, the first one faint and muffled, then more: one, two, three, small-caliber and raggedly spaced, and finally the short stuttering burst of full-auto.

She watched, momentarily frozen, and forgotten by the cops as they piled into their cruiser. The white grabbed the microphone but the black caught his hand. "Wait, man! I'm sure that was junior-bad's car pulled into that lot up there! Best we check it out fore callin backup!" He dropped the car in gear and burned away, letting the door slam shut by itself.

Markita had seen Deek's Trans-Am motoring by, heard Too Short's old raunchy rap about cool Oaktown and all the bad bad niggers—and white people on TV worried about heavy metal turning *their* kids into twisted little suckers! —and noted Ty's tall profile in the car. She was sure he'd noticed her too. But then the cops had curbed her, smirking like dogs eating shit when they recognized her as the Burger King girl with the attitude, and she'd forgotten about Ty in her anger. But now she didn't hesitate. She bolted up the sidewalk for the car-wash lot. A hundred yards ahead she saw the cruiser slew sideways, tires whimpering, lurch nose-down for an instant as if undecided, then hit the chain head-on with its heavy push bars, snapping it like a cheap necklace.

Ty discovered he wasn't dead, and that the glistening ebony angels swarming over the fence were only wet kids. Danny had shot him in the shoulder . . . in that stupid showtime spot where every TV hero always took his lead. Ty lay on his back for a minute, dazed, with all hell busting loose on every side, and the only thing he could think was that Danny had even managed to miss bone. Ty felt his sleeve soaking with fresh blood, but the wound wouldn't kill him. Maybe that was luck. His arm didn't even hurt anymore; in fact, he could hardly feel it at all. He concentrated on getting his breath back. The shot seemed to have cleared the fog from his mind, as if something inside him had decided to throw all its remaining resources into survival. Still, for those first few seconds of ass-kicked reality, it was like being totally drunk and trying to follow some fast-action kid's game or skate moves from the sidelines.

The strange-eyed slender boy was the first over the fence . . . which was stupid because he wasn't even armed. But *he* at least still looked like some sort of small avenging angel. He actually seemed to fly for a second as he leaped from the mesh, which was bent almost double under the weight of Gordon, the fat boy, and the twins scrambling over. He landed lightly on the vac box. Gordon hung by his elbows long enough to aim his .22 pistol and fire three orange-flashing pops in Deek's direction. The bullets must have cut past just inches from the slender boy's ear but he never flinched.

Ty's hearing, dulled after he'd hit the ground, now came

back with a crash. He heard all the kids screaming and yelling on every side while their leaders bawled commands and curses. It sounded like a major schoolyard fight. Danny's voice called, "Lion," and Ty saw him toss the nickel revolver to the slender boy. It took Ty a second to realize what that meant.

"YOU!" he yelled to the fragile-looking kid. "*You* set this up!"

The slender boy turned and met Ty's eyes for an instant. Maybe there weren't little black werewolves any more than there were ebony angels, but the name, Lion, came close enough. Then the boy was gone, not vanished exactly but blurring away as if only half real. Danny snatched the .45 from the top of the box and aimed double-handed for Deek.

"Danny! No!" Ty found he could move. He lunged for his brother. Deek's Uzi blasted a short burst of fire, yellow-orange flame licking out from its muzzle. Bullets thunked the vac box, spraying paint flakes and rust before the gun's recoil bucked its barrel skyward in Deek's hands and sent shots slicing the air over Ty's head. One bullet twanged off the fence mesh. From the edge of sight, Ty saw Deek spin in a frantic circle as the gang boys tried to move on him from all sides, some wielding knives. The Uzi spit another burst of flame and noise.

"Bail!" Wesley bawled to his dudes. He swung the unloaded carbine butt-first at Deek's head, but Deek dodged away and the boys scattered like windblown trash. Deek fired a few more rounds, trying to target one of the running kids. The small boy in the huge Army shirt yelped and pitched forward on the pavement, but scrambled up fast and darted away, one hand clutching his side.

Deek was no fool, Ty thought, even as he grabbed for Danny. Deek knew how fast his clip would empty on full-

auto and wasn't wasting shots until he marked the odds.
Danny managed to fire the .45 once before Ty got a grip
on his arm and pulled him down. The bullet went wild over
Deek's head to rake paint chips from the wash structure's
roof.

Danny screamed curses, tears still streaming down his
face as he fought and bit at his brother. But Ty twisted the
gun from his hands. A heavy bulk crashed onto the top of
the box, buckling the thin sheet metal: Gordon. Ty slapped
Danny aside and tried to grab Gordon's leg as the fat kid
fired another .22 pop at Deek. But Gordon, seeing the shot
miss, leaped down and pounded away after the Lion, his
wet jeans slipping low while his shoes squished and spurted
water.

Danny's small fist smashed into Ty's cheek, striking
sparks in his brain. Ty backhanded his brother out of the
way, then saw with horror that the Lion kid had dived into
Deek's car and snagged the other Uzi off the back seat. He
threw it to one of the twins. Now he'd found the two loaded
magazines and bailed out with one in each paw. Ty tried
to get a shot at him, but then Danny was clawing for the
gun before he could aim. Ty jerked the trigger anyway, and
the bullet starred the 'Am's windshield, sputting glass
shards that glittered ice-blue as they scattered. The Lion
hit the ground and rolled, yet managed to fling one clip to
a twin and the other to Wesley, who leaped up and caught
it one-handed from the air. The twins dropped to a crouch,
frantically trying to figure out how to get their gun loaded.

Deek saw them, and whipped his Uzi around to cut them
down. Wesley had his magazine in, but was struggling with
the bolt, forgetting to hold in the safety lever so the gun
would cock. Gordon roared something at him, and Wesley
found the problem. The bolt snicked back, ready. Ty tried

to target Wesley, barely feeling Danny battering at him or hearing his pleading screams. The boy didn't understand! Deek *couldn't* die now!

Deek shouldered his gun to shoot down the twins, who had managed to get their Uzi loaded and cocked but were now, unbelievably, fighting over which one would fire it! All around, the unarmed boys of Wesley's gang were scooping up rocks and bottles and anything else throwable and hurling them at Deek. The small camouflaged kid had a bloodstain on his shirt but darted in to fling a rock. Most of the stuff missed Deek, and he didn't seem to notice when something did hit him, but the jiggly-fat boy heaved a Bud bottle that clunked the Uzi aside so the burst of bullets ripped up asphalt a foot from the twins instead of tearing into them. They stopped arguing. One let the other have the gun.

Then Ty saw the lanky boy break from the wash structure and dash toward Deek from behind, the .38 clutched ready in both hands. Desperately, Ty drove an elbow into Danny's stomach and broke free of his grip. He swung the .45, steadying it on top of the box for a straight shot at the kid. Something small and wet and savage crashed down on Ty's back. He glimpsed dripping dreadlocks framing a furious little-boy face and bared teeth. Then there were four small hands clamped on his gun arm and twisting it sideways.

Suddenly a shotgun blast roared out over the shouting and yelling of the kids. The lanky boy seemed to leap into the air. Bloody spray, black as oil in the moonlight, exploded from his chest. The shotgun blasted again, knocking the kid another yard before he hit the ground. He smashed face-down on the pavement, the .38 skidding away from his outflung hand. The boy's body quivered and twitched for a few seconds before going totally still.

Ty's ears were ringing from the gun roar, but there might have been silence for a moment or two. Danny and the Rasta kid had frozen and were no longer fighting him. Then Danny's cry cut the quiet, sounding as if it were ripped from his heart: "Turbo!"

Ty glanced at the body; dead kids always looked so small. Then he saw the crouching bulks of the two cops in the wash-bay shadows. The white one whipped the smoking shotgun around to target Gordon, who had his .22 aimed at Deek. The man pumped another shell into the chamber and sighted, while the black cop aimed his pistol at Wesley. Ty expected them to yell "Freeze!" but they didn't. A dark blur flashed at the edge of Ty's vision. He saw the slender little Lion, silver revolver in hand, leap to the Trans-Am's hood. Big teeth gleamed in a stark white snarl. The boy's voice was a pure animal scream, seeming too huge to come from his fragile frame at all. "THEY ON DEEK'S SIDE!"

It was true! Ty saw Deek bring the Uzi to his shoulder, aiming for the Lion. Then both cops swung their guns at him too. A voice echoed in Ty's mind, like the voice that had kept him from pulling the trigger last night. *"You be sellin ALL your little brothers, fool!"*

All three guns fired.

Markita had come running into the front of the lot just in time to see the two cops melt into the shadows of a wash bay. Their dark uniforms were perfect camouflage, except for the helmets, which looked like pale skulls floating. One carried a shotgun. Markita skidded to a stop on the gravelly asphalt, panting back her breath, and not sure why she'd come or what she expected to do now. Nearby, halfway between the wash structure and the street, the cruiser idled quietly. From beyond the flimsy tin building came the screams and the shouting of what could have been a wild kid's game except for the gunshots. Markita had heard many gang fights before, but no one she cared about had ever been involved.

The cruiser's radio spat code words and static, tuned low. It took Markita a moment to realize what was wrong with the picture. The cops hadn't called in at the first sounds of shooting; they hadn't used their siren or strobes, and now both doors stood open and all the lights were off. Only a tiny green eye that was probably the radio's pilot lamp glowed from the dark interior.

Moving warily, moon shadow going before her, Markita came up to the car. The cop had called him "junior-bad," but Markita had known he'd meant Deek. For sure there was always word about cops who took money from dealers, mostly to turn their backs but sometimes to protect them. But then there was word about everything in the city, and if it didn't touch you, you let it slide by. There was plenty of trouble going around without borrowing any.

Reaching the driver's door, scenting the cop smells she'd hated and feared half her life, Markita saw her Mace can still lying on the dash. Suddenly she wanted to run for home, like last night with Ty in the alley, and have her mother hold and comfort her even as she comforted J'row. Her mother would murmur the old words, promising that some-day everything would be all right. And in another year, when her son would be old enough to discover the street and run crying home from its terrors, she would whisper those same goddamned old promises to him. And nothing cut a kid deeper than getting promises broken.

And *nothing* was all right! Day by day the cage seemed to close in tighter around her, crowded with things that clawed and tore at each other in a blind fight for a freedom they *knew* existed but saw only as secondhand shadows behind a TV screen. It was like the ancient cartoon where a starving wolf tried to eat a picture of a Thanksgiving turkey.

She trembled at the car door. She could feel her heart pounding as the alien smells and the radio's unknown language warned her away. Then her nostrils flared: "serve and protect"! The law had just helped itself to a serving of *her*, and then stolen her only protection! More shots sounded from the rear of the lot. She scented gunpowder smoke in the air. Stay clear, girl, her instincts warned . . . be cool; steal back what's yours by right, and then run home. She thought of what Leroy had said; maybe she did just have a thing for bad-acting dudes. But that's all Ty was doing . . . acting a part that the world wrote for black kids. Bad. Cool. The only protection, pitiful as it was, that couldn't be stolen; like children not allowed to play in the real game so they made up one of their own and pretended they didn't give a shit.

Two shotgun blasts roared out. An instant later came a warning scream. It hardly seemed human, more like something Markita had heard at the zoo or maybe in an old horror movie. But the words were plain, and so was their meaning: she'd known who *they* were for a long, long time. Snatching the Mace from the dashboard, she ran for the wash structure.

Danny and the Rasta boy had stopped fighting Ty when Turbo had died. Now they were both clinging to Ty as if he alone could save them from the same. The words still echoed in Ty's head: not the warning scream, but the other words, the ones meant only for him. Maybe they'd come from God, or maybe they'd been inside him all the time and it took the little Lion's magic to set them free. It didn't matter: what is, *is*, and what ain't, ain't worth nothing. And no magic could save the little Lion.

Ty fired his .45 just as the three other guns blasted at the slender boy. Ty caught only an eye-corner glimpse of the Trans-Am's windshield exploding inward and spraying slivers of glittering glass. But the fragile little Lion was gone!

Ty had no time for miracles. His first three bullets took Deek in the chest, where his heart would have been a long time ago. Whatever had replaced it was probably cool as hell, but it wasn't black. Deek spun half around, staggering backward, two of the bullets tearing on through him. His mouth opened but no sound came out. His eyes found Ty's an instant before he fell. Ty swore they looked disappointed. The Uzi's fire cut off, its empty brass still spinning across the pavement as Deek's dead hand unclenched from the safety. But Ty didn't wait to see him go down: he emptied the rest of the .45's clip at the cops, then yelled at the small boys beside him to run. Amazingly, both obeyed, darting in opposite directions along the fence line. Ty couldn't tell if he'd hit the cops, and they were armored anyway. Again the shotgun roared. The fence mesh twanged and a strand blew out just behind Danny, but the boy kept going.

The other kids of both gangs were dashing for shelter behind Deek's car. The black cop's pistol boomed again and again. The jiggly-fat boy screamed and went down, clutching one side of the chub roll at his waist. Gordon and Wesley both grabbed him and dragged him to safety. Another shotgun blast channeled asphalt inches from the Rasta kid's feet as he doubled back to snatch up Turbo's .38 before joining the other boys behind the Trans-Am. Were these kids really that brave, Ty wondered, or just too stupid to know any better? Then he remembered the Lion. He jerked his head around, expecting to see him blown apart like Turbo. Instead, the slender boy was just leaping down from the roof of the car . . . or the sky? No miracles in Oaktown; maybe just a way past cool skate move.

The cops were still firing, bullets and shotgun loads spewing gravel and pavement chunks, some slashing the water beyond the fence. Another blast from the shotgun crashed into the vac box, slamming the sheet-metal cover against Ty's chest. The big buckshot pellets clanged something solid inside, but one ripped through and tore into Ty's leg above the knee. Ty clutched at the place, blood running hot between his fingers. He fought back the pain and stared toward the car. Would those kids let him come?

Yes! Danny and the Lion were both signaling him to run. Gordon stood, bawling orders. One twin and another of Wesley's dudes had the roly-poly kid's shirt off and were crouching beside him as he sat against the car door. Wesley and the other twin were scrambling up along the 'Am's front fender with their Uzis. Both stood and opened fire across the hood at the cops. Gordon aimed the .22 around the shattered windshield and tugged on the trigger but it seemed to be jammed. "Ty!" screamed Danny. "C'mon!"

Ty shoved the crumpled cover away, but agony lashed up his leg when he tried to put weight on it. Another bullet banged the box. Wesley and the twin must have fired half their clips, the big carbines bucking upward in their small hands, their bullets raking the wash structure's sheet metal, ricochets clanging and whining away off the heavier trusses and brace beams. The shotgun roared in return. The Trans-Am rocked on its springs as the blast blew a huge hole in the left front fender and a headlight exploded in a spray of shards. Blood spurted from Ty's leg as he tried to get up. No way!

"Bail!" he shouted to the other boys. "Run, you stupid

little suckers!" He sank down, crying, and whispered, "You poor little niggers!" He looked back toward the car. The boys were all watching him, waiting for him. Why? *What is.*

Using his good leg, gripping the box cover with one hand, Ty stood, exposed to fire from the waist up, his empty gun hot in bloody fingers. The gang kids were staring at him, wide-eyed now. Tears gleamed on Danny's face. Ty stabbed the gun at Deek's body. "Game over!" He aimed at the cops.

Markita saw Ty through the wash bay's short tunnel, over the crouching cops' shoulders. She stood at the front entrance, Mace can in hand, flinching back as full-auto fire raked the wall above the cops' heads. Moonbeams stabbed through the holes like light-show lasers while ricochets rattled and screamed all around. She'd seen Ty shoot Deek down, and then the muzzle flame from his .45 spurt out at the cops. One had grunted when a bullet hit his armor. Other bullets had hissed past her toward the street. One had thunked into the cruiser. She thought she could smell hot antifreeze. A quick glance over her shoulder showed steam ghosting up from the front of the car. Then the white cop snarled, "It's over! Bastard's own bodyguard took him out! *Animals!* Get that backup now!" Then he'd fired at Ty's little brother.

The black cop shot at the other running boys as they dashed for cover behind the dealer's car. "Got one!" he'd muttered when a fat kid went down, then cursed as he'd had to reload, and two other boys dragged the wounded kid away. He jerked the walkie-talkie from his belt, thumbed a button, and called some words, then cursed again. "Goddamn steel all around! Like a motherfuckin cage in here!"

More Uzi fire blasted from over the Trans-Am's hood.

"Get back to the car!" yelled the white cop. "Those little shitheads ain't gonna run!"

The black started to scuttle away. "Move yourself, man! We outgunned an a half!"

The white backed deeper into the bay, but suddenly stood and shouldered his shotgun. Markita gasped, seeing Ty stand unprotected.

"*He* knows!" the white cop snarled. "Nobody'll listen to those little suckers, but *he* can shit all over us!"

"So take him! Who's gonna care?" The black turned to bolt for the cruiser.

Markita leaped in front of the man, Mace can out in both hands, and sprayed him full in the face.

The big man screamed, dropping his gun and clawing at his eyes. Markita flung the can at the white cop, then tore the black's club from his belt and ran at the white. His head had whipped around when the Mace can bounced off his back, and now he ducked in time to take Markita's wild swing on his helmet.

"Nigger BITCH!" The man jammed the shotgun butt into Markita's stomach, slamming her back, then jerked up the shotgun to blow Ty away.

"Ty! DOWN!"

It was the little Lion. Ty saw him break from behind the car and race for the cop. The stupid little sucker was going try taking out a shotgun with that pussy piece of shit! To save *him!*

The other boys saw it too. Gordon roared a warning. Wesley and the twin aimed their Uzis at the cop but couldn't shoot now without hitting the Lion. The Rasta kid dashed after him with the .38. Ty saw the shotgun swing from him to the Lion. The slender boy's shape was strangely blurred, like some sort of double image of something bigger around him. The kid would vanish, Ty thought, believe!

The little nickel-plated revolver spat one flash of fire just as the shotgun blasted. Above the roar, Ty heard the Rasta boy scream the Lion's name, and Danny's voice echo it. The shotgun load blew the Lion's slim chest apart and flung his body backward against the Trans-Am's grille.

Sudden silence switched on. The shotgun slipped from the white cop's hands and hit the concrete. The man groped at his throat where the one little bullet had buried itself. Blood pumped in gushes through his fingers. He made wet, strangled sounds as he crumpled face-down beside his gun.

Ty saw the other kids gathering around the little Lion's body. From beyond the wash structure came a man's cries and curses and the sounds of puking. Then Ty saw Markita come running to him from the shadows.

Ty tried to move to her, but his leg buckled under him. He grabbed the box to keep from falling. Pain shot up his arm like he'd dipped it in fire. His sight blurred. Blackness rushed in from the edges, almost familiar now. The fog was coming back.

Dimly, Ty felt Markita take hold of him. Then a small figure appeared from nowhere to help: Danny. Ty took a few stumbling steps, one arm over Markita's shoulders, the other around his brother. Maybe this fog *was* real, he thought, the kind that drifted in off the Bay. Real or not, it was getting hard to see. Small forms surrounded him: not little angels, only kids. There were Wesley and Gordon, standing together, the other gang boys all around—except for the little Rasta, who stayed crying at the Lion's side. Scents of gunpowder and blood and kid sweat filled Ty's nostrils. Wesley was pointing. "You want we do him, man?"

It took Ty a second to realize what Wesley meant. The black cop was staggering in blind circles, trying to find the cruiser. Ty noticed two things in Markita's hand: a cop's belt radio and a microphone with a broken cord, little colored wires sticking out. That reminded him of something, but the fog was thickening, closing in, and he couldn't think very good. "No," he heard himself say. "He can't hurt us no more."

Ty tried to focus his eyes on all the young faces. For the moment there was no need to be cool or bad and they were just kids again.

"Game over," said Ty. "Go home."

The blackness took him away.

Ty woke to the sound of a young child's laughter. It wasn't an angel but it was close enough for Oaktown, and probably the closest he'd ever get to the real thing. He opened his eyes, blinking in the soft golden sunlight streaming through the window. It had that pure, clean sparkle of early morning. A square of it fell on the floor nearby, and J'row sat in the center, laughing. The little boy was naked except for baby-blue Huggies, and the sunlight shone warm and beautiful on his ebony velvet skin.

Ty blinked again as his vision came into focus like the opening scene of a movie. Danny was on the floor with J'row, his legs in a V around the child. He was beautiful too. It took Ty a second before he noticed Danny's new clothes . . . nothing showtime, just 501s that fit him right, the big Nikes he'd always wanted, and a black satin tank top his own size. His hair was still a wild bush, but it glistened now in the sun. He was sharing bites of a grape Popsicle with J'row, and both were bent over the little Speak 'N Spell

computer. Ty tried to make words, but his throat and lips
were swollen and dry and his tongue felt thick and clumsy.
He gave it up and looked around.

He was in Markita's apartment . . . in her bed. The scent
of her lingered on the pillow and sheets, waking a warmth
in his loins that surprised him. The frilly spread was folded
neatly at his feet, and he was naked beneath the single
blanket. His body felt clean, as if he'd just been bathed.
There were stiff new bandages on his forearm and around
his biceps and leg. They smelled and felt professional. There
was a tightness to the skin of his forearm that had to be
stitches . . . at least he supposed that's what stitches would
feel like. There wasn't much pain but he felt weak all over,
like when he'd had the flu and the fever had finally broken.
His eyes roamed the room; even by daylight it looked warm
and safe. Against the wall by the hallway door two skateboards stood together, his and Danny's.

Then he heard Markita laugh. "Oh, Danny, you can't
program it to *say* them kinda words."

Danny giggled . . . not a smart-ass snicker, but a sound
as innocent as J'row's, who joined in too.

Ty turned his head, squinting at the computer's little
screen. "Danny!" he croaked. "Jesus Christ, that ain't no
kinda word to be teachin a baby!"

"TY!" Danny hurled himself at the bed, all arms and
legs and elbows, landing flat on top of his brother and
hugging him in the awkward, brutal way that boys hug other
boys they love. Maybe it hurt, but Ty didn't notice. He
locked his arms around the boy and pulled him even tighter.
Danny winced a little, though he tried to hide it, and Ty
felt the bandages under his shirt. "You been shot!"

Danny smiled. "Naw. Just a cracked rib when they kick
me. Ain't nuthin."

Ty scowled. "When WHO kick you, man?" he demanded.

Danny only smiled again. "Don't matter. My heart ain't busted."

Ty studied his brother carefully, then kissed his cheek. "Yeah. Your heart be warm an strong an black, man." He added a kiss to Danny's notched ear. It was good to see the boy blush. Then he noticed that Danny's lips were almost healed and that the bruises on his face had faded.

Markita came over with J'row in her arms. She was smiling happily, but looked tired, like she hadn't slept much. "So how you feelin . . . boy?"

Ty tried to wet his lips with a dry tongue, feeling them crack when he smiled in return. "Okay . . . girl." His voice sounded like sandpaper. "Thirsty," he added.

Markita's smile brightened even more. "Just like the doctor say you be. I get you some orange juice." She turned, about to set J'row back on the floor.

"Put him here," said Ty, pushing the covers off his chest as Danny stood up.

Markita gave him the little boy. Tiny fingers, warm, sticky, and perfect, grasped Ty's, then found the little silver medallion and jingled it on its chain.

Danny slipped the Popsicle between Ty's lips. It tasted way past good. "Gots any beer?" Ty called to Markita.

Danny snickered. "Yo! Now we know he okay for sure. Word!"

Markita turned, frowning slightly. "You . . . ain't gonna keep on drinkin, Ty?"

Ty smiled, getting his lips used to it again. "Not like I done."

"Mmm." Markita opened the fridge and took out a can of Bud. "Doctor prob'ly have a cow, but it likely do you more good than orange juice right now."

Danny laughed. "He give you a testicle shot, Ty. In the butt!"

"You mean tetanus."

"Yeah. For cause why?"

"For cause rabies."

"Oh."

Markita came back with the beer. "Ty gots no probs with his balls."

Ty felt his face flush, but there was pride in Danny's eyes.

"Yo, *memsaab*, I have me a *pombe* too," said Danny.

"Huh?" said Ty.

"That Swahili for a beer an a lady you spect. Doctor dude talk like that all the time."

"Oh." Ty didn't insult the boy's dignity by saying okay. Markita handed him the beer and went back for another. Ty studied Danny's face once more. "How long it been? Almost seem like a kinda bad dream."

"Three days," said Markita, returning. "It Sunday mornin." She gave Danny the Bud and glanced out the window. "Even this goddamn city look a little better on Sunday mornins. It my day off. Mom in church."

Ty sipped beer. It opened his throat and tasted as good as the Popsicle.

"Got some soup ready for you too," Markita added. "Make it up myself."

Ty smiled. "Chicken, right?"

"Course. Everbody know chicken soup be the thing when you sick."

Danny snorted, sipping his Bud slow, like Ty. "Shit! Somebody oughta cook up bout a zillion gallons an feed it to Oaktown, man!"

Ty gave Markita an uneasy glance. "Um, what church you mom go to?"

"That big ole churchy-lookin one with the steeple, bout six blocks over. Why?"

"Oh," said Ty, feeling relieved. "Nuthin." He considered, watching J'row play with the medallion. "Guess if God ain't everwhere, He ain't nowhere. But you still gotta look for Him."

Markita gave Ty a look of speculation. "Mmm. Spose that sound right enough. Now, for sure you feelin proper, Ty? I mean, you been talkin out your head for most three days . . . angels an stuff."

"Lions an werewoofs too, man," added Danny.

Markita nodded. "Course, doctor say you likely gonna do that, what with all the blood you lose an the infection fever."

"Um, I sorry, Ty," said Danny. "I give you that affection."

"It cool, man," said Ty. "Gonna get some, best it come from my own brother." Ty glanced at his arm. "Ain't there a law say doctors gotta report all gunshot wounds?"

Markita shrugged. She sat down on the bed. One hand went to Danny's shoulder, the other stroked J'row's curls. "Used to be a law sayin we gotta ride the ass end of buses too. My mom always say they get more laws everday, an less justice. Sides, I told you bout this doctor bein from South Africa. Best believe *he* know the difference tween a law an the right thing to do!"

"But how I pay for all this fancy-ass bandage shit an shots? Man gotta live, don't he? He live round here, for sure he can't be rich."

Danny grinned, digging in his pocket and pulling out a wad of bills. "Yo! Curtis come over next mornin. Give us five bucks, man!"

"Curtis?"

"The little dude with the dreads."

"Oh."

Markita looked sad. "Poor kid. He been comin here everday. Stay a while. Seem like he crazy or somethin . . . always talkin bout lions in Jamaica."

"Lyon was his homey," said Danny. "Lyon, with a y. He the dude what help me. Make the plan to save your ass when it woulda been a lot easier just to do us both fore takin out Deek."

"Yeah," said Ty. "That woulda been the coolest way."

"Curtis one grade down from me, but I gots him in PE. I used to figure him an Lyon was homos, for cause Lyon was always so . . . I don't know, gentle, I spose I mean. Course, for sure he weren't that night! Maybe he was on somethin? He was drunk most of the time, but only Curtis knew."

"Maybe it was love?"

Danny thought a moment. "Yeah, I guess that could do it. Anyhow, Curtis always talkin up how him an his folks gonna move to Jamaica someday, when they save emselfs back enough bucks. Now Curtis tellin everbody that Lyon already gone there. That a island somewheres, ain't it?"

"Yeah," said Ty. He looked up at Markita. "What bout them other kids? What happen, after?"

"Well, they help me bring you here. It seem best, bein only a block away." She snagged a paper off the coffee table. "Made page four next day. Same ole shit bout gang violence, an how all gangs should oughta be busted up."

Ty snorted. "Be like tryin to bust up them Little Rascals."

Markita shrugged. "Seem like nobody out there see it that way. Or know what happenin in places like this. Everbody blamin it on the drugs an guns . . . like the doctor

say, treatin the symptoms stead the disease. Anyways, that
black cop sucker never know he owe his life to *you* . . . for
what it worth. He been s'pended till some sorta 'vestigation
done . . . somethin bout unproper procedures. But mostly
the paper people screamin over that white cop gettin killed.
Gonna be a big ole funeral. With honors." She offered the
paper. "Wanna read it?"

Ty shook his head. "Wonder what kinda funeral they
gonna give Turbo. Or Lyon. An what happen to them other
two dudes, the fat boy and the little one?"

"Game-Boy an Tunk?" said Danny. "Weren't nuthin major bad. Doctor fix em right here. After you. Take the
bullet out Game-Boy's chub. Shit, man, he even shake their
hands! Say, where he from, kids younger than they be
fightin! Say '*Uhuru!*' " Danny reached under the mattress
and pulled out Ty's .45. "I take it all apart, Ty. Clean it
total. Better'n new. Word! Score you new bullets too."

"He bought himself a gun book," said Markita.

Ty took the gun, but only because Danny seemed so
proud. J'row dropped the medallion and reached for it. Ty
frowned and laid it aside. "Mmm. Spose it words in a row.
Maybe kids read more if it bout stuff relate to real-time."
Then Ty smiled and gave Danny the gun. "Ain't sure now
just what I gonna do with it. Maybe you get good at fixin
our ole truck too."

Danny turned the big gun over in his small hands. "You
ain't gonna stop fightin, Ty?"

Ty touched the medallion J'row had picked up again.
"No, Danny. Word. But there other ways to fight this shit,
man. You can't just go round shootin down every hungry
kid dealin on the corners. Most of em wouldn't be if they
had some kinda . . . a . . . ."

"Option," said Markita.

Ty nodded. "Um, you figure Leroy talk to me bout that night school he goin to?"

"Course he would. Fact is, he just bout to graduate with his high school diploma. Gonna be quittin the King pretty soon to take a computer job." Markita hesitated. "Danny here been tellin me you a way past cool cook . . . if you call Burger King cookin."

"Ty ain't gonna wear him no goddamn lame little uniform!" said Danny. "We gonna score us that truck! Do us some real work!" He turned to Ty. "Huh, man? Markita tell me all bout it. Yo, Ty, me an her, we talk over all kinda shit these last days. We even went an did that uptown shoppin. Markita come an talk to Mom, tell her enough what it is so's not to worry. We even score stuff for the little kids too. Yo! We score us that truck, man. Believe! I help you after school." He flexed his thin arm. "Yo. Check it, Ty, I *need* me some buildin up! Course, you wanna go night school, that make me proud too."

Ty smiled. "Yeah? So what happen to chump change not bein cool?"

Danny shrugged. "Well, there cool, and there way past cool, Ty. So, fuck cool."

"Fuck coo," laughed J'row.

"Jesus, Danny!" said Ty.

Markita smiled. "Maybe I can get Leroy to program that into his Speak 'N Spell."

"Mmm," said Ty. "So how much of that five bucks we got us left, Danny?"

Danny's smile faded. "Only bout two. Spose that ain't enough for a truck, huh?"

"You needed them clothes, man. Same's all our brothers an sisters deserve nice stuff." Clumsily with his bandaged arm, Ty slipped off the medallion and put it on his brother.

"Here, man. This yours now. Might be some magic in it, who in hell know?"

There was a knock on the door.

Danny gripped the .45. "Motherfuckin cops been goin apeshit all over the hood!"

Finger to her lips, Markita rose and crossed quietly to the door. She peered through the peephole. Ty watched her face, but she only looked surprised. Shooting back the bolts, she pulled the door open. The Friends filed into the room, carrying their boards, Gordon leading, his eyes casually wary. There were four boys behind him, Ty saw. One was the small camouflaged kid. He wore his huge shirt open to show the white bandage, already grimy, around his ribs. Ignoring Markita—she was only a girl—they came over to the bed. Markita smiled and went to the fridge, returning with Buds for all. The kids accepted them by right, with murmured thanks.

Gordon yanked up his sagging jeans. "Yo, Ty. You cool now, man?"

Ty smiled and nodded. "I flash your sign if I knowed what it was."

Gordon shuffled his feet a moment. "Um, we ain't figured one out yet, man. It like, there only so much you can do with five fingers, y'know?" He took a gulp of beer. "Anyways, we come to, um, tell you thanks for savin our asses, man. Word! An Wesley, he say the same." He pointed out the window. "This, um, our ground now. Wesley trade us a block so's we get Tunk." He glanced at Markita. "We be watchin for dealers an shit." He turned back to Ty. "Yo, an Furball can join us, he want."

Danny looked at his brother. "Maybe part-time?"

Ty smiled. "That be cool. The right kind."

Curtis stood at Gordon's side. Gordon nudged him forward.

"Um," said the small boy. "We 'cide to give you this, man."

Ty stiffened slightly, seeing Deek's pouch. There were dark, rusty-colored stains on it.

"We took some," added Gordon. "'Spenses. But there still most five grand." He shrugged and drained his beer can. "Yo! I mean, what the fuck *we* gonna do with all that buck? Stay drunk a year? Shit, then what good we be? Only scare hell out our parents, we give it to them. An just a lotta trouble, man, if word go round we gots mega-money!"

Ty accepted the pouch from Curtis. "Thanks, man." Then he met the small boy's eyes. "I sorry over Lyon."

Curtis only shrugged. "He in Jamaica now. I see him when I get there."

Ty nodded.

Gordon set his beer can on the coffee table. The other boys chugged theirs and did the same. One of the twins burped.

"Rac, you fucker!" bawled Gordon. "Say 'scuse me, asshole!"

"I'm Ric. 'Scuse me, asshole."

Gordon sighed. "Well, see you round, Ty. Um . . . maybe, sometime we need big-dude a'vice bout somethin, we ask ya, okay?"

"Believe, Gordon. Take care now, all you dudes."

The boys turned to go. Ty saw the little nickel revolver just showing under Curtis' shirt. "Yo. What happen to the Uzis?"

The small boy faced Ty once more and shoved the dreads out of his face. "We keep one. The Crew get the other. Number three hid by for 'mergencies in neutral ground. We make a rule over it."

Ty took the .45 from Danny. "I still might be needin me a gun sometime, but maybe this one be better for you. Danny here go all through it. Trade me, man?"

Slowly, Curtis pulled out the little revolver and fingered it. "Um . . . well, it hard to score bullets for this . . . an it pretty old."

"Aw, go for it, man," advised Rac. "Heart magic's cool, but there ain't very much of it goin round."

"Or comin round neither," added Ric. "Lyon-o woulda said you need a good gun."

Curtis turned to Danny. "You figure he woulda, man?"

Danny smiled. "Believe, homey. Just cause that's what it is."

"Okay, Ty." Curtis traded guns and stuffed the big pistol in the back of his jeans. Tunk helped him cover it. "Um, see you round, Ty," said Curtis. "An, thanks, brother."

The boys filed out.

"Maybe I'm a fool," said Markita as she closed and bolted the door. "But I think I gonna feel a little bit safer walkin home nights."

"You ain't no fool," said Ty. "Believe." He studied the bloodstained pouch in his hand. "Yo, Danny. You talk to Curtis. You find out how much more money his folks need for movin to Jamaica. I think he really find his Lion-brother there."

Danny considered that. "Naw. Prob'ly just some cool dude *like* Lyon. Hell, maybe there a lot of em in Jamaica. Or somewheres. I mean, he never really belong *here*, know what I sayin? Maybe he just finally got to go home?"

Ty glanced out the window. He heard skate wheels clicking sidewalk cracks. He looked over at his own board by the door. "Mmm. Maybe you right, Danny. But I wish there was more of em here . . . whatever they are."

Danny nodded, then took a last bite of Popsicle and a

gulp of beer. "Yo, Ty! Know what? Grape Popsicle an beer sound like shit but taste way past cool!" He stared at his brother, then moved close. "Yo! Why you cryin now, man? Game over."

Ty took his brother's hand and smiled up at Markita. "Maybe it really just startin."

DIXIANA MOON

WILLIAM PRICE FOX

THE VIKING PRESS   NEW YORK

Library of Congress Cataloging in Publication Data
Fox, William Price.
Dixiana moon.
I. Title.
PS3556.O97D5   813'.54   80–51770
ISBN 0–670–27453–4

*Grateful acknowledgment is made to the following for permission to reprint
copyrighted material from other sources:*
Bourne Co. Music Publishers: Portions of lyrics from "The World Owes
Me a Living," words by Larry Morey, music by Leigh Harline.
Copyright © 1934 by Bourne Co. Copyright renewed. All rights
reserved. Portions of lyrics from "Hi-Diddle-Dee-Dee," lyrics by Ned
Washington, music by Leigh Harline. Copyright © 1940 by Bourne
Co. Copyright renewed. Used by permission.
Chappell Music Company: Portions of lyrics from "Falling in Love with
Love," by Rodgers & Hart. Copyright © 1938 by Chappell & Co., Inc.
Copyright renewed. International copyright secured. All rights re-
served. Used by permission.
Hallnote Music: Portions of lyrics from "Me and Jesus," written by Tom
T. Hall. Copyright © 1971 by Hallnote Music. International copy-
right secured. All rights reserved. Used by permission.
Edward B. Marks Music Corporation: Portions of lyrics from "Manhat-
tan," written by Richard Rodgers and Lorenz Hart. Copyright Ed-
ward B. Marks Music Corporation.
Warner Bros. Music: Portions of lyrics from "New York, New York," by
Betty Comden, Adolph Green, and Leonard Bernstein. Copyright ©
1945 by Warner Bros. Inc. Copyright renewed. All rights reserved.
Used by permission.

With love
for Sarah and Kathy and Colin.

"They tell me that in some places out on the edge they still buy lightning-rods and almost everyone you meet will be wearing the Little Wonder Electric Tibetan rheumatism ring. I know because I sold them."
—Harry Leon
Professor, How Could You!

CHAPTER

1

Some mornings my old man would sit on the edge of the bed with so many plans and so much energy he'd pick up the phone and dial seven numbers. Any numbers. Someone would answer. Then he'd roll into his master-of-ceremonies delivery. "O.K., world, Joe Mahaffey here. Get your flat ass ready!" And Mom would groan, "Jesus, Joe, knock it off. When are you going to grow up?" She might as well have been talking to a tornado.

We owned this nightclub in Lorraine, about an hour out from Pittsburgh. Mom hopped the tables and did the salads, and when Dad went up on stage she'd handle the bar. When she was younger she'd sung a little and danced a little. She always said she'd peaked too early. I remember one night she was up to her elbows in a sinkful of beer glasses and Dad was mopping down the duckboards and she said, "There's no business like the fringe of show business. Right, Joe?" Then she pushed her hair back with her wrists and took a long hard look at me. My name's Joe too. "I hope you're smarter than this idiot." Don't get me wrong, Mom loved him and she still loves him, but back then she definitely had other plans for me.

Dad took us through a Spanish-period "Granada" where the walls were covered with bullfighters and dancing senoritas on black velvet. He tried "Gay Paree" with red-checked tablecloths and Toulouse-Lautrec wallpaper and Edith Piaf on the juke. Some Philadelphia hustler unloaded 144 salt and pepper shakers on us shaped like the Eiffel Tower; they're still around. Then it was "Broadway Nights" with a Manhattan-skyline shot and the big-band sound. We ran through the Irish look, the Italian look, the Hollywood look. If there'd been an Eskimo troupe or a gypsy caravan coming through he would probably have jumped on that too. Everyone kept telling him to go straight country-and-western and keep it there. But he hated country. He hated western. He'd load up the juke with old Sinatras, old Benny Goodmans, old Glen Millers. If it was old enough and a disaster enough, we had it. But through it all our regular customers and the Happy Hour crowd stayed loyal. To them it didn't matter if it was Maurice Chevalier on the juke or Nanook of the North. One time he had it set up like a Swiss village with the Matterhorn in the background; we were all dressed up in lederhosen. There was this customer on the bar looking it over and grimacing. "Joe, what in the hell goes on with you? No one's paying good money to see this crap." Dad winked at him. "Stick around, cowboy, you just don't know class when you see it. You watch, they're going to love this concept. Let me tell you something, customers aren't stupid." The guy finished his drink. Then he slid his glass back for a refill. "The hell they ain't."

Dad played the trumpet, piano, and guitar and did the MC'ing. He even did a little singing. Up under the pin light with his cigar and waggling his yellow skimmer and telling Vegas jokes he looked great. And every move he made I was mimicking as I swept the floor, did the glasses, and polished down the backbar. Dad broke me in on the sound and light board before I was eleven and on my twelfth birthday gave me my first shot at MC'ing.

Some nights when it was late and the crowd was thin he'd let me stay out there on the mike under the lights. And every time I did I'd get this great feeling that everyone was dead wrong and he was dead right. With the right combination and a little luck we could make it work and really make some money.

In the wintertime Lorraine is pretty grim. All you can do is shoot baskets at the gym or hang around the Burger King or hit the movies out at the mall. About twice a month the Pico ran a cartoon festival: eight, nine, ten of them all back to back. I guess I really loved them all, but way back then there was one that hit me right between the eyes with what Mom called the mark of the gypsy. It was "The Grasshopper and the Ants," the oldest story going. Ants work; grasshopper play. Ants live; grasshopper die. In the Disney version the fun-loving grasshopper gets caught in a snowstorm with a pretty stiff windchill factor and freezes solid. Mom said if he'd been a member of ASCAP he could have picked up some Florida bookings. Anyhow, the hardworking ants feel sorry for him and bring him inside to the fire and thaw him out. When he comes to and limbers up he picks up his fiddle and starts sawing away on his old summer song.

"Oh the world owes me a living . . .
Zooma-Zooma-Zooma-Zooma-Zoom."

The ants join in the chorus and they all sit around little mushroom tables drinking out of acorn cups and having a great old time until the credits start rolling and the lights come up.

Once in a while four or five bars of a song will get in your head and just seem to stay there. Well, that grasshopper's "zooma-zooma" got in on me and never came out. At first I thought it was just a little patter I'd picked up to step over sidewalk cracks and practice chip shots with. But deep down it was setting up like cement. I'd sing it going to school. I'd whistle it out at second base. On a slow grounder I'd time it out with a slow zooma-zoom. On a fast one, I'd speed it up. I was on the high-school golf team and I'd whisper an easy zooma on the backswing and a long zooma on the follow-through. It's also the greatest thing in the world for getting the short putts down. We lived about a hundred yards from the club and at night I'd lie there sticking my fingers in under my eyes and moving the moon from one side of the Coca-Cola sign to the other with that grasshopper rhythm ticking through my teeth, making plans. I had it figured I'd be holding down second base for the Yankees in the spring and summertime, and then after the Series I'd pick up the golf tour until spring training started down in Fort Lauderdale. When I hit thirty-five I'd hang up the spikes but I'd stay on the tour; meanwhile I'd be checked out as chief pilot for Pan American on the New York to Paris run.

One night when I had the moon balanced dead level with the *a* in COLA and doing my old "zooma-zooma" it hit me that the greatest name in the world for our place was just that: "Coca-Cola Moon." In the morning Dad said he liked it but there was no way he could build a club around it. He said to forget it. If Mom and Dad ever get divorced it will be about something like this. She liked it and billed it up on the backbar mirror in purple, pink, and yellow as the latest thing up from Jamaica. It was rum, Coke syrup, and orange juice over cracked ice garnished with a pineapple wedge and a cherry and served in a coconut shell. It was a red-hot item with the college kids for about ten days, and then, whap! Nothing. Dad said we were too far north for exotic drinks. But Mom wouldn't let go. It's funny how they'd argue sometimes about everything: the menu, the music, even the setting on the damn air conditioner until they wouldn't even be looking at each other. And then later, in the middle of a show, Dad would hop off the stage and drag Mom out from behind the bar into some great time step or some old slow-beat samba. Their fights were the best floor shows we had going, and the beer crowd said it was a marriage made in heaven.

The day I finished high school I decided to make some actual money and got a bellhop job at the Hotel Holiday up in the Catskills. It was a big place with four hundred rooms, two pools, and a seven-thousand-yard golf course. After the club hours the ten hours on the floor were like a vacation. The money was great. The food was great. The women were great. My first month there I met Dolores. She was five foot ten plus her five-inch Puerto Rican beehive and five-inch stiletto heels, which shot her up to a cool six foot eight. She had raven hair, brown eyes, and legs so long and slim and smooth they'd drive you to the wall. At night in her black Latin satin with orange panels, lapels, and trim she looked like a New Orleans float. Dolores worked in the coffee shop and hooked on the side. She taught me the samba, the rumba, the cha-cha-cha, and the tango. God, could she tango. One day she got lucky and met Bennie Ross, this big New York tycoon. Bennie asked Jerry, the superintendent, if she was hooking. Jerry said no. He asked me and I told him she'd been raised in a convent. Bennie decided to believe this and it became the Big Love. Not Dolores's; Bennie's. Now he had to have her. He started camping out in the coffee shop all morning, every morning. He'd sit on the counter eating bagels and cream cheese and writing her notes on the back of his calling cards. She showed them to me. "Dolores, I love you. $350, Room 306. Bennie." "Dolores, I love you. $400, Room 306. Bennie." He kept running up the ante. But Dolores kept saying no. Finally it hit $700 and she couldn't turn it down. That night they went to Bennie's three-room, $200-a-night corner suite overlooking the mountains. God knows what happened in the bed, but in the morning they had breakfast together. Then it was lunch, then dinner, and then breakfast again. Bennie and Dolores had become a couple.

Bennie was five foot two with eyes of blue and a flat sixty. Next to Dolores he looked like a dachshund following a full-grown Doberman. You'd see them every-

where. On the golf course. At the pool. At the midnight
snack. Strolling along the nature trail. You'd see little
Bennie and big Dolores sitting at the bar. She'd be
knocking down six-dollar champagne cocktails and he'd
be sipping Manhattans. Dad says people who drink
Manhattans are out of their heads. I've seen him actually
refuse to make them. Anyhow, it was kind of funny and
kind of sad seeing little Bennie there with Dolores. He'd
have to reach up to put his arm around her shoulder, and
he'd cock his head up like a puppy and sing to her. It was
a golden oldie: "Falling in love with love is wonderful . . ."

Bennie had this murder Seventh Avenue accent. The *g*
in "falling" would hang out there long enough to make the
brandy glasses tremble. The "wonderful" would come
through like he had a mouthful of hot beets. But it was
music for Bennie, and Dolores didn't seem to mind. With
those eyes and lashes and that dark Latin look there was
no telling what she was thinking. Once in a while when
the bar wasn't busy she'd call me over. "Joe, how about
we do a little cha-cha-cha?"

I'd say, "O.K."

She'd say, "Bennie say it's O.K. with him."

Bennie would nod.

And out on the floor she'd say what she always said:
"For as you know Bennie doesn't dance." It wasn't so
much the accent as it was the "for as you know" that got
me. It had a formal English quality that had come a long
way from the sugarcane fields of old Puerto Rico.

Two years at the Holiday were enough. I'd learned a
lot. How to spot the big tippers. The no-tippers. Whether
they were married or living together. If they were fag,
dike, horny, or dangerous, or just poker players in from
the Midwest looking for an honest game. If you bellhop
too many years you get caught up in it. You either go all
the way and become superintendent, which is straight
hustle—car washes and waxes, laundry, dry cleaning,
late booze, late food, and women—or you start getting
service stripes out on the floor running errands and

starving. I went home and took Ma's advice and put in my time out at State College. I came out with a straight C average in business administration and couldn't even make the golf team. I'd wasted four good years. Then it was back to the club. The place had a North African look with big glossies of Bogart and Bergman and was called "The Casablanca." In the old days, Mom and Dad would have had everyone wearing French Foreign Legion hats with white scarves and the wallpaper would be desert fortifications and stacked M-1 rifles. But the Globe Tool and Die Plant down the road had folded and the seventeen thousand Lorrainians had dropped to fifteen thousand. The town was dying. Except for the glossies and the Casablanca red neon it was the same old place with the same old clientele on the same old stools watching television. And they were still calling it what they always called it, "Joe's."

A month later it officially became Joe's. There was no big ceremony or announcement in the papers. It was just a simple name change in the Yellow Pages and THE CASABLANCA sign coming down and JOE'S going up. Mom said it would save a fortune in neon and decorations but I'll never forget the trapped look on Dad's face when they slid in the pinball machines and shuffleboard where the stage had been. I'd never seen the look before. It was saying something we'd always known but none of us had ever admitted. Joe's had simply become what it always had been, a friendly neighborhood bar out on Route 40 next to the Burger King and three hundred yards from the cutoff.

That night I lay awake watching the moon coming up over the Coca-Cola sign and decided I was going to leave. Chicago was three hundred miles west, New York four hundred and fifty east. It would be easier getting a job in Chicago. It was closer to home and I had friends there from school. But New York City was New York City. I decided to decide at the exact moment the moon cleared the sign. The moon made its move and I made mine. As it pulled away from the red border I knew where I was going was four hundred and fifty miles east and it was New York City.

The first night view of Manhattan from the plane set me up forever. I picked out the Empire State Building, the World Trade Center, the United Nations. Even the Statue of Liberty. And the minute I saw the skyline, the way it was on every postcard and every movie I'd ever seen, I knew that this was it. This was where I was going to live and love and marry and make a million dollars. They could even bury me out in Queens.

The cabbie was a New York fast talker. His name was George. I liked the way he whipped across the six lanes like he owned them. I even liked the machine-gun chatter of the meter heading for fifteen dollars. And then I realized it was midnight.

"George?"

"Yeah."

"How'd you like to make ten bucks in thirty seconds?"

He glared in the mirror. "Forget it, buddy."

I laughed and elbowed up. "I'm straight. It's something else." I handed him the ten. He slowed down to see if it was real and hear the catch.

"I know it's crazy but it's my first trip in. It's my damn birthday."

"And?"

"And I want you to sing 'Happy Birthday.' "

"Jesus! I really get the creeps." He thought about it for a minute. "O.K., what's your name?"

"Joe."

He sang it straight through. I said, "Terrific. Now pull into the next booze store. You and me are going to drink a couple bottles of champagne." I told him I wanted to drink it in the absolute center of the absolute center of town. We wound up on the Public Library steps at Fifth Avenue and Forty-second Street up between the lions. The store on Third Avenue had stiffed me twenty-six dollars a bottle for Mumm's '69, but it was worth it.

George gave me a cigar and we sat there like kids, yakking about the Yankees and the Jets and the Knicks. I couldn't believe all the cabs coming down Fifth. I counted seventeen in a row before the first real car came along. It was a big black Mercedes 600 with drawn shades. When George left we shook hands like long-lost brothers. Then I just sat there draped over the steps and staring up at the two o'clock moon sliding across the slot down Forty-first Street. I kept working on the champagne and smoking the cigar and thanking God I was out of school and out of Lorraine and on my own and right here in the middle of the middle of everything. I kept saying, "Jesus! Jesus! New York City! *New York City!*" Everything was backlighted like Dad's wallpaper and stage curtains during his Broadway Nights period, and it was so great I could hardly stand it. The cabs with their yellow running lights were barreling along south going sixty. And the mix of rubber and gas and exhaust smelled like fast cars and big money and the tall furred women waiting for the limos up at the Plaza. Up and down Fifth Avenue I counted nine or ten blocks of lights staying green and staying green. Crosstown they were staggered: Madison green, Park red, Lexington green. In Manhattan it's red and green. *Stop* and *Go*. There's no *Caution*, and it was exactly what I wanted. I stretched out on the steps with my feet up on my suitcases and my hands behind my head, looking straight up at the sky where the stars would be if there wasn't so much ground light, and absolutely knew, I absolutely *knew*, that this was where I belonged. Then I got up and cupped my hands around my mouth and roared so loud I almost tore my throat out. "O.K., out there! It's Joe Mahaffey! *Get your flat ass ready!*"

I was so cranked up I trotted up to the top step. Then I did one of Dad's little six-beat crossovers between the pillars. And then it was like I was behind a camera and watching myself coming down the steps. Two steps down and one step back. Then two more down and one more back. I had to look crazy and ready for the net and the

paper slippers. But it's the kind of thing you can do in
Manhattan. People think you're hyperventilating. Or
trying out for Broadway. Or high on hash, or in love, or
you have a reservation for a river-view room down at
Bellevue. I had the phantom fiddle tucked in under my
chin and I was sawing away. It was the old "Grasshopper
and the Ants" song, and it never sounded better.

> Oh the world owes me a living . . .
> Zooma-Zooma-Zooma-Zooma-Zoom.

Two days later I dropped into Careers Unlimited on
Forty-second Street across from Bryant Park. The manager, Carson Miller, had some hard facts about life in the
big city. With my B.A. in nothing and two years at the
Holiday and working with Dad I was qualified for assistant bartender and there were no openings. Carson Miller
didn't waste any words.

"Mahaffey, in New York it's best to have a job. Any
job." He let the "any" hang in the air for three or four
beats. "It keeps you from looking unemployed." I was
carrying about eight hundred dollars, but with New York
prices it was going fast. I made some rapid rearrange-
ments downward. "Well, how about this 'any' job?"

"That, I can do for you." He shook out two cigarettes
and lit them. I figured it was some grim delivery job and a
great chance to start at the bottom. It was assistant
manager of a hustle called Danceland, and I jumped for it
like a trout.

For a first job in Manhattan, Danceland was perfect.
The staff was sharp and good-looking and they all seemed
to be going places. A lot of them had Off-Broadway parts
and every girl was a looker. The hundred dollars a week
was tough, but if you nailed a customer to a Silver Plan or
a Gold Plan it was a flat twenty-five bucks commission.
But the best news at Danceland Fifty-seventh Street was
Monica Murphy, a tall, dark-haired, darked-lashed beauty with Miss America legs and a smile that could wipe you

out. She had this half-inch snow-white birthmark running through her hair and it was gorgeous. She also had this great ballroom carriage and when she crossed the floor people took a long, long look. She was also as Irish as Hogan.

One day I saw her sitting alone at the counter at Chock Full O'Nuts on Fifty-ninth Street. I'd decided to come on strong and avoid the old question-and-answer routine, which can bog down fast and stay there. As I came up I gave the stool next to her a hard spin. "You know what my old man calls this?" It was a low, vinyl-covered, chrome-trimmed backless job.

She looked up like I was a shade crazy. "Calls what?"

"This stool." I sat down and did a full revolution like an idiot. "Fast seat. He calls them fast seats. Greatest thing in the world for turnover. You see, a drunk will slide off and a bum can't handle the back pain."

I pointed at her feet. Beautiful ankles. "Now, if you didn't have a footrest, the circulation would get cut off. That speeds things up, too."

She sipped her coffee and watched me in the mirror. Then she cocked her head. "How do you come by so much fascinating information?"

I let the sarcasm slide by and kept on talking about how the wall-to-wall mirrors in Chock Full O'Nuts keep everybody on edge and staring straight ahead. Then I pointed at a brooder hunched in over two hot dogs and a cup of coffee. "He won't be here five minutes. Watch." I timed him. During the four minutes it took him to leave we isolated and timed three or four other cases and clocked them. And then all of a sudden we were getting along like bandits.

We had dinner that night. The next day was Saturday and we did every stupid thing a hick tourist does on a package plan. We went to Coney Island. We climbed the Statue of Liberty and magic-marked our names and hometowns in behind the eyes. We went around Manhattan on the Circle Line and even paid four dollars to check

out the skyline from the top of the Empire State Building.
That night we were down at Nick's in the Village. I got
her in a back booth and was telling her about Dad
breaking me in on the stage and how I'd never been the
same since. She was probably glassy-eyed from my
nonstop talking, but all of a sudden she lit up and put her
hand over my mouth. "I got to tell you how I got started.
You're not going to believe this."

Monica was from Lima, Ohio, and she'd been here for
three years trying to make it on Broadway. She'd had a
couple small parts Off-Broadway but each time the show
closed and nothing came of it. She told me that when she
was seven her father, in storybook fashion, went out one
night for a loaf of bread and never came back. Her mother
worked, and that stuck Monica with babysitting three
kids from five years old down to two. She pushed her hair
back with her little fingers. God, she was beautiful. "I'd
be Spider-Man one week, then Road Runner the next. I'll
bet I logged in four thousand hours of Bugs Bunny. Then
some nights I'd come on with a cigarette and a holder and
a cloche hat and kill the house with a medley of Cole
Porters." She leaned on her elbows and closed her eyes
and sang the top four lines of "I Love Paris." She sat back
and sipped her beer. Then she laughed. "Well, Joe, so
much for humble show-biz beginnings."

All of a sudden I wanted a lot more than just getting her
in bed. I held my hand over my heart and cut my eyes at
the ceiling. It was one of Dad's old routines. "Madame, I
believe I'm falling in love with you." I was joking, but I
was pretty close to meaning it. Dad taught me how to
work a stage and time a joke. He also taught me the old
six-card dodge where you pick a guy's card by watching
his pupils. It comes in handy in poker and handling the
bar drunks. It's also a pretty good weather vane when
you're dealing with women. Something happened in her
eyes. Something had scared her. Like a fool I asked her,
"What's wrong?"

"You really want to know?"

And like a bigger fool I said, "Yes."

"Joe, don't be making any plans about us." She took my hands. "No, I don't mean it like that. I mean . . . Joe, I'm living with somebody and . . ."

I raised my hands like I was stopping traffic and snapped my fingers four or five times. Then I gave her my biggest grin. "Hey, don't worry about it. I thought it was something serious."

I started taking her out to the ball games and we kept going to the movies and trying out the small cheap restaurants. But every night stopped at the door. She was living with this director, and everything was still sitting on dead center. Summer rolled in, and I went home for my vacation. For two weeks I listened to Dad's plans about taking the JOE'S neon down and reopening as the "Club Zanzibar." The idea sounded fine, but the hooker was he wanted me to stay out there and help out. Mom backed me up when I said no, but I still felt pretty guilty about pulling out and heading back to Danceland.

And then it was fall '76 and the Yankees were in the Series and even the Jets were looking good. October is a great month in Manhattan. There's a snap in the air and the women dress sharper in their fall outfits. The new shows open and everyone seems to have more money and everything seems to be happening at once. It must have rubbed off, because all of a sudden I decided what I needed to make Monica forget the director was to get the hell out of Danceland and get me a real job. I began checking the want ads and went out on a string of interviews. And then, just as I had decided to take a job as an advertising trainee, Carson Miller over at Careers Unlimited called me in with a red-hot lead. He shook out two cigarettes. This time I lighted them. "Mahaffey, I think I can double your salary. Maybe triple it. Can you sell?"

"Damn right. Hey, it's not insurance?"

"No. No insurance."

He slid me a sales quiz. "Standard procedure. It keeps

the nuts out." He gave me a pencil and pointed me at a cubicle. I could have passed it with sticks from across the room.

Do you like to be in crowds? Yes.

Do you prefer baseball to listening to music? Yes.

Do you like being at the end of the line? No.

Carson checked the answers. "O.K., Joe, I'm saying you've been in the city five years. I'm scratching off Danceland. They might think you're a fag. You've sold hardware and encyclopedias and done a little ad work. If they want to check it out I'll handle the background, O.K.?"

"You're the doctor."

Then he spun his Roto-File for the phone number and slung his feet up on the desk. "How soon can you move?"

With the money Miller was talking about I figured I'd wear Monica out with dinners, shows, champagne, roses. "Give me about twelve minutes."

"Now you're talking." He winked. "Bet you a double Scotch I'll close this right now."

"You're on."

He dialed Pioneer Packaging out in Omaha and asked for Edgar Greene, the V.P. "Edgar! Carson Miller. On that trainee slot. I've got you a live one. You'll love him." He paused to listen.

"No, this one's mature. He's twenty-six, five ten, blond, and good-looking. The receptionists will eat him up."

He listened again.

"Sure he's sold. Done advertising work. Even bell-hopped. Edgar, if this son of a bitch can't ask for an order, nobody can. . . ." He drummed his fingers as he listened. Then he smiled. "Does Mahaffey sound Jewish? Joe Mahaffey, an apple-pie name you can't forget." He winked at me.

"O.K., Edgar, we're in business." He hung up, stood up, and we shook hands.

"They're paying the agency fee. Joe, you play your cards right and you got the best sales job in the country. This is a first-class outfit. O.K., let's have that drink."

CHAPTER

2

Pioneer Printing and Packaging is based in Omaha and their big accounts are out there in the Big Eight country: Ralston Purina, General Mills, Quaker Oats, and the meat and candy companies around Chicago. From the New York office we handle everything east of Pittsburgh, which means I can whip out to see the folks when I make any calls in Pennsylvania. Herb Bronson, who had been with Pioneer for seven years, had quit to go with Klear-tone Printing in Yonkers. I was his replacement, and they gave me his office in a building on Park and Forty-seventh with this great view of everything. South, the Brooklyn Bridge; north, the Triboro. I could see right down the stacks of Sunshine Biscuits and American Chicle out in Long Island City and when it was clear all the way out the Northern State Parkway to Jones Beach. I also had a break here that Carson Miller forgot to tell me about. Every June, Ben Costo and Jake Muller, the other two salesmen, and I take turns and go out to the plant to see the new equipment and spend some time with Ernie Wayne, our sales correspondent. When we head back east, it's in a brand-new air-conditioned Olds 88 with a

15

tape deck for doing call reports, power seats, power
windows, power everything.

Costo took me out on my first call. I was trying to learn
how to figure ink coverage. How to price. How to pitch.
We made only two calls that first day before we slid into a
deli, bought a picnic spread, and drove out to a park
overlooking the Hudson. Costo had a four-inch-high
sandwich: a double order of corned beef, a double order of
mozzarella cheese. He knocked down a kosher pickle as
thick as my wrist, a quart of chocolate milk, and a big
twin-pack of Fig Newtons. Costo was fat. Lying out there
on the grass his zipper was over a foot long of solid strain,
and I knew he'd never worked hard. He had to be smart.
Costo says there's only one way to sell and that's to go out
and get in trouble and then dig your way out. Of all the
advice I've ever heard and the sales aids I've ever read
this is the only thing that ever stuck. Costo also liked
selling. He knew packaging machinery and bags and
laminations and was sharp on analyzing process work.
People liked him; they could count on him. But Costo had
two killer problems. One was his 240 pounds on his five
foot seven frame. The other was he was a sweater.

One day we're pulling into the parking lot at Elgin
Bread over in Newark. It was cold—twenty, twenty-five
degrees—and here he was drying his hands on his pants.
The steering wheel was soaked, and he hadn't even cut
the engine. The purchasing agent, Tom Horner, had a
sign on his desk: "Salesmen will confine their presenta-
tions to five minutes or less." *Five minutes* was underlined
in red. The minute we came in he turned over an egg
timer. Sand operated. With the sand running and Costo
sweating it was a damn circus. I sat there watching
Horner grind him down and wondered why I'd ever left
Danceland. Costo spent two full minutes discussing the
weather. The roads. The inflation. By the time he'd laid
out his printing samples he was down to two. The sweat
was beading on his nose. It was dripping on his cellophane samples and shining there. Right in the middle of

the pitch the time ran out. I figured Horner would flip the timer over and give him five more. Wrong. He stood up and stuck his hand out. Then, left-handed, he pressed the buzzer to send in the next peddler. Costo got his handshake in. Then he started scooping up his samples. I got his hat and coat. Out in the hall the samples were sliding. He couldn't hold them. He had to kneel down to get them back in his case. Then he mopped down, blowing. "One of these days I'm going to crawl over that desk and make him eat that goddamn timer." Out in the car he gripped the wheel until his fingers turned white.

"Kid, you want that goddamn account?"

"Costo, you don't want to do that."

"The hell I don't. Take the son of a bitch. Take him, he's yours."

There were accounts that Costo made me wait out in the car on. He'd wink. "No hard feelings, kid, but this is my old ace in the hole. When you start landing the big ones keep the damn office out. Keep everyone out. The day you leave Pioneer you want to be able to go out like Bronson. Go out smart. You want to be able to go down the list and say, 'This is my account, this is my account, and this is my account, and they're all going with me.' " He slid his sample and attaché cases out of the back seat. "You think about it. I won't be long. Play the radio if you want to."

After a week with Costo I had a week with Jake Muller. Making a call with old Jake was a nonstop running lecture. Every move had a reason. Every reason had a reason. He'd read every sales book and sales manual ever printed and he kept a list of what he called "sales tools." How to look into the purchasing agent's eyes. How to sit. How to cross your legs. What to do with your hands. How to carry your sample case left-handed to keep your right pants legs from getting slick. How to move from generalities to hard specifics. How to stay there. He kept another list of one-liners he'd heard on TV and clipped out of *Reader's Digest*. He even had a system for checking them off to prevent repeating. He had pads and notebooks and date books and about nine ball-points riding in a vinyl sleeve in his shirt pocket. But his long ball was a steno book with a red line down the center. On the left he'd write positive. On the right negative. For every account he'd have two lists in descending order of importance. "Kid, this way I always know where I am. This way there's no surprises; no embarrassments. You know what my motto is?"

"What's that, Jake?"

"Cover yourself. Always cover yourself."

Jake was also one killer dresser. One day we were sitting in the bullpen at Union Stores on Forty-second Street and he flicked his pants up to show me he was wearing four-inch black socks. The receptionist thought he was crazy and dove back into her magazine. "Kid, you've got to dress down. Way down. You wear those hundred-dollar Italian shoes and socks that run up to your knees and they think you're too good for them." He sat closer, whispering faster. "You better listen to me. I'm telling you something important." We went into the purchasing agent and got a color approval on a polyethylene bread overwrap. Later at lunch he was having his one watered bourbon for the day. "Kid, when I first started selling I used to love to have it rain. I mean it. I'd get my ass so wet I'd come in looking like a cocker spaniel. I'd let the purchasing agent know that I didn't mind getting wet. They don't forget something like that. Of course I'm a little too old for that game now. But if I was in your shoes I'd be listening to the weather report. If it's going to rain, lay you out an old suit."

Except for my trouble with Monica, who was still living with her director, who was still promising her he would get her on Broadway, my first two years at Pioneer were pretty smooth. Mom had eased Dad into delaying the Club Zanzibar move and they were still clicking along with Joe's. But in the third year everything started changing. The Japanese had gone into the converting business, and sales and profits began dropping like a stone. In two months I lost United Shirts, which was good for $60,000 a year every year, Helm's Pretzels out in Wilkes-Barre for another $48,000, and Soft Weave Knit Wear, $26,000. And then it was December and all of a sudden I was right in the middle of losing Fried Rite Potato Chips out in Riverhead, New York. The problem with Fried Rite wasn't the Japanese; it was this local printer, AAA Packaging in Brooklyn, who can ship five hundred pounds with no upcharge. We have to ship five thousand or the freight eats us up.

Most companies have their big party at Christmas and there's a lot of promotions and bonuses floating around. But in sales, forget it. December 25 means you've got one more week to ship and get your billings up. So while there's some tinsel and streamers and eggnog pouring, and maybe some ass-grabbing in the supply room, most sales parties are pretty grim because there's always some guy with a bad territory over at the water cooler sweating out when the boss is going to tell him about the ghost of Christmas future. We were too small to really have a party, but Costo lugged in a tree and Jake rounded up some flowers. I picked up some Scotch and we all chipped in and bought Ethel Bernstein, over at the answering service, a sweater set with pearls around the collar and cuffs. As we stood around drinking and eating the hors d'oeuvres that Ethel had brought in, listening to Costo bitch about the Jets, I knew Fried Rite was dead and that if I didn't land a volume account pretty soon this might be my last Christmas with old Pioneer.

It was Thursday and I'd driven out the 120 miles to tell Fried Rite the sad story. I got it over with fast and headed for the first bar down the road. Rudolph's is your standard neighborhood bar. A couple of pinball machines, a shuffleboard down the side, and two windows of beer neon. An old Joan Crawford movie was on TV, but the sound had been cut off and the picture was flickering. Hard-boiled eggs, cheese crackers, and small-bore breath cleaners were lined up down the backbar. I checked over the snack items, but there wasn't anything new. When you're in packaging you look at things differently and you wind up seeing things differently. Once in a while I catch myself walking in the gutter looking for wrappers and bags. The average person looking at an angle rack of Beech-Nut chewing gum probably sees the yellow cellophane and the tear-tape tab. Me, I see the red-and-green Beech-Nut logo with the white registration on the trademark. Beech-Nut is a bitch on specs. If that hairline registration on the acorn isn't right they ship the whole thing back. They buy a hundred thousand pounds at a crack. I've called on Beech-Nut about a dozen times now. They're as nice as they can be to salesmen. Hell, they ought to be, it's up in Canojoharie, New York, three hundred miles from nowhere and in the middle of the snow belt. You can buy them drinks and they'll tell you all about the Baseball Hall of Fame over in Cooperstown. As for getting business, forget it. But it looks good on the call reports and makes Omaha think I'm breaking my ass getting up there and smooth enough to get them out for lunch. As I signaled Rudolph for another draft I saw a calling card Scotch-taped to the mirror. It read Brody Bags, Inc., Riverhead, New York.

"You know Brody?"

"Sure thing."

He told me Brody was an inventor and his plant was only three blocks away. I tore open a Slim Jim hot sausage and checked the printing code on the back seam. It was Bestprint out of Asbury Park. "He been out here long? I never heard of him."

"About a year. He's up from Georgia or Carolina. One of them jungles." He drew himself a short beer, "He used to be in show biz. Carnivals or something."

"What's his line?"

"Bags. Plastic bags." He finished his beer and rinsed his glass. Dad does this; the second he finishes a beer he washes the glass and puts it in the rack. "That's all that crazy bastard's got on his mind. That and some moron circus he keeps talking about."

Most people take bags for granted. They probably think of them as extensions of socks, or something the gypsies whipped off crossing the deserts, or don't even think about them at all. They can't tell a back-seamed bag from a tube bag, and wouldn't know a satchel bottom or a tin-tie duplex if it bit them. But in packaging you've got to figure over half the market uses some kind of bag, so you damn well better know them.

I phoned Brody from Rudolph's and he said if I hurried over he'd spend a few minutes with me. At first I thought he was the janitor. His right forefinger had been cut off at the second knuckle and his nose looked like it had been broken three or four times. He had red curly hair and freckles back to his ears, and propped on the back of his head was a tan Fort Worth Stetson that must have set him back two hundred bucks. Danceland wouldn't have let him in the door. But in a big, rough-cut way he was good-looking. He was on the phone. I figured him for around forty-five, about six foot one and 210 pounds. He was giving the other guy about ten percent of his attention. The rest was on some legal paper he was reading and frowning at. Finally he said, "Ben, old buddy. A customer just came in and he's waving an order right in my face. Let me ring you back. . . . Sure I'll call. Now don't move, boy. Be right back at you."

He was southern. A real mush-mouth. He hung up and stood up. He had big hands and shook so hard I forgot about the finger. I said I was sorry it was so late because it would have been nice having lunch together. He popped his hands together. "Hot damn, I knew I was forgetting something. I ain't eaten." He flipped the folder open and showed me the gold sheriff's seal. Then he hooked his head and winced. "Women. They'll bring you down. They'll get you every time."

I thought of Monica sleeping with that damn director. "Yeah, I know what you mean." He shoved the folder in the drawer. "Let me take a leak. Then I'll take you to a first-class eating establishment. And little buddy, everything's on Buck Brody. Call me Buck, O.K.?"

"O.K., Buck."

Buck Brody had fourteen calendars of long-legged nudes on the walls from Kleartone and Rose Hill Printing, which meant he was buying printed cellophane or polyethylene. On the back wall was an old circus photograph. A troupe was lined up with the front rows on their knees and the back row standing. I looked for him in the back. Then I found him in the middle of the front. He was grinning out from under one of those foot-high white shako hats the drum majors wear. He seemed to be in charge. Brody didn't flush the john and I didn't hear him until he slapped me on the back. "You like the circus?"

"Sure. I catch Ringling every year at the Garden."

He steered me through the door, frowning. He had on black cowboy boots with ruby and rhinestone inserts in the toe. He called them "Mexican fence climbers." As he locked the door he said, "Ringling! Shit man, Ringling's like a halftime show at a football game. One of these days I'll show you a real circus. Let's roll."

The 29A Diner was a half mile away. From the corner booth we could watch the plant. Buck introduced me to Fred, the owner. He ordered a steak with two orders of hash browns and four kinds of vegetables. He talked loud, but with his mush-mouth delivery, I had to listen close. "Fine place, right?" He repeated himself a lot. "Ain't this a fine place?"

"Right. Looks good to me."

Buck held his fork like a trowel and ate fast. When the steak was gone he mopped the plate down with a piece of bread until it was shining. I figured him from Mississippi or Alabama. He lit a cigar, took two long puffs, and sighed and closed his eyes. And then for no reason except the meal was over he launched into a story. "Friend, let me tell you something. I was in Savannah, Georgia, one time and I saw a wharf rat sitting on a trash can eating an onion." He drummed his fingers for more of my attention. "Now a wharf rat, friend, is the smartest animal on four feet. And that there rat was sitting there eating that onion and I want you to know that that rat was crying. I mean tears. Real tears. Tears like you and me cry. And I stood there and I watched that rat and I said that things have really got to be pretty tough if a rat can't make out any better than that." Fred took the plates away and Buck forked into his apple pie. "Whenever things get rough in this business I always remind myself of that rat."

He slid a quarter in the juke and punched down two country-and-western bleeders. Then he ordered another beer. Suddenly he whipped around. A customer was buying a bag of O.K. Potato Chips. He whispered quickly, "Watch! Watch this!" The man was biting off the blue corner of the bag and Buck was on his feet. He rushed across the room with his hand raised. "Mister! You there!"

The customer jumped back, petrified. Buck closed in smiling, calming him down. "Friend, I've got to show you something. Fred! Give me another bag here."

Fred shook his head, groaning. Buck showed the guy how to open a bag from the heat-seal fin. "See, once you see how, you'll never forget it. Am I right? Or am I wrong?" The man nodded. "And when you want it closed just fold it back down. There you go, a perfect seal." He patted the man's shoulder. "You take care now."

He sat back down and finished the chips and smoothed the bag flat. "Here's one of the best bags in the industry and he's massacring it." He relit his cigar and rolled on about the potato-chip field. How they design their bags from the top down using solid ink coverage to hide the breakage, the burns, and the short measure. I could have told him about Fried Rite but I lay back. He opened his knife and began scraping at the printing. The blue ink flaked. "They're hitting it with too much heat. Now, if you're smart you'll go see these boys. Show them how they're getting screwed."

He tapped his cheek with one finger and blew out a perfect smoke ring and then another. "I always say, first you got to be an engineer. Then you can be a salesman." He handed me a cigar. "Boy, you stick with Buck Brody. He'll show you the ropes." He checked the bag again. "Wonder who prints this crap, anyhow."

I found the code at the bottom of the fin. "Coe and Roberts out of Philly. They've got O.K. Chips in their back pocket."

He grinned. "Hey, all right! I'll be damned if you don't know a little bit about this business."

Buck Brody sat back. He was waiting for me to move in on him with my "quality, loyalty, service" pitch about Pioneer. But I didn't. A lot of times the best way to sell is to change the subject. Then let them bring it back to you. That way they think you're a pretty good guy and aren't crowding them. I lit my cigar. "Damn, it must have been something being in that circus outfit."

His eyes softened. Then he began examining the cigar label as if he was checking the printing registration. "Bo." From that time on he called me Bo. "There's nothing like it in the world. Absolutely nothing."

He talked about the fifties. The sixties. About the old circus days. How he had thirty-nine trucks, eighteen elephants, and a troupe of 140. How his tent sat over six thousand and how they made so much money it took them two days to count it. I asked him why he left it. He puffed his cigar.

"Money." Then he said it again, slowly with two long southern syllables. "Mon-ey. I ran out." He said he couldn't get out of winter quarters near Sarasota and had wound up trading most of his trucks for four Simplex bag machines and moving to Riverhead.

I'd had three beers and was feeling mellow. "But how could you go from something like that to running a damn bag plant. It doesn't make sense." It was the right thing to say. His face went hard and his lips tightened. He'd have made a lousy poker player. I'd hit what Jake called his "hot button." His lips tightened.

"You know what ruined the circus? Television. People don't know what a live show is anymore." He calmed down as he relit his cigar. Then with a flourish he held it out at a gambler's angle. "TV's done to the mud circus what panty hose has done for finger fucking."

We laughed, but the humor didn't stay in his eyes too long. "No lie, one of these days I'm going to put something together that's going to play and play and keep on playing. Something different. Something big." Buck's eyes were slits and he was nodding. "I've still got some stock and some props and a few trucks. All I need is a little time and a little money. Then, Bo, it's the big time. The goddamn big, big time." For a moment I thought I was back listening to Dad describing the zebra stripes and the tom-toms of the Club Zanzibar he was still planning. The check came and Buck Brody began picking his teeth with the corner of a matchbook.

Outside on the blacktop he slapped my back. "Look!" All I could see were parking-slot lines and the RIVER-HEAD CITY LIMIT sign. Buck's hand was on my shoulder. "No shadow, right? Bo, right there is what's wrong with your north country. Six months a year you don't see your shadow." He was all wound up again. I eased him toward the car, but there was no stopping him. He did about five minutes on different clouds. Northern clouds. Western clouds. Southern clouds. "Bo, if a man don't see his shadow something happens to him. He forgets who in the hell he is. Tell you what. Take a look the next bad day you get. I'll guaran-damn-tee it will be solid cloud cover."

Back at the plant he let the phone ring. I figured it was Ben. In the back room I heard the Simplexes banging away at sixty bags a minute. But then I picked up a different sound. A high clicking whine I'd never heard before. It was something big. Something fast. He saw me counting the strokes. "You don't miss much, do you?"

"What the hell is it?"

"Come on back."

Buck Brody had a high-speed polyethylene drawstring bag machine. It was brand new and stretched across the room like a locomotive. It must have cost sixty thousand dollars.

He slapped my back. "Take a guess how fast."

"Ninety, maybe a hundred."

"One-sixty a minute and I can push it to two hundred." He introduced me to a tall blond girl named Helen. She was shy and seemed awkward. She smiled quickly and then ducked her head back in to feed the drawstring.

In the office the phone was still ringing. He ignored it, sat down, and slapped both hands on the desk. "All right, Bo, let's talk some business." We did. But it wasn't me selling him. He was selling me. Brody didn't print. He was making drawstring bags for the Mills and Mills chain and wanted us to print the polyethylene for him. What he needed was a twenty-thousand-dollar line of credit. It was a cinch, and I called Greene for the approval. He was out of town, but Ernie Wayne said it was routine and we put the order through.

That night my luck kept running and Monica said O.K. to dinner. I took her to Charley's on East Fifty-fourth. Great place: heavy silver, heavy linen, fresh candles and flowers, and a twelve-page wine list. I told her she was Buck Brody and the sky was the limit. We had to have a big bill for the expense report. She picked out an eight-dollar white wine. A ten-dollar red. Finally a twenty-four-dollar Dom Perignon champagne. And then another. The bill was $124, but with Brody's name riding it there would be no problem. I told her about Buck and the potato-chip buyer. About the wharf rat and the onion. Monica's a great laugher, and when I hit her with the panty-hose line she couldn't stop. She kept drying her eyes and pushing her hair back. She was wearing it down to her waist, and in the orange light from the candles the white streak was knocking me out. When she crossed the room to the john I watched the men looking her over.

Monica wasn't having any luck on Broadway or Off-Broadway or even Off-Off-Broadway, but Danceland had given her a raise and her new title was "executive dancer." We used to call it a "skimmer," and the job is to handle the fresh meat dumb enough to win the ten free lessons on the "Name This Tune" telephone hustle. She was laughing about making an advertising V.P. sweat and tremble and promise her a fortune for private lessons and how she'd signed him up for a Gold Plan during his first lesson. Danceland has a Bronze Plan for one year. A Silver for five. A Gold for ten. The Life Plan takes you all the way. But the top of the line is the Double Life, which allows you to dance all day and all night forever.

We sat there drinking champagne and making up our own plans. The Perpetual Plan, which went in your will and passed on to your sons and daughters. The Double Perpetual, with no cutoffs, which stayed alive as long as your family line survived. And finally the Eternal Plan, where you flashed your solid-gold card to Saint Peter and he ushered you around the line at the Pearly Gates and in toward the hardwood floor and the Muzak.

I was feeling great about Monica and the night and the Brody business. New York salesmen will kill you for an account that far out on the island near the beaches. I was also dying to dance. The champagne and the music were getting to me. All of a sudden I'm out in the center of the floor with my arms spread out for a pin light. It came. Then I did one of Dad's double spins and snapped my fingers. "Is there anyone in the room who will dance with the great Mahaffey." Monica came camping out in a running tap dance. The bandleader applauded. Two or three tables picked it up. Someone shouted, "Let's see something."

It was a good band and I wanted to show her off. I was also as horny as a goat. We did two big demonstrator turns and I swung her out. She stayed out on the break and did a gorgeous spin. She slid back in. "Let's give them a tango."

I said, "Hell yeah. Hey! How about it, maestro? A tango!"

The drummer grabbed the mike. "Man! No one does the tango anymore."

But the piano-playing leader had other plans. He came

in on top of "A Rose in Spanish Harlem." The electric bass filled in behind. The sound was great, and we were drunk enough to try anything. We arched our backs like Brazilians and began popping our hands and clicking our heels. The piano man had the mike. "Hey now! Olé!"

We used half the floor. Then all of it. I stamped my heels and clapped my hands. The tables were throwing flowers. Monica had her arms high over her head, snapping her fingers and looking like Rita Hayworth in her old Carmen movie. Then she tucked a rose in behind her ear and another in her teeth and we swooped across the floor. Her hair made a soft hissing sound and smelled of this great clove shampoo that costs a fortune and drives me crazy. The room was with us. I dropped her down in a deep dip. Then I spun her around in a crossover so she could flash her legs. Her skirt flared up and she tossed the roses with a circus flourish. The band shouted, "Olé," and we were off again. We did a profile turn. Then another. Then a big stylized stalking walkover and two big spins like we were doing it for a living. We finished in a deep dip with her head thrown back and her hair spread out on the floor. The piano player was still shouting, "More. More!"

My thigh was between her legs. I held it there. The crowd had joined the piano player and everyone was applauding. I slid her up. She shook her hair and tucked her blouse in. "I'm smashed."

"Want to stop?"

"No, one more."

"Terrific."

After two more numbers I pressed her to the mirror wall. I was sweating like a ditchdigger. "I'm out of shape."

She pushed her hair back from her face. "Me too."

"Listen, what say I take you home tonight?"

"No, Joe. Not tonight." But it wasn't a definite no.

After the break we came back out on the floor. We danced closer. I didn't want to press too hard and scare her off. But I had to keep after her. "Great, isn't it?"

"Never better, baby." It was the baby that did it. Something clicked inside. Maybe Mister Director was out of town or running out of luck. Or maybe she was through with him and looking me over again. The back of my hand was on the back of her neck. I pushed her against the mirror. "This is the move I used to put on the blue-rinse set."

She slid her leg in tight between mine. "Here's my old trademark."

From Monica's bed we could see the Empire State Building. Up on the tower the high-intensity lights, to keep the birds from crashing, were bouncing off the clouds, and the Union Square clock was striking four. Her head was on my shoulder, the way I'd been dreaming one night it would be, and we lay there watching the clouds and the city and the lights of the big jets heading out from LaGuardia. I'd been telling her about the club and growing up in Lorraine. It's funny how you'll talk a lot less after you make love but it will usually make more sense. The more I told her the more I wanted to tell her. I told her about Dad's group called the "Royal Hawaiians" who knew only two Hawaiian songs and faked the rest in Spanish. About the 144 salt-and-pepper Eiffel Towers. And then I told her about the ants and the grasshopper song and how I'd sung it on the library steps the night I came to town. She begged me to sing it. I sat up cross-legged and with an ashtray and pencil fiddle under my chin I began sawing away.

"Do it again, Joe, please." I did it again. And then we did it together.

> Oh the world owes me a living . . .
> Zooma-Zooma-Zooma-Zooma-Zoom.

And then she kissed me hard and flopped back on the bed laughing so hard she was crying. "Joe, you nutty bastard. You're great. You're like a goddamn musical comedy."

Her hair was in her face and I pushed it back and held it

back while I kissed her. God, I was in love with her. It was all I could do to keep from proposing.

In the morning I made the coffee. Colombian and mocha, a great aroma. Monica's hair was covering her face and the pillow. Her hip was raised and round and if I'd had another ten minutes sleep I'd have crawled back in. She moved, made a triangle in her hair and peered out. Then she raised one finger and snuggled down in the warm spot I'd left behind. During the night we hadn't talked about the director but we'd figured a couple of things out. While we'd been together at Danceland we had had enough in common to talk about. A lot to laugh about. It was all crap and a fast buck and we were really bloodsuckers, but we'd managed to make it funny. But with me at Pioneer and her still dancing, all we had was each other. We needed more. Not much more; but more.

I hadn't seen any men's clothes in the closet. I checked under the bed for shoes. In the bathroom I went through the medicine chest like a jewel thief. Maybe the guy had finally moved out. The deodorant was hers. So were the creams and lotions. The razor was a Lady Gillette. After the shower I was drying myself and feeling great about everything. And then on a back shelf I saw the Old Spice shaving cream, the Old Spice after shave, and the Wilkinson razor. A cold hand gripped my stomach from the inside. The bastard was still living there.

Outside, the rain was freezing as it hit, and I headed for the subway. In the office I checked in with Ethel. Omaha had called at nine sharp. It was bad news. Rather than telling it to me, Ernie had left word that it was no-go on a credit line for Buck Brody. He suggested we ship C.O.D. I knew Buck couldn't do it but I called him anyway.

"Sorry, Bo. I just don't have that kind of cash right now."

"Buck, they're crazy. Something's wrong. I just don't understand what in the hell they're doing out there."

"It's O.K., Bo. It's O.K. These things happen. Listen, there's no problem. Keep in touch now, you hear?"

I sat there watching the office building going up across the street and blocking out my view of the bridges. I was talking to myself out loud. "Yeah, keep in touch." It was going to be a bitch pushing through the expense report. But then I began thinking about Monica. We'd been so close at Charley's and making love and singing together and watching the skyline and the clouds. I just couldn't believe there was room in her life for this other guy, no matter who he was.

Jake had said a lot of things about sales which I never listened to, but one thing began coming back. He said that when he'd lost an order and things were crashing down he'd go over to the Bowery and watch the bums. He'd see how well off he was and know that except for his sales ability and his knowledge of what he called "human relationships" he could be one of them wiping down the windshields and begging dimes for wine. I guess Jake's Bowery trips were a little like Buck's wharf-rat idea. Anyhow, Jake said I needed something like that for the times when I "bottomed out." Well, with losing Fried Rite and now Brody and worrying myself sick about Monica I guess I was bottoming out.

Where Jake went to the Bowery I went to the movies. The Tivoli, on Forty-second Street, was full of salesmen. The cold rain had driven them in. They were all taking up three seats each. One for their overcoat and hat. One for themselves. One for their samples.

These Times Square freaks will steal your cases if you put them on the floor. They sell them for luggage. And you don't want those winos getting too close. You might get mugged. Or propositioned. Or thrown up on. But it was cold outside and you had to go somewhere. New York can get grim in January. It's the month when the old folks stroke out and the suicide rate jumps. Maybe it's the cloud cover, like Buck said. It's also the month when casket sales peak. Every year we ship heavy-duty poly bags to the mortician crowd. When it comes to packaging, this is the place we should all go to school. Retail prices on the bronze coffins run up higher than a new Cadillac.

Then they bill you for the flowers. Matter of fact, if you're in packaging you get to know a helluva lot about a helluva lot of things.

Like about once a month I'll cruise into Sultan Rubber, Inc., down near the Battery. I never got an order or even a quote request. But I like to watch the girls on the production line. Here they are, all bright-eyed and nimble-fingered, lined up skinning rubbers on plastic dicks. Checking them out for strength and holes. Well, somebody's got to do it.

The feature movie was a dark Italian job with a child's death up front and about nine suicides. I should have walked out and found a musical comedy or a cartoon festival or a good porn. But that's the way I am. I have to see how everything comes out. I don't believe I've ever walked out on a movie, and I mean I have seen the dogs.

CHAPTER

3

It was one-thirty when the movie broke. I didn't want to
face Costo or Jake with the Buck Brody news, and I sure
as hell didn't want to sit down and crank out a long memo
explaining the $124 dinner at Charley's. There wasn't
anything else to do, so I decided to eat. Looking out the
Chock Full O'Nuts window on Forty-second Street I saw
a bus go by advertising a revival of *Guys and Dolls*. The
matinee was at 2:30. It was one of my all-time favorites,
so I paid the bill, tipped a quarter, and headed out for
Forty-seventh Street. The theater was packed and the
play was great, the band was great, and the cast was
great. During Dad's Broadway Nights period he used to
sing every one of the songs, and they were still holding
up, and it was exactly what I needed. And then, during
the intermission, when I was peeling back the carton
wings of one of those four-ounce orange juices they stiff
you a buck for out in the lobby, I heard a giggle. I felt a tap
on my shoulder. "Joe." It sounded Spanish.

"Jesus Christ! Dolores!"

I couldn't believe it. We jumped around like idiots,

bear-hugging and kissing each other. She had on a mink coat that came to her ankles. She kissed me again and I hugged her so tight I thought I'd break her ribs. "Damn, honey, where you been? How've you been?"

We must have looked crazy because people were stepping back and giving us plenty of room. She twisted her hips three or four beats with the intermission music. "Only sensational." She did a rumba with one deep bump and I thought she'd landed a lead in a Broadway show. She flipped back twenty or thirty minks down the long panel that reached the floor. "Look." It was a Neiman-Marcus label with *Dolores* running through it in Puerto Rican black and orange.

"Twenty-four thousand, Joe. Wild?"

"I guess so. Dolores, you look fantastic."

She fluttered eight fingers of rings and about a dozen gold and platinum bracelets. A five-strand choker of pearls was around her neck, and her dark blue lashes were longer than the chorus girls'. She pushed back a dozen more minks from her watch. "Tiffany, baby. Nine thousand dollars."

"Jesus, I can't take all this in."

She opened an accordion file of color shots: two kids, a sixteen-room house in Larchmont, six horses, a Rolls-Royce, and two big Mercedes.

"Damn, how'd you do it?"

"Remember little Bennie?"

"Sure. Seven hundred dollars."

She grinned. "Nine hundred. We got married. Joe, you got to come see the kids. You got to see the pool. We got one man all he does is cut the grass. Bennie even let me bring up Mama and my sisters. I belong to a country club. Ain't that a kick? Me in a country club!"

"This is incredible. I swear it is. Is he with you? God, I'd really love to see him."

Her smile vanished. "Oh, baby." Her big smile flattened and vanished. "Little Bennie's dead."

"I'm sorry, Dolores. I'm really sorry."

"Nothing to get upset about." Her eyes were soft as she squeezed my shoulder. "He was a nice little fellow, wasn't he Joe?"

"He was, Dolores. He really was."

It was an absolute cookies-and-milk ending. Bennie got Dolores and Dolores got the house, the kids, the cars, the furs, and her family up out of the sugarcane. Some women let furs and diamonds wear them. But Dolores was way out in front of hers and staying there. She looked great rich. She was made to be rich, and the American economy wasn't going to suffer, because she was damn well going to spend it.

We had drinks after the show. I began putting a move on her, but she smiled and waved me off. She told me she was engaged to Bennie's best friend, Harry Abramowitz. I didn't recognize the name until I heard the company. It was Bunny Tissue, Inc. Harry T. Abramowitz was the chairman of the board. I've called on his purchasing agent, Manny Stevens, about a dozen times and haven't even had a ripple. Dolores said she would tell Harry about me. "They've got to buy from somebody, baby. It might as well be you." She grinned and winked. "We'll keep it in the family." She touched her finger to my chin. "Joe, it's just terrific seeing you again. Some night we go out and dance." She kissed my cheek. "We do a little cha-cha-cha."

In the morning at 10:30 sharp Manny Stevens called. At 10:45 I was in the Empire State Building elevator heading for Bunny Tissue on the twenty-fourth floor. They had the whole floor. Bunny Tissue only distributes in the Midwest and down in the Bible Belt, but they're one of the biggest tissue companies in the country. Their salesmen's policy is under glass in the lobby with their trademark. It's this two-foot-high stuffed rabbit standing on his hind legs. He's leaning on a fence post, reading a scroll: "Bunny Tissue is first and foremost a sales company. *Without your help we would be nothing.* We believe that every salesman is a human being and should be given as much time and courtesy as the personnel can afford. Coffee and donuts courtesy Bunny Tissue. Signed, Harry T. Abramowitz, Chairman of the Board."

Manny Stevens is about four foot six tops, which brings him in close to being a midget or a dwarf. I get those two mixed up. He had lifts going and he pushed his hair straight up and at you in one of those old fifties pompadours. This gave him a couple more inches. It's interesting about Manny. I mean, here he is with his little one-button blazer and his kid's-sized necktie and his cut-down green desk blotter, and for a long time I really didn't notice how really short he was. But when you're selling a guy like this, a guy who with one stroke of the old ball-point can jump your commissions four or five thousand, you see him about the way he wants you to see him. You also do a helluva lot of reacting. Like you smoke only when he smokes. You laugh when he laughs. Costo calls it "pipe conversation." Both ends are kept open. You've got to see which way he wants to go. Then you go with it. You've also got to look him in the eye when you think he wants you to. A little fellow like that can get sore at the damnedest things.

Manny let me rattle on about the weather and then bitch about the subway. He was in a good mood so I kept him off business as long as I could. Finally he raised his hand and cut me off. "Can you print this?" He unrolled a design of a twenty-inch-high rabbit holding a black-and-white scroll reading, 12 ROLLS, DOUBLE STRENGTH. It was six-color process plus two back-up whites; eight colors. As I said we could, I checked Manny's eyes. So could Bestprint and Rose Hill and AAA in Brooklyn. Manny liked to work with locals and there had to be a catch. There was. He wanted it made into 24-by-36-inch-long drawstring poly bags. No one in the East had the machinery. We didn't either. Then I remembered Buck's and I asked him how many he wanted. "One million. Can you handle it?"

I said I thought we could but I had to check a few things

out. He rolled the artwork up and snapped a rubber band around it. "O.K., get back to me before five."

I called Buck. He said he could run it in three days and he'd give me ten percent of everything. But there was a catch. I needed two orders from Bunny Tissue: one for the printing from Pioneer, one for the bags from Buck. It would be hard selling Manny on this, but with Dolores pushing Abramowitz we had a good chance. I made up Jake's positive and negative lists. I arranged the points carefully and dialed. As I waited on hold I kept underlining *two orders*. TWO ORDERS. I put a star next to it. I drew a box around it. Manny came on the line and said O.K. to everything and to come pick up the order and the artwork. I couldn't believe it was going to be this easy.

Manny had both orders made out to Pioneer. I handed it back. "Sorry, Manny. But I've got to have two. I told you that on the phone. Remember? Just make the bags out for Brody."

He shook his head and stared me down. "I never heard of Brody. I barely heard of Pioneer."

I took two beats, three beats, four. I had to keep calm. I had to be firm. "Manny, Buck Brody's guaranteeing everything. And we're standing behind him one hundred percent. Buck makes the best drawstring bag in the country."

"Bullshit." His voice dropped. "If you want this business, Buster, this is the way you get it. Otherwise, I'm tearing it up."

Even his paper knife was three-quarter size. He was balancing it on the edge of the blotter.

"Name it."

The price was twelve cents a bag. Total first order, one hundred and twenty thousand dollars. My Brody commission was a flat twelve thousand. If I said no, I'd be out. If I said yes, I'd be in trouble. But I'd have the order in my hand. Maybe I could work something out. I could smell the coffee and donuts out in the reception room. Manny pointed the knife. "What's it going to be, Mahaffey?"

I said we could do it and promised delivery in four
plants in three weeks. Then I took the artwork and the
order and headed back for the office. I had to be alone to
think it out. I had to clear my head and I had to plan. I sat
back counting the twenty-two stories they'd floored in the
office building across the way. It was going up to fifty-four
and I wouldn't even be able to see the sky. I swung
around to the big painting of the Pioneer trademark: a
Conestoga wagon heading into the western sun. I kept
looking for some message. All I knew was that nothing
mattered now but Bunny Tissue, Inc. I lit a cigarette and
tried to make a list. Nothing came; I was drawing blanks.
Then I realized they weren't blanks. There was simply no
way of handling it. All I had was an order I simply
couldn't fill. I'd have to go crawling back past the stuffed
rabbit and Abramowitz's message to the sales world. I'd
have to face Manny. "I'm sorry, Manny, but we just can't
do it."

It was raining. It was dark. Cars coming out of the Park
Avenue tunnel had their lights and windshield wipers on.
I decided not to call Omaha. I'd get a flat no and I'd be
dead. I'd go out and sell them. Why not? Why the hell not?
It was twelve thousand dollars. My twelve thousand
dollars. It was enough to take Monica to Europe for two
or three months, or Hawaii, or Japan, and I'd be damned
if I was going to let them blow it. Once they heard the
story about Dolores and Abramowitz they would have to
go along with it.

I called United and got on the seven o'clock through
Chicago. I called Ernie and told him to meet me. Then I
called Monica. She hadn't come in to work. Maybe she
was sick. I tried her at home. There was no answer. I'd
call her again from LaGuardia. Maybe she went to a
movie or was out shopping, or maybe she was staying
with a girlfriend. I could always call from Omaha and
leave a callback number.

Danceland, the health clubs, and magazine subscrip-
tion hustles like to work the phone and use the mail. It's

cheap, and they can back off fast if they get in trouble. But for leverage it's hard beating the old stand-up demo and hard eye contact. I flew out and checked in at the Ramada Inn at the airport. I set my watch back an hour and met Ernie in the bar. We had two fast drinks. Ernie agreed with me on everything. "Joe, it's a natural." He had a slight tick in his left eye. He drank fast. "There's no way for the old man to say no."

Ernie Wayne had started with Pioneer in high school and worked his way into sales and out into the Illinois territory. He always said he was billing over half a million dollars when they brought him in for punching out a purchasing agent. I'd heard it different; he'd never cracked two hundred thousand, and it wasn't his temper that brought him back in, it was his drinking. Four years back Greene had tried him out again in the Chicago area, but it was no use. In three weeks he was drinking. In four he was picked up for drunken driving in Evanston. Five weeks after Ernie had gone out with his samples, his order book, and his company car he was back down in the mail room figuring out Zip codes and working the stamp machine. Since then he'd worked back up to sales correspondent.

Over dinner, Ernie told me how Greene was promising him a territory. It was only a matter of a few weeks before he was back out on the road. "Joe, I loved that old territory. No one worked it the way I did. No one."

His speech was slurring and he was calling himself "Old Ernie." "Joe, Old Ernie loved every jerkwater town and moron purchasing agent he had to pry an order out from under. I mean it, Joe. I mean it."

He was looking into his drink as if he could still see the white line down Interstate 55 or was out on the Skokie heading north out of Chicago.

"I know you did, Ern."

Ernie wasn't going to be any help, and I was wondering how I was going to pitch Drayton. What would he think of subcontracting on Brody's shaky credit? What would he

think of Brody? Maybe he'd fire my ass for coming out
with no authorization.

In the meeting with Drayton and Greene and the staff I
did twenty minutes on what Brody could do and what it
would mean for Bunny Tissue. I told them the volume had
to be over half a million dollars and with any luck would
probably go higher. Greene seemed to like it but he kept
quiet. I couldn't tell what the staff thought. Drayton stood
up, arranging his Phi Beta Kappa key. When he hooked
his thumbs in his vest pockets I knew it was a big fat no.

He did about eight minutes on how the Pioneer label
represented thirty years of quality and service and
integrity and how subcontracting would go against everything his father and grandfather had stood for. Greene
was sitting downwind. When Drayton sat down he got up
and picked up the refrain. The staff was nodding like they
were on the same connecting rod. It was a long meeting;
it was painful. The answer was no, and I was sorry I had
even gone out there. I flew back that night drinking
double Scotches and watching the lights of the prairie
towns. I knew that Omaha hadn't only said no to subcontracting; it was no to New York. Omaha had never
understood New York. Now I knew they never would.
They would come to town with their tan shoes and their
traveler's checks, hoping to shake hands with Dempsey
and see Joe Namath and check out the central buying of
National Biscuit and American Tobacco. But they would
always be suspicious of the dark clothes and the lightning
ways of the East. In Nebraska and the Big Eight,
subcontracting and shaky credit was like the tin plate of
the leper. In New York it was just another way of doing
business. Omaha was pulling back. Back behind the
soybeans and the hog futures to the old reliables: Ralston
Purina, Kellogg's, P&G, and the friendly Farm Coops
who paid their bills in ten days and never gave them any
trouble. We were passing over the lights of Pittsburgh. I
unsnapped my seat belt and squeezed up against the
window, watching for Route 40. I thought of Mom and

Dad down there in the club. Maybe I ought to go back and help them open up the Zanzibar. I'd be my own boss and I'd know exactly where I stood. Lorraine was down there in the dark, but I couldn't find it. As I kept watching for the green lights and the red neon I decided there were other fields besides sales, and I made up my mind to call Carson Miller in the morning and look into advertising and public relations.

CHAPTER

4

The next day Greene called. He was excited. He'd talked Drayton into taking the whole order from Bunny, and we were back in business. Pioneer would print the polyethylene and ship to Brody Bags. We'd also ship Pioneer cartons, Pioneer labels, Pioneer sealing tape, and a Pioneer engineer east. Our truck would wait for the bags. Then it would head west for Minneapolis, Green Bay, Portland, and Seattle. It was perfect! It was incredible! I would make twelve thousand dollars and it was absolutely terrific! Greene had finally stuck his neck out. He'd finally come through. I called Buck.

"Hot damn! Fantastic Bo! Fan-damn-tastic! I knew you could do it."

"And Buck, I want fifteen percent, O.K.?"

He laughed. "Damn right! You goddamn earned it." My commission was now eighteen thousand dollars.

I wrote out a confirmation for Manny and headed out. I was too up to ride the bus. Too nervous to flag a cab. I wanted to walk. I wasn't carrying anything. No satchel. No attaché. No manila envelope. Only the confirmation in my pocket. I stepped over a sidewalk crack. And then another. My stride was right, my timing was right, and I stepped over every one and zooma-zooma-zoomed over to Fifth Avenue. Everything had come together. I'd stepped into a gold mine. I jammed my hands in my pockets. I wanted to rub them together like a miser and cackle like a fiend. Instead I did a little tap dance up to my old friend the right lion on the Public Library steps and across to the one on the left. I jumped down. My stride was longer, tighter. I waited for the light at Fortieth Street, snapping my fingers and doing little four-beat zooma-zoomas behind my teeth and looking over the girls. A tall model came oozing by and I saluted her like a member of the Cold Stream Guards. "Madame, you are gorgeous." It was Dad's old line. Another cruised by and I simply whispered, "Absolutely stunning." She smiled and I grinned and two cops looked over and I eased on down Fifth thinking about what kind of present I'd buy Dolores. Maybe Monica and I would get her a date from Danceland and we'd go out and cha-cha-cha all night. Bunny had really come up with something revolutionary. People don't buy too much john paper. It bulks too much. But the new twelve-pack was a natural. They could sling it under the shopping cart. They could carry it with one finger. It was one hell of an idea, and the country was going to line up for it. There was no telling what the reorders would be. Two million? Three million? Four? I did a broken field run through the crowd at Thirty-fourth Street. When I hit the revolving doors at the Empire State Building I stayed in for three revolutions. I came out grinning.

After leaving Bunny with the purchase order, I was back at the Public Library steps watching the traffic and the crowd. The sun had broken through the exhaust fumes and a hook-and-ladder fire truck was screaming. A religious zappo wearing a sandwich sign with about a thousand lines of copy was giving away New Testaments to any Jew who promised to read it. Another freako windmilling his arms, like he was working an aircraft carrier, was parking the buses. And in front of the newsstand, another winner with a World War II officer's coat and black tennis shoes was nonchalantly pissing on a fireplug. It was my territory and it was beautiful and I loved every steaming, crawling inch of it. I had Drayton and Greene and Manny Stevens in my back pocket, and if anything went wrong I had Dolores taking care of it with Abramowitz. The only thing missing was Monica, and with this kind of money coming in that was only a matter of time.

A week passed, the plates were ready, and Omaha pulled the proofs. Manny loved them. He said he'd never seen the tones around the Bunny's eyes done better. I was proud of Pioneer and proud of being a salesman for them. I told him we were one of the few companies in the country that could do it. Then he handed me a Xerox of a letter from Abramowitz to Drayton. Enclosed were the TV and magazine ads announcing that the new twelve-pack 500-count double-ply tissue roll would be packaged in a new poly drawstring bag exclusively produced by Pioneer Packaging in Omaha. Manny had underlined the last line in red. "We will be reordering an additional two million bags for our initial sale and are happily forecasting using one million bags per month for the first year."

Outside in the lobby I whipped out my computer. On twelve million bags a year my commission from Brody would be over two hundred and sixteen thousand dollars. I checked it again. And again. It was right. Now I could do anything I wanted. Anything. Monica and I could commute from Hawaii. Or Acapulco. Or Europe. Or if she really wanted to stay in show business we could live in Hollywood and really do it right. That phony Off-Broadway director could never compete with me now.

I got a ticket for doing eighty on the way out to Buck's. When I told him the twelve-million news he went crazy. He slung his arms around me and cut loose with a rebel yell that almost tore my ears out. "Hot damn! This is fan-damn-tastic. We've got it made in the shade." He kept hugging me and bouncing around and slamming on the desk and pounding on the walls. "This time we're going all the way. All the goddamn way. If you want a Rolls-Royce or a Chris-Craft go at it. This is only the beginning. Only the beginning."

Omaha made up twenty handmade Bunny Tissue twelve-pack bags and packed them with twelve rolls of tissue and sent them in. Manny and Abramowitz were ecstatic. They rigged up a demo counter in the lobby right next to the stuffed rabbit. I couldn't believe it, but there it was, stacked up in a six-foot-high triangle display under the simulated store aisle lights. It looked like a shrine. It was quality. It was convenient. It was competitive. And I'll be damned if it wasn't beautiful. Customers would have to buy it. There was no way for them not to buy it. The stores would have to put a limit of maybe two or three to a customer until we could ship more bags and Bunny Tissue could produce more tissue. Every day I'd drop in for coffee and a donut. I'd hang around watching the salesmen looking it over and then watch them realizing I was the one that had the business.

Buck was handling everything beautifully. The draw-string bag machine was running beautifully. He had spare parts in case it broke down. That was beautiful too. Everything was beautiful. The organization. The flow chart. The conveyor belts. Even the cotton drawstring cord wound up on the overhead spools was beautiful.

It was Tuesday night, and I took a bath as hot as I could stand it. Then I drank two beers and got in bed. The Bunny Tissue shipment was on its way east. I lay there hoping the beer would take hold. Maybe I'd take two Valiums. But I wanted to wake up sharp. I had to have my wits about me. I relaxed and let my hands and feet dangle off the edge of the bed and tried to clear my head. But it was no use, I kept seeing the Pioneer truck coming in on the interstate. It was in Iowa. Tomorrow it would be Illinois and Ohio and into Pennsylvania. On Thursday it

would be out on Long Island, being unloaded. I began to
relax. I was drifting off. "Fine" was ringing in my head. I
was saying it over and over again. "Fine. Fine. Fine."

It was after midnight when the phone rang. It was
Buck. At first I could barely hear him.

"Bo? Bo? You there?"

"Yeah. For God's sake, what's up?"

All I could hear were screeching drill presses and big
machinery. "You there, Bo?"

"I'm here. What the hell's up?"

He closed a door and I could hear everything. "Bo?"

"Yeah."

"The sheriff showed up. It's that damn subpoena."

"What subpoena?"

"The one I showed you."

"Buck, you never showed me any subpoena." Then I
remembered. "Damn, Buck, you said that was a divorce
thing or something." I was panicking. "Buck, you said it
was a woman."

I heard him sigh. "O.K., O.K., I'll fill you in later. It's
gotten a little more complicated."

I didn't know how to say it. "How about Bunny?"

"No problem. No problem. I got it all worked out." The
noise was getting louder. He was shouting. "Bo, can you
meet me?"

We met in an all-night machine shop down on Spring
Street. Overhead, cranes and three-foot-wide belt pulleys
lined the ceiling along with heavy-duty monorails for big
equipment. It had been used to service subway cars and
snowplow equipment. I didn't ask him why he was there.
I didn't care about anything except Bunny. He kept
saying how simple it all was, but the more he explained,
the worse it sounded. The sheriff had closed him down
and padlocked the plant. They were auctioning off his
equipment to his creditors. All I could say was "Damn,
Buck. Damn."

His arm was around me and he was telling me how
everything was going to be all right in the morning. All we

had to do was run a couple errands. Then he spelled it out. We were going to move the drawstring machine to Jersey City. Buck had everything ready. A panel truck was loaded down with two dollies, a tripod hoist, and enough heavy tools to lay sewer pipe. We headed out with me driving. It was freezing. Our first stop was an all-night Whelan's drugstore. He came out with a shopping bag filled with flashlights. "They probably cut the juice. We might need these."

We started out again. The muffler had rusted out, and in the Midtown Tunnel we sounded like a tractor. At the toll gate I had to promise the officer I'd get it fixed in the morning. It was almost one and we had 120 miles to go. The heater was barely working and the wind was whistling through the door gaskets and the window seals. I'd forgotten my gloves and drove with one hand on the wheel and the other under my crotch. I kept shifting hands and jiggling my feet trying to keep warm. Buck slid close, shouting that the sheriff had a warrant out for his arrest. That's why I was driving. He cupped his hand over my ear. "It's O.K., though, Bo. It's going to be O.K. Once we get to Jersey they can't lay a hand on us."

He'd said us. At sixty-five the old truck had a shimmy. I eased it up to seventy and it smoothed out. He said a machinist friend had broken the machine down. It was ready for us on the back siding. All we had to do was pick it up, take it to a warehouse in Jersey City, and set it up again. Buck kept saying nothing had really changed except our location. The sheriff couldn't do a thing in Jersey. It sounded simple. Too simple. Then it sounded crazy. But it could work. It should work. And with the exhaust roaring and me swapping hands and jiggling my feet to keep from freezing and holding the truck on seventy to keep it from falling apart and sweating out the Bunny Tissue shipment and the eighteen thousand dollars, I knew it had to work. It was almost three when we pulled in behind the plant. It was pitch dark, fifteen degrees, and blowing snow. Buck groaned. He'd seen something. Then I saw it, too. The machine wasn't on the siding. "Bo, we've got to get it out of there."

I was getting a chill. "Fred's open. Let's get some coffee first."

"No, we got to hurry. I've got to break in my own damn place."

I had a cold, sinking feeling as we climbed in the back window. Buck turned on a flashlight. It was a disaster. The machine hadn't been touched. "Jesus, Buck! What happened?"

"Beats hell out of me." He was circling it, shining the light on the carriage and up at the belts. "It's O.K., though." He slapped me on the back. "No problem. Nothing we can't handle."

The sinking feeling had settled in my stomach. It was staying there. We pulled the blinds, switched on the flashlights, and lined them up around the floor. For some reason I was counting the flashlights. There were twenty-two of them.

"Bo, grab that wrench. I want you to unbolt this baby. I'll tear her down."

I had to lie on my back and work left-handed. Everything felt cold and clammy and smelled of heavy-duty machine oil. I leaned on the first bolt. It was stuck. I pounded it with a heavy-duty hammer. It wouldn't budge. Cotton lint from the drawstring and grease dirt kept dropping in my eyes. I slid a pipe over the wrench handle and banged it with the sledge. It popped loose. As I unscrewed it I realized there hadn't been any machinist because there *wasn't* any machinist. I banged on the second bolt.

"Buck, damn it, why'd you have to lie for?"

"Not so loud!" He was whispering. "Easy, Bo. Hell, I didn't lie. I swear I didn't."

"How come these lights? These tools?"

"I told you. In case something went wrong. Bo, I'd never lie to you. Come on, we got work to do."

I was on the fourth bolt, I had twelve more to go. I

checked my watch. It was 4:30. I scraped at the grease crust with a putty knife and started again. Buck was moving fast, dismantling the cutters and feeders and stacking the parts near the door. Who would meet the Pioneer truck? Who would explain the move? What if we didn't get set up in Jersey City? I didn't want to think about anything. I kept concentrating on the lug bolts. My back was solid grease and I could taste the machine oil on my back teeth. I kept my eyes closed to keep the oil and dirt out and worked by feel. I stayed on my back, working left-handed, taking eighth and quarter turns with the big wrench. It was slow, it was cold, and it was painful. But the bolts were coming and I could feel the big rig easing up from the floor.

At 5:45 I had one more bolt to go. Buck was carrying cartons of parts out to the truck. We were almost through. As I leaned on the wrench I heard a car on the gravel. I slid out and crawled over to the door. I couldn't see anything. Suddenly I was scared and began crawling around the machine and cutting off the lights. Then I eased up and called out. "Buck? Buck?" And then I saw it. A black-and-white patrol car was circling the plant. It was running its light over the loading platform. As it turned the corner I shot through the door and jumped down. I streaked across the lot to Buck. His hand was on my shoulder, but this time he kept quiet. The car came around again as we hid behind the truck. They stopped. They'd seen the jimmied window, the open door, the machinery.

Buck made a hissing sound through his teeth. "Shit fire!"

I was cursing and praying they'd change their minds and go someplace else. But no one moved. Then two more cars pulled in with their red lights flashing. Buck punched me. "Let's get out of here."

We cut down an alley and across a lot and out onto Route 29A heading for Fred's. We walked along the road shoulder. It was colder, much colder, and the wind was

up. Dawn was breaking, and all I could think about was
Manny Stevens. Who was going to tell him? I knew the
answer. Me. Me. I had to tell him.

"Damn, Buck! We got the order. We got the machinery
and the materials and the money. Isn't there somebody
you can talk to and work something out?" I was sounding
like a child. Buck knew it and didn't answer.

We sat at Fred's watching the plant and the police cars
with their red lights spinning. I tried to think. Right now
the Pioneer driver was barreling through Pennsylvania
on the turnpike, and Omaha was sitting back waiting for
their big two-million reorder, and Manny Stevens was
waiting for his bags. And all out there at the Bunny
Tissue plants—Green Bay, Minneapolis, Portland, and
Seattle—the warehouses were backed up with 500-count
john paper waiting for the big production to start. It was
terrible, and I had to stop thinking about it.

Buck's face was smooth and his eyes were calm. I
looked at him close. Maybe the strain had finally flipped
him out. The subpoenas and the sherriff had finally
finished him off, and he was ready for the graveled walks
and the paper slippers. He pulled a napkin out and
dipped it in his beer.

"Lean here, Bo. I'll get that grease off for you."

It was beginning to snow. It looked colder, bleaker.
The commuters heading for the station were hunched
over into the wind. They all had on dark hats and
overcoats and it looked like an Italian funeral. I pushed
away my coffee and ordered a beer. Buck was on his
fourth and was scratching the label off. "They've nailed
me to the cross, Bo."

Suddenly I was mad. "You? Bullshit! How about me?
What in the hell do you think they're going to do to me?
My ass is fired the minute they get the call through!"

"Bo, I'll tell you a little something. If this thing had
worked we'd have really made it." He sighed and whistled
a long clear note. "Yeah, we almost made it." We sat there
like idiots drinking Miller High Life and eating O.K.
Potato Chips. We were waiting for nothing. Buck had

loaded the juke with straight country-and-westerns. Every song was coming through weeping steel and real tears. Music to slash your wrists or strangle yourself by. I had had no sleep and no breakfast and was now on my third beer and listening to a child-visitation-and-alimony bleeder and watching the patrol cars. I knew if I didn't go off the deep end this time I never would. I saw stacks and stacks of Bunny Tissue out at the warehouses waiting for their poly bags. Then I saw rolls of it unwinding. It was dropping through space. A roll weighs only two ounces, but it bulks up like cotton candy. The only thing bigger in the market is dog and cat food or peat moss out in garden supply. I took out my pocket calculator. I converted one 500 double-ply tissue roll to linear feet. Then I converted the feet to miles. I began multiplying. Dividing.

"Buck, figuring just the million on the first order, take a guess how much john paper that is?"

"Probably a helluva lot."

I did one more division. "If you lay it out single layer it'll go to the moon and come back." I sounded like a schoolteacher.

"You're kidding?"

"That's it. And there's over two hundred thousand miles left over. That's rough, of course." Now I was sounding crazy.

Buck seemed to be reading his beer label. "To the moon and back. Damn, that's really something, isn't it."

I began wondering how I would tell the news to Manny. Maybe he would call Abramowitz in. They would sit side by side and I would stand. Or they would stand and I would sit. There had to be a better way. I could write him. I could wire him. Maybe I could give the elevator boy five bucks to go up and tell him to stick his head out the window. Then I'd stand on the corner and holler up to the twenty-fourth floor. He could stack up a couple phone books so he could see out. . . . I was whispering through my teeth. "Screw you, Manny. Screw you!"

Buck was sound asleep. His head was back on the seat back. His mouth was open, and the gold crowns on his

molars were shining. I started to wake him up. Then I
decided to have one more beer. I had to keep awake and
keep everything straight. I snapped my ball-point down
and made a list.

> Call Ernie
> Call Greene
> Ask Dad what he'd do
> Talk to Manny
> Call Monica

And then I sat there crossing out Monica, and then
Dad, and then Greene and Ernie. I underlined *Talk to
Manny*. Then I drew a box around it. What would I say?
How would I say it? I had to think. I was too tired to think
carefully. But I had to. I had to. I laid my head on the
table and began going over what I would say to him.
"Manny, something has come up." No. "Manny, you aren't
going to believe this."

At 11 A.M. I got off the subway at Sixth Avenue and
Thirty-fourth Street. The snow had turned to rain and as I
walked over to Fifth I got soaked. I was taking Jake's
advice about using the rain as a sales tool. Maybe Manny
would feel sorry for me. I stopped at Walgreen's. I had
three aspirins and a coffee. I had another coffee. Manny
would never come in the drugstore. I sat there looking in
the mirror at the reflections of the candy and greeting-
card display and my bleary eyes. I needed a shave. The
Whitman's Sampler for Valentine's Day had a new gold
band. I wondered who printed it. I made my notes of what
to say to Manny. "Some rain, right Manny?" No. Too
upbeat. I started off again and copied it on an envelope.
"Manny, I really feel sick about what I've got to tell you.
Sick." That was it. I wrote it out again in caps. I
underlined it. It was the truth. I really was sick. I turned
it over and finished up the message.

I paid the bill and headed out. At the candy display I
checked the Whitman's job. It was Kleartone out of

Yonkers, Bronson's outfit. Then I headed for the twenty-fourth floor. I decided to wear my coat in and look wetter. If I left in a hurry I didn't want to stop and have them screaming at me in front of the other salesmen.

Manny was smiling. He was actually standing up. Waiting to shake my hand. I shook and crouched low and sat down fast. "Manny."

He interrupted. "Joe, I got some great news for you. Sales is really excited about the twelve-pack. Hey, you don't look too good."

"I know." My speech had caught in my throat. I had to hurry or I'd never get it out. "I think I got the flu."

"Well, there's a lot of it around. Maybe this will make you feel better." He had the new order for two million bags. Manny was beaming. "We're going into every market in the country on this one. And I want to thank you for working so close with us. Joe, you've really done a great job."

In my head I was rattling on, "Manny, if you were to tell me to get out of here and never come back, I'd understand. Because this has got to be the worst thing . . ." But nothing was coming out. I was sitting there bobbing up and down and smiling over the two-million order like I was in deep senility. Now it was too late. It was too late to tell him anything. I had to get out of there. I had to go out and come back with a fresh start. Maybe I could rest a couple hours. I needed rest. Sleep. Deep sleep. Maybe some steam? Maybe a movie? I'd go to the movies and get some steam and drink some orange juice. Then I'd be ready for him. That was it. I needed a movie. I lurched up.

"Manny! I've got to see a doctor. I've got to shake this stuff." He was up and around the desk. I'd never seen him in front of it. His arm was around my waist. "O.K., Joe. You do that. And get some rest." I'd never realized how small his hands and feet were. How tiny his ears. "You look like you haven't slept in a week."

"Thanks, Manny. Good-bye."

"So long, Joe."

I took a large orange juice and a Giant Baby Ruth into a Charles Bronson feature. When it was over I had two more large oranges and a Mister Goodbar. The sugar would give me energy. Then I crossed the street and with still another orange went in on the middle of a Clint Eastwood. When it was over I felt worse. I headed for the subway. It was almost four. At home my temperature was 103. I lay down soaking wet with sweat and shaking with a chill. But I was happy. Now I could let my voice settle into a deep croaking bronchitis. He would know I was sick when I called. At ten to five I tested my voice. "Manny. Manny." It was strained, pained. It was great. I dialed.

"Manny Stevens, please."

He answered. "Stevens here."

"Hello, Manny."

"That you, Joe?"

"What's left of me." I didn't laugh. "I'm really sick."

"You sound it."

It was almost five. I'd get it over with. Then I wouldn't answer the phone.

"Listen, Manny." I slowed down to let my voice roll deeper, sicker. "I've got some bad news. It's about the bags."

He was in a hurry. "O.K., Joe, you want another few days? Take it. Take it. I'll understand. Now you've got to let me go. I've got a train to catch."

"It's worse than that, Manny." My voice went lower as I headed for the grim fact on the other side of the envelope. "Manny, it's bad."

"How bad?"

"The worst, Manny. I really feel sick about what I've got to tell you. And if you tell me never to call on Bunny again I'm going to understand." I read it straight from the envelope. There was no need to think. I'd already done that. All I had to do was read the lines. Slowly, with feeling. "Because what I've got to say to you is the hardest and the worst thing I've ever had to tell a purchasing agent in my whole life." I turned it over. Manny was waiting. I could hear him breathing. There it was. In caps. Underlined. "Manny, I'm sorry but there's not going to be any drawstrings."

His voice changed. I could barely hear him. He asked me how. I told him how. He couldn't believe it. He asked again. I repeated it. Then he believed it. His voice was faint but it sounded calm.

"What do I tell Abramowitz?"

"Tell him the truth. Tell him I screwed up. Tell him the whole thing was my fault."

There was a pause. "Manny?"

He didn't answer.

"Manny, you there?"

Suddenly he was screaming. Raging. "I'm here! You miserable son of a bitch! If you ever set foot in this building I'm having the goddamn Pinkertons on your ass. You understand?"

I croaked, "I understand."

He kept on screaming, "As for Pioneer, I'm hitting them with the biggest fucking lawsuit you ever heard of! . . . You hear that?"

"I hear it. I don't blame you. . . . Listen Manny, I've got to get back in bed."

"Well, Buster, you better damn well stay there. Because when you get up you've got one helluva lot of answering to do to our lawyers. What's that moron president's name?" I cleared my throat. "Drayton. Sorry, Manny. . . . Can't talk." I hung up. I was soaking wet. I staggered to the bed and spread out. I was shaking again. The room was beginning to turn. I had to get to the bathroom while I still had the strength. I inched over, holding onto the bed. The chair. Along the wall. In the john I sat on the floor. I pushed the seat back. I pressed my cheek to the china. It was cool there. It was safe there. Then I realized I was smiling at my reflection in the toilet bowl. I'd told the news to Manny. The hard part was over.

CHAPTER

5

Four days later I was back in the office. I tore out the days from the calendar and squared up my desk blotter. It felt more like home here than the apartment and I realized how much I missed it. How much I wanted to hold on to it. I lined up my stapler, my ball-points, my paper clips. My coffee cup with my name on it felt like an old friend. I didn't even mind the building's shadow that had crossed the floor and was climbing up the wall. I'd buy a lamp and turn the desk around and face the Conestoga wagon. The mail was mostly trade flyers and packaging magazines. No orders, no cancellations, but there was a sealed memo from Greene that had been addressed by hand. I tucked it under the blotter frame and began polishing my paper scale and sharpening my pencils. Then with a red one, a blue one, and a yellow one I began highlighting who I'd call first, who second, who third.

I slid the phone onto the window seat and dialed Ethel. It was 8:30 and the sun was dead center behind the building across the street. "Ethel, this is Joe Mahaf-fey."

"Hello, dearie. You been out of town?"

"Yes. . . . Well, no. I've been sick."

"Are you better now?"

"Yes thanks. Any calls?"

"A few. Only a few." Manny had called only once. Greene hadn't called at all. There was no word from Buck. No word from Monica.

"Mr. Mahaffey, if you don't want to talk to people for a few days, I mean until you feel better, I'll be glad to tell them something."

"Like what?"

"On vacation. Having root-canal work done. Death in the family. You let me know, I'll handle it. After all, that's what I'm here for."

"I'll think about it. Thanks again. Good-bye now."

"Bye-bye, dearie."

I called Buck. There was no answer. The building's shadow had joined Pan Am's. Down below it was solid shade. Nothing would ever grow on the median. Maybe they'd Astroturf it. I tried his home number. A woman answered. When I asked for Buck Brody, she repeated his name twice and then began cursing him in machine-gun Scandinavian and slammed the phone down.

I called the weather number. It was going to snow again. I'd see an early movie. Then come back and take care of everything. Then I figured I might as well get Greene's memo behind me. It was a help-wanted page torn from *Modern Packaging*—Greene's way of saying you'd better start looking. An ad was circled: "New York and Pennsylvania territory for right man. Heavy travel, top money for producer." It sounded like straight commission and three thousand miles a week. In the top-left corner was "Joe." At the bottom right, "No hard feelings. Edgar Greene."

I didn't want to see Costo or Jake, so at 8:45 A.M. I headed out for the movies. At six, after Costo and Jake had left, I came back and sat in the window watching the traffic. Down below people were driving home with their girlfriends and wives. Or guys were getting together to watch Monday-night football. I kept the lights off and sat there and sat there and sat there. It was after seven when the phone rang. Ethel was off and it kept ringing. Omaha would never call this late. It might be Monica. It might be Buck. If it was Greene I'd fake a high voice, say wrong number, and hang up. I picked it up like it was red hot. It was Buck. He was whispering. At first I couldn't understand him. I asked him where he was. He said he couldn't say.

"In town?"

"Yes."

"Below Forty-second Street?"

"Don't ask me. I can't talk."

"You in jail?"

"No. Listen, I'm in a hurry. I gotta go. Wait for me, O.K.?"

"O.K., Buck."

At eight o'clock Buck came in. It had been only five days but he was heavier. He had on a suit so tight across the chest he couldn't button it. His eyes were crazy red.

"Damn, Buck. You O.K.?"

He grinned and hooked his head. "Never better."

At the Roosevelt Grill we drank Scotch and water and ate peanuts. After that we had sirloin steaks. He was tense. Nervous. He kept watching the doors. During the soup he shoved all the matches he could find in his pockets.

After the steak he told me the story. A creditor had given him a job, eight hundred a week. But all the money went back to them. Buck got carfare and twenty dollars in cash. The hours were from seven to seven, seven days a week, and he had lunch at the bench. I asked him if it was the Mafia. He wouldn't say. I tried to get him angry so he would tell me.

"Bo, let's drop it, O.K.? Let's drop it."

"O.K. with me."

He ordered strawberry cheesecake. I told him we were

unloading the Bunny poly stock for scrap and that Pioneer had lost eighteen thousand dollars. Manny was buying regular plain bags and glue-on labels with E-Z-Stick. He winced when I mentioned the lawsuit. When I told him about his wife screaming, he stopped chewing and swallowed. He pointed his fork at me. "Know something? She's the only person I couldn't handle." His smile was thin, as if he knew it wasn't funny. "Hrugla, ain't that a helluva name for a woman. Not enough goddamn vowels." He dumped his brandy in his coffee and flashed a grin like the old Brody. "Bo, never marry a woman with not enough vowels in her name." He told me how she couldn't, or wouldn't, cook. How she was cold in bed and all she wanted to do was watch TV and bitch about going back to Oslo. He bit his bottom lip and pushed his hair back. It was covering his ears and curling up two inches on his collar. "I think I ran that business into the ground just so I could put in more hours to keep out of the goddamn house." He had moved out and was living with Helen, the machine operator.

By the time he'd wound down I'd drunk too much. At first I didn't tell him how they were trying to get rid of me. But I told him everything else. How the window had gone dark. How when it did, something had leaked out of me. How I was dodging Costo and Jake and didn't even have the nerve to answer the phone. I had the feeling I'd never see him again. That he'd vanish in the machine shop or be shipped away to another part of the country. Another part of the world. I'd probably seen too many Italian movies. It was like talking to a stranger on a plane. You tell them more than they can handle; always more than you'd planned.

We had another brandy. I told him about the movies. How I'd just seen five. He said if he was around Times Square he would have done the same thing. He said in sales it's either the cathouses or the movie houses. Then I told him about the grass dying on Park Avenue and that Greene was trying to fire me. And then for no reason that

I could think of I was laughing. Tears were running, and I had to go for the napkins. "Crazy, isn't it?"

He slapped his hands on the table. The ashtray bounced, the salt and pepper fell over. "Bo!" He laughed and hooked a southern whoop on the end. "Bo, we almost made it." He punched me on the shoulder. "We almost goddamn made it."

We sat there going over every agonizing step. But this time, for some zany reason, everything—the Omaha trip, Abramowitz's rabbit, Manny's tiny ears, the subpoena, the police cars, the cold night at the plant, and the morning at Fred's—was funny. Finally I told him about my 103-degree fever and the "Sorry Manny, there will be no drawstring bag" phone call. His face was flat on the table and I could see the tears. He raised his hand. "Stop, Bo! Stop. No more. I can't take it."

But I kept on. And when I stopped, he started in on his wife and the plant and how we would have to change his name to keep from being prosecuted. It was wild, here we were half drunk and half out of our heads, cracking up on everything. How I'd planned on making a hundred and fifty thousand a year and commuting from Hawaii and how now I was seeing five movies a day and watching TV all night and waiting for the ax to fall. How he'd planned on eating at only four- and five-star restaurants and was lucky to be taking a sack lunch to a bench job.

It was after midnight when I pulled out my credit cards. I discarded the Shell Oil and telephone charge cards and fanned my Master Charge, American Express, Visa, and Diners Club cards out like a poker hand. Then I closed my eyes and elaborately drew the Master Charge.

Buck said, "Things that bad?"

"They're getting there fast." I began laughing again and couldn't stop. "Any chance of that money? Old Greene would do a double backflip."

He grabbed the waiter's sleeve. "Buddy, give me a couple handfuls of those peppermint jobs from the cashier, O.K.?"

"Yes, sir."

The waiter was working us for a big tip and served him twenty or thirty Mason Mints on a silver tray. When Buck dumped them out on the tablecloth they looked like a half-dollar jackpot. "No, Bo. I'm broke. Stone broke."

He began sliding the mints in his pocket. "Sorry."

"Then how about another brandy? Might as well go down in flames."

"Now you're talking." He rocked forward and palmed my shoulder. Something new was in his eyes. "Bo, you ought to get the hell out of here." He tried not to smile but it came through anyway. "It's dragging your ass down. Tell you what, I'm going to fix you up with something that'll put some blood back in your face." He glanced around the room to make sure no one was listening. "I'm getting ready to make me a move. Tonight. You hear that? Tonight! That's why I called you. I'm heading back to Sarasota."

"The hell you are. I thought you were broke?"

"I got some stock and some props. And I think I got me some credit." He was talking fast about a small show in winter quarters. He said he'd kept it from the sheriff by incorporating it in a dead man's name. He leaned in closer, whispering. His wallet was out and he unfolded a Delta night-coach ticket.

"Bo, all it takes is a handshake and you're in. I'll buy the ticket."

"What in the hell could I do?"

"Front man. Promo work. Greatest job in the world. That's where the money is. Hell, we used to make so much we'd carry it out in pillowcases. Bo, I'm telling you, you'd be a goddamn natural."

"No, Buck. I've got to stick this out."

"You sure?" His teeth flashed as he bit into one of his mints.

"I'm sure. Buck, you'll keep in touch won't you?"

He opened two more mints. "Damn right. Bo, you're going to be hearing again from this old mongoose."

For the next two weeks I was in the office before eight and out before nine. I never saw Jake or Costo. I didn't open a single piece of mail. I didn't answer a single phone call. All I did was go to the movies. On Forty-second Street, between Sixth and Eighth, there are nineteen shows side by side, and they change features every other day. I'd hit two and then have lunch. Then two or three more. Then I'd call Ethel, make a list of the shrinking callbacks, and head home to drink beer and watch TV until I could sleep.

It was Saturday, and I'd seen every ball game on the tube; even the Spanish soccer on the Puerto Rican channel. I kept the telephone and a jar of peanut butter on the set. I'd made a little nest there, to save steps, and it was loaded down with Saltines and cigarettes, an ashtray, and a memo pad in case I had any red-hot ideas. The pad stayed blank. When the ball scores ended at eight I opened two beers and sharpened the focus on the cable movie. Suddenly I realized the phone was in my lap and I'd dialed the first six numbers for Monica. I took a long pull on the beer and spun the seventh. A man answered. He had the golden tone of a disc jockey; it had to be the director. When he went to get her I hung up. I cut the movie off and sat there in the dark, listening to the couple arguing in the next apartment and the traffic going by on Columbus Avenue. Then I heated up a can of Campbell's chicken-and-rice soup. I call on Campbell's down in Camden about once a month on my way to Whitman's Candy outside Philadelphia. No business, but it's like Beech-Nut; it looks good on the call reports. They're a big, smart company and their red-and-white can label with the gold seal in the middle is as famous as Coca-Cola red and the red, white, and blue of National Biscuit. Tomato soup and chicken-and-rice soup are their biggest sellers, but they've got one out now with little donut-shaped hamburgers sliding around in it that's a dog's dog. They'll probably pull it off the market in the spring. I watched the *Late Show* and then the *Late Late*.

And then it was Monday morning. I was in the office, calling the weather number. It was cold: nineteen degrees. It was snowing in Yonkers. I called for the correct time; 8:22. Then I called traffic information. Then I just sat there. Across the street they were flooring in the twenty-seventh and twenty-eighth floors. The Triboro Bridge, the Whitestone, the Con Edison stacks, everything had vanished forever. If I pressed my face against the glass I could see a slot of sky up Park Avenue. It was like being in an air shaft.

Making phone calls in sales is like putting together a string of good golf shots. You hit one, and then, if things are clicking, the next one is easier, and the one after that is just routine. I hadn't made any, and it didn't look like I was going to make any. But I had to. I had to call something besides the weather recording and the traffic recording and the goddamn time. I decided to call Dad. About a month back Mom had convinced him that the Club Zanzibar would be a disaster and he agreed to forget it and stick with Joe's. He came on like a Roman candle. "Joey! Joey! What a great surprise! Damn, am I glad you called!"

He said Mom was fine, and the weather was great, and then he told me two quick jokes. Then he dropped in a plug about business. "Listen kid, I want you back out here. I *need* you out here. These Pirates and Steelers have turned this whole country around. It's booming, kid. It's booming."

I could hear him pouring a beer and figured Mom was out shopping. "Kid, sticking with Joe's was the smartest move I ever made. See, I figured it out. Club Zanzibar had to mean disco, and disco has to mean trouble. That bunch don't buy drinks and they don't buy food. All they want to do is get laid. Who the hell needs the grief."

As he rattled on I had a quick flash that maybe I really did belong out there. There'd be plenty of women around the bar, and in a couple months maybe I'd forget Monica. But as he kept on about how great everything was and how wonderful it was going to keep on being, I realized

I'd marked down four verticals and a slash for the greats and seven more for the wonderfuls. There were too many. Something was wrong, big wrong. And then I knew what it was. He was lying. The old boy missed the lights and the mike and the nights out in front of the crowd. I also knew that every time he looked over and saw the pinball machines, where the stage had been, it had to bring him down. As he wound down, and we finally said good-bye, I decided that that was my last call for the day.

By nine o'clock I was in the movies with my knees jammed into the seat in front. My hands were in my overcoat pockets, my hat was down low. I'd left my sample cases at home. From ten feet away I was just another wino sleeping it off. After the double feature I had an orange juice at the hot-dog stand. Oranges were sky-high, and a six-ounce cup was seventy-five cents. I slid a dollar out. "Easy on the squeezer. I can't go that rind taste." It was the first person I'd spoken to in a long time.

"O.K., doctor, you're the boss."

You've got to watch this bunch. They'll lean down to get that extra drop and you get all the coloring and the chemicals.

It was colder as I crossed Sixth Avenue to this new health store. These all-organic, all-protein places always look like they just moved in or are just moving out. The shelves are one-deep, and they're big on bulletin boards: free kittens, free dogs, gerbils, abortions. I ordered a fruit drink and watched the counter girl wash out the blender. Women in these places are usually knocked up under their muu-muus and the guys are a little too close to Charles Manson to suit my taste. Three were in a booth eating salads and black bread. Their plates were about nine inches deep with sprouts, radishes, carrots; helluva meal for twenty-degree weather. It would be an ideal spot for old Jake. He liked to talk customers into big salads; then he'd head for the meat loaf. While they chewed he could talk.

I drank my juice and checked the racks for a decent package. Potato chips, banana chips, carrot chips were all in hand-packed bags with stick-on labels and cheap closures. Most of the stuff was shipped out of Salinas Valley, California. Then I got the feeling I was being watched. The guys in the booth were looking me over. Maybe I looked lonely. Maybe they had something else in mind. No, this is the kind of guy who gets all the pussy he can handle but can't buy a pack of cigarettes. One of them smiled. Then the other. They were inviting me over. Probably wanted me to slip on a poncho and get in behind a bowl of sprouts and start "rapping." Everybody has to belong to something, but I'll be damned if I was ready for this one yet. I drank up, smiled, tipped a quarter, and got the hell out of there.

I called Ethel from the pay phone on Forty-sixth Street next to the Orange Julius. No calls. Ethel sounded like a mother hen. "You still feeling bad, dearie?"

"I'm afraid so."

"I thought so. Well, don't go rushing it. I have this sister-in-law out in Bensonhurst who really got in a lot of trouble that way. Why don't you go home and I'll just tell everyone that you had to go back to bed and you'll be in touch just as soon as you're up."

"Maybe that's a good idea."

"Of course it is. And you heat up a cup of milk before you lie down. It's the best thing in the world to relax you."

"Maybe I'll do that too."

"Good. Bye-bye now, dearie."

There was no place to go, so I headed back to Forty-second Street. The wind was swinging the stoplights and cutting through me like a knife. I turned into the first movie without even looking up at the marquee or the starting time. I'd decided to see one more show, and only one. Then I'd catch lunch with Costo or Jake. I had to talk to someone besides Ethel. Anyone. The movie was an old John Wayne in the cheap orange when Technicolor was just coming in. *The Quiet Man* with Maureen O'Hara. It was solid Wayne. No bullshit or singing in the saddle. No indecisions or screwing around, and I'll be damned if it didn't do something to me. I came out slow, walking like Wayne. Long-striding like Wayne. Swinging my arms, like I was wearing leather chaps and 44s, like Wayne. The cold wind didn't bother me, and everyone I walked at moved out of the way. I was even thinking like Wayne when I pulled into the phone booth at the cigar store and called Greene. I told him I needed two weeks to go to Sarasota and I could guarantee Brody's eighteen thousand dollars. If I didn't collect, I'd resign and forfeit my vacation. Greene cleared his throat. "Joe, you've got guts. I'll say that for you. I like you, I've always liked you. But you've got to understand I really stuck my neck out for you and . . ."

It was the old "nice try, but no" routine. He wanted to give me two weeks to look around for another job and then turn in the car and the office key.

I broke in. "You want the money? I'm telling you I can get it."

"And I'm telling you why should I believe you? You want it any straighter than that?"

The sun was clearing the building on the corner, and I squinted into it like Wayne. "It's two weeks and you get the money or two weeks and you don't." I paused and took three beats, four beats, five. It came out slow and drawn out like Wayne. "O.K., Mister Greene, it's your move." Then I waited.

"All right Joe. You've got it. Try and hold the expenses down."

I hung up and did a machine-gun drum solo on the shelf. Two weeks with the car and expenses in Sarasota. It was wild. It was great. It was a license to steal. And then I decided if I could sell Greene on two weeks I could sure as hell sell Monica on one. With the John Wayne delivery still ringing in my ears it made sense. The hell with finding Buck. I'd take her down and we'd stay on the beach. When I got back it would be easy getting a job with a tan. O.K., by God, Sarasota! One last fling before they dropped the curtain. I'd dine her and dance her and screw her until she couldn't walk. Then I'd propose. She'd accept and we'd get married down in the great boondocks where all you need is three bucks and proof you aren't brother and sister. All I had to do was get her out of town.

I didn't need the Wayne delivery but I had to stay up. I had to be positive. I had to be absolutely on top of everything. I didn't want to call from the inside booth. I wanted it outside. Outside so I could let her know how everything was up and how fantastic Joe Mahaffey had become since she saw him last. I found a phone that worked at a gas station on Eighth Avenue. A bum had taken a leak and it was still stinking of ammonia, but it didn't bother me. I was up and laughing as she came on the phone. I told her I'd just made eighteen thousand dollars on the Bunny Tissue job and I was going to make another eighteen next month and the month after that. It was a great story. A wonderful story. And as I winged it along I was almost believing it. I raved on how Buck and I were both drunk and running around drinking champagne and celebrating at every bar we could find. I told her he wanted to say hello. I shouted "Hey, Buck!" Then I told her he was too stoned. I raved on how he was buying champagne for everyone. I asked her if she could hear the music. The crowd. The noise. I told her we had gone into business together. That I'd resigned from Pioneer. Then I told her I was taking off two weeks and running down to Sarasota to play golf and get a tan. I asked her to come along.

"I'm sorry, Joe. It sounds like fun, but I'd better pass."

"Come on, Mon. Tell them you've got a virus or need root-canal work or something. Hell, tell them to go to hell. I'm telling you we're rolling in dough."

"No, Joe, I can't. I just can't."

I raved on about the beach, the nightclubs, the dog races, the jai alai, the dancing. She kept saying no and I kept on. And on. Finally she paused. She was quiet. Then she said it. "Yes. Yes, damn it, yes. I'm coming. The hell with this meat rack. If they don't like it I'll quit."

I grinned at the receiver like a madman. "Terrific! Terrific! Absolutely terrific! We'll leave now and beat the traffic."

"O.K., but I've got to stop. I need some things."

I was so up and wild and happy and crazy I didn't know what to do. If the phone cord was longer I'd have spun around in this great new disco step. Instead, I closed my eyes and tapped out the rhythm on the steel floor and did it with my shoulders, my elbows, my knees. A week with Monica. Three or four thousand miles with her. Seven days and seven nights with her. Maybe fourteen. Maybe a lifetime. It was all I wanted. It was everything.

"Joe, you there?"

"Sure, baby. Right here." I wanted to say a hundred things, but all that came out was, "Terrific! Terrific! Monica, we are going to have one terrific time."

When I picked Monica up I was ready. I'd bought a dozen tapes: the Beatles; the Eagles; Emmy Lou Harris; Crosby, Stills, and Nash; and for laughs some of the crap we used at Danceland. The back seat was like an explosion at Bloomingdale's. An ice bucket, ice, glasses, twelve bottles of Dom Perignon champagne, and a thirty-four-dollar round of assorted French cheeses. No National Biscuit or Sunshine Biscuit here; it was Cadbury's Olde English Stone Grounds and white water biscuits packed in Coldstream Guards tins with copper hinges and friction closures. Also a fruit basket, about nine kinds of nuts, and thirty-six American Beauty roses with the longest goddamn stems I've ever seen.

As we came out of the Holland Tunnel Monica was drinking champagne and singing along with the Beatles. Her hair was in ponytails with blue ribbons, and when she cocked her head for a high note she looked so great I couldn't stand it. I didn't know whether to go a hundred miles an hour and get there in a hurry or slow down to twenty and wallow in every second of it. She had on tight tan Levi's, a blue cashmere sweater, and half boots the color of peanut butter. On top at a hard angle was a long-billed New York Yankees cap.

She jumped the tape to "Hard Day's Night," refilled the glasses, and proposed a toast to the Statue of Liberty. We toasted the Pulaski Skyway, the Verrazano-Narrows Bridge, and, as we banked around the big cloverleaf into the New Jersey Turnpike, we toasted the wild and great and fantastic fifteen-hundred-mile trip south. The smell of the roses, the champagne, and Monica herself were driving me crazy. I eased the Olds to thirty in the slow lane and kissed her with one eye on the road. Then I dropped to ten and kissed her with both eyes closed. And then I pulled onto the shoulder and stopped and kissed her so long and hard I thought I'd pass out. I was in love with her. And crazy as a banshee for her. And horny as a goat for her. I wanted to pull off the turnpike and hit the first motel. Or whip in behind a Coca-Cola sign and make love in the back seat with her feet on the ceiling, ripping out the upholstery.

And then I had another idea. A great idea. The Newark exit was coming up and I was saying, "Damn right, damn right, damn right."

Monica said, "Damn right what?"

"You'll see."

In another three minutes we were pulling into Elgin Bread. I told her I'd be right back and grinned in the window with Costo's old line, "Play the radio if you want to."

There's no high like a champagne high, and I cruised by the receptionist like I was chairman of the board. Marty Rosenbaum from Bestprint was in Horner's office with a leather standup demo. He was in the middle of a pitch. Horner looked up, furious. "Just what in the hell do you think you're doing?"

I touched Marty's shoulder with one hand. With the other I pointed at the egg timer. Horner looked at it. Marty looked at it. It was half empty, down to two and a

half minutes. No one spoke. I reached over and with two
delicate fingers picked it up and smiled my sweetest
smile. Then I snapped the bastard in half and poured the
sand in a big X across the desk. Horner crouched up. I
was so ready for him I was shaking. "Keep your seat,
shithead."

I had a speech rehearsed, but I forgot it. Instead, I
slapped Marty on the back. "Hang in there, sport. If you
can sell this prick you're a better man than I am."

When I left I was higher than when I came in.

The sun was just setting when we hit the first bridge.
Monica sighed. "It's beautiful, Joe. Just beautiful."

Unless you live on the West Side with a view of the
Hudson, or hit the Happy Hours at the top of Rockefeller
Center or the World Trade Center, you don't really see
too many sunsets in the city. She touched my knee with
one finger. "Know something, I really didn't think you had
it in you."

In my head I was saying, "Me neither." But what came
out was perfect. "All it takes is a little luck. And a little
money."

In my head I was going a mile a minute. *Mahaffey,
remind me to give you a medal. And every hour on the hour
let's pause thirty seconds so I can tell you you're a goddamn
genius.* I squeezed her knee. Maybe we'd hit Sarasota and
keep on going. Down to the Keys. Get a job bartending.
Or working on a sailboat. Or selling conch shells or
whatever it is that washes up there that the tourists buy.
But before we hit the Keys it was going to be wild. We'd
probably go down in flames like Bonnie and Clyde or
those two Mississippi crazies that flashed from state to
state sticking up Mini-Marts and wrecking cars and
making love. But first we were going to do it right. She
kissed my ear and had me crooning like a puppy when we
started up the bridge. The rigging shadows were
stretched out over the bay. She touched my cheek with
the back of her wrist. "You know what's going to be even
nicer than all this?"

I wanted her to say it. "What?"

The sun had cooled and you could look directly into it. About nine or ten shades of orange and red all bleeding into an orange-yellow-gold center. Sea gulls were wheeling and gliding through the bridge's superstructure. They were gold, then silver, then gold again. Her fingers grazed my chin. "Me and you in a great big king-size bed with the TV picture on and the sound off. It makes the room nice." Then she kissed my ear. When she tipped her tongue in I almost jumped into the oncoming lane.

We arranged the roses on the table when we had dinner. And on the headboard and nightstands when we made love. And in the bathroom when we showered, and in the foyer when we dried each other off. And then back around the bed where we made love again. And then, with the picture on and the sound off, we slept together coiled so tight we could have used a single.

When I woke I turned the TV set on from the headboard. We'd slept through the "Today" show and into the local news. Monica stretched and opened her eyes; I'd never seen her prettier. She touched my cheek with one finger.

"Morning, Joe."

I did a push-up over her and kissed her nose, her lips, her chin, and then each breast three times. "Morning, Mon." What a great way to wake up. She was watching the television show, trying to figure out where she was and what time it was. I pushed the sheet down to the foot of the bed. I wanted to see the small of her back, the back of her knees, underneath her breasts, her toenails. I left the picture on and cut the sound off. And then, as if I'd been planning it all my life, I made the longest, smoothest, coolest, finest love I'd ever made to anyone. Each time we'd made love it had been better than the last time. But this time was brand new. She horseshoed up into a high arch like a baton twirler. Her legs were longer. Her arms were stronger. We swooped and dipped and sailed together and she stretched her legs in a wide V, holding her feet with her hands, and she scared me with her strength. Her eyes were deep and wild and I was with her and wanted to stay there forever. When it was finally over, and finally over again, I hooked the sheet with my toes and pulled it up and reached for the champagne. It was warm, but it was perfect. Everything was perfect. Then I lay back with the bottle balanced on my stomach, telling her I'd sprained my arches and pulled loose every small bone in my body.

She was laughing. "You're crazy, Joe. You're really crazy. I guess that's what I like about you."

I handed her the bottle. "You know what I feel like right this second?"

"I'll bite."

"Like I've melted and if I move I'll just pour off the bed and go oozing across the room about an inch high and a yard wide."

She was laughing as she filled my navel with champagne. We were both giggling and couldn't stop as she sucked it up and filled it up again.

She was right, the color from the TV did do something to the room. She'd read about it in *Cosmopolitan*. And then, just as it hit me that I had never been happier, something cut in. I tried not to think about her holding her feet like that. But it kept flashing back. It was something new since the night of our dinner at Charley's. Probably something the director had just taught her.

The sheet label was loose and I pulled it off. It was a Cannon queen size: sixty percent cotton, forty percent polyester. Cannon Mills is in North Carolina, but their purchasing is down on Worth Street in Manhattan. They buy a lot of polyethylene for overwrapping sheets and pillowcases. Monica walked her fingers up my stomach and skimmed them around my nipples. Maybe she'd read about the big V in another magazine. Or a girlfriend had told her about it in the bathroom. Or she'd seen it on triple X on the cable.

She slid up and kissed my ear. "You know what I want,

Joe?" She bit it softly and pronounced every word very slowly and very clearly. "Some nice, ice-cold orange juice and about nine slices of bacon. And I want it as crisp as they can get it." She kept her lips in my ear. "And two eggs over light, and some coffee, and some home fries, and some toast, and some butter." Hot and cold flashes were trilling down my spine and my heart was hammering in my throat. There were two things that I now knew were certain: as soon as we got a few more miles from Manhattan I was going to propose, and what she and the director had done in bed was going to be the easiest thing in the world for me to forget.

CHAPTER

It took three great days and three great nights to get to the Florida line. We'd finished nine champagnes. Half of the cheese. All of the nuts. The roses were still holding up as we cruised down Route 8, the old road running along the Gulf of Mexico. Long stretches of ocean down one side. Long stretches of swamp down the other. Stopped and skinny dipped. Dried off on the car roof and made love in the back seat. As we headed on south, the temperature kept moving up. In Tallahassee it was eighty-five. Near Tampa, ninety. The wind was from due south, and gardenias and camellias and azaleas were everywhere. I could smell the salt, the fish, the swamp. Rod-and-reel fishing from the bridges, the causeways, and the culverts; pole fishing and trotlines back on the creeks. Everyone and his brother had a pickup truck with two tall dogs in the back and a shotgun in the window rack. Violent country: road signs used for target practice; shotgun patterns in the mailboxes. More Fords than General Motors; almost no imports.

The sun was setting out over Tampa Bay, and up in the

oaks the birds were settling down for the night. Pelicans were skimming along about two feet above the water, and out on the horizon the ship lights began coming on. And then it was dark all over and the fast food and honky-tonk neon was lighting up like a giant pinball machine. AL'S . . . DICK'S . . . MARY'S . . . JIMMY'S PIG 'N' WHISTLE . . . The names reminded me of Lorraine, and suddenly I was thinking about Dad being stuck out there with Joe's.

We stopped at a honky-tonk built right on the beach with the neon sputtering SHANGRI-LA. An orange cat was in the window under a Miller High Life sign and four dogs were lying out in the yard. Some of the customers were sitting on old bus seats facing the shrimp boats in the distance. Inside, at the bar, I kept my right hand over Monica's left knee and drank left-handed. Dancing still in the sixties down here: Twist, Watusi, heavy-beat faking, and spontaneous breakdowns that had nothing to do with anything. A tall high-stepper in a silver-piped powder-blue cowboy suit was dancing alone, doing a combination clog and tap routine. Monica couldn't believe him. "We could use that one at the studio. Watch him."

When the music slowed he kept his eyes on the Miller High Life sign in the window for isolation and concentration. When the beat picked up he hairpinned down, studying his feet as if they belonged to someone else. He was wearing white vinyl boots complete with metal plates, and when he swooped across the floor his heel-and-toe work sounded like a stick being dragged along a picket fence. "Your Cheatin' Heart" came on, and a mother and daughter with identical beehive hairdos and matching tight-fitting purple pantsuits came out on the floor holding hands.

He circled them warily with his hands in his pockets and then eased in smiling, trying to cut in. They shook their heads and kicked into an old double-time Lindy. The mother had a lot of moves, and out on the breakaway she slowed down with her eyes closed, her face soft, feeling the words behind the words or remembering some red-rimmed neon honky-tonk, some old and long-gone love. The daughter finally had to bring her in. The cowboy closed in again, but this time something else was on his mind. His face creased into a look of tender pain as he chorded an invisible guitar and circled them, slow-tapping and singing every word as if he was there when Hank Williams wrote it.

The record changed. It was Willie Nelson and Waylon Jennings doing "Good-Hearted Woman." Suddenly, as if on signal, the room rose and crowded the floor. They came from the booths and the corners and the bus seats out front. They came out carrying cigars and beer and mixed drinks, and one old lady was dancing along with her knitting. Each one had their own move. There were pump-handlers, eyes-closed dreamers, dippers, sliders, and swoopers, and the cowboy dropped backward on his hands in a wild humping hootch that scared every woman under forty back to the wall. A leather-backed greaser with DAYTONA SPEEDWAY on his jacket and STP on his cap wrapped his arms around the old lady, and they sailed across the room in a high-stepping triple spin.

Monica pushed her hair back from her face and in the same move lifted it from her neck and fluffed it out. "You know something, I really like this place." The beer was getting to her. "I mean, I really like this place."

I grinned in the backbar mirror. "O.K., we'll buy it." I printed out JOE AND MONICA'S on the back of a Florida Gators football schedule. "How's this?" I scalloped on a border. "Red neon, blue trim. Like it?"

"Let me." She sketched in two bubbling glasses of champagne in the bottom corners and four exploding firecrackers across the top.

I snapped my fingers. "Perfecto." I surveyed the room. "And we'll move the juke back. It'll keep from crowding the door like that."

She shook her head. "No. No juke." She sat erect and elaborately pointed her cigarette at the corner. "Live music, over there. Maybe some tapes behind the counter." She paused and winked in the backbar mirror. "The right tapes."

She was wearing a black turtleneck, and a gardenia I'd picked was tucked in over her left ear. With her chin cocked and her brown eyes bigger than I'd ever seen them and the gesture with the cigarette, she looked like one of the great lingerie models they use for the Saks ads in *The New Yorker*. We kept planning "Joe and Monica's" and decided to go French, and ship in Dad's Eiffel Tower salt-and-peppers and his red-checked tablecloths. We'd do the ceiling, the walls, and the backbar in Toulouse-Lautrec prints. There would be low wine bottles with running candle wax and hanging cheese and salamis, and on the juke would be every old French show tune we could find. And next winter we'd bring Mom and Dad down to help plan the menu.

I flipped over a Budweiser beer pad and carefully centered and printed out COCA-COLA MOON.

"Joe! Hey, that's nice." She looked at it again and then at me. "It really is. Where'd you get it?"

"I made it up a long time ago. You sure you like it?"

She kissed me on the cheek. "Forget 'Joe and Monica's.' It's 'Coca-Cola Moon,' and anyone who doesn't like it, well, they can keep on driving."

I winked at myself in the mirror and did a little bongo pattern on the bar. Then I cupped both hands over her ears. "I love you. I love you. And I've got a rip-roaring sensational idea."

I pulled her chin around so I could see her eyes and, more important, so she could see mine. "Listen, Mon, we can go outside and pick oranges and tangerines right off the trees. Hell, we can pick gardenias, thousands of them, millions of them. You ever think you could do that? Tangerines off a tree? Gardenias off a damn bush?" I didn't give her a chance to answer. I jumped ahead, way ahead. "Let's stay down here. Screw New York. Screw everything." I took two beats and plunged on. "Let's get married. I mean really get married. You and me. Me and

you. You'll be Monica Murphy Mahaffey. I'll still be Joe."
I stopped. I had to be serious. I had to look serious. I *was*
serious. "No kidding, Monica. I'm not kidding. I want to
marry you right here and right now. How about it?"

Her eyes were shining, and if she hadn't waited that
extra second she would have said yes. Her hand was on
the back of my neck. She squirreled around and kissed
me on the lips. I held her there. "Ask me tomorrow, will
you, Joe."

I mimed "I love you" in the mirror. She smiled and
squeezed my knee. "Me too, Joe."

Out on the floor the mother and daughter were still
doing Lindy turns and breakaways. The cowboy with his
eyes closed and his thumbs and first fingers in little O's
was dancing alone. He had given up on them and was
staying close to the juke. Monica traced her fingers over
my hand. Something else was on her mind. "You haven't
asked me about Gordon." She kept watching me in the
mirror. "Want to know about him?" It was the first time I'd
heard his name.

"No, baby, I don't think so."

She sipped her beer. "You know something, you have
changed. I thought you'd want to know everything."

"Maybe I have." Inside I was the same old churning
liar. I wanted to know everything about him. How tall?
Was he better looking? Better in bed? Funnier? A better
dancer? Did he fill out a short form on income tax or a long
one? But what I really wanted to know was what she had
ever seen in him that was missing in me. I made a soft fist
and pushed against her cheek. "It's called success." I
winked at her in the mirror. God, how I loved that white
streak. At the next Roadside America or Crazy Cal's
Fireworks we'd buy a Joe-and-Monica two-hearts-
entwined bumper sticker and a wooden plaque for the
mantelpiece. And in the morning we'd pick up a ring in
Sarasota and find a justice of the peace in the Yellow
Pages. As far as I was concerned we were as good as
married.

But then a small voice came cutting through about the eighteen thousand dollars a month, every month. I began making new plans fast. I'd find Buck and get the damn money. If that didn't work, I'd hock everything in the apartment that wasn't nailed down and get a twenty-four-month loan for the rest. Then I'd send the check to Greene and get back on the Pioneer payroll. She would understand, and she would love me even more. I slid my arm around her waist and pulled her close.

Sarasota outskirts. Red and yellow neon was bouncing off the clouds and every other radio station was Spanish. Great sounds. Trumpets, flamenco guitars, and cha-cha-cha. Talk and call-in shows same as New York, New Jersey, Pennsylvania; same old husband playing around, wife playing around. Same old senior citizens sweating out the Red Menace and disfranchised youth trying to wring some intrinsic meaning from it all. Back to the Spanish. Had the air conditioner on high and all four windows open. Could smell the salt and feel the cold. Best of both worlds. Along the road, the real estate sharks were filling in the swamps and trying to unload them before they sank. Quadruplex movies and high-rises going up where the armadillo and the iguana used to roam, and cement mixers working three shifts were pouring K-Marts, S-Marts, Woolcos side by side by side. The trees and the wild jungle cabbage were highlighted against the night with red and pink and blue floods. Everything was thicker, denser, greener, and mockingbirds were up on the orange-tiled roofs and TV antennas, singing everything but the theme song from *Doctor Zhivago*. Saw the big red, yellow, and blue Holiday Inn star and headed for it.

Holiday Inn good deal as steady place to stay. Good food, pool, plenty of hot water and towels, color TV, and if you check out during the rush they never run your credit card through the computer check. You can also register as a single and no questions asked.

I was in the pool on a plastic raft. There was no breeze.
There were no clouds. No birds. It was like the desert.
Monica was greased down with coconut oil and stretched
out on a chaise reading a paperback novel. She had on a
white bikini that was cut so deep and close it made me
nervous. Every time she shifted her legs or turned a page,
four guys playing gin rummy had her in the cross hairs. I
was floating around on the raft trying to sort things out.
I'd proposed twice since the honky-tonk, and each time
she was closer to yes. One more day, one more time,
maybe two more times would do it. But right now what I
really wanted to do was get alone for about two hours in a
phone booth. I wanted to try for Brody. Then I saw that
she was watching me. There was a funny look in her eyes,
as if she'd seen something. My throat tightened. Something cold was moving in my stomach. I forced a smile.
Jesus, she'd found out. It was all over. But how? And then
she winked. Slowly she closed her eyes, and then, even
slower, she ran her tongue over her top lip. I grinned like
an ape and nodded. Then I checked the card sharks. They
hadn't missed a beat.

After we made love I lay with the ashtray on my
stomach, watching the air conditioner suck the smoke
across the room. It was the first time she had wanted me
more than I did her. Usually I get a big voltage drop right
after I make love. I want to take a shower or go for a walk.
A drink. A pack of cigarettes. But with Monica, as the old
song went, it was all brand new. I'd stay inside until she
got tired of my weight. Then I'd snug her head up on my
shoulder and hold her. I couldn't get enough of her. I
couldn't turn her loose. Sometimes I'd wake up and look
at her. I'd just lie there, grinning and grateful, whispering
"I love you" just loud enough not to wake her and loving
her more than ever. But this was the first time I had to get
away. It was Buck; I had to find out where he was. I had
to see him. "Monica, I've got to get the car checked."

"Anything important?"

"Just points, maybe plugs. Might take an hour." I

wanted to go alone but I wanted to cover myself. "Come on. Come on along."

"No thanks. I'll work on my tan some more. Pick up a paper. I want to see how everybody else is freezing."

I pulled into the first bar and took a beer into the phone booth. I opened the Yellow Pages to Entertainers. Buck had too many creditors to use his real name, and he hadn't been South long enough, but I had to start somewhere. I drew a block around three possibilities: Ace Shows, Acme Shows, Consolidated Exhibitors. In Manhattan, in printing, packaging, bail bonds, and small loans there's a big scramble for first listing in the Yellow Pages. Usually it runs AAAAA then AAAA then AAA. Then it drops to real names: Acme, Acorn, All Right. If they figured a purchasing agent could pronounce Aardvaark they'd have slugged it in fifty years ago. No one knew Brody. No one had ever even heard of him, and I finally gave up.

I ordered a Mai Tai, the specialty of the house. It's sweet with rum and fruit juices and they serve it in a small flowerpot with a stalk of pineapple, a gardenia, and a little Japanese parasol. I began twirling the parasol. Monica, Monica, Monica; it was all Monica. I had to come up with something. Maybe I'd simply tell her the truth. That would sure as hell be the easiest. Then I could concentrate on Buck. There was an outside chance he had the money. An outside chance I could hang on at Pioneer. If I told her the truth I wouldn't have to be lying every time I opened my mouth. Yes, that was it. I'd tell her everything. Then we'd run him down together.

I'd simply tell her. And she'd laugh and say she knew it all along. I'd be the prodigal son. The lost sheep. Like one of those fifties movies where the girl is sharper than the guy and sees through the muck he's gotten himself into and helps him out. And each discovers some deeper quality in the other. Yeah, that would damn well do it. Truth and honesty and direct eye contact. Truth would out. It would make you free. All of the old clichés were true. If they weren't true they wouldn't be clichés. I had another Mai Tai. And then another. I'd bring her here. Tonight. I'd load up the juke with soft songs. Yes. I spun the paper umbrella: red, yellow, green, purple. Terrific. Fantastic. Wonderful. In that chair. The Mai Tais would set her up. Yes. The music would help. I'd have the waitress light the candles and bring more gardenias. Yes. Everything would be perfect. Yes, yes, yes. I tipped the waitress five dollars.

Outside it was so white and blinding I forgot I had on sunglasses. Traffic was bumper to bumper, and the air conditioner wasn't putting out enough. Inside in the dark and cool with the gardenias everything was possible, but out here with the truckers shouting and the red-necks revving up and laying down rubber, it was another story. Everything was leaking away. I could no more tell her the whole truth than I could go waltzing in to see Manny Stevens and Abramowitz as if nothing had happened. I'd have to wait for a better time. A voice cut in, "When?" I was talking through my teeth. "I don't know. I don't know. Damn it, leave me alone!" A driver behind me was leaning on a three-tone horn. In front, an orange bumper was glowing HONK IF YOU LOVE JESUS.

The last bottle of Dom Perignon was in the ice bucket. But I didn't want to drink. I didn't want to watch the *Late Show.* I didn't want to make love. What I wanted was to get the hell out of the room. I had to find out about Buck and what was happening in Omaha. "Honey, I need some cigarettes, you want something?" My voice cracked as if I couldn't get enough air. She was watching a Warren Beatty movie. I'd missed the title but it looked like a loser.

She smiled. "I think I'd like some chocolate." She kissed two fingers and blew it at me. "Any kind. Surprise me."

It was a relief getting out on the gravel path. I headed for the bar. I needed to be alone. Why had she let me see her holding her feet like that? It was bad enough living with that son-of-a-bitching Gordon, but it was pretty damn crude showing me how they screwed. I kicked the gravel. Everything would have been all right if she hadn't come on like the goddamn *Kama Sutra*. The hell with it. If she found out, so much the better. Maybe I'd just tell her and end the damn thing and mark it off as a piece of first-class ass and nothing else. In a few weeks, when I'd worked things out, maybe I'd try again. But right now I had more important things to deal with. I figured Ernie might have heard from Buck, and I called his home. The line was busy, and I told the boy to try again in a few minutes and call me. I slid onto a bar stool and flipped through the Miami *Herald*. Nice paper, with smooth printing stock that holds the colors. It was cold back in the territory. Pittsburgh, twenty degrees; New York City, eighteen; Philadelphia, eighteen. Good-looking sports page. The Celtics were on another streak. The Knicks were doing their usual nothing. I kept seeing Monica stretched out with that long reach for her feet. You don't read that stuff in the magazines. I ordered another drink and picked up the phone.

"This is Mahaffey. How about hitting that Omaha number again."

"Oh! You're in the bar! I'm sorry, I put the call through to the room. Mrs. Mahaffey took it."

My voice shot up. "The room?"

"Yes, sir, you said room."

"The hell I did. Jesus!" My heart sank. I couldn't remember what I'd told him.

"Well, I'm sure sorry. I'm really sorry. They've been talking for five or ten minutes."

I sat there, stunned.

"You want me to cut in?"

"Yes! No! I mean, no, you'd better not."

There was nothing to do but wait. I'd call Ernie back and find out how much he'd told her. Five minutes later they were still talking. I had a double Scotch. Maybe I had said "room." Maybe I'd wanted Ernie to do the dirty work I couldn't. But I could have sworn I said "bar." Finally they hung up. I called Ernie. He'd been drinking. He'd told her the whole Brody story. The whole Bunny Tissue story. I asked him why.

"Why? Joe, you asking me why? Because you're the damn best field man we've got. Boy, if Old Ernie was in your shoes he'd tell them to kiss his ass."

"O.K., Ern, O.K." There was a long pause. "Joe, there's something else." He took a deep breath. "It's like this. Greene's letting me out in the territory."

"O.K., great."

He was apologizing. "Yeah, but guess whose territory?" I didn't have to. "When you coming in?"

"Soon, a week, maybe two. I've got to break in my replacement out here. Joe, I feel like hell about this. You got to believe me, I feel terrible."

He sounded like me whining to Manny. "It's O.K., Ern. It had to be someone. Listen, I'm glad for you. I'm really glad."

"Joe, any chance you getting that money? This bunch would turn on a dime if you brought it in."

"I'm working on it."

"Damn, I sure wish you could. They're going to farm old Jake out next year. Boy, me and you could really rack them up in the old Big Apple."

I covered the speaker. I had to hear it out loud. "The Big Apple. Jesus!" Ernie had been in once for the packaging convention at the Americana. "You driving in?"

"No, flying. They want me to use your car. I'll need the keys and the registration slips. Joe, you ain't mad at me, are you?"

"No, Ern, it's O.K. So long now."

"Hang in there, Joe."

I dropped every quarter and every dime I was carrying in the vending machine. Three Hershey's with almonds, three Hershey's plain, two Reese's Peanut Butter Cups. Then I just stood there feeling the almonds in the

Hershey and trying to think. The bar seemed bigger. For thirty-five cents it ought to be. What could I tell her? "I'm sorry" would get me in the door. Then what? I checked the label; it was a new size. The candy market is grim on keeping you in the dark. They'll increase the weight and raise the price and you need a ten-place calculator to figure out how you're getting screwed. Same thing on soap powders, frozen foods, and six-packs of everything. I dried my palms on my pants. I had to keep cool. I had to be firm. I had to make her understand that it was all because I loved her and wanted to marry her. I came in grinning and snapping my fingers. I fanned the candy out on the foot of the bed like a poker hand. "How was the movie?"

She sat on the edge of the bed, brushing her hair. "O.K." Her voice was flat. I opened the last champagne and filled two glasses. I had to keep moving. I had to keep talking. I raised my glass. "Cheers."

She tipped hers at the screen. The news was coming on.

"Mon, you mad?"

She shook her head. "No, Joe."

"I did it because." I finished my glass and poured another. "Well, damn it, because I love you. I wasn't kidding, honey. I wasn't. I really want to marry you."

She was at the dresser, brushing her hair and trying to get it to stay up. I thought she was getting ready for bed. "You didn't have to be a goddamn millionaire."

"I know. But it just got loose. Mon, I'm sorry. I'm really sorry."

I sat on the luggage rack, slowly stacking the candy. The Hershey's plain on the bottom, then the almonds, then the Reese's. If you ask people what's number one on the candy counters of America, nine out of ten will jump for Hershey's almond or Hershey's plain. Not so. Reese's Peanut Butter Cups have been there for thirty years. Number two is M&M's. Then Hershey's plain. Then Hershey's almonds. I offered her another drink, but she shook her head. Her hair kept slipping loose. Finally, she tied it down with a scarf. "Joe, I want you to take me to the airport."

"Listen, baby, you've got to listen."

"There's nothing to listen to."

"I'm serious. I've never been more serious in my life. I want you to marry me."

"Marry you?" She sounded as if she'd just heard it for the first time. She unzipped her jeans to tuck in her blouse. "Come on, are you taking me or do I have to call a cab?"

"But why not, Monica. Why not? O.K., I lied. But Jesus, it was because I love you. I want to marry you and be with you. Monica, you've got to have a reason."

"Joe, damn it." She zipped her jeans up. "If you don't *know* the reason, you'll never know it."

On the way to the airport she sat as far away as she could get. Neither of us spoke. I plugged in the Beatles tape and jumped the tracks to "Hard Day's Night." All it did was make everything worse. I cut it off. As I turned onto Route 17 I laughed. It sounded hollow. "Pretty funny about me wanting to marry you." Everything I said sounded like I was in an echo chamber. She kept staring out the window at the billboards and the orange and grapefruit shippers lining the road. "O.K., so I lied. Mon, that doesn't mean I don't love you."

"Listen." She swung around. "Oh God, there's nothing to say to you. Nothing."

At the airport, I pulled the car into a slot and cut the engine. "Let me at least buy the ticket."

"Oh Christ, no." She was out of the car with her bag.

"Well, let me carry the bags."

"No! Just stay where you are."

"Oh God, Mon, just listen to me. Listen, I'm going to make something happen. I'll call you, O.K.?"

She didn't answer.

"You hear me, Monica? I'm going to call you."

Her voice was cold, flat. "O.K., Joe, you do that."

She took four steps and dropped her bag. Then she turned around screaming. "Why? Why in the hell didn't you tell me?" She tore her kerchief off and threw it at me. "Jesus, Joe! Jesus!"

The Eastern flight moved out on the runway, and I sat there watching the wing lights. I turned the Beatles tape on. As the sound came up I turned it off. Then I began peeling the label off the Hershey's almond. Jake said in the old days Hershey's had a foil liner but had gone to glassine in the sixties to save money and the bar had never been the same. The wing lights of the plane vanished and another jet was coming in. I finished the Hershey's and opened a Reese's Peanut Butter Cup. Then I cut the engine on and headed back.

I kept asking myself, why had she done it? Why? Why? It didn't make any sense. Maybe she was still in love with that asshole Gordon and was just testing it out. Or maybe she was just horny and wanted to get out of town for a few days. Women. Who in the hell can figure them out? Maybe I could pick something up at the bar. I had to do something to keep her off my mind. It was going to be a long, hard night.

CHAPTER

7

By breakfast my head had cleared. The strain of lying every time I went to the john was gone, and I was beginning to feel better about everything. I pushed away the grits; I didn't feel that good. Southerners eat this crap three times a day, every day. I ate my bacon and eggs, wishing I had an English muffin and an order of home fries on the side. After breakfast I began going through the Yellow Pages under Booking Agents. Brody, or someone who knew him, had to be out there someplace. If I could run him down and get the money, the rest would fall into place. Monica could wait. The hell with her. Let her sweat me out for a few days. Maybe they'd hit some turbulence, or had a hijack scare, and she was already on the phone trying to apologize.

Cruised into Sarasota. Good-looking town. Sixty-foot yachts in the marina from Long Island, Connecticut, and Rhode Island. Downtown is built in a circle. Shops and restaurants are low Spanish adobe set back in under the live oaks and the bougainvillea. It looked like money. It felt like money. And with the azaleas and gardenias blooming, it smelled like money. Blue rinse set very thin, very old, very rich. Men in crested blazers and madras slacks. Gucci, Pucci, Yves Saint Laurent. No polyester or K-Marts here. No Buck Brody either.

Two hundred yards south of Sarasota it turns into a retirement colony. Big pitch for golden-agers. Billboards featuring aluminum walkers, ambulance services, funeral arrangements. For keeping a customer on the books you'd have to go a long way to beat this crowd. I've seen Tums, Rolaids, and Bromo Seltzer in the Pennsylvania Turnpike vending machines, but first time for Geritol and iron tablets. Picked up flyer advertising Ringling Museum two miles away.

Decided to drive up and look in. Asked the ticket taker and the groundkeeper if they'd heard of Buck Brody. Both said check the tour guide. Guide too busy so followed him along, listening to spiel. He had a running lecture about how John North Ringling's wife had fallen in love with Venice and he had simply built her a Venetian palace here, complete with grottos, canals, a gondola, and a mandolin-strumming gondolier. On moonlit nights the gondolier would take her for a cruise, and while she trailed her hand in the lagoon, he sang of love, and vino, and his native land across the seas. Things done in style back then. Up in Ringling's room I cornered the guide. He'd never heard of Brody but said I should check the winter quarters back in around Fruitland and Deland. Ringling's room was covered in red velvet with gold stripes. Exhibit of his wardrobe, his shoes, his shaving mugs, his favorite walking canes. Also on exhibit, a six-color litho of his famous partner, old Phineas Taylor Barnum. Beautiful face tones and fine hairline work on eyes and fingernails. Poster shows P. T. in the center of wheel with illuminated spokes running out to six-color illustrations of his many accomplishments. P. T. addressing the joint meeting of U.S. House and Senate. P. T. founding the city of Bridgeport. P. T. discovering Tom Thumb, Jenny Lind, Gargantua, and four or five other

show-biz firsts. Sent Mom and Dad a 24-by-36-inch copy
in a paper-tube mailer. Started to send one to Monica but
decided to wait and get something nicer.

Took guide's advice and headed for winter quarters
back toward Fruitland. Kept driving; kept asking questions. Everyone was connected to the circus or the
carnivals, but no one seemed to know anyone else. The
bullshit was about a foot deep. Circus people look down
on carnies, carnies look down on everyone. Elephants,
male or female, are called bulls. The "ope" in calliope is
pronounced like it is in "hope" so they know you're on the
inside, and no one has a straight name. One guy was
Sanitary Ike. Another, Birdliver Baker. Unemployment
doesn't exist; it's called "at liberty." One wino who told
me he starred for Ringling for twenty years, on the high
wire, said the only eastern state he wasn't wanted in was
Delaware. He was in semi-retirement until the statute of
limitations ran out. He hit me for a dollar for a pint of red.
He didn't know Brody but told me to see a tent-and-sail
man in St. Petersburg. The tent man said he heard that a
Brody had come through town. He told me to see a
coin-operated-machine man in Tampa. The Tampa man
said he knew for a fact he had moved on to California and
was following the migrant workers. Three hundred miles
and ten hours later I was about to give up. Finally, at an
International House of Pancakes, a waitress with a
nameplate that said MARY ANNE and a chrome beehive,
told me circus people never know anyone. "Honey, there
ain't a one of them that someone ain't looking for. I mean,
if it ain't an ex-wife or an ex-husband, it's got to be a
subpoena server. That's why you get all these crazy
names. These people are wonderful people. But honey,
they change their names every time the wind blows." I
told her about Brody's broken nose and red hair and
missing finger. She shook her head. "I know a lot of them
like that. You want some more coffee?"

"Might as well."

She brought over another waitress. Her nameplate

read CARLOTTA. I described him again and she said, "He's real smart and talks a lot?"

"That's him."

"And he's from Mississippi?" She pushed her hair forward. "And he wears his hair kind of like this?"

"Yeah. Yeah."

"I used to know him. But his name wasn't Brody. Four or five years back it was Rabon. Rick Rabon."

"Any idea what it is now?" I pushed her five dollars. She pushed it back.

"Calling himself Mozingo now. I think he used it a long time ago. But this time it's 'The Great Mozingo' and he's just as full of shit now as he ever was. Hooked up with some religious crazy up in Georgia." She snapped her fingers. "Jericho, that's it. Jericho, Georgia. Up on the Dixiana Highway near the Carolina line. My sister-in-law married a Driggers boy from there. I wish I could remember that preacher's name. Arlo something. Seems like I heard they'd taken his license away. Mary Anne, what do you call them then?"

She laughed, "How about an ex-preacher?" I left the bill on the table and headed north.

Two hours of North Florida and another four of Georgia later, I caught the first sign: a twelve-foot-high cross with GET RIGHT across the horizontal and WITH GOD coming down the post. It was painted red where Jesus's head and feet had rested. Backing it up in six-inch black on white was:

BIBLELAND, GEORGIA
A CHRISTIAN COMMUNITY
60 MILES
TWO MILES PAST JERICHO
CAMPERS WELCOME
FREE HOOKUPS
FREE FISHING
FREE SWIMMING

Another fifty miles and the notices were at every road crossing and big turn. Pitches were stapled to the phone poles and fence posts and whitewashed onto smooth rocks and run-off culverts:

TRIPS TO THE HOLY LAND
SPECIAL RATES FOR SENIOR CITIZENS
SPECIAL RATES FOR CHURCH GROUPS

R U READY FOR ETERNITY?
GOD LIVES! DO YOU?
SIGN UP NOW FOR THE JUBILEE CRUSADE!!

Five miles from Bibleland I had to stop to take it in. On a forty-foot billboard standing on a rock was Buck's partner, the Reverend Arlo Waters. He was in white robes playing Jesus looking out over the multitudes. Sun rays stretched out to big egg-shaped insert panels showing the Trial Before Pontius Pilate, the March to the Cross, the Crucifixion. It was a lot like P. T. Barnum's salute to himself. Across the top in two-foot-high letters ran WORLD'S LARGEST AND MOST FAMOUS PASSION PLAY. CAST OF 200. Across the bottom was a ten-foot flyer: FAMOUS LIFE OF CHRIST PAGEANT APPEARING IN VALDOSTA, GEORGIA, MARCH 1–2. And underneath was what I was looking for: UNDER NEW MANAGEMENT. Buck Brody, alias Rick Rabon, alias the Great Mozingo was in the passion-play business.

Jericho, Georgia, was on the roadmap, but Bibleland wasn't. It was exactly one block long, with a Gulf station at one end and a deserted drive-in at the other. Six elephants were grazing in the drive-in. There were three signs in town. The first two were DIXIANA HIGHWAY and LET'S KEEP GEORGIA GREEN! But the one on the end was the kicker: THE GREAT MOZINGO'S FAMOUS POISONOUS SNAKES. SEE THE 16-FOOT KILLER COBRA. Campers, trailers, and semi rigs were parked on cement beds around a fifty-foot-high radio tower with A . . . R . . . L . . . O running down the spine. There was a small lake for fishing, but no fishermen. A small stream for swimming, but no swimmers. The stream looked like a chemical-plant runoff, the kind people pass by fast and small animals and birds avoid. The only shade was at the Gulf station, and I pulled into the Premium pump and flipped the hood latch up. The men's room door had been ripped off at the hinges; the women's was padlocked. The soft-drink machine was empty. The attendant had on a fishing cap with a nine-inch green visor bill sticking straight out. He had to be over eighty. Stitched in red over his left pocket was his full name, A. J. CARTWRIGHT. I had my credit cards out and he was shaking his head, "Sorry, son. All we take is cash."

I hadn't been called son in a long time. "O.K. Cash it is."

He washed the windows and checked the water level in the battery. He even ran his fingers over the fan belts looking for nicks and heavy wear. As he closed the hood he told me Buck Mozingo had bought in with Reverend Arlo Waters and they were partners in the biggest disaster in South Georgia. He described Buck Mozingo's fast talk and missing finger and said he owned the elephants and the old Winnebago Chieftain parked out under the trees and the Spanish moss. He and Arlo Waters were in Savannah.

"Any chance of a room around here?"

" 'Fraid not son. Tell you what. You hightail it in to Jericho. You get you a poolside at the Quality Courts. Now, that's living. And they got a first-class buffet—all you can eat for three dollars."

The coffee machine was working and I slid in a quarter. "How about a coffee?"

"Naw, I can't go that instant crap."

I asked him if Arlo Waters owned Bibleland.

"Used to. Went broke. Mozingo and the bank's got him by the short hairs now." He nudged his long-billed cap at my coffee. "Sorry, ain't it?"

"For sure."

"Listen, that Quality Courts buffet is a deal. Now, you talk about some people that can fry some chicken!"

I asked about the cast of two hundred in the passion play. He laughed and pointed his nose at the radio tower. Five horses and two camels were grazing around the base. "Maybe they count the livestock. Hell, there ain't been two hundred people here in a year. Ain't no money in passion plays anymore. Ain't no money in nothing anymore down in here." Tall white birds were walking along with the animals. A. J. said they were cow egrets and that they fed on the crickets and grasshoppers the animals nosed up. Across the field an amphitheater had been bulldozed out of the red clay. Wooden seats that looked more like steps ran up to the stage sinking in the weeds.

"That where you have the passion plays?"

He was wiping grease from his hands. "That's where we used to have them."

I checked in at the Quality Courts and had a fast drink at the bar. After a swim and two more drinks, on the patio, I had the fried-chicken buffet. A. J. was right, it was good chicken. But as I was eating, it hit me how alone I was beginning to feel without Monica. The hash browns weren't brown, but I ate them anyway. If she'd been along, I would have probably kidded around with the waitress and sent them back.

It was almost dark when I got back to Bibleland. A. J. was squatting by a charcoal fire at a Hibachi grate, heating water for cereal. A. J. was from Louisiana. He had a '62 Cadillac pulling a '69 Airstream and lived with two black Labradors and four cats. His dogs and cats were eating dry kibble. He bought it in fifty-pound bags. Good, heavy-duty, triple-ply bag with a built-in tear-string. World Wide Paper has some board-of-directors deal on this business and no one even tries to compete. A. J. said he had property near St. Petersburg and he had been planning on going back eventually, but when the Great Mozingo arrived with his Jubilee Crusade idea, he said he knew that was the time to go.

I thanked him for the Quality Courts tip. "That was the best chicken I ever had."

A. J. grinned. "Ain't it though. And how about that gravy?"

"Terrific."

"Here, have some coffee." He poured me a mug. "That's fresh. Like I said, I draw the line on that instant crap. Damn stuff tastes like some kind of wood."

"You got any sugar?"

He slid over a one-pound spout box. The water was boiling, and he stirred in a cup of Cream of Wheat. "Mozingo owe you some money?"

The hot cereal smelled good, but I wasn't hungry. "Yeah, a little bit."

"I thought so. He's a hustler all right."

"You can say that again. What's the story on Arlo Waters?"

He kept stirring. "Ain't got a pot to piss in. They're all hustlers, but now there ain't no one around to hustle but each other." He tapped his spoon on the pot. "I got me a couple buddies I slide the shuffleboards with. We're all pulling out in a couple days." He spooned up a mouthful. "Son, you get yourself a good night's sleep, but tomorrow morning you get your tail out of here. Those two get their hooks in you, you ain't going nowhere." Two people were out on the shuffleboard courts, and I could hear the tap of the sticks and the click-click of the discs. A Labrador came over and I scratched her head. A. J. was lacing the cereal down with sugar. "That's Molly. Other one's Trailer. Mother and son."

I poured some more coffee. "Why you leaving, A. J.?"

"Ain't nothing here for me. It's pure-out hustle. That's all it is, and I say the hell with it." A. J. was quiet until he finished his cereal. "Son, when I was your age I could spurt sperm three times without uncoupling." He cackled and grinned up. "No offense, is there?"

"Hell no. Wish I could."

He slid the bowl to Molly and Trailer and I asked him

why he was so hard on the good reverend. When he stood up his knees cracked. He rolled his shoulders to get the stiffness out.

"I'm from South Louisiana. New Iberia, Louisiana. That's where we make all the Tabasco sauce that's fit to put in your mouth. I know my Bible frontwards, backwards, and sideways. Arlo Waters don't know nothing. He comes to me for quotes and scriptural help. Then he turns around and preaches, and I ain't even mentioned. I guess you'd call that a problem about the size of a field pea, but son that really gets me right down in the old craw."

"Hell, I don't blame you. That kind of information is valuable. Why don't you just bill him?"

He laughed one dry note. "I wouldn't give that son of a bitch the satisfaction. No, I'm pulling out. The hell with this graveyard."

I asked him what Reverend Arlo Waters was like.

He opened two beers and gave me one. "Well, I guess he's about forty, give or take a few years. Served in the Marines, and he's hard as a stone. Got a couple tattoos on him. And he's seen a lot of foreign shores and knows a lot of foreign customs. I'll tell you one solid thing about him. If he had any business sense he'd be a multimillionaire. He had this place going like a house afire. It could have been another Disney World. You seen them weeds on that stage?"

"Yeah."

"Well, there's your sorriness. Lord, I mean this place was booming. People were coming from all over the country. You should have seen the license plates: Texas, California, New York; I mean everywhere. Then one day he just ups and gets tired of it and it was all over."

I figured it was a woman behind it. "Is he married?"

"No. He'll go to a cathouse every now and then. Says he can't stand women. Says he hates them. I tell you someone else he hates."

"Who's that?"

"You ain't Jewish, are you?"

"No."

"The Jews. He spots one sniffing around he'll run their ass right off the premises."

"He'd be great in New York."

"But that scutter had him a following. He'd get up on that stage and he'd have that crowd swaying back and forth and believing every lie he poured out. Son, that man's a born preacher and a born salesman. I'll bet you anything that's why your buddy Mozingo bought in with him." He pushed a cat off the table. "How about some more coffee?"

"Yeah, thanks."

"Hey! Speak of the devil." A yellow school bus with REV. ARLO WATERS FAMOUS PASSION PLAYERS printed under the windows was pulling in under the shuffle-board lights. A. J. cackled as he rinsed his bowl and poured water for the dogs and cats. "Here he comes, Jesus of Nazareth."

He was fifty yards away and badly lighted, but I could tell the long stride and the way he cocked his head. It was Buck Brody, and he was still talking. He saw me and shouted. "Bo!" He rushed up, rubbing his hands together, and picked me up in a bear hug. Then he pushed me back and gripped my shoulders. "Bo! Where in the hell you been?" He shook my hand, still beaming. He didn't give me a chance to say anything. "I been trying to call your ass!" He slapped my shoulder and backed up and popped his hands together. "Hot damn, looka here. I'll just be goddamned if it ain't great seeing you."

He introduced Arlo Waters as his best friend and partner. With his crew cut, tight T-shirt, and long side-burns he looked like a drill sergeant and bad news. He had a weird smile, about one-third teeth and two-thirds gums, and a crazy cast in his eyes. A. J.'s yellow insect-repellent light didn't improve things. "Pleased to meet you." He had a deep disc-jockey delivery covering his accent. I figured he was from the bottom of something: Georgia, Alabama, or Mississippi. He squeezed his kidneys and stretched. "A. J., remind me to have them ball joints checked. We picked up a shimmy coming in." He was racehorse thin and wore his blue jeans low with no belt.

A. J. spoke flat, hard. "Remind yourself, Arlo."

Arlo grinned back, and his gums flashed. "Don't sass me, A. J." Then he turned to me. "Where you staying?"

"Quality Courts, A. J. here recommended it."

He kept looking at me. He didn't seem to blink. "How long you aiming on staying with us?"

I didn't like him. "Couple days, maybe three. I'm just passing through."

Buck moved in between us. "Bo, you come with me." He was squeezing my elbow, signaling something. "Got somebody I want you to meet. See you, Arlo. Take care, A. J."

A. J. tipped his cup. "I always do."

Buck pulled me into the dark. He was whispering fast. "Listen, Bo. Listen fast. No more Buck Brody, get me. It's Buck Mozingo. Got it? Mozingo. M-O-Z-I-N-G-O. You got to hit the Z. Mozingo."

"O.K. with me."

"And I got me a new girlfriend."

"I met her in Riverhead. Helen."

"Naw. It's Loretta. You mention Helen or Hrugla and I'm sunk. So keep your mouth shut, O.K.?"

"But where's Helen?"

"Back on Long Island. It wasn't working out. I was a damn fool to marry her."

"Marry her?" Everything was coming too fast. "You divorce Hrugla?"

"Never got around to it. She went back to Minneapolis."

"You told me Oslo."

"Same thing."

He had lied to everyone about everything. "Damn, Buck."

He tapped my arm. "Mozingo."

"O.K., I got it, Buck Mozingo." Nothing had changed. I felt like I was in a Marx Brothers skit. He looked back to make sure no one could hear us and started filling me in.

He was living with Loretta and swearing he'd never marry again. I listened to the wild story, wondering how many women were lined up behind Helen and Hrugla and Loretta, sweating out alimony and child-support checks. Loretta had worked for him on the high-wire act in his old show. Now she was too old and heavy to be a flyer and worked as a perch-pole artist, whatever that was. Buck pulled out a pint of whiskey from his back pocket.

"Have a snort." He was drinking six-dollars-a-pint Wild Turkey. Things couldn't be too bad.

"What's this Arlo Waters business?"

He wiped his mouth with the back of his hand. "A gold mine. Crazier than a hoot owl but a goddamn gold mine."

"He gives me the creeps."

"Me too. But that son of a bitch can solid sell a crowd. Boy, we got something that's going to make us all millionaires."

"All I want's eighteen thousand dollars." I took a drink. "Buck, they're firing my ass. I need that money."

"That's peanuts. Peanuts."

"You got it?"

"No, but I'll damn well have it Friday. Boy, this Life of Christ and Jubilee Crusade is going to turn the circus business upside down and inside out."

"Can I tell Omaha we're getting the money?"

"Friday for sure. No, make that Saturday. We'll be too busy counting it. Bo, we're going to be making so much we're going to have to carry it in pillowcases."

"I heard that one before."

"Bo, listen, this time it's a lead-pipe cinch. You see the promos on the highway?" He looped his arm around my shoulder. "I swear before God if it ain't good to see you. Look!" He slapped his stomach. "Lost eight pounds and I'm hard as a rock."

"Yeah, great." I took another drink. "Buck Mozingo, that it?"

"Thataboy. Now you're talking. Come on now, I want you to meet the little woman."

Loretta wasn't exactly the little woman. She was close to forty and looked it. Her hair was up in torpedo curlers and she had the red, rough look of an alky. She was spread out on the couch with a can of Blue Ribbon watching the *Wednesday Night Movie* and eating pretzels. It didn't make any sense why he'd traded Helen for her.

Buck said, "Honey bun, this is Bo Mahaffey. He's down from New York."

She looked me over like I was a subpoena server. "How much we owe you?"

"Nothing. We're just good friends. I happened to be passing through."

"I'll bet." She sipped her beer. She kept looking and not approving. "What business you in?"

"Packaging. I'm a salesman. Cellophane, paper, foil. Anything that goes into packaging."

Buck was in the bathroom with the door open. He kept talking as he pissed. "Bo, you have a good ride down?"

"Pretty good."

He raised his voice. "What say?"

Loretta laughed. "Better speak up. This is a class place." She handed me a beer and I asked her what a perch-pole artist did. When she smiled she looked better, younger.

"Artist? Buck tell you I was an artist? Marvelous. There ain't much art to it. I'm on the bottom. I hold the damn thing still. Next time out I'll give you a demonstration."

Buck tucked his shirt in and zipped his fly. He had lost weight. Whatever life he was leading was agreeing with him. I began eating the pretzels. A few years back National Biscuit used reverse-printed seven-color cellophane as an overwrap. One of the best-looking packages on the shelves. But when the sugar market tightened they went to a printed carton and have been there ever since. I pulled the inner wrap out, skinned the two laminations apart, and showed them to Loretta. I told her pretzels needed more protection down South because of the high humidity. She was interested and wanted to know how

tear-tape was put on cigarette packages. I showed her
how the machine fed it in under the wrap and peeled back
the paper and foil. I even told her the Camel on the pack
was designed back when a lot of people couldn't read.
The same as Shell gas, Blue Cross, Red Devil Lye. I
winked at Buck as she opened two more beers.

Loretta smiled. "This bird's O.K. Come on now, how
much do we owe him?"

Buck grinned. "Not much, baby. Just a few bucks."

He was getting nervous with me doing all the talking.
He was probably scared I'd mention New York. Or screw
up on Mozingo or call her Helen. He punched me on the
shoulder. "Come on, Bo. I'll show you around."

Loretta got up. "Bull! It's pitch dark out there. I'm just
getting to like him."

Buck turned the TV volume up and patted her shoulder. "Watch your show, baby. Come on, Bo."

Outside, we headed for the shuffleboard lights and the
high back wall of the drive-in. The marquee still had the
last movie up, *Godzilla vs. Rodan.* The letters had
dropped sideways; the a's and o's were missing. Out in
the moonlight the speaker stations were bent over and
two-foot-high weeds had split big cracks in the parking
ramps. The elephants seemed to be sleeping. A vine had
filled the concession stand and had pushed out the
windows and doors. It was as thick as a garden hose and
looked like something out of a monster movie. "Jesus,
Buck, what's that?"

"Kudzu. Damn stuff will knock you down and strangle
you."

"Kudzu?"

"That's it. Bo, I'm going to make a southerner out of you
yet."

"You better hurry. You got three days."

His arm was back around my shoulder. "That's all I
need, little buddy. That's all I need."

Buck's cover story was that he'd been with a West
Coast outfit called Daniels and Foster for the past year

and a half. I moved his arm away. "They believe you?"

"Arlo does. That's all that matters."

"How about Loretta?"

"Naw, you can't fool her. But my ass is mud if she hears I'm married."

"Twice."

"Yeah, twice. You be careful now. You never heard of Buck Brody, right?"

"O.K., I'll go along with anything. But Buck, I've got to have that money."

"You're going to get it. Now just relax. Listen."

He was excited and walking faster, talking faster. He had combined his circus and Arlo's passion players into the Mozingo–Arlo Waters Famous Life of Christ and Jubilee Crusade Corporation, a nonprofit religious enterprise that was exempt from state and federal amusement taxes. "Bo, I had this idea fifteen years ago. I just never ran into the right minister. Wait till you see this son of a bitch in action. I'm telling you, this crusade is a gold mine. No taxes, no social security, we don't even have to pay minimum wage." The Famous Life of Christ Festival was playing Valdosta Friday and Saturday as the big premiere before the Jubilee Crusade march across South Carolina and on up to Charlotte. "Bo, we're sweeping right through the center of the Bible Belt. We're going to have to beat them off with sticks. I'm telling you, the money is going to roll in."

The idea sounded grim. "Who you getting to march like that?"

"Arlo's got this wild following. That's why I need him." A. J. Cartwright's lights were still on and a dog was barking. Buck's arm looped over my shoulder. "I didn't like old Arlo the first time I met him either. But he'll grow on you. Bo, I want you to do me a favor and try and get along with him." He was sounding like I was going to be there longer than Saturday. I pushed his arm away.

"Hold it, Buck. Just hold it a damn minute. All I want is that money. Then I'm clearing out. Understand?"

"I understand, but try and give me a hand on Arlo, O.K.?"

"I'll try."

"Bo, I'm going to tell you a little something. You're going to be pulling out of here a goddamn hero. I mean it."

We climbed up the road shoulder and walked along the Dixiana Highway. The moon was rising, and a sweet chemical smell was coming up from the creek. "You know, if you look at it in the wrong light you might say I screwed you pretty raw on that Bunny deal. But Bo, I got hurt too."

I didn't say anything.

Buck kept talking. "All I want is the air clear between us, that's all. And as far as I'm concerned you're still in for that fifteen percent we shook on. O.K. with you?"

I said it slowly, overarticulating every syllable: "After the eighteen thousand on Saturday."

He repeated it. "After the eighteen thousand on Saturday." He was sliding the cellophane from a cigar and lighting it. "O.K., now let me hear you say it."

"Say what?"

"You know, Mozingo. Buck Mozingo."

"Buck Mozingo. I never heard of Buck Brody."

"Thataway, Bo. That'll do it."

I laughed and couldn't stop it. "And I never heard of Rick Rabon."

He stopped. "Now where in the hell did you hear that?"

I paused and lit a cigarette. "Well Buck, I just don't want you to think I'm stupid."

He puffed on his cigar and looked up at the radio tower. Then he looked at me. "No, Bo, I never thought you were stupid."

CHAPTER

In the morning Buck had on brand-new everything: a safari jacket, a pith helmet, riding knickers with leather knees, and a pair of black circus boots with a mirror finish. He touched his baton to his helmet, British style. "Morning, Bo."

"Morning, Buck. You look like the great white hunter."

He grinned. "Glad you like it, old man, because you're going to be seeing a great deal of it. Come on, I want to show you around."

We stopped by a novelty shop, the kind you see hooked onto fireworks stands all over Georgia. It had been closed for months, and you could write your name in the red dust. Cement yard animals were still on sale at sacrifice prices: two frogs lounging under a mushroom umbrella, a duck family, a chicken family, a deer family, silver reflector balls, and three-tiered pink birdbaths supported by arching flamingos and seahorses. Buck said, "If you see anything you want, just holler."

The tour continued. Kudzu was springing up through the Passion Play stage planking and covering Arlo's old centerpiece, "The Grotto of the Nativity." The kid's motorcycle, car, and airplane rides were broken down and rusting out. Everything standing needed painting.

"Look at that radio tower." Buck frowned. "Seventy thousand dollars and he didn't broadcast once. Ain't that a crime."

At the top, a buzzard was looking out toward Jericho, two miles away. I told him A. J. Cartwright had said the place had failed when Arlo lost his religion. Buck shrugged and spat. "A. J.'s a romantic. What beat Arlo was the interstate." He whipped his baton against his leg. "Only thing moving on these back roads is the kudzu and the truckers skipping the weigh stations."

The place looked like a junkyard, and a green, evil-looking mist was hanging low over the creek. The semis needed painting and tires, and every transmission I saw was leaking oil. But Buck's energy was up and staying up. He kept whipping his baton. "Once we play Valdosta we're going to be in clover. Wait till you see the acts. They're going to knock you down." He changed subjects without catching his breath. "You tell Omaha you'd mail the money?"

I opened my first beer of the day and watched the elephants and camels grazing around the radio tower. "Yeah, I called them after breakfast." I was lying, but I had to keep the pressure on. "I said Saturday, Buck."

"No problem, Bo. No problem."

As long as Buck talked it made a little sense. With a few beers it moved from it might work to it could work to it would work. With the eighteen thousand dollars I could call Greene and get squared away. Then I'd call Monica and get back on the road north. Jesus, it had to work. I had to get her back. I was missing her more than ever.

A. J. was right, Buck and Arlo were having problems. A. J. had said the crew was down to the bone. Down to the gypsies and the winos and the ex-cons who changed their name every time they crossed a state line. Buck took me over to the sleeper wagon. I'd never seen one. It

was grim. One door on the end, no windows. The only
plumbing was a canvas pot in the back. At night they'd
piss out the door. Most of the bunks were empty and most
of the shelves had been cleaned out. He introduced me to
Lou McIntire, saying he had known him for seventeen
years.

Lou nodded. "Nice meeting you." His hair was down to
his shoulders and he wore an earring carved out of a
silver dollar. His bed had been stripped down and his
mattress was rolled. Buck acted surprised. "What's up?
Damn, Lou, you ain't leaving me?"

The mop boy was coming through and Lou slung his
suitcase over the springs. His suitcase handle was missing and he looped a rope around the middle. "I've had it
Buck. Had it."

Buck hooked his thumbs in his belt loops. He couldn't
believe what was happening. "Lou, I tell you Valdosta is
going to turn the whole thing around. It's a gold mine.
There's no way on earth for it to miss."

"Not for me, Buck."

Buck soft-punched his shoulder. "Come on, Lou. We're
almost over the hump."

He tightened the bowline knot. "Buck, give me a
break."

"O.K., Lou, I guess you know your own mind." He
pulled out the pint of Wild Turkey. He shook it. Then he
studied the bead like he was looking for a message. "One
for the road, old buddy."

Lou drank and passed it to me.

Buck said, "Where you heading, Lou?"

"Tallahassee. Bob McCoy says he can use me. I'm
riding down with A. J."

Buck drank and wiped his mouth. "You tell Bob hello
for me, O.K.? And when you see old Alice, you slip her a
little goose. Say I sent it."

Lou eased his bag down. "Buck, you're into me for two
hundred. How about it?"

"Sure thing." He pulled his wallet out. Then his face
tightened. "Damn it! I forgot. I just paid the feed bill." He

spat. "You any idea what they're charging for a goddamn load of third-rate feed these days?"

Lou saw it coming. "I'll take a hundred."

"I haven't got it, Lou." He opened his wallet on a twenty-dollar bill and three tens. "Sorry, good buddy. But that's it." He gave him the fifty. "Now listen, I don't want you worrying about it, hear. I'll send it on down. The way A. J. drives, it'll beat you there." He tightened the cap and gave him the bottle. "Here, Lou, this will get you through Georgia."

As we crossed back over to the camper, A. J. Cartwright came hotfooting over in a fast half-step. For eighty he could move. "Mister Mozingo."

Buck touched his baton to his hat and clicked his heels, British style. "Mister Cartwright, I presume."

A. J. cracked a smile and mopped his forehead. "Got a Nashville charter bus out front. They want to see the snake show." He counted out thirty-seven dollars, a dollar a head. "Three or four of them look drunk to me."

"Ain't nothing wrong with that, Mister C." Buck handed him back ten dollars. "Tell them I'll be right along. And A. J. . . ."

"Yessir."

"We're going to miss your old salty ass around here."

They shook hands and A. J. grinned. "You get back down near St. Pete, you look me up."

Buck slung his arm around A. J.'s thin shoulders. "I'll do that thing." Buck grinned. "Now you be good. And if you can't be good, I want you to be careful. And A. J., old buddy, if you can't be careful, may the good Lord take a liking to your soul."

A. J. and I shook hands. "Take care, son."

In the camper, Buck changed his boots and had two quick drinks. "Bo, you ain't seen my snake show yet. Come on, this might even prove educational." Buck climbed into the Great Mozingo Famous Poisonous Snakes booth and nonchalantly emptied out five wire baskets of snakes. It was as if he had done it a thousand times. The snakes looked doped and sluggish. He announced that the hot weather was beating them down and they were just tired. But if angered or if they took a notion, they could strike as fast as they could in the springtime. He picked up the first one with a hooked stick and identified it as a cottonmouth moccasin. Then he eased his fingers in behind the jaws and gave a short lecture about its markings and characteristics. He swung the snake back to the ground and waved the crowd in closer.

"Yall come on in here. I want to show you something. Come on. Come on. Ain't nothing to be afraid of." He pronged a coral snake behind the head and lifted it by its tail. "Now, this little lady here doesn't have a backbone. So she can't be striking from this position. But I'll let yall in on a little secret. I don't recommend it too highly." He held it up. "See how this red cuts in and out like that. Well if you see one of these jobs lying around and somebody says, 'Oh, my! What a nice play pretty!' Well right there, podner, I want you to start backing off fast." He held it higher. "Everybody see it? Now take a good look. Because this little scutter here will kill you quicker than a train. For my money I'd put her up against my king cobra any day of the week."

He explained how most people and the experts believe that Florida has more poisonous snakes than Georgia. "Folks, that's all wrong. All wrong. The great state of Georgia is second to none in the poison-snakes department. We are, and always have been"—he held up a single finger—"number one. And I'm going to tell you why." He fingered the coral behind its jaw. "Deadly. Deadly. Now a lot of people figure this little darling is strictly a Florida resident. Well, that's right where they are all wrong. Dead wrong. And any of yall from Glynn County or from down in there around Savannah will back me up. How about it. Anyone here ever seen one?"

A short, fat man with a "Happiness Is a Warm Place to Take a Crap" T-shirt stretched across his stomach elbowed in. "You can say that again! If I ain't seen one, I seen fifty. Found a whole nest one day with a backhoe."

"What did you do?"

"Got me my twelve-gauge and blew their asses out. That's what."

"Easy, cowboy, ladies present here."

"Sorry, sir. But we got 'em. I'll grab aholt of the Bible on that one."

Buck lowered the coral and picked up a big rattler. "Now, here's one that Florida doesn't have because Florida doesn't have our mountains. Ladies and gentlemen and boys and girls, the dreaded timber rattler. We get them up in Jasper County and on up there around the Chattooga. This old fellow tips the scales at twenty-four pounds. Anybody want to hold him?"

There were no takers. A man with a "Willie Nelson Fan Club" straw skimmer moved in to the rail with a can of beer in one hand and four more dangling from a six-pack carrier. He grinned. "Hey, Jungle Jim, I hear the boa constrictor don't actually strangle a man." He had a high-pitched nasal accent and he looked like trouble. "I hear they wrap themselves around you. Then when you exhale they just take up the slack."

He whooped and two of his friends slapped him on the back. Buck didn't like being upstaged. "Friend, I heard that one in Tacoma, Washington, the day we landed on the moon. But it still sounds good." He tipped his hat with the tip of his baton. There was no doubt about it, the son of a bitch was smooth. He was also good. His voice was deep, and with his jungle khakis he even looked good. But the thing Buck did that doesn't come out of sales-training films was to key his pitch and jokes and chatter to the white-sock and red-neck level of the charter crowd. "This timber rattler has a peculiar marking and I want you to take a close look at it. For it may, God forbid, be the difference between life and death. . . . if you will sort of spread out here I'll bring him in closer." He touched the black area just above the long rattles. "See right there.

Look close now, right there. It's black, and that's not like
any other rattler." He held it closer to the crowd. A
ten-year-old girl who was trying to get her teeth out of a
candy apple frowned. He pulled back. "Sorry, little lady.
Didn't mean to scare you. But this old granddaddy's
sound asleep."

She pulled the candy loose. "I ain't scared of that old
snake. . . . When you going to milk it?"

"Now folks, you hear that? Now how's that for being
brought up and not even knowing the meaning of fear?
What's your name, honey?"

"Rebecca Wheeler and I'm the baton twirler and fancy
strutter for Morehead Junior High."

Buck held the snake at the back of its jaws. "And
honey, I will cold guarantee you're a good one. Rebecca
Wheeler, in your honor I will now milk this old boy
down." With a shot glass under its mouth he squeezed the
fangs. The yellow venom dripped. He held it high so the
back row could see.

Rebecca was beaming, "That's the part I like best."

Buck slid the snake down with one hand and gave
Rebecca a rabbit's-foot keychain souvenir with the other.
"Ladies and gentlemen, boys and girls, this concludes our
show. Drive carefully. And have yourselves a good time
in Music City. And hey, if you see Waylon or Tom T. Hall,
you tell them old Buck Mozingo says stay loose."

Buck was stretched out on his double hammock and
Loretta was sitting in the door tuning her guitar. Except
for the shuffleboard lights, Bibleland was dark. As I sat
there clicking my beer can against my teeth, I knew the
Crusade would never work. Something was wrong with it.
Dead wrong. "Buck, if this is such a red-hot damn idea,
why hasn't it been done before?"

He mixed a sigh with a low yodel. "Because everyone's
stupid, that's why. They hang on to something that works
and they milk it till they kill it. What we got's new, brand
new."

Loretta was picking out a Kristofferson song that I couldn't place. "You tell him, baby." She'd been drinking beer since dinner.

He rocked the hammock with his foot and rolled on about playing in the old days before the Jehovah's Witnesses and the big Baptist conventions. How the big groups had filled his tents to see the show but wouldn't spend a dime. "Hell, they'd bring in peanut butter and bread and make their own sandwiches. Wouldn't even spring for a damn Coke. But then I figured it out. It took me five years to figure it out and then ten years to find the right preacher. But now, hot damn it, I got him."

He got up and opened three more beers. One for Loretta. One for me. One for him. "This time it's going to work. And this time it's going to keep on working." He crossed the dirt patio in four strides and spun around waving his beer like he was addressing a thousand. "Here I am, the Great Mozingo, one of the greatest showmen in the world, and my ass is sucking wind down here in the Georgia turpentine." He was almost shouting. "Zorog, Beaty-Cole, Bob McCoy, and me. We're the last of the last. The last of the goddamn last. When we're gone, it's all gone."

I said, "How about Ringling?"

"Bo, I'm talking about a tent show. A set-'em-up, and play-hell-out-of-'em, and tear-it-down, and move-'em-out, canvas-and-dirt-and-sawdust tent show. Bo, I'm talking about the old mud circus. *The only goddamn circus!*" He slapped the side of the camper. "When we're gone, it's all gone."

The beer was hitting Loretta. She was slurring her words and repeating everything. "It's sad, honey. Sad. I mean it's really sad when you think about it." I thought she was going to cry.

"You bet your sweet ass it's sad." He pointed at me. "I play one night. Maybe two. Then I got to knock down, move out, drive two hundred damn miles, and set up again. That's what kills us." He slammed his fist in his palm. "What I want to know is where in the hell does it say we have to keep moving around like a pack of goddamn gypsies?" It was a question he wasn't looking for an answer to. He took a deep pull on the beer and slid a canvas chair in close. He was looking me straight in the eye. "Billy Graham and Oral Roberts and that screamer, old what's-his-name, out in Tulsa, hit a town and stay there until they've got every red cent rolling. And it's tax free. Not one damn penny is taxed or accounted for. And what kind of show do they give the crowd? I'll tell you, it's crap. They give it crap. Choirs and finger snappers and those 4-H kids who sing for nothing and buy their own uniforms. It's enough to make you puke." He glared out at the amphitheater shining in the moonlight. "TV's ruined it all. Ruined it. People want to see plane crashes and the National Guard shooting the damn looters. That's what they really want. Hell, they killed Lee Harvey Oswald like it was a network special." He snapped out of it, sat down, and slapped his knees. "But I got it knocked now. I'm going to beat the whole damn system. . . . Now listen. . . ."

I was listening, but I was also planning my Saturday-night trip north. I'd take the Dixiana Highway to Savannah. Then I'd pick up I-95 north.

Buck rolled on, "We got the bulls in the Long Mount and the cats are in ring three. We got the gals up on the swings and ladders." He squared his hands and framed the scene. "Got the picture, Bo?"

I hadn't seen any cats or girls. I hadn't even seen any ladders. "I got it." It would be a straight drive from Savannah to Richmond. Ten or twelve hours.

Buck was excited. "O.K., hold it right there. Because right there is where Ringling ends. That's where the circus has always ended. But Bo, from now on that's where we start. That's our base."

He was up again and popping beers. "We're going to bring that mother up and keep it up. People want a message. We'll give them a message. And I don't mean no salute to Alexander Graham Bell or the landing on the moon bullshit. Hell, people done forgot that anyway." He gripped the table and shook it. "We're going to give them 'The Life of Christ.' And if we ain't got ourselves a winner, hell ain't hot. Am I right or am I wrong?"

I said it, but I didn't believe it: "Right." If I took I-95, I could drive on through the first night. With any luck I'd be in Manhattan Monday morning. Maybe I'd pick up Monica on her way to work. Maybe I'd bring her some gardenias. Loretta wasn't very steady on her feet. She came over and kissed him.

"You're right, Buck. You're dead right."

He calmed down and sat down. He was quiet for a while. The crickets and bullfrogs began hammering away. Something big down in the swamp made a heavy adjustment and cleared its throat. "What's that?"

Buck got up and dropped back in the hammock. "Bull gator, probably horny."

Loretta strummed her guitar. "Babe, you want to hear something?"

"Yeah, hon. You know the one, 'Spanish Eyes.'"

Loretta tuned the E string. She'd had too many beers to sing, but it didn't bother her playing. Buck stretched back out on the hammock, holding the beer on his stomach. "Bo, there's no music like Spanish music." He asked her to play it again. He put his feet up higher on the hammock and said it reminded him of Texas. He talked on about San Antonio and the Mexican dancers. About the chili peppers and the great nights they'd played at the state fair in Dallas and about a tear-down a long time ago in Austin in the rain. I'd skipped dinner, and the beer was hitting me hard. I knew if I didn't eat something soon, I'd be sick. Buck was humming along with the music. He held his beer up. "We had us some times, Bo. We had us some times."

The more Buck drank, the more he believed it. Hell, maybe he believed it cold sober. Anyhow, as I sat there, the pieces were coming together. I realized he was sounding exactly like Dad. I guess I'd known it all along, but it took the beer to hold it still. They were the same dreamers and schemers, and the same losers; they had the same pitch and believed the same crap. How the old days were the great days. How right now they were being screwed or misunderstood, or both. And how all they needed was a little time and a little money and a little break and it was going to be a brand-new horse race. And here I was sitting there in the beer and the music and the moonlight taking it in again and almost believing it again. Now, talk about your basic patterns!

A jet plane was crossing over and bats were flickering around the shuffleboard lights. The sky was overcast and the wind was up. The song ended and Buck sighed. "Bo, you should have heard them goddamn trumpets. That right, baby?"

"You said it, lover." She strummed awhile, then stopped. "Babe."

"Yeah, doll."

"I'm hitting the sack."

"Sleep tight, sugarfoot. Thanks for the music."

"Good-night, Bo."

"Good-night, Loretta."

When the light went off inside I said, "Buck, what if we don't make it in Valdosta?"

His fingernails were clicking on the beer can. "There's no way not to. No way."

"But let's just say we don't. What if—"

He interrupted. "Bo, I don't want to hear any 'if this' or 'if that' crap. If, if, if. If the frog had wings, there'd be some readjustments in the trees. Forget it. Forget it, it'll drive you crazy. It's going to work and keep on working." He pointed his beer at me. "You got my word, good buddy."

"Buck, I've told Omaha the money's coming. My ass is on the line."

"Bo, you worry too much. Wait till you see this crowd pulling in. We're going to have to beat them off with sticks." He sighed. "I've just got this feeling that it's going to be fantastic."

Mosquitoes were buzzing but they weren't biting. I drank another beer and sat there watching the moon and the elephants and the radio tower.

"Bo."

"Yeah, Buck."

"She's a great gal, ain't she?"

"Yeah, Buck."

"Maybe a little heavy across the beam and she'll solid hit that gin. But, damn it, you can count on her. You can really count on her."

"I like her, Buck. She's O.K."

"Yeah." He was stretching out in the hammock with one hand behind his head and his beer and potato chips on his stomach. "She's a cunt, no doubt about it. But, damn it, she's a lady."

He lay still for a while. "Bo."

"Yeah, Buck."

"Any more beer over there?"

"Sure, I'll get you one."

I popped it open for him and he lay back with his feet high up in the hammock. The moon was out and lighting up the drive-in and the radio tower. The stars were reflecting in the creek. Buck was quiet for a long time and I thought he was asleep. But then he finally spoke. "Bo."

"Yeah, Buck."

"You should have heard them goddamn trumpets."

CHAPTER

It was raining. It was cold. Buck didn't have a license in the name of Mozingo, so I was driving the Chuck Wagon as we headed for Valdosta. Kids going to school stayed down in the drain ditch out of the wind and waved up as we rolled by. Buck sat in the middle, trying to get the weather report, but all that was coming through was static and engine noise. He hunched in over the dial and kept watching the skyline. "Maybe it'll blow over."

Loretta had a hangover and was trying to cure it with bourbon. "We won't be able to set the goddamn stakes. Look!" She pointed at a garbage-can lid rolling down the road shoulder and then sailing across a field. "This is crazy, Buck. Crazy."

Buck snapped, "How about shutting up." He cut the radio off and sat back, whistling through his teeth. It was "Red River Valley."

They had been to Valdosta six times promoting the Mozingo–Arlo Waters Famous Life of Christ Festival. They had hit every church, every mission, and every prayer-meeting club in town. Blue-and-white posters had been printed up for the Baptists and the Methodists. For the Pentecostals and the Church of God, who like their fundamentalism strong, the announcements were in bright red. But the churches and the clubs hadn't bought the blocks of one hundred or fifty or even ten seats. They took only the half-price coupons, and we knew the money had to be made at the gate. The clouds were touching the telephone poles and the rain was coming in surges. I kept the windshield wipers on fast speed, but it wasn't fast enough. There was just too much rain, too much wind, and I had to drop to twenty to even see the white line.

In Valdosta, on the lot marked off with red flags for the tent and white for the midway, it was running mud and sheeting rain. The wind was howling through the window channels. The cab was rocking. We had nine hours to get ready for the seven o'clock show. Buck stubbed his cigar out and shook his head. "What a mess."

Loretta wiped the glass down. "I think it's getting worse."

Buck grimaced and spoke through his teeth. "Brilliant." But he wasn't giving up. "It can't last. There's no way for this to last."

In the Howard Johnson's motel room Buck was pacing back and forth. The two nights in Valdosta where he had planned on netting forty to fifty thousand dollars weren't going to happen. He finished his drink. He poured another. He kept pacing. Loretta was sitting on the luggage rack, eating pork fried rice from a tapered pint carton and watching a rerun of *Star Trek*. Across the bottom of the picture, an emergency storm warning was flashing. She rocked her head and clicked her tongue in syncopation. "Here's the pitch. We build a big wooden ark. Then we send out for the animals. Then two by two by two . . . Shit! This is the goddamn end." She took Buck's hand. "Babe, how about the auditorium?"

"It's too late. It's too late for anything."

Arlo, in a see-through plastic raincoat, was standing in the door. The rain was sheeting across the Astroturf lawn and down the orange-tiled roofs. It was overflowing the pool. He whistled one note and twisted his fist in his palm. He sounded in pain. Real pain. "This is terrible. Terrible. What are we going to do?"

Buck was pouring his third drink. The bottle was almost empty. "Tell the drivers we're heading back. We're going to need the goddamn Coast Guard out here."

Loretta had gone to the bar to watch a basketball game on the big screen. Buck was lying across the bed. His hands were behind his head and his shoes were off. I poured out the last drink and sat on the rack. Buck's socks were riddled with tiny holes; it looked as if he'd stepped in battery acid. I knew from now on it would only get worse. Buck was absolutely and exactly like Dad: a loser. It didn't matter what he sold or stole or promoted, he was a born and total loser. He would never make it in Valdosta. Or in the circus business, or in bags or snakes or anything. He was great on ideas, and maybe a genius born fifty years too soon or fifty years too late, but there was no counting on him. The crowd who chained him to the workbench and made him bring a sack lunch probably knew him better than anyone.

I had to get out. Everything I owned and cared about was hooked up to the son of a bitch. My job. My car. My apartment. Monica. Monica; I couldn't bear thinking about her. God, I loved her. God, I really missed her. "Buck, I still got to have that money."

He kept his arm over his eyes. "You'll get it."

"I mean today."

His arm was still over his eyes. "I said you'll get it. Now leave me alone for a while, I got to think."

We parked the rigs and the crew back in Bibleland. Then Buck and I took the Oldsmobile and headed south for the Florida line and Bob McCoy's circus. Buck was going to sell off his elephants, his camels and horses, and some of his rigs. He brought along three six-packs of Blue Ribbon and a grocery bag of pretzels, potato chips, and peanut-butter crackers for the long drive back through the Low Country. Near the Florida state line, gravel began rattling under the fenders. I slowed down to keep the exhaust pipe from banging. "How much of this?"

He checked the map. "Ten, fifteen miles. Watch for Number 8."

I almost stopped. "Look!"

A sign was painted on an automobile tire and nailed to a tree: "Madame Dubose reads heads and works roots." All of the s's were backwards.

He snapped his fingers and pointed a pistol finger. "Now, that's the gal we need."

I felt bad making him sell his stock, but there wasn't any choice. If I stuck with him I'd get buried with him.

We were going through the back country. The two-strand power lines had tapered to one and the doorjambs and window frames were trimmed in blue. Buck said it was called "haint blue" and it kept the evil spirits off the porch and Doctor Death on his side of the drain ditch during his rambles down the road at night. Poultry was flapping on the porches, and car radiators and universals were pulleyed up on the thick limbs of the oaks and the chinaberries. One house with fishing poles racked up above the door was studded with hubcaps and license plates. In the yard a man was crouching in over a car engine, grinding valves. His wife and child were feeding the chickens from her apron. It could have been ten years ago, twenty years ago, thirty.

The flash flooding that had hit Valdosta hadn't touched North Florida. It was warm, clear. There was no wind. It was almost dark when we spotted McCoy's red arrows stapled to a deer crossing. Three more signs were stacked at a crossroads, indicating a turn. Then we saw the big twenty-four-sheeter on a tobacco-curing house. It was red, blue, and yellow trimmed in bright silver. The printing plates had to have cost four thousand dollars.

"Be Not Deceived by Envious Competitors!
This Is the Original Bob 'The Real' McCoy.
Presenting the World's Greatest Showcase of
European and International Acts and Artists.

17 BULL ELEPHANTS. . . . 11 NUBIAN LIONS
14 BENGAL TIGERS. . . . 12 GIANT POLAR BEARS
HORSES. . . . CLOWNS. . . . PARADE
THE GREATEST CIRCUS UNDER ONE TENT IN THE
UNITED STATES AND ALL OF EUROPE"

Buck laughed. "That paper's fifteen years old. He hasn't had a polar bear since Cleveland." We made two turns and saw the show sitting out in a big parking lot. Buck groaned. He was really hurt. "A K-Mart mall. A goddamn K-Mart mall."

We walked along the midway. I was eating an Ice Cream Delight, a square of ice cream on a stick dipped in chocolate and rolled in nuts. Buck was cleaning his fingernails with the big blade of his knife and looking over the three-card monte and the chuck-a-luck operations. He said there was too much carnival and too much hustle. We stopped in front of Bo-Lo-Mo, the Bird Woman of Madagascar. She had feathers on her arms and shoulders and a strange tapered face. She was looking at Buck curiously. Buck winked. "That you, Alice?"

Bo-Lo-Mo closed her eyes and nodded. "Things are rough all over."

"I'll check you later. Hang in there."

We moved down to the two-headed-baby show and Buck said a legitimate show wouldn't be caught dead with an act like this. It was a low-rent half stall with a sawdust floor. The ticket taker, who looked like he was wanted for armed robbery, was announcing to a crowd of eight that they had just joined forces with the medical profession in its heroic fight against birth defects and mental retardation. Above him a hand-printed sign announced that doctors and nurses with proper credentials were admitted free.

We bought a Coke and kept walking around the midway. Suddenly, Bob McCoy was at our side with his arm around Buck's waist. "Great seeing you, Buck. Just great."

Buck introduced us. McCoy looked me over. "Pleased to meet you. Come on, let's get some coffee. I gotta take me some pills."

I figured Buck wanted to get him alone. "I'll catch you people later. I've got to pick up some shaving cream." I also wanted to pick up a gift for Monica.

Buck grabbed my arm. "No, come on. I want you along."

McCoy laughed and slapped his back. "Think I'm going to put it to you, don't you?"

He led us into the K-Mart, keeping up a steady singsong about the poor crowds, the bad weather, and the high prices. In the cafeteria line he picked up a low-calorie cottage cheese and a cup of coffee. He insisted on paying for our coffee and donuts and led us over to a red booth overlooking the men's socks and underwear section. I wanted to see how Fruit of the Loom packaged their shorts and undershirts for the southern market but decided to check it later.

Bob McCoy, who billed himself as the Real McCoy, looked terrible. Too much booze. Too many miles. Too many years. He was wearing dark sunglasses. So dark it looked like he had black eyes, or had just come out of surgery. Buck saw it too. "You O.K., Bob? You look kind of green around the gills."

I thought it was a stupid way to begin negotiations. McCoy hooked his head and winced. "Stomach, Buck. Always the stomach." He licked his lips in a thin smile. "I think I got me a bleeding ulcer this time." He pried the styrene lid from his cottage cheese.

"You remember Horace, that brother of mine down in Deland? We went to the dog races one night?"

Buck was watching him close, trying to figure if he was broke or flush. "Yeah. Yeah, I got him."

He scraped the cheese from the lid. "Heart attack. Buck, I'm going to level with you. He wants me to help him run them orange groves."

He lined up two red pills, two whites, and a green. He

chased them with the coffee. "Buck, I'm getting too old for
this route. Forty years. Damn, they slide by, don't they?"
He took his glasses off and rubbed his eyes. They were
small and pale as a rabbit's and were glued to Buck's as if
he was begging. I felt like an idiot sitting there. McCoy
leaned closer, smiling. "It's nice seeing you again, boy.
I'll be damned if it ain't. There ain't many of us around
anymore." He spooned up a mouthful of cheese. "You
hear about Buzz Borden's stroke?"

"No, he O.K.?"

McCoy dropped his eyes. "We figure him for about one
more white shirt." He shook his head slowly. "Buck, I'm
telling you they're all going. All of them." Before Buck
could stop him he was off remembering the old days. Bob
McCoy had ridden with Ringling and Carson-Rogers and
had seen the great days of the train shows. But now,
eating cottage cheese with a plastic spoon and a nervous
tic flickering in his cheek, he knew he would make only a
few more musters. His eyes flashed. "Remember that one
I pulled off in Wichita?" His face was brighter, younger.
"We came limping in there with no feed for the stock and
no gas for the trucks and . . ." McCoy, with his eyes a
thousand miles and twenty-five years away, rolled on
about how he had talked the police into a permit and two
hundred tickets, the schools into a location and four hundred tickets, and the Lions and the Shriners for the rest.
How he had left in three days with over fifty-five thousand dollars clear profit. "Yeah, Buck, them were the days.
I tell you these kids coming up nowadays can't find their
ass with both hands. They missed it. They missed it all."

Buck rapped his knuckles on the table to stop him.
"Bob, how in the hell can you advertise seventeen bulls
and twelve polar bears?"

"Old paper, pal. Can't afford the printing." He grinned.
"And who in the hell could print quality like that these
days?"

"How many bulls you carrying?"

"Five. I still got Betsy and Joe." He loaded his coffee up

with five spoons of sugar and two dairy-mixes. "And I got Wilma and Ben and Charley."

"How many horses?"

"Twelve. That son of a bitch Stilliphant's been sniffing around. He's got him some deal with the dog-food people."

McCoy waited until Buck looked at him. "You ever think you'd live to see the day when Bob McCoy, the Real McCoy"—he tried to smile but it went thin and faded —"played a K-Mart mall?"

My coffee was cold, but I sipped it anyway. I couldn't stand looking at him. McCoy reached over and took both of Buck's hands. "They're breaking my heart out there. I tell you they're breaking my heart." He looked out over the men's socks and underwear. The green light was flashing and K-Mart was marking down dish towels from ninety-nine cents to forty-nine. McCoy's voice was strained and grinding down. "Buck, I used to go into rehearsals and whole acts would stop just for me to say hello. I used to get all the pretty girls. Any girl I wanted. You remember Gloria? Shirl? You remember that little flyer Fern? All gone. Gone. Now they got my ass so spread they could drive a pole wagon through it."

Buck lit a cigar and exhaled. "Come on, Bob, come on. Get ahold of yourself. Everything's going to be all right. . . . Come on, now."

"I'm sorry Buck. I'm sorry." He scraped up the last of his cottage cheese and snapped the lid back on. "Let's go back to the trailer. We can't do business in a place like this."

McCoy lived in an old Airstream. Oriental rugs were on the floor and dark Turkish lamps were hanging from the ceiling and bubbling in the corners. Everything was old and wearing out, but it seemed expensive. Circus posters and eight-by-ten glossies of old acts and old stars covered every foot of wall space.

Buck was in front of a pair of Buffalo Bill Wild West advertisements. "Now here's the beauts I like. Look here,

Bo." They were curled and cracked at the corners, but the litho colors were strong and bright.

McCoy slid a bottle of Scotch out on the table for us. He poured himself a warm Coke. "Nice, ain't they?"

I took a close look, checking the opaque blue and the hairline registration.

"Damn right."

The printer's date was 1889, and Bill Cody in his tasseled leather and flowing beard was up on his rearing horse. He was waving his white hat with one hand and a smoking forty-four with the other. Around him, Indians, cowboys, Conestoga wagons, and riders and flags of all nations were swirling in an Apache circle. The announcement read, MY LAST AND FINAL APPEARANCE IN THE SADDLE, and no one had stopped the artist from stacking a hundred thousand people in the bleachers. The second poster, stretching into the same clouds and the mountains in the distance, was posthumous. In the middle of the circle and the waving crowd, the ghost of Cody sat tall in his silver saddle with his white hat raised to the heavy promo: LET MY SHOW GO ON!!!

McCoy was nearsighted and got in close. He pointed at Cody as if he knew him. "Those were the days, Buck, I swear they were." And then he sounded as if he'd been thinking about it for a long, long time. "They won't be seeing times like that again. Not around here they ain't."

I kept looking at the Apache circle, the wild riders, and Cody's eyes. McCoy was right. They were all dying off and being driven to the wall by rising prices and the dog-food people. The old mud circus would soon be gone, and the big tents would be heading in for the circus museums and the Halls of Fames that were lining the roads like fast-food franchises, or being auctioned off to the screaming evangelists. As I looked at the old poster, I knew that if Buck was like anyone he was like Buffalo Bill Cody and he would stay in the saddle and stay in the saddle. He would do one more show. Then one more. And then, finally, one more. And I also knew that Buck Brody, alias Buck Mozingo, alias Rick Rabon, and alias whatever else he was, was exactly like the old man. He was a dreamer and a charmer. But he was mostly a loser, a born and total loser. And there was one hard fact that stayed right in the middle of my head, and that was that I had to get my money out of that trailer and get the hell out of there.

Buck was licking down a fresh cigar. "O.K., Bob, let's get on with it." McCoy loosened his belt. "Well, I could use some bulls. You still carrying six?"

"Yeah, but I'm only selling four." He had told me they were big Africans worth seventeen thousand dollars a head.

"Buck, if I had the money I'd pay the market." With his dark glasses there was no telling what he was up to. "I can swing four thousand a head."

"You're kidding."

McCoy said, "I know that's pretty grim. But that's it. Four thousand cash. No checks, no notes, nothing."

Buck lit his cigar and shook his head. McCoy sat forward. "You know I wouldn't shaft you while you're down. We go back too far for that."

"Who said I was down?" Buck studied the flame. Then he shook it out. "Bob, what if I said yes?"

McCoy cocked his head like a bird. "Let me hear the 'if' part."

Buck said he'd sell him four elephants now for four thousand dollars apiece and two more later. For ten thousand more he'd throw in his camels and horses, his tent, and three of his trucks.

"Sounds too good, Buck. What's the catch?"

"No catch." He held his cigar at the gambler's angle I'd seen back at Fred's. "I need your show for two dates. Two dates, Bob, and then everything's yours. And you pick up the other two bulls for eight thousand."

"What dates? What in the hell you talking about?"

"Charles City on the seventh and eighth and Summerville on the ninth. A forty-mile jump, that's all."

Buck was on his feet, telling McCoy about the

Mozingo–Arlo Waters Jubilee Crusade and the Famous Life of Christ Festival. McCoy smiled when he heard there was no state or federal entertainment tax. But he was still behind his shades. There was no telling what he was thinking. Buck told him they would split the profits. After Charles City and Summerville, McCoy could take the last two bulls and be back on the spring tour by the tenth. McCoy didn't like it. "Buck, those people are broke. They're always broke. They always will be broke."

"No, Bob, you still don't get it. I need them for atmosphere. That's all." Slowly he balanced his cigar on the table edge and slowly he spelled it out. "What I want me is a couple fat cats. The old medicine show dodge. Break even out front and take a Howard Hughes to the back tent."

McCoy seemed to be losing interest fast. "Why didn't you tell me this on the phone? The hell with this noise."

Buck gripped McCoy's shoulders. "Two dates, Bob, that's all. Then it's all yours. Lock, stock, and barrel. This is it Bob, the big one, and you're coming out with six of the best bulls on the road."

Slowly Buck moved him into a 180-degree turnaround, and in another ten minutes a cigar box of money and a bill of sale were on the table. McCoy had agreed to send his drivers back to Bibleland to pick up the rigs and the four bulls. He would get the other two after Summerville. It was Buck's move. At first I thought he'd back down, or stall to think it over. But he stuck his hand out and didn't bat an eye. "Bob, you'll never regret it."

McCoy copied the dates in his black book. Suddenly his eyebrows creased together. "Hold it! This is too tight. I'm playing Buford, Georgia. I'm looking at three hundred miles. Can you handle the stakes?"

Buck relit his cigar. "No pain, no strain. Just give me a blueprint." McCoy began pulling out drawers and checking the shelves. "I've got one around here someplace. Now, get me something decent. That South Carolina crap down in there is like coffee grounds." He found one. Then he slid Buck the bill of sale. "Sign this." He counted out twenty-six thousand dollars.

As Buck signed the bill of sale he cut his eyes at McCoy's. "Just be sure you make it on time, old buddy."

McCoy looked angry, then hurt. "I've never missed a show date in my life."

Buck pushed the money over to me. "Count it, Bo." Then he tapped McCoy's shoulder. "I'm sorry, Bob. Just kidding."

We had another drink and this time McCoy joined us. I sat back with the money as they began talking about the old days when Ringling Brothers and Haggenback and Wallace and Clyde Beatty and a dozen names I'd never heard were crossing the country. They kept drinking and rolled on about the old medicine shows. One out of Texas was called "Rabbitfoot." Another was "Silas Greene from New Orleans" with a cast of two hundred; their stars were Bessie Smith, Carmen Miranda, Stepin Fetchit, Mickey Rooney, and Red Skelton.

I sat there half drunk, listening to the old stories, and the old lies, and feeling absolutely great about everything. Buck had come through, as he said he would, and the money was bulked up and heavy in my jacket. The only thing missing now was Monica. In the morning I'd call Greene and tell him the news. Then I'd call Monica. And then about eleven o'clock, after a good night's sleep, I'd say farewell to Buck and Loretta and Arlo and the Jubilee Crusade and get the hell out of here and head back to civilization.

The whiskey was hitting McCoy, and his face was beginning to flush. He was mad and getting madder, but he was talking slower as he bitched about how when the circus stopped using tents, and went inside, it was the end of the class acts. "Buck, I saw a show in Cedar Rapids that would have dropped you to your knees. The top rows were higher than the trapeze platforms. Those goddamn people were looking *down* on the flyers. Now if that ain't pathetic, I'll eat it."

Buck was listening, but I could tell he wasn't really listening. He had poured out three more drinks and was shaking out another tray of ice cubes. "The Sherrys working tonight?"

McCoy grinned, "You better believe it. I got me a red-hot show out there. Best show this jackrabbit town ever saw. Stick around, the gang would love to see you."

Buck was dropping ice cubes in the drinks. "Who else is on?"

McCoy raised five fingers. "I got them all. I got Don Castelleone. I got the Rodriguezes. Hey, I even got little Freddy Logan on the wagon."

Buck interrupted. "How about Borovelski?"

"Lost him. The bastard took off on me. Poland, Czechoslovakia, one of them damn places. But listen, I got the Borodinos and Commodore Onslow. You boys have got to see it. Come on, I'll let you sit with the band." He smiled at Buck. "Buck, they'd love to see you out there."

Buck took a big drink, wiped his mouth, and set his glass down carefully. His eyes were bright, and I knew he was planning something. He winked at me and hitched his pants up with the inside of his wrists. "I got a better idea."

McCoy lurched to his feet and slapped him on the back. "Man, you would! It'll be like old times." He turned to me. "Kid, you ever see this fellow work a crowd?"

"Only a snake show." And then I winked at Buck. "And Pioneer and Bunny Tissue."

McCoy had been drinking too much to question anything. "Well, you're in for a surprise. He's the best there is, and I've damn well seen them all. Hey! I got some stuff you can wear." He opened a closet and began dragging out star-spangled jackets, stovepipe hats, and four different pairs of boots. "It's that bastard Borovelski's."

Buck looked terrific. Everything fit. The gold gloves, the boots, even the foot-high white shako hat with the gold chin strap. He buttoned up a red velvet jacket with silver frog latches and mica-trimmed lapels and wrapped his waist in a black-sequined cummerbund. Then McCoy rolled out his big piece. A six-foot-long, high-collared black cape with a crimson lining. The great Mozingo minced and pranced and showboated in front of the mirror, flexing his leather baton and popping it against Borovelski's patent-leather boots. "Bo. . . . This is the goddamn greatest."

Then he swung his hat up until it hit the low ceiling. *Ladies and gentlemen, boys and girls, and children of all ages . . . welcome to the circus.* He swung it down and out in a big circle. Then he squared it on his head, clicked his heels, and saluted himself in the mirror. "Come on, Bo."

Outside, we headed for the big tent. He was walking faster, talking faster. He kept slapping his leg with the baton. The cape sailed out behind him like Count Dracula, and he was talking like a streak. How the tent was more than just canvas. How it had to be cared for and watched over. How wooden stakes were used for dirt and steel for asphalt. And how the indoor shows, even Madison Square Garden, couldn't touch the old mud show. "Bo, when that canvas gets wet it's the greatest soundboard for music in the world. It smooths it out and holds it in and the crowd feels it. Then the acts feel the crowd and then, whap! everything works and keeps on working. Madison Square Garden is like playing in the goddamn subway. There's no feeling there. Get me? It's all feeling." I'd seen him up when I'd hit him with the twelve-million Bunny Tissue bag news, but this was different. It was a whole new kind of excitement. I said I thought I did. He stopped and shook his head. "No, you don't. Nobody knows but old bastards like McCoy and me. You've got to be doing it. And this bunch of half-asses are doing it. And it's something they ain't ever going to turn loose."

It was a brand-new Buck. "You watch tonight. Watch close. Those people are doing double and triple turns. When they finish their acts they'll shovel elephant shit, sell Cokes, popcorn, snow-cones, you name it. Now don't tell me they ain't a group. Far as I'm concerned they're the goddamn greatest people breathing."

The Great Mozingo sucked his stomach into his chest and stepped into the spotlight in the center ring. He blew his whistle. Then, with a long smooth flurry, he swept his white shako down. Then out. Then up. *Ladies and gentlemen, boys and girls, and children of all ages . . . welcome to the circus.* He circled the center ring with the mike cord trailing out behind. *For your entertainment and edification we are proud to announce in ring number one, which is on my immediate left, the fabulous, world-renowned perch-pole family, the Flying Del Marcos. In the third ring, which is on my right, on the dangerous and death-defying teeter board, the Gonzales Family and Señor Enrico Valdez.*

A thin pin light came from the ceiling. It splashed on the silver revolving ball. *And in the center ring, our feature during this portion of our show, the unbelievable, the incredible Don Manuel Del Castelleone, who will attempt and no doubt complete the freehand stand on the silver ball you see before you, using only one finger of one hand.*

The actors bowed and flourished. The drumroll started. The audience was in the palm of his hand, and he spread his arms. *Ladies and gentlemen, boys and girls . . . the Wonderful World of Bob McCoy! . . .*

McCoy's hand was on my shoulder. "Bo, he's the goddamn best there is!"

I couldn't believe any of it. "He might damn well be."

Buck's baton came down, and the cornets, the trombones, and the cymbals split the air as if they had been paid that morning. With his half-stepping and strutting before the tiny bandstand, the nine pieces sounded like thirty. They were playing to a full house set up by the Shriners, who were getting forty percent of the gross.

Vendors hawking Cokes, peanuts, snow-cones, and Pronto-Pups were streaking in and out of the packed grandstand and the overflowing kids in the bleachers. The lights caught the spinning, the leaping, and the cartwheeling of the overture. Then three pink pins zeroed in on Don Manuel Del Castelleone handstanding onto his slowly turning silver ball in the center ring. He raised himself carefully on two hands. Then one. And then slowly, and with the snare drums underlining it, onto his famous one-finger stand. McCoy's breath smelled like toenails. He kept holding on to me and talking about Sidney Weiss, who with charges against him of interstate flight in Arkansas and Tennessee had grown a mustache and changed his name to Don Manuel Del Castelleone. "They think he's Spanish. He told one woman he was the grandson of Rudolph Valentino."

Buck had called it. Everyone was doing double and triple turns. The Del Marcos changed costumes and appeared later on the trapeze as Phil, Annette, and Francine Salvatore. The Gonzales, changing from red tights to white, became the Hungarian Motoronzos on the fire-lighted trampoline, and Don Manuel Del Castelleone came back dressed in Cossack blue with black fur trim as Count Borodovsky, hanging from his heels and holding Francine Borodino by her teeth for the Iron Jaw Spin. Buck introduced the Rodriguez family as the foremost tumbling act in the known world in ring number one. In the center he announced Commodore Onslow McGregor and His Leaping Dalmatians. Then he stepped back into the shadow of the king post.

McCoy was gripping my shoulder and lisping his words. "He's hot tonight. He's really hot. Kid, that fellow is the best I've ever seen, and I've seen them all."

I kept watching Buck and wondering about everything. "But why hasn't he made it? With all that going for him, why isn't he on top?"

"It's simple, kid." McCoy laughed. "He just don't care about money. Never has and never will. All he likes is the action. But I'll tell you something, that son of a bitch can do it. You name it, electronics, canvas work, handle animals, snakes, he can do it all. But when it comes to money, forget it. I saw him with over two hundred thousand dollars in five- and ten-dollar bills down in Clearwater. Damn stuff was bouncing around in his damn car trunk. He didn't even have it banded. Hell, you opened it up and it would be flying all over the place." He shook his head. "That's the kind of guy old Buck is. But I'll tell you something, I wish to hell I could hire him."

The cats were ready, and Buck stepped into the spotlight. He blew three short blasts and raised his gold-gloved hands. *And now, ladies and gentlemen, boys and girls . . . in ring number three, none other than Captain Dave Hoover and his mixed ensemble of royal Bengal tigers and black Nubian lions . . . Untamed! . . . Wild! . . . Incredible!* The snare drum set it up. Then the trumpets and trombones charged into "Burma Patrol." Captain Dave Hoover in his white uniform, and with his chair and whip, twirled into the ring of cats. He seated them on their stools as Buck cautioned through the microphone, *Watch now! Watch now! That second cat, Sabu, is a killer. . . .*

The act built until the finale, and Sabu, a toothless twenty-year-old, faked a sudden return to savage fury. He made a quick move at Dave Hoover. Then he stopped. He was glaring, spitting. Buck hushed his voice and dampered his hands down. *Ladies and gentlemen . . . at this time I'd like for you to be as quiet as possible. . . .*

The big cat inched forward, low, menacing, about to spring. He stopped and slowly raised one paw as if he was going to take Hoover's face off. He crouched lower. Closer. Hoover stood his ground. Then he backed carefully. The big cat kept coming. His shoulder muscles bunching, quivering. Hoover stopped. He jabbed with his chair and flourished his whip out behind him. Then he stepped forward. They were face to face. The cat's paw shot out, the audience screamed, and Hoover jumped back with his whip popping. Sabu roared and rushed again. Again he stopped and, rearing up ten feet tall, screamed and clawed the air above him. Then, slowly and with condescending majesty, he whipped around and joined the line of cats whirling around the cage and thundered out the runway.

The crowd was whistling, shouting, and applauding.

The band held them there with "Under the Double Eagle" as Dave Hoover bowed and raised his hands. He bowed again and Buck shouted, *The fantastic Captain Dave Hoover!* A dirt farmer at the edge of the reserved seat section hooked his head. "Yeah! Yeah now! That's all right!"

The show rolled on through the flying acts, the trained seals, and into the intermission, where the clowns sold *Wonderful World of Bob McCoy* coloring books for two dollars and jumbo Cokes for one. At the circus there is no such thing as a small or regular Coke. Buck came forward again. *Ladies and gentlemen, boys and girls, direct to you from Paris, Moscow, and command performances before the crowned heads of Europe, we are happy to bring to you the most famous high-wire act in the world today . . . Les Sherrys!*

The music flared into "Midnight in Paris." The lights picked up the father, mother, two sons, and one daughter in pink and gold posing at the top of the tent. *Ladies and gentlemen, you will notice the Sherrys do not work with a net. So I must beg you to remain in your seats and be absolutely quiet during this portion of the show.* He nodded for the drumroll.

The Sherrys were stacked three deep to cross over the high wire. As the pink and blue pins outlined them, they seemed higher than fifty feet, smaller, more vulnerable. The snare drummer worked with only the brushes as they moved out. Suddenly, halfway across, one long balancing pole dipped. Monsieur Sherry shouted. A woman screamed and the crowd leaped to its feet. Buck's arms shot up for silence, as the Sherrys windmilled their arms, straining for balance. The poles leveled. The crowd sighed and eased back in their seats as the band picked it up and segued into "Ramona." Then the Sherrys moved on across, and, timing it perfectly, with the cornets punching out the grace notes, McCoy's finest group ended their act with a leaping circus finish to the high platform. The crowd was back on its feet, going wild as they bowed and flourished and threw kisses from the pink-and-gold top of the tent. Buck popped his baton and swung his gold hands. *Ladies and gentlemen, boys and girls . . . the Sherrys! Yowza! Yowza! Yowza!*

The cat act and the Sherrys had tuned the crowd to the perfect circus pitch Buck had told me about. I could feel it building. They were straining forward, wanting more and more, and still more. McCoy kept saying, "Great show. Great show. Great show." I kept saying, "Yeah. Yeah." Buck waved to the wings and blew his whistle. Another whistle answered from the dark, and the drummer leaned in on the tom-toms. The ground began to rumble. The cornets staircased quickly, topping out to ping away on the B's and high C's of "Jungle Drums" as the prancing Captain Freddy Logan came high-stepping in from the shadows, leading the elephants. Don Manuel Del Castelleone, alias Sidney Weiss, who out in the dark had helped the elephants clear their bowels by rearing them up on their back legs, was whipping them from the rear. The crowd was roaring. After running the herd around the circle, Captain Freddy Logan stretched them down one side of the tent. He made them stand on their front legs and then their hind legs. They rolled over and did single turns and doubles. Then they lay on their sides to let the kids, planted in the bleachers, climb them and slide down their stomachs. And then with the tom-toms pounding and the brass weaving in and out of the heavy rhythm of "Burma Patrol," the lead bull reared up on his hind legs. It was the signal. The others followed him up and into the spectacular Long Mount as the music filled every crack and seam and panel in the place. Captain Freddy's whistle sounded again. And leading the elephants, still up on their hind legs, he swept them out into the dark as the band peaked and held and showered bright and perfect music on the whistling, shouting, screaming fans. Buck stepped forward and, with a long smooth bow, bent low. He held it for a measured moment. And then pointing his white shako at the top of the tent he boomed, *Ladies and gentlemen, boys and girls, and children of all ages . . . this concludes our show.*

McCoy was gripping me so tight I had to pry his hands loose. "Just a goddamn perfect show. Jesus. Jesus, I wish I had him."

The show was over and the tent rigging and the high wires were down. The Bible trucks, whose slides lowered to form seat galleries, had pulled out. Freddy Logan, with two elephants, was at the end, stacking the bleachers. Buck was dropping the tent and he wanted me to see it. The side flaps were down. The stakes had been pulled. All that held it up were the queen poles and the kings. He led me through the ropes and across the sawdust to the center pole.

"Close now. Stand close." He held the fifty-foot line from the tops. "See the slot?"

I looked up. "Not yet. Yeah, I got it."

"Well, keep an eye on it." He shouted. "O.K., boys!"

The men stopped talking and moving around.

Buck shouted, "Who's on one?"

"Johnny."

"Well, where the hell is he? Johnny, I can't see you."

He called out from the shadows. "Taking a leak. All set now."

Buck shouted, "O.K., ready! Number four?"

"Ready."

"Number three?"

"Ready."

"And number two?"

"Ready."

He tapped my shoulder. "Set?"

"Yeah."

"O.K., watch the slot." He boomed out, "And let's bring her *down*."

Buck's line tightened. The king pole slipped the grommet and the big tent shuddered. It rippled out from the long spine. Then it ballooned and stopped and started

down again, faster. Suddenly I froze, looking straight up.
I couldn't see the slot. The light vanished like black ink
poured in clear water as a deep *whoosh* held in the air and
a million feet of space collapsed at a hundred thousand
feet a second. It closed in around us. Buck grabbed my
elbow. "See the slot?"

"No." Then I thought I saw it. Then I really saw it.
"Yeah! Yeah!"

He was busy with the rope. I aimed him at it. "There!"

It grazed our heads. We ducked in. We stood up. The
canvas was billowing out, rolling out and flowing in all
directions. Slowly it sank. The only sound was the
whisper of the air. Against the Tallahassee lights the
canvas looked silver as it stretched out to the skyline and
the low moon. Buck paused and stripped the cellophane
from a fresh cigar. "This is what I miss. It's something,
ain't it?"

"Buck, it's just great."

Buck lined up twenty men to fold the gray duck down to
six feet wide for the spool truck. He waved them into a
straight line. His voice ran down the canvas and echoed
off the cage wagon, the pole wagon, the sleeper, the cook
house, the Bibles.

"O.K. . . . Now, let's walk it off. . . . All right . . . lay
it down. . . . Down . . . down . . . That's it. . . . Fine . . .
Back up."

It was a lower voice, a slower voice, and it keyed in
with the men stooping, kneeling, crawling.

"One more time. . . . O.K., let's walk her in. On in.
Keep those ropes in the middle. . . . All right, one more
fold. Keep it smooth. . . . Smooth. Yeah, all right!"

The canvas was narrowed down and smoothed out. The
spool truck backed onto it and wound it up. Everything
was ready for the pullout. The cages were stacked; the
seats, the stakes, the steel. The wagons were ready to
strike out for the red-arrow markers leading them north
to Macon.

Buck boomed out. "O.K., pole wagons, let's go."

The big wagon, its valves clacking wildly, ground out. "Keep it moving. Keep it moving."

The wagons pulled out in double low. He shouted at the cage-wagon driver. "Low! Keep her low. Low! You dumb son of a bitch! Freddy! See if Jo-Jo's drunk! O.K., Bible wagon. Roll it! Come on, cage! . . . Roll! Let's go *spool*."

Buck was right; it was like nothing I'd ever seen or would ever see again. For a moment I really saw why it was pulling on him. Why it would never let him go. The moon was low and full, and the skyline and the low clouds were backlighted in black and silver and I knew it was something I would never forget. I also knew that if I had my arm around Monica's waist, feeling her tremble with the night and everything around us, I'd be the happiest bastard in the world.

We stood there watching the red trailing lights of the spool truck vanishing down the road and the crew lined up side by side coming forward picking up the Dixie Cups and the snow-cone sleeves and the popcorn boxes. In the morning the only thing left on the lot would be the stake holes and the sawdust where the entrance of the tent had been. Buck was cocking his hands up as if he was framing the Tallahassee skyline for a photograph. "Beautiful, ain't it? Ain't that the most beautiful thing you ever saw?"

"It sure as hell is."

He kept his arms up and his hands squared. "Ain't but one thing prettier, Bo, and that's the Wendy Van Hooten Circus. Ever heard of it?"

"Can't say that I have. Hey, didn't Disney do a movie on something like that?"

"No, ain't nobody even written it down. It's inside stuff. The circus crowd tells them to their kids and they pass it on down."

We stood there looking at the crew and the skyline as if we owned it all. My hand was on his shoulder. "Buck, let me have one of those cigars."

I bit the end off and lit up as the men cleared the

lot and the moon slid along the edge of the clouds. Buck
puffed on his cigar. "Bo, I grew up on the damn stories. I
guess they never leave you." His voice went softer as he
told me how Wendy Van Hooten was only nine years old
and his red, white, and blue rubber tent could shrink to
seat five hundred or expand for five thousand or fifty
thousand, and how it was floated from town to town by
colored balloons. He went on about how the center poles
were glass, with goldfish swimming inside, and the
quarter poles and stakes were solid brass that gleamed in
a sun that always shined when Wendy came to town.
Buck relit his cigar. "Nice story, isn't it?" He didn't wait
for an answer. Instead he reared back as if he wanted to
see how far the Milky Way stretched. "One more month,
Bo. Yessir, that's all I need. Once I get a stake out of this
Crusade mess, I'm going to buy me a circus and I'm never
going to leave it." We stood there smoking and watching
the men.

Buck sighed, "Bo, in one more month we're going to be
standing on our own lot, with our own trucks, with our
own cats and bulls and everything."

I heard the "we're" but didn't say anything. He kept
puffing on his cigar. "Two weeks from now and we're in
the clear and sailing. And Bo, let me tell you something.
You're in for a third of everything. That's thirty-three and
a third of everything, right off the top, and a goddamn
unlimited expense account."

For a split second I liked the idea. Maybe it was the
night. Maybe it was the tent coming down like that, or the
Wendy Van Hooten goldfish in the center poles. Or maybe
it was the feeling of belonging to something that would set
up one day, and tear down that night, and play the next
night two hundred miles away, and then tear down and
strike out again. And then I remembered that morning at
Fred's. "Forget it, Buck. Damn it, don't jack me off like
this. I'm getting out of here."

Buck said, "Don't get mad. Jesus. Now, listen to me.
I've given this some strong thought. The way I figure it,

you can go and break your ass in that Klondike and you might just make out fine. Maybe in ten years you'll be pulling down thirty thousand and a Christmas bonus. You'll have a couple cars, a color TV, and maybe a house out in Jersey." He held my elbow as if he was helping me cross the street. "But Bo, that ain't nothing. You still got to grin every time a purchasing agent cuts a fart. Now, I ask you, what in the hell kind of life is that for a great guy like you? Bo, you got potential. The way I see it, a man ain't worth a damn until he's got about a hundred thousand dollars salted away in the bank. Then you don't kiss any ass."

I puffed on my cigar and spoke through the smoke. "When was the last time you had a hundred thousand in the bank?"

Buck held his cigar out and tapped the ashes off. "A long time. A long, long time." He laughed. "But I'll tell you something, little buddy. There ain't nothing like it in the world. Nothing."

Later, we were heading back to Bibleland with Mc-Coy's trucks following us. Buck had his shirt and shoes off and was stretched across the back seat with a baseball cap over his eyes. It was midnight, and the only show I could get on the radio was the Grand Ole Opry from Nashville. It seemed to be on four or five stations. It sounded better on AM, and I turned up the treble on a whanging bluegrass bleeder with about twenty-six words per line. A real loser. I've never liked the stuff, but down here with the mules and the red clay and the R.U. Ready for Eternities painted on automobile tires and nailed to the fence posts it made more sense than when you're whipping up the F.D.R. Drive or sweating out the Lincoln Tunnel. Maybe Buck was right. Maybe the place did have something besides the hookworm and the rock-bottom per-capita income. If it did, I didn't want any part of it. All I wanted was out of here in the morning. When the song ended, I kept the station on. Buck tapped me on the shoulder.

"That's WSM. Down here we get that station set on the dial and tear off the knob." He lit a cigar and leaned up with his elbows hooked over the seat. "Getting so you kind of like it, don't you?"

"It's all you can get."

He laughed, "That's for sure."

As we came around a big curve I saw about a dozen bullfrogs blinking in the headlights. I slowed down. "Look!"

Buck said, "Damn if they don't always look like little tombstones. Big, ain't they?"

I drove on through the Spanish moss, watching for frogs and snakes and alligators. Buck sat forward again and cocked his hat back. "Cut that volume down a tad. Yeah, that's it. Bo, I'm going to tell you a little something. The way I see it, you're getting yourself a first-class education on the South. I mean it." He relit his cigar. It was going to be another lecture. "Bo, people up north figure we're still wiping our ass with corncobs down here. No lie, the average New Yorker knows about as much about the South as a hog knows about the Lord's plan for salvation. We've got it all over you people. Always have and always will have."

I turned around. "Come off it."

"Bo, I wouldn't steer you wrong. Now hear me out. First of all, we've got more imagination."

I was laughing. "You're not going to hit me with the wharf rat in Savannah bit are you?"

"No, nothing like that." He laughed. Buck leaned forward with his beer. "Bo, down in Palermo, which is about as far south as you can get in Europe, I started checking out Saint George and the Dragon paintings. O.K., so here's what I found out. In Palermo, Saint George was about five foot ten and built like a wide receiver, and the dragon was coming in bigger than the Seagram Building and throwing out about a sixty-foot sheet of raw flame. Got me?"

"I guess so." We were going through a crossroads town.

The only light was on a Texaco gas pump. The town passed and we were running through a tunnel of thick oaks and Spanish moss. When the lights hit the bullfrogs they did look like little tombstones.

"O.K. When you hit southern Italy that dragon is about the same. But when you get up into northern Italy, where they get a little snow every now and then, and into Germany, that dragon starts getting smaller. I'd say five hundred miles north and he's down to about half the size he was in Palermo. But here's the big ripple. Up in Copenhagen and Oslo, that Palermo dragon that's weighing in at about ninety thousand tons, with a Pittsburgh furnace coming out of his mouth, has shrunk to a good-sized jackrabbit. No lie, in Copenhagen old George is holding him up by one ear, and I mean that mother wouldn't dress out more than eight or nine pounds. And no flame, not even any smoke. What I'm saying is that southern folks just have bigger visions and they stretch things out a little more. You know, you get on down in South America and it's three growing seasons a year. Hell, I hear the women have two periods a month. You think that one over, Bo."

"O.K., Buck. I'll give it some strong thought." I was beginning to sound like him. I had to get out, fast.

Then he angled his cap down over his eyes and said, "End of sermon." Then he went to sleep.

An hour later we were still sliding through the swamp, and I was still listening to WSM. The trees were thinning out and the moon was popping in and out of the moss and lighting up the white line and the reflectors on up the highway. An old Elvis record came on and I adjusted the tuner to get the static out. Buck stirred, "Little louder there, Bo. I heard him introduce that thing in Memphis."

When the song ended, I said, "Wish I'd seen him. Wonder what he was like, anyway."

Buck opened two warm beers and handed me one. "He wasn't like anyone. You start trying to compare Elvis to something and you can forget it." He began humming the melody. "Bo, all you can do with a talent that big and that different is sort of point at it when you see it going by, and maybe listen for the ricochet."

He was quiet for a moment and then he elbowed up in behind me. "I saw that scutter in Jackson, Mississippi, one night and I was sitting next to two old biddies. I mean they had to be over seventy, and those old gals didn't sit down once during the whole show. Damnedest thing I ever saw. One of them just kept saying, 'Lordy! Lordy! Lordy!' But the other one said something that I'll just be damned if I'll ever forget. You see, when it was all over, and she knew he wasn't going to be doing any more encores, she just looked up at him, smiling. Bo, that was one of the most beautiful smiles I've ever seen in my life. And that old sweetheart said, 'Oh, if I could only just do his sewing.'"

I guess Buck had brought me around a little on the South. I was beginning to like the damn country. Maybe it was the flowers all blooming in February and the gardenia smell at night. Maybe it was the way the dogs stood around in threes and fours in the small towns. Buck called them dead-in-the-road-Georgia-dogs. But there was something wrong with it all. The sun had been baking everyone's brains out too long. They seemed slacker-jawed, duller-eyed. New Yorkers were sharper. They dressed better. They talked faster. Things really buzzed and clicked in Manhattan; there was more energy in the air. As far as sales was concerned, it was like the Sahara. They'd even missed the Sun Belt cut. Hell, you'd need a two-thousand-mile territory to even touch Manhattan south of Fourteenth Street. Even the Midwest had Ralston Purina, P&G and General Mills, and the meat-and-candy field around Chicago. But down in here they had nothing going but third-rate insurance companies and lightweight industries turning out urinal filters. I'd only been gone nine days, but it felt like ninety. I couldn't wait to get back. I missed Monica, and the restaurants, and the noise, and the lights. But most of all I missed the action. Winter was half over now, and in a few more weeks it would warm up and the balloon men and the Italian-ice vendors would be out at Central Park, and Monica and I would be cruising through the zoo and heading over for the Tavern on the Green.

CHAPTER

10

In the morning I packed up at Quality Courts, checked out, and went over to say good-bye. Buck was on the patio. He'd slept late and hadn't shaved. He handed me a beer. "Here you go, Bo. So cold it's got ice in it."

I didn't want it but I took it anyway and dropped in the hammock. There's nothing like that first cold beer in the morning, and I stretched out, promising myself that the minute I hit I-95 north I was going on the wagon.

Buck said, "Bo, you sure you know what you're doing? I mean, damn, I'm going to miss your Yankee ass."

"My mind's made up."

"O.K., but I'm telling you we're going to clean up with old McCoy. Christ, ain't you even curious?"

"Yeah, I guess I am. But I got to get back, you know how it is." He rubbed his beard. "How about one more favor old buddy? Just one, then I'll let you go. I've got to get into Savannah."

"Be glad to. What's up?"

"I've got to see this Arab. We need some props for the march. Tell you what, let me grab a shave. Have another

144

beer, there's some potato chips around here someplace."

Buck came out in his jodhpur pants and safari jacket. I could smell the after-shave lotion.

We pulled out on the Dixiana Highway for Savannah. It was an old two-lane blacktop. The road they would take on the Crusade. Out on the interstate the law keeps advertising fifty and one hundred yards back from the road shoulders, but down in here it was still World War II. Signs were plastered on the sides of smokehouses and stapled to the fences. Most were JESUS SAVES and scriptural quotes. But there was also hardware and soft goods: TAKE 666 COLD TABLETS . . . NITE CRAWLERS . . . CRICKETS . . . SHE-CRAB SOUP. At a crossroads, REPENT was stenciled in red on a whitewashed smooth rock riding low in a rusted-out wheelbarrow. FEAR GOD was everywhere. Buck sharpened up a station with a high-pitched preacher coming down on birth-control devices and mini-bottles. He cut him off. "They used to scream about chewing gum and dancing. Now they've moved into the bedroom. Guess that's progress. Hey! Slow down. I want you to see this."

I pulled off on the red clay shoulder. A cow pasture was full of egrets. Buck said they'd worked out an interesting arrangement with the cows that never varied. One bird would ride the cow's back, cleaning off ticks and discouraging the hornets. Two others would high-step alongside, eating the crickets and grasshoppers she nosed up. "Go on. Count them."

I counted. He was right. There were three egrets to every cow.

"I could watch those scutters all day," Buck laughed. "Now, Bo, that's something you don't see on Times Square or up on the Cross-Bronx Expressway."

We hit Savannah at noon and caught the lunchtime traffic. Grim city on the outskirts: blocks of used-car lots, burnt-out mattresses, overturned trash cans, and bedsprings leaning on the fireplugs. Then a long row of storefront churches, small loans, detective agencies, and bail-bond setups all side by side. A guy could get married, stick up a loan shark, get arrested and bailed out, and never leave the block. Beautiful downtown in the old section: wood sidings, cobblestones, fancy wrought-iron work, gaslights, and twenty-foot solid banks of azaleas. Great squares every other block that looked like Gramercy Park but had about ten times more flowers. Buck said I wouldn't believe it but the town was a dead copy of the city of Peking. I didn't.

The Arab's company, Transoceanic Manufacturing, was down on the docks. The name sounded like a heroin mill and looked like a shoe factory bricked up for air conditioning. There were about forty cars in the lot, and I pulled into Visitor's Parking. I locked the windows and the doors. "Give me that name again."

"Kabaar. Harun El Kabaar. I'm saying we're partners."

"Be my guest."

As we opened the glass door he touched my elbow. "I do all the talking."

The only thing Arabian about Harun El Kabaar was the red fez he had on his narrow and oily head. I pegged him for East Bronx, close to 248th Street. He had on hundred-and-fifty-dollar green-and-red Gucci shoes, beltless slacks, and an open-collared golf shirt. He smiled and rubbed his fingers together as if that was what was expected of an Arab in Savannah. Like Arlo, he had a lot of gum in his smile. Harun made us mint juleps from a small refrigerator. Frozen glasses and fresh mint were ready. "The trick, Mister Mozingo, Mister Mahaffey, to the julep is in the mint. . . . You must crush it so."

He was your basic Seventh Avenue–type pain in the ass who'd seen too many Peter Lorre movies. As he drank, he studied Buck's card. "Tell me, Mister Mozingo. As a student of commerce, I find this very curious. Doesn't 'The Great Mozingo' make it, say, rather difficult for you to bargain?" He gave the z a long beat as if he knew it was phony. Buck sipped his julep. I could tell he didn't like him.

"My purchasing agent usually takes care of things like this. But this time it's a little different."

Harun nodded slowly. "I understand."

The office was carpeted with Persian rugs and overlooked a long, two-storied factory and a windowless warehouse. The bridge over the Savannah River was about a mile away. Even through the air conditioning we could smell the United Paper Company. Now, talk about a company owning everything! United owns the land, the trees, the mills. The only packaging they're in is kraft bags for the food chains. But they make *all* the kraft bags. If they wanted to go into anything else they could wipe us all out. They were also doing a good job of wiping out the good townspeople of old Savannah town. Buck said the sulfite had killed every oyster and clam within forty miles and ruined the river for everything but water skiing. Buck didn't waste any time with small talk. He drank fast and slapped his knees. "Come on, Harun, let's do some business."

"Excellent. Excellent." He set his drink down carefully as if it might spill. "Now, I think you ought to tell me what you have in mind. I'm in a position to save you a lot of money." Harun smiled with only his mouth; nothing happened in his eyes. "Do you agree?"

"Absolutely." Buck had good eye contact going and was enjoying the in-fighting. "It's for a religious grotto for the Easter crowd. It's free, so I've got to buy cheap."

"Naturally."

Harun led us down the stairs toward the warehouse and the factory. Buck tried to get him off balance. "How old are those Cleopatra statues you told me about?"

"Oh, let's see. Ten, maybe fifteen. I forget."

"Let's say twenty-five, baby."

Harun looked disappointed. "Please, no 'baby.'" He forced his phony smile again. "With material like that you can fiberglass the cracks and spray-paint. It's so big no one gets too close." We were in a long hall. "As a matter of fact, that's the property C. M. Hill was looking at."

Buck was looking around. "Well, I had it in mind for a doorway, but maybe there's something else. Something cheaper?"

Harun spoke softly. "There always is." He was like a funeral director hustling you away from the plain woodens and the plastics and on to the bronze. He led us into a dark storage room and switched on the lights. It was wild. Statues of Roman emperors, Roman senators, and lounging and leaping lions were lined up for inspection. Against the wall were twelve- and fifteen-foot columns, aqueduct sections, and twenty-foot-high fronts of Roman buildings. It was from a movie set he'd bought in Italy when one of the studios folded. He waved his hand delicately. "Over here." He led us through an arch to the Coliseum to a ten-foot-high plaster reproduction of the *Pietà*. "One second." He flipped on a switch and red neon began humming as it rose and etched itself up and around Mary and Jesus.

"Personally, I don't care for this. But you can never tell. Some Texas oilman ordered it for his ranch. He'd just been converted and wanted to see it at night."

I asked, "Why didn't you ship it?"

Harun smiled smoothly. "Unfortunately, the conversion didn't last."

Buck was circling the statue. "He pay you?"

"Everyone pays me." He cleared his throat with one note. "Gentlemen, I assume you have cash."

"Always, Harun, always. A neon-trimmed *Pietà*. Well, Harun." Buck slid his hand down the robe draped over Jesus's feet. "You're going to be seeing this operation for a long time."

Harun smiled; his eyes were closed. "Mister Mozingo, if you want it, I'll give you a very nice price. Say, four hundred and fifty dollars, delivered."

"How about three hundred?"

"Mister Mozingo, you may have it."

"Let me think about it."

He led us into the factory. It was low and modern with

indirect lighting, Muzak, and Peter Max landscapes on the walls. There were no windows. Forty or fifty workers were on four long tables doing close work with strange hooks, magnifying glasses, and surgical tweezers. They were making relics: prayer blankets, robes, and metal trinkets. When the items left them, they went down a slow conveyor belt to six technicians in masks and rubber gloves. They were working with acids and a vat of solvent, giving the relics their first treatment on their two-thousand-year journey back to the time of Christ. One of Harun's hands was on Buck's shoulder. The other was on mine. "This is, of course, highly confidential. . . ."

Buck whistled a long clean note. "Absolutely. . . . Nice equipment."

He said simply, "The best." Then he snapped his fingers twice and a man hurried up. Harun spoke in rapid something and the man pulled a glass box from a shelf. Quickly he spread pieces of black wood onto a white cloth. He angled his head and spread his arms in crucifixion. Harun said, "Parts of the true cross." The slivers looked like pieces of fence post that had been left out in the sun for a long time. As Buck studied the price list, Harun, with one finger, signaled the man to replace the case. "Twenty percent off to professional people."

Buck said, "Well, this wasn't exactly what I had in mind. Damn, you really get a long price on this stuff."

"Mister Mozingo, you must realize this is all specialty work. We are the only operation like this in the entire country." Harun owned the plant. He did all the planning and promotion and could make a price concession on the spot. But he had too many items for machine packaging. His products would be sold in black velvet pouches with gold braid pucker strings, or papier-mâché cosmetic boxes made in France. In another case were other samples. The true robe was in three fabrics with three price lines. The pieces of silver that Judas collected came in silver or alloy in job lots of not less than a hundred. I pointed over at four cages of small dogs and cats that were suspiciously close to the exhibit of the highly polished bones of the saints and skins of the martyrs. "What're the animals for?"

Harun dismissed me with a shrug. "Oh, that's nothing. Nothing. Ah, but here!" He held up a vial of clear liquid mounted on a three-color cardboard slug. "A natural for what you have in mind. They're small, easily handled, easily stored. Water taken from the River Jordan on the exact day of the Crucifixion. Some minister out in Little Rock is cleaning up on this one. Mister Mozingo, for you, I'll give you my rock-bottom price. On eight gross and up, ninety dollars."

He handed me one. The polypropylene tube was two inches long with a solid-color acrylic closure. They were skin-packed to discourage pilferage and could be clipped onto a potato-chip rack or exhibited on a novelty tray. I must have been frowning. Harun smiled at me. "It offends you, I understand. In my country there is absolutely no problem with this kind of merchandise. Of course we have our other prejudices. . . . But this"—he shook the vial and watched it foam—"would be considered quite tasteful. . . . But come. One last item. My pièce de résistance." We moved through a maze of acid baths, drying racks, and slow-moving conveyor belts. He explained how he paid top money for his help. How they were the best in the world. "I had an operation similar to this in Connecticut, but the unions moved in and tried to take over. Southerners don't buy that union propaganda. They're too independent. Mister Mozingo, Mister Mahaffey, I don't care what they say, the average southerner, for my money, is one smart son of a bitch when it comes to the things that count. Mark my word, one day all of your manufacturing will be done down here."

Buck said, "Put me down for ten gross of that Jordan water. And I'll take that *Pietà* at three hundred. That's delivered."

Harun smiled. "Wonderful. You won't regret it."

We were in a blue-lighted room. The Muzak was playing "Lovely Hula Hands." Harun snapped his fingers once and two workers in the corner vanished. We were standing at a projector facing a screen. His voice was excited. "This is it, gentlemen. As they say in the trade, the top of the line. Through a new scientific lifting technique, we have been able to raise this impression." He threw two switches. One dropped the room into a dark grayness; the other threw a bluish light against the screen. "It will take but a moment to heat up." As the Muzak oozed around us I heard Buck humming along. And then the screen lighted. It came slowly but it came clearly. It was the head shape and hairline from Da Vinci's *Last Supper*, but the serene eyes and full lips were those of Kahlil Gibran. There's an old shopping-bag gal hangs around the Village who claims she went to school with Gibran up in the Bronx. Most people think he was the original Persian, but he hung out in the East Bronx and the Village. She said he had a helluva problem getting women because he was so moist. Well, moist or not, the son of a bitch has really raked in the money. Books, place mats, thoughtful sayings for the wall, praying hands—you name it. Probably sold more books than the Beatles sold records. Harun was whispering as if he was deeply moved. "Nice, isn't it? It was raised from the winding sheets. Or so the story goes. Mister Mozingo, for one hundred or five hundred I will give you my one-thousand price, three dollars per print."

"Too high."

"I'll take off another fifty cents. It's a very slow process and it has to be very closely monitored. I use a lot of labor."

Buck nodded. "For two bucks I'll take three thousand. Take it or leave it."

Harun threw both switches at once. "Sold, Mister Mozingo. And you won't regret a penny of it."

Going back through the warehouse, Buck bought two Coliseum arches and four six-foot statues of Julius

Caesar and the emperors Augustus, Tiberius, and Claudius. He decided he would flank them on each side of the *Pietà*. On the way out, Harun patted the leg of Nero leaning on his four-foot-high harp. "Mister Mozingo, take this off my hands. We can cut this off and put in a sun dial."

"It's Nero, right?"

"Yes. But who's going to know him?"

Buck shook his head. "Some high-school kid would show up with a history book. I'd look like hell. Hey, who's this?"

"Caligula."

"Well I'll be damned. He doesn't look too bad. What say, Bo?"

I couldn't resist it. "Take him."

Buck smiled, "Harun, old buddy, I'll knock you down with twenty-five bucks. I'll bill him as Pontius Pilate."

"Mister Mozingo, you can have him for nothing. And I'd like to say it's been a distinct pleasure doing business with people who know what they are doing. Gentlemen, I'll have this whole shipment out of here in the morning."

Buck tore across the lot, jumped in the car, and rolled the window up. As I started the engine he let out an ear-splitting yell. "Ooooo*HAH*!" He slapped his leg and began pounding on the dash. Then he whooped again. . . . "Fantastic stuff! Fantastic! Bo . . . we're going to make Billy Graham and Oral Roberts and that Tulsa bastard who's claiming he can raise the dead look like a Mississippi mud act. . . ."

Buck's couple of hours had turned out to be six, and we were driving back into the sun. He'd quit leaning on me about staying. He had other things on his mind. He kept drawing sketches on my call-report pad: how he would arrange the *Pietà*, the emperors, the arches, the lions. He'd make a sketch. Then he'd tear it up. Then he'd make another. He was trying to coordinate the Sherrys, Captain Dave Hoover and his cats, Captain Freddy Logan and his elephants, and Commodore Onslow McGregor's Leaping Dalmatians.

"Buck, how the hell you going to get them all in there?"

He kept sketching. "Wish I had the Texas Rangerettes and the Marine Corps Marching Band. That tent is big!" He glanced at me. "Hell, you ought to know that."

We were going through some pretty weird country. Most of the shacks were cocked up on brickbats and stump corners and had no windows, just shutters. Even from the road you could see the seams in the siding and knew that the light would leak through at night. The only thing I saw moving were the dogs shifting around to keep in the shade. Buck made me stop a couple times to read the old circus posters. Carson Barnes . . . Hugo and Johnson . . . Bartok's Minstrels . . . .Neat, how they left up the posters. In Manhattan, where space is at a premium, they'd have plastered fifteen more on top. He finally gave up on the choreography, pushed his shoes off, and pulled his baseball cap down over his eyes. "Put me on some music. If you can't get Spanish, I'll take country."

Miami came in with a lot of static. I had to settle for country-and-western from Savannah. Chewing tobacco and snuff signs were big down here, and REPENT and JESUS SAVES were everywhere. We flushed up a pair of buzzards working over a dead possum in the middle of the road. Ugly bastards up close. Long scaly legs, red scabby heads. The sun was directly in front, and I had to slow and keep way to the right. We'd be in Bibleland in another hour. By eight I'd be pulling out. In the morning I'd be three or four hundred miles north. Probably North Carolina. Maybe Virginia. The sun would be on my right. The music would be some good jazz out of Washington or Baltimore. Maybe I could even pick up WOR in Manhattan.

CHAPTER

11

It was dark by the time I'd said good-bye to Buck and Loretta and all the good folks of Bibleland. I told them I'd keep in touch and swung back on the Dixiana to Savannah. At Savannah I picked up I-85 and set the cruise control on sixty heading north. Diamond Reos, GMCs, and Peterbilts loaded down with fresh citrus and frozen orange juice were in a convoy in the left lane doing eighty. Allied Transfer, Cooper Motors, Trans-American, Roadway: all the carriers we used at Pioneer. I hadn't called Greene with the news about the eighteen thousand dollars. In the middle of the night I'd decided to just send it in a memo in the morning. I'd be letting him know it was just another routine due bill, just another routine collection.

As I watched the convoy lights beginning to blur in the distance, I pulled my yellow pad out of the glove compartment and snapped down a ball-point. I began making up one of Jake's "What to do for more sales" lists.

> Make more calls
> Get in early

Leave late
No booze
No movies

I underlined "No movies." Yes, that was it. I'd turn over
a brand-new, green new leaf. I'd make more hard calls.
Maybe I'd buy some new clothes. Jake said, "If you can
handle the hard calls, the rest are a piece of cake." I was
talking to myself. Out loud. "O.K., hot shot, we'll go for
the hards."

The first call would be Manny Stevens at Bunny. Why
not? Get it the hell over with. Maybe Monica and I would
take Dolores and Abramowitz out to dinner. We'd show
him our old tango or five or six cha-cha-cha moves. And
then I'd go waltzing in to see Horner. I'd have to
apologize, but so what? He'd have to listen. I'd have my
five minutes. Hell, he might even like me better for it.
Maybe I'd follow him home and study his house. Cruise
around his neighborhood and try to learn something about
him. I began laughing. Would I do that? Sure I would.
Why the hell not? Maybe I'd sneak up on his kids and ask
them what the old man did for a hobby. Woodwork?
Sailing? Football trivia? All I needed was a couple big
ones like him. What kind of hobby would Manny have?
Probably something tiny: collecting stamps or old coins.
Probably went to the movies and sat up on a booster. I
decided it was Horner, Manny, and Abramowitz—The
Big Three. I'd keep plugging away at Hershey's and
Campbell's Soups and Beech-Nut. You never can tell
when someone's going to stroke out and you're sitting
there in the lobby and they need you.

Each mile north I felt better. It was clearer, colder, and
I started singing:

"East Side, West Side,
All around the town . . ."

I sang it again, louder. Then again. It felt like New York.
It was New York. Then I tried:

"New York, New York, it's a beautiful town.
The Bronx is up and the Battery's down . . ."

But I didn't know the rest of it. And then I found the song I wanted. It reminded me of Monica and Central Park and Fifth and Fifty-ninth and the great martinis at the Oak Room at the Plaza:

"I'll take Manhattan, the Bronx and Staten Island too . . ."

I held the lines as long as I could hold them and as loud as I could get them. I did it over and over and over again. And then, coming around a long curve, I saw the North Star straight up the road. It was pulsing and pulling me home. I flicked off the cruise control, gunned it to eighty, and sang it again.

And then I got an idea. I'd call Monica from the next phone. No one hangs up on long distance. It was brilliant. I'd tell her I'd gotten my job back at Pioneer and the whole Bibleland story. Then I'd tell her I was exactly eleven hundred miles from the Holland Tunnel and was driving straight through. I'd call her every two hundred miles so I could keep awake; I'd tell her I was hurrying back to her. Maybe I wouldn't say it quite like that. I'd call from nine hundred miles, seven hundred miles, five hundred miles. I'd wear her down. She'd be begging me to stop and get some sleep or pull off and take a nap. Women are like that. But I'd hang in there. I'd keep driving. I'd keep calling. A Texaco station was shining at the next exit and I pulled off and up to the phone.

The call went through and she answered on the second ring. She sounded glad to hear from me, and I began rattling on about Buck and the money and Pioneer. Then I said, "Guess where I'm calling from? Georgia. And I'm heading north on the interstate. Listen now, I'm going to call you every two hundred miles. I've been up all night and I've got to stay awake. O.K., honey?"

"No, Joe, I don't think so. Why don't you get a room for the night?"

"No, honey, I've got to get in. I'm dying to see you and I've just got to stay awake." Something was going wrong. "Is there somebody there with you, you sound funny."

"No, it's not that. I just don't want you calling me all night. I've had a tough day and I'm beat. Call me when you get in."

"O.K., if that's the way you want it. Can we go out tonight? We'll go to Charley's."

"No, I'm busy, but call me anyway."

"Well then, how about Wednesday? I'll be in good shape then and—"

"Joe, I'm sorry, but I'm afraid not."

There was a long pause. I started to say something, but nothing came out. Finally, she broke the ice. . . . "I'm sorry, Joe, watch your driving, and call me, please."

"Sure, sure."

"Good-night, Joe."

"Good-night."

She hung up and I slammed the booth door open. Everything had suddenly turned sour. She thought I was crazy or still a jerk or both. What in the hell was I thinking about, calling her like that? If I called back, Gordon would probably answer and announce that she was in the bathroom greasing up her diaphragm. The hell with her. I had to keep going. I had to think about other things first. I cranked up the Olds and aimed the trim on the hood right back at the North Star.

I hadn't eaten since Savannah and McDonald's golden arch was shining up the road. Pulled in and washed up. McDonald's is a great chain but lousy in the washrooms. No towels; electric blowers. They're billed as a big hygienic breakthrough, but all it is is a piss-poor way to save on towels. Christ, no one washes their face anymore. Unrolled about ten yards of john paper and had to pick the lint from my face. From now on I'd carry a handkerchief or a small hand towel. Had a double cheese, a side

of fries, coffee, and a fried cherry pie. McDonald's is a
salesman's dream: forty billion hamburgers. Forty billion
everything. French-fry package is an eight-point sulfite
sleeve printed red, yellow, and black. Probably a hundred million every month; if you had it, you could retire
on it. Finished up and pulled out of the driveway with a
cup of coffee on the dashboard for the I-85 entrance.

And then it was as if I was in slow motion and I was
watching what I was doing from a long way off. I wasn't
slowing down. I wasn't turning into the northbound lane.
I was heading across for the southbound. The southbound, Savannah lane! I grabbed the coffee to keep from
spilling and stopped. "Jesus! Now what in the hell are you
doing?"

I wouldn't answer. I wasn't listening. It didn't make any
sense. The money was in my pocket. And the North Star
was shining up where I wanted to be—with Pioneer, and
Monica, and the Giants, and the Jets, and Fifty-ninth and
Fifth, and the music, and the tall furred exotics sweeping
by the fountain at the Plaza. "What in the hell are you
doing?" I knew what I was doing. But I wouldn't talk. I
just sat there. Paralyzed from the neck down. Paralyzed
from the neck up. I was shouting, "Mahaffey, are you
crazy?" I cut the engine and just sat there. I knew if I
picked the coffee up I'd spill it.

Sometimes we never know why in the hell we do things.
Like one time I'm zipping along the Pennsylvania Turnpike, going to see White Rose Potato Chips, out near
Lancaster. All of a sudden I knew I'd turned wrong and
was going in the wrong direction. A cloverleaf was
coming up. All I had to do was bend around it and get
back right. What did I do? I went right by it going eighty.
Then I sailed by four more cutoffs, still doing eighty. To
solve the problem I doubled it. Then I tripled it. Maybe
something in the magnification made it real. Hell, I don't
know.

I guess a lot of it was being pissed off at Monica. She
probably thought I was coming back up there with my hat

in my hand to beg her for another goddamn chance. Well,
if that's the way she was seeing me, the hell with her. I
didn't want her and I damn well didn't need her. As a
matter of ice-cold fact, right now, I didn't need anybody,
or anything. But there was something else going on while
I was sitting there. On down a side road was a honky-
tonk. You see them all over the South. Red neon: Al's or
Ben's or Flo's. There's a three-quarter-size pool table in
the back with short sticks because of the room size, a
beer license, and a jukebox. A place to dance; a place to
fight. It was the damn neon. Something in me wanted to
see that red-trimmed *Pietà* sell those Jesus prints. Jesus,
was that it? A couple years back this moron sock maker
down on Twenty-third Street designed a plastic globe and
hung socks on it from all over the world. It looked
terrible, and he called it Sockorama-Unisphere. It was a
dog's dog from every angle and an immortal bitch to deal
with at the department store. But all it did was sell socks.

Anyhow, looking down that black Georgia road, it hit
me. The neon-trimmed *Pietà* might just be the greatest
thing since hula hoops. Why not? It was a first, for damn
sure. It was big enough; you sure as hell couldn't ignore
it. People would want to get in close to take another look.
They'd be moved by it and maybe buy the Jesus prints and
the Jordan water. God knows what the religious freaks
would do. Pose before it? Hold their kids up to it?
Scotch-tape ten- and twenty-dollar bills to it? There had
to be a dozen ways to make it pay off. I poured the coffee
out. I didn't need any. I started up and drove another fifty
yards and headed back down the southbound side. I
turned the air conditioner to SUPER COOL, sucked all
four windows down, and pushed the Olds to the floor-
board. The wind was howling and I joined it:

> "Row, row, row your boat
> Gently down the stream.
> Merrily, merrily, merrily, merrily
> Life is but a dream."

It was a dumb song, but I didn't have to think of the words. I sang it again and then again. And then one more time so loud my throat collapsed. I cut on a Spanish station, and when this wild stack of trumpets did a "Malagueña" chorus I bellowed out Buck's favorite swamp shout: "Hot damn! *All right!*"

In three hundred miles I'd own one-third of everything: the neon-trimmed *Pietà*, the Roman emperors, the Coliseum arches, and the leaping lions. I'd also own one-third of the Jesus prints and the Jordan water and the flatbed and the Chuck Wagon, and—damn, I'd forgotten—I'd own one-third of two full-grown African elephants. I'd call them bulls. Buck and Arlo and I would pose before it all. I'd send an eight-by-ten glossy to Monica signed and dated. The Jubilee Crusade. Years from now I'd open the album on my lap with our kids. Monica would be in the corner knitting and watching TV and I'd be telling them about the great old days with The Great Mozingo and Arlo and the elephants and the Jubilee Crusade. . . . I mean, like what if I'm seventy and telling the kids how I didn't sell Horner. Or how I had to kiss Manny Stevens's ass for nothing and schlepping around New York in March having to use the subway stations to take a piss while I looked for a job. Screw it. This was the way to do it. This was the way to go.

Every mile south, the music was clearer. The air was warmer, softer. I could smell the honeysuckle and the gardenias. Even the diesel smoke coming out of the Cooper Warren sixty-footer in front smelled great. For a minute I wanted Monica to be with me holding my dick and pouring champagne. But there was too much to do ahead. She'd only get in the way. I'd have to be explaining to her, or apologizing to her, or trying to cut loose from her. I'd read someplace or heard somewhere, or probably saw it on *Gunsmoke,* that a woman loves the drunkard and the wild man. Maybe it's the black sheep coming home after having seen the elephant and heard the lion. Well, I'd seen the elephant and I'd damn well heard the lion. That was me, the drunkard, the wild man, the roaring, shouting, screaming, crazy man whipping down the highway into sudden disaster or fantastic riches, or both, or nothing. Now talk about a cold call. "Mahaffey's the name, Joe Mahaffey, and I'm here to tell you about our neon-trimmed *Pietà* and our Jubilee Crusade, which may very well change your whole life. . . ."

No, it wasn't like a cold call. It was like some great chase scene in the movies. Only this time I wasn't out there with the peddlers and the winos looking up. I was up there on the screen starring in the goddamn thing. What made it even hairier was the timing. It was so tight you couldn't drive a nail through it. In a few more days Ernie would be flying east to pick up his car, his sample cases, his office, and to check out his Big Apple. And in a few more days the Mozingo, Waters, and Mahaffey Jubilee Crusade would be swinging down Main Street in Charles City, South Carolina, meeting Bob McCoy's three-ring circus for the first appearance of the Jubilee Crusade in the goddamn Western world. And, oh, sweet Jesus, the horses are lined up and they are ready. And ladies and gentlemen, boys and girls, and children of all ages, they are off.

> "Oh, the world owes me a living,
> Zooma-zooma-zooma-zooma-zoom."

CHAPTER

12

In the morning I was chauffeuring Buck into Charles City to see the sheriff and put up posters in the store windows. During the night and over breakfast I'd come to my senses and decided to hedge my bets with the Crusade and The Great Mozingo. What I would do was hang on to the money and stall Greene until we rolled into Charles City. Then I'd decide what I was going to do about everything.

There was no doubt about it, Buck was really glad to see me back. Some of it had to be the money I was carrying, but he also liked having a licensed driver and the air-conditioned Olds. He also needed someone he could get excited with about the Crusade and the big meeting with Bob McCoy. He had most of it already worked out. Captain Dave Hoover and his lions and tigers were going to be "Daniel in the Lion's Den" and Freddy Logan and his elephants were the Roman Coliseum entertainment. He was still working on where he would place Commodore Onslow McKenzie and His Leaping Dalmatians. The other acts were "The Betrayal in the

Garden," "The Trial Before Pontius Pilate," "The Crucifixion," and the big finale built around "The Resurrec-
tion."

I listened to it all a couple times and then I asked him,
"Is Arlo playing Jesus?"

"Yeah. What do you think?"

Charles City was only seventeen miles from Bibleland
and we were almost there. "Well, it's not exactly a
musical comedy."

But when he described the center ring with the Roman
arches and the Coliseum fronts and the emperors around
the neon-trimmed *Pietà* it sounded like it couldn't miss.
"O.K., Buck, it sounds good."

Buck said, "And listen, we're going to sell those prints
and that Jordan water hand over fist. Don't forget, we're
billing this as religious drama. And Bo, no one, I mean *no
one*, pans a passion play."

Charles City, population, 2,004, had two stoplights,
two service stations, a Woolworth's, a Burger King,
and a radar trap set at twenty-nine miles an hour. We
hit the town at eleven A.M. The temperature was
ninety-six. Sheriff T. T. Littlejohn's office, in the two-story
Permastone-fronted Littlejohn Building, was up a long
flight of stairs above the All-American Finance Company,
which he also owned. We shook hands and he adjusted
the venetian blinds to keep the sun out. From his big
window he could see all four blocks of Charles City and
tend his radar trap. Littlejohn was small and his light
pink skin was stretched too tight. He kept moving his
mouth as if he was chewing something. I've never seen
two southern con men in action. There's nothing like it.
When you see them whispering, they're talking pussy.
When they shake their heads, it's money. And when
they're telling jokes, it could be anything. Littlejohn had
a string of Jewish and Polish one-liners that had been
around for a while. They sounded like cable television.
Then Buck told one. Then Littlejohn told another. And
then Buck leaned in and looked around to make sure the

secretary couldn't hear. "T. T., this is going to wipe your butt out. You heard about the New York couple going to the Savannah barbecue?"

"No. Let me have it."

"Well, it was a pretty wild party. Everybody stone drunk and dancing and raising hell. Anyhow, it gets to be about two in the morning and this guy George starts looking for his wife. He looks in the kitchen and the downstairs rooms and he can't find her. Well sir, he puts his drink down and goes upstairs and starts checking the bedrooms. He tries them all, and he still can't find her. I mean she has flat-out disappeared. Well, about an hour later he's still looking for her and he decides to try the barn."

T. T. Littlejohn grinned. "The barn?"

"Yeah. Well, he goes in and there she is." Buck's voice dropped. "Lying face up, right under an old milk cow. And she doesn't have a living stitch on. She is stark raving buck-assed naked." T. T. was leaning closer, loving it.

"And he says, 'Elizabeth! Jesus H. Sebastian Christ! Just what do you think you're doing?'

"And she looks up with her eyes closed and she gives him this real sweet smile and she says, 'Hon-ey, why don't you just go on home by yourself. I just feel certain that one of these nice gentlemen will give me a ride.' "

Littlejohn exploded and jumped up whooping. "Lord! That is outstanding! Outstanding! Wait till I tell Leonard!" He kept laughing and heaving and drying his eyes. He repeated the last line at the window, memorizing it. Then he stuck his handkerchief back in his pocket. "Hot son of a bitch, ain't it?" Outside, the street was deserted. "There ain't a living soul out there. Damn, that was one outstanding story." He tucked his shirt in tight. "Well, Buck, what's on your mind?"

I wasn't ready for the 180-degree swing, but Buck was. "T. T., we just need a little help. Just a tad."

T. T. sat down and crossed his feet up high on the desk. His eyes were even with the incoming-mail basket. "Name it, Buck."

"Well, old buddy, we'd like to march in here with the McCoy circus. That's one of the really big ones. One of the all-time greats. Elephants, lions, tigers, high-wire acts, the works; mostly stuff for the kids. We'll probably have a few church services from the center ring, and we'll probably want to sell a few trinkets. Then we'd move on out the next day. See any problems?"

"Sounds reasonable. Tell me about those trinkets."

"Just a few religious items, T. T. Some nice tasteful things. And they're cheap. No hustling, no gouging. And absolutely no dinging." Dinging's when you wrap a balloon string around a two-year-old's finger and then hit the parent for fifty cents. Buck told him about the "Last Supper" banners and the "Betrayal in the Garden" paintings on black velvet, which didn't exist. "It's really the same old stuff, T. T., only this time it's for a worthy cause. Every penny goes into the Jubilee Crusade."

T. T. waited a minute and kept looking me over. "Buck, me and you are good friends, so I'm not going to beat around the bush. We had that cold spell, and we're going to be sucking wind on the peach crop. And hell, you know yourself it don't pay shit to ship melons anymore. But I tell you what, I'm willing to cooperate. I'll give you a four-motorcycle escort coming in. And four more going out. I'll keep the kids off your ass and get the Chamber of Commerce to do a little marching and put up the posters. I'll also give you a prime lot right off downtown. How's that sound?"

"How much, T. T.?"

"Well, I've got this campaign coming up. I've got to be thinking ahead." He raised both hands as if stopping traffic. "But I'm willing to be reasonable. Let's say twenty percent."

Buck said, "Ten."

T. T. shook his head and began scanning his calendar.

Buck was up on his feet, looking tight-faced and worried. "It's costing a fortune just to get this show here. Come on T. T., fifteen."

T. T. Littlejohn looked disappointed. He squared his

blotter and looked at me again. "You ain't from around in here, are you?"

"No, New York. But I've got a lot of friends down here."

"O.K., Buck, fifteen. Let's say you put down three hundred dollars and I get a look at the books and the ticket count. How's that strike you?"

"Perfect, T. T." Buck slapped the desk and shook Littlejohn's hand. "I knew you'd be fair. Didn't I tell you that, Bo?"

"You sure did."

Buck counted out three hundred dollars. T. T. folded it into his shirt pocket. "I got some pole beans coming in pretty soon. Any chance your bunch doing a little picking for me?"

"Come on, T. T., you know I don't have that kind of crowd."

"No harm in asking." He led us to the door. "Give me that Elizabeth gal's last line again."

Buck did.

T. T. said, "I got it now." His hand was on my shoulder. "New York. I had me a buddy in the Marines from New York. Seems like he lived right down in there. Had him a dry-cleaning business. Next time we got to sit down and talk about it, O.K.?"

"O.K. with me."

"And listen"—he looked around to make sure no one was listening—"I can't be fixing your parking and speeding tickets while you're around here. But I'll tell you what, good buddy, if you get in any real trouble you come see old T. T., O.K.?"

"Yessir, I appreciate it. I really do."

Littlejohn was easy. All he wanted was money and his pole beans picked. Arlo was going to be the hard one. I remembered this old black-and-white movie about the Crusades. This creep who called himself Walter the Penniless claimed he had a written message from the Virgin Mary in his right hand. Every time the camera hit him he had his fist raised and pointing east toward the

Infidel. The people believed him and followed him
through thick and thin. It was more thin than thick,
because they had a helluva time keeping this bunch fed.
In the second reel there was trouble about whether
Walter was holy or not. They finally decided to try him by
fire. If he lived, he was a saint; if he didn't, he wasn't: the
swift sword of justice. He lived through the flames, but
when they passed him around so everyone could feel him
he stroked out. Walter was buried with full ecclesiastical
honors with both sides claiming victory. Anyhow, they
regrouped and marched on into the Holy Land where
they really screwed up. Arlo reminded me a lot of old
Walter.

He lived in a short one-room trailer propped up with
concrete blocks at the corners. If he had any money, none
of it was showing. He was sitting on the floor in a tight
black bathing suit, cutting his toenails. Buck spun a chair
around and straddled it. "Ain't you hot with the damn
windows closed like that?"

He pried his small toe out and clipped the nail. Tiny
muscles rippled down his spine and shot along his rib
cage. He was built like a greyhound, and with his
red-and-blue tattoos he reminded me of the lead stud in a
porno movie. "Heat don't bother me." He looked at me
and his top lip curled. "Cold neither." He didn't seem to
blink. "Yall a team now?"

Buck didn't give an inch. "You might say that."

They sat there not saying anything. A. J. Cartwright
was right. Arlo had lost his religion. His life story was
told in his tattoos. On his left arm was a rising sun with
orange-red rays reaching up to a blue WIN WITH JESUS.
The orange and blue were old and fading. A small
two-color eagle clutching the Marine Corps globe and
anchor and his serial number was across his chest. The
latest installment, a hangman's noose with BORN TO
LOSE in the loop, was in fresh colors on his right arm.

I couldn't stand the tension. "Arlo, how do you keep in
such good shape?"

He kept looking at Buck as he spoke to me. "I don't do

nothing. What's on your mind, Mister Mozingo?" He had dropped the Buck and was acting like he wanted to fight. "What yall want from me?"

They had agreed from the beginning that Charles City, South Carolina, would be the first stop on the road to Charlotte. They had also agreed that the big problem was how to bring the media out. The Crusade was a natural for TV and radio, and maybe the fat cat we were looking for would come tooling up in his Mercedes 600, or dropping out of the Carolina sky in his Lear jet. But now Arlo was acting like it was all brand-new news. It didn't seem to bother Buck, but it was bothering hell out of me. Buck hooked his heels in the chair rung and rocked back. "Arlo, old buddy. Main thing right now is seeing if you have any ideas about the gig we're on."

Arlo examined the points of the scissors. He snapped them. "Gig?"

Buck was mad, but he was managing to sit on it. "Act. Show. Anything you want to call it. Arlo, let's try and not split hairs and wind up in a damn argument."

Arlo's eyebrows stayed flat, his face blank. "What you got in mind?"

"We need those marchers. Today, right now. I'm thinking about the media. And the collections."

"Nickels and dimes." Arlo kept clipping. "You got to give them a heap more than a march these days to make any money down in here."

Buck kept rocking his chair. I could tell he wanted to get up and move around. "That's what we're doing. We're giving them a pick 'em up and lay 'em down, good old-fashioned Crusade. We dress them up in monk's clothes and promo the hell out of it."

It was the first time I'd heard monk's clothes.

Arlo examined his big toe. "Monk's clothes? The heat will kill them." His eyes narrowed. "And your circus man, this McCoy. He's meeting us right downtown?"

Buck smiled. "About as downtown as you can get. Sheriff Littlejohn is giving us the red carpet. Twelve motorcycles and all the fire department's equipment, a free tent lot, free help from the Chamber of Commerce, and eight high-school marching bands. Arlo, it's going to be the biggest thing to hit the Palmetto State since William Tecumseh Sherman." Littlejohn's four motorcycles had jumped to twelve. The eight bands were red-hot news, and Charles City didn't even have a fire department.

Arlo nodded. "Sounds big."

"It is big. Come on now, Arlo. How about it? Can we get the damn marchers?"

He stabbed the scissors in the floor. "I can get them. But I want me something out of this."

"Name it."

He put on his socks. They were short black stretch Dacron that fit any size from six to twelve. "Where we heading after Charles City?"

Buck couldn't believe it. "Fellow, what's going on with you? We've agreed on Charlotte. The Astrodome. My best buddy handles the bookings."

Arlo's lips tubed. "Ain't no Astrodome in Charlotte. The Astrodome's in Houston, Texas. All Charlotte's got is a two-bit Coliseum and that roller-coaster park out at Carowinds."

Buck said, "Well, they must have closed it or something. I can make some arrangements."

Arlo ignored him. "Mister Mozingo, we got to feed this bunch, and state law says we got to provide sanitary toilets." He was hunched over, tying his shoes. "I say we forget Charlotte. I say we go to the Darlington 500. The original Sodom and Gomorrah."

"Darlington? That damn race ain't till Labor Day."

Arlo tightened his laces. "We get there early and set up out there on the infield. Then when they get there, we're ready for them."

Buck groaned. "Six months! That sure as hell ought to be early enough." Then he began backing down. "Well, maybe it makes some sense. People will be coming to see how we're getting ready for them. That the way you see it?"

"Precisely." He nodded. "When you have a Crusade you've got to have a challenge. That's the best challenge we're going to be getting. Those people fornicate right out there on the infield."

Buck would have agreed to march to Nome, Alaska, to get the bastard moving. "O.K., Arlo, you got a deal. It's Darlington. That cuts it down to about a hundred and forty, a hundred and fifty miles. Yeah, you're right. Dead right. I like that a helluva lot better."

Buck's voice softened. Almost too much. "Arlo, you sure you can get your crowd to do this kind of marching?"

Arlo skinned on a tight black T-shirt and pulled on a pair of jeans over his bathing suit. "I've already made a few telephone calls, and a couple, three groups are heading in. I'm going to make a few more."

"Terrific, Arlo! Terrific. Yeah, I like that Darlington. Bo, what do you think?"

"Sounds great to me. Great."

Arlo tightened his belt an extra cinch. "One more thing. That woman you're living with in the same trailer. Miss Loretta Jane Reynolds."

"What about her?"

"What if I was to call on her. I mean a social call?"

Buck smiled. "She'd be glad to see you. Be my guest."

Arlo smiled for the first time. "Would you tell her I'll be coming by a little later on?"

"Be glad to. And those marchers, you sure they're going to show?"

"They're on the way."

When I told Loretta that Arlo was coming to see her she started laughing. "Sweet mothering Jesus! That's all I need." She was stretched out on the hammock, drinking iced tea and doing a crossword puzzle.

"Boy, I really attract them. Know a five-letter word for movie?"

"Afraid not. Want me to stick around? He might be trouble."

"No, it's all right. He's been giving me the big eye since we got here. I'd kinda like to see his moves."

"You're the boss. Where's Buck?"

"Probably out with his damn snakes. Sit down and have a beer."

Ten minutes later we saw Arlo cutting across the lot. His shirt was tucked in as tight as he could get it, and he was wearing a narrow red string tie. He was carrying a white shoe box. Loretta laughed. "He's all dressed up. God, now if this ain't going to be a study."

Arlo leaned on the camper and squinted in the sun. His hair was soaked in a sweet-smelling pomade. I asked him if he'd made the phone calls.

"Yes, I have." He sounded formal. "I didn't come over here to talk about that."

Loretta slipped on her sandals. "I'll bet you'll talk to me." She looked at the shoe box and smiled. "You bake me some cookies?" He slid his eyes over me as if I was intruding on a private conversation. I pulled another beer from the cooler. "O.K., I was just leaving."

But Loretta had changed her mind. "Wait a second, Bo. Stick around. Arlo, baby, you don't care if Bo hears your little speech, now do you?"

Arlo frowned and spoke through his teeth. "I ain't got no speech, miss. Don't matter to me one way or the other." We filed into the kitchen and sat down around the horseshoe booth like we were going to play gin rummy. Loretta kept clicking her ball-point up and down.

"Arlo, you know a five-letter word for movies?"

"I ain't studying that, miss."

She snapped her fingers. "Flick. That's it. Flick."

When Loretta was filling in the squares, Arlo leaned over and looked right down her blouse. "Miss Loretta, you ain't wearing no brassiere." One thing about the son of a bitch, he was direct.

"No, hot shot, I'm not. It's cooler this way." She dipped

her fingertips in her iced tea. "Now these," she touched her nipples, "are called tits. That's t-i-t-s. Now this is my right tit. And this is my left tit. Cute, ain't they?"

"Don't be mocking me, miss. I ain't no Buck Mozingo."

They were heading for an argument. I got up fast. "Why don't we all go back outside?"

Arlo whipped around, thin-lipped and burning. "Why don't you go on back outside by yourself?"

Loretta slapped the table. "He's staying! O.K., Arlo. What's on your mind? That is, as if I didn't know."

He calmed down fast and pulled out a pint of whiskey in a brown kraft bag and set it in the middle of the table. Then he carefully placed the shoe box on the floor. He pulled out his wallet. Loretta said, "You're looking for romance. That right?"

He whipped his wallet back and forth across his hand. He wasn't carrying any credit cards and the leather was flexible. "No, no romance. Just straight dollars and cents."

He pulled out four twenties. As he counted them out he watched her eyes carefully. "Three or four minutes. That's all I need. I'll be in and out of you like a jackrabbit. I don't go in for that before-play business."

She cocked her head and fluttered her eyes for my benefit. "Oh, my Rosenkavalier."

"Don't be mocking me, miss. I'll spread you out like a quartered pullet."

Loretta was still playing and dropped her eyes coyly. "Well, I'll have to think about that. What's in the box?"

Arlo let the question slide by. He looked at me and then back at her. "Maybe I scare you? You can have Mahaffey sit right there in that ladder-back if it'll make you feel better." He didn't blink. "Miss, I been craving you since you sashayed in here licking your lips and swinging your hips like a Jezebel and I'm willing to pay top dollar."

"I understand, Arlo. But what makes you think I charge?"

Arlo's eyes narrowed. "Because I've been studying you. I know you better than you know yourself. The way I got it ciphered out you been charging Buck Mozingo by the day. You're getting you a stake up so you can pull out of here. You got ambition. You're an artist."

She smiled at me. "That's what Bo here said. I guess that's me all right."

He studied his fingernails carefully. "I can pay more than eighty. More than a hundred if I have to. That's a lot of money for just laying back and spreading out."

Loretta was biting her bottom lip to keep from laughing. "Nothing fancy, right?"

"No. Straight fornication."

She knew he was dangerous if she pushed him. But she was curious. "Maybe you won't be able to get it up with company in the room like that?"

His eyes were fixed on hers. Peering, watching for any change of light. Any glint of anything. "Miss, all I do is touch myself and I'm like a ball peen hammer."

A cold shiver ran down my spine, and I looked around the room for a baseball bat or a crowbar. This bastard was capable of arson, multiple rape, mass murder. But Loretta kept playing with him. "Arlo, I just can't believe a fellow like you has to be paying for it."

"Miss, I keep it on a straight business basis. To me it's just like going to the grocery store. I'll hit the massage parlors now and then. But I don't feature all that fancy wallpaper and those black lights and Japanese sex gadgets they try to unload on you. That's where you come in." His eyes were on her like a snake. He didn't know I was there. He didn't care. "Miss, I like it straight. Fast. Machine-gun style. Zap. Zap. Zap. I like to get it over with and forgotten about. I got other fish to fry."

It didn't seem to bother Loretta. "Tell you what, Arlo. I'll think about it. Right now, it's my time of the month and you know yourself how a girl can feel."

He eased the box up on the table. His voice went softer, stranger. Like it was coming through cellophane. "Miss, that mean you'd do it if you were clean?"

His teeth and gums flashed when he pronounced "clean" and he drummed his fingers on the box top. I was expecting cookies or peanut brittle or divinity fudge; something for the table. Loretta watched it. "I guess so."

Slyly and slowly he peeled back the tape. He peered in as if they were baby chicks. "You're lying, miss. Lying like a dog. Here, I been saving these."

In the box, displayed on black velvet, were three Kotex napkins. "Them's yours. I got them dated from last week."

Loretta was disgusted. "Lord, Arlo."

He looked at them proudly. "I learned this little trick in high school."

I was laughing when I said it. "Arlo, they must have given you a helluva write-up under your yearbook picture."

He gripped the table to keep from swinging at me. "You keep out of this, you sap-sucking bastard."

Loretta calmed him down. "Listen, Arlo, now listen. Now you know I think you're pretty cute. I mean, I really kind of like you. But I'm just not quite in the right mood right now. I want you to come see me next week. We'll have a nice drink, and then we'll start all over, and well, we'll just see what happens."

"O.K., miss." Suddenly he was smiling, friendly and easygoing. He could have come by to check the plumbing or read the water meter. He pushed the bottle to her. "Miss, I'm going to make you a present of this Wild Turkey."

"Arlo, that's mighty nice of you. Thanks."

"Don't mention it. I know it's your favorite."

I was wondering what else the bastard had dug up in their garbage can but I kept quiet. He retaped the shoe box, and, as if he had a house call on down the line, he left. We heard him open and close the garbage can. Then he went whistling off across the lot. Loretta was pouring a large drink. "Jesus suffering Christ on the cross. Imagine sliding in between the sheets with that lizard." She drank the whiskey neat. "Probably have nightmares for a month."

I said, "And that creep's a minister?"

"Mail order. He clipped a coupon and paid his money. The woods are full of them down in here. But Lord, don't you feel sorry for the kid who draws that lucky number at the massage parlor? Bo"—she poured another drink and looked pensive—"there are some hard, hard dollars in this old world."

It was after dark when Arlo told us he had four or five groups coming in to do the marching. He didn't say who they were or where they were from. Just that they were coming in. Buck was delighted. He opened a bottle of bourbon, a bottle of Scotch, and shook out three trays of ice in the beer cooler. Arlo stuck with the beer. He was in a good mood and hunkered back against the trailer. Buck kept after him about how many were coming. Whether they had any money. If he was sure they weren't too old to march. Arlo drank his beer. "When they get here you'll see them. I told you I'd get them, and I'm getting them."

It took Loretta to get him talking. "Come on Arlo, tell us about them."

"Tell you what?"

"Anything you want. Just something. Lord!"

He cleared his throat. "Well."

Loretta motioned. "Come sit over here where somebody can see you."

He leaned on the picnic table and began picking at the pretzels. "Well, these people are going to be different than the type yall are used to. But I'm telling you something, they got strong wills. They'll be ideal for this kind of march and camping out at Darlington." He told about a group he tried to reach but couldn't. They were called the Silent Brothers and Sisters of Christ and came out of East Tennessee. They spoke only on Mondays, which was also the day they dug three spades of dirt from their own graves. He popped open another beer and slid the ring pull in his pocket as if he was saving them.

"I featured them out front leading the way. Damn, I wish I could've gotten ahold of them."

Loretta held her knees, trying not to laugh. "Too bad."

Arlo's voice curled. "I ain't sitting here to be mocked at, miss."

Buck waved his hand. "Ignore her, she's drunk. Damn it Loretta, straighten out."

I couldn't help thinking about the congregation digging their own graves. "Damn women and children digging!"

Arlo held up his hand. "Only the men over thirty-three years of age. That's how old our blessed Savior was when the Jews cut him down."

Loretta asked him, "They have Jews in that church?"

"No, they draw the line there. Besides, that's farm country." He jutted his jaw at her. "You ever heard tell of a Jew farmer?"

Loretta said, "I'll have to think about it."

I wanted to keep him talking. "I never have. Why's that, Arlo?"

Arlo said, "Too busy stealing. Too busy plotting. Too busy loaning money out at thirty-three and a third percent interest. There are facts and figures proving that the Jews are to blame for ninety-nine percent of the misery of the world."

Loretta popped open a beer and watched the foam run down. "Arlo, you are ninety-nine percent full of shit. What do you think Jesus was, a goddamn Chinaman?"

Arlo had a hair trigger. "Jesus wasn't Jewish." He crushed his empty can. Then he leaned on it, flattening it. "That's the biggest Jew trick in the world, making folks swallow that one."

Loretta yodeled two notes and sighed. "I'd better pass."

Buck lit a fresh cigar. "Know any more strange ones?"

"Well, I wouldn't call them strange, Mister Mozingo. I'd call them different. They just see things different than me and you."

Loretta yodeled a low note that broke in half.

Buck asked him. "How about snake chunkers? I'll bet they're pretty thick up in there?"

Arlo dropped his eyes and shook his head. "No, that's kind of dying off too. People get tired of the same old things. They want new stuff." He studied the Miller High Life label. "And they're getting it. Looks like every time you turn around, some fellow's got a new way of looking at Scripture and off he's running with a whole new flock." He stopped. "Now you take up near Shelby. I guess that's kind of old and kind of new at the same time. They call themselves the Church of the Chained Christ."

I said, "Chained Christ?"

"Yeah. They take a man who's been seized by the Holy Ghost and when he wants the chains, they wrap him up."

I asked, "In what?"

"Nothing but the chains. They wrap him up and they lock him up. Then they put him across four of the deacons' shoulders and the whole church promenades outside. They march around the church three times. Once for the Father, once for the Son"—he sipped his beer—"once for the Holy Ghost. Then they head on down the road." Arlo was a born storyteller. His voice went soft and sly. He almost whispered. "To the river."

Loretta made a low strangling sound and Buck whistled. Arlo took a deep pull on his beer and wiped his mouth. "They get down there and sing a couple or three songs. Then the minister blesses the man, and the chains, and the locks, and the water, and then everyone gets down on their knees and starts in to praying." He sipped and clicked his teeth on the can rim. "Then they throw him in. If Jesus has laid his hands on him, he snaps those chains and shoots right back up and they have themselves a Jubilee celebration."

Loretta groaned. "You ever seen one?"

"Only one."

Loretta didn't want to ask him. "And?"

"He stayed down. We waited around for about an hour but he stayed down. Preacher said the man had sins that hadn't been purged. But he claimed the sanctified drowning had washed him out as clean as a newborn babe."

Buck sucked in. "I've heard them all now. Whew! Chained!"

Arlo spoke softly, philosophically. "I checked it out in Scripture, and it's all there. You know, the older I get, the more tolerant I get. Twenty years ago I'd have called that flat-out murder. But today I say that's just their way of looking at things. They might be dead right and we might be dead wrong. And if it gives them the satisfaction they're looking for, I say, who am I to cast the first stone." He belched. "Excuse me. . . . The only place I draw the line is that crazy bunch up near Asheville."

Loretta's top lip curled back. She shivered. "I ain't listening to any more of this."

He ignored her. "Call themselves the Church of the Crucified Jesus. Every few Sundays they get these sanctified chrome nails out." He paused. "Maybe they're silver. I wonder who makes them things, anyway. That keeps the blood poisoning down. Anyway, they get them some poor fellow that ain't too bright and, well, I swear, I kind of believe they take advantage of him. You know, like promising him he can be some sort of a hero. Then when he agrees, they put him up. They only nail him through the hands and feet. But Lord, all that weight coming down. You know for yourself that's bound to tear hell out of a man." He pulled out another beer. "I guess that and a lot of those crazy things the Chinese and the Indians do. That gets a little too far out for me."

Buck sucked in. "I'll damn well buy that."

We heard a noise and watched a school bus passing in under the lights of the shuffleboard courts. A hand-printed sign ran under the windows, REVEALED CHURCH OF THE NAZARENE. Buck moved over to get a better look. "That your crowd, Arlo?"

He nodded. "Let's leave them alone tonight. They'll come out when they're ready."

Loretta sighed. "Oh, boy."

I sat there drinking beer and swearing I had to start cutting down. I was up to ten and twelve cans a day and was hitting the vending machine for chips and crackers every three or four hours. As I watched the bus, a snow-white egret came gliding down the dark creek bed. For some reason it reminded me of Monica, and I realized how much I missed her. Arlo and the time-coded Kotex would have been something to joke around about if she was here. She could probably have talked old Arlo into a Gold Plan or one of our Perpetual Plans we'd come up with back at Charley's. With her here the whole Jubilee Crusade, the snake show, Arlo Waters and Buck Mozingo, and now the Revealed Church of the Nazarene, whoever they were, would have been funny; without her, all it had going was a grim Jonestown feeling.

Arlo held his beer can out, wiggling it so the silver caught the moonlight. "You know something?"

I kept watching the long, dark bus. All of the shades were drawn, and things were getting spooky. "What's that?" Arlo crushed the can flat. "I think that bunch up near Asheville is Jews."

CHAPTER

13

The Revealed Church of the Nazarene turned out to be snake handlers out of Rifle, Alabama. In five screened-in boxes at the back of the bus were copperheads, cottonmouth moccasins, diamondback rattlers, and fourteen coral snakes from a swamp near Mobile. All of the members had been bitten at least twice and claimed their strength was spelled out in Mark 16, verses 17 and 18, and that they were living in rapture, unable to express their joy and thanksgiving to the Lord. Eudora Gulley, the Mistress of the Serpents and their leader, was big and wore a white flowing robe. She was originally a Mennonite from Berwick, Pennsylvania, and had worked on the Wise Potato Chip line. Eudora said they were afraid of the Georgia law on snake handling and hoped they could change their outlaw status by going on the Jubilee Crusade and taking their problem to the public. I didn't care who they were, or what they did, as long as the show was getting on the road.

All during the next day Arlo's crowd kept coming. They were strange people that made you laugh one minute and think you were heading for Bellevue the next. One bus brought in the entire congregation of the Stark Valley Pentecostal Church, from Stark Valley, Mississippi. The eleven men and eight women were lean and haggard looking. They had driven from the Mississippi Petrified Forest and had been living on hard-boiled eggs and condemned tuna fish. They'd been driven out of Stark Valley for conducting services using Drano and strychnine that had resulted in two official deaths right on the altar. One of the recoverees, Jessee Royal Stamps, a tall mechanic in bright white coveralls, had been ordained their deacon. He also drove and serviced the bus. Jessee Royal, with small blue eyes and thick, snow-white eyebrows, said the minute he had received his friend Arlo's plea for help he had made the decision and headed for the Tidewater lands and Bibleland. At the back of their bus in a doorless refrigerator was a two-foot-high statue of Jesus. At his feet were children's wind-up birds and farm animals. A horseshoe arched over him spelling out JESUS LOVES in soft-drink caps, and a single rose in Lucite sat above him in the ice-cube compartment.

Six Hare Krishnas in a twenty-seven-year-old Cadillac hearse pulled in with blue-and-tan New Jersey license plates. Arlo wouldn't say how he got in touch with them. They seemed harmless and smiled when they spoke. They also smiled when they listened; they didn't want to offend anyone. They wore brown gauze robes and thonged sandals and each one had a long oiled and waxed pigtail growing from his shaved head. After they shook hands smiling, and bowed smiling, they kept on smiling as they passed out tracts explaining the glories of the Upanishads. Later they tried unloading a twelve-dollar book on the good life in India, but there were no takers.

Another group came in just before dark, marching in Indian file. They announced that they were the first ordained Walking Baptists in the world and they had walked over singing hymns from the Winn-Dixie mall in Dover.

Most of the people were mill workers, secretaries, house painters, carpenters, Tupperware and Avon women, and retirees. A few lived on government pensions for service disabilities; others on food stamps and church suppers. All of them had prayed, and walked, and taken up their snakes in concrete-block churches where collection plates were seldom passed. They were all broke. But for Buck and me, their names on the marching list were like gold. Around the campfire they were the strongest voices on "We Shall Overcome" and "Onward, Christian Soldiers," which not only hyped up the march that lay ahead but filled us in on what they'd left behind. Loretta, who had spent half her life living with freaks and geeks and homosexual clowns, hated them. She stayed in the trailer in front of the TV set. At night she wouldn't come out. When they drifted over to the patio she'd run them off.

"They're terrible! Terrible! Look at them, Buck. Look at them. They ain't even freaks. You seen the one with no nose? Oh God, their eyes just scare me to death." Buck kept saying, "They're human beings." Loretta kept saying, "Bullshit."

While the Stark Valley Pentecostals and the Walking Baptists and the Nazarene group were quiet people who kept to themselves, the Church of the Flaming Cross, an independent group out of Rodell, Florida, hit Bibleland like a Hell's Angels convention. The men wore white shirts and black pants. The women, white blouses and black skirts. They arrived standing up in the back of two pickup trucks with GO WITH GOD and KNOCK-KNOCK. WHO'S THERE? JESUS! stickers on their bumpers. They were ringing big clapper bells for attention and waving long-barreled blowtorches and screaming, "Fire hallelujah! Fire hallelujah!" They drove up and down the street shouting how they would light up at night and pass the raw flames over their bodies and how their faith had quenched the violence and the fear of the flames. Finally, they parked down by the creek. The smell didn't seem to bother them, and all night they roasted hot dogs and toasted rolls and sang songs that no one had ever heard.

At times I found it funny. Then sad. Then I didn't know what I felt. I drank a lot. I ate a lot. And I watched a lot of TV with Loretta. Every time I caught a glimpse of New York I knew I'd made a terrible mistake. If I was on Times Square I'd get right down with it and roll around in it like a dog. I'd go dizzy with the neon. I'd make friends with the pimps. The whores. The gays. Even the creeps around the porn shops. I'd even buy a triple carrot juice at the health-food store and join those bearded wonders behind the bean sprouts. This was crazy, warped, stupid. And every day it was getting worse.

I'd plotted out the campground as if it were a no-man's-land. I avoided the Stark Valley and the Flaming Cross crowds as if they were machine-gun batteries. Also, the smiling Hare Krishnas with their never-ending supply of books and temple bells and finger cymbals. I'd begun to like the Walking Baptists and a new group of eight blacks from a local Free Will Abyssinian Church who lived on Kentucky Fried Chicken and old Ray Charles tapes. But the group that put me off most were the strangest—the Groats. They camped in a small Volkswagen Cutaway and kept moving around. One night they would be at the lake. The next, by the drive-in. The next, down by the creek. The parents and a pair of twenty-year-old twin boys were all heavy-necked, short-armed people with high foreheads and wide-set eyes. They were always standing side by side as if facing a common disaster or an invisible photographer. They had signed up for the Crusade giving their home as Old Dog, Georgia. Loretta and I had checked it out on the map, hoping they were joking. But they weren't.

Old Dog was down in the southwest corner near the Alabama line. Even Buck was afraid of the Groats. He found out that they believed the world was coming to an end on Labor Day at high noon, and that they were the ones that had engineered Arlo into moving the march to the infield of the Darlington 500. Buck said, "They're the only group I can't stand. They look like rapists to me. Even the old lady. I tell you what, Bo, once we get through Charles City we red-light their asses."

"Red-light?"

"An old train-show wrinkle. We'd give the conductor ten bucks to stop out in the swamp or out on the prairie and open the door. See, it looks like a regular water stop. Then we'd take some son of a bitch we couldn't live with and shove his butt out, close up, and move on out. Took about twenty seconds. They wouldn't know what hit them."

"Damn, in the wintertime?"

"Anytime."

"Be a good way to get rid of old Arlo one of these dark nights."

"Don't think I haven't thought about it."

Buck was up and shaved every morning by six. He had put away his cowboy boots and jeans and denim jacket and was dressing in his circus jodhpurs, safari jacket, and a leather Stetson. He still wore his ringmaster boots and carried his baton. When the Crusade and McCoy's show hit Charles City he'd be ready for the center ring. He kept telling me we'd tapped a whole new market. That it was tax free and a guaranteed money-maker and that the prints and Jordan water were going to move like hotcakes. For a while I needed three beers to believe him. Then it went to four, to five, and on to six. On the sixth it made sense: no one big had ever pulled it off and combined the circus and the Christ story. It was a natural, and when the right churches stepped forward, we'd be able to play forever. But then a small voice kept cutting through and asking me why John North Ringling and old Phineas Taylor Barnum had never done it. And at night when the beer and Buck's hype wore off I knew the answer. They were simpler times back then; there was no radio back then; there was no television. But the big reason was simply that they didn't have to.

On Sunday morning three church buses, carrying the congregation from the Jericho Second Baptist Church, drove out the two miles to look us over. Each bus was packed, and Buck, Arlo, Loretta, and I came out on the road shoulder to greet them and welcome them on the Crusade. They cruised up the street in double low, peering out at the Crusaders, and us, and the *Pietà* tableaux spread out on the flatbed. By the time they reached the drive-in at the end their minds were made up. The drivers made a big U-turn, shifted to high, and headed back to town. Suddenly, as they were rumbling by, I realized I wanted to join them and get the hell out. But I didn't. I just stood there and stood there.

Buck had to be feeling what I felt. It was fear. We kept busy to keep from thinking and worrying about it. We polished the popcorn machine in the Chuck Wagon. We sharpened the ice-maker blades and refiled the distributor points. We changed the oil and painted a border on the Jubilee Crusade sign running along the sixty-foot skirt of the flatbed. But I couldn't stop worrying. I knew that whatever motive Arlo and his followers had, whether it was prayer, or power, or straight profit, or the salvation they sang and prayed about, it didn't matter. Because they believed it. They knew the same songs. The same prayers. They spoke the same language. Buck and I were the outsiders. And now Buck was beginning to sound like one of them. I was the loner. The real loner. Every time I closed my eyes at night I saw the scene at McDonald's. I'd pull back like a camera and watch the Olds slow down at the northbound lane and hear myself shout, "North! North! Turn north!" Then I'd watch the car slide over the viaduct and drop down the southbound lane and a cold chill would run down my spine and stay there. I'd lie there talking to myself. "Listen, stupid, you got your money, pack your bag and get the hell out. Get out!" But I wouldn't, or I couldn't, and all I'd do was get up, dress, and head out for the beer cooler.

CHAPTER

14

We put up one-sheets and posters imprinted with CHARLES CITY—MARCH 3 AND 4 on the barn sides and the smokehouses and in the storefronts of Jericho, Georgia, and Charles City, South Carolina. Over Arlo's forty-foot Passion Play panorama on the Dixiana we hung a big leader that the Jubilee Crusade's destination was now the Darlington 500 and announced there would be twelve high-school marching bands and a balloon ascension, and that everything would be featured on prime-time television. Out on the interstate the dynamite-style circus lettering told the story: BE AMONG THE FIRST TO SIGN UP FOR THE GLORIOUS JUBILEE CRUSADE. ONLY 9 SHORT MILES. ONLY 9 SHORT MINUTES. TAKE EXIT 14, CROSS OVER TO THE DIXIANA HIGHWAY. FOLLOW SIGNS TO BIBLELAND, U.S.A. But the Winnebagos and the Airstream camper cruisers kept on rolling. They were used to Holiday Inns, Quality Courts, Howard Johnson's. They knew that state-inspected rest areas, horseshoeing up under the trees on the pull-offs, had running water and toilet paper. They also knew that nine short miles probably meant nineteen. And with a camper loaded down with kids, dogs, and in-laws, there was no such thing as nine short minutes. Only a few stopped, and they stayed only long enough to ask directions and then got the hell out. And I'd stand there like an idiot wishing I was smart enough to follow them.

The pressure was mounting, and Buck and I were drinking as much as Loretta. It was the only way to take it. The Abyssinian Free Will group discovered that the Stark Valley school bus was carrying ninety-six snakes and had a quick meeting and left for Atlanta. The Groats were grumbling about something, and the Flaming Cross people were acting strange and crazy and getting louder. The only decent group left were the Walking Baptists. They were cheerful people, and at night they'd build a bonfire and sing old barbershop songs like "My Indiana Home" and "I'll Take You Home Again, Kathleen" and "Roses of Picardy," one of Dad's favorites.

Loretta and I began calling them all Baptists: the Snake-Chunking Baptists, the Drano Baptists, the Blow-torch Baptists, the End-of-the-World Baptists, the Hare Krishna Baptists. When the last group, "Jesus' Brother-hood of Chosen Messengers," came in in a twenty-year-old panel truck with scriptural quotes covering the doors, the fenders, and the hood, they became the "Phone-Pole Baptists." They were the Robards out of Tampa, Florida. The mother, Maude, who called all the shots, said Jesus had appeared in a vision at the foot of her bed one night with a can of white paint and a half-inch brush and demonstrated a revolutionary way of spreading his Gospel message to the world. The medium was old—the telephone poles—but the process was new. Instead of standard horizontal signs, they were to print the message vertically. In the morning she and her husband, Leo, a refrigeration mechanic, and their two daughters had set out for Key West. There, on the first telephone pole at the tip of the Keys, they had printed IN THE BEGINNING down the pole. Slowly they had started north, determined to print out the entire Old and New Testaments. The plan was to travel up Route One to the Canadian border and then head west. After three weeks, something happened at the outskirts of Miami that they wouldn't talk about, and they had abandoned their project. Luckily, two days after the incident, they had heard about the Jubilee Crusade and had driven up to join us. On the first evening, they gathered with their paint and brushes at the first pole in town. Maude painted a white cross up as high as she could reach. Then under it she started again, IN THE BEGINNING. Leo had moved out to the second pole and was on GOD CREATED. The daughters were up the drain ditch on the third and fourth poles heading north, and the Robards were back in business.

It was the night before the pullout and we were trying out the acts. The *Pietà* was centered up on the flatbed between the emperors, the Coliseum arches, and the lions. Arlo was leaning on Caligula and bitching about his ecclesiastical collar and the heat. He had a towel and was mopping down. "Let's break. Whew! I've never seen it so hot!"

I was too up to play him back his "heat didn't bother him" crap he'd pulled in the trailer. Everything was finally going right. Everything was finally falling into place. In the morning—with eighty-four marchers, the flatbed tableaux, two elephants, the Chuck Wagon, the Jesus prints, and the Jordan waters—we were finally marching. The media would have to take us seriously. They had too many Baptists and Methodists and Pentecostal subscribers and advertisers; they couldn't afford to laugh at us or ignore us. It was all numbers and economics, and Buck was dead right: no one pans a passion play. As I watched Arlo rehearsing up under the lights with the Coliseum arches behind him and the emperors on the end and the red neon of the *Pietà* flickering over everything, I knew that if only half of what we were expecting actually happened we were going to make it big and keep on making it.

The heat was rolling in from the swamp. It had been

black flies all day and black mosquitoes all night. Buck
called them "no-see-ums," and they slid through screens
like water through a sieve. Flying ants were swirling
around the floodlights.

Buck tossed Arlo a can of insecticide. "You need more
air on that third line. Suck it up on the bridge. Then
pause. Then slap it to them." He waved at Loretta. "How
about it hon?"

Loretta grinned. "Looks great. Hey, stud! Unbutton
that jacket. I don't want you getting it all sweated up."

Arlo didn't like taking instructions. He jutted his jaw
and hooked his thumbs in his belt loops.

Buck reached up and grabbed his ankle. "Steady now.
We're about through. This one's for insurance. That's all.
O.K. Ready?"

"All right. O.K."

Arlo wrapped the mike cord around his wrist. He
rolled it out and let it trail. He had all the moves. Frank
Sinatra. Johnny Carson. Tom Jones. He was leaning
forward and spelling it out softly. "Love. . . .
L . . . O . . . V . . . E. . . ." He stood up and reared back,
reaching for more volume. "That was Jesus' middle
name." He took two exaggerated steps and turned around
slowly. The cord dropped smoothly. He was louder now,
shriller. "Jesus didn't dance. Jesus didn't sing. And
there ain't one word in Scripture about him even
playing a musical instrument. . . . All that man had on
his mind was love. That's all!" The mike was in his left
hand. His right fist was in his kidney. He was Mick
Jagger, stomping his foot and whipping his head and
screaming. "And that, folks, is what we got out here on
this Crusade and what we're keeping as we go all the
way to the original Sodom and Gomorrah, the infield of
the Darlington 500 in Darlington, South Carolina."

Buck changed the red pin lights to blue and played
them over the *Pietà*, the emperors, the arches, the lions.
He slapped his hands together. "Hot damn! Arlo, you are
the living greatest!"

I felt terrific about everything. I had one arm around

Buck and one around Loretta. "Damn it, we're really going to do it."

Buck was sweating and grinning. "You mighty right."

As I stood there with my arms around Buck and Loretta I knew we were going to make it and make it big. I knew that some of it was the beer, and some of it was the great way old Arlo looked up there on the stage. But it was more than that, much more. The whole thing was just too big, and just too damn good, not to make it. The Crusade and the circus and the Jubilee Pageant cut across too many nerve endings and touched too many people where they lived. As far as I was concerned, we could roll it into any town in the country and compete with anything, or anybody; the Jesus prints and the Jordan water were just icing on the cake.

As Arlo hopped down from the stage, Buck gave him a fresh towel and a cold beer. "Terrific, Arlo, just absolutely terrific. I've never seen you better."

Arlo was shaking his head as if he wasn't quite sure. "Naw, that didn't feel right. I got to have me a crowd out there. I got to hear the feedback, then I can get me a roll going." Arlo kept talking about how he liked a back-up guitar or a tambourine when he preached. But Buck and I weren't listening. We were looking down the road as two Georgia sheriff's patrol cars were slowing down and turning in.

Buck spat and shook his head. "Shit fire!"

I said, "What the hell's going on? We haven't done anything illegal." I grabbed Buck's arm. "We haven't broken any laws, have we?"

Buck didn't seem too surprised. "I guess we'll know pretty soon."

It was a Georgia sheriff and four deputies with a Florida collection subpoena for an old bill of Buck's from Sarasota. It was for twenty thousand dollars. I had had just enough to drink to begin sounding off about how I'd read a little law in school and I knew that Florida had to collect its own bills and we were out of their jurisdiction.

Buck tried to keep me quiet, but this time I knew I was right and I wouldn't give a damn inch.

The sheriff listened very carefully, then he said, "Son, you're right, you're absolutely right, that's about how the law reads. And if you want to take this to court you'll make the ACLU boys in Atlanta very happy, and it just might turn out to be a great legal milestone." Then he smiled. "But you boys ain't got that kind of time, now have you?"

I was making him mad but I just couldn't stop it. "And what if we don't?"

"Well then, I guess I'd just be forced to call in the tow trucks. And then maybe in, say, about thirty or sixty days from now, you boys can have your little parade and your little tent meeting in Charles City."

Buck eased me away and began telling him how the flatbed and the statuary wouldn't bring a penny on the dollar at an auction. The sheriff seemed to be listening to the lyrics of a country song that was coming from his radio.

Buck kept on. "Sheriff, I tell you that crap's worthless."

He smiled. "Well, it must be worth something to you people. Sorry, Mister Mozingo, I've got my orders, and you know how it is."

Buck shrugged his shoulders and began counting out his last sixty-one hundred dollars on the sheriff's car hood. "Sorry, but that's all we're holding." He smiled thinly and hooked his head. "I don't suppose you'd take an IOU?"

"Afraid not, Mister Mozingo." He looked at the money and shook his head. "And I'm afraid that that ain't going to be good enough."

It was just like the night out at the bag plant, but this time I wasn't going to let it happen. For some reason I wanted to spare Buck the embarrassment of having to ask me for it; I stepped up to the car hood and started counting out one hundred and thirty-nine hundred-dollar bills right next to Buck's. The sheriff was delighted with

the arrangement, and, after giving us a receipt, he told us
to have fun in Charles City and to be sure and say hello to
T. T. Littlejohn for him.

As he pulled out, Buck said, "Bo, you saved our hat and
our ass. That was mighty nice of you. Mighty nice."

Loretta kissed me on the cheek. "Thanks, Bo, you were
wonderful. Just wonderful."

All of a sudden it was as if the sheriff hadn't even
showed up. Buck and I were shaking hands and slapping
each other on the shoulders. Then I was shaking with
Arlo and pounding him on the back. Then I was jumping
around and hugging Loretta and reaching over to shake
with Buck and Arlo again. "There's no way for them to
stop us now. No damn way!"

Buck was beaming and popping open four beers. "Now
you're talking, Bo. Now you're talking."

Later he told me he was considering my money a flat
loan to the Jubilee Crusade Corporation, and I would be
the first one paid in Charles City.

Four hours later I was doing 180-degree mood swings.
From red hot to go one minute, to ice cold to pulling out
the next. I'd been drinking too much and eating too much.
Three meals a day at the buffet plus five or six trips to the
vending machines: corn curls, potato chips, peanut-
butter crackers. I told myself I was buying them for
research. To see where the cellophane was printed.
The beer smoothed things out. It made me forget Omaha and Ernie and Monica and the seventeen miles to
Charles City. And then I'd sober up and the doubts
would crash back down. I asked Buck again about
what happened when McCoy left us and we were on our
own.

"That's the least of our worries."

I knew the worst. "Arlo, right?"

"Bo, he's a savage. He might as well have a goddamn
bone in his nose."

I wondered if Loretta had told him about the social call
with the shoe box.

Buck smoothed his hands on each side of his beer can. He rotated it slowly. "Bo, I been meaning to tell you something. But there just hasn't been the right time. The bastard wants to go on to Washington. The Groats got to him again. They figure they want to be on the White House lawn when the damn world ends."

"Damn it, Buck! What are you talking about?"

He held up his hands. "Hold it. Hold it. Now listen, it makes sense. He wants to march on the back roads. He's calling it God's Line. It takes thirty-three days to get there. One day for each year Jesus lived. Bo, it ain't a bad idea."

"Damn it, Buck! Oh Jesus, what's going on around here?"

"He had me over a barrel. He owns these people. You see me negotiating with those Groats or that blowtorch group?"

"Well, where in the hell's my opinion? I just dropped in almost fourteen thousand bucks and I'm like a leper around here. Nobody tells me nothing."

"Come on, Bo, I figured you'd back me up."

"I'm not spending no month on the road doing this crap. You hear me? You hear me?" I was shouting.

"Easy Bo, settle down. Don't get all worked up." He glanced over his shoulder. His voice dropped.

"Now listen, in Charles City we're talking about sixty, maybe seventy thousand bucks clear profit. Here's the wrinkle: we take that money and knock old McCoy down. Freddy Logan, the Sherrys, Dave Hoover, old Onslow are all dying to come with us. McCoy can't last another month."

I said it slowly. Clearly. So I could hear it. So I could really believe it was a possibility. "We *buy* the McCoy show? *We buy it?*"

"Damn right. Mozingo-Mahaffey. Or the Mahaffey-Mozingo Show. How's that sound? Terrific, right?"

I was mad and talking fast and almost screaming at him. "What in the flying hell are you doing?"

"Simmer down. Simmer down. Tell me now, what is it you want anyway? Name it. Name it, just name it."

"I want my money back and I want out of this godfor-saken crazy-ass country."

"O.K., O.K., ease up." He laughed. "I was just kidding you. I was just trying it out for size."

"The hell you were. Listen, Buck, I can't stand it anymore. My damn health is cracking."

I jammed my hands in my pockets to keep from hitting him. Then I kicked the door open. Outside I slammed my beer can against the trailer. I picked up two more and tried to break a window. Both missed.

Back at the motel I turned the TV on. I turned it off before the picture settled. I had to think. I had to plan. I had two, maybe three more days. Then it would all come crashing down. Greene would wire me I'd been fired. The sheriff and the Pinkerton men would come charging in to pick up the Olds and the office key. I was trapped. I was through. I didn't want to drink beer or watch TV, and the only thing to read was the Gideon Bible.

I picked it up, wondering how far the Robards would get before it ran out. Some philanthropic society had donated a King James giant-print edition to the room. The book ran eighteen hundred pages, and with roughly six hundred words per page the total count was over a million. With two or three words per pole it was going to be a helluva lot of phone poles. Maybe they'd really get to Maine and make the big turn west. How far would they get? Ohio? Montana? California? Someone should warn them not to head too far north. Donner Pass was out there someplace. I needed to know the distance between the poles. Maybe they'd only make it to Boston. It was easy enough to check. I took my beer out on the highway and began stepping off three poles. A possum was sitting at the third pole, and I could see his pink eyes and rat's tail when a car came by. The average was fifty yards from pole to pole. Maybe up north they were closer because of the ice, but fifty would do for my calculation. It came out to thirty-five poles per mile, and I couldn't believe it. If they used two words it was over fifteen thousand miles. If three, ten thousand. They would cross the country, come down the West Coast, and get all the way back here to Bibleland. Maybe that was what they had in mind. But they'd be painting forever. It would take years. Maybe they could speed it up and go four and five words per pole. Or carry a lightweight stepladder and go seven and eight. I had to talk to them. I had to show them what they were doing. At least I could tell them the facts and they'd be able to plan better. I checked myself in the mirror, worrying about the Robards. I couldn't believe what was happening to me. I sat down and gripped my knees. I squeezed hard. I had to get hold of myself. I had to calm down. I'd take a swim. Yes. A nice, long, cool swim. Yes, that was it. Then I'd be able to think better.

My suit didn't fit. I had to wear it low. At the pool I lowered myself on the ladder. I was too dizzy with beer and vending-machine food to dive. I'd probably aged five or ten years. I slid up on a kid's raft and spread-eagled out with my hands and feet dangling. I had to relax. I had to get things back in focus. I cupped my hands around my eyes like blinders and concentrated on the North Star. Then I traced the Big Dipper handle out to the Milky Way. With ten or twelve key stars I sketched in New York State, New Jersey, and Pennsylvania out to the Ohio line. It was my territory and I missed it. I knew it cold and I loved it. I wanted to be back out there now more than ever. I wanted to have lunch out there, and dinner out there, and check in at the motels, and have breakfast out there. I could call on General Electric in Schenectady. Beech-Nut in Canojoharie. Schuler's out in Buffalo, and Eastman Kodak in Rochester. Their doors were always open to salesmen. I'd call on Johnson and Johnson in New Brunswick and Campbell's Soups in Camden. I'd go out to Hershey, where the streets are named for ingredients —Chocolate Boulevard, Mocha Road, Cocoa Drive—and the streetlamps are shaped like six-foot-high silver bells. Maybe I'd never sell them, but that didn't matter. They were mine. I could see the call report: "Lunch with

General Electric. $38. No new business now, but Bud Arnold advises we keep in close contact for new products coming up. Will call back next month."

It was my account. They were all my accounts. I knew their products. Their packaging machinery. Their secretaries. Their receptionists. Where the men's rooms were. What jokes to hit the purchasing agents with, and the steak and the go-go places in the area in case they wanted to go out for dinner and a night on the town. I lay there sketching out the Pennsylvania Turnpike. The New Jersey Turnpike. The New York Thruway. It was probably beautiful up around Syracuse. The snow would be six feet deep and cut away like angel-food cake. In the north country they have sharp seasons. And the people match the seasons: they make sharp decisions. Down here nothing was straight. Everything was laid back and fuzzy. They'd grin and shuffle and "aw shit" and "aw shucks" you to the wall. No one would give you a straight answer on anything. Ernie, out at the Ramada, had missed it all too. He'd wanted to ride back over it and say hello to the purchasing agents, the receptionists, the secretaries. Now I was feeling the same way. My wildness was gone. I was as low and as sorry as old Ernie, and probably had his same bad breath and the five o'clock shakes before my first drink. Then I picked out a red star west of Pittsburgh and Chicago. It was Omaha, and I wondered if I would ever get back there again.

I dangled my hands and feet in the water as I drifted out to the center. I knew I had no choice. I had to stick with Buck through Charles City. I was talking out loud. "And then what are you going to do?"

I answered, "I don't know."

"Well damn it, you got to know. You got to *do* something." I was getting louder. "Well, what in the hell do you want? Answer me that. Come on, answer me that one!" I screamed out, "I want my job back. I want my money back! Damn it, I want my girl back!"

I went back to Buck's trailer. He had gone to bed, but

Loretta was still up. I opened a beer and a bag of chips. It was the jumbo, six-ounce size. A few years back regular was six ounces, large was eight, and jumbo ten. Since then regular has been taken off the market, jumbo is regular, and everything's gone to hell. We sat there popping beers and watching an old black-and-white World War II movie. I knew I'd never sleep. I'd just lay there replaying the McDonald's scene, wishing I'd kept on north on I-85. Then I'd crank up the fourteen-thousand-dollar donation scene. I couldn't stand facing all the bad decisions again. But tomorrow, Charles City, South Carolina, would tell the story. We were going to make the money. Or lose our ass. Or get locked up or fire-bombed. Or maybe old Harun's oilman would buzz down in his Lear jet and take us back to his Texas ranch where we would set up the *Pietà* out with the longhorn cattle and live happily ever after eating barbecue and drinking Genesee Twelve Horse, or Schlitz, or Coors or whatever swill they brew out there on the lone prairie. But a couple of things were dead certain. Tomorrow we were going to Charles City down the Dixiana. We'd be there around two or three, and McCoy would be there by four. The show would start at eight. A cold hand was gripping my stomach from the inside. In sixteen hours we would know everything. Everything.

The movie was over. The *Late Late Show* was starting. Loretta said she couldn't take any more and patted my head. "Don't drink too much more, O.K.? Night now."

"Good-night, Loretta."

I'd seen the movie too many times to go it again and switched channels. The only thing operating was an all-sports network out of Mid-America featuring a football game between Evangel University and Central Arkansas State. The game was played on a grassless field, and after every play there was a cloud of dust and a long delay while they determined who had the ball and where the forward progress had stopped. Only a handful of support- ers were seated on the fifty-yard line, and there seemed to be cars parked in the end zone. During the halftime the coach made a pitch for Christian athletes to come out to Evangel U., and then he sang a beautiful hymn about the next world. As I sat there opening another beer, I realized we'd done it all wrong. This was the crowd we should have contacted. We didn't need the freaks and the bunch who missed the cut at Jonestown. There were plenty of straight, God-fearing Christians out there who would have been glad to march. They sure as hell would have looked better. I decided to call the eight-hundred number for Evangel and tell them our story. And then I saw that it was three o'clock and realized just how drunk I was. There were beer cans on the table, the floor, the chairs, on every flat surface. I started to count them. And then I knew I didn't want to.

As I headed back to my room I saw a car parked down in the drain ditch. The headlights were on. It was the Robard family working the phone poles. They were probably trying to get enough ahead so they could be ready to march in the morning. I shouted down, "How's it going?"

"Wonderful, Mr. Mahaffey. Wonderful. Tomorrow's going to be a glorious day. Glorious." Leo Robard paused and came closer with his head cocked. "Are you all right?"

"I'm fine. Fine. Hey, I'd like to talk to you sometime. There's some facts and figures I think we ought to be going over."

"Wonderful, Mr. Mahaffey. We'll be here. You sure you don't need some help?"

"No thanks, everything's perfect. Perfect. Good-night now, and take it easy."

"Good-night, Mr. Mahaffey."

CHAPTER

15

The switchboard called at eight. It had to be wrong. It couldn't be eight. I'd just gone to bed. Or had a fast dream that I'd been sleeping. I sat up, but I had no strength. My head was pounding and I had to lie back down. Outside, the sun was blazing on the pea gravel and bouncing off the pool. I eased along in the shadows trying to keep cool and balance the hangover. I had to keep from throwing up. Maybe it was too hot for the Crusade. Maybe they would delay it a couple days. A day? A few hours? I was like some religious madman looking for a sign. Some shape in the clouds. Some configuration in the trees. Some sound in the wind. But there were no clouds; there was no wind: only the blinding white sun and the rising heat. But it was more than the heat. More than the fear and the galloping hangover. My heart was thumping in my throat and my pulse was coming in violent rushes. In a few minutes I'd step over the line into terminal delirium tremens and a one-way ticket to madness.

By nine o'clock it was eighty. By ten, eighty-six. The Robards were right in starting out at night to beat the

heat. At eleven o'clock it was ninety-four degrees and we
were moving out of Bibleland. We were out on the
Dixiana. The world's first Jubilee Crusade was heading
north. It was stark raving mad, and I was not only smack
in the middle of it, I was paying for it. Arlo and the
elephants were leading the way. The Chuck Wagon was
next, pulling the flatbed. Everything was there: the *Pietà*,
the emperors, the arches, the lions. Then the marchers:
eighty-four were from Bibleland. Littlejohn had drafted
fourteen from the American Legion and the Chamber of
Commerce. Buck, Loretta, and I were pulling up the rear
in the Oldsmobile.

I kept the Olds around five miles an hour. The air
conditioning was off, and the doors were wedged open
with beer cans. What was I doing? How in the hell did I
get here? My hangover was worse, and now it was mixed
with straight fear. Hot flashes one minute; cold chills the
next. Maybe I had something serious? Polio? Pneumonia?
Suddenly the heat light began flashing. I stopped and
pulled the hood latch. As the engine cooled, we watched
the caravan crawling along. It was long: over a hundred
yards. Arlo in his blue serge suit, white shirt, and red
string tie was out front leading the way. Dogs and kids
were zipping in and out between the elephants' legs.
Buck had promised twelve high-school bands and a
balloon ascension: also minute-by-minute coverage on
prime-time television. Everyone seemed to have counted
on it, but no one seemed disappointed. I began feeling
sorry for the marchers. They weren't used to the heat. A
few were too old and too fat for it. Just as I decided they
were the walking wounded of the world, Buck tapped my
arm. "Looks great, doesn't it?"

"Are you kidding?"

"Hell no, they're the greatest. Look at them!"

Maybe I'd missed something. I examined them carefully. They looked awful. If there was a God in the sky,
something terrible was going to happen. There was no
way he'd allow this kind of shakedown without sending a

flood or a fire or a famine. But maybe the famine was on its way. When we started feeding them, the money was going to fly.

The heat-gauge needle dropped back down, and I started up. It seemed hotter. The humidity had soaked the blacktop and was dripping from the phone poles and the green-glass insulators. It was a flat one hundred degrees and the disc jockey was warning people with respiratory troubles to stay indoors. It was going higher, and Littlejohn's marchers were bitching.

"This is crazy. What in the hell were we drinking?"

A fat man was fanning himself with a piece of cardboard. "This is the dumbest thing I've ever seen."

His partner, a short, lizardy-looking man, looked up at him. "We told you to leave them onion rings alone. Ain't nothing but pure-out grease. What'd you expect?"

"I didn't expect this."

Behind them a heavyset American Legionnaire had his shirt off and was mopping down his chest with it. He squinted up at the fireball sun as if someone had played a dirty trick on him. "Man, would I love to have me a nice ice-cold beer!" He made a sharp right turn and headed into a soybean field.

"Where you going, Paul?"

"Home. I've had it."

"But you gave T. T. your word, man. What are we going to tell him?"

"Screw him. Tell him I lied."

The sun was boiling and the heat snakes were rippling on the road. Littlejohn's volunteers were spitting, kicking the dirt, and cursing. They were getting down to the hard fact that there were other things they'd rather be doing than marching seventeen miles in the Carolina heat. One group stopped, said good-bye, and headed for an Exxon station to call a cab. They were all peeling off. A woman in the last twosome to go said it flatly: "We made a terrible mistake. Just terrible."

The ranks moved up. They filled in. The Stark Valley

Baptists. The Revealed Nazarenes. The Groats. The Hare Krishnas had started off walking in single file right down the white line, but the hot blacktop had driven them to the road shoulder. They had put away their finger bells and were limping along the red clay. A Nazarene snake handler, curious about the trailing robes and pigtails, slapped one on the back. "Hey there, amigo! I hear it gets pretty hot over there in old India."

He smiled faintly. "Not like this."

At noon we stopped for lunch. Southerners call it dinner. Each marcher got a Kentucky Fried dinner. Three pieces of chicken, mashed potatoes and gravy, and a half pint of three-bean salad and a soft drink. All I could keep down was ginger ale.

Littlejohn drove up and began apologizing for his volunteers pulling out. Buck said it was O.K. and handed him a Kentucky Fried box and a large Coke. Littlejohn sprung a chicken wing open and bit. He talked as he chewed. He was excited about everything and told us how everyone in town was ready for the circus.

Littlejohn was on his third piece of chicken and reaching for another Coke. "Where's your buddy? You know, the Real McCoy?"

Buck said, "He'll be along. T. T., you know something, I was just thinking, this is really going to be a red-letter day for you."

T. T. wiped his mouth with his sleeve. "It sure looks that way. You ought to see that crowd. Four deep all the way down Main."

Buck looked up the road as he opened another beer. "T. T., can I use your phone for a second?"

"Sure, help yourself. Key's under the mat. Loretta honey, hand me over another one of them boxes. I'm about to starve."

Buck dragged me along to Littlejohn's office. I could barely walk but maybe there would be some ice water there and a place to lie down. He said McCoy was cutting it too close for comfort, and he dialed a number in Buford.

His face flushed as he listened. When he hung up he said, "Something's wrong. Something's really wrong." McCoy hadn't played there, and the only circus on the books was Beaty-Cole coming in for the Shriners in June. Buck called the Chamber of Commerce in Milledgeville. In Griffin. In Covington. No one had even scheduled McCoy. A few hadn't even heard of him. Buck's face was getting redder. "The bastard's pulling a fast one. There's no telling where he's holing up." He kept calling until finally he found an old friend in Atlanta who had seen McCoy's ads. He was playing at a shopping mall and was booked to stay there two more days. Buck dropped into Littlejohn's chair. "Jesus!" He slammed both hands on the desk. "Goddamn it, I knew things were going too smooth."

My throat closed and my heart sank. We were through. We were dead. We were going broke so fast it was pathetic. Buck's fists were white. His eyes were closed. "Listen, you got to hold that Charles City crowd. Hot damn, what a mess. What a goddamn mess." He paced up and down, popping his hands. He wiped the sweat from his face. "Hey, and don't tell Littlejohn anything." He leaned on the window. He drummed his fingers on the pane. Then he swung around as if he had something. "Maybe Arlo can find a guitar group or a bunch of cloggers. He can preach to them. But listen, none of that passion-play crap. This crowd is waiting for the goddamn circus." He looked back up the street. We could see four miles down the Dixiana, and the Crusade was still out of sight. "Bo, I want you to talk to Arlo. If we lose that crowd, we're wiped out."

Littlejohn had a glass-topped desk, and I pressed my face to it for the coolness and closed my eyes. "How, Buck?" Every word was painful. Every thought was painful. "Exactly how do I talk to him? What do I say?"

"Feel him out. The bastard's got to want something. Money, center stage, women, his name in lights. It's got to be something."

I was too weak and sick to get mad at Buck. Hell, it wasn't his fault. I should never have gotten involved with any of it. Every time I thought of the money, and what I'd tell Omaha, I almost threw up.

Buck was crossing and recrossing the room. "Bo, you got to sell him on something." He was back at the window, talking through his teeth. "I gotta catch that McCoy. I'm going to take his last dime and every head of stock that's walking and every piece of equipment that can roll. And then I'm going to haul off and kick his ass until it goddamn rains, right in front of his whole goddamn cast."

I could hear him, but his voice seemed to be coming from a mile away. "Sure, Buck, sure. We'll get him." When I opened my eyes the room was spinning. And then I felt Buck's hand on my elbow, lifting and steering me to the toilet. "Come on Bo, get with it. Run your finger down your throat. Couple minutes and you'll be a brand-new man."

It was painful, but after nine or ten false starts and thinking I'd ripped loose some vital organ I finally threw up. But Buck was wrong. I didn't feel any better.

Back at the caravan, Loretta aimed the Olds for Atlanta and took off with Buck. I climbed up on the flatbed. I'll be damned if I was going to march. I pushed back against the bulkhead between a Coliseum arch and Caligula and closed my eyes and tried to rest and tried to think. I tried to think of something pleasant—Monica. But the thing that came through was that the Crusade and my job were absolutely doomed. It was going to be one grim, humiliating day introducing Ernie around as my replacement. I'd probably tell everyone how I was moving on to some other company. That I'd keep in touch. Probably some red-hot, ice-cold joke about how Ernie and I would be in friendly competition. Then I'd show him how to use the tunnels and bridges and where to park. And then it would come—the final moment. We'd be in the parking lot and I'd give him the keys. "Here you go, Ern. Square one's ignition. Round one's for the trunk. Grease and oil checklist is right there on the doorpost. There's a little lifter noise, but don't sweat it." We'd shake hands. "Good luck, Ernie."

"Hang in there, Joe. You'll come by, won't you?"

"Sure. You take care now."

Would I look back to see if he was watching me? Or trot out and flag down the first cab? Or would I just put my hands in my pocket, skip a couple sidewalk cracks, and go zooma-zooma-zooming on down the street? Where in the hell would I go?

I wouldn't have a car. But I wouldn't need one. I wouldn't have anyplace to go. Nowhere. Where would I get my mail? Read the paper? Every time I took a leak I'd have to plan it. Taking a crap would be a nightmare. I could always drop into American Tobacco or Nabisco or Lever Brothers. I had friends there. "Hello, Harry. Just in the neighborhood. Thought I'd drop by."

Harry would send out for the coffee and Danish wagon. Maybe we'd do the weather. The subways. The Yankees. The Jets. But then it would taper off. He'd roll his wrist to check his watch. "Well, Joe, anything I can do for you?"

"Not a thing, Harry. Not a thing. Just wanted to stop by and say hello." I'd slap my knees. I wouldn't have a sample case on my lap. "Well, Harry, you take care of yourself now."

"You too, Joe. Nice seeing you. Come by anytime."

And then out in the hall I'd meet someone from Cleartone or AAA out of Philadelphia, or see Marty Rosenbaum bouncing down the hall with a sample of a job they had on the press. Where would I go in the mornings? I'd still get the subway at Seventy-second Street. But why the express? I could take a local and get a seat. Would I get off at Times Square for a movie? Or shuttle over to the office to use the phone and borrow the washroom key? If Costo and Jake were out I'd be locked out. I wouldn't want anyone seeing me trying the door or hanging around. I remembered Carson Miller's painful warning, "Mahaffey, you don't want to *look* unemployed."

I opened my eyes as a South Carolina State Police

patrol car cruised by slow. It stopped and backed up. I thought he was going to pull us over. The patrolman nodded at me. Then he shook his head and went on by. I closed my eyes again.

I was almost asleep when Arlo slid up on the flatbed. "Where's Buck?"

"Went to see McCoy." I didn't want him seeing my eyes. "Slight delay. Nothing serious."

"Is that so?" His voice flattened. He'd smelled something. "Exactly what time is McCoy getting here?"

"Around seven. Maybe sooner. Something busted on his power plant."

"Well then, how come Buck Mozingo didn't tell me about it?"

"Hell, I don't know."

He shifted around to get a good look at me. The old hard eye contact. "Ain't nothing funny going on, is there?"

It didn't matter how hard I tried, I just couldn't stand the bastard. "You mean funny ha-ha? Or just funny."

Suddenly, he grabbed my arm. "You New York Jew sapsucker! I ain't trusted you since you came in here. And I don't aim to start in now." I wanted to knock him on his ass, but I knew I had to wait. He backed off, looking sly and suspicious. "You and Buck Mozingo are pulling something, ain't you? Ain't you?"

"Yeah. I just sunk fourteen thousand dollars into this leper parade and we're pulling something. Just what in the hell you think we're pulling?"

I could tell he was clicking off possibilities. "Well, next time he does something sudden-like I want to be told."

"Tell him about it. Listen, just leave me alone, will you?"

The caravan had caught up with the Robards and was slowly passing them. They were only averaging three and four words per pole. I'd have to talk to them and give them my calculations. I read their message: "And all the days . . . of Enos were . . . nine hundred and five . . . And he died . . . And Cain lived." The Charles City water tower was shining in the distance. It looked like another two miles. I lay back and closed my eyes against the glare. There was no way on earth of selling this zappo on anything. "Arlo?"

"Yeah."

"Why don't you go out in the woods and strangle yourself."

But Arlo wouldn't leave. We rode along for ten minutes not saying anything. Then I thought I'd give it another shot. "Arlo." My eyes were still closed and I tried to keep the edge out of my voice. "Think we could hold the crowd if McCoy and Buck show up late?"

"Don't give me that *we* business, Mahaffey. You couldn't do nothing."

"O.K. Think *you* could do it?"

"If I wanted to hold a crowd I could do it"—he snapped his fingers—"like that."

I propped up one elbow. "Yeah, I bet."

His eyes narrowed hard. "I got me a couple pieces of talent out there that can hold any crowd breathing. That tall old boy, Jessee Royal Stamps. That's one. The other's out there behind the Groats. Got on that yellow shirt." Henderson Moke was wearing a yellow see-through shirt on the outside of his pants. His other crowd-stopping feature was that he had only one ear. A smile eased across Arlo's face like a zipper sliding open. His eyes narrowed and brightened. "You're trying to suck me into something, ain't you?"

It was no use. "Arlo, I don't give a flying shit what you do. Come on, move back, I'm trying to get me a tan." We were passing a KEEP SOUTH CAROLINA GREEN sign. The e's and o's had been used for target practice. I could feel him peering at me. Breathing on me.

"Mahaffey, you been having sexual congress with Miss Loretta Jane Reynolds, ain't you?"

I said, "Never heard it called that."

"Call it what you want. Well, ain't you?"

"No, I'm afraid not."

"You're lying. I been seeing that satisfied look she's got on her face when yall are together. Mahaffey, I ain't stupid." The marchers had started "Onward, Christian Soldiers" again. Arlo was humming along, waiting for an answer. "Come on, Mahaffey. You can level with me."

"Why in the hell should I tell you anything?"

It was the right tone. He came back sounding like a boy scout. "If it was me, I'd tell you."

"O.K., Arlo, anyway you want it. I had her three or four times. No, make that five. Once on the kitchen table."

His voice cracked and shot up. "Kitchen table?"

I stretched out again with my arm over my eyes. It was all I could do to keep from laughing. "Sure. She likes to watch it going in. Arlo, now don't tell me you're not getting it?"

"No, I ain't been back."

I raised up and shaded my eyes. "Come on, for a hundred bucks? I figured you'd been in there three or four times."

"No, I swear I ain't."

I had to keep it going. I had to keep it open. "You were right about one thing. Buck isn't getting it."

He grinned and nodded like an ape. "Yeah, I laid my hand right on that one."

We were going through a crossroads community of eight houses all painted the same bright yellow with "haint blue" trim. They were out of plumb and cocked and twisted on their brickbat corners. In the pounding heat they looked like kids' drawings. The families were out on their porches and in their yards watching us. It's not every day you look out and see a pair of elephants and enough statuary to reshoot *Cleopatra* coming down the Dixiana Highway. They were nodding at us. They seemed to be saying it was all right. None of them waved. Somehow the Crusade was something you didn't wave at. You looked at it and liked it. Or you looked at it and hated it. But you didn't wave at it.

Arlo shifted closer. "Mahaffey, if I was to give you a hundred dollars, could you set me up? I don't like all that negotiating and all."

That was it. I'd lucked into it. Loretta was old Arlo's hot button. I waited a few beats. I had to play it cool. "Maybe I could." I took two beats. "I'm just saying maybe now."

His voice dipped low. "I wouldn't expect no blood oath guarantee." He was almost whispering. "Women are funny when it comes to things like that."

I didn't want to say anything smart-ass. I kept my mouth shut and watched a kid wearing a Carolina Game-cock cap skipping alongside Alexander the elephant.

"Mahaffey, if I hold that crowd, you think you could do it?"

"Listen, you're not doing nothing for me. I don't care what you do."

I was easing off so he could move back in. I wanted it to be his idea.

"O.K., Mahaffey, I'll hold that crowd for Mozingo and McCoy. What do you say?"

I had him on the offensive. I had to keep him there. Caligula's shade had shifted and I slid over and stretched out. "Let me think about it, Arlo."

He dropped off and went out to lead the marchers. The families were still watching, and two kids and three dogs were loping alongside the caravan. Maybe I was too close to see the effect the Crusade was having on them. Maybe we really did have something. Julius Caesar and the three emperors were on the corners looking out over the swamp and the tin roofs of the shotgun houses as if they had come this way before, and had disapproved, and now were back again to take another look. If a person from a hundred yards away telescoped his hands over his eyes and blocked out the phone poles and the TV antenna, it could really be happening a thousand years ago, or even two thousand. There was no doubt about it; in the right light it was biblical, and for the Georgia and South Carolina

Nazarenes and Pentecostals and the Church of God it might be the biggest religious juggernaut they would ever see.

In ten minutes Arlo was back. The water tower was less than a mile away. He sat up against the bulkhead. "You decided yet?" I kept my eyes closed in the sun and tried to act bored with it all. "O.K., Arlo, you hold the crowd and I'll fix you up with Loretta."

"You can?"

"You want me to guarantee it?"

He smiled like a clam being pried open. "You'll guarantee it?"

"She owes me a couple favors. You want me to get it in writing?"

He was grinning and shaking his head. "No, that might get touchy. She might back off. I'll take your word for it. Lord, and you really put it to her on the kitchen table?"

I nodded and kept my voice calm. "What are you going to do until McCoy shows?"

He smiled again. "Mahaffey, what do you think of a live, in-the-flesh serpent handling?"

The water tower was close enough to read. CLASS OF 78 was in black and red spray paint and bright orange Clemson Tiger paw prints were scalloped around the bottom. We'd be there in thirty minutes. Out on the lot in forty. "I thought snake handling was illegal?"

"Not in South Carolina."

"You sure?"

"Sure I'm sure. Eudora Gulley can quote you legal statutes. Chapter, verse, and line. They're more liberal down in here. Better informed. Georgia's like the Middle Ages. You can't do nothing there."

If anything could hold the red-necks and bring the media out, this would be the ticket. But I didn't want him seeing me jump for it.

"I don't know, Arlo. Something just doesn't seem right."

He was shaking his head. "You just ain't ever seen a good one. They get wild." He grabbed my arm. His eyes were flashing. "Wild! Dancing, screaming, stomping, shouting! Those people get *loose.*"

It sounded better and better. It was also the only thing we had.

"Arlo, I still don't like it."

He was excited. His eyes were shining like new dimes. He looked crazy. "If you ain't pleased one hundred percent, I don't get Miss Loretta Jane Reynolds. If that ain't fair, nothing is." He was beaming. "You ain't going to believe this show. You know something? I don't believe it's ever been done onstage. I got the idea when we crossed that South Carolina line." His hand was out. We pumped two firm times. It was a deal. It was based on mutual distrust and mutual disgust: the perfect sale. Arlo moved in closer. "Mahaffey, something else. When you talk to Miss Loretta Jane Reynolds, I'd appreciate it if you'd kind of mention I'd be partial to doing it on the kitchen table. Can you handle that?"

"Sure. I'll pass it along."

Sheriff T. T. Littlejohn met us at the caution light. The Charles City High School Band with a drum major and three high-stepping fancy twirlers were pounding out "Under the Double Eagle." He had flushed the people out of their houses and off their farms, and they were lined up three and four deep down the hot block waiting for the circus. Littlejohn was red-faced and excited. A blue-and-white band was around his hat, campaigning VOTE FOR ME IN JUNE AND DON'T FORGET ME IN NOVEMBER. There were too many words for any distance. A radio announcer and two newspapers were already there and Charleston TV was on its way. Littlejohn said it would be great for his campaign if he could ride in on an elephant, and we helped him mount Alexander from the flatbed. His legs were too short for the thick neck, and he had to hold both ears to get balanced.

I shouted up, "You O.K., T. T.?"

He was scared but he grinned anyway. "Wow! It's high

up here. . . . O.K., I got her. Let her rip." And then, waving his hat and hollering to his friends as the trumpets pinged away and the cymbals banged together, he led the Crusade and the crowd down the street and out onto the lot behind the school.

The big grass lot was flagged off for McCoy. Red flags for the big top. White for the midway. Black for the cook house, the light wagon, the sleepers, and the elephant wagons. Arlo took over like a drill sergeant and parked the flatbed at the edge at the lowest point. The crowd could sit down and look down. Then he swung the Chuck Wagon parallel to it a hundred feet away. He climbed up on the flatbed between the emperors and the *Pietà*. He liked to work it big, and when he spoke people stopped talking. He told them how the churches that were marching with us had been driven from one state to the next. How the great Palmetto State of South Carolina was the only state that stood behind the religious freedom guaranteed in the Constitution. Then, with no pause or buildup, he brought on the Reverend Jessee Royal Stamps. Jessee set up a card table and laid out his Bible and a flat railroad watch. He stood at parade rest while Arlo announced he was going to recite the Lord's Prayer one thousand times before the sun set at 8:17. Jessee kept smiling at the crowd that had come to see the circus as if they were old friends. He cleared his throat. "Number one. Our Father Who art in Heaven . . ."

A reporter from Augusta handed me his card. McClain Switzer. "I missed that name."

"Jessee Royal Stamps." I spelled it out, "S-t-a-m-p-s."

He clicked his ball-point down. "Thanks, this is the kind of stuff the wire service eats up. Where's the circus?"

I said, "They're running a little late. Few more hours, but don't go away, they'll be here."

Jessee Royal did six prayers in the first minute, but he was a disaster. The crowd was shifting around and not paying attention. Two kids were throwing a Frisbee between the emperors and the arches and the back rows were breaking up. Arlo took the microphone. "Hey out there! Let's give these folks a chance. We just got here."

The crowd hesitated. Arlo knew his people and announced there would be no collection and that the best stuff was coming up. They came forward slowly as he slid out a wooden frame of two-by-fours. It had a plywood bottom and looked like a miniature sandbox. He then waved Henderson Moke in out of the wings. Henderson was in his yellow shirt and Bermuda shorts. The shorts were so tight the pockets had sprung open. He had on white-striped jogging shoes and red socks and was carrying a case of Coca-Cola bottles in one hand. Two brand-new brickbats were in the other. Arlo patted his back and raised his hands for quiet. He introduced him, and the curious crowd came closer. Henderson knelt down and began smashing the bottles into the frame. Then he re-smashed the bigger pieces. He stacked the brickbats and dusted his hands on his pants. He pushed off his shoes and socks. The crowd was quiet. Then he smoothed his black hair straight back and closed his eyes in concentration. Suddenly he leaped in the box, screaming, "Here I am, *Jesus! Here! Right here!*" With short furious stomps and high leaping jumps he pounded on the glass for a full fifteen seconds. "*Jesus! Jesus! Jeeeesus!*" He stopped, stepped out, did a military box step, and came to attention facing the crowd. There was no blood. He didn't even limp. Arlo pumped in the applause until it peaked. When it ended, and Henderson had slid his box offstage, Arlo raised his hands again.

"Ladies and gentlemen! Only a small sample of what we got planned for yall. Yall going to stick with me now?"

The crowd applauded and whistled *yes*. A softball player for Charles City Service with HARLAN stitched to his cap raised his cap. "By God, I am. Hey! I got a question."

Arlo was hyped up, and he shouted down. "Name it, partner."

He pointed at Jessee Royal. "That bird hitting the toilet? He taking any breaks?"

Arlo smiled. "No, sir. No breaks. He's on a food-and-water fast for the Jubilee Crusade. Jessee Royal Stamps has come prepared to pray right on through to sunset."

Arlo introduced six members of the Stark Valley Pentecostal Church. They spread a white sheet over another card table and began lining up brown bottles, glasses, and a pitcher of water. At the side was an army cot made up with military corners. A GOD LIVES pillow was at each end. Arlo raised his hands with his palms out. "Yall scootch in here a little tighter. Yall in the back row! Come on in here. There's plenty of room. This is something you've got to see to believe." He paused while the crowd tightened. "Brother Ethan Deloache and his twin brother Billy are going to drink off two ounces of undiluted strychnine."

He held up the four-ounce bottle. "I'm pouring two ounces into each one of these water glasses. Then I'm going to be giving them each another full glass of water to chase down that taste." His lip curled back over his gums in his best joking smile. "I don't suppose many of yall know what strychnine tastes like?"

It was the wrong question. Harlan down front cocked his cap and raised his hand.

Arlo said, "Yessir?"

"How we know that stuff's strychnine?"

A woman's voice cut through. "Knock down a chicken. If it's strychnine she'll drop like a rock."

Arlo unscrewed the cap. He began pouring. "You'll have to take me and the Lord's word for it."

Harlan's elbows were on the stage. "Bull, mister. I ain't seen no halos floating around. That could be Diet Pepsi."

The woman moved in closer. "Get some stuff from the drugstore. Then everybody's happy. Mister, nobody knows you. You just pulled into town."

Arlo stalked over to the Deloache twins. They talked and nodded. Arlo got back on the mike. He was mad. "Get it! Go on, get it then."

Out on the lot Loretta was parking the Olds. When she saw me she hooked her thumb down the road. Buck was shimmying up in a GMC elephant wagon pouring smoke. She told me the story. It was grim. McCoy had gone broke. Everything he owned—stock, props, rigs, canvas —had been sold or repossessed. Buck had salvaged a truck with only two forward gears and no reverse. No money, no stock, nothing. We'd been screwed. Royally. Loretta touched my elbow. "Bo, take it easy on him. He's in real bad shape."

Buck climbed down from the cab. I saw his face. He was really down. Not the crazy cornered down from the Roosevelt Grill but a beaten down, whipped down, bitter down. I said, "Loretta told me the good news." He nodded his head. "Yeah, Bo, he really put it to us." He winked and punched my arm. "But this old mongoose still has a couple tricks up his sleeve."

"Like what? Jesus Christ, Buck, we advertised a circus and we don't have a circus. We're in trouble. At least admit it."

He looked confused, hurt. Then his face creased and he hooked his head.

"Yeah, I'm going to have to admit that one. O.K., we're in a little bit of trouble. But I've been doing some thinking." He was watching Arlo and paused to light his cigar.

"Good, isn't he?"

"Fooled hell out of me. People really listen to that crap down here."

He smiled and signed. "I told you he was good."

"He's also crazier than goose shit. Listen, Buck, if you got any red-hot ideas, let's hear them right now. This is a goddamn disaster. You've got to tell these people something."

His arm was around my shoulder. "You didn't tell Littlejohn anything did you?"

"No, he's in the dark."

Buck puffed on his cigar. "Fine. Fine. If we can unload those Jesus prints and that Jordan water we can still make out. Hell, maybe we don't even need McCoy." He slapped my back. "Bo, you did a good job on Arlo. I swear you did. We're going to make this thing work yet. You watch. You just watch."

"That's what I thought I'd do."

Up on stage Arlo raised his hands. "Ladies and gentlemen, Mr. Harlan Estee here has an announcement to make." Harlan loved being on stage. "Howdy, folks. Well, Doc Gleason says we can't buy strychnine or laudanum without a prescription. I told him it was for the Lord's work, but that didn't cut no ice." He grinned out and waved to his teammates. "Said if Jesus went to medical school, the Bible sure kept it secret."

He held up a one-pound tin-tied bag of "Sudden Death Rat Killer." It was a standard duplex bag with a thirty-pound glassine liner. It's used in packing fresh-ground coffee and specialty teas. He held it higher and read the label. "Twenty percent arsenic. Fifteen percent strychnine. And sixty-five percent of something I can't pronounce. Guaranteed to kill any rat in five seconds." He grinned to his friends. "Or within twenty feet of the spot where he eats it. Whichever one comes first." He whooped and slapped his thigh.

Arlo spooned out four round tablespoons of the dark gray powder into the eight-ounce glasses. Then he poured in the water. It foamed up like beer. The Deloache twins listened to three more Lord's Prayers. Then they nodded and picked up the glasses. Without taking it from their lips they drank it off and wiped their mouths left-handed. As they stepped back, Arlo came forward. His eyes were burning. "The Lord spoke of faith that moves mountains. *Mountains!* Amen hallelujah!" He hugged a Deloache in each arm, and the applause rolled in. Hallelujah! They were pale. Their eyes were closed and their hands were clenched. They were praying along hard with Jessee Royal Stamps.

When the applause stopped, Arlo was back on center stage. "Ladies and gentlemen, I'd like to call your attention to the Jesus Brotherhood of Chosen Messengers, who are spreading the Holy Gospel along the

Dixiana Highway. I'd also like to welcome you to feel free
to pass through the Great Mozingo Famous Killer Snakes
of the World exhibit, which won't cost you a penny. And
also, when you get a chance, please visit our Chuck
Wagon for foot-long chili dogs, popcorn, cold drinks, and
snow-cones. . . . In the meantime, let's hear it once again
for Henderson Moke, the Deloache brothers, and the
Reverend Jessee Royal Stamps, who is now on Lord's
Prayer number two hundred and fifty-six."

Loretta and I were selling the kids popcorn, snow-
cones, and cold drinks. The adults were lined up for chili
dogs. Behind us, Buck was changing clothes for his snake
show. He was trying to tell me how to adjust the burner
on the popcorn machine. "Keep it on four-fifty. I don't
care what it looks like. Just don't let it burn." Buck
claimed he had built the Chuck Wagon himself. Outside it
was a pots-and-pans old-time gypsy wagon. Inside it was
expensive hardwood and chrome and as tight as a Mc-
Donald's kitchen. The snow-cone and popcorn machines
and infrared-ray warm-up lamps were on one end. On the
other were wire-clip racks for potato chips and pretzels
and flat racks for candy, gum, and breath fresheners. The
backbar was for stock: hot-dog buns, corn, salt, and a
product called "Butterin." Hot buttered popcorn doesn't
mean butter. It doesn't mean margarine. It means Butterin, and it's the only way to go in the concession-stand
business. Like canned soup, it requires no refrigeration
and can be served at the Equator or the North Pole.
Under the backbar was the refrigeration unit and the
control panel for the lights and the public-address system. On the end was a small dressing room and a
chemical toilet.

Arlo had left the Groats up on stage playing a medley of
bluegrass hymns and joined us in the Chuck Wagon. He
popped open a beer and poured it in a milk-shake cup.
He'd seen the smoking elephant wagon and figured out
the rest. He was trying hard not to grin. "Well, Mister

Mozingo. Now I reckon you're going to tell me we ain't going to be getting no circus? Ain't that about the way the field plows?"

Buck angled his safari hat back with his baton tip. "Arlo, you're a damn mind reader. Yes, we have had what you might call a temporary setback. But only temporary. Come on, walk me over. I'll fill you in. Arlo, I swear it's a pure-out pleasure watching you work a crowd like that. Now listen. . . ."

I kept making snow-cones and working the popcorn machine. Buck had showed me how to squeeze forty-eight open cartons under the popper. When the corn dropped, all I had to do was sprinkle salt and close the lids. Loretta was on the foot-longs. Out on the lot, Arlo and Buck were shaking hands. Buck's arm was around his shoulders. They were more than partners; they were buddies. Buck slapped him on the back. Then, whipping his baton on his pants leg, he headed for the snake show. Loretta said it was the same as the Georgia show except that now he would be billing South Carolina as number one in the poison-snake race. When he came back to the Chuck Wagon she asked him, "What in the hell did you promise him?"

"Nothing, baby. We just came to an understanding."

"Well, as long as it ain't no meal ticket on my ass."

Buck grinned and kissed her cheek. "Sugarfoot, Arlo Waters ain't studying women."

Buck made himself a foot-long and loaded it down with chili and mustard and sprinkled red peppers on top. He poured beer into an eighteen-ounce Jumbo Freeze cup. Then he slid up on the backbar with his legs crossed under him, Indian style. With the hot dog and the big cup he looked just like a kid. He might as well have been one. He had absolutely stopped worrying. It was as if McCoy, the circus, and the elephants had never happened. I've never seen anyone get rid of the past so fast. Right there I decided I knew what made a good salesman. All you had to do was pick out a target, then go for it. Just forget the negatives and keep on selling. It was like the car commercials. They don't mention the seventy-two monthly payments or the fine print in the warranty. They take the positive side. The sales side. They show you driving that brand-new sweetheart along like you just won it in a crap game. And next to you is some half-wild half child with her hair blowing and her tits out, giving you a hand job while you're cruising along the California coastline. Buck had told Arlo that McCoy was getting there in the morning. And Arlo believed it. And there was a good chance that even Buck believed it. And when McCoy didn't show up in the morning he would simply sell him on something else.

Littlejohn drove up with Rydell Mitchell, the chief newscaster from Charleston television. A big Ford mobile unit was behind them. Littlejohn had conned him into announcing that Charles City was one-hundred percent behind the Jubilee Crusade. The cameraman shot footage of Littlejohn talking to Buck, Littlejohn up on the stage with Arlo, Littlejohn singing along with the Walking Baptists, and Littlejohn listening to the Groats' red-hot newsbreak about how they would be down on their knees on the White House lawn when the world came to an end. Littlejohn wanted to pose with Buck at the snake show, but Rydell Mitchell said the county was already too famous for moccasins and rattlesnakes. All it would do was scare off the tourists. He kept shaking hands and passing out campaign buttons and bumper stickers. Suddenly he waved to me from his car. It was a phone call. "It's for you. It's long distance."

"Where's it from?"

"Hell, I don't know. It's a woman. Says she can hold until I get you. If you want some privacy, take it in the office."

If it was Monica I'd want to be alone. "Good idea. Thanks. Hey, is she young?"

"Can't tell." He grinned. "You people all sound the same to me."

The call was from Ethel. There were sixteen callbacks

from Omaha in the last twenty-four hours. Ernie had called eleven times. Greene five. Greene calling was the bad news. But Ethel wasn't upset. "I told Mr. Greene how hard it is to find anybody down South. Dearie, I don't want to stick my nose into this, but Mr. Greene sounded very nice this time. He sounded as if he wanted to do something very nice with you." I wrote down "Greene very nice" on the police memo. As she talked on about Greene and Ernie I drew a scalloped frame and carefully printed "Monica" in it. It looked like the Coca-Cola Moon neon sign we had drawn back at the North Florida honky-tonk.

"You sure there's no calls from Miss Murphy? Miss Monica Murphy?"

"No, I'm afraid not. I know her voice as well as I know yours. Your cold sounds better. I'll bet you've been eating those Florida oranges and grapefruits, haven't you?"

I shaded in the box until "Monica" vanished. I told her I had and apologized for not calling her more. Ethel said she understood. She had learned never to get upset with salesmen. "Mr. Mahaffey, you boys have so many pressures on you, I just can't imagine how you ever get any peace."

"Ethel, you aren't telling anyone I'm down here?"

"Oh no! I'd never do that. I just say you're on the road and between calls. I would never tell anyone where you were."

I wrote down "oranges and grapefruit." I'd send her a basket from the next roadside shipper. "Tell Mr. Greene you're still trying to reach me. O.K.?"

"All right. And how about Mr. Ernie? He sounded so upset. Something terrible's going on with him. I couldn't get him to talk about it."

I said, "O.K., I'll call him. Take care of yourself. And listen, if Monica calls, you can give her this number."

"Oh, I know that. . . . Bye-bye now, dearie."

Outside, I caught myself looking up the road. I figured Greene had contacted the police to pick up the car. As I

headed back for the crowd and the Chuck Wagon, I kept
looking up and down the road for the blue flashing lights.
I'd seen too many cop stories on TV. Too many Kojaks.

Up on stage, the Groat family, with two guitars, a
banjo, and a mouth harp, were doing an old hymn about
the next world. When they finished, Arlo eased the mikes
away from them before they could get started preaching
about the end of the world. "Ladies and gentlemen, all of
us except Jessee Royal Stamps are going to take a supper
break in a few minutes. But at eight sharp our big
attraction goes on. So be sure and be out here in plenty of
time and get you a good spot. Now don't forget. The TV
crowd are here from Charleston. So if you got any bright
clothes at home, get them on. Let's really make it look
good. Also, if you got something to say for the live
interviews, copy it down so you won't forget it or get
tongue-tied on camera. And something else: bring a
blanket along in case it turns cool."

The Groats began picking three chords, softly, over and
over again, and Arlo shoved his hands in his pockets. As
he came forward to the edge, the music slowed. "Ladies
and gentlemen, I guess I don't have to tell you that
nothing in this here world is free." He paused, waiting for
the back rows to settle. "But we ain't passing the plate.
Or we ain't passing the washtub like every other bingo
minister in the country is doing these days. And we ain't
loading you up on some tapeworm cure or nerve tonic
that's half alcohol and half codeine with a little shot of
coloring. No sir. What we have here are two very, very
special items. Items you can take home with you. Items
you can proudly put up on your mantelpiece. Items that in
the days and years to come will mean something to you
and your loved ones. Ladies and gentlemen, I'm talking
about genuine religious items." He held up a vial of the
Jordan water.

Buck popped open a beer under a towel to keep the
noise down. "Here it comes. Watch him now."

Arlo told how Jesus' friends went down to the Jordan on

the day he died and scooped up buckets of the water, and
that it had been stored for almost two thousand years in
underground vaults. He rolled on about how, now that the
Arabs had pulled out of Galilee, they were able to get it
out of the country. Then he picked up a rolled Jesus print
and began speaking in a new voice—lower, slower. Buck
put the beer down. "Bo, this bastard is fantastic." Arlo
was letting them in on a great secret. He was talking
about mummification. How when the winding sheets
were unwrapped, there on the linen was the impression of
the face. It was only a matter of getting equipment
sophisticated enough, sensitive enough, to lift it. He
compared it to the Xerox process. He keyed his delivery
to a slow wide pendulum motion and told them how there
were only a few very vague references to this great secret
in the Bible. They were swaying with him. They were
straining forward, cupping their hands to their ears. The
sermon had ended. The pitch had started. We had the
prints and the Jordan water ready. Buck was in my ear,
translating the lines, the moves. I had never seen it
before or even heard of it before. Arlo had key phrases
which told the Lions that he was a Lion. The Rotarians
that he was one of them. "Deep down, dead level" was the
password for the Masons. The raised fingers behind the
head was the sign of the Moose. The fingers touching in a
small steeple, the white knights of the Ku Klux Klan. He
let them know he was with them in the Eagles, the
Optimists, the Kiwanis, the KOC, the BPOE. "Bo, I've
never seen a crowd worked better. Watch that pendulum.
Smooth, ain't it? That son of a bitch could sell refrigerators to the Eskimos."

Arlo stalked up and down the sixty-foot flatbed, telling
about the Jubilee Crusade. About the wonderful days that
lay ahead. He skipped the payments and the refinancing.
He skipped the hills, the mosquitoes, the blackflies, and
the cottonmouths down in the slug slime in the drain
ditch. He told about the good times on up the road. About
camping out. About singing around the campfire on the

Darlington 500 infield. About the picnic on the White House lawn with the president and the members of the cabinet. The more he talked, the more he believed it. He was like Buck, exactly like Buck. A born salesman. And like Buck and me and all the salesmen schlepping demo kits and sample cases around the country, the biggest suckers out here on the pike.

Buck skinned the Saran Wrap off a ham-and-cheese sandwich. "Bo, you really nailed that son of a bitch. I'm really proud of you. I don't know how you did it, but that freak would walk on hot coals." I was thinking about how I'd break the news to Loretta.

Buck wiped mustard from his lips. "Let me tell you a little something about salesmanship." Here he was, fresh from the biggest screwing he'd ever had, and he had a lecture ready on selling. He held his beer can up delicately. "Selling is like getting a fresh piece of ass. You try everything. And nothing works." He dropped the can in the trash. "Then all of a sudden you notice something's working and you move in on it and stick with it. Bo, am I right or am I wrong?"

I slid into a sing-song delivery, "Right, Mister Bones. You're right on Arlo. But something sure as hell slipped loose on McCoy."

He popped open another beer and watched the foam run over his knuckles.

Arlo had a vial of Jordan water in his left hand. A Jesus print was in his right. He placed the water on the table. With the rolled print in both hands he came forward. He described a great secret meeting in Jerusalem. It sounded as if he had been there. Buck was whispering, "Watch him now. He's almost ready. We'll unload this junk so fast you're going to think it's a Macy's rush at Christmastime."

Arlo described the radiologists, the archaeologists, and the religious leaders of the world crouched in over the sacred cloth. They were voting that the world had waited long enough for the picture of the blessed Lord. The crowd was hushed. Still. They were frozen. Buck nudged me. "They're beginning to sound like bees. Listen." I did. They were.

"They're almost ready. Now he'll get them on their feet so they can get to their wallets faster. A man sitting down's got too much time to think. Watch the women. They'll get up with their pocketbooks."

Arlo had taken them to the top of the mountain. He was holding them there. They wanted a release. He told them how the prints were smuggled out of the Mideast. Secretly. Illegally. He mentioned the FBI. The CIA. How they had fooled them all. He laughed. The crowd laughed with him. They didn't know why. Probably afraid he would change his mind and not sell them. They were on their feet. Buck was right, the women rose with their pocketbooks. The men had their hands on their wallets. Some had their money out and were looking around. They were ready. But Arlo wasn't. His voice was louder, clearer. "I was down in New Orleans, Louisiana. I went down there to see that King Tut's tomb. All that is, folks, is Egyptian mummies." They were bobbing their heads together and whispering, "Yes, yes, yes."

Arlo paused. "Let me hear an Amen."

"Amen."

Arlo shouted, *"Let me hear a Yes Lord."*

"Yes Lord!"

"And I looked down on those mummy faces. And you know what I saw? I saw that they were just as human as you and just as human as me standing right out here tonight under God's own stars. Ladies and gentlemen, it's the exact same process." He paused. "Amen and Yes Lord."

It came back. "Amen. Yes Lord."

"Well, folks!" He unrolled the print. He held it up. He thundered, *"Here he is! Our Blessed Savior!"*

The crowd believed it. They loved it. They wanted it.

Arlo was at fever pitch and was holding it there. "We have it! We have it! And it's our God-given right for yall to have one too if you want one. Can I get an Amen on that?"

It sounded like Yankee Stadium. *"Amen!"*

"We don't care if it's illegal. We don't care if the FBI and the CIA and the United States Treasury Department likes it or not. Is that good enough for a Yes Lord?"

"Yes Lord. Yes Lord. Yes Lord!"

Buck nudged me. "Watch him now. Watch him."

Arlo mentioned a limited time, and one to a customer, and ten dollars for the print and five for the Jordan water. He opened two buttons on his shirt and then the high sign came. He brushed his nose twice and pulled his ear. Buck said, "That's it. Let's roll."

Buck, Loretta, and I came forward selling. We tried to keep a path open to the flatbed, but the crowd was waving their money and jamming us in. We sold as fast as we could take in the money. Arlo kept shouting, "I'm sorry folks but only one to a customer. Only one to a customer." It was a stampede. After we sold the first batch we regrouped behind the Chuck Wagon counter. The crowd was lined up six and seven deep with their tens and twenties waving. Now there was no limit. One man bought four prints. Another six. Another five prints and five Jordan waters. One woman with a flat straw hat with a spray of wooden cherries on top gave me five twenty-dollar bills.

"I want me ten Jesuses."

"Yes, ma'am. Here you are."

The money was coming in too fast to handle. We dropped it in the beer case on the floor. Buck had said you never want people to see money piling up. They think they're being stiffed. Or you're doing it for profit. And there was always some interstate-flight type sitting out on the edge of things with a .38 Smith & Wesson and a fast car.

In less than an hour we were out of Jordan waters and down to the last couple dozen prints. Buck pulled me back to the toilet. Loretta was on the counter. "Bo, we're sitting on a gold mine. There's about thirty thousand bucks right there on the floor. And it's peanuts. Peanuts, you hear that?"

"I know, I know. Jesus, I've never seen anything like it."

He was pouring a drink. "Think we could move five thousand more?"

"Five? Make that ten. Hell, Buck, we could sell twenty."

"Now you're talking." He drank the whiskey neat and poured another. Then he slapped his wallet down. "Take the thirty and here's my last thousand. I'm saying we buy every print and Jordan water that Arab's sitting on."

"We can't miss, Buck. We can't." I pulled out my wallet. "Here's four more. Let's shoot the damn works."

"Fine, Bo, fine." He knocked down his second drink. "O.K., I've gotta see Arlo. Go call Harun. Tell him if he can deliver tonight we're buying. But he's got to deliver. He's got to deliver!"

It was about sixty miles to Savannah. Harun could make it by ten o'clock. "He can do it, Buck. I know he can."

"O.K., call him. Try and get that price down if you can. But the main thing is delivery. We've got to have it now. Bo"—his arm was around my shoulders—"if we pull this off, it's going to put us right up there in the big time. I mean the big, big time."

I streaked the whole two blocks to Littlejohn's and slid the key out from under the mat. Harun's office didn't answer, but he wasn't hard to find in the phone book. He was out of Jordan water but he had a good supply of Jesus prints. I couldn't move him off of the two dollars a print, but he promised delivery of fifteen thousand in a half hour.

Back on the counter we told the customers we would have prints in fifteen minutes and to be sure and tell their friends. More cars were pulling in. The problem was going to be to hold them. We decided to stretch the slim acts out with medical testimony. Even Arlo liked the idea. Buck flipped up the toggle on the PA system and announced that we were looking for a doctor.

Dr. Omar Stuckey, in a Buick Electra, pulling a silver Airstream trailer out of Barnwell, South Carolina, had

pulled off the road to see the McCoy circus. He said he
would be glad to identify strychnine for the crowd and the
television audience. Buck asked him if he would wear a
white jacket and a headband mirror.

He shook his head. "I'd look like a fool out there."

But Buck stayed with him. "Dr. Stuckey, I know you
boys can't advertise, but this thing is going on prime-time
TV. If you get on that camera you can say anything that's
on your mind. Never can tell, it might do you some good
on down the line."

Dr. Stuckey thought about it. "O.K., I'll wear the
jacket. But no mirror. Wait a minute, I thought you
couldn't wear white on TV?"

"That's for black and white. It's O.K. on color. But you
might want to powder down some of that sunburn."

After Dr. Stuckey left I poured four beers into Jumbo
Freeze cups and Loretta began serving the Kentucky
Fried dinners. Buck wanted Arlo to hype up the show to
make sure it got on the eleven o'clock news. "We need
something hot for those cameras."

Arlo was hunched in over his chicken, tearing off the
meat. "I told Mahaffey here I was hitting them with a
serpent handling. They'll sit up and take notice of that."

Buck tubed his lips and looked thoughtful. "Maybe for
you and me, good buddy, but TV's spoiled them out there.
They've seen open-heart surgery. They've seen airplane
crashes and looters shot right out there on the scene.
Hell, I saw one that had a live rape on it. Arlo, to get on
network news, you got to damn well *make* the news.
You've got to go all out."

Arlo smiled at Loretta. "Any more biscuits, Miss
Loretta? I got shortchanged here." It was the strange
smile of a soft crazy.

Loretta looked at him carefully, trying to figure it out.
"Sure, Arlo. Here you go. You feeling O.K.?"

"I've never felt better in my life." He turned and pointed
his chicken leg at Buck. "You just ain't ever seen a good
snake handling."

Buck said he'd been dealing with snakes all his life and

hadn't seen one move fast yet. Arlo bit the bone and sucked out the marrow. "Well, damn it, name me something else then."

Buck mentioned a gasoline-immolation trick and said he could pick up a Nomex suit from a local dirt track and no one would get hurt.

Arlo spooned up a mouthful of three-bean salad. "No, I've been that route before." He talked while he chewed. "I saw the real thing up in Harlan County. It was horrible. Right there is where I draw the line."

"Well, let's rig up a real snakebite. Something's got to happen or you're going to be looking like *National Geographic* out there."

Loretta reached for the salt, and Arlo's eyes dipped down the V in her blouse and stayed there. Then he looked back at Buck. "Something's going to happen."

Buck sighed. "Tell you what, old buddy. I'll milk down my diamondback. Then you hit him with a little sandpaper before your man takes hold of him. That'll move his ass."

Arlo shook his head solemnly. "Eudora says a milked snake ain't no snake for religious handling."

I said, "But why tell her? Hell, who's going to know?"

His eyes screwed down tight. "It would impotenize the service."

I kept after him. "O.K., no milking. But how about the cobra? Think you could handle that?"

He slipped the sleeve back on a fried cherry pie. "Yeah, now maybe that's O.K. That's something these people down in here might never get another chance to see."

"He's sixteen feet, Arlo. He'll sure be different."

He finished in two bites and was licking his fingers. "Yeah, we'll take him on."

Buck said, "And you can have my diamondback. That old boy will look great in color."

"Yeah, that's good too. Miss Loretta?"

"Yeah, Arlo."

He smiled softly and cocked his head coyly as if they'd already discussed the kitchen table scene. "You got any more of them little bitty pies back there? I don't know when I've been so hungry."

"Sure. Here you go, stud."

Littlejohn had talked Rydell Mitchell into giving us a monitor in the Chuck Wagon so we could see the show while we sold the prints. The plan was to film everything and cut it down to four or five minutes for the eleven o'clock news. During the sixty-second countdown, Mitchell fooled around, following a dog working his way through the garbage. With twenty seconds he went to black. Then he came up with all three cameras on Arlo up on the middle of the flatbed stage.

The show was on, and Arlo came forward with his arms raised. The hot lights were turning him red. He blinked and wiped the sweat down and smiled grimly. "This is my first time on a national TV show, so I reckon I got me a right to be a little nervous and high-strung." He repeated himself. "Yeah, a little nervous and a little high-strung." As he crossed over to Jessee Royal he was swinging his arms too wide for his stride. He slapped Jessee on the back. "This is my good friend Jessee Royal Stamps, who hails out of Montgomery, Alabama."

The TV crew had rigged a tripod and a stack of flash cards to show Jessee's progress. Arlo held a card up high. "See that! See that! Number eight hundred and seventy-eight! That's how many Lord's Prayers this old boy has done since four-forty this afternoon. He's breaking one thousand before the sun goes down. So what we'll just do is keep checking on him." One camera was on Jessee and Arlo, one was on the flash card, and the third was measuring the angle between the sun and the soybean field in the distance. When I saw the field, I swung around to check the road for Harun and his delivery truck.

Rydell Mitchell's boys had done a good job on the sound system. When Arlo came downstage with the microphone you could hear Jessee droning on in the background. Arlo was calming down. "Ladies and gentlemen, our first testimonial of faith is from Mr. Henderson Moke from Stark Valley Baptist out of Stark Valley, Mississippi. Mr.

Moke will demonstrate how deep and abiding his faith has been since he finished high school."

Henderson came forward, dragging his two-by-four frame. He was carrying another case of bottles and his brickbats. A few people complained that they'd seen his act. Henderson still wore his yellow shirt, but for television he'd changed his Bermuda shorts for green bell-bottoms. As he rolled his pants above his knees, a fiddle player with an amplified hookup and a young girl named Lee Anne on ringing tambourine stepped in close. They were playing "The Man from Galilee." Henderson didn't waste any time. He began smashing the bottles. The crowd squeezed forward as he stacked the bricks on the empty case. His shoes were off and the tambourine was ringing. The fiddle was playing the refrain faster and faster. Suddenly Henderson shouted, "Here, Jesus! Here! Here I am!" He jumped onto the glass and began his leaping, chin high, stomping. He screamed. "Jesus! Jesus! *Jeeeeeesus Chhhhhhrrriiiiiist!!*"

The short act ended and the crowd applauded. The music softened and slowed down as Henderson showed them his feet. Arlo was slapping him on the back and shouting.

"Pure faith! Pure and unadulterated faith! Any of yall like to come up here and try and match it? How about it?"

The crowd was whistling, shouting, and applauding as the cameras zoomed in for tight shots of Henderson's feet and the rapture in his eyes.

It was 8:05, twelve minutes from official sunset, when Littlejohn joined us in the Chuck Wagon. He sat up on the backbar, sipping on a pint of whiskey in a paper bag. "You can hear better here than in the doggone front row. That Rydell knows his stuff doesn't he?"

Buck said, "Damn right. T. T., before this night's over you're going to be wishing you'd run for Congress."

T. T. was quiet. You could tell he was thinking about it. Then he snapped out of it. "Hey! Where's this Real McCoy bird?"

Buck set his beer down and counted out ten twenty-dollar bills. "He'll be here. Here's your cut so far, and there's plenty more coming." He gave him another hundred dollars. "And that's for all this fine promo work. T. T., by God, you should have been a circus man."

T. T. folded the money in his shirt pocket. "Thanks, Buck. But damn it, where's McCoy?"

"He's coming. He's coming. We ought to be seeing his trucks any second now. Come on, get yourself something to drink before you dehydrate."

Arlo had both hands raised. "Folks, for yall in the back, Jessee Royal Stamps is now on Lord's Prayer number nine hundred and ninety. That's it, folks! Ten more! That's all he's got to do and he's got six more minutes to do it in. So now while we're waiting for the glorious finish I'm going to introduce a few members of the congregations that are represented here tonight."

He introduced the Groats, Eudora Gulley, the Deloaches, and Lee Anne Strickland, the nine-year-old girl on tambourine. He pointed out the Robards, who had just surfaced from behind the Littlejohn Feed and Seed Store. "And speaking of world-wide records, right out there in that drain ditch is one that's not going to be taking a back seat to nobody. That's Leo and Maude Robard and their fine daughters Lou-Anne and Gwendolyn, copying out the whole Bible. That's right, folks, and they're prepared to get the thing done if it means going all the way to the California coastline." I wondered if they really had any idea that California wasn't even halfway. When the show was over I'd talk to them and show them the figures. The applause rang out and Arlo shouted, "Amen hallelujah!"

At three minutes before sundown, Jessee Royal Stamps smiled and shut his eyes in the dying sun. He was leaning hard on the podium. I thought he was in pain or had lost his voice.

Buck laughed, "Look at that grass-eater hamming it up."

Jessee cleared his throat and went on in a brand-new

voice. It was deeper, louder; it had more authority. He cruised on by one thgusand and was on one thousand and seven with the last slice of sun dropping over the soybean field. As it vanished, and he rushed through one thousafd and eight, Arlo began hoking around like a master gf ceremonies on a quiz show. "That's it! That's it! Official sunset! One thousand and eight Lord's Prayers. Amen hallelujah! Amen hallelujah!" He bear-hugged Jessee as if he'd won a deep freezer, a new station wagon, and a trip around the world.

"Yessir! Yessir! Yessir! And it happened right here in Charles City, South Carolina." He waved the applause in. "Let's hear it now for Jessee Royal Stamps!" The applause finally died. Arlo came forward and looked out over the crowd. "Jessee says he wants to thank you in his own way."

Jessee moved up and peered into the cameras. "I'd like to let you all in on number one thousand and nine." His voice was faint and scratching and the crowd had to pass the message back.

"He's doing one more. Join in."

"Join in what?"

"Prayer, you fool."

The heads went down and Jessee in tears led them into number one thousand and nine. "Our Father Who art in heaven . . ."

Out on the shoulder of the road, the Robards slipped their brushes into their cans and bowed their heads.

CHAPTER

16

It was dark, and we switched the Chuck Wagon neon on. It was a single red script line spelling out CHUCK WAGON and it reminded me of Pioneer's Conestoga wagon. But I didn't think about it too long. I had so many things on my mind I'd forgotten my hangover. Would Harun get here before the crowd broke? Could we jack up the price to fifteen dollars? Arlo could tell them the Arabs were sticking it to us, the way they did on the oil embargo. And then suddenly I remembered the damn cobra. I'd talked Arlo into it. What if something happened? There was no "if" to it. Something terrible was going to happen. After the next act I'd get him aside and make him take it out. It was a stupid idea, and now he didn't even need it. And then I saw a panel truck with the lights off easing into the back of the lot. It was Harun's Transoceanic Manufacturing, and I wasn't the only one who saw it; Buck was hotfooting it across the lot with the money in the beer case.

I was so relieved I had to have a drink. It tasted great, and I had another, and suddenly I felt wonderful. I would have given my eye teeth if only Monica was here. She

would have loved it. We were going to make so much
money we would damn well need pillowcases to carry it.
The transaction between Buck and Harun went fast, and
in a few minutes they were lugging the stacks of prints to
the Chuck Wagon. I sipped on my drink, remembering the
way Monica had toasted the Verrazano-Narrows Bridge
and the great turnpike trip south, and I raised my glass.
"*Ladies and gentlemen, boys and girls, and children of all
ages, I give you The Great Mozingo.*"

Up on stage, Dr. Omar Stuckey, in his white jacket,
winked at his wife and children. Arlo was pumping his
hand. "Dr. Omar Stuckey here is from Barnwell, South
Carolina, where he is a practicing medical doctor. Is that
right, sir?"

Dr. Stuckey smiled brightly into the middle camera.
"Yes, that's absolutely correct. I've been there eight
years."

"And you went to medical school in Charleston, South
Carolina, for six years and have been practicing your
trade for over fourteen years? Is that right, too?"

"Yessir. Six years in Atlanta, eight years in Barnwell,
that's fourteen."

Rydell Mitchell went to a split screen. One camera was
on the doctor. The other on his family up on the end of the
flatbed. Dr. Stuckey had joined them.

"And I'd like for you to meet my wife who was a
Browder from Greenville, South Carolina. . . . Now this
is Dawn; she's five. . . . This is Kimberly; she's three.
And this is our little Chippie who will be two on June
fifteenth."

Arlo moved into the shot. "What a fine-looking family.
I'll bet you're just as proud as you can be."

Dr. Stuckey had warmed up. "And I'd like to say hello
to all my in-laws in Savannah and Augusta and the great
gang out in the plutonium-recycling wing in Barnwell."

"Wonderful. Now, Dr. Stuckey, we'd like for you to
identify the medicine in this bottle that I am now placing
in your hand."

Dr. Stuckey read the label. "It says oil of strychnine,

and the Pure Food and Drugs Act very clearly states that the material inside must be exactly what it purports to be on the outside or it will be in violation—"

Arlo cut him off. "Yessir, we understand all that, but can't you run some little test on it for the good folks?" He smiled down at Harlan Estee. "We've got a couple doubting Thomases out here with us tonight."

Dr. Stuckey uncapped the bottle. Professionally, he wedged the cap between two fingers and poured a few drops in his hand. He cupped it to his nose and frowned. "It's straight strychnine. One hundred percent. I'd stake my reputation on it."

Arlo raised both hands and took over. "There you have it folks. Here's a bona-fide medical doctor with over twenty years total experience and he's staking his reputation on it. Now is there anyone out there that needs any more proof?"

He pointed at Harlan. "How about you, sir?"

Harlan tipped his cap. "O.K. with me, sport."

"One more thing. Dr. Stuckey here says he is absolutely in no way prescribing this for anybody. His appearance here is strictly for the public service of identification. Is that correct, sir?"

"Absolutely correct. Absolutely."

Harun had left for Savannah, and Buck and I were stacking the prints on the counter. Everything was falling into place. Everything was perfect. Even the weather was perfect. No clouds, no wind, no mosquitoes, and it was going to be a full moon. The plan was to sell the prints from the counter before the snake-handling exhibit. With no purchase limit, Buck said they would move faster than red-necks at a white-sock sale. I told Buck my fifteen-dollar idea, but he shook his head. "Bo, this ain't New York. You can't pull that crap down in here. These people will tear you up." He punched my shoulder. "Good idea, though. Listen, I told Harun to tune us up another batch. When this hits the news we're going to have to beat them off with sticks."

I said, "Great. How many?"

"Twenty thousand."

"How much time?"

"Two days. Maybe three. We'll have them mail in the money to Bibleland."

I laughed, "Well, so much for his hard work and slow drying."

The stage lights were flickering, and two guitar pickers and Lee Anne on tambourine were leading a slow procession up the steps, singing, "I Walked and Jesus Talked," and lining up behind the card table. Henderson Moke was in the middle. Next were the Deloaches and the Groats. On the end, singing louder than anyone, was Jessee Royal Stamps. Arlo moved in on the mike. "Ladies and gentlemen, for Sheriff T. T. Littlejohn, who helped make this presentation possible, and for all yall out there from Charles City and out there in videoland, we are going to show our appreciation for your understanding with a revealed test of our faith. I'm now going to ask one of our members to step forward and drink down this strychnine."

Littlejohn was hissing through his teeth. "Wish he'd quit mentioning my name like that. Buck, when in the hell's McCoy getting here?"

Buck cupped his hand on his shoulder. "Won't be long now. Come on, grab yourself a beer."

Arlo had called for a volunteer. As if on signal the whole row stepped forward. Littlejohn groaned. "Lord, I hope that sweet little Lee Anne don't do it. Damn, I don't like this."

Arlo selected a short, swarthy man who introduced himself as T. Poole Denny, a sheet-metal worker from Tuxedo Flats, Georgia. T. Poole Denny had big biceps and triceps and looked like a weight lifter. He stood on an angle, keeping his pectorals pumped up and his legs rigid. He was wearing a tight T-shirt with the arms ripped out and had oiled himself for the camera.

Arlo asked him, "Mr. T. Poole Denny, have you ever drunk strychnine before?"

"Five times, Reverend Arlo. Five times for the Lord Jesus." Despite his clothes, T. Poole Denny kept it formal.

Buck nudged Littlejohn, trying to calm him down. "Probably a geek. Hell, I've seen those mothers scarf down whole chickens. I mean bones, feet, feathers, and all. Nothing bothers them."

Littlejohn was biting his bottom lip and twitching. "This is terrible. Terrible."

Arlo raised his voice. "You people in the back back there, you hear that? T. Poole Denny here says he's drunk it five times for the Lord."

T. T. was getting more and more nervous. "What's a geek?"

Buck said, "Some people call them gommlers. They put a live chicken between him and a bottle of Thunderbird. He eats the bird before he gets the juice."

Littlejohn swallowed. "All of it?"

"Hell, it's only a pullet. One and a half, maybe two pounds. But you know, T. T., you don't see many around like you used to. But I'll tell you something, if this recession keeps going they'll be coming around. I can cold guarantee that."

T. T. couldn't bear watching Arlo, and he wanted Buck to keep talking. "How come they call them gommlers?"

"Guess it was the first guy's name." He laughed and popped a beer open. "Maybe he sold the franchise."

Arlo's arm was around T. Poole's heavy shoulders. "Well, boy." He nodded at the bottle. "I can't speak for the people watching this show on their color television sets at home. But I'd say that the good people of Charles City are ready when you are." T. Poole nodded once. He took the bottle and dropped to one knee in a combination genuflection and sprint position. He stared at the floor, getting ready. Then, raising his hands straight, up he rose with it, screaming, "*Jeeeeeeeesuuuuus! I love you!*" T. Poole Denny drank the two ounces down. Then, smacking his lips, as if he wanted more, he reached for the water. Dr.

Omar Stuckey came loping across the stage. He had his stethoscope and his stopwatch. He took his pulse. He checked his pupils, then his heart. He flicked his pencil light on and depressed his tongue and peered in. Suddenly, T. Poole dropped to the floor. The audience sucked in and raised up on their toes to see him. He was on his fingertips doing push-ups, and he was picking up the pace. He was going too fast to count. He shot back up and, standing at parade rest, he was barely breathing hard. Stuckey examined him again. "This man is as healthy as anyone here. This is amazing!"

Arlo moved in shouting, "A miracle! A miracle! Right here before your eyes and ears. A genuine miracle! And don't forget you saw it here tonight in Charles City, South Carolina, on the first night of The Jubilee Crusade."

The crowd loved it. Buck loved it. I loved it. The word was out on the radio, and cars were backed up a solid block in the parking lot. The print sale was going to be wild. When the eleven o'clock TV news broke we'd be famous all over South Carolina, all over Georgia and the whole Bible-pounding hard-lard belt. We'd go national. I jotted a note down for Arlo to announce: "All mail orders to Bibleland, Georgia. Ten dollars will cover packaging, handling, shipping. One week delivery." I had to find out the Zip code. Fifteen thousand prints would barely scratch the surface. We'd hit them with the Jordan water. Then the pieces of silver and the black velvet banners. Maybe the splinters from the cross. The customer list would be a gold mine. I was doing my zooma-zooma through my teeth as I stacked the prints on the counter and got the beer cases in position. It was going to be great. It was going to be fantastic, incredible, and we were both going to be rip-roaring millionaires.

The beer wasn't doing anything for Littlejohn, and he opened a pint of Buck's Wild Turkey. "Buck, damn it, level with me. Where's McCoy? People are asking me too many questions."

"T. T., the old boy is just running a little late. That's all.

Keep an eye out for his lights." He slapped his knees and slid down from the backbar. "Last act coming up. Come on, let's get this stock ready."

Up on the stage the entire sixteen-member congregation of the Christ Revealed in Flames Church were lighting their blowtorches from a single torch in the center. They seemed paler than the other Crusaders, and their clothes looked like they'd been made a long time ago. The men wore white shirts and clip-on bow ties. The women's hems were at their knees, and their shoes looked orthopedic. The crowd pulled back as the flames shot out and the nine men and seven women with their sleeves rolled up came forward. They were adjusting the jets from blue to the cooler yellow. They were absolutely nonchalant as they passed the flames over their forearms as if they were stripping furniture or taking off wallpaper. The group behind them kept singing as if nothing was happening. One demonstrator fanned the yellow flame over his head and the singed-hair smell held in the air all the way back to the Chuck Wagon. Another pushed her shoes off. She flexed her arches and moved the flame around her ankles, down the foot, and across the toes. The fire-baptism celebration was silent and confined to the small area by the card table. It was also short. It was over before some people even knew it had started. Arlo came forward. "Not even singed! Not a sign of a burn or a blister! Lord! Lord! They're not even red! Praise Jesus!"

Dr. Omar Stuckey with his black bag joined him. Arlo shoved the mike in his face. "What do you say, Doctor?"

"I can't believe it. Not even a blister. I just cannot believe it!"

Arlo was long-striding up and down the flatbed. He was shouting. "Well, we believe it! We believe it! By the almighty living lights of our sweet Lord Jesus Christ, *yes Lord, we believe it!*"

The short blowtorch act had ended, and Arlo came forward. He was talking about the Crusade and what would happen when they marched out onto the infield at

Darlington, and what would happen on the White House lawn in Washington. In another minute he would start pitching the prints and the money would be rolling in. I'd arranged three stacks of prints down the counter and three beer cases underneath. One for Buck. One for Loretta. One for me. Each stack was a six-inch-high five-hundred ream. Each stack was worth five thousand dollars, and behind us on the backbar were thirteen thousand and five hundred more, and backing that was Harun running up another twenty thousand on twenty-pound, glossy-finished poster paper on some oversized Xerox.

But something was going on with Arlo. He seemed funny on the monitor. Different. Maybe he could see Loretta spread out on the kitchen table. Maybe he'd been thinking about her too long and didn't want to spoil the dream? He was afraid of her? Loved her? Hated her? A. J. had said the only person he'd ever loved was Jesus. But he'd even managed to walk out on him. The son of a bitch was so spooky there was no telling what was going on. I tapped Buck. "Look at him."

Littlejohn elbowed in. "Anything wrong?"

Buck laughed. "He's saving himself for the pitch. T. T., wait till you see this boy in action."

I was watching the monitor for a close-up. It came. There was a new luster in his eyes. "Glycerine! He's using glycerine. That's an old show-biz trick."

"You're right Bo. T. T., all that old boy wants to do is go to Hollywood." He adjusted the color and the fine tuner. "Hell, he's been marching all day and screaming all night. Something's probably gotten loose." He looked over the stock. "Bo, you ready?"

"Almost. How about Arlo?"

"This is it. Yeah, this is it."

I cleared the end of the counter. "O.K., we're set. Open their cages. O.K., Arlo . . . Sell their asses."

Except for a pin light on the *Pietà* the stage was dark. Two singers were humming in the mike. There was a pause. It was a long pause. Then another pin came on and Arlo stepped into it like he was announcing a fight at Madison Square Garden. His hands were raised. His palms were up and out. His shadow formed a cross behind him on the Coliseum arch. This was it. Buck nodded. Loretta nodded. I nodded. And T. T. Littlejohn moved back on the backbar out of the way.

Arlo was speaking. " 'My faith shall quench the fires. . . . And I shall feel no pain.' Luke 14, verse 12. When you get home, read it. Study it. It's Gospel Scripture, word and text. And it's what we're doing out here tonight under God's own stars." Buck explained to Littlejohn that going from Egyptian mummification to the Jesus prints was too easy for Arlo Waters. He was an artist and had worked out a new twist. Littlejohn was breathing through his teeth. "I'm going backstage. I want to keep an eye on this bird."

Buck waved him off. "Look at that crowd. They're eating this stuff up. He'll start selling now. Watch. . . . Watch."

Arlo stepped back into the shadows. The choir moved back in on the mike. As the refrain ended, Arlo came back into the light. His lips were on the mike. You could hear him breathe. His voice was richer, lower, deeper—deep down where Orson Welles and the boys who do life-insurance voice-overs work. "The Lord also spoke in Exodus. . . . And in John. . . ."

There was a knock on the Chuck Wagon door. It was Lee Anne Strickland, the tambourine girl, with a memo-rized message from Arlo. "Mr. Mozingo, Reverend Waters doesn't want to sell those pictures of Jesus until after the exhibit. He says he doesn't want to break the mood."

Buck said, "Fine, honey. Here, take a box of popcorn. Thanks now."

When she left he said, "Crap! What in the hell's he up to?"

The camera was in on a tight close-up of Arlo's eyes. I realized the shine wasn't glycerine; it was something else.

But what? What was it? Onstage, the hummers had closed in around Arlo again. The pin light brightened. Then it slowly tracked over to a screened box being slid out of the wings.

Loretta had seen it. "Oh Lord."

Buck was scratching the backs of his hands. "Hot damn."

Littlejohn's elbows were on the counter. He was leaning forward, trying to get closer. "Is that what I think it is? How in the hell did I get mixed up in this, anyway?"

"Don't sweat it, T. T. It's all rehearsed. Listen, just sit back and enjoy it."

Loretta was laughing. I couldn't tell if she was drunk or hysterical. Or if she really liked it. "Yeah, T. T., you do that. Enjoy it."

Arlo's voice was peaking. " 'I shall take up the serpents of death.' Ladies and gentlemen, it's right there in the Bible. Matthew 16, verse 4. 'I shall take up the serpents of death and I shall have no fear.' You hear that? No fear! I'll say it again. *No fear!* I'll shout it out, NO FEAR!" He screamed so loud the glass in the popcorn and snow-cone machines rattled. "NO FEAR!!!"

Almost on cue Dr. Omar Stuckey's Buick Electra pulling the silver Airstream eased out on the lot and up onto the Dixiana. He was heading back to Barnwell.

Eudora Gulley was at Arlo's side. The choir was humming. Behind them were the Deloaches, Henderson Moke, T. Poole Denny, and Jessee Royal Stamps. Eudora, the mistress of the serpents, led the ceremony off. She was in a long white gown with a small white beanie on the back of her head. It looked like something a confectioner from the chocolate room at Hershey's would wear. She said a quick prayer, with her hands folded in her full sleeves, and then nodded for the music. Two amplified guitars, a fiddle, and Lee Anne on tambourine moved in on the mike. It was a top-forty Gospel song, "Me and Jesus Got Our Own Thing Going." They started it off slow, with Lee Anne whispering the words. As she finished the first refrain, Eudora slid the screen top back. The crowd sucked in and pulled back. The first snake came out. The second. Then two at a time. Then three at a time. Fourteen. Seventeen. Twenty-six. Twenty-nine.

Loretta said, "Oh my God."

T. T. Littlejohn said, "Lordy."

Buck was soft-talking Littlejohn to take it easy. I couldn't believe any of it and kept looking for the cobra. Thirty-five. Thirty-eight. Forty-one. Before the second refrain was over, over fifty snakes were on stage being passed back and forth. The music was building, climbing. The small corals were held like tiny birds' nests. The heavy rattlers and moccasins were supported with both hands. They were wound around their waists and draped over their shoulders. I couldn't find the cobra. The music was picking up and the congregation was doing little shuffles and soft clogs. Then quick heel-and-toe tap dancing. They were handing the snakes back and forth faster and faster. They were snatching them, tossing and catching them as if they were red hot. The music went faster, almost bluegrass. Every few seconds a loud yip or yodel ripped out as they danced and whirled and filled every foot of the stage. Then I saw the cobra whipping around and looking around and my teeth began chattering. I almost threw up as I watched his rising, swaying head.

Arlo had gone back in the shadows and I knew there was no way for him to pitch the prints now. When he came back he had taken his shirt off. He came on, flexing his muscles in time with the music. He had picked up T. Poole Denny's moves and was improving on them. He had oiled himself for the cameras. Probably Vaseline, maybe Buttrin. He nodded to Eudora that he was ready, and, smiling, she handed him a cottonmouth moccasin.

Littlejohn was breathing hard. "I didn't know he did that."

Buck spat. "Just showing his ass."

But something else was going on. Arlo was feeding on

the cameras. The chance to go national was too much for
him. He was doing silly things, crazy things. He wrapped
the snake around his neck. He let it glide across his
stomach. He was holding his breath for the cameras and
shooting his pectoral cuts out like a Mr. Universe candi-
date. The snake eased into the stomach cavity and wound
around his waist. It climbed up his back. Arlo was
grinning and leering and bobbing up and down with the
music. His tenseness and the heat and the grease had
made the snake nervous. It was moving fast, too fast.
People in the front row were trying to get back. Eudora
moved over and took the snake. She swayed with it and
began humming and talking to it. Her heavyset body was
rocking as she calmed it and eased it back across the
stage. Then she stooped and poured the long moccasin
back into the box. I couldn't keep my eyes off the monitor.
Arlo didn't like being upstaged by Eudora. With one hand
he scooped up a coral from a Deloache twin and wound it
around his wrist like a bracelet. He strutted downstage
toward a camera, draping it over his neck. He grinned in
the lens. A second camera moved in to get him in profile
and Rydell went back and forth with one-shots. Arlo
pumped his bicep up and the tiny coral slid inside his
elbow and up and over the big blue vein. He rolled his
eyes, pretending he was scared. Littlejohn was wheez-
ing. "This is getting to me."

Buck shook his head. "It's a dumb act. He couldn't do
two minutes in a truck stop." I didn't care what he could
do in a truck stop. I was petrified watching the cobra
rising up three and four feet and looking around. Arlo
would never pitch the prints now. There was also a
chance we would have to eat every damn one of them.
Buck was biting his bottom lip and scratching his knuckles. Loretta mixed a low yodel with a long sigh. "Crazy
time, right?"

On stage Arlo was planning higher things. He bowed
elaborately and presented the coral to Eudora. Then
he took the diamondback from Henderson Moke. The

twenty-six-pound snake was five feet long and big around as an orange-juice can. It had a three-inch set of rattles. Arlo held it in front of the camera as he scratched it and rubbed it like a long dog. He tickled its chin until the black tongue flickered. Then he held it close to his grinning face as he began sassing and mincing around in a fast heel-and-toe step, shouting, "All right, Jesus! All right!"

The Groats and Lee Anne were singing,

"Me and Jesus got our own thing going,
Me and Jesus got it all worked out. . . ."

The music went faster, wilder. Arlo caught up with it and, holding the snake in front like a partner, did the old Twist. Eudora raised her hand and slowed the beat. Then she started for Arlo. He saw her coming and dropped into a weight lifter's crouch. He stretched the snake out to its full five feet and pushed him straight up over his head shouting, "Jesus! Jesus! Jesus!"

Littlejohn was frantic. "Goddamn it, Buck. We got to stop it. Somebody's going to get hurt."

"Easy T. T. Easy now."

"Easy, shit. I got to live here."

Eudora gave quick instructions. She picked up the swaying cobra like he was an old friend and slid him in a box. The other snakes were put away. Then she glided over to reason with Arlo. The screen was split. Rydell had them both on close-ups. Eudora was trying to smile. The mike picked her up. "Hush now, Arlo. Hush now. You're all worked up. Jesus don't mind you calming down."

Arlo jumped back. He held the rattler like a pitchfork. One end was wrapped around his left arm. His right held the head. He minced around, mocking her. He jabbed again and backed up, laughing at her. Eudora's hand was on Arlo's shoulder. "You've got to simmer down now, son. You're making a spectacle of yourself out here." Arlo pulled away with his sly and crafty look.

Littlejohn said it slowly. "That son of a bitch is crazy."

No one argued with him. Maybe Arlo was crazy. But something else was going on. He had moved from selling to being sold. The cameras and the lights and the crowd, and the chance to go national, had pushed him to the edge. But he had made the big next step all by himself. It didn't have anything to do with Loretta, or sex, or money, or his name in lights, or immortality. It was simple. Whatever the Stark Valley Church and the Revealed Church of the Nazarene and the Flaming Cross believed, he believed. He had fallen two years behind, but now he was catching up, and we were going to eat thirty-five thousand dollars worth of twelve-by-twenty-four Xerox prints of Jesus.

All Buck said was, "Oh boy." But it was the hollow way he said it, and I knew we were doomed.

Eudora grabbed Arlo by the shoulders. Her voice was smooth, soothing. "Easy, Arlo. Remember what I told you, Arlo? Remember, Arlo? Arlo?" But Arlo wasn't listening. Or couldn't hear. He jerked away. The camera zoomed in on his eyes. He looked like he'd just climbed the wall at Bellevue; like the famous shot of Charles Manson. Suddenly he cracked out a crazy laugh and rushed at Harlan Estee. He was at the edge, jabbing the snake's head down. The crowd was screaming and panicking below. They were trapped at the flatbed, looking straight up at Arlo leering straight down.

Harlan shouted. "Back! That moron's crazy. Back!"

But the crowd was pressing forward to see, and no one would move. Littlejohn unbuttoned his holster. "Screw this. I'm fixing his ass."

Buck held him down. "It's O.K., T. T. It's the old clown's rush. We do it all the time."

Arlo had the snake over his head. He dropped to one knee shouting "Jesus! I love you!" Eudora moved in quickly. But Arlo was quicker. He leaped to his feet and held it over his head. He paused for another screaming "Jesus!" Then he slammed it to the floor. The crowd

gasped. No one moved. No one spoke. They were paralyzed. Petrified. The camera zoomed in on the diamondback and held it. The only sound was the buzzing of the
generator and the beetles clicking against the lights. And
then in a quick convulsion the snake was coiling and its
rattles were rising. The microphone picked it up. The
twin two-hundred-watt speakers pushed it out over the
crowd and up into the chinaberry trees. It sounded like
BB shot in a Ping-Pong ball. The dry *tick, tick, tick* of a
tiny doll's rattle. It went faster, higher, louder. The
snake's scooped head was flatter; he was puffing up,
tightening up, and his black eyes and tongue were
glistening. Arlo dropped to his knees before him. "Jesus!
Jesus!" He spread his arms and chest and throat screaming, "Strike! You demon of the dark! In Jesus's name, I
command you! *Strike!*"

The snake did.

Arlo took three steps back, then three forward. His
knees were suddenly gone, and he staggered, held out his
hands to break the fall, and dropped. The camera came in
tight on his red face and the pounding pulse in his neck.
Suddenly, Rydell cut to another camera to catch the
fast-moving diamondback streaking off the front of the
stage into the absolute center of the crowd.

I've been in a New York City bomb scare and the
rushes at Grand Central. But this was different. Women
screaming. Men cursing. Kids crying. They were shouting that the snake had bitten two more people. That it
was closing in on a third. That there were three more
snakes—four more. It was a stampede. And then suddenly the crowd was gone. The only thing on the monitor was
the lot and the big diamondback. Littlejohn, with his
pistol, and Buck, with his forked stick, were on him. The
camera zoomed in tight as Buck pronged the snake to the
ground. He lifted him up and they headed for the box. Up
on stage Eudora was holding Arlo's head in her lap. She
was stroking him and humming. Rydell picked up a shot
of the *Pietà* to show the resemblance. He must have

figured it was tasteless and cut back to Arlo's pulse and
the eager faces around him. Buck, Littlejohn, and Loretta were squatting by him. They looked relieved. Buck
said, "How do you feel, boy? You really gave us a scare
there."

Littlejohn was nodding and trying to keep his back to
the camera. The camera zoomed in on Arlo's pale lips.
"Mr. Mozingo, I feel wonderful."

"Fine, we've sent for a doctor. That Stuckey fellow got
an emergency call."

Arlo shook his head once. "No, Mr. Mozingo. No
medical attention. This one's my business."

"Come on, Arlo. All he needs is a couple minutes. Hell
boy, you might die. Then what?"

Arlo raised a finger and tried to smile. "That's the
question, ain't it? I tell you, I'm ready. If He wants to pull
me on through this to do his work, I'm ready. If He wants
to bring me on home, I'm ready for that, too."

Loretta was leaning in. "Come on, stud, listen to Buck.
Maybe you can buy me that drink you promised."

Arlo's eyes met hers. "No ma'am, I ain't studying you
now. I got other fish to fry."

Buck was worried. "At least let me get the snakebite
kit."

Arlo shook his head again. He was getting weaker. "It's
out of my hands. It's out of all yall's hands. It's entirely up
to Him now."

Eudora was whispering in his ear and he nodded. Then
he closed his eyes and began trembling.

CHAPTER

17

Buck, Littlejohn, Loretta, and I were sitting in front of the Chuck Wagon, waiting. We'd been drinking since they'd carried Arlo to the school bus. Rydell Mitchell and his crew had gone back to Savannah. If Arlo died, the film would be solid-gold news. If he lived, it was nothing but another snakebite session they could lay off to an anthropological society. It was nine-thirty and still light. Enough breeze to move the candy wraps and snow-cone sleeves. But not enough for the popcorn boxes. Out on the lot, a guy with basketball knee pads and a metal detector was sweeping where the crowd had panicked. He was built for his work—low to the ground, with thick legs and solid arms. Littlejohn, slumped low in his canvas chair, had finished a pint of Wild Turkey by himself and was on his second. He was still sober, still worried. He was watching the coin man digging in the flat grass. "Maybe that's the profession I could try. I could move around at night and no one would know me." Buck slung his leg over his chair arm. "Knock it off, T. T. That boy's going to be fine. Hell, you couldn't kill him with a crowbar."

All I could think about was Arlo dying. It was my fault.
I'd pushed him into it. If it hadn't been for me pimping it
wouldn't have happened. I was also thinking about the
fifteen thousand Jesus prints and what in the hell I was
going to do in the morning.

We sat there watching four kids up on the flatbed.
They'd seen a lot of television and had a gift for panto-
mime. They were acting out Arlo's death scene. A tall,
serious, moon-faced girl was the snake. They were
arguing about how Arlo had fallen. "Damn it, Ralph, you
did a stupid swan dive! Quit trying to hog everything!
Reverend Arlo Waters sort of crumbled. You saw him.
Now do it right!"

They did it again. This time Ralph crumbled and the
snake slithered over him and in a series of fast S's moved
downstage. Suddenly, a trailer mother was running
across the lot, hollering, "Elgin, you little snot! Get down
from there!" She climbed the flatbed and grabbed him by
the ear. "You ape! Wait till your father hears this one.
He's going to beat your little ass until you can't walk."

A dog was crossing the lot with a foot-long wrapper in
his mouth. The metal-detector man was on his knees,
digging. And then we heard a guitar tuning up in the bus.

Loretta sighed. "Oh Lord. I bet he's dying right this
second."

Buck swung over. "Will you hush that."

I felt terrible and kept staring at the ground. "Buck, tell
me the truth. Just once."

Buck spat, "I've already told you, he's going to be all
right. Now leave me alone."

While Arlo was fighting the forces of darkness, Buck
began talking. Nonstop. He couldn't have stopped if he
wanted to. He said the cameras were the cause of it all. "I
tell you it's television. The whole country's camera crazy.
And the preachers are the worst. Time was they'd settle
for a chicken dinner and a piece of ass from the soprano.
Nowadays they've got recording studios and satellite
hookups. Everybody's got to be a goddamn superstar." He

reached over and squeezed Loretta's knee. "Hon, run over and see how he's doing."

He kept on drinking and rolled on about how he was running a drive-in theater when JFK and Lee Harvey Oswald were killed. "That right there was the biggest week in drive-in history. And you know why? Every damn network kept replaying the assassination. Hell, they thought they were performing a public service. But let me tell you something, no one was watching. The minute they were cut off from their regular crap they panicked. Hell, we had them lined up four blocks before the sun went down. I had to let the overflow sit out on the grass." I didn't see the connection with Arlo, but it kept me from thinking about him. Buck eased the ashes from his cigar as Loretta crossed over the lot from the bus. She raised her shoulders and shrugged. Nothing had happened. Buck popped open a beer for her as she sat down, sighing. "They'll know something around midnight."

Buck sucked in through his teeth. I wanted him to keep on talking. But something else was on his mind. He kept watching the metal-detector man and drinking. When his beer can was empty he squeezed it flat. Then he folded it back and forth until it snapped.

I drifted out on the road shoulder and kicked a beer can two or three times. I threw it at a phone pole. The Robards had left a message: "And Eban begat." The can missed and I heard it splash down in the drain ditch. I sat down in the phone booth in the Gulf station driveway, drumming my fingers on the metal shelf. Up on the ceiling a local had carefully printed out JIMMY HOFFA PLEASE CALL YOUR OFFICE. The guitar picker was still working the four chords over and over again, and I began keeping time with it. The wind had died, but now it was coming back up and I could smell some late eaters frying chicken. Maybe Arlo was resting. Maybe now was the time to call Ernie and Greene and get it over with. Why not? Life goes on. The coin man was still going on. The Charles City lights were going on. Little squares of light.

Inside, people were getting up from dinner and turning on
the news or the movie of the week. They were feeding the
dog and thinking about making love after the kids went to
sleep. They were planning things in twos and threes and
fours with houses and cars and kids and jobs. Everybody
had somebody; everybody had something. Buck had
Loretta. Littlejohn had Mrs. Littlejohn. Everyone had
somebody. But me, I had no one. Nothing. Not even a job.
I banged my fist on the phone-book shelf. I had to get
ahold of myself. I had to do something positive. The
negatives were taking over. I dialed the operator and read
off my credit-card number. As I sat there waiting for the
intercept and the announcement that the card had been
revoked and I should mail it in immediately or suffer
egregious action, I tried to squeeze out a zooma-zooma.
But it wouldn't come. The call went through and Ernie
answered.

"Joe! It's great hearing your voice. Where the hell are
you?"

"South Carolina."

"Great! God's country! Sock it to the bastards. Boy, if
Old Ernie was in your shoes he'd damn well do it."

It was Old Ernie. He was stone drunk. "Do what,
Ernie?"

"Living like a king, that's what."

"Sure, Ernie, sure. What's going on?"

His voice dropped. "Well, Joe, they're screwing me
over again. O.K., straight from the old shoulder. I had a
couple knocks at the Legion. O.K., I got in a little trouble
and I had to spend the night down at the station. They
didn't lock me up—just made me sit on the bench until
Greene got me out. Well, the long and the short of it is
they've got Old Ernie in a holding pattern on the Big
Apple. They want you to stay with them for three or four
more weeks."

I made a quick adjustment. "Well, Ernie, I've had a few
offers. I'd have to think about it."

"Joe, damn it, tell them to screw off. You don't need
them. Get out while you can. I'm telling you it's all over in

this country for the salesman. Mavericks like Bronson and you and Old Ernie, we've got to go. We bring in the big accounts, but then they've got to sweat us keeping them. Joe, they don't want any wild men anymore. They want order takers, that's all."

"O.K., Ernie, maybe you're right. I'll give it some thgught."

"Thataboy, Joe. You know something, me and you, we're exactly alike. We just don't take the bullshit."

"You're right, Ern. Take care now."

"You too, Joe. Good-night now."

A month. At least I'd have my office. A place to make phone calls and go to the john. A car. My expense account. It's easier finding a job when you've got one. When you don't, they treat you like a leper.

The moon was edging up down the road and the tin roofs were shining. It was getting lighter out on the Dixiana and in the bean fields, but back in the shadows the school bus was dark. Arlo would be dead by midnight. Here he was dying and I was sweating out a stupid phone call to Omaha. Things were getting into perspective fast, and I checked Greene's home number in my black book and dialed the bastard. He was surprised, and while he was clearing his throat I got the jump and laid it in flat. "Ernie said you wanted to talk."

Then I leaned back in the booth, watching the moon as he song-and-danced about Pioneer being a sound company and respecting the feelings of their employees. It sounded like he was reading it from a promotional flyer. He finally came to the point. "Joe, we're on the spot with Ernie right now." His voice was smooth and forceful. Right out of the old sales manual. "I'm sure you can appreciate that?" He wanted me to stay on for one more month.

I told him I was on the spot too. That I didn't want to rush into another job until it was the right one. I said I needed three months. He understood, and suggested two. I said, "No, it wouldn't be worth it. Let's forget it."

He came back fast. "O.K., Joe, you're right. You want

three months? Three months it is. I'll send you a letter."

"O.K., Mr. Greene. That will do it."

"Call me Edgar."

"O.K., Edgar."

"And you'll be back in New York in a few days?"

"I'll be there."

"Joe, we've had our little differences, but I've always liked you and I've always admired you. I always knew when it came right down to it I could count on you." He was off on a long "honesty, loyalty, integrity" pitch, and I let him run it out. When he ended, I kept the edge out of my voice.

"Anything else on your mind?" I was way ahead, and I was going to stay there.

His voice dropped, but it stayed firm and he didn't rush it. "No, that's it, Joe. Thanks again."

"O.K., take it easy now, Edgar, and say hello to Ernie for me."

I hung up and sat there trying to sort things out. The moon was higher, and the bright marmalade color was flickering over the tin roofs and the bean fields and the mailboxes. I might be able to stretch the three months to six. Maybe longer. It would give me time to look around. The thing to do was call Carson Miller at Careers Unlimited in the morning. And then a chill hit me; the music had stopped. It was all over; Arlo Waters was dead. The bus lights were weaker, the trailing lights were out. I stood up, then I sat back down with my heart pounding in my throat. This was it, and I couldn't handle it. I knew I had to go over and pay my respects. What could I say? As I sat there with my teeth chattering, trying to phrase something to say to Eudora, and something else for the reporters, and something else for the police, I knew I had to talk to someone. Costo? Jake? Ethel Bernstein? No, I needed more than sympathy, more than advice. I had to really talk the whole thing out. And then without even realizing it I was dialing 0 and 814, the code for Lorraine; I was calling Dad person-to-person.

In five seconds I knew Dad was too up and excited for me to bring him down with my snakebite-and-heading-for-poverty news, and I decided to wait. "Joey, I got a whole new game plan out here. First off, I checked out a few disco spots. Jesus Christ, you can't hear yourself think. And the owners are starving; this bunch doesn't buy anything. Like I said, all they want to do is get laid. So I said, Mahaffey, this crap can't last. People want to relax and hear the music and maybe a few jokes and a little patter. I've been in this business too long and I know what I'm talking about."

He'd figured that the best listening music was Spanish and had come up with a whole new club—"South of the Border." The new neon was a bullfighter and a charging bull in red, black, and yellow. Inside, the decor was serapes and ponchos and a six-foot painting of a Mexican taking a siesta under a big sombrero.

I finally said, "It sounds like the old Granada."

"Naw, that was a dog to end all dogs. It was too sophisticated for these monkeys out here. You got to hit them over the head. South of the Border means Mexican, and everybody knows it. And Joey, this time it's working; we took in over two thousand bucks Saturday."

He was talking faster and sounding even more excited. "We got this little three-piece Mexican band that came in the last two Saturdays; they were terrific. If this business keeps up I'm going to try them out on Fridays. And listen, I got this gal, she lives in a trailer down the road, and she can sing her ass off. She plays her own guitar. Joey, she's dark, and people think she's really Mexican, but would you believe it, she's from Altoona."

"Sounds good."

"Damn right it's good. She's only worked one weekend, but next week I'm putting her on full-time."

There was absolutely no "wonderfuls" and no "greats" and no hype, and I figured it all had to be true. There was also not one word about my coming back out there to help out. Finally, after another ten minutes of my not saying anything about Arlo or Buck, or even telling him where I was calling from, we said good-night.

As I sat there kicking my ass for not asking him what he thought I should do, and at the same time glad that I didn't, something happened. Something inside clicked on, and all of a sudden I had this nice smooth feeling that I used to get when I was hitting great tee shots and had my big follow-through going. My voltage was up, and staying up, and, without even thinking, I was dialing Greene again. I even remembered the bastard's number.

"It's me, Edgar." It was a cinch calling him Edgar. "I'm sorry, old man, but three months won't do it. Six won't do it either. I've been giving it some thought, and, Edgar, it's like this: I need a one-year contract."

"Jesus, Joe, you just agreed. I've got your word on three months."

"Scratch it, forget it, I've changed my mind. Listen, Edgar, I know this is too quick a decision for you. Call me back. Here, I'll give you the phone number."

"Forget it, Joe. O.K., you got it. One year. I'll draft a letter in the morning." I waited a few beats. Then I said, "Terrific, Edgar, you're doing the right thing."

"And you'll be in New York in a couple of days?"

"Yeah, I'm pulling out of this swamp in the morning. Take care now."

I'd come out on top of the son of a bitch. One year. In that time anything could happen and probably would. I sat in the phone booth, drumming my fingers on the steel shelf and thinking about Arlo. And then I saw Buck and Eudora out on the highway. The moon was coming up directly behind them. It was Coca-Cola red and looked like it was out of an old Road Runner cartoon. Eudora was doing all the talking. Buck was nodding his head, agreeing with everything. I knew it was Arlo. They were deciding where to bury him. What to tell the papers. I trotted over. "What happened? What happened? What happened to Arlo?"

Buck said, "He's fine. Fine. He'll be O.K."

Eudora moved in quick. "Don't be lying like that. That boy's in there fighting the death tremens right this second."

Buck's hand was on my shoulder. I pushed it away but he put it back. "Bo, she's exaggerating. People don't die from a damn snakebite anymore."

She snapped back, "The Elder brothers did back in Brighton. Both bit the same night. Both died the next morning. Within ten minutes of each other."

Buck grimaced and shook his head. "I mean people like Arlo Waters. Eudora, go tend to him. I got to talk to my partner here."

Eudora shrugged, "Suit yourself. But I'm telling you something and you better be listening. We can use yall in there praying."

Buck's hand was still on my shoulder. "Bo, they want the Chuck Wagon and the flatbed crap. They want to go on without us." He paused and almost apologized. "I'm afraid I had to level with them about McCoy."

All I could think about was Arlo Waters. "How about Arlo?"

"Forget him, will you? He'll have a few bad hours. Then it'll be like it never happened."

"Buck, for God's sake tell me the truth for once, just once." I grabbed his arm. "Please, Buck, please!"

"He's going to pull through. Now listen, every now and then I'll throw you a slider. O.K., I'm admitting that. But right now you're worried. So why in the hell would I lie at a time like this? Bo, I've been handling diamondbacks for seventeen years."

"Buck, this is really getting to me. I talked him into it."

"We both did."

I was sounding like a child. "Yeah, but you're used to this stuff. You do it all the time." But Buck was doing something else. He stopped, popped his hands, and framed them around the moon like he was going to take a picture of it. "If that ain't the prettiest thing in the whole damn world, grits ain't groceries, chicken ain't poultry, and, good buddy, old Mona Lisa was a man." Buck had forgotten all about Arlo Waters, the way he had forgotten McCoy and every other disaster that lay behind him, and was looking on down the white line into the middle of the moon, and I'll be damned if he wasn't planning something new. He pounded me on the back. "Bo, right there is your basic southern moon."

"Oh Buck, Jesus! I can't take this."

He looped his arm around my shoulder and squeezed. "Ease up, Bo, ease up. I want you to put everything out of your head for a minute. Now, I want you to listen. We've got about four thousand dollars and we've got the elephants and the snakes. And there's a few bucks back at Bibleland in stocks and props. And on top of all that we still got the Jesus prints."

"Hell! Give it to them. I don't care what you do. I want out. I'm getting the hell out of here." I couldn't see his eyes in the dark, but I kept looking at them anyway. "I've had it. I just got my job back. I'm not screwing around in this jungle anymore."

His hand was back on my shoulder. I left it there this time. "Come on, Bo, I got to talk to you."

I decided to listen to kill the time. It would keep my mind off Arlo.

"O.K., Buck, tell me how beautiful and wonderful everything is."

He laughed once. "Yeah, it's been a long night."

I bit it off. "And it's not over yet."

We started back down the white line. Right into the moon. It was fire orange with deep red highlights and would make a great litho print if you used good heavy rag stock and didn't spare the ink. It seemed to be rolling toward us. Buck's hand firmed. The pitch was coming. "Bo, maybe if I was your age I'd shag on back to New York and get on the Blue Cross and hernia plan with some big corporation. Hell's bells, maybe there ain't nothing like a steady payroll and steady pussy and not having to sweat out the rent every month." He rolled on. He said he'd grown fond of me. At first I'd been too careful for his taste. I worried too much. But now I was beginning to loosen up. I'd handled Arlo like a pro. I had great potential as a front man. With enough time he could train me to read the towns and do the promos. I could sell the Shriners, the Eagles, the Lions, the Elks. He would show me all his tricks and all of Arlo's. I could make a fortune, and with our own corporation it was an unlimited expense account and no withholding tax. Then he got into specifics. . . . With the Jesus prints and the money, we had a base to build on. We could rent a tent. Freddy Logan and Dave Horner were dying to join us. None of it made any sense, and I was dividing everything by four.

I shook my head. "No Buck, no." But he kept on. And on.

For a while I just watched the moon and didn't even listen. If I believed any of it I'd believe that Arlo Waters was out there in the soybeans masturbating and doing wind sprints. He rattled on about how we could save the mud circus from vanishing from the great American scene, about Dallas and Mexico City and Denver and San Francisco. About the money and the women and the champagne and the silk sheets and a hotel suite over-looking the Pacific at Acapulco. Down the road in front of us, the moon was balanced against the black sky, and I could feel it pulling me. Buck's grip tightened. He was believing every possibility. We kept walking. He kept talking. And then I knew where I'd seen the scene. It was Pinocchio. All I had to do was say "maybe" and the fiddle music would start. We'd sing, "Hi-did-dle-de-dee-an-actor's-life-for-me. . . ." Then I'd leap up against the cartoon moon and click my heels and throw away my sales books and sample cases. And then The Great Mozingo would laugh and roar. He'd leap higher and click his heels faster and roar louder and we'd sing the second verse together. Then, arm in arm, we'd go tap dancing down the white line and the silver-spangled trail into the tangerine moon and fame and riches and our

names in lights that would burn forever. All we needed
were top hats and walking canes.

"No, Buck. I'm sorry, but it's got to be no." In my head it
was "Capital N, Capital O: NO." I had had it with the
great swamp and the hard-lard belt. It would make great
sales stories. The snake handlers. The poison drinkers.
The blowtorch people. The phone-pole Baptists, the
end-of-the-world Baptists. I'd be able to hold the buyers'
attention. They'd get to like me and give me their
business. Maybe I'd get a videotape of the snakebite
session from Rydell Mitchell. I'd have Horner from Elgin
Bakery and Murphy from National Biscuit over to see it.
Manny and Abramowitz and Dolores might even come.
"Now, folks, here we are in Charles City, South Carolina.
Right there is Arlo Waters. Now keep your eye on him,
because when this thing starts moving, it moves fast.
That fellow on the end is Henderson Moke. He's worth
watching, too. You won't believe the names down here."
First I'd lay out a few sample shots on their desks. "Mr.
Horner, why don't you and the little woman come out and
see the movies. No trouble at all. I'd love to show them to
you."

And then it began to sour. Buck had said that the South
was like sweet potatoes and peaches. You could only ship
the green ones and the culls north; you had to eat the ripe
ones down here near the patch. He was right. Maybe in
five years Arlo's getting bitten like a lunatic and the
whole Crusade fiasco might be funny. But for now it was
as crazy and as grim as the Jonestown mess. There was
absolutely nothing I could take back to Manhattan.
Nothing would travel. They wouldn't know whether it
was funny or sad or both or what. In the end I'd be the one
that was heading for the Thorazine shots and the pajamas
that tied in the back.

Suddenly Eudora shouted from the school-bus door.
"Yall come! Come! Come see this!"

Buck shook his head. "I ain't going to no prayer
meeting." I stood still. Paralyzed. I wanted to be in there

with him. But I didn't want to see him die. The music was louder, wilder. They were clapping hands. I couldn't tell if it was happy or sad. Suddenly I felt weak and exhausted, like I'd just given a pint of blood and had stood up too fast. Someone should have made him see a doctor. Maybe Buck wanted the publicity and wanted him dead? Rydell Mitchell sure as hell did. Wasn't there some law that a person couldn't refuse treatment? Some wild California transfusion case where the Supreme Court stepped in? I just stood there. I couldn't go forward; I couldn't go back. Arlo had tried to help us, there was no doubt about that. I'd pushed him. He'd sure as hell sold those prints and Jordan water. Maybe he was being punished for it. Maybe we all were. Jesus, I was getting as bad as the rest of them.

The tempo had picked up and everyone was stomping. Everyone was singing. Everyone was clapping and shouting, and the trailing lights were back on and bouncing. It had to be the crisis, and I knew I couldn't face it. I walked out on the lot. Out where it was darkest. There wasn't much ground light and the stars were bright and blue. I used the Big Dipper handle as the Canadian border and traced out my territory. Out in the northwest, west of Chicago, west of Omaha, I picked out a yellow star. "Come on, Lord. One time. I've never asked you for anything much, and you know it. But that poor sap's in there counting on you." I tried to rephrase it, but nothing came. All I could say was, "Come on, Lord. Come on. Forget Monica and Pioneer. I can handle that. But you've just got to give that poor loony a break."

A red star out west of the yellow star was throbbing. A sign? My heart was pumping in my throat. But there it was, red and pulsing. If it kept pulsing, Arlo would live. If it stopped, he'd go to whatever heaven there is that takes in zappo snake handlers. But it was moving too fast, and then I realized it was a jet up around forty thousand feet heading for Atlanta. Suddenly, Arlo was screaming, and my heart dropped. I rushed to the door and eased in.

Eudora took my hand. The only light was the red amplifier pinpoint for Jessee's electric guitar. Arlo was squatting on a pallet in front of the refrigerator Jesus. The rose in the block of Lucite was shining. She whispered that I was just in time. He was freezing one minute and burning up the next. He screamed. "No! No!" His eyes were wild and crazy, then sly and suspicious. He smiled and whispered as he watched the shadows. "I see you. I see you sliding in over there."

Eudora said the devil was stalking him. Arlo followed the vision over one bank of seats and down the other. The devil was circling him, and he was turning with him. "You ain't getting in behind me. Ain't no use even trying."

His muscles and ribs were outlined in the red light like a skinned rabbit. He had rolled the sheet into a long, thick roll—the same shape as a diamondback. He gripped and squeezed it like he was back up on the stage as he followed the stalking devil moving in and out of the shadows. He was smiling. Eudora gave the word, and the music picked up. It was faster, wilder. Almost breakdown bluegrass. She shouted that everyone was with him. That they had enough power to cast out a legion of demons. Arlo didn't hear her or the music. His eyes and ears were on the devil. His big blue arm veins were bulging as if they were arm wrestling. His teeth ground together and his knees began to jerk. Suddenly he was jerking all over.

Eudora shouted, "It's the demons! It's the demons! Pray, yall! Join hands and pray!" We joined hands. We all were praying. I was praying, "Come on, Lord. Come on, Lord."

Arlo leaped up and slung the snake at the wall. Then he dropped to his knees with his hands in a karate position. The spasms moved from his neck down his chest. His whole body was shaking. Eudora sang out, "He's chunking! He's chunking out the demons! He's working them down!"

They had moved from his chest to his legs. She shouted,

"Look, yall! Look!" They moved from his legs to his feet. Suddenly they stopped. His color was coming back. He raised his hand and pointed back out at the red amp light. "Get back! Get on back! Get on back where you belong!"

Eudora was shouting, "Praise Jesus! Praise his name! Arlo's home! He's back to lead us! Amen hallelujah!" She was ecstatic. The room went wild. They were screaming, dancing, clapping, and thanking Jesus. I thanked him too: "Thank you, Lord. I mean it. I really mean it. Thank you. Thank you. Thank you."

Arlo was sitting up. He was soaking wet and smiling. Jessee Royal Stamps was on his knees in front of him, plugging a hole in an orange. Arlo sucked the juice as Eudora mopped down the back of his neck with a cold cloth. He reached out and took Jessee's ball-point. "I made me a pact with Jesus." His voice was clear and firm, and we crowded in close. He drew two small x's where the snake had bit. He dated it. Then he began printing in, "Charles City, S.C." "Every snakebite I get from here on out will be written down as testimony. Just like this." The printing was on an angle, but Arlo's hand was steady. He finished the "S.C." "When we hit a town, I'm having the tattoo man set it up in red and blue." He clicked the ball-point. "That's the way *He* wants it."

Eudora said, "Amen."

Arlo looked at me. "That you, Mahaffey?"

"Yeah, Arlo. I'm really proud of you. Really proud."

"Thanks for being with me. I won't forget it."

I started to say I'd been there all night, but Eudora was too close.

Arlo's hand was out. "Shake, Mahaffey."

I did, hard.

He grinned. "I don't care where you came from or what you are. All I know is you done me the greatest favor in the world." He grinned and held up two fingers side by side. "Me and Jesus. That's the way it's going to be from here on out."

"That's great, Arlo. Fantastic. Man, am I glad."

His face went serious. "And on that other matter, I'd consider it a personal favor if you just forgot it. Can we shake on that?"

"We sure can." I gripped his hand so hard I almost broke it.

The music started again.

> "Me and Jesus got our own thing going,
>   Me and Jesus got it all worked out,
>   Me and Jesus don't need nobody,
>   To tell us what it's all about. . . ."

Eudora was singing with her arm around Jessee Royal Stamps. The Groats were picking and grinning, and Henderson Moke was pounding his foot on the floor so hard the bus was rocking. The Robards had left their work and joined in, and the Hare Krishnas were doing a long monotone vowel and sounding like backup bass. There was no harmony because everyone was singing at the top of their lungs. Including me. Ten more minutes on that bus and I'd come out stone raving mad and ready to march all the way to Washington. Out on the Dixiana I was so up and happy and alert and alive I didn't know what to do. At first I thought I'd run a mile down the road as fast as I could. Then I'd do a hundred push-ups and then two hundred side-straddle hops and then get out in the bean rows and jack off. It would clean me out. It would get me started. But then I decided I didn't feel like running a mile or doing side-straddle hops or jacking off. What I really wanted was a nice ice-cold Miller High Life or an old-fashioned tall brown bottle of Bud.

CHAPTER 18

In the morning it was a simple deal. We split the money down the middle—Arlo's Jubilee Crusade, twenty-six hundred dollars; Buck and me, twenty-six hundred dollars. Arlo took the Chuck Wagon, the flatbed, the statuary, and the elephant wagon, which he would convert to a sleeper. It was ten o'clock and they were ready to pull out. The Robards had left at dawn, and you could see their scriptural trail on the black poles running up the road. The sun was high, the shadows sharp, and two spotted dogs were working over the garbage. Arlo, Eudora, Henderson Moke, the Groats, the Deloaches, Jessee Royal Stamps, and the others were lining up in a reception line, and Lee Anne Strickland, with a mouthful of green bubble gum, was bouncing a tennis ball against the elephant wagon. Buck, Loretta, Littlejohn, and I walked along the line, shaking hands and wishing them well and promising to keep in touch. As they climbed up on the flatbed, Buck told Arlo to drop him a card from Washington. Arlo said he would. The Roman emperors were still holding down the corners and the *Pietà* was still in the center, but the Coliseum arches were stacked to make room for the Crusaders. Arlo's conversion had sharpened him up. He didn't believe in straight walking anymore. He wanted to get on to the next town and take another shot at the snakes. The plan was to ride to within a mile of each town and then parade in behind the flatbed and set up on the first shopping mall they could find. By the time they reached Washington, Arlo figured the American people would have seen serpent handling and poison drinking for what it truly was.

"It's revealed truth, that's all. You'd think a country as big as the United States of America would have a place for us."

Buck agreed. I did too. When I shook hands with Arlo the last time, I made him promise to tell the Robards that if they went to five words per pole they would finish up somewhere out in California. If they stayed with three they'd have to come all the way back across to South Carolina. Arlo thanked me and punched me on the shoulder. "So long, Mahaffey."

"So long, Arlo."

Arlo led them out in the Chuck Wagon. Eudora was sitting next to him, and hooked behind them was the flatbed loaded down with Crusaders and statuary. George Groat had plugged his electric guitar into the neon outlet and was warming up with "Wildwood Flower." A Deloache twin was driving the elephant wagon, and at the rear, the Stark Valley school bus was whining along in low gear with Henderson Moke behind the wheel. The caravan pulled out onto the Dixiana. They would sleep on the road tonight and hit Ridgeland tomorrow. Then it would be on to Yemassee, Walterboro, and Grover, and on north and east to Darlington. They would be five months too early for the Darlington 500. But they were planning a revival on the empty infield, leaving posters behind announcing that on Labor Day they would be down on their knees on the White House lawn, praying for the fans and the drivers. Arlo said he would stick with his new "Pure Faith Exhibitions and Revealed Demonstrations," but he would be keeping an open mind about the Groats and their end-of-the-world prediction. After Darlington, it was a four-day march to Charlotte. Then on to Raleigh. Then on to Washington and a Crusade picnic on the White House lawn. They had a toilet in the wagon and the weather report was clear for the next week. But the money wouldn't last. Maybe they would pass the hat. Maybe if they ran into an emergency the Red Cross would step in or the Salvation Army or the United Way. Or maybe some philosophical Baptists or Methodists would take a long view of things and set up sawhorse tables with hot covered dishes on the road shoulder and welcome them with open arms. Anyhow, when I wished them well, I really meant it. So did Loretta. So did Buck.

Littlejohn cocked his hat on, grinning like he was going to lower a joke on us or do a quick time step. But he had other things in mind. "Buck, it's been a pleasure doing business with you people." He stuck his hand out. "But what say we don't be doing it again too soon, O.K.?"

They shook. "O.K., T. T. You take care of yourself."

"I'm going to be doing that, you hear?"

He shook hands with Loretta and then me. Out on the highway he turned his siren and blue lights on and went wailing around the big bend east doing seventy. Buck was peeling an orange. "There goes one bird that knows a little something about revealed truth."

Buck and I divided the twenty-six hundred dollars. Pioneer had given up on their eighteen thousand, so my thirteen hundred was straight profit. I agreed to take them back to Bibleland. This time there would be no McDonald's scene in the middle of the night. A full year with Pioneer was perfect. I'd spend twelve solid months getting the ideal job in Manhattan and getting Monica back. There was no way to make it any better. We had packed the snake show in the trunk and I was getting nervous about them getting loose. When we got back to Bibleland I'd leave the motor on while Buck got the damn things out. And then it would be so long Buck, and so long Loretta; I love you people but the season's over. Then I'd make a U-turn, wave a couple times like I was going to miss them, and head north, and the farthest south I ever wanted to see again was South Philadelphia.

I couldn't wait to pull out. I asked Buck how he was going to handle the elephants. He leaned over and wiped the orange juice on his socks. "No sweat, Bo." And there wasn't. He hooked the elephants' chains to the front axles as if he'd done it a hundred times, and we moved out with the engine off. Side by side they were too wide for the right lane, and I pulled over on the shoulder. We were going too slow for the needle to register, but I knew I could make up the time out on I-95.

Loretta was in the back seat with the beer cooler and her guitar. She began strumming. "Any requests?"

Buck opened a beer. "Yeah, you know—that Spanish job."

She tuned the E string and went into "Spanish Eyes." I finished one beer and popped open another. With the music and the beer and the elephants blocking out the sun we didn't see the patrol car until the blue light flashed. The patrolman cruised by and stopped. He came back with his thumbs hitched under his belt. He tipped his hat. "Hot, ain't it." He was young, with a fresh crew cut. Right out of training school.

Buck was out of the car, steadying the elephants. "No argument there."

The patrolman looked at Loretta. "Anything I can do for you, ma'am?"

"No, officer." She smiled up at him. "We're in pretty good shape."

He nodded at Buck. "Where yall heading?"

"Back to Bibleland, son."

The officer kept checking over the elephants and the hitch and the Olds. Then he looked at Loretta again. "Ma'am, you want to put that beer in a paper sack." It was almost an apology. "There's a lot of school kids around and you know how it is."

"Sure thing, officer."

He touched Ben's leg, then patted it. "How much one of these operations weigh?"

Buck said, "About eight thousand pounds. Give or take five hundred."

"Well, how about that?" He didn't know what else to ask. "Well, they sure do seem peaceful." He tipped his hat again. "O.K., if yall need any help or anything just tie a handkerchief to the aerial. Good luck to you now."

We rode on another fifty yards and I clicked the elephants to stop. "Be right back." I trotted back to the patrol car. "Officer"—I felt like an idiot but it didn't slow me down—"officer, when you saw that rig, what did you think? I mean do we look as crazy as I think we do?"

Loretta had started playing again, and he cocked his head. "That gal can play that thing, can't she?" He flashed a grin. "Yeah, I guess you look like you're missing on a couple cylinders. But that ain't why I stopped you."

For some reason I had to get another opinion. "What I've got to know is do you think that whole thing's crazy?"

He looked back over the Olds and the elephants. Then he looked at me as if it was the kind of question he fielded three or four times a day. "Mister, there's a whole lot of things in this world that's a lot crazier than what yall got."

Loretta was playing Buck's Spanish music. The officer kept cutting his eyes from the elephants to me and back to the elephants. "But I'll be dogged if that wouldn't be a real nice way to make a living."

"Thanks, officer. Let me give you a couple cold beers."

"No thanks, they watch us pretty close on that. Thanks anyway. And hey, good luck."

"Same to you."

As I got in under the wheel it dawned on me exactly what was really crazy. Number one was getting back in that dark office with the air-shaft view of Park Avenue. Number two was buying forty subway tokens for the week. Three, four, and five were Manny and Abramowitz, and Horner out at Elgin Bread, and three movies a day on

Times Square was right out of the recreation-room scene from *One Flew Over the Cuckoo's Nest.* At Pioneer it would be the same old sweat of a territory split. Or a merge with a conglomerate that believed salesmen were like anybody else and should be kept on straight salary. Ernie was right; the old peddlers were dying off. Maybe we were already dead. But the tent circus was dead, too. And the circus-and-religion combination wasn't going to cut it either. But Buck wasn't worried. Loretta wasn't worried. They both knew that down the road was something new. Something bigger and wilder and better, with more money and more fun and more everything of everything. And right there, steering the Olds down the Dixiana Highway, with the elephants blocking out the sun and the guitar sound and that great smell of cold beer, I knew exactly what I was going to do. I told Buck to slide in under the wheel. I had to make a phone call.

At the Gulf station I phoned Monica at work. "Hey, Mon. It's me."

"Oh for God's sake. You back in town?"

"Nope. South Carolina. We're heading for Georgia. First I'm going to tell you what I'm doing."

"Oh Jesus."

"Just listen, O.K.?"

Monica groaned, "It's your dime."

"I'm in the circus business." I started in about the elephants. How in the trade we called them bulls and how we were heading back to Bibleland to get the show rehearsed before going on the road. "Baby, things are really rolling. There's just no way I can tell you how great everything is." I was sounding like Buck. I'd even picked up the bastard's accent. "We've got lions, tigers, elephants. I mean babydoll, we got everything." McCoy's poster was on the side of the gas station. I began reading her the lineup. "Seventeen elephants. None of those Asiatics; Africans. The ones with big ears and long tusks. Kids eat them up. We've got the greatest cat act ever put together. Fourteen Nubian lions; thirteen Siberian tigers. We've got seals, bears, kangaroos. Hell, we've got eight polar bears. Big ones." I told her there was nothing like the old tent show. That Ringling Brothers playing Madison Square Garden was like a Vegas act and that Buck and I were bringing the real circus back. I was wilder than Buck. Crazier than Arlo Waters. "Check this motto: 'Be not deceived by envious competitors. This is the one and only Great Mozingo-Mahaffey Show. The most famous show ever assembled under one tent on the North American continent.' "

Out on the Dixiana the bulls and the Olds were moving along. Behind them, kids were tacking back and forth on bicycles and dogs were yapping down the drain ditch. They looked great. They looked wonderful. They looked fantastic. And I loved every bit of it. I'd picked up my old wildness. It had come back stronger than ever, and I knew I'd turn in the car at Budget Rental and forget Pioneer. If I ever collected the money I'd keep it for the embarrassment of working for them. I raved on. About how the Sherrys were under contract with us, along with Captain Dave Hoover and Captain Freddy Logan and Commodore Onslow McGregor and His Leaping Dalmatians. I told her half of Ringling Brothers were ready to sign including the Christianis and the Great Wallendas. I was lying, but I couldn't stop it. I didn't want to stop it. They weren't sales lies, or real lies; they were circus lies. They were different. As a matter of fact they weren't really lies at all; the essential facts were there. I wasn't telling her we were playing Madison Square Garden on Monday, or we were booking the Superbowl for Havana. I was telling her what I knew we could damn well do.

After running out of McCoy's poster material and Buck's hyperventilation, I began telling her about the South. But the country I was describing was more like Polynesia than the bean rows and the slug slime of the Tidewater country. Suddenly Monica was laughing. "Joe, Joe, Joe."

The minute she started laughing, I realized she wasn't

believing any of it. And then it hit me right between the eyes why she'd walked out on me. It was simple, so damned simple. With the instinct God gives women, and holds out on men, she figured I wanted to protect her and take care of her. Monica didn't want and didn't need any protection or taking care of. What she wanted was coming through the laughter and the "Joe, Joe, Joe."

She wanted in on the zappo madness; she wanted to be a partner in the insanity, and if there really was a Mozingo-Mahaffey Traveling Tent Show she damn well wanted to be there in the third ring with a dance act.

She tried to speak but she couldn't stop laughing. "Joe, you sound crazier than ever."

I said, "Maybe I am. But goddamn it, this time it's for real."

She could barely get it out. "And you got dates for this crazy stuff?"

"Damn right. Macon, Augusta, Birmingham. Just the South right now until we get it set the way we want it. Then we're heading for Atlanta and Houston and Dallas." I slid into my John Wayne delivery. But this time I couldn't hold it. Now I was giggling. "Well, babe, it's your move."

I could see her pushing her hair back from her face with her little fingers. I could see the white streak. She started giggling again, and this time she couldn't stop. "You're lying and I know it. I can just see you standing there like a son of a bitch and lying. Joe, it does sound like fun, though."

"O.K., maybe I stretched it a little." I had to dry my eyes with the inside of my sleeve. "O.K., we don't have the polar bears yet. But we've picked them out and we're getting them."

"Hold it, I need some Kleenex." She came back. "Oh Jesus, this is just too crazy. Does this mean you're staying down there?"

"Damn right I'm staying. People got the South all wrong. It's a helluva place to live. Great people. Great food. Great scenery. You've got to see the damn moon down here. Monica, no lie, in another twenty years everybody with any sense is going to be living down here. It's like a garden."

She'd been listening close. She hadn't said yes but she hadn't said no.

"Come on, Mon, you'll love Buck and Loretta and the rest of the gang. They're the greatest people in the world."

"Oh Joe." She was blowing her nose and still giggling. She was on the fence. She was swaying. She kept giggling and kept saying, "Stop, stop, stop it."

But I kept on, "And Monica, we've booked this fantastic Spanish group. Marimbas, guitars, trumpets, maracas. I mean the works." I took two long beats, but I had to force myself not to laugh. "Monica, wait till you hear these goddamn trumpets."

She waited. I could hear her breathing. The giggling was finally tapering off. And then she said it. "O.K., Joe, I've got another week's vacation."

"Terrific! Absolutely terrific! That's all we need. And honey, something else." I slowed down, took a deep breath, and said it with all the feeling I could manage. "Monica, there's not a day that passes . . ." It was sounding like a line out of the movies and I cut it off and jumped on ahead. "What I mean is I've never stopped loving you. Never."

"O.K., Joe, I don't believe any of it, but we'll try it." Her voice was soft, and beautiful, and she was laughing through it. "I've been thinking about you, too."

"Fantastic, honey, just absolutely fantastic. Listen, Monica."

"What?"

I leaned in, whispering. "I love you, Monica. I love you, Monica." And then I held the phone out as far as the cord would stretch and shouted as loud as I could, "I love you, Monica. I love you, Monica! *I love you, Monica!*"

I streaked back through the soybeans. "O.K., Buck, I'm

back in. We're partners. By God, you got yourself a deal. Fifty-fifty, right?"

"Right." We shook hands. Loretta hugged me from the back and squirreled around and kissed me on the lips. "Great, Joe, absolutely great."

Buck was beaming. "We're going to knock 'em dead, Bo. I mean dead." I told them I was meeting Monica in the morning at the Savannah airport.

"Hot damn! Terrific! Women love the circus. Right, babe?"

"Right. That's wonderful. Wonderful!" She laughed. "What are you saying when she sees this spread?" She waved at the bulls.

I said it almost automatically, "I'll think of something."

She laughed and groaned. "I'll be damned if yall ain't going to make a pair."

Buck sang out. "Yowza! Bo, when I get through with your dusty butt you're going to be the greatest man out front since Phineas Taylor Barnum. The best of the best. Nu-mer-o uno!"

I was grinning like an idiot. "The best of the best. Yeah, that's what I want to be."

Buck laughed, "And we're going to make more money and drink more champagne and buy more Cadillacs than the law allows. And Bo, damn it, we're going to put on a show they're going to damn well remember." He rubbed his hands together like he was drying them. "I got an idea for three rings that's going to knock you down. I mean it's never been done before. Listen. No, hold it. Hold it!" He stuck his hand out the window and click-clicked the bulls to stop. "Come on, give me a hand."

I stepped on the parking brake.

"Let's give them about twenty more feet. That way we won't have to be looking up their asses for the next seventeen miles."

I grinned and gave him one of Dad's favorite lines, "O.K., Buck, break out the champagne and the caviar. Let's go first class."

Buck hooked his head and popped his hands. "All right! Now you're talking, Bo. Now, damn it, you're saying something." He looped his arm over my shoulder, and I knew I was in the club. He began rolling on about three rings of fire, with six acts going at the same time, and a twenty-piece band, and thirty-six Miss Americas up on the swings and hanging in the webbing, and thirty-two African bulls thundering in with Captain Freddy Logan out front in his skin-tight silver suit, and while the Great Mozingo was flooding out over the levee, and rushing on to the sea, and I was nodding like one of those drinking birds you see on the backbars, and counting the house of the silver-spangled and gold-trimmed Great Mozingo-Mahaffey Exhibitions and Traveling Tent Show, I was also listening to another tune, an older tune. It was my old tried and true. Right. You got it.

"Oh, the world owes me a living . . .
Zooma-Zooma-Zooma-Zooma-Zoom."